THE YEAR'S BEST

Fantasy & Horror

Also Edited by Ellen Datlow

Blood Is Not Enough

A Whisper of Blood

Alien Sex

Vanishing Acts

The Dark

With Terri Windling

THE ADULT FAIRY TALE SERIES

Snow White, Blood Red

Black Thorn, White Rose

Ruby Slippers, Golden Tears

Black Swan, White Raven

Silver Birch, Blood Moon

Black Heart, Ivory Bones

A Wolf at the Door

Swan Sister

Sirens

The Green Man

The Faery Reel

The Year's Best Fantasy
First and Second Annual Collections

The Year's Best Fantasy and Horror:
Third through Sixteenth Annual Collections

Edited by Ellen Datlow and Kelly Link & Gavin J. Grant

The Year's Best Fantasy and Horror:
Seventeenth Annual Collection

Also by Kelly Link

Stranger Things Happen (collection)

Trampoline (editor)

Magic for Beginners (collection)

THE YEAR'S BEST

Fantasy & Horror

EIGHTEENTH ANNUAL COLLECTION

Edited by

Ellen Datlow and

Kelly Link & Gavin J. Grant

St. Martin's Griffin ☀ New York

www.stmartins.com

Summation Fantasy: 2004 copyright © 2005 by Kelly Link and Gavin J. Grant
Summation Horror: 2004 copyright © 2005 by Ellen Datlow
Media of the Fantastic: 2004 copyright © 2005 by Edward Bryant
Comics and Graphic Novels: 2004 copyright © 2005 by Charles Vess
Anime and Manga: 2004 copyright © by 2005 Joan D. Vinge
Fantasy and Horror in Music: 2004 copyright © 2005 by Charles de Lint

ISBN 0-312-34193-8 (hc)
EAN 978-0-312-34193-0
ISBN 0-312-34194-6 (pbk)
EAN 978-0-312-34194-7

First Edition: August 2005

10 9 8 7 6 5 4 3 2 1

Contents

Acknowledgments

Thanks to the editors, publishers, publicists, authors, artists, and readers who sent us review material and suggestions—especially Terri Windling, Ellen Datlow, Jim Frenkel, Charles N. Brown, and all at *Locus*, *Rain Taxi*, and *Publishers Weekly*.

We could not have proceeded without the generous assistance of the following people: Diane Kelly, Jim Cambias, Deb Tomaselli, Jonathan Strahan, Colleen Lindsay, Elizabeth LaVelle, Mark and Cindy Ziesing and their essential catalog, and interns Jedediah Berry and Gwyneth Merner.

Any omissions or mistakes are always, of course, our own.

To submit fantasy material for this anthology, please visit www.lcrw.net/yearsbest.

—G. J. G. and K. D. L.

Thanks to Karen Haber, Todd Mason, Will Smith, Thomas M. Disch, Bill Congreve, Steve Jones, Sheila Williams, and Stefan Dziemianowicz. Special thanks to Jim Frenkel, our hardworking packager, his assistant Antoni Stosh Jonjak, and interns Michael Gorwitz, John Payne, and David Polsky. And always, a very special thanks to Tom Canty for his unflagging visual imagination. Finally, thanks to my coeditors, Kelly Link and Gavin J. Grant.

I'd like to acknowledge the following magazines and catalogs for invaluable information and descriptions of material I was unable to obtain: *Locus*, *Chronicle*, *Publishers Weekly*, *Washington Post Book World* Web site, *The New York Times Book Review*, *Hellnotes*, *Darkecho*, *Prism* (the quarterly journal of fantasy given with membership to the British Fantasy Society), and *All Hallows*. I'd also like to thank all the magazine editors who made sure I saw their magazines during the year and the publishers who got me review copies in a timely manner.

—E. D.

My heartfelt thanks to editors Ellen Datlow, Gavin J. Grant, and Kelly Link. Their fine editorial judgment and hard work makes this volume the pleasure it is for me to read. Thanks, too, to our editor at St. Martin's Press, Marc Resnick, his assistant Rebecca Heller, and the St. Martin's production staff, for their help and patience with what is too often a difficult process. My thanks to Stosh Jonjak, who now understands what it means to make one of these, and who has contributed immeasurably to its successful completion; and thanks to our interns, Michael Gorwitz, John Payne, and David Polsky, with special thanks to volunteer Derek Tiefenthaler, all of whom worked on this. Thanks, also, to the agents, editors, rights people, and authors who have cooperated in granting permission to reprint the fiction and poetry within these pages. Lastly, my thanks and appreciation to Ed Bryant, our two wonderful Charleses—de Lint and Vess—and Joan D. Vinge, for their columns, which enrich this yearly project with their informed and helpful guides to the fantastic in all its diverse splendor.

—J. F.

Summation 2004: Fantasy

Kelly Link and Gavin J. Grant

Welcome to the summation of the year in fantasy for the eighteenth annual edition of *The Year's Best Fantasy and Horror*.

This year we have slimmed down this summary to allow more space for fiction. All the same, there is still a list of stories at the end of the summary we wish we could have included. Seek them out.

Because so many readers of this anthology have access to the Internet (if not at home, then at libraries, work, or school), we felt it was unnecessary to duplicate resources such as *The Magazine of Fantasy and Science Fiction's* online columns, as well as the thorough—and thoroughly admirable—year's-best summaries available at *Locus Online, SF Site, The Alien Online, Emerald City,* and many other Web sites. We will continue to recommend books that represent the whole broad cloth of the fantastic genre and to point attention to notable novels, collections, and nonfiction. But this is a large and lively genre, and even between the two of us, we don't manage (or even want) to read every novel published in the genre. When it comes to short stories, however, we read as widely as possible. This year our starter list of honorable mentions was well over three hundred stories and poems. While this was only perhaps 10 percent of what we read, next year we *intend* to be even more discriminating.

Thanks in no small part to the Internet, fantasy is a field where a reader can easily find a favorite author's recent books (or a recent discovery's backlist) on Amazon, Bookfinder, or other search engines as well as on publisher, author, magazine, and independent bookstore Web sites and blogs. The Random House imprints (Del Rey, Bantam Dell, Spectra, Ballantine, etc.) Web site is very good (as is their e-mail newsletter) while Tor's is slowly improving. Meanwhile, the smaller publishers—like Night Shade, PS Publishing, Tachyon, Prime, Wheatland Press—are well established online. Night Shade, TTA Press, and *Strange Horizons* offer readers lively discussion boards where new readers as well as authors and editors join the conversations. Similarly, while Tor is still the largest publisher in the field, the smaller presses, such as Prime and Wheatland Press, are publishing some of the most interesting work including debuts, translations, and anthologies. Although publication dates may not be completely reliable (but whose are?), the books are looking better and better and it's worth keeping an eye on their Web sites to see what's coming down the line. In other small-press happenings, despite the dissolution of the Ministry of Whimsy's association with Night Shade, and although the Ministry is on hiatus for now, the good news is that the *Leviathan* series (see Favorite Books) will continue with Jeff VanderMeer and Ann Kennedy at the helm. Forrest Aguirre, editor of *Leviathan 4*, is going on to edit his own anthology series.

We note that many magazines (from the smallest through the genre digests to *The New Yorker*) still have incredible gender imbalances in the number of contributors. Writers' advocacy group Broad Universe offers a useful page on their Web site concerning this subject (www.broaduniverse.org). Editors (and we can attest to this ourselves) report that submissions run between 60 and 70 percent from male writers, but that doesn't explain tables of contents that run 90 percent plus male. *The New York Times Book Review* was the latest newspaper to cut down on single book reviews and introduce more summations. Considering that large review magazines are inundated with fifty thousand–plus books per year, we can understand that urge, although our preferences run to more and longer single-title reviews. The *Times* also reduced their Notable Books to one hundred titles and dropped the genre breakout listing. Some books of genre interest were on the list, including David Mitchell's *Cloud Atlas*, Karen Joy Fowler's *The Jane Austen Book Club*, Susanna Clarke's *Jonathan Strange and Mr. Norrell*, Jonathan Lethem's *Men and Cartoons*, and Philip Roth's alternate history *The Plot Against America*. Since we are intent on slimming down this introduction, we won't comment further.

Resources

We could not put this book together without *Locus* magazine and Mark R. Kelly's *Locus Online* (www.locusmag.com). Both Mark Ziesing's fantastic catalog and *Rain Taxi Review of Books* were invaluable sources for finding wonderful books. *Chronicle* had some scheduling fluctuations; however, they cover a lot of ground. We were sad to see *The Women's Review of Books* placed on hiatus while they explore alternate funding solutions—we wish it a speedy reappearance. *The Ruminator Review*, meanwhile, was energetically relaunched and, along with *Entertainment Weekly*(!), introduced more genre reviews. *Prism*, the newsletter of the British Fantasy Society, dropped its color covers, but kept up its chatty coverage of the U.K. scene. Online resources include (and are obviously not limited to): *Ansible, The Alien Online, Green Man Review, The Internet Review of Science Fiction, Newpages, Revolution SF, Rambles, SF Site, Speculations,* and a reborn *Tangent*.

Disclosure: We are the editors and publishers of Small Beer Press and the zine *Lady Churchill's Rosebud Wristlet*.

Favorite Books of 2004

One of the best books of the year, and one of our favorite collections of the last several years, was from Australia: Margo Lanagan's *Black Juice* (Allen & Unwin), a remarkable, eclectic, and haunting selection of short stories. *Black Juice* has already won several awards and of the ten original stories that it collects, we picked two stories for this anthology. This collection is a feast: these stories are so good, so fresh, funny and warm and beautiful. The good news for American readers is that Eos has recently republished Lanagan's collection as a young-adult book, and that she has a second science-fiction-themed collection, *White Time*, also forthcoming in the U.S.

Susanna Clarke's *Jonathan Strange and Mr. Norrell* (Bloomsbury) is one of the best novels (first novels, historical novels, best sellers, etc.) that we read this year. We hope you have already read it, but if not, you are in for many delightful hours of reading. Kelly has loved Susanna Clarke's writing since first reading her short stories in the *Starlight* anthologies and in Terri Windling's selections for *The Year's Best Fantasy and Horror*; she's been waiting more or less patiently to read *Jonathan Strange and Mr. Norrell* for several years. (It was even better and stranger and longer than she'd hoped.)

Ursula K. Le Guin's *Gifts* (Harcourt) is, like the Earthsea series, nominally a young-adult book. However, adult readers should seek out Le Guin's short, compelling novel of those born with "gifts" and their responsibilities to themselves, their families, and their communities. Le Guin's deft prose never skimps on emotional richness.

Nancy Farmer's *The Sea of Trolls* (Atheneum) is an excellent young-adult novel set in eighth-century England and Scandinavia, in which a boy and his sister must survive after being taken prisoner by Viking raiders. The narrative is playful, magical, and deeply moving. Farmer puts Norse mythology and a great deal of historical research to use, and her characterizations are never simple or flat. This was one of Kelly's favorite novels of the year. Highly recommended for both adults and young adults.

The Faery Reel: Tales from the Twilight Realm (Viking), beautifully illustrated by Charles Vess, is Terri Windling and Ellen Datlow's follow-up to the excellent young-adult anthology, *The Green Man*. The writers used the widest possible interpretation of the faery theme, and as well as the story "The Oakthing" by Gregory Maguire, reprinted here, there are wonderful stories from Jeffrey Ford, Gregory Frost, Holly Black, Delia Sherman, Katherine Vaz, and *many* others, as well as poetry by Charles de Lint and Neil Gaiman, a list of resources, and an Introduction on "The Faeries" by Windling.

Air: Or, Have Not Have (St. Martin's Griffin) by Geoff Ryman was one of Kelly's favorite novels of the year. Strictly speaking, it's science fiction, but it has the texture, richness, and fantastical complications (ghosts, visions, layering of mythology and folklore and history) of other slipstream Ryman novels like *Was*. In a rural, mountainous province of China, Chung Mae, a fashion expert, is changed by the testing of an experimental communications technology designed to bring the whole world simultaneously online. *Air* is a remarkable and magical act of transformation; it has the feel of a fable, but we care deeply for the characters. *Air* is not only profound, it's also marvelously written, deeply joyful, and—even more rare—optimistic.

Tobias Seamon's *The Magician's Study: A Guided Tour of the Life, Times, and Memorabilia of Robert "The Great" Rouncival* (Turtle Point) was one of Gavin's favorites. It is a quiet, engrossing tale that slowly intensifies into a powerful tale of love and magic. Set in bustling, early-twentieth-century New York and surrounds, Seamon gradually unwinds the story of a magician, Rouncival, and his circle, as he goes from penny-ante attraction to a popularity that rivals Houdini.

Mother Aegypt (Night Shade) by Kage Baker includes thirteen stories—the title story is original to the collection. Baker is the author of several novels about "The Company" as well as last year's fantasy novel *Anvil of the World*, and her short fiction is as engaging as her novels. Baker is an old-fashioned storyteller in the best possible sense: sly, witty, strong on character and world building, and firmly in the heart of genre. If you're unfamiliar with Baker, this is an excellent starting place.

Mortal Love (Morrow) is the richest and most accomplished novel yet from Elizabeth Hand. The prose here dazzles: this is a deeply sensual book. Hand moves between present-day London and late Victorian England, pulling together the lives of pre-Raphaelite artists, rock stars, journalists, and an otherworldly muse in a story of obsession, art, madness, and magic.

David Mitchell deftly slices up genres to great effect in his Russian-doll-structured novel *Cloud Atlas* (Random House). Six narratives ranging from the 1850s to the present day to the future slowly (and sometimes abruptly) interweave, come together, and split apart. It's a bravura performance and highly recommended to anyone who likes page-turners and gorgeous prose. Strong political underpinnings don't distract or detract from the narrative; they only make the story richer.

Earth Logic (Tor) is the second book in Laurie J. Marks's Elemental Logic series, following *Fire Logic*. This is a political novel in the broadest possible sense, meaning a novel of people and the place they live. Marks is writing a traditional fantasy series that never becomes simply escape fiction, although it's always enjoyable to read. Her characters are living in a period of occupation and great changes; there are heroes, but their actions and decisions have real consequences. Marks's characters have the needs, contradictory impulses, and moral weight of real people.

Maria Tatar's *The Annotated Brothers Grimm* (Norton) collects and provides extensive notes on over forty of the brothers' tales from their 1857 edition. A. S. Byatt gives an Introduction, and the whole production—as with the other titles in this series—is as beautiful an object as one could wish. This is a book that will be read over and over again.

The Wizard Knight (Tor) by Gene Wolfe is a novel in two volumes. The first volume, *The Knight*, is a marvelous, old-fashioned epic fantasy about a boy named Able who steps into another world, with knights, giants, fairy women, and flashes of something far stranger. The second volume, *The Wizard*, seems slower, more recursive and digressive, although this may in part be the effect of reading the two books after a gap of many months. Readers who are simply looking for a good story will enjoy the two books, but Wolfe's novels also reward repeated and close readings. Wolfe is a master of both novel and short-story forms. His collection *Innocents Aboard* (Tor) was also one of our favorite books of the year.

The Hamilton Case (Little, Brown) by Michelle de Kretser is a bewitching, beautiful, interstitial book set in Ceylon. The novel is framed as a colonial mystery, but there are ghosts here as well, and readers of all persuasions should be entranced from the first page by de Kretser's language, her characters, and her insights into human nature.

Leviathan 4: Cities (Ministry of Whimsy/Night Shade), edited by Forrest Aguirre, collected ten novellas on the title subject of cities. Jay Lake, K. J. Bishop, and Ursula Pflug's stories were standouts, as well as the Stepan Chapman story, reprinted here.

In the excellent twenty-ninth installment of the Discworld series, *Going Postal* (HarperCollins), Terry Pratchett takes on the post office, golem rights, recidivism, and the importance of physical mail. Pratchett's second young adult Tiffany Aching/Discworld novel, *A Hat Full of Sky* (HarperCollins), was also one of our favorite books of the year. Year after year after year, Pratchett somehow manages to remain trenchant, moving, relevant, and always read-aloud funny.

Elizabeth Lynn's *Dragon's Treasure* (Ace) is a sequel to her earlier novel, *Dragon's Winter*. Readers of this anthology note that her story "The Silver Dragon" is set in the same world. This is rich, appealing fantasy in the traditional mold, with shape-changers, believable magic, and strong female characters. New readers needn't fear picking up this sequel. It stands on its own.

Iron Council (Del Rey) by China Miéville, like his earlier Bas-Lag novels, *Perdido Street Station* and *The Scar*, is set in the world of New Crobuzon. It's a dense, language-rich, subversive, and nuanced work of fantasy in which a crew of train workers escape from and then return to New Crobuzon. The image of the train—which undergoes several fantastical metamorphoses, travels on tracks that its crew continuously lay down and then pick back up again as the train moves on—is one of the most striking images in any novel we read this year. It's also a workable metaphor for the kind of work that Miéville does as a writer.

Flights edited by Al Sarrantonio is a mixed bag of an anthology. Twice as long as any other anthology we read this year, it would have been even better if it were significantly shorter. There are outstanding fantasy stories by Elizabeth Lynn, Patricia A. McKillip, Gene Wolfe, Neil Gaiman, Elizabeth Hand, and others. There are also some real duds. Sarrantonio's somewhat bombastic introduction and story notes suggest that these stories are revolutionary and groundbreaking. This is stretching the truth: much here is familiar traditional fantasy territory, albeit excellent traditional fantasy at that. If you're looking for cutting-edge fantasy, try Forrest Aguirre's much slimmer *Leviathan 4: Cities* or one of the Wheatland Press anthologies instead.

Alphabet of Thorn (Ace) is another of Patricia A. McKillip's intricate and graceful fantasies. Nepenthe, a foundling made ward of the Royal Library of Raine, is given a book written in the language of thorns. The library setting is a wonderful choice, and McKillip's usual gifts of characterization, dry humor, and elegant prose are on display.

Trujillo (PS Publishing) by Lucius Shepard is a handsome book. It weighs in at over six hundred pages, and contains one short novel, six novellas, and four novelettes, as well as an introduction by Michael Swanwick. The title work is original to the collection. Other standout stories include "Only Partly Here," "The Park Sweeper," and "Jailwise." In the last few years, Shepard has been producing some of the finest stories of his career. These are allusive, startling, sumptuous, and unclassifiable works of fiction. Readers of this collection should also seek out Shepard's recent novel, *The Handbook of American Prayer* (Thunder's Mouth) as well as the fascinating short collection, *Two Trains Running* (Golden Gryphon), which comprises an essay (expanded from a *Spin* magazine piece) and two stories, one of which appears here for the first time.

First published in Germany in 1870, then in Italy in 2000, *Beautiful Angiola: The Great Treasury of Sicilian Folk and Fairy Tales Collected by Laura Gonzenbach* (Routledge), translated and introduced by Jack Zipes and illustrated by Joellyn Rock is—amazingly—published here in English for the first time. Gonzenbach, most of whose papers were lost in an earthquake in 1908, collected her stories from working-class Sicilian women and their voices and concerns are central in this unique and alluring collection.

Magazines and Journals

Locus reported that subscription numbers are falling for many magazines. We hope short-story fans and readers of this anthology will subscribe to some of the following magazines in the following year.

The top speculative fiction magazine is now Scifi.com's *SCI FICTION*, edited by Ellen Datlow. While readership figures are hard to evaluate, the quality of the stories and the number of award nominations and wins are inarguable. We had at least half a dozen stories in our short list of outstanding short stories, and were hard-pressed to cut that to only two. We enthusiastically recommend their free online archive where you'll find some of the year's best stories by Richard Butner, Robert Reed, Howard Waldrop, Susan Palwick, Terry Bisson, Suzy McKee Charnas, and Paul Witcover, as well as *SCI FICTION*'s ongoing series of reprinted classics.

The Magazine of Fantasy and Science Fiction had an excellent year and we especially enjoyed stories from Carol Emshwiller, newcomer Ysabeau S. Wilce, Kit Reed, Charles Coleman Finlay, Ray Vukcevich, M. Rickert, Lisa Goldstein, and Robert Reed. Sheila Williams took over editorial duties at *Asimov's* from long-time stalwart Gardner Dozois who—happily—is concentrating on more anthologies and more writing. Despite its heavy tilt? bias? toward science fiction, we saw good fantasy stories from Lynette Aspey, Michael Swanwick, and Benjamin Rosenbaum among others. *Realms of Fantasy* again had a terrific year with fiction from all corners of the fantastic. Stories that stood out included those by Ian McDowell, Joe Murphy, Nina Kiriki Hoffman, and Rudi Dornemann.

The U.K. magazine *The 3rd Alternative* remains an excellent source of more risky slipstream, fantasy, horror, and science fiction. With publisher Andy Cox's takeover of *Interzone*, *The 3rd Alternative* may become more focused on darker fiction. In the meantime we particularly enjoyed work by Daniel Kaysen, Damien Kilby, Jay Lake, and Vandana Singh. The new, glossy *Interzone* immediately looked healthier and livelier, although the fiction still tends toward science fiction.

Amazing was glossily resurrected as a half fiction, half media-coverage hybrid. The fiction tended to be SF but we enjoyed a number of stories, especially those by Leslie What and Ray Vukcevich. The magazine was put on hold in early 2005 and we hope that it will reappear once again.

PS Publishing launched a new genre magazine, *Postscripts*. The first issue skewed toward SF and horror but the second issue found more space for fantasy. *Paradox* tried adding an annual PDF issue but decided against it and switched to two issues a year. Their fiction tends toward the historical over the speculative, but for the most part the editor's eye is good and clichés are generally at a minimum. There was one issue of *Black Gate*, which, as with *Paradox*, has a great amount of nonfiction reading. There was an excellent story from Judith Berman, among others. *Argosy*, a magazine with its own long and sometimes complicated history, produced one issue, which we did not find as strong as the first. The following titles appeared with regularity but are best enjoyed as additions to the top-level magazines, with the best being *On Spec* and *Weird Tales*. We also enjoyed stories from *Space and Time*, *Leading Edge*, *Tales of the Unanticipated*, *Nemonymous*, *Full Unit Hookup*, *Harpur Palate*, *Scheherazade*, and *Premonitions*.

After a banner year in 2003, in 2004 the three weekly literary magazines,

Harper's, The Atlantic, and *The New Yorker,* ran very little fantastic fiction—however, Kevin McIlvoy's November *Harper's* story, "Permission," is worth seeking out. The evolution of the newsstand magazine continues with *The Atlantic* announcing that they are cutting their monthly fiction and instead collecting it into an annual subscriber-only publication.

Online, *Strange Horizons* is a reliable, impressive, continuously evolving, volunteer-staffed venture that weekly posts free fiction, poetry, and nonfiction. (They are supported by reader donations.) The fiction is thought provoking and frequently cutting edge. Standouts this year came from Vandana Singh, Tom Doyle, Barth Anderson, Alan DeNiro, and Leslie What. There was also a hilarious nonfiction piece by Lucy A. Snyder, "Installing Linux on a Dead Badger: User's Notes."

Also worth reading are bimonthly *Lenox Avenue* and quarterlies *Fortean Bureau, Ideomancer,* and *Chizine.* All have a very wide remit. (*Chizine* mostly falls under our coeditor's watch.) These e-zines are an excellent bet for readers looking for new writers and new waves. *The Infinite Matrix* continues under the guidance of polymath Eileen Gunn, offering fiction from Karen Fishler and others, and a blog by none other than the legendary Howard Waldrop. Other enjoyable online zines include *Fantastic Metropolis, Would That It Were* (now published on an irregular schedule), and *Abyss and Apex.*

We were again impressed by the breadth and quality of Australian magazines. *Borderlands* is the most interesting. *Aurealis, Orb,* and *Andromeda Spaceways Inflight Magazine* are all solid with occasional flashes of brilliance.

In the mini- or micropresses, Tim Pratt and Heather Shaw published two excellent issues of *Flytrap,* full of "divers oddments" and memorable stories from Benjamin Rosenbaum (who published four breathtaking stories this year), David Moles, and Sarah Prineas.

Christopher Rowe, author of one of the best stories of the year, "The Voluntary State" (we would have reprinted it in this anthology if we could have defined it as fantasy), and coeditor Gwenda Bond published one issue of their themed-issue zine, *Say . . . Why Aren't We Crying?* in which the outstanding story was Janet Chui's "Black Fish." Edgewood Press's *Alchemy* published half a dozen high-quality fantasies in their second issue, including strong work from Sarah Monette and Theodora Goss.

Small Beer Press published one issue of *Lady Churchill's Rosebud Wristlet* with stories by Douglas Lain and Deborah Roggie among others. One of the most energetic and self-aware (in the best sense) of this set of publishers, John Klima, produced two issues of *Electric Velocipede.* Although his taste runs more toward SF than fantasy, stories by Alan DeNiro, Jodee Rubins, and Liz Williams stood out.

Lori Selke's *Problem Child's* strong second issue was best summed up by its own subtitle: *A Group Home for Well-Loved but Unruly Literature.* William Smith's *Trunk Stories* number 2 is recommended for those who enjoy slightly retro dark fantasy. We recommend collectors choose the special edition, which includes a handmade pop-up centerfold. *The Dogtown Review,* from writers David J. Schwartz and Keith Demanche, made an auspicious debut. *Talebones* tends toward darker fiction, but we still find more than a few stories of interest. *Zahir* produced three issues with story quality slowly rising to approach their accomplished production level. Many of these zines are labors of love begun by writers wanting to publish quirkier fare. Now many of the authors published in, for instance, *Flytrap* and *Electric Velocipede* are also being published in more prominent magazines. We look forward to the next round of high-quality zines and to seeing how the experience of publishing affects these editor/writers in their future career choices.

While it is literally impossible to keep up with all the magazines published each year, we had a great deal of fun reading established journals such as *The Harvard Review*, *The Paris Review*, *StoryQuarterly*, *One Story*, *Agni*, *Tin House*, *McSweeney's*, *Conjunctions*, as well as punchy newcomers like *Hobart*, *The Land-Grant College Review* (especially recommended for their art), and *3rd Bed*, all of which had a great year. Especially of note is *Ninth Letter*, a beautiful production that included an excellent story by Carol Emshwiller among others—they also have an attractive and substantial Web site. In the year's first issue of *Marvels and Tales Journal of Fairy-Tale Studies* there were articles on Robert Coover's *Briar Rose*, "Escape from Wonderland: Disney and the Female Imagination," Salman Rushdie and fairy-tale utopias, among others. The second issue was a celebration of the three-hundredth anniversary of the introduction of the *Arabian Nights* to the West, an event also celebrated in *Fabula* (not seen). Literary journals that had some level of genre fiction or poetry included *The Georgia Review*, *The Denver Review*, *Black Warrior Review*, *The Kenyon Review*, and *Prairie Schooner*. New literary magazines that included a smidgeon of speculative fiction included the single issue of *Swink*; North Carolina's *Backwards City Review* (which included an excerpt from Cory Doctorow's novel *Someone Comes to Town, Someone Leaves Town*), and Steve Erickson's Cal Arts–sponsored, themed literary journal *Black Clock* (from which we selected Shelley Jackson's story). The two issues that we read this year included an in-depth interview with Samuel R. Delany, fiction from Jonathan Lethem and Aimee Bender, as well as a wonderful nongenre story by Lewis Shiner. New to us was Boston-based journal *Post Road*, which had some wonderful poetry and fiction as well as a unique series of writers' recommendations.

Single-Author Story Collections

The standout collection was Margo Lanagan's *Black Juice*, a remarkable, eclectic, and haunting selection of award-winning short stories; two stories are reprinted in this anthology.

John Crowley's *Novelties and Souvenirs* (Perennial) collects most of Crowley's short fiction. Crowley is the author of the seminal fantasy novel *Little, Big*, as well as the Aegypt series. He is a master of short fiction, and these stories are luminous, profound, and haunting. Highly recommended.

The new James Sallis collection, *A City Equal to My Desire* (Point Blank), is a treat. Sallis, who also writes mystery novels and is a regular reviewer for *F&SF* and *The Boston Globe*, writes elegiac and thoughtful explorations of the human condition. Best enjoyed with a glass of wine close to hand, on a porch as the sun is sinking.

Eileen Gunn's *Stable Strategies and Others* (Tachyon) is an excellent and dapper debut from a writer who doesn't write nearly enough. *Stable Strategies*, a cross- or multigenre set of stories, contains one new fantasy story, "Coming to Terms," nine more stories by Gunn, and two collaborations. Gunn is a funny, striking, and original writer and this is a knockout collection.

Gene Wolfe's *Innocents Aboard* (Tor) collects twenty-two stories from 1988 to 2004. Highlights (of this amazingly strong collection) include "The Tree Is My Hat" and the semiautobiographical and unnerving "Houston 1943." Highly recommended, as is the reprint of his collection *Endangered Species* (Orb).

Ray Bradbury provided the cover art for his latest collection, *The Cat's Pajamas* (Morrow), which includes only two previously published stories.

Suzy McKee Charnas's *Stagestruck Vampires and Other Phantasms* (Tachyon) is a fantastically strong cross-genre collection that includes stories from the last twenty-five years (including a Hugo- and a Nebula Award–winner) as well as two new essays by the author. Charnas's humor, empathy, and intelligence are all on display.

Alice Hoffman's *Blackbird House* (Doubleday) slips occasionally into the fantastic. Hoffman is a writer with an earthy, intelligent way with words and these dozen tales will please many readers.

A. S. Byatt's *Little Black Book of Stories* (Knopf) collects five rather dark, fantastic-tinged tales from *The New Yorker* and other such venues. Byatt is a master of the short-story form.

Jay Lake's *American Sorrows* (Wheatland Press) is an accomplished collection of four novellas. At his best, Lake is a gutsy, vigorous writer with a flair for physical description, and *American Sorrows* is a solid introduction to one of the top new writers in the field. Fans can also search out Lake's chapbook, *Green Grow the Rushes-Oh* (Fairwood Press), which reprints a series of stories from *Strange Horizons.com*.

Jeff VanderMeer's accomplished second collection, *Secret Life* (Golden Gryphon), includes five stories set in the imaginary city of Ambergris, as well as three new stories. VanderMeer, one of the hardest-working writers and editors in or out of the genre, brings his obsessions—language and story, what it is to be human, and, overarchingly, individual mortality—to the force, and acknowledges and explores them from many different angles. This is a quirky, rewarding, and strongly recommended collection.

Hiromi Goto won the James Tiptree, Jr. Award recently for her novel *The Kappa Child*. In her debut collection, *Hopeful Monsters* (Arsenal Pulp Press), Goto explores race, identity, gender, and history, examining the fantastic minutiae of everyday family life. She uses mythology and a strong sense of humor, and is always enthusiastic—curious, never squeamish—about the fantastical strangeness of the human body.

L. Timmel Duchamp's excellent debut collection, *Love's Body, Dancing in Time*, is also the debut title from Aqueduct Press, which has quickly established itself as a home of fascinating and strongly feminist speculative fiction. The five love stories mix science fiction and fantasy into something unique to this author. Duchamp is a daring, intelligent, and innovative writer.

From the U.K., Liz Williams's mixed-genre debut collection, *Banquet of the Lords of Night and Other Stories* (Night Shade), shows off her sure voice in these stories, many of which see their first U.S. publication here. Night Shade are to be commended for their beautiful new edition of Lord Dunsany's club tales, *The Collected Jorkens*, a series of stories told by a man who will only accept a drink as stimulant to tell a story. This first volume collects the first two Jorkens titles, *The Travel Tales of Mr. Joseph Jorkens* and *Jorkens Remembers Africa*, and features an Introduction by S. T. Joshi and an essay by Sir Arthur C. Clarke.

Ignacio Padilla's first collection translated into English, *Antipodes* (Farrar, Straus & Giroux), is a collection of alternate, secret, and historical fantasies.

Daniel A. Olivas's enjoyable cross-genre collection *Devil Talk* (Bilingual Press) brings together twenty-six stories and vignettes often involving the choice between good and evil.

Joanne Harris's first collection, *Jigs and Reels* (Morrow), showcases both her sense of humor and her enthusiasm for the traditional speculative short story. Four of the stories can be found on her U.K. Web site.

James Purdy's latest collection, *Moe's Villa and Other Stories* (Carroll & Graf), contains a few light fantasies. Purdy is an acquired taste, but for those with the patience, there are gems to be discovered.

Bison Books continues their wonderful reprint series with Francis Stevens's *The Nightmare and Other Tales of Dark Fantasy* which collects stories from 1917–23.

Also noted: Alasdair Gray's *The Ends of Our Tethers*, wonderfully subtitled "Thirteen Sorry Stories" (Canongate); Jim Shepard's excellent and occasionally surreal *Love and Hydrogen* (Vintage); Jonathan Lethem's genre-cracking *Men and Cartoons* (Doubleday); Hannah Tinti's fantasias in *Animal Crackers* (The Dial Press); Mark Helprin's *The Pacific and Other Stories* (Penguin); Brian Evenson's dark and beautifully strange *The Wavering Knife* (Fiction Collective Two); Witold Gombrowicz's ingenious collection *Bacacy* (Archipelago); World Fantasy Award–winner Ian R. MacLeod's *Breathmoss and Other Exhalations* (Golden Gryphon); Adam Roberts's first U. S. collection, *Swiftly: Stories That Never Were and Might Not Be* (Night Shade). Penguin Classics reprinted Jorge Luis Borges's *The Aleph and Other Stories*. "All That Remains Is You" is the stand-out story in Steven Savile's *Angel Road* (Elastic Press).

Also, Allen Ashley's U.K. collection, *Somnambulists* (Elastic Press); Kay Green's *Jung's People* (Elastic) uses archetypes and myth to somewhat successfully probe the human psyche; recent World Fantasy Award–winner Bruce Holland Rogers's third collection, *Thirteen Ways to Water* (Panisphere/Wheatland Press); John M. Ford's wide-ranging and somewhat staggering *Heat of Fusion* (Tor), which collects over twenty years of stories and poems; *The Facts Behind the Helsinki Roccamatios* (Harcourt), an early collection by Yann Martel (*Life of Pi*) in which the last story leans to the surreal; *Eighty-Sixed: A Compendium of the Hapless* (Word Riot), a dark and cutting collection by Brian Ames, shows very occasional flashes of surrealism; *The Sound of White Ants* by Brian Howell (Elastic Press) included a few dark fantasy stories, one set in an almost Lovecraftian Japan; John Grant's collection, *Take No Prisoners* (Willowgate), collects stories mostly published in anthologies, nicely balanced with a number of original stories. James Morrow's mostly SF collection *The Cat's Pajamas* should still appeal to fantasy readers (Tachyon); Theodora Goss's *The Rose in Twelve Petals* (Small Beer Press) is a chapbook (with an original cover illustration by Charles Vess) that collects stories and poems from one of the genre's rising stars. Richard Butner's *Horses Blow Up Dog City* (Small Beer Press) is a mixed-genre chapbook that includes several excellent new and reprint fantasy stories.

Anthologies

See *The Faery Reel*, *Leviathan 4: Cities* and *Flights* in Favorite Books. The year's most enjoyable surprise was the high quality and all-around fun of *All-Star Zeppelin*

Stories (Wheatland Press), edited by David Moles and Jay Lake (although it was oddly lacking contributors' notes). As with *The Faery Reel*, the writers took the theme as far as possible—while there are, of course, a couple of Hindenburg stories, Benjamin Rosenbaum stood head and shoulders above the other stories with his highly creative metafiction, "Biographical notes to 'A Discourse on the Nature of Causality, with Air-Planes' by Benjamin Rosenbaum." There were also strong stories from Paul Berger, Elizabeth Bear, and Lawrence M. Schoen (whose story was a deliciously Damon Runyonesque pastiche), among others.

The fourth in the *Polyphony* (Wheatland Press) series, edited by Deborah Layne and Jay Lake, was a standout collection of work from the weird, surreal, and slipstream edges. We especially appreciated stories by Greg van Eekhout (anthologized within), Eliot Fintushel, Tim Pratt (whose excellent story "Hart and Boot" will be reprinted in the *Best American Short Stories*), and the collaboration between Bruce Holland Rogers, Ray Vukcevich, and Holly Arrow.

Gothic! is a spooky and terrific young-adult anthology edited by Deborah Noyes (Candlewick) with stories by Garth Nix, Gregory Maguire, Joan Aiken, and Vivian Vande Velde that had us on the edge of our seats. We're reprinting M. T. Anderson's darkish reworking of a classic tale.

McSweeney's Enchanted Chamber of Astonishing Stories (Vintage) is a literacy fund-raiser and worth handing over your hard-earned cash for. Hardworking and estimable editor Michael Chabon, determined to cross-pollinate genres and introduce the joys of genre fiction to more mainstream audiences, gave us China Miéville's story, reprinted here, as well as a great spooky story from new writer Jason Roberts, a pulp story from Daniel Handler, and a number of literary writers' forays into genre fiction, some of which were more successful than others, but all pleasingly enthusiastic.

Sheree R. Thomas's second broad-based and cross-genre "Dark Matter" anthology, *Reading the Bones* (Warner Aspect), showcases "speculative fiction from the African diaspora" and is recommended to our readers. There are standout stories from David Findlay and Kiini Ibura Salaam, as well as dark, challenging, and very enjoyable stories from Cherene Sherrard, Nalo Hopkinson, and Kalamu ya Salaam. The stories here range from traditional genre work to more experimental shores.

So Long Been Dreaming: Postcolonial Science Fiction and Fantasy (Arsenal Pulp Press), edited by Nalo Hopkinson and Uppinder Mehan, is wide-ranging in subject, tone, and style. Split into five sections and with an Introduction and Summary from the editors, *So Long* is a thought-provoking collection that we hope will inspire more such focused and provocative anthologies. While many stories tilted toward science fiction, there are some strong fantasy stories here.

Girls Who Bite Back (Sumach Press), edited by Hugo-winner Emily Pohl-Weary, is one of our favorite anthologies of the year. It energetically and positively presents fiction, nonfiction, comics, and art about women either in control or taking control of their lives. Recommended for fans of *Buffy the Vampire Slayer*, Nancy Drew, and teens and adults of all genders.

F. Brett Cox and Andy Duncan came up with an interesting regional concept and built a flavorful anthology around it in *Crossroads: Tales of the Southern Literary Fantastic* (Tor). Excellent original work from Richard Butner, Honorée Fanonne Jeffers, James Sallis, and reprints from Duncan, Fred Chappell, and Sena Jeter Naslund made this anthology a standout.

The James Tiptree Award Anthology 1: Sex, the Future, and Chocolate Chip Cookies (Tachyon), edited by Karen Joy Fowler, Pat Murphy, Debbie Notkin, and Jeffrey D. Smith, reprints winners and short-listed works along with new essays by the editors. While this is the second Tiptree anthology, it is numbered as the first of what is a promising new series.

The Ratbastards' third annual chapbook, *Rabid Transit: Petting Zoo* (Velocity Press), included three of the best stories of the year, by David Moles, John Aegard, and David Lomax, making it, percentagewise, well worth your dollars. John Aegard's story was one of Gavin's favorites, while David Moles's story inspired a whole anthology, *Twenty Epics*, to be edited by Moles and Susan Marie Groppi.

The Ratbastard editors are also writers and we applaud their ongoing publishing efforts.

Cities, edited by Peter Crowther (Four Walls Eight Windows), collects novellas by China Miéville, Paul Di Filippo, Michael Moorcock, and Geoff Ryman, which were originally published separately by PS Publishing.

You will find Tanith Lee's "Speir-Bhan" from *Emerald Magic: Great Tales of Irish Fantasy*, edited by Andrew M. Greeley, reprinted in this anthology. There were also good stories by writers including Jacqueline Carey, Charles de Lint, and Judith Tarr.

Legends II (Del Rey), edited by Robert Silverberg, is a hefty doorstop volume containing almost-novel-length works by best-selling series writers including Robin Hobb, Neil Gaiman, George R. R. Martin, and others.

Harry Turtledove and Noreen Doyle put together *The First Heroes: New Tales of the Bronze Age* (Tor), which included two of Kelly's favorite long stories: "Gilead," by Gregory Feeley, and Gene Wolfe's "The Lost Pilgrim."

We were not able to get copies of every anthology DAW Books published. Of those we saw, the two alternate history anthologies, *Conqueror Fantastic*, edited by Pamela Sargent, and *ReVisions*, edited by Julie E. Czerneda and Isaac Szpindel, were the best. Kij Johnson and James Morrow's stories from the former were worth seeking out.

For a fascinating glimpse into a different fantastic tradition, readers should not miss *The Dedalus Book of Greek Fantasy* edited by David Connelly (Dedalus), which brings together a broad selection of stories from the last one hundred years or so. *The Anchor Book of New American Short Stories* (Anchor Books) edited by Ben Marcus is a reprint anthology, containing some work that occasionally slips into the fantastic or horrific, such as George Saunders's wonderful and terrifying story "Sea Oaks." There's also a good deal of inventively experimental fiction here. Marcus's Introduction alone is worth the cost of the anthology.

Also noted: Patricia A. McKillip had a wonderful novella in the romance/fantasy crossover anthology, *To Weave a Web of Magic* (Berkley); Patrick Nielsen Hayden's *New Magics* (Tor) is an impressive young-adult fantasy primer. Effective both as an introduction to the best of the past three decades of genre fiction and a great fiction collection, *The Locus Awards* (Eos), edited by *Locus* founder/publisher Charles N. Brown and reviews editor Jonathan Strahan, is a particularly strong "best of" anthology, covering thirty years of award-winning stories. Gordon Van Gelder's latest anthology from the pages of *F&SF* is *In Lands That Never Were: Tales of Swords and Sorcery* (Thunder's Mouth); *The Alsiso Project* (Elastic Press), edited by Andrew Hook, contains enough good stories to ensure the reader will take note of Elastic

Press and a number of the newer authors; *Agog! Smashing Stories* (Agog! Press), edited by Cat Sparks, is an original anthology of Australian speculative fiction with several excellent stories; first paperback publication of Nicola Griffith and Stephen Pagel's *Bending the Landscape: Fantasy* (Overlook); Jason Eric Lundberg makes his editorial debut with *Scattered Covered Smothered* (Two Cranes Press), a wirebound anthology that deliciously pushed the limits of its "food" theme.

First Novels

See Tobias Seamon in Favorites. We published Jennifer Stevenson's *Trash Sex Magic* (Small Beer), a lovely, bawdy contemporary fantasy set along the banks of the Fox River. There are tree spirits, mysterious rains of fish, feral twins, and a mother and daughter who can seduce a man just by looking at him, as well as magical transformations and a dollop of social commentary. Stevenson's characters are formidable and her writing is droll, lush, and dazzling. Sarah Micklem's *Firethorn* (Scribner) was the standout in traditional fantasy debuts in part for the way it subverted the once-dominant norms by giving us a servant girl's take on the fantasy staple of men at war. *Firethorn* is the first in a series that is recommended to fans of writers as diverse as Karen Joy Fowler, Marion Zimmer Bradley, and Diana Gabaldon. Steph Swainston's *The Year of Our War* (Gollancz) debuted in the U.K. (U.S.: Eos, 2005) to much acclaim. It is a dark novel of switching realities, drugs, war, and a winged messenger upon whom, yes, the fate of more than one world depends. The story rushes toward the end, where it becomes clear there will be more stories to follow. Also: Robert Freeman Wexler's *Circus of the Grand Design* (Prime) is the tale of a man to whom some strange things happen; Catherynne M. Valente's ornate and complex tale of the Minotaur, *The Labyrinth* (Prime); Minister Faust's *The Coyote Kings of the Space-Age Bachelor Pad* (Ballantine/Del Rey) is a language-rich and inventive fantasy novel of two likable computer geeks; Leslie What's first fantasy novel *Olympic Games* (Tachyon) is a lovely, zany contemporary soufflé in which gods and mortals do what gods and mortals do best: fall in love, fall into further complications, and so on. As lightly sketched as a Thorne Smith novel, What's prose and characters also offer more substantial pleasures. One of Kelly's favorite novels of 2003, *The Etched City*, by K. J. Bishop—she called it "baroque, digressive, deeply strange, and compulsively readable"—was reprinted by Bantam.

Traditional Fantasy

Robin Hobb's *Fool's Fate* (Bantam Spectra) is the rich and multifaceted conclusion of the Tawny Man trilogy. It's reminiscent of Ursula K. Le Guin's *The Other Wind* and the finest moments of Anne McCaffrey's Pern series. Rosemary Kirstein continues her successful blending of fantasy and science fiction in the latest of the wonderful Steersman series, *The Language of Power* (Del Rey). Greg Keyes, *The Charnel Prince* (Ballantine), second in The Kingdoms of Thorn and Bone series, is a gripping dark fantasy where the king is dead, and murder most foul walks the land. Keyes is one of the best writers working this territory. The dark first entry in Canadian writer Steven Erikson's epic ten-novel series (so you can't say you don't know what you're getting yourself in for!), "Malazan Book of the Fallen," *Gardens of the Moon* (Tor), lives up to its advance billing from the U.K., where it has drawn comparisons to everyone from George R. R. Martin to Roger Zelazny, Guy Gavriel Kay to Jack Vance. Erikson's newest Malazan novella (almost a vignette compared to the series) is *The Healthy Dead* (PS Publishing). Likewise, Mary Gentle's secret history novella *Under the Penitence* (PS Publishing) takes place in the world of her Book of Ash series. Juliet E. McKenna's *Turns and Chances* (PS Publishing) is a traditional tale of conspiracy, intrigue, and possibly, a revolution. Charles Stross begins a new series, The Merchant Princes, with *The Family Trade* (Tor). This is one of the recent novels from Tor which suffers from being cut into smaller novels in order to comply with chain bookstore policies suggesting that hardcover books be priced under $25: while a fun take on an old story—an abandoned baby is, of course, heir to a mighty kingdom—it's best read with the second book (*The Hidden Family*) near to hand. Guy Gavriel Kay's *The Last Light of the Sun* (Roc) is an unexpectedly dark story of clashes and magic between Vikings, Celts, and Anglo-Saxons. Steve Cockayne's transposition of modern British life into a fantastical setting, "Legends of the Land," cries out for U.S. publication. In the meantime, savvy readers can pick up the terrific everything-is-falling-apart third book, *The Seagull Drovers* (Orbit). "What if the bad guy was right?" asks Jacqueline Carey in *Banewreaker* (Tor), the first in a new series, The Sundering, where human events mirror the battles of the gods. A *Scholar of Magics* (Tor) by Caroline Stevermer is an enjoyably frothy sequel to her earlier A *College of Magics*. Robert E. Howard fans should snap up the new illustrated edition of *The Savage Tales of Solomon Kane* (Del Rey). The sixteen stories (and one variant) are mostly from *Weird Tales*. An added bonus is H. P. Lovecraft's essay in memoriam of Howard. Another illustrated edition, *The Bloody Crown of Conan* (Del Rey), has three Conan tales as well as many extras (untitled drafts, synopses, etc.) that will delight fans.

Also noted: Dave Duncan's *The Jaguar Knights: A Chronicle of the King's Blades* (Eos); Martha Wells's *The Ships of the Air* (Eos); Katya Reimann completed Cherry Wilder's fourth book in her Rulers of Hylor series, *The Wanderer* (Tor), after Wilder's death; Kelly enjoyed the mixed fantasy/science fiction novel *Moonrise* by Mitchell Smith so much that she tracked down his earlier books (Forge); Jane Lindskold's energetic and more complex fourth book in her Firekeeper series is *Wolf Captured* (Tor); Tad Williams's new trilogy begins in *Shadowmarch* (Daw); Stephen R. Donaldson restarted The Chronicles of Thomas Covenant with *The Runes of the Earth* (Putnam); Leah R. Cutter's *The Caves of Buda* (Roc) is something much better than your usual demons-in-WWII novel; *Monument* (Ace) is Ian Graham's dark quest tale of an antihero; debut novelist Boban Knezevic's *Black Blossom* (Prime) seems to be a postmodern traditional fantasy of knights, quests, and retold fairy tales. Also see Sarah Micklem in First Novels herein.

Contemporary and Urban Fantasy

We published Sean Stewart's dark fantasy novel *Perfect Circle* (Small Beer Press). Stewart's narrator, Will "Dead" Kennedy, wants two things: to stop seeing ghosts, and to see more of his ex-wife and their daughter, Megan. *Perfect Circle* is set in Texas, and like Stewart's earlier novel *Mockingbird*, it's a page-turner and also a moving, funny, note-perfect exploration of family, personal responsibility, and magic.

Jim Munroe is both a leading light in speculative fiction independent presses (see his group blog theculturalgutter.com and his inspiring Web site nomediakings.com) and a successful novelist. His latest novel, *An Opening Act of Unspeakable Evil* (No Media Kings), is a dark yet hilarious journal-style fantasy of a woman's encounters with her roommate who may or may not be enacting demonic rituals. We're not exactly sure how to classify Stephen King's latest Dark Tower novels. They're westerns, Tolkien-influenced fantasies, contemporary fantasies as well, certainly horror, and excellent fun. So who cares? He capped (as far as we know) the series with the last two volumes, *Song of Susannah* and the eponymously titled seventh volume (both Donald M. Grant/Scribner). King draws his own career and many of his nonfantastic novels into the many-worlds tale of the Gunslinger and his quest companions.

Oracles by Melissa Tantaquidgeon Zobel (U. of New Mexico) is set a few years in the future and considers the friction between traditional and nonnative lifestyles in a fictional Native American tribe. *Tainaron: Mail from Another City* (Prime) marks Finnish writer Leena Krohn's U.S. debut. A woman arrives in Tainaron, a city of insects, and sends letters back to her lover. She does not question the city, the insects, nor her failure to remember what brought her there or why her lover never answers. As winter approaches, she comes to understand the inevitability of change. *A Girl Like Sugar* (McGilligan Books) is editor, writer, and zinester Emily Pohl-Weary's debut novel, in which a girl is haunted by her late boyfriend. Ghosts also haunt a newly married couple in M. A. Harper's chatty New Orleans–based *The Year of Past Things* (Harcourt). A temp haunted by the cat he drowned is the lead character in James Hynes's *Kings of Infinite Space* (St. Martin's), an excellent novel that will please fans of William Browning Spencer's *Resumé with Monsters*. Nina Marie Martínez's *¡Caramba!* (Knopf) is an excellent debut novel offering ghosts, volcano cults, and strong, likable female characters.

Also noted: *No Traveller Returns* (PS Publishing) by Paul Park, in which a man attempts to follow his mentor into the afterlife to bring him back to life. This is a mesmerizing, dreamlike, and utterly strange novella. *Jigsaw Men* by Gary Greenwood (PS Publishing), an imaginative alternate nineteenth-century London fantasy reminiscent of *The League of Extraordinary Gentlemen*; in Anthony Doerr's slow and dreamy *About Grace* (Scribner), David Winkler tries to avoid the future that he reluctantly sees; Lily Prior's "novel of enchantment" and magic seeds, *Ardor* (Ecco); Andrew Sean Greer's *The Confessions of Max Tivoli* (FSG), a gentle novel of a life lived backwards; painter and sculptor Dorothea Tanning's wonderful surrealist first novel, *Chasm: A Weekend* (Overlook); time, art, sex, and death are the subjects of *My Death* by Lisa Tuttle (PS Publishing); Kelley Armstrong gave us two books in her fast-paced, smart Women of the Otherworld series, *Dime Store Magic* and *Industrial Magic* (both Bantam Spectra); Stephen Policoff's *Beautiful Somewhere Else* (Carroll & Graf) was an engaging if open-ended first novel; Night Shade published the first U.S. edition of M. John Harrison's wonderful novel *The Course of the Heart*; Small Beer brought Carol Emshwiller's debut novel, *Carmen Dog*, back into print as the first title in their Peapod Classics reprint series.

Historical, Alternate History, and Arthurian Fantasy

Robert Holdstock's Arthurian Merlin Codex series continues in *The Iron Grail* (Tor), wherein Merlin returns to a future fantastical England and has to deal with Jason (of the Argonauts fame), King Urtha, and a war with the Otherworld. Alex xxviii ·→· Summation 2004: Fantasy

Irvine mixes fact and fantasy, baseball, beat poets, and the Arthurian myth in the 1950s U.S.A. in his second novel, a fast-moving adventure, *One King, One Soldier* (Del Rey). Elizabeth E. Wein's young adult novel, *The Sunbird* (Viking), is the third in her African/Arthurian series. Telemakos is grandson of both Arthur and Kidane, a member of the Aksum parliament; his bifurcated history and loyalties are tested to the core.

Also recommended: Cecelia Holland's second Viking tale, *The Witches' Kitchen* (Forge); *Merlin and the Making of the King* by Margaret Hodges and Trina Schart Hyman (Holiday House); Charles Stross's *The Atrocity Archives* (Golden Gryphon) will appeal to fans of Tim Powers as well as readers of Lovecraft and spy thrillers. *Winter on the Plain of Ghosts* by Eileen Kernaghan (Neville Books) is an appealing epic-fantasy novel set in the prehistory of the Indus Valley. James A. Hetley's dark post-Arthurian series continued in *The Winter Oak* (Ace). New writer Jules Watson begins a series filled with love and war in first-century northern Europe with *The White Mare* (Overlook). Caitlín R. Kiernan's *Murder of Angels* (Roc) is a dark but beautifully written sequel to her earlier *Silk*. Ludvig Holberg's *The Journey of Niels Klim to the World Underground* (Bison) is a reprint of a Hollow Earth novel from 1741.

Humorous Fantasy

Besides Terry Pratchett's two excellent Discworld novels, *Going Postal* and *A Hat Full of Sky* (HarperCollins), and Leslie What's terrific *Olympic Games* (Tachyon), we recommend the following humorous fantasy novels. Gideon Dafoe's slim *The Pirates! In an Adventure with Scientists* (Pantheon) brings together a band of seemingly nameless pirates and Charles Darwin. Romance writer Katie MacAlister's paranormal romance *You Slay Me* (Onyx) is a fast, fun story of Paris, dragons, and missing packages. Stephan Zielinski's *Bad Magic* (Tor) is funny from cover to cover so don't miss any of it. Jasper Fforde produced the fourth in his Thursday Next series, *Something Rotten* (Viking). However, unlike Pratchett, the lack of rules in Fforde's fantasy seems to make the world smaller rather than larger as the series goes on. Christopher Moore's *The Stupidest Angel* (Morrow) features zombies, which pleased Kelly enormously.

Fantasy in the Mainstream

Samantha Hunt's debut, *The Seas* (MacAdam/Cage), tells the story of a girl who believes herself to be a mermaid. There are echoes of "The Little Mermaid" and the novel *Undine*, but Hunt's contemporary tale is far stranger. Beautifully written, playful, and highly recommended.

Rudolfo Anaya's *Serafina's Stories* (U. of New Mexico) is a lovely and surprisingly gentle translation of a dozen *cuentos*, or folktales, in the style of *The Thousand and One Nights*. Set in 1680 in Santa Fe, where a woman tells the governor of New Mexico a series of stories to save the lives of her fellow Pueblo Indians. (Interested readers are also recommended to David Roberts's nonfiction account, *The Pueblo Revolt: The Secret Rebellion That Drove the Spaniards out of the Southwest* (Simon & Schuster)).

A recent winner of the James Tiptree Award, Johanna Sinisalo's wonderful

Finnish novel *Troll* (Grove) has been gaining fans since its Finnish and U.K. publications.

Paul Fattaruso's *Travel in the Mouth of the Wolf* (Soft Skull) is a short, occasionally astonishing, hard-to-describe novel about psychics, dinosaurs, baseball, and postdeath experiences.

In Patrick Neate's *The London Pigeon Wars* (FSG), London pigeons split into two camps who begin a war over a scrap of chicken in Trafalgar Square. The human tale hung around the pigeon war is a little absurd but does not distract from the wonderful fun Neate has with his pidgin English.

Joanne Harris's dark, intense tale of superstition and witchcraft, *Holy Fools* (Morrow), is superficially reminiscent of her earlier best seller, *Chocolat*, but this is a darker tale of group hypnosis and the strictures of belief in a small community.

In the latest of his Stay More series of novels, *With* (Toby), Donald Harington tells the story of a kidnapped girl who is taken at the age of eight to an almost inescapable mountaintop. She survives both her kidnapper, and, with the help of a ghost, many years alone.

Fay Weldon adds chunks of autobiography to *Mantrapped* (Grove), her tale of young and handsome Peter and middle-aged and tired Trisha, unwitting and unwilling bodyswappers. Longtime readers will enjoy Weldon's asides, newer readers may be surprised.

Also noted: Keith Miller's love story/quest fantasy *The Book of Flying* (Riverhead); José Saramago's doppelgänger tale, *The Double* (Harcourt); Carlos Ruiz Zafón's sentimental best seller about bookselling, *The Shadow of the Wind* (Penguin); Erik Orsenna's *Grammar Is a Sweet, Gentle Song* (translated by Moishe Black) (George Braziller), a whimsical fantasy about two children marooned on an island where words have physical form; finally, Salley Vickers's *Mr. Golightly's Holiday* (FSG) is a story of two age-old competitors gently having it out for the future of us puny humans. Genre readers will enjoy Vickers's writing, although the story is a familiar one.

Poetry

In literary magazines we particularly enjoyed *Jubilat*, *Conjuctions*, and *Lit*, even as we found poems with intrusions into or by the fantastic in almost every journal we read. Speculative poetry shows new energy with Prime Books's announcement of a new poetry (and fiction) magazine, *Jabberwocky*, to debut in 2005, and Sam's Dot Publishing debuted *Illumen* in late 2004. *The Magazine of Speculative Poetry*, *Star*Line*, and *Mythic Delirium* are all ongoing and worthy projects interested in actively reaching out to more readers and writers. The Science Fiction Poetry Association's first book, Suzette Haden Elgin's *The Science Fiction Poetry Handbook* (Sam's Dot Publishing) will be published in 2005. Mario Milosevic, whose poetry has appeared in many genre and nongenre magazines, self-published two enjoyable collections, *Fantasy Life* and *Animal Life*, through Lulu.com—a recommended site for those wishing to take control of the means of production one unit at a time. Stephen Mitchell produced an interesting modernized version of *Gilgamesh* (Free Press) in which he pieced together previous translations—and even added pieces— to keep the narrative going. Neither an academic nor a free translation, this version has the flaws and vigor of a mongrel. Even more interesting is the attempt at updating *Dante's Inferno*, illustrated by Sandow Birk and translated and adapted by Birk and Marcus Sanders (Chronicle). Also noted: James Tate's *Return to the City of White Donkeys* (Ecco); Rad Smith's *Distant Early Warning* (Mira Press), or "Frankenstein's Monster," among others.

More from Elsewhere

McSweeney's gives us Robert Coover's outstanding novella "Stepmother" (originally published in *Conjunctions*) in a beautifully illustrated (and made) hardcover. A fantastic gift. McSweeney's also published *The Future Dictionary of America*, a book and CD set to benefit progressive causes, which has enough straight-out fantasy to fill a trilogy or two. *Molvanîa: A Land Untouched by Modern Dentistry* (Overlook) by Santo Cilauro, Tom Gleisner, and Rob Sitch riffs on the language of travel guides and stretches the idea of a guide to an underdeveloped Eastern European country as far as it can go. R. J. Carter annotates *Alice's Journey Beyond the Moon* (Telos) as if it were a newly found Lewis Carroll manuscript. Brian Hicks's *Ghost Ship: The Mysterious True Story of the Mary Celeste and Her Missing Crew* (Ballantine) is a fresh look at an old mystery; *The Dark Horse Book of Witchcraft* edited by Scott Allie (Dark Horse).

Children's/Teen/Young-Adult Fantasy

See the Best of the Year list for *The Faery Reel*, *The Sea Trolls*, and *Gifts*.

In a note-perfect pastiche and homage to turn-of-the-century children's novels, Boston-based writer M. T. Anderson's *The Game of Sunken Places* (Scholastic) involves a board game, two firm friends, various supernatural characters, and evil that can only be defeated by two young boys in short pants. Highly recommended.

Unexpected Magics by Diana Wynne Jones (Greenwillow) is an excellent collection of young-adult stories by one of the best and most reliably energetic writers working in genre. Fans of Diana Wynne Jones's novels should seek out this collection immediately, and if you haven't read her novels, well then, you have a great deal of catching up to do.

Eva Ibbotson's latest, *The Star of Kazan* (Dutton), is an old-fashioned pleasure complete with a falling-apart castle, wicked relatives, reversals, and triumphs. Although, strictly speaking, it isn't fantasy, it should appeal to readers of fantasy. A beautifully put-together novel with lovely illustrations by Kevin Hawkes.

Donna Jo Napoli places the Cinderella story in fourteenth-century China in *Bound* (Atheneum), a generous and compassionate retelling that will please readers of all ages.

The hardest-working author in the field of young-adult fiction, Scott Westerfeld, debuted a new trilogy, Midnighters, with *The Secret Hour* (Eos). This is a wonderful, fast-paced page-turner about a group of five children who stay awake during the twenty-fifth hour of the day (at midnight, of course!). Readers will be on the edge of their seats and then, needless to say, stay there waiting for the next two books.

Terry Pratchett's *A Hat Full of Sky* (HarperCollins) is the third of his young-adult Discworld novels—although Pratchett readers ahead of their age group are recommended to begin the adult series, too—and the second featuring capable young heroine Tiffany Aching.

Shannon Hale follows up last year's lovely debut *The Goose Girl* with a much darker and fascinating if not always successful sequel, *Enna Burning* (Bloomsbury). Enna learns the language of fire and pays the price. Power, manipulation, and love are crisscrossed in interesting patterns.

Readers of Meredith Ann Pierce (author of the wonderful Dark Angel trilogy) will be pleased by *Waters Luminous and Deep* (Viking), a collection of stories of strong women, fairy tales, and magic—half of which are new to this collection.

Gregory Maguire's charming and hilarious screwball *Leaping Beauty and Other Animal Fairy Tales* (HarperChildren's) is a collection of fables, tall tales, and yes, fairy tales, that have been stood on their heads to very good effect. Recommended for adults and fans of *The Stinky Cheese Man*.

Holly Black and Tony DiTerlizzi produced two more volumes in their action-packed and best-selling middle-grade series, The Spiderwick Chronicles: *The Ironwood Tree*, Book 4 and *The Wrath of Mulgarath*, Book 5.

Charles De Lint's astute turn to young-adult novels has paid off for himself and his readers. His latest spirited novel, *The Blue Girl* (Viking), brings a new set of high-school-age characters to his ongoing imagined city Newford. Ghosts, dalliances, and a frightening ratcheting up of tension will keep the reader turning pages until well after dark.

The Shamer's Daughter by Lene Kaaberol (Holt) is the first in an interesting-looking trilogy translated from Danish. Shamers see every guilty deed of anyone who looks into their eyes—a dangerous talent if those in power are not using their power for the common good. Should appeal to fans of Tamora Pierce.

Philip Reeve's books now have a series title, The Hungry City Chronicles. *Predator's Gold* (Eos), sequel to *Mortal Engines*, is another inventive, dark, and enjoyable novel recounting the wars of roaming cities, and the various adventures of their inhabitants. Recommended for slightly older readers.

Clive Barker's heavily illustrated second *Arabat* book, *Days of Magic, Nights of War* (Cotler/HarperCollins), picks up the story from the first novel, so don't try reading this on its own.

David Fickling/Random House published the first three volumes in The Edge Chronicles by Paul Stewart and Chris Riddell. Longtime bestsellers in the U.K., the books should please young fans of Terry Pratchett and readers of the Spiderwick Chronicles.

Dastardly twists of fate are overcome in the nick of time in pseudonymous Australian writer Lian Hearn's third and final book in the Asian-influenced Tales of the Otori trilogy, *Brilliance of the Moon* (Riverhead).

Eileen Kernaghan's second novel of the year (see the Historical section), *The Alchemist's Daughter* (Thistledown), continues the popular use of John Dee in historical fantasy. Despite her preference for natural philosophy and science, a young Renaissance woman is forced to use both alchemy and her scrying talent (inherited from her late mother) in a search for hard-to-find alchemical ingredients.

Patricia C. Wrede and Caroline Stevermer's *The Grand Tour* (Harcourt) is a sequel to their much-beloved epistolary novel *Sorcery and Cecilia*. Although the new book is slower, readers will be pleased to reconnect with these protagonists on their honeymoon tour of a conspiracy-and-magic-riddled Continent.

Also noted: *Girls Who Bite Back* in anthologies; E. Rose Sabin's *A Perilous Power* and *When the Beast Ravens* complete the boarding-school-magic trilogy begun in *A*

School for Sorcery (all published by Tor); Lois Lowry's *Messenger* (Houghton Mifflin) follows *The Giver* and satisfyingly answers more questions than it raises about the gifted children from the earlier book; history and Haitian magic come together in *Stormwitch* by Susan Vaught (Bloomsbury); older readers will enjoy the inconsistencies and possibilities hinted at in *A Fast and Brutal Wing* (Roaring Brook) by Kathleen Jeffrie Johnson; bestseller Philip Kerr's enjoyable genie tale, *Children of the Lamp* (Scholastic); Welsh poet and author Catherine Fisher's Norse-mythology-influenced trilogy is collected in *Snow Walker* (Greenwillow); Cornelia Funke's *Dragon Rider* (Scholastic); Garth Nix offers the compelling second volume of a rather ghastly week, *The Keys to the Kingdom: Grim Tuesday* (Scholastic); also from Australia, Kate Constable's *The Singer of All Songs* (Arthur Levine/Scholastic) is reminiscent of Anne McCaffrey's singer novels; Katherine Langrish's *Troll Fell* (HarperCollins); David Almond's *The Fire Eaters* (Delacorte) is another beautifully written novel from the author of *Skellig*; Keith Oppel's *Airborn* (Eos) is filled with zeppelin lore and plucky young heroes; Steve Augarde's *The Various* (Fickling/Random House) is the first in a trilogy where a young girl discovers that fairies and other "little people" are real; a boy has to save his mother—and avoid the seven deadly sins!—in *Jack and the Seven Deadly Giants* by Sam Swope (illustrated by Carll Cneut) (FSG); Dave Barry and Ridley Pearson's sequel to *Peter Pan*, *Peter and the Starcatchers* (Hyperion); Brain Jacques's latest Redwall novel, *Rakkety Tam* (Philomel); Isabel Allende's second young-adult fantasy, *Kingdom of the Golden Dragon* (HarperCollins), received mixed reviews; midtrilogy novels from Clare B. Dunkle, *Close Kin* (Holt), and Jonathan Stroud, *The Golem's Eye* (Hyperion); T.A. Barron's latest tale of Avalon, *Child of the Dark Prophet* (Philomel); Chris Wooding's *The Haunting of Alaizabel Cray* (Scholastic), a dark tale of a "wych-hunter"; Mike Davis's second "science mystery," *Pirates, Bats, and Dragons* (Perceval Press); and Verónica Uribe's hand-sized *Little Book of Fairy Tales* (Groundwood).

Picture Books

Anthea Bell provides a nonbowdlerized translation of Hans Christian Andersen's *The Little Mermaid* (minedition) for Lisbeth Zwerger's lovely, pellucid illustrations. If you are unfamiliar with Zwerger's art, we recommend you seek her out. Charles Vess's beautiful illustrated ballad tales are collected in *The Book of Ballads* (Tor), which features stories and poems by Delia Sherman, Neil Gaiman, Midori Snyder, and Lee Smith, among others, as well as an introduction by Terri Windling. Doris Orgel's new translations are wonderfully illustrated by Bert Kitchen in *The Bremen Town Musicians and Other Animal Tales from Grimm* (Roaring Brook); Caldecott Award–winning artist David Wiesner illustrates a Fritz Leiber story in *Gonna Roll the Bones* (iBooks); Brian Froud turns Joni Mitchell's 1969 song *Chelsea Morning* (iBooks) into a whimsical book. Randy Cecil's take on fairy tales *One Dark and Dreadful Night* (Holt) is both splintered and side-splitting. Leo and Diane Dillon provide illustrations for a new edition of Virginia Hamilton's *The People Could Fly* (Knopf). P. Craig Russell returns to his series of illustrated Oscar Wilde fairy tales with the by turns sentimental and cynical (but always highly moral) *The Devoted Friend & The Nightingale and the Rose* (NBM). Benoît Peeters's *The Book of Schuiten* (NBM) is a striking collection of fantastic illustrations collected from Schuiten's comics, posters, and scenery designs. Much of the book is being published in the U.S. for the first time and that will inspire readers to search out his other work. (NBM also published the second half of Schuiten and Peeters's sexy and fantastical political allegory, *The Invisible Frontier*.) As always, we recommend the annual *Spectrum* anthology by Cathy and Arnie Fenner (Underwood), now in its eleventh year. Underwood also published *The Best of Gahan Wilson*, a terrific collection of illustrated essays and cartoons. David B.'s graphic novel *Epileptic* (Pantheon) is an amazing journey through a family dealing with epilepsy and the young David's retreat into (often fantastical) art. *Krazy and Ignatz 1933–1934: Necromancy by the Blue Bean Bush* (Fantagraphics) is the last black-and-white and the fifth in the series of George Herriman's collected Sunday comics as edited by Bill Blackbeard and Derya Ataker. Paul Kidby's *The Art of Discworld* (Gollancz) is energetic and fun and belongs on the ever-extending Discworld shelf. *The Deceiving Eye: The Art of Richard Hescox* by Randy M. Dannenfelser (Paper Tiger) collects the artist's favorite pieces, including many fantasy book covers. Also noted: *Kingsgate: The Art of Keith Parkinson* by Keith Parkinson (SQP); *Amazona* by Chris Achilleos (Titan); *Ilene Meyer: Paintings, Drawings, Perceptions* by Ilene Meyer, Cathy and Arnie Fenner (Underwood).

General Nonfiction

See Maria Tatar in Favorites. *The Wave in the Mind: Talks and Essays on the Writer, the Reader, and the Imagination* (Shambhala) is Ursula K. Le Guin's second collection of nonfiction and includes essays on writing, reading, libraries, her family, and other subjects. Le Guin's writing is, as always, individual, entertaining, and instructive, and highly recommended. *You Are Here: Personal Geographies* by Katherine Harmon (Princeton Architectural Press) is a lovely book of one hundred maps, including some very fantastical ones. *The Dharma of Dragons and Daemons: Buddhist Themes in Modern Fantasy* by David R. Loy and Linda Goodhew (Wisdom) finds Buddhist subtexts and patterns in work by Tolkien, Le Guin, Hayao Miyazaki, and others. Joseph McCabe's *Hanging Out with the Dream King* (Fantagraphic) contains an opening and closing interview with Neil Gaiman. In between are interviews with the best-selling author's many collaborators—artists, inkers, pencillers, musicians, and writers—that create a sort of informal biography. Brian Rosebury's revised *Tolkien: A Cultural Phenomenon* (Palgrave) is a study of Tolkien's full body of work as well as the ongoing cultural relevance of *The Lord of the Rings*. David Sinclair's *The Land That Never Was* (Da Capo) is a history of a country that never existed, the man who invented it, and the consequences. In his exploration of writing and mental health, *Nervous System* (Raincoast), Jan Lars Jensen tells the moving, insightful, and often surprisingly funny story of his nervous breakdown, which occurred just as his SF novel *Shiva 3000* was published.

Also: Editor Sean Howe put together a wonderful selection of writers writing on comics, *Give Our Regards to the Atomsmashers* (Pantheon); Bev Vincent, who writes a column on Stephen King in *Cemetery Dance*, analyzes the thirty-five-year, seven-book series in *The Road to the Dark Tower* (NAL); *Ursula K. Le Guin: Beyond Genre: Fiction for Children and Adults* by Mike Cadden (Routledge); Michael Moorcock's *Wizardy and Wild Romance: A Study of Epic Fantasy* (Monkeybrain) was reprinted with an introduction by China Miéville and an afterword by Jeff VanderMeer; *Why Should I Cut Your Throat for Free* (Monkeybrain) is an often entertaining collection of writer/editor Jeff VanderMeer's reviews, convention reports, and miscellaneous nonfiction writings. *Conversations with Ray Bradbury* (University Press of Mississippi), edited by Steven L. Aggelis; *Pulp Fictioneers*, edited by John Locke (Adventure House), gathers behind-the-scenes articles about the business of writing and publishing for the pulp magazines; *Ray Bradbury: The Life of Fiction* by Jonathan R. Eller and William F. Touponce (Kent State); a new, expanded edition of *Terry Pratchett: Guilty of Literature*, edited by Andrew M. Butler (Old Earth); *Speaking of the Fantastic II*, edited by Darrell Schweitzer (Wildside); in *A Blazing World* (MonkeyBrain) Jess Nevins continues his remarkable job of annotating Alan Moore and Kevin O'Neill's *The League of Extraordinary Gentlemen*; *Robert E. Howard: Power of the Writing Mind*, edited by Ben Szumskyi (Mythos Books) collects some writing by Howard and pieces about him; *Spectral America: Phantoms and the National Imagination* (University of Wisconsin Press) edited by Jeffrey Andrew Weinstock collects essays on North American ghosts from the last few centuries; David Willis McCullough's *The Unending Mystery: A Journey Through Labyrinths and Mazes* (Pantheon) is expansive but perhaps a little lacking in focus; a new edition of *The Sorcerer's Companion* (Broadway) by Allan Zola Kronzek and Elizabeth Kronzek will keep young Harry Potter fans happy.

Myth, Folklore, and Fairy Tales

See Maria Tatar and Jack Zipes in Favorite Books and Alex Irvine in Fantasy. Deborah Grabien's second mystery based on old English ballads is *The Famous Flower of Serving Men* (Minotaur); Sheldon Oberman's appropriately scary *Island of the Minotaur: Greek Myths of Ancient Crete* (Interlink) is illustrated by Blair Dawson; Joyce Carol Oates adapts folktales by Zora Neale Hurston in *What's the Hurry, Fox? and Other Animal Stories*, illustrated by Bryan Collier (HarperCollins); Tatiana Zunshine's retelling of a Russian tale, *A Little Story about a Big Turnip*, illustrated by Evgeny Antonenkov (Pumpkin). Dietrich Varez's *The Legend of La'ieikawai* (University of Hawaii Press) retells the legend of the separated-at-birth twins La'ieikawai and La'ielohelohe and their many adventures. *Pancha Tantra—Five Wise Lessons: A Vivid Retelling of India's Most Famous Collection of Fables* by Krishna Dharma (Torchlight). Editor Brian Swann gathered stories and songs from thirty-one Native American groups in *Voices from Four Directions: Contemporary Translations of the Native Literatures of North America* (Bison Books).

Awards

The Thirtieth World Fantasy Convention was held in Tempe, Arizona. Ellen Datlow, Gwyneth Jones, Janny Wurts, and Betty Ballantine were the guests of honor. The following awards were given out: Life Achievement: Stephen King and Gahan Wilson; Novel: *Tooth and Claw*, Jo Walton (Tor); Novella: "A Crowd of Bone," Greer Gilman (*Trampoline: An Anthology*); Short Story: "Don Ysidro," Bruce Holland Rogers (*Polyphony* 3); Anthology: *Strange Tales*, Rosalie Parker, editor (Tartarus); Collection: *Bibliomancy*, Elizabeth Hand (PS Publishing); Artist: Donato Giancola and Jason Van Hollander (tie); Special Award, Professional: Peter Crowther (for PS Publishing); Special Award, Nonprofessional: Ray Russell and Rosalie Parker (for Tartarus Press).

The James Tiptree, Jr. Memorial Award for genre fiction that expands or explores our understanding of gender was awarded to Matt Ruff for *Set This House in Order: A Romance of Souls* (HarperCollins). Ruff received the award at WisCon 28 in Madison, Wisconsin. The judges also provided an additional short list of works that they found interesting, relevant to the award, and worthy of note: "Knapsack Poems," Eleanor Arnason (*Asimov's*, May '02); "Boys," Carol Emshwiller (*SCI FICTION*); "Birth Days," Geoff Ryman (*Interzone*, April '03); "Lady of the Ice Garden," Kara Dalkey (*Firebirds*, Sharyn November, ed.); *Fudoki*, Kij Johnson (Tor); *Coyote Cowgirl*, Kim Antieau (Forge); *A Fistful of Sky*, Nina Kiriki Hoffman (Ace); "The Catgirl Manifesto," Richard Calder (as Christina Flook) (*Album Zutique #1*, Jeff VanderMeer, ed.); "Looking Through Lace," Ruth Nestvold (*Asimov's*, Sept. '03); "The Ghost Girls of Rumney Mill," Sandra McDonald (*Realms of Fantasy*, Aug '03); and *Maul*, Tricia Sullivan (Orbit). WisCon 28 guests of honor were Patricia A. McKillip and Eleanor Arnason.

The International Association for the Fantastic's William L. Crawford Fantasy Award went to K. J. Bishop for *The Etched City* (Prime) and the IAFA Distinguished Scholarship Award was given to Marcial Souto.

The Mythopoeic Award winners were announced during Mythcon 35, July 30–August 2, in Ann Arbor, Michigan: Adult Literature: *Sunshine*, Robin McKinley (Berkley); Children's Literature: *The Hollow Kingdom*, Clare B. Dunkle (Holt); Scholarship Award in Inklings Studies: *Tolkien and the Great War: The Threshold of Middle-earth*, John Garth (Houghton Mifflin); Scholarship Award in General Myth and Fantasy Studies: *The Myth of the American Superhero*, John Shelton Lawrence and Robert Jewett (Eerdmans).

The Science Fiction Poetry Association 2004 Rhysling Awards: Short Poem: "Just Distance," Roger Dutcher (*Tales of the Unanticipated*, July '03); Long Poem: "Octavia Is Lost in the Hall of Masks," Theodora Goss (*Mythic Delirium*, winter/spring '03).

The stories listed below are those that we were unable, for reasons of length, to reprint, but which were among our favorite stories of the year. Seek them out.

John Aegard, "The Golden Age of Fire Escapes," *Rabid Transit: Petting Zoo*
Richard Butner, "The Rules of Gambling," *Horses Blow Up Dog City*
A. S. Byatt, "The Pink Ribbon," *Little Black Book of Stories*
Suzy McKee Charnas, "Peregrines," *SCI FICTION*
Rebecca Curtis, "The Wolf at the Door," *StoryQuarterly* 40
Jeffrey Ford, "The Annals of Eelin-Ok," *The Faery Reel*
Randa Jarrar, "The Lunatics' Eclipse," *Ploughshares* 94
Jay Lake, "The Soul Bottles," *Leviathan 4*
Kevin McIlvoy, "Permission," *Harper's*
Patricia A. McKillip, "Out of the Woods," *Flights*
Benjamin Rosenbaum, "Biographical Notes to 'A Discourse on the Nature of Causality, with Air-Planes' by Benjamin Rosenbaum," *All-Star Zeppelin Adventure Stories*
Howard Waldrop, "The Wolf Man of Alcatraz" *SCI FICTION*
Gene Wolfe, "Golden City Far," *Flights*

We keep a small Web page for The Year's Best Fantasy & Horror at www.lcrw. net/yearsbest and we encourage e-mail recommendations of works for consideration in next year's volume. However, please check the Summation and Honorable Mentions list to see the types of material we are already reading. Thank you, and we hope you enjoy the following stories as much as we did.

—Kelly Link and Gavin J. Grant

Northampton, Massachusetts

Summation 2004: Horror

Ellen Datlow

Publishing News

There were no major upheavals in horror during 2004, although there were some changes in publishing that will surely have an impact on the field in the long run.

Two companies announced plans to create new television networks dedicated to horror, suspense, and thriller programming to the genre audience: Silver Pictures and Orchid Ventures teamed up to create Scream, and there was an announcement of The Horror Channel, a subsidiary of Terrorvision Television, LLC. As of the end of 2004, only The Horror Channel had a functioning Web site.

Lone Wolf Publications ceased operations. Owner Brian Hopkins stated, "Despite the fact that I think Lone Wolf offered the highest-quality multimedia titles since its inception in 1999, the sales figures just do not justify the continued investment of my time and energy. Clearly, the genre has little interest in electronic formats. It's not just Lone Wolf, as I've compared notes with other electronic publishers and have watched many electronic titles to which I've contributed sink quietly into oblivion."

On November 17, Monica O'Rourke, publisher of Medium Rare Books, advised its authors that it was dissolving all current contracts.

David Longhorn, editor of the U.K. magazine *Supernatural Tales*, announced that future issues would be published once a year as a small paperback anthology of about 150 pages beginning 2005.

Avalon Publishing Group acquired independent publisher Four Walls Eight Windows at the end of May, with Four Walls merging into Avalon under the Thunder's Mouth Press imprint. Four Walls publisher John Oakes was named publisher of Avalon imprints and the Thunder's Mouth Press imprint. The acquisition of Four Walls includes about two hundred books—the firm's backlist and frontlist as well as their unpublished inventory, all of which will be absorbed into the Thunder's Mouth list. A number of genre titles were published and will continue to be published by Oakes.

The newest incarnation of *Argosy*, published by James A. Owen and edited by Lou Anders, officially debuted with a January/February issue (although it was shown off at the 2003 World Fantasy Convention) and made a splash with its beautiful packaging, looking more like an anthology than a magazine. But just after its second issue shipped, Lou Anders resigned in order to devote full attention to his new duties as editorial director of Pyr, a new SF and fantasy imprint of Prometheus Books. Publisher James Owen asserted that issue number three (edited by Anders) was ready to go and most of number four was also ready. There was talk of distribution problems, and problems getting the magazine into bookstores with its format. But by November, Owen announced *Argosy* 3, renamed *Argosy Quarterly*, would be published in spring 2005. It would be designed and edited by Owen, and distributed by Publishers Group West.

Infrapress, an imprint of Writers.com Books, launched in November with their republication of Dennis Etchison's retrospective collection *Talking in the Dark* and Peter Atkins's novel *Morningstar*. Paula Guran is the publisher.

Paizo Publishing announced in early October that Jeff Berkwits would replace Dave Gross as editor in chief of *Amazing Stories* magazine. Berkwits left his position as senior writer at Wolfson Public Relations to take the helm. Previously he had worked as a freelance correspondent covering the music and entertainment industries for several publications. But in mid-December rumors were circulating on the Web that Paizo Publishing had ceased publication of *Amazing Stories*, which was first published in 1926 and was resurrected this year as a broad-based entertainment publication. Berkwits denied to Sci Fi Wire rumors that it has closed after starting back up in September, but admitted that the monthly magazine would take a break from publishing.

Effective January 1, 2005, the Ministry of Whimsy's association with Night Shade Books ends and the press will go on hiatus for the foreseeable future. Ministry of Whimsy and Night Shade had an amicable parting of the ways. Founder Jeff VanderMeer cited an inability to continue to juggle a day job, writing, publishing, and editing. VanderMeer will now focus his attention primarily on his own writing and on individual editing projects.

David Pringle, longtime editor and publisher of the U.K. science fiction magazine *Interzone*, stepped down after issue number 193 for familial and financial reasons. Andy Cox, publisher and editor of the magazines *The 3rd Alternative*, *Crimewave*, and *The Fix*, took over all the duties of running the magazine with issue 194, which came out in September. Cox plans to publish *Interzone* initially on a bimonthly schedule, with the possibility of returning to monthly at a future date.

Short fiction review zine *Tangent Online*'s managing editor Chris Markwyn announced that he would step down effective January 31, 2005, after having filled in for senior editor Dave Truesdale the past year. He cited increasing personal and professional needs that prevented him from devoting the time needed to run *Tangent*. By the end of the year the Web site was in the capable hands of Eugie Foster, who caught up with most of the reviews and by the New Year had it all running smoothly, with reviews being posted in a timely manner.

Sean Wallace's Prime Books, Inc., made a distribution and sales agreement with Wildside Press, which will assume marketing and back-office tasks for the critically acclaimed small press. Prime also became an imprint of Wildside Press. "This decision provides me with the opportunity and means to properly print, market, and distribute my authors," noted Wallace, who continued as senior editor at Prime Books.

Awards

The International Horror Guild Awards, now in their tenth year, recognize outstanding achievements in the field of horror and dark fantasy. The 2003 awards were presented at the World Horror Convention on Saturday, April 10, 2004, in Phoenix, Arizona.

Nominations were derived from recommendations made by the public and the judges' knowledge of the field. Edward Bryant, Stefan R. Dziemianowicz, Bill Sheehan, and Hank Wagner adjudicated the 2003 awards.

Recipients of the 2003 awards:

Novel: *lost boy lost girl* by Peter Straub (Random House); First Novel: *Jinn* by Matthew B. J. Delaney (St. Martin's Press); Collection: (tie) *The Two Sams: Ghost Stories* by Glen Hirshberg (Carroll & Graf) and *More Tomorrow and Other Stories* by Michael Marshall Smith (Earthling Publications); Anthology: *The Dark: New Ghost Stories*, edited by Ellen Datlow (Tor); Long Fiction: *Louisiana Breakdown* by Lucius Shepard (Golden Gryphon); Medium Fiction: "Dancing Men" by Glen Hirshberg (*The Dark*); Short Fiction: "With Acknowledgments to Sun Tzu" by Brian Hodge (*The 3rd Alternative* 33); Periodical: *All Hallows: The Journal of the Ghost Story Society* (The Ghost Story Society); Illustrated Narrative: *The Goon*, issues 1–4, words and art by Eric Powell (Dark Horse); Nonfiction: *The Devil in the White City: Murder, Magic, and Madness at the Fair That Changed America* by Erik Larson (Crown); Art: Caniglia. Film: *Spider*, directed by David Cronenberg, screenplay by Patrick McGrath, based on his novel; Television: *Carnivale*, created by Daniel Knauf (Home Box Office).

Honored as Living Legends were Stephen King and Everett F. Bleiler. IHG Living Legends are individuals who have made meritorious and notable contributions and/or have substantially influenced the field of horror/dark fantasy. Jack Cady was recognized posthumously with a special award.

The Bram Stoker Award weekend took place in New York City at the Park Central Hotel June 4–6 and the awards were given out Saturday evening, June 5, at a banquet. Winners for Superior Achievement are:

Novel: *lost boy lost girl* by Peter Straub; First Novel: *The Rising* by Brian Keene; Long Fiction: "Closing Time" by Jack Ketchum; Short Fiction: "Duty" by Gary A. Braunbeck; Fiction Collection: *Peaceable Kingdom* by Jack Ketchum; Anthology: *Borderlands 5* edited by Elizabeth and Thomas Monteleone; Nonfiction: *The Mothers and Fathers Italian Association* by Thomas F. Monteleone; Illustrated Narrative: *The Sandman: Endless Nights* (collection) by Neil Gaiman; Screenplay: *Bubba Ho-Tep* by Don Coscarelli; Work for Young Readers: *Harry Potter and the Order of the Phoenix* by J. K. Rowling; Poetry Collection: *Pitchblende* by Bruce Boston; Alternative Forms: *The Goreletter* (e-mail newsletter) by Michael Arnzen; Lifetime Achievement Award: Martin H. Greenberg and Anne Rice. The HWA Trustee Award (a.k.a. the Silver Hammer) was given to Robert Weinberg for service to the organization. Lee Thomas was given the Richard Laymon President's Award for Service. Paul Miller of Earthling Press won the Specialty Press Award.

The members of the Science Fiction Poetry Association have chosen the winners of the 2004 Rhysling Awards for achievement in speculative poetry. The membership voted on nominees in two categories: Short Poem (up to forty-nine lines long) and Long Poem (fifty lines and over). The winners are, in Short Poem category: First Place: "Just Distance" by Roger Dutcher (*Tales of the Unanticipated*, July 2003), Second Place: "'Observe the Month of Spring'" by Lucy Cohen Schmeidler (*The Magazine of Speculative Poetry*, spring 2003), Third Place (tie): "How I Will Outwit the Time Thieves" by Mike Allen (*Strange Horizons*, December 2003), "Nursery Ghosts" by Sandra Lindow (*Raven Electrick*, June 2003); Long Poem category: First Place: "Octavia Is Lost in the Hall of Masks" by Theodora Goss (*Mythic Delirium*, winter/spring 2003); Second Place: "A Portrait of the Artist" by Vandana Singh (*Strange Horizons*, July 2003); Third Place: "Hugo Schizophrenica" by Charlee Jacob (Miniature Sun Press broadside, 2003).

Notable Novels of 2004

Dead Lines by Greg Bear (Ballantine) is a terrific novel about a maker of porn films whose adolescent daughter was murdered by a serial killer a couple of years before the book opens. He is approached by a young, energetic businessman who is raising investment funds for a new type of phone called the trans. Unfortunately, this remarkable device does more than help the living to communicate more easily. There are some genuinely creepy bits.

Perfect Circle by Sean Stewart (Small Beer) is an absorbing story about a Texan loser paralyzed by his lifelong ability to see ghosts. William "Dead" Kennedy's wife left him soon after their child was born and Kennedy has spent the next twelve years haunted by dead relatives and refusing to grow up or take control of his life. But his complacency is about to be challenged when in desperation he agrees to meet a cousin and the cousin's ghost.

Iron Council by China Miéville (Del Rey/Ballantine) is about revolution and mythmaking. A rich industrialist dreams of building a great railroad to connect New Crobuzon to the rest of the land. The workers are made up of a motley of races, volunteers, and conscripts. The story took a while to get into this reader's bones the way *Perdido Street Station* and *The Scar* did, but it does build and there are dazzling moments of beautiful and shocking images.

Troll: A Love Story by Johanna Sinisalo, translated from the Finnish by Herbert Lomas (Grove), is a terrific story about a photographer who takes home a troll cub being abused by a gang of vicious teenagers. It's a quick read and has a lot of troll lore. Published in the U.K. in 2003 under the title *Not Before Sundown*. Co-winner of the James Tiptree, Jr. Award.

Move Under Ground by Nick Mamatas (Night Shade) is an excellent first novel that combines the beats of the '50s and their experiences on the road with the Cthulhu mythos. Imagine that the Elder Gods are taking over America, city by city, and only the alcoholic emotional wreck Jack Kerouac, his junkie friend Bill Burroughs, and Neal Casady stand between them and human annihilation. It's a crazy idea and it works by the sheer force of will and by the marvelous ability of Mamatas to capture the voices of the beat trio (with a guest appearance by Allen Ginsberg).

London Revenant by Conrad Williams (The Do-Not Press) is an absorbing and grim contemporary urban novel about two Londons: the one that narcoleptic Adam Buckley inhabits with friends who are becoming increasingly alienated from their city, and a mysterious underground one, where one of its denizens is pushing people riding the tube (subway) under trains.

Stevenson under the Palm Trees by Alberto Manguel (Canongate) is a brief, nicely dark fantasy blending bits of biography and fiction about Robert Louis Stevenson's final months on Samoa, where he encounters a missionary who preaches brimstone and hellfire against the natives and must face his own repressed desires, as a rash of violence breaks out.

The Arcanum by Thomas Wheeler (Bantam) is a first novel in the tradition of William Hjortsborg's *Nevermore* and Alan Moore's graphic novel *The League of Extraordinary Gentlemen*. A dangerous book has been stolen from the British Museum and Sir Arthur Conan Doyle enlists his colleagues Harry Houdini, H. P. Lovecraft, and Marie Laveau to save the world. Some nice touches.

Some Danger Involved by Will Thomas (Simon & Schuster Touchstone) is a richly detailed, entertaining debut, with two interesting characters: an inquiry agent and the young, desperate man he hires as an assistant. They are soon called upon to solve a brutal murder that may signal a rise in anti-Semitism in Victorian London.

Chasm: A Weekend by Dorothea Tanning (Overlook Press) is more a novella than a novel about an increasingly surreal weekend spent on an isolated ranch owned by an arrogant, sinister, and a controlling man.

Hell at the Breech by Tom Franklin (Morrow) an excellent dark western based on true events that took place in 1897 in rural southwestern Alabama. A group of men create a secret gang to avenge the death of a friend and terrorize the whole area. First novel by the author of the acclaimed collection *Poachers*.

A Carnivore's Inquiry by Sabina Murray (Grove) is about a monstrous young woman whose only interesting characteristic is an obsession with (and predilection for) cannibalism, apparently inherited from her crazy mother. The book picks up a bit about halfway through, but by then it's too late.

Mortal Love by Elizabeth Hand (Morrow) is a dark, sumptuously written novel about a dangerous woman who is muse to writers, artists, and musicians over two centuries. The book moves back and forth between time and between worlds and draws the reader into each one with ease.

Other Novels

Tartarus Press published new editions of long-out-of-print novels: *The Haunted Woman* by David Lindsay is a later novel than the author's better known *A Voyage to Arcturus*. Douglas A. Anderson wrote the Afterword. *Miss Hargreaves* by Frank Baker, first published in 1940, is a dark, funny, and moving fantasy about an imaginary acquaintance who comes to life. Glen Cavaliero introduces the novel and its author. *The Purple Cloud* by M. P. Shiel is about a man who, after becoming the first human to reach the North Pole, then survives the poisoning of the world by a mysterious purple cloud. This is a reprint of the novel's first 1901 edition, and it uses reproductions of illustrations from the original magazine serial. Brian Stableford wrote the introduction. *The Golem* by Gustav Meyrink, translated by Mike Mitchell, retells the sixteenth-century legend about Rabbi Lowe's creation. There are twenty-five illustrations by Hugo Steiner-Prag, eight from the original 1915 edition of the book and the rest from the artist's later portfolio. There is a new introduction by the translator.

Delirium Press published *Host*, a novel by Bryan Eytcheson about a parasite harbored in a mutilated pig's head. Jacket art is by Frank Forte. This book debuted the press's Exclusive series of extremely limited (maximum edition: one hundred copies) hardcover editions, only available by preorder within a limited-time reservation period. Delirium also published *Sleepwalker* by Michael Laimo, a novel about a man whose dreams and the waking world become confused. Cover art is by Alan M. Clark and the foil-stamp design is by Colleen Crary.

Night Shade Books published a beautiful new hardcover edition of M. John Harrison's marvelous dark fantasy *The Course of the Heart*, with evocative, mythologically inspired jacket art.

Cemetery Dance Publications published the following: a reissue of Ray Garton's erotic horror novel *The New Neighbor* in its first trade edition, with attractive new jacket art and effective interior illustrations by Caniglia; Jay Bonansinga's novel *Oblivion*, with jacket art by Alan M. Clark; Michael Slade's *Death Door*, with disturbing yet attractive cover art by Alan M. Clark; *Revenant Savior*, a short novel by Dominick Cancilla about various outside and inside forces that conspire to destroy a small town, with jacket art by J. K. Potter; *The Mountains of Madness* by Hugh B. Cave, an adventure tale of voodoo and greed that takes place on a Caribbean island, with jacket art by Keith Minnion; *Midnight Mass* by F. Paul Wilson, an expansion of his 1990 vampire novella. The limited edition has jacket and interior art by Harry O. Morris. There is also a trade edition published by Tor Books. All the dust jacket designs are by the talented Gail Cross.

Also Noted

Dust of Eden by Thomas Sullivan (Onyx), about a mysterious red dust stolen from its Middle East resting place; *Antwerp* by Nicholas Royle (Serpent's Tail), a dark crime novel; *The Boys Are Back in Town* by Christopher Golden (Bantam); *Rage* by Steve Gerlach (Leisure); *The Donor*, a medical thriller by Frank M. Robinson; *Through Violet Eyes*, a first novel by Stephen Woodworth (Dell) in which violet-eyed people can channel the dead; *Deep in the Darkness* by Michael Laimo (Flesh and Blood Press) in a limited edition, with cover art by Alan M. Clark, also published as a mass market by Leisure; *The Resort* by Bentley Little (Signet). Stephen King finished off his Dark Tower series with *The Dark Tower VI: Song of Susannah* and *The Dark Tower VII: The Dark Tower* (Donald M. Grant/Scribner). *Song of Susannah* has color illustrations by Darrel Anderson and *The Dark Tower* has color plates by Michael Whelan. Also, *Mirror Me* by Yvonne Navarro (Overlook Connection Press), a supernatural serial-killer novel; *Survivor* by J. F. Gonzalez (Midnight Library) which expands the author's novella "Maternal Instinct"; *The King of Ice Cream*, a first novel by Robert Wayne McCoy (Five Star), about fallen angels residing near a Kentucky college town; *Covenant*, John Everson's first novel (Delirium Press), about a former newsman searching for calm in a quiet coastal town and the truth he uncovers about the rash of teenage suicides; *Black Fire*, a first novel by James Kidman (Cemetery Dance Publications) about a young man who is haunted by an act of violence he committed years before the book begins; *The Lebo Coven* by Stephen Mark Rainey (Five Star), about the struggle between a satanist and those in a small town who oppose him; *Banquet for the Damned* by Adam L. G. Nevill (PS Publishing), about witchcraft and murder in contemporary Scotland; *Deep Blue* by David Niall Wilson (Five Star), about a man who longs to play the blues the way they were meant to be played; *Midnight Rain* by James Newman (Earthling Publications), a dark coming-of-age story that begins with the discovery of a murder, with illustrations by Alex McVey and Foreword by Ed Gorman, and also published in mass market by Leisure; *Murder of Angels* by Caitlín R. Kiernan, a sequel to her first novel, *Silk*, is about some of those same characters ten years on; *The Upright Man* (Jove) is Michael Marshall's sequel to his dark suspense novel *The Straw Men*; *Necropolis* by Tim Waggoner (Five Star), is about a zombie private eye whose beat is a city where vampires, werewolves, witches, and other dark folk dwell; *The Overnight* by Ramsey Campbell (PS Publishing), concerns what happens when a bookstore is opened in a business park. Mark Morris wrote the Introduction to the limited edition, with nicely eerie cover art by J. K. Potter — Tor published the trade edition in the U.S.; a new translation of *The Phantom of the Opera* by Gaston Leroux, adapted in English by Jean-Marc and Randy Lofficier (A Black Coat Press Book) with forty new black-and-white illustrations throughout; *The Soft Room* by Karen Heuler (Livingston Press); *Night Cage* by Andrew Harper (Leisure); *Missing Monday* by Matthew Costello (Berkley); *The Ghost Writer* by John Harwood (Harcourt) is about a boy growing up in an Australian town who, during many years of living with his mother, discovers ghost stories written by his mysterious great-grandmother; *The Midnight Band of Mercy* by Michael Blaine (Soho Press); *Borrowed Flesh* by Sèphera Girón (Leisure); *Blood Road* by Edo van Belkom (Pinnacle). *The Reckoning* by Jeff Long (Atria); *In the Night Room* by Peter Straub (Random House), related to his novel *lost boy lost girl*; *The Nebuly Coat* by John Meade Falkner (Ash-Tree Press), a mystery novel first published in 1903, with Introduction by Mark Valentine, and jacket painting by Paul Lowe; *House of Blood* by Bryan Smith (Leisure); *Scarab* by Don D'Ammassa (Five Star); *Bride of the Fat White Vampire* by Andrew Fox (Ballantine); *The Tolltaker* by James Sneddon (Five Star); *The Hidden* by Sarah Pinborough (Leisure); *Eye for an Eye* by Joel Ross (Leisure); *The Book of Dead Days* by Marcus Sedgwick (Wendy Lamb Books/Random); *A Handbook of American Prayer* by Lucius Shepard (Thunder's Mouth Press); *Family Inheritance* by Deborah LeBlanc (Leisure); *Messenger* by Edward Lee (Leisure). Charnel House published *The Taking* and *Life Expectancy*, two new Dean Koontz novels in expensive limited editions; *Hallows Eve* by Al Sarrantonio (Leisure); *The Devil in Gray* by Graham Masterton (Leisure); *A Boy* by Jonathan Trigell (Serpent's Tail); *Dime Store Magic* and *Industrial Magic* by Kelley Armstrong (Bantam); *In This Skin* by Simon Clark (Leisure); *Possessions* by James A. Moore (Leisure); *Sleep* by Kat Meads (Livingston Press); *Body Parts* by Vicki Stiefel (Leisure); *The Secret* by Eva Hoffman (Ballantine); *The Hunted* and *The Awakening* by L. A. Banks (St. Martin's); *In Silent Graves* by Gary A. Braunbeck (Leisure); *The Lake* by Richard Laymon (Leisure hardcover); *Kings of Infinite Space* by James Hynes (St. Martin's); *Stained* by Lee Thomas (Dominion), a supernatural murder mystery that marks a notable debut; *The Quick* by Dan Vining (Jove); *Incubus Dreams* by Laurell K. Hamilton (Berkley); *Black Creek Crossing* by John Saul (Ballantine); *Criss Cross*, a new Repairman Jack novel by F. Paul Wilson (Forge); *Face of Death*, a Civil War vampire story by Chelsea Quinn Yarbro (Hidden Knowledge e-book); *The Journal of Professor Abraham Van Helsing* by Allen C. Kupfer (Forge); *Dark Corner* by Brandon Massey (Da Fina); *Trouble in the Forest, Book 2 — A Bright Winter Sun* by Trystam Kith (Fire Star); and *Wind Caller*, a Native American novel by P. D. Cacek (Dorchester).

2004 was another surprisingly strong year for the horror short story, and again, I could have taken twice the wordage I was allowed and been quite happy. However, there were also more mediocre or just plain bad anthologies published mostly by the micropresses that keep sprouting up like mushrooms and then dropping out of sight after a year or two.

Anthologies

Gothic! Ten Original Dark Tales, edited by Deborah Noyes (Candlewick), is aimed at young adults, but some of the stories will also appeal to adults. Contributors include Neil Gaiman, Gregory Maguire, Caitlín R. Kiernan, Joan Aiken, Garth Nix, and five others.

The Many Faces of Van Helsing, edited by Jeanne Cavelos (Ace) was timed to be released simultaneously with the movie *Van Helsing*. The twenty-one stories are all readable, but the most interesting are those by Brian Hodge, Tanith Lee, Steve Rasnic Tem and Melanie Tem, and an SF tale by A. M. Dellamonica.

The Mammoth Book of Vampires, edited by Stephen Jones (Carroll & Graf) is a reprint anthology originally published in 1992, but has three new stories, one of which, by Tina Rath, is reprinted herein.

The Mammoth Book of New Terror, edited by Stephen Jones (Robinson, U.K.), is a follow-up to Jones's 1991 volume *The Mammoth Book of Terror*. Most of the excellent stories are reprints, but a few, such as those by Graham Masterton, Christopher Fowler, Brian Mooney, David J. Schow, and a collaboration by Tanith Lee and John Kaiine, are published for the first time.

A Walk on the Darkside: Visions of Horror, edited by John Pelan (Roc), is a solid, all-original anthology with twenty-one stories by a strong roster of writers including Steve Rasnic Tem, Michael Shea, Brian Hodge, Mehitobel Wilson, Caitlín R. Kiernan, and others.

Dark Dreams, edited by Brandon Massey (Kensington/Dafina Books), is an uneven all-original anthology of horror and suspense stories by black writers. The strongest stories are by Joy M. Copeland, Robert Fleming, D. S. Fox, Terence Taylor, and a collaboration by Steven Barnes and Tananarive Due.

Dark Thirst, edited by Angela C. Allen (Pocket Books), has six vampire novelettes, all by black writers, most pretty standard fare. The best is by Kevin S. Brockenbrough.

Quietly Now: An Anthology in Tribute to Charles L. Grant, edited by Kealan Patrick Burke (Borderlands Press), is a limited-edition book honoring the chronically ill Charles L. Grant for his contribution to the subgenre of "quiet" horror. Most of the stories are original, and some of those are very good, particularly those by P. D. Cacek, Steve Rasnic Tem, Scott Edelman, Chet Williamson, Paul Finch, Kathryn Ptacek, David B. Silva, and Kim Newman. There are also tributes to Grant, an interview with him, and a bibliography.

Damned: An Anthology of the Lost, edited by David G. Barnett (Necro Publications), is a good themed anthology on the subject of heaven and hell, consisting of eleven stories and one short novel by a varied group of writers including Jack Ketchum, Brian Hodge, Gary Braunbeck, Tom Piccirilli, Charlee Jacob, and others.

The Last Pentacle of the Sun: Writings in Support of the West Memphis 3 (Arsenal Pulp Press) is a mixed reprint/original charity anthology edited by M. W. Anderson and Brett Alexander Savory to raise money for three teenage Goths found guilty of murdering three young boys, on spurious evidence. The book has very good fiction and interesting nonfiction about murders and miscarriages of justice. The interior black-and-white illustrations are by Clive Barker.

Tales from a Gas-Lit Graveyard, edited by Hugh Lamb (Dover), is the first North American publication of an anthology originally published in the U.K. in 1979.

Tales From the Gorezone, edited by Kealan Patrick Burke (Apartment 42 Productions), is an all-original (but one), nontheme charity anthology, with 100 percent of the net profits going to PROTECT, an organization that helps abused children. There are some very good stories by writers such as Chesya Burke, Mike E. Purfield, Harry Shannon, Chad L. Smith, and others. The cover art is by Deena Holland Warner. Introduction by Mark Sieber, and foreword by Brian Keene.

The Parasitorium, edited by Del Stone Jr. (Cyber-Pulp), is named after the Yahoo writing group to which the contributors belong. The fifteen stories are all original except for the titular story by the editor. The best are by Richard A. Bamberg, Charles A. Gramlich, and Ryan Michael Thompson.

Cloaked in Shadow: Dark Tales of Elves, edited by W. H. Horner (Fantasist Enterprises), has noteworthy stories by Gerard Houarner, Erin Mackay, and a few other contributors but on the whole there isn't enough meat to most of the plots.

Strange Bedfellows: The Hot Blood Series, edited by Jeff Gelb and Michael Garrett (Kensington), is the twelfth volume of erotic horror in the series. As usual, there are only a handful of stories that are more than a sexual gotcha. The best are by Greg Kihn, Ilsa J. Bick, Christa Faust, Graham Masterton, Stephen Gresham, and Marv Wolfman.

Haunted Holidays, edited by Martin H. Greenberg and Russell Davis (DAW), is a lightweight original anthology of mostly supernatural ghost stories taking place around holidays. Notable contributions by Peter Crowther (not horrific though) and Brian A. Hopkins.

Peep Show, volume 1, edited by Paul Fry (Short, Scary Tales Publications) has twenty original sexual horror stories. Cover art is by Caniglia.

The Book of Monsters, edited by C. Dennis Moore (Scrybe Press), has ten original stories about different kinds of monsters.

Small Bites, edited by Garrett Peck and Keith Gouveia (Coscom), is a book of almost two hundred short-short stories of cannibalism, with the proceeds going to Charles L. Grant's medical fund.

The Dead Walk!, edited by Vincent Sneed (Die Monster Die! Books), is a zombie anthology with illustrations by Jason Whitley and zombie stories by Robert M. Price, Brian Keene, C. J. Henderson, and others.

Spooks!, edited by Tina L. Jens and John Everson (Twilight Tales), is a mixed reprint and original ghost story anthology with stories and poems. There were good original stories by Tina L. Jens, Bruce Hoff, and Lisa Mannetti. The cover art and design is by John Everson.

Eldritch Blue: Love & Sex in the Cthulhu Mythos, edited by Kevin O'Brien (Lindesfarne Press), has twenty erotic Lovecraftian stories, about half original. Lovecraft is probably turning in his grave but fans should enjoy at least some of the stories. Introduction by Robert M. Price.

Delirium Books published two anthologies: *New Dark Voices*, edited by Shane Ryan Staley, presents original novellas by Michael Oliveri, Gene O'Neil, and John Urbancik. This is the first in a series intended to showcase the work by newer horror writers. Brian Keene has written the introduction and Shane Ryan Staley wrote the afterword. The jacket art is by the ever-imaginative Mike Bohatch. Also, *Deathrealms: Selected Tales from the Land Where Horror Dwells*, edited by Stephen Mark Rainey, features a sampling of fiction from a decade (thirty-one issues) of the late, respected magazine. The fifteen stories include work by Elizabeth Massie, Wayne Allen Sallee, Jeff VanderMeer, Jeffrey Thomas, and others.

Maelstrom, Volume 1, edited by Paul Calvin Wilson (Calvin House), is an anthology of thirty-four horror and dark crime stories, the best by R. J. Sevin, John Rector, Gary McMahon, and Gary Fry. This trade paperback has cover art by Allen Koszowski.

Carnival Circus, edited by Jean Rabe (Lone Wolf Publications CD-ROM), is a double disk of original stories by Lee Thomas, Paul G. Tremblay, John Urbancik, Patrick Lestewka, Robert E. Vardeman, James S. Dorr, and a host of others. It features the artwork of M. W. Anderson and music by John Everson.

Night Visions 11, edited by Bill Sheehan (Subterranean Press), is a worthy successor to previous volumes in the series (originally begun by Dark Harvest and taken over by Subterranean with volume ten in 2001). This volume contains a Richard Jepperson novella by Kim Newman, with a villain dubbed Swellhead. Tim Lebbon's dark novella is about a collector of rarities who blackmails mortals to add to his collection by holding their loved ones hostage. And Lucius Shepard writes about sex, crime, and violence as an ex-con hooks up with a mysterious trio in the Florida backwoods.

Great Ghost Stories, selected by R. Chetwynd-Hayes and Stephen Jones (Carroll & Graf), has twenty-five stories chosen from the *Fontana Book of Great Ghost Stories* series, edited from 1972 to 1984 by Chetwynd-Hayes.

The Ash-Tree Press Annual Macabre 2004: The Last "Queer Stories from Truth," edited by Jack Adrian, presents thirty-one short, sharp shocks originally published in the weekly U.K. magazine over a forty-year period, from the 1880s through the early 1950s.

Best New Horror 15, edited by Stephen Jones (Robinson), has twenty-six horror stories and one novella. The book overlapped with *YBFH: Seventeenth Annual Collection* with five stories. Jones also provides a summary of the year and a necrology.

Mixed-Genre Anthologies

The Urban Bizarre, edited by Nick Mamatas (Prime Books), is an odd mix of freaky stories about urban life. A few are dark; most are entertaining. Good stories by Ian Grey, Michael Hemmingson, Jeff Somers, and Ann Sterzinge. *Dark Matter: Reading the Bones*, edited by Sheree R. Thomas (Warner), follows up the World Fantasy Award–winning anthology of original and reprinted speculative fiction by black writers. This volume has some very good dark stories by Pam Noles, Cherene Sherrard, and Ibi Aanu Zoboi. *Agog! Smashing Stories*, edited by Cat Sparks (Agog! Press), is the third in a series that is becoming known for the reliability of its quality. There are some excellent darker stories by Simon Brown, Deborah Biancotti, Paul Haines, Richard Harland, Justine Larbalestier, Robert Hood, Martin Livings, and Ben Peek. It's got a witty cover design by the editor. The Simon Brown is reprinted herein. *Flights: Extreme Visions of Fantasy*, edited by Al Sarrantonio (Roc), has some very good dark stories, although none of the stories in the book are "extreme" in any way, shape, or form. My favorite dark tales were those by Tim Powers and Joyce Carol Oates. *McSweeney's Enchanted Chamber of Astonishing Stories*, edited by Michael Chabon (Vintage), is an interesting mix of original genre and mainstream stories. Unfortunately, not enough of the stories are in fact "astonishing" although there *is* an utterly charming London fantasy by China Miéville (picked by my coeditors for their half of this anthology). The best of the darker stories are by Stephen King, Peter Straub, and Joyce Carol Oates. The Straub is reprinted herein. *Crossroads: Tales of Southern Literary Fantasy*, edited by F. Brett Cox and Andy Duncan (Tor), is a mixture of fantasy and dark fantasy, reprints and originals. The three best darker originals are by Richard Butner, F. Brett Cox, and Kalamu Ya Salaam. *The Locus Awards: Thirty Years of the Best in Science Fiction and Fantasy*, edited by Charles N. Brown and Jonathan Strahan (Eos), gives a taste of the field's evolution with eighteen stories, novelettes, and novellas culled from the thirty years that *Locus* magazine has been providing its readers a forum in which to vote for their favorite stories of the year. Most of the stories are SF, although there is a bit of darkness throughout. *Encounters*, edited by Maxine McArthur and Donna Maree Hanson (CSFG Publishing, Australia), is the third in a series of original mixed-genre anthologies produced by the Canberra Science Fiction Guild and it's got good dark stories by Richard Harland, Ben Payne, Gillian Polack, Nigel Read, and Michael Barry. The attractive cover art is by Les Peterson. *Salome and Other Decadent Fantasies*, edited by Brian Stableford (Cosmos), has eleven stories, all originally published between 1992 and 2000. With an introduction by Stableford about the decadent movement of literature. *Powers of Detection: Stories of Mystery and Fantasy*, edited by Dana Stabenow (Ace), has dark stories by Michael Armstrong, John Straley, and Anne Bishop. *Punktown: Third Eye*, edited by Jeffrey Thomas (Prime), is an interesting bunch of original stories written about the editor's nightmarish creation, first introduced in his collection *Punktown*. The best stories are by the editor himself and by his brother Scott Thomas. The good-looking cover art is by Travis Anthony Soumis. *The Alsiso Project*, edited by Andrew Hook (Elastic Press), is an intriguing idea that works rather well. Using a typographical error made by writer Marion Arnott, twenty-three contributors created stories using a nonexistent word: alsiso. *Sick: An Anthology of Illness*, edited by John Edward Lawson (Raw Dog Screaming Press), is a mixed original and reprint anthology of stories about sickness that came out late in 2003. Included are stories by Jeffrey Thomas, Jack Fisher, Mark McLaughlin, Greg Beatty, Michael A. Arnzen, and Scott Thomas. *Shades of Black*, edited by Eleanor Taylor Bland (Berkley), is a terrific anthology of original crime and mystery stories by Black writers with a reprint by Walter Mosley. *Leviathan 4: Cities*, edited by Forrest Aguirre (Ministry of Whimsy Press), has ten stories of SF, fantasy, and dark fantasy. Jay Lake's story is particularly good and dark. The cover art is by Myrtle Vondamitz III and cover design is by Jonathan Edwards. *Scattered Covered Smothered: An Anthology of Food and Fiction*, edited by Jason Erik Lundberg (Two Cranes Press), is a clever oddity of stories and poems, some of them including recipes and some of them dark. Some of the better-known contributors are Nalo Hopkinson, Christopher Rowe, Jeff VanderMeer, D. F. Lewis, Bruce Boston, and Rhys Hughes. The amusing cover art is by Janet Chui. *Writers of the Future*, volume XX, edited by Algis Budrys (Galaxy Press), always has a good mix of science fiction, fantasy, and horror.

The artists who work in the small press toil hard and receive too little credit, and it's important to recognize their good work. The following artists created art that I thought noteworthy during 2004:

Karen Tristao, Paul Lowe, Douglas Walters, Russell Dickerson, A. R. Menne, Denis Tiani, Allen Koszowski, Oliver James Crowther, Edward Noon, Chris Nurse, Dennis Sibeijn, Chad Michael Ward, D. Canada, Phil Wrigglesworth, Vincent Chong, Julia Morgan-Scott, Alex McVey, John Myroshnychenko, Rob Suggs, Nick Maloret, Robert Dunn, Michael J. King, James Ordolis, Richard Marchand, Stephen Fabian, Jill Bauman, Maral Agnerian, Hugo Martin, Dallas Goffin, R&D Studios, Kerri Valkova, Cat Sparks, Adam Duncan, Les Petersen, Bernie Wrightson, Travis Anthony Soumis, Ben Baldwin, Mike Bohatch, Bob Libby, Keith Minion, Chad Savage, Jesse Young, Caniglia, Dennis Calero, Augie Wiedemann, H. E. Fassl, Keith Boulger, Tom Simonton, Bob Hobbs, Teresa Tunaley, Eric Turnmire, David Kendall, Brian Smith, Renee Dillon, Shaun Tan, Claire McKenna, Brian Horton, Josh Finney, Krzysztof Biernacki, Jason Van Hollander, Dion Hamill, Tom Kelly, Emily Percy, Cathy Buburuz, Dave Senecal, Bob Bryson, Craig Mrusek, Kirk Alberts, Lauren Halkon, Carole Carmen, Ken Usanami, Bruce Carter, Randy Russo, Andrea Wicklund, Michael Gibbs, Sandra Scholes, and Jorge Hausmann.

Magazines and Newsletters

Small-press magazines come and go with amazing rapidity so it's difficult to recommend buying a subscription to those that haven't proven their longevity. But I urge readers to at least buy single issues of those that sound interesting. The following are those I thought the best in 2004.

Some of the most important magazines/Web zines are those specializing in news of the field, market reports, and reviews. *Hellnotes*, the e-mail and print newsletter, edited by Judi Rohrig, is indispensable for overall information, news, and reviews of the horror field. It also runs interviews and has a weekly best-seller list. *The Gila Queen's Guide to Markets*, edited by Kathryn Ptacek, was on hiatus for nine months because of personal difficulties but managed to get one big e-mail newsletter out before the end of the year. Ptacek hopes to get back onto a regular schedule in 2005. The guide is an excellent font of information for markets in and outside the horror field. Ralan.com is *the* Web site to go to for up-to-date market information. Paula Guran's knowledgeable and interesting *Darkecho* is currently being sent out as an irregular e-mail newsletter. The only major venues specializing in reviewing short fiction are *The Fix*, *Tangent Online* (www.tangentonline.com), *The Internet Review of Science Fiction* (www.irosf.com/), *Locus* and Locus online (www.locusmag.com), but none of them specialize in horror.

Most magazines have Web sites with subscription information, eliminating the need to include it here. For those magazines that do *not* have a Web site, I have provided that information:

Video Watchdog,® edited by Tim Lucas, is going strong as it hit its hundredth issue in the middle of 2003. It's got to be the most exuberant film magazine around, and seems especially gleeful when its reviewers discover variant versions of videos and DVDs. The magazine is invaluable for the connoisseur of trashy, pulp, and horror movies and enjoyable for just about everyone.

Rue Morgue, edited by Rod Gudino, is an entertaining bimonthly that is graphic in its coverage of horror and mayhem. Although it focuses on movies and video, there *is* a regular book column. In 2004 there was a brief but insightful discussion with filmmaker Douglas Buck, who in 1997 made the chilling and unforgettable twenty-three minute film, *Cutting Moments*. His movies *Home* and *Prologue*, along with *Cutting Moments*, make up *Family Portraits: A Trilogy of America*. Also, a profile of Mark Ryden, whose fantasy paintings portray Keene-eyed innocents with bloody tears and wounds. An article and interview with David Cronenberg about his "Cinema of Science and Disease" and an interview with Clive Barker updating readers on his forthcoming return to the horror fold after a detour into fantasy. The magazine also ran brief profiles/interviews with Jack Ketchum and Brian Keene.

Scarlet Street, edited by Richard Valley, is more restrained than *Rue Morgue*, and covers older rather than contemporary horror and other B-movie genres. In 2004 it showcased an excerpt from David J. Skal's revised and updated Dracula chronicle *Hollywood Gothic*, a two-part article about the character Van Helsing's appearance in various movies, and "Attack of the Horror Hags, Part Two," Ken Hanke's major article about big-name actresses who ended their careers by playing nasty, evil characters and/or crazies in '60s horror movies. It also has DVD and book reviews.

Wormwood: Literature of the Fantastic, Supernatural and Decadent, edited by Mark Valentine, is an excellent, accessible critical journal. In 2004, two issues came out, rich in articles about Mervyn Peake's Lonely World, "John Wyndham and the Fantastic," "The Dark Houses of Cornell Woolrich," Oliver Onions, "The Godwin Family," and other articles and reviews. Contributors include Glen Cavaliero, Brian Aldiss, Joel Lane, Andy Sawyer, Brian Stableford, and others.

Studies in Modern Horror: A Scholarly Journal of Contemporary Weird Fiction, edited by NGChristakos (sic), published two issues in 2004. Issue two held a symposium, with five writers discussing who were/are the most important influences on contemporary horror fiction. There was an article by the editor (continued in issue three) on Miéville's *The Scar*, and essays by Steffen Hantke and Nick Curtis. Issue three completed the editor's article on *The Scar*, had pieces by Dr. Robert Waugh and Drew Williams, and also had an annotated fiction reprint. The journal is meant to come out quarterly, but only two issues were published in 2004.

Necropsy: The Review of Horror Fiction, edited by June Pulliam is a Web site with new issues up every few months. The sometimes uneven reviews are mostly of horror literature and also occasionally take on movies. The best reviews are smart, coherent, and analytical, the worst are wrongheaded.

Weirdly Supernatural: Journal of the Bizarre, edited by Christopher Barker, is an excellent little magazine that launched with one issue in 2002 and one in 2004. Issue two has five original stories, a reprint by Joan Aiken, several essays, plus book and movie reviews. The cover art (from the chilling Reggie Oliver story) is by the author.

Argosy, the classic U.S. pulp magazine published (under various titles) from 1882 through 1943, has been revived by Coppervale International under publisher James A. Owen. The first and second issues, edited by Lou Anders, had excellent original dark fiction by Jeffrey Ford, Caitlín R. Kiernan, Emily Raboteau, and Ann Cummins. The Ford is reprinted herein. Leo and Diane Dillon's art is on the first cover, and the interior illustrations are by Steve Rude. The trade paperback–sized magazine and a separately bound novella are packaged in an illustrated slipcase. The second issue came out in October and is as impressive as the first in looks, although there are fewer stories that I'd judge horrific. The colorful interior illustrations are by

Dr. Seuss, and there is also old advertising and other interesting ephemera through-out. A pair of stories by Charles Stross and Cory Doctorow (one previously pub-lished) make up the separate booklet-sized novel. The cover illustration is by Gregory Manchess. Anders left the magazine after the second issue came out but the stories for the next issue were bought by him.

Postscripts, edited by Peter Crowther, published its first two issues in 2004 and it had enough dark fiction to attract horror readers. In addition to new horror stories by Joyce Carol Oates, Ramsey Campbell, and Stephen Gallagher, there are weird, unclassifiable stories by Rhys Hughes, Jeff VanderMeer, and Zoran Zivkovic. Christopher Fowler supplies an introductory essay adapted from his Guest of Honor speech given at the British Fantasy Society's annual convention in 2003. There are a few nonfiction pieces, and interviews with James P. Blaylock and Kage Baker. This is a magazine to watch. The Gallagher and Oates stories are reprinted herein.

Not One of Us, edited by John Benson, brought out two good issues in '04. Not all of the stories are dark but they're at the very least strange, and most of them are well worth reading. Some of the best are by Sonya Taaffe, Mark Steensland, Danny Adams, Marc Lecard, and Patricia Russo. Also, *Subnatural*, Benson's annual one-off, had good mixed-genre work.

Supernatural Tales, edited by David Longhorn, continued its impressive run with two issues in 2004. There were excellent stories by Christopher Harmon, Adam Go-laski, Jane Jakeman, D. Siddall, Joel Lane, Iain Rowan, and Geoffrey Warburton, and good ones by other contributors. Beginning in 2005, the magazine moves to an-nual publication as an anthology.

Inhuman, edited and illustrated by artist Allen Koszowski, is a fun throwback to an earlier era in its concentration on monster stories. There were good stories in the first issue by Paul W. Finch and Jeffrey Thomas, and suitable artwork by the editor.

Black October, edited by Joe DiDomenico, looks good and ran some good horror stories in its two 2004 issues. The best stories were by John Everson, Richard D. We-ber, Lou Kemp, Bill Mingin, and Chris Roberson. The art of Mike Bohatch was fea-tured in issue six. There were interviews with Thomas F. Monteleone and Poppy Z. Brite, and essays on the beginning of science fiction and on the evolution of vam-pire fiction.

Weird Tales, edited by George H. Scithers and Darrell Schweitzer, is over eighty years old, and is a mix of heroic fantasy, dark fantasy, and the occasional horror story. In addition to fiction, the magazine runs book reviews and interviews (one with Terry Pratchett). There were good dark stories by Ian Watson, Melinda Thielbar, and some good, lighter stories by Tanith Lee, Barbara Krasnoff, and collaborators Batya Swift Yasgur and Barry N. Malzberg. There were good-looking covers by Rowena Morrill, Tom Kidd, and Marianne Plumridge. *Weird Tales* has a new sister magazine, *Weird Trails: The Magazine of Supernatural Cowboy Stories*, edited by George H. Scithers and Darrell Schweitzer, with a lot of fun stories. Designed to look like the old pulps, with old advertising about, for example, using yeast as a pim-ple cure, a telegraph set, and just what the world needs now—an auto scare bomb! Anyway, the concept works remarkably well and should be a big hit with readers looking for that old-time kind of story. Some of the contributors are P. D. Cacek, Gregory Frost, Ron Goulart, and Mike Resnick.

John Betancourt's Wildside Press has been busy creating a stable of new magazines including the above-mentioned *Weird Trails*. *H. P. Lovecraft's Magazine of Horror*, edited by Marvin Kaye, officially debuted in 2004 although advance copies were out in the fall of 2003. The first issue's fiction, most of which was assembled by publisher John Betancourt and editors Darrell Schweitzer and George Scithers, is virtually indistinguishable from (although heftier than) *Weird Tales*—with the same authors and mostly the same artists (although there's a fine Bob Eggleton cover on the first issue). One hopes that editor Marvin Kaye will take the magazine into darker realms as promised and provide it with a different voice from its sister magazine. The second issue came out in the fall and had five stories, one less than half a page long.

Wildside also published facsimiles of some of the more popular pulp magazines of the 1930s. It brought out *Spicy Mystery Stories, February 1937, Ghost Stories, June 1931*, edited by Harold Hersey, and *Strange Tales of Mystery and Terror, issue 7*, edited by Harry Bates. Also, an updated version of *Strange Tales of Mystery and Terror*, edited by Robert M. Price, came out with attractive cover art by Jason Van Hollander, seven original stories, and a reprint. The glossy perfect-bound cover look complements the two-column interior text. Also published was *Adventure Tales, #1*, edited by John Betancourt, with eleven stories, most originally published in the pulp era, and a new interview with Hugh B. Cave.

Cemetery Dance, edited by Robert Morrish, had a good year, with four issues out in 2004. In addition to regular columns by Thomas F. Monteleone and Bev Vincent, interviews with small-press publishers and with horror writers such as Stewart O'Nan, David B. Silva, Elizabeth Massie, and others, there were excellent new stories by James Ireland Baker, Sherry Decker, Glen Hirshberg, J. A. Konrath, Tony Richard, David B. Silva, Bentley Little, and Jack Slay Jr., and a very good poem by Ray Bradbury.

Midnight Street, edited by Trevor Denyer, is a British magazine that mutated from the editor's earlier magazine, *Roadworks*. *Midnight Street* specializes in dark, mixed-genre stories and showed promise in its first year of publication, with good stories by Joel Lane, Antony Mann, Andrew Humphrey, Peter Tennant, David Penn, and Lisa Tate.

Underworlds, edited by Sean Wallace and William P. Simmons, had a rocky start when its original editor was replaced after the first issue, published in early 2003. The second issue was edited by publisher Sean Wallace. The February issue had a suitably appropriate dark and slick-looking cover and the interiors are designed for readability. The fiction was uneven although there were notable original stories by Darren Speegle, David Ireland, and Paul Bates, and a very good poem by C. S. Thompson.

Terror Tales, issue 2, edited by John B. Ford and Paul Kane (Rainfall Books), is a trade-paperback magazine that looks more like an anthology but has fiction, an interview with Paul Miller of Earthling Books, and several book and movie reviews. There are some very good original stories by Paul Finch, Lisa Negus, and Jeffrey Thomas.

Horror Garage, edited by Rich Black, published one issue in 2004. There were three original stories, none particularly interesting, but two good reprints by Norman Partridge and Brian Keene. Also, along with the usual rock 'n' roll columns, there was an interview with Dennis Etchison plus book and movie columns by

Hank Wagner and Norman Partridge, respectively. The magazine now has a Web site that features a regular original column by Mark McLaughlin plus reprints from earlier issues of the print zine.

Albedo One, edited by John Kenny, Bob Neilson, David Murphy, and Roelof Goudriaan, has a new look for issue twenty-eight and a full-color cover. Celebrating its tenth year of publication, this Irish magazine, which publishes science fiction and horror, has some very good dark fiction plus an interview with Ken Macleod. Philip Raines and Harvey Welles's story is reprinted herein.

Flesh and Blood, edited by Jack Fisher, published two issues in 2004. The cover art has been improving with each issue but the washed-out-looking fantasy art on issue number fourteen just seemed wrong. Justin Maylone's art for number fifteen was nicely, subtly horrific. Along with the poetry and fiction, there was a publisher's spotlight on PS Publishing, articles by Darrell Schweitzer on vanity publication and small-press publications, book reviews, and an interview with China Miéville. There were good stories by K. D. Wentworth, Douglas Clegg, Gerard Houarner, and Holly Phillips and notable poems by Marge Simon and Bruce Boston.

Bare Bone, edited by Kevin Donihe (Raw Dog Screaming Press), started as a magazine but now looks more like an anthology with its perfect-bound design. The best stories and poems in number six, the one issue published in 2004, were by Tim Emswiler, Gene O'Neill, Daniel C. Smith, and Andrew Humphrey.

All Hallows: The Journal of the Ghost Story Society, edited by Barbara and Christopher Roden, is an attractive perfect-bound magazine published in February, June, and October. As it's only available to members of the Ghost Story Society, this is another good reason to join the organization dedicated to providing admirers of the classic ghost story with an outlet for their interest. *All Hallows* is an excellent source of news, articles, and ghostly fiction. For more information on how to join visit the Ash-Tree Press Web site. Address provided at the end of the summary. During 2004 there were very good stories by Tina Rath, Aaron Albrecht, Michael Dirda, Paul Finch, David McVey, David Mills, Sarah Monette, Anthony Oldknow, Iain Rowen, Paul J. Shaw, J. J. Travis, Don Tumasonis, and David Williams.

Book of Dark Wisdom, edited by William Jones, is a nice-looking magazine specializing in Lovecraftian horror. Most of the stories in the two 2004 issues were silly—almost parodies of Lovecraft rather than homage.

For pulp lovers, try *Lovercraft's Weird Mysteries*, edited by John Navroth, where you'll find reprints and originals, reproduced ads for shrunken heads, spicy photographs and cover art poorly reproduced (intentionally or not, it's hard to tell).

Mixed-Genre Magazines

Many of the best of the current crop of magazines, zines, and Web sites that publish horror are not strictly horror magazines. Over the past several years *The Magazine of Fantasy and Science Fiction*, *The 3rd Alternative*, *Interzone*, *Crimewave*, and others have done a marvelous job of mixing dark and light, SF and fantasy and horror.

The 3rd Alternative, edited by Andy Cox, has always used excellent artists inside the magazine and on its covers. This trend has continued in 2004 with gorgeous covers by Dennis Sibeijn on the spring and summer issues. The art on the autumn issue was by Richard Marchand, and Vincent Chong's art was on the winter issue.

Liz Williams, Paula Guran, and Nicholas Royle wrote guest editorials. Guran's was about horror and the announced movement in that direction by Andy Cox. There was very good dark fiction by Graham Joyce, Joel Lane, Daniel Kaysen, Joe Hill, Paul Meloy, Steve Mohn, David J. Schwartz, Melanie Fazi, Mike O'Driscoll, and Jeremy Minton and less horrific but no less high quality by John Grant, Al Robertson, Damien Kilby, Eugie Foster, and others. Melanie Fazi's story is reprinted herein. Christopher Fowler contributed his last film column for the magazine, and screenwriter Steven Volk succeeded him. Issue thirty-nine celebrated *TTA's* tenth anniversary. Here's hoping for another ten—at least. The one issue of the Pringle-edited *Interzone* had notable dark stories by John Meaney and Darrell Schweitzer. The two issues taken over by Andy Cox didn't publish anything I'd consider horror. *Alchemy, No. 2*, edited by Steve Pasechnick, has lovely cover art by James Christiansen and is beautifully designed by Bryon Cholfin. Of the six stories, at least half are dark enough to be enjoyed by the dark fantasy enthusiast. *Nemonymous Four (Part 3)*, edited by D. F. Lewis, continues his experiment with "late labeling," that is, providing author names in the next issue of the magazine. There's less dark fiction this time around and more just plain weird stuff, although there were notable dark stories by Adrian Fry, Gary McMahon, Jamie Rosen, Jay Lake, and Scott Tullis. What with no author names and no obvious editorial presence anywhere on or within each volume, Lewis seems to have thrown the entire idea of marketing out the window. His decision to use a blank white cover this time around seems to confirm that belief. *Asimov's Science Fiction* published notable dark fiction by Robert Reed, Ian McDowell, and James Van Pelt. *Zahir: Unforgettable Tales*, edited by Sheryl Tempchin, is a simply but attractively produced triennial magazine of SF/F/H. There were good dark stories by Davin Ireland and Mark Patrick Lynch. John Klima's zine *Electric Velocipede* came out twice in 2004 and has impressive dark fiction in number six by Edd Vick, Neil Ayres, and Liz Williams, but not much in number seven. *Space and Time*, edited by Gordon Linzner, published its ninety-eighth issue, which was heavy on horror. It had some very good stories and poems by Harley Stroh, Tess Collins, Sherry Decker, and Richard William Pierce, and I liked the cover art by Katherine Hasell. *Talebones*, edited by Patrick and Honna Swenson, is a well-produced perfect-bound magazine that showcases science fiction and dark fantasy stories and poetry. In the two issues published in 2004, Ken Rand interviewed Kay Kenyon and Tom Piccirilli and there was the usual selection of brief book reviews. There were also good stories and poems by Sandra McDonald, Paul Melko, Sarah Prineas, Carrie Vaughn, and T. J. Berg. *Borderlands*, edited by Stephen Dedman, is an Australian magazine of science fiction, fantasy, and horror. Only one issue was published in 2004. It contained good dark stories by Simon Brown and Claire McKenna. *On Spec*, edited by Diane L. Walton, is the premiere Canadian science SF/F/H magazine. It's an attractive perfect-bound quarterly. In 2004 there were a number of good dark stories, including those by Jack Skillingstead, Laurie Channer, E. L. Chen, Jean-Claude Dunyach, Ron Horsley, Holly Phillips, Wes Smiderle, and Angelo Niles. *Orb Speculative Fiction*, edited by Sarah Endacott in Australia, always has beautiful cover art. There was one issue published in 2004 and it had good dark fiction by Geoffrey Maloney, Nathan Burrage, and Deborah Biancotti. An SF story from it by Cat Sparks won the 2004 Aurealis Award. *Tales of the Unanticipated*, edited by Eric M. Heideman, published its twenty-fifth issue and celebrated with a "Strange Romance" theme, with some very good dark stories by S. C. Lofton, Whitt Pond, Lee Battersby, and Manfred Gabriel, and a poem by Christine Butterworth.

Dark Horizons, edited by Debbie Bennett (Marie O'Regan is taking over the editorship in 2005), is a wonderful bonus for members of the British Fantasy Society. The magazine is published twice a year (although I only saw one issue in '04) and the stories and poems are always readable—highly recommended for those interested in traditional supernatural fiction. The British Fantasy Society is open to everyone. Members also receive the informative quarterly magazine, *Prism* (being taken over by Bennett), which has opinionated magazine, book, and movie reviews plus interviews with U.K. writers. Both magazines will be revamped in 2005. *Dark Horizons* will expand to three or four times a year and may be renamed. The society organizes Fantasycon, the annual British Fantasy Convention, and its membership votes on the British Fantasy Awards. For information write the British Fantasy Society, the BFS Secretary, 201 Reddish Road, Stockport SK5 7HR, England. Or check out the Web site at: www.britishfantasysociety.org.uk

Single-Author Collections

Elvisland by John Farris (Babbage Press) is the second collection by the author of *The Fury, All Heads Turn When the Hunt Goes By, Son of the Endless Night*, and the classic '50s sex and high school novel *Harrison High*. *Elvisland* has thirteen stories, four of them original to the collection. One, "Hunting Meth Zombies in the Great Nebraskan Wasteland," is reprinted herein.

A Hazy Shade of Winter by Simon Bestwick (Ash-Tree) is an excellent first collection of supernatural stories that's going to make a splash come awards time. Nine of the fourteen stories are original to the collection and most of them are terrific. Joel Lane wrote the Introduction. The ghoulish jacket art is by Paul Lowe. The title story is reprinted herein.

Out of His Mind by Stephen Gallagher (PS Publishing) collects twenty-two stories and novelettes published since 1985, with one finely rendered original tale. Gallagher's a terrific storyteller and this first collection is long overdue. Some of the stories have been reprinted in previous volumes of *YBFH*. The introduction is by Brian Clemens, a television scriptwriter and director. The author's end notes explain the genesis of each story.

Nightworlds by William F. Nolan (Leisure) is an abridged version of the author's 2001 Stealth Press collection *Dark Universe*, which was subsequently published in mass market by Leisure.

Demonized by Christopher Fowler (Serpent's Tail) is a partly original collection by the multiple-award-winning author of numerous disturbing stories. It includes "The Green Man," reprinted in an earlier *YBFH* and "American Waitress," winner of the British Fantasy Society Award. The originals are all strong and one, "Seven Feet," is reprinted herein.

Fears Unnamed by Tim Lebbon (Leisure) contains four novellas, including the brilliant, award-winning "White" (reprinted in an earlier edition of *YBFH*) and a very well-wrought and thought-provoking original called "Remnants," about the discovery of a "city of the dead" in the desert.

The Machinery of Night by Douglas Clegg (Cemetery Dance) contains almost

250,000 words of Clegg's short fiction, including the novella *Purity* and a harrowing stand-alone prequel to his novel *The Hour Before Dark*. Thirteen of the stories made up the paperback collection *The Nightmare Chronicles*. Ten poems, vignettes, and stories are original to the collection. One story is reprinted herein.

Nocturnes by John Connolly (Hodder & Stoughton) is an excellent collection of traditional supernatural stories by the noted Irish crime writer. Some of the stories were first broadcast on BBC radio, and a few have appeared on his Web site, but many are original to the book.

Falling into Heaven by L. H. Maynard and M.P.N. Sims (Sarob Press) showcases fourteen horror stories by the longtime U.K. writing team. It's their best collection yet, with some subtle, unnerving ghost stories, most appearing for the first time. Gerald Gaubert illustrated the cover. William P. Simmons provided the Introduction.

Use Once, Then Destroy by Conrad Williams (Night Shade Books) is a selection of the author's stories over the past ten years. Williams is expert at portraying depressives in bleak surroundings. There are three new stories, including "The Owl," which is reprinted herein.

The Worm in Every Heart by Gemma Files (Prime Books) is the up-and-coming author's second collection of fifteen stories. Several of them are original to the collection. Nancy Kilpatrick provides the Introduction (not seen).

Bumper Crop by Joe R. Lansdale (Golden Gryphon) and *High Cotton* (2000) represent the definitive volumes of the author's short fiction. All the earlier stories in the new collection were originally published between 1982 and 2003. Imaginative and attractive jacket art by John Picacio. Also, *The Atrocity Archives* by Charles Stross, a collection of two short novels, one the title story, the other "The Jungle." The jacket art and design by Steve Montiglio and Lynne Condellone respectively, are beautiful and effective.

Alone with the Horrors by Ramsey Campbell (Tor) is the first U.S. trade edition of this book collecting Campbell's short fiction between 1961 and 1991. With an updated introduction by the author and one early story not published in the 1993 Arkham House edition.

100 Jolts: Shockingly Short Stories by Michael A. Arnzen (Raw Dog Screaming Press) features one hundred pieces of flash fiction, a mode of prose I don't really care for. A few here do actually pack a punch. Some are published for the first time. The cover art is by Matt Sesow.

Midnight House published *The Shining Hand and Other Tales of Terror*, the horror fiction of J. E. Muddock. It is the first time since 1889 that the collection, originally called *Stories Weird and Wonderful*, has been available. This expanded edition includes a novella published under a pseudonym in 1926. Editor John Pelan provides an introduction to the author and his writings. Jacket art and frontispiece by Allen Koszowski. Also, *Horrible Imaginings* by Fritz Leiber, the third in a series of volumes dedicated to preserving the author's weird and macabre tales. This volume has fifteen stories, including one, "Skinny's Wonderful," recently discovered.

Charnel Wine by Richard Gavin (Rainfall Books) is the debut collection of an interesting writer whose work is sometimes reminiscent of Thomas Ligotti. Of the twenty-three stories and vignettes, five appear for the first time. Steve Lines illustrated the cover and the interiors.

Compositions for the Young and Old by Paul G. Tremblay (House of Dominion) is an impressive first collection by a talented newcomer. Seven of the stories are original to the collection. The attractive cover art is by David Ho and the cover design is by Luis Rodriquez.

Chocolate Park by Chesya Burke (Undaunted Press) is a minicollection of four related stories (one reprint) about three orphaned sisters, the eldest a junkie whose habit threatens the other two. The cover art is by Deena Warner.

The Extremist and Other Tales of Conflict by Paul Finch (Pendragon Press) brings together five horrific war stories, one published for the first time. Introduction by the author.

Darker Places by Richard Matheson (Gauntlet Publications) has two novellas and four short stories written (and in one case, forgotten) early in the author's career. None have previously been published. One, "Cassidy's Shoes," is a classic of its type and would have fit comfortably in the original *Twilight Zone* television series. Also included is the never-filmed screenplay of John Saul's novel *Creature*. The cover art is by Harry O. Morris.

Madman Stan and Other Stories by Richard Laymon (Cemetery Dance Publications) has twenty stories reprinted from magazines and anthologies. The book comes with a brief introduction by Stanley Wiater and an afterword by Laymon's U.S. editor, Don D'Auria. There is no previous publication information provided for any of the stories. Alan M. Clark is the jacket artist.

Fearful Symmetries by Thomas F. Monteleone (Cemetery Dance Publications) showcases twenty-six of the author's stories and novelettes from the past two decades. The earlier stories occasionally reveal Monteleone's science fictional roots. The book is a good overview of his short work. Illustrations by Matt Eames. Rick Hautala provides an introduction and the author provides a preface and story notes.

One Hand Screaming by Mark Leslie (Stark Publishing) has twenty-three stories, vignettes, and poems, two written with other writers, and a couple published for the first time.

Tartarus Press published *The Suicide Club and Other Dark Adventures* by Robert Louis Stevenson, a more than five-hundred-page collection of the author's fantastic and macabre stories. Some of the highlights are "The Strange Case of Dr. Jekyll and Mr. Hyde," "The Body Snatcher," "Markheim," and "Olalla." The Introduction is by Mark Valentine. Also, from Tartarus, *Morbid Tales*, a good new collection of five stories and three novellas by the contemporary gothic writer Quentin S. Crisp. It has a brief Foreword by Mark Samuels. The cover illustration (of "Cousin X") is by R. B. Russell. Also published was an enhanced edition (with two additional stories) of Ralph Adams Cram's six-story collection from 1895, *Black Spirits and White*, edited by Stefan Dziemianowicz and Doug Anderson. One of the stories, "The Dark Valley," was singled out for praise by H. P. Lovecraft in his essay "Supernatural Horror in Literature."

Gauntlet Press published *As Timeless as Infinity: The Complete Twilight Zone Scripts of Rod Serling, Volume One*, which contains nine scripts, one with two alternate versions. Edited and with commentary by Tony Albarella. Appreciations by Richard Matheson and Rockne S. O'Bannon. Also, *The Twilight Zone Scripts of Charles Beaumont, Volume One*, edited by Roger Anker, has a Preface by Beaumont's son Christopher Beaumont, and a Prologue and commentary by Anker about each of the nine solo scripts included.

Sleep Disorder by Jack Ketchum and Edward Lee (Gauntlet Press, 2003) is a collaboration between the two writers on five stories, one published for the first time.

Also, first drafts by each author for two stories on which they originally collaborated. The jacket and interior art is by Harry O. Morris.

Angel Road by Steven Savile (Elastic Press) is an excellent collection of eleven stories and two poems, about half of which are published for the first time. Savile writes with grace and originality. The cover art is by Robert Sammelin.

Incredible Adventures by Algernon Blackwood (Hippocampus Press) collects five novellas with an Introduction by S. T. Joshi, analyzing the author's influence on H. P. Lovecraft.

Darren Speegle had two very good collections published in 2004: *Gothic Wine* (Aardwolf Press) and *A Dirge for the Temporal* (Raw Dog Screaming Press). It's rare for a relatively new writer to have written enough good stories to create one satisfying collection, let alone two in one year. Yet Speegle had forty stories—eleven published for the first time—and each is well written, with control over the material. He's someone to watch.

The Sword of Zagan and Other Writings by Clark Ashton Smith (Hippocampus Press) heralds the first publication of this 39,000-word adventure, several stories, and poems. Edited by W. C. Farmer and with an Introduction by S. T. Joshi.

Howling Hounds, the Haunting Tales of Phil Locascio (Sarob Press), is the author's first collection, with thirteen stories, three original. The jacket art is by Thomas M. Arensberg.

The Dreams in the Witch House and Other Weird Stories by H. P. Lovecraft (Penguin Classics) has twenty-one stories with Introduction and notes by S. T. Joshi, with some corrections to the texts of the original 1984–86 Arkham House collections.

Dead Souls by David G. Barnett (Shocklines Press) is the first collection by a writer better known for being the publisher of Necro Press. There's a good mix of ten original and reprint stories, most written during Barnett's college years. The Introduction by Gerard Houarner, personal story notes, and good-looking cover and interior art by Chris Trammell make for an attractive package.

Strange Stars and Alien Shadows, by Ann K. Schwader (Lindesfarne Press, 2003) showcases twenty mostly Lovecraftian mythos stories. About half the stories are original to the collection and some are quite good. Suitably illustrated by Steve Lines. Each story has an Introduction written by publisher Kevin L. O'Brien.

Delirium Books published several collections, including *Shadows of Flesh* by Scott Thomas, collecting the author's erotic horror, with fifteen stories, six of them original to the collection. The others were previously published in the chapbook *The Shadows of the Flesh* or in small-press magazines. Alan M. Clark did the jacket art. *Honey Is Sweeter Than Blood* by Jeffrey Thomas (brother to Scott) has eight tales of erotic horror, a couple quite disturbing, and six of them original to the collection. Alan M. Clark did the jacket art. *Dreadful Delineations: The Best of John Maclay* features thirty stories, most very short, five original to the collection. The stories are from throughout his career, beginning in 1984. William F. Nolan wrote the introduction. Mike Bohatch did the cover artwork. *Fear of Gravity* by Brian Keene is the author's second collection. It has ten stories, more than half of them original to the collection, and most written since 2002. Keene writes on a variety of subjects and themes and styles. From graphic zombie and monsters chowing down on humans to the subtle slash of a cold killer. There's something for every taste in horror. There is an Introduction, Afterword, and individual story notes by the author. The cover art is by Alan M. Clark. *Down to Sleep* by Greg F. Gifune is the second in the Delirium Books very limited series of "exclusives." It is a hardcover reprint of the author's first collection, with three new stories and new jacket art by Mike Bohatch. *Motivational Shrieker* by Mark McLaughlin is number three in the series and has seventeen humorous horror stories, three of them new. The cover art is by the author.

Midnight Tableaux by Michael McCrann (Double Dragon Publishing) features twelve stories by this new writer.

By Reason of Darkness by William P. Simmons (House of Dominion) is an attractive collection of twenty-three stories, twelve of them published for the first time. Gary A. Braunbeck wrote the Introduction and T.M. Wright wrote the Afterword. The cover art is by Joakim Back.

Havoc after Dark by Robert Fleming (Dafina) has fourteen horror stories that mostly concentrate on the African-American experience. There is a short Foreword by Tananarive Due and an Introduction by the author.

Ancestral Shadows: An Anthology of Ghostly Tales by Russell Kirk (Eerdmans Publishing Company) has a Foreword by Vigen Guroian.

Nightmare Dreams by Steve Vernon (Cyber-Pulp) is the first collection of this promising Canadian writer and has twenty-five stories, several appearing for the first time.

Dark Water by Koji Suzuki (Vertical) has seven stories with a framing Prologue and Epilogue. First English publication (not seen).

Claw Foot Bath Dog published *Unspeakable Vitrine*, Victoria Elizabeth Garcia's chapbook of five stories. Three of the stories are original. Ray Vukcevich has written a brief Inroduction.

Ash-Tree Press continues to publish attractive collections of classic and contemporary fiction: *Dancing on Air* by Frances Oliver showcases ten ghostly, well-told, and spooky stories, written over four decades by this still-active writer. Two of the stories are originals, including the haunting title story, which is reprinted herein. *Tales of the Uneasy* by Violet Hunt demonstrates the influence of M. R. James on her work, and is the first of a projected two volumes containing all her supernatural fiction. This volume has all the stories from her 1911 collection *Tales of the Uneasy*. Introduction by John Pelan. Jacket art by Allen Koszowski. *The Devil of the Marsh and Other Stories* by H. B. Marriott Watson showcases fifteen stories by a prolific author who, although better known for his adventure and historical fiction, also wrote many tales of the supernatural including the vampire story "The Stone Chamber," one of the earliest and considered by some the best written soon after *Dracula*. Edited and with an Introduction by James Doig. The excellent jacket art is by Keith Minnion. *Satan's Circus* by Lady Eleanor Smith collects all the author's supernatural fiction in one volume for the first time, including everything from the first American edition of *Satan's Circus*, plus two previously uncollected stories. Christopher Roden has provided an extensive Introduction to her relatively brief life (she died at forty-three) and work. The jacket painting is by Paul Lowe. *The Captain of the Polestar: Weird and Imaginative Fiction* by Arthur Conan Doyle edited, and with an Introduction by Christopher Roden and Barbara Roden. With a Preface by Michael Dirda. This is the most complete volume of Doyle's weird fiction published, showcasing thirty-seven stories of the mysterious and the macabre.

Night Shade Books published *The Collected Jorkens*, volume one, by Lord Dunsany, edited by S. T. Joshi, the first in the proposed three-volume set of tall tales told by Mr. Joseph Jorkens. With a Foreword by Sir Arthur C. Clarke. Volume two has an Introduction by T.E.D. Klein. Also, *Red World of Polaris: The Adventures of Captain Volmar* by Clark Ashton Smith, presented with two other classic stories about the captain. The volume is edited and with an Introduction by Ronald S. Hilger and Scott Connors, Afterword by Donald Sidney-Fryer. The colorful jacket art and black-and-white interior illustrations are by Jason Van Hollander. *The House on the Borderland and Other Mysterious Places* is the second volume of *The Collected Fiction of William Hope Hodgson*, bringing together the author's most famous novel, *The House on the Borderland*, his creation Carnacki, the Ghost-Finder, and a section of stories that seem to be supernatural but end up having natural explanations. The book is edited and with an Introduction by Jeremy Lassen. The silver-foil-stamped cover art and the interior artwork is by Jason Van Hollander.

The Fear Report by Elizabeth Massie (Bloodletting Press) is a hefty overview of Massie's career so far, with twenty-nine reprints, including the Stoker Award–winning "Stephen," and one chilling original. The jacket art and three interior illustrations by Cortney Skinner are nicely rendered. Unfortunately, the publisher neglected to provide publication information on the reprints. And for a $45 trade edition and a $275 deluxe edition, it would also have been nice to have had an Introduction or commentary by the author.

The Scaffold and Other Cruel Tales by Villiers de l'Isle-Adam (Black Coat Press) has twenty-seven stories translated from the original French, with notes and biographical information by Brian Stableford. *The Vampire Soul and Other Sardonic Tales*, also by l'Isle-Adam, and translated by Stableford, has eleven stories.

Oddest Yet: Even Odder Stories to Chill the Heart by Steve Burt (Burt Creations) is the third in a series of ghostly and creepy stories for young readers. There are nine stories, most appearing for the first time. The best is the novella, "The French Acre."

Subterranean Press published Brian Lumley's *Freaks*, a slender collection of five stories, one original to the collection. The jacket art is by Allen Koszowski. They also published *Nightscape* by David Morrell. This terrific writer's second collection includes eight stories, two of them novellas, each with his commentary. Most of the stories were published after 1992.

Dead Man's Hand: Five Tales of the Weird West by Nancy A. Collins (Two Wolf Press) has four reprints and one original novella.

Ancient Exhumations +2 by Stanley C. Sargent (Elder Signs Press) is a second edition, revised and expanded with two more reprints.

Iguana Publications debuted the first of a projected series of chapbooks. *Masque of the Small Town Oddball*, edited by Jon Weagly, has seven odd, original stories.

Naked Snake Press published a series of chapbook collections by new writers including *Harvest of Horrors* by Tim Johnson, reprinting four of his stories. The cover art on this chapbook is by Donna Taylor Burgess. The press published three chapbooks by Eric S. Brown: *Zombies: The War Stories* by Eric S. Brown with six brief zombie stories, two published for the first time; *Flashes of Death*, with ten very short stories, one original; and *Still Dead*, with six stories. Diavolo illustrated all three chapbooks by Brown. *Blood Freaks: Vampires, Ghouls, and Sanguine Hedonists* by Octavio Ramos Jr. has twelve brief stories, four original to the chapbook. And *Cold Comfort* has two stories of betrayal by Amy Grech.

Bloc Press published two chapbooks: *Crap Ghosts*, presenting ten brief stories by Gavin Inglis and *The Chronicles of Vinegar Tom* by Stefan Pearson, with three horror stories about a resilient cat that has better luck than some of the people he encounters.

Borderlands Press continues its successful series of attractive, signed and numbered limited-edition undersized hardcover titles. 2004 titles included *A Little Purple Book of Peculiar Stories*, five reprints by Craig Shaw Gardner; *A Little Blue Book of Rose Stories* by Peter Straub collecting his classics "Blue Rose" and "The Juniper Tree"; *A Little Yellow Book of Fevered Stories* by Al Sarrantonio with eight horror tales about childhood; *A Little Beige Book of Nondescript Stories* by F. Paul Wilson, with three short novel prequels, two stories, and one and a half drabbles (a story of exactly one hundred words). The story Introductions by the author make this one an extra-nice little package. *A Little Gray Book of Alien Stories* by John DeChancie with five reprints, an original story, and an original "fight song" dedicated to Miskatonic University. Also includes an Introduction by the author. *A Little Brown Book of Bizarre Stories* by Thomas F. Monteleone has two originals and five reprints, plus an Introduction explaining the genesis of each story.

Mixed-Genre Collections

Innocents Aboard by Gene Wolfe (Tor) features twenty-two fantasy, dark fantasy, and horror stories originally published between 1988 and 2003. There is one story published for the first time in 2004. The amazing "The Tree Is My Hat," reprinted in an earlier *YBFH* is included, as are other dark stories from anthologies and magazines and Web sites. *Black Juice* by Margo Lanagan (Allen & Unwin, Australia) is a marvelous collection that dances gracefully between the science fiction, fantasy, and horror genres. Very Australian in language and tone, Lanagan is a writer to watch. One of the stories "Singing My Sister Down" is included herein. *Little Black Book of Stories* by A. S. Byatt (Alfred A. Knopf, first U.S. publication) has five stories, three original to the collection. Byatt's short fiction, while firmly rooted in the mainstream, often contains fantasy moments and dark undercurrents. *Thumbprints* by Pamela Sargent (Golden Gryphon) has a dozen stories ranging over the author's career from the classic SF/horror story "Gather Blue Roses" of 1972 to a story published for the first time. *The Cat's Pajamas+5* by Ray Bradbury (Hill House, Publishers) has twenty-seven stories by a master of the fantastic, five more than the William Morrow trade edition (which was published first). Most of the stories appear for the first time. They range over the author's sixty-year career, including a few from as recently as 2003. The limited edition is gorgeous, with early-'60s-type cover art by Bradbury that shows through the peephole of the slipcase. *Jigs and Reels* by Joanna Harris (HarperCollins) is a collection of mostly originals (with eight reprints) by the author best known for her novel *Chocolat* (made into a movie). There is one very good dark story, "The Little Mermaid," and some other notable ones. *Two Trains Running* by Lucius Shepard (Golden Gryphon) is a gorgeous hardcover collecting Shepard's article for *Spin* magazine about riding the rails with hobos, the Sturgeon Award–winning cross-genre novella "Over Yonder," and an original, dark-tinged story about a hobo and the young girl with whom he rides the rails. The book's beautiful jacket art is by John Picacio and the jacket design is by Lynn Condellone. *Somnambulists* by Allen Ashley (Elastic Press) has sixteen stories, four published for the first time. The attractive cover is by Dean Harkness. *The Night Orchid: Conan Doyle in Toulouse* by Jean-Claude Dunyach, adapted in English by Sheryl Curtis, Jean-Louis Trudel, Dominique Bennett, and Ann Cale (A Black Coat Press Book) is mostly science fiction, but a few of the fourteen stories are dark (included is "Watch Me While I Sleep," which was reprinted in *YBFH 15*). With a Foreword by David Brin and an Afterword by the author. The wonderful cover illustration is by Gilles Francescano. *Secret Life* by Jeff VanderMeer (Golden Gryphon) is a cornucopia of imaginative phantasms that often seem hallucinogenic in their vibrancy and dislocation. Some of the work is dark, two of the stories original to the collection. The jewel-like jacket art is by Scott Eagle. *Nations of the Living, Nations of the Dead* by Mort Castle (Prime) has twenty-five stories and poems (published in 2003 but not seen until 2004). *Matrix Dreams and Other Stories* by James C. Glass (Fairwood Press) has twenty-one stories, four original to the collection. *Waltzing with the Dead* by Russell Davis (Wildside Press) has four poems and fourteen short stories. *Not in Kansas* by Janet Fox (Dark Regions Press) showcases five fantasy and dark fantasy stories and twenty poems. One story is original. There is a gracious Introduction by A. R. Morlan, and Allen Koszowski did the cover art and interior illustrations. *Novelties and Souvenirs* by John Crowley (Perennial) collects all of the master fantasist's short fiction from 1977 through 2002. (Unfortunately, it misses his terrific recently published story from *Conjunctions*.) Crowley ranges from dark, bittersweet SF to fantasy to almost mainstream. *Mad Dog Summer and Other Stories* by Joe R. Lansdale (Subterranean Press) is a really wonderful mix of genres from a man who can write everything from noirish crime fiction to steampunk. The book includes a collaboration with Andrew Vachss, another collaboration with Karen Lansdale, his wife, and a very odd original novella. *Stagestruck Vampires and Other Phantasms* by Suzy McKee Charnas (Tachyon Books) is a retrospective of Charnas's all-too-rare short fiction, including her award-winning short story "Boobs," her classic SF novelette "Listening to Brahms," six other stories, and two essays about adapting fiction for theater. Introduction by Paul Di Filippo, jacket art by John Picacio. *The Voices in My Head Don't Like You* by Derek J. Goodman (1st Books—2003) has eleven fantasy and dark fantasy stories by a new writer. *The John Varley Reader: Thirty Years of Short Fiction* by John Varley (Ace) is a solid retrospective of this fine author's work and includes such classics as "Overdrawn at the Memory Bank," "The Persistence of Vision," "Air Raid," "Options," and others. One, "The Bellman," was published in 2004 for the first time. Varley provides a Preface and Introduction to each story. *Iron Mosaic* by Michael Cobley (Immanion Press) has seventeen pieces of fiction ranging from dark ghost stories to cyberpunk. Ian McDonald provides a short Introduction. *Daydreams Undertaken* by Steve L. Antczak (Marietta Publishing) has fifteen stories, four of them original, and a number of them dark, if not out-and-out horror. *Devil Talk* by Daniel A. Olivas (Bilingual Press) has twenty-six very short stories. Most are reprints from literary magazines and a few are dark. *The Wavering Knife* is Brian Evenson's fifth collection (FC2) of dark fiction with stories published mostly in literary journals/anthologies such as *Conjunctions*, *The Quarterly*, and *McSweeney's*. *Swiftly* by Adam Roberts (Night Shade) has twelve stories, mostly science fiction, a few pretty dark. Eight of the stories appear for the first time. The jacket design by Garry Nurrish is exceptionally classy. *The Banquet of the Lords of Night and other Stories* by Liz Williams (Night Shade) is an excellent debut collection with eighteen stories, one original. The striking jacket art is by Tom Kidd. A signed limited edition has an extra story. Night Shade Books also published a new edition of Iain M. Banks's *The*

State of the Art, collecting eight stories, including the title novella. Cover art by Les Edwards. Night Shade started a new series of Manly Wade Wellman books, each collecting two tales, some novella length. The first two are *Strangers on the Height*, comprising "Strangers on the Heights" (a.k.a. "Beasts from Beyond") and "Nuisance Value" (a.k.a. "The Dark Destroyers") with cover art by Colleen Doran and *Giants from Eternity*, comprising "Giants from Eternity" and "The Timeless Tomorrow," with cover art by Vincent Di Fate. Both volumes were edited by Jeremiah Rickert. *Take No Prisoners* by John Grant (Willowgate Press) has fifteen stories showing the author's great range, shifting easily from alternate history, space SF, and fantasy to the supernatural, and crime. Two of the stories are original to the collection. *Trujillo* by Lucius Shepard (PS Publishing) is a huge collection of eleven stories comprising about 250,000 words and includes one original, the novel-length *Trujillo*. The novelettes and novellas were all originally published after 1999 and the book leads off with "Only Partly Here," Shepard's powerful 9/11 story (reprinted in *YBFH 17*). Michael Swanwick wrote the Introduction. The cover art is by J. K. Potter. *Animal Crackers* by Hannah Tinti (Dial Press) has a wonderful mix of stories that are often strange, sometimes horrific, sometimes magical. *Another Green World* by Henry Wessells (Temporary Culture) has nine mysterious, often dreamlike stories, some with darker tones. A few are published for the first time. The book itself is a lovely piece of production: simple yet elegant. *American Sorrows* by Jay Lake (Wheatland Press) has three novelettes and an original novella by the prolific John W. Campbell Award–winning writer. With an Introduction by James Van Pelt. *We Would be Heroes* by Robert N. Stephenson (Altair Books and Magellan Books, Australia) has eighteen stories, five of them original, two of the reprints completely rewritten. A few of the stories are dark. *Stable Strategies and Others* by Eileen Gunn (Tachyon Publications) has been publishing stories for almost twenty-five years and finally has enough for a collection. From the sharp, dark, satirical bug-eyed view of big business to a heartbreaking tale about a woman and her dying father, Gunn's stories are always engaging. William Gibson introduces the collection. Howard Waldrop supplies the Afterword. *On Account of Darkness and other SF Stories* by Barry N. Malzberg and Bill Pronzini (Five Star) collects all the SF collaborations by the two authors, most written between 1975 and early 1982. Many of the twenty stories combine elements of SF and crime or horror. Also included is one solo story by Malzberg and four by Pronzini. *The Heisenberg Mutation* by Steve Redwood (D-Press) has four mixed-genre stories, one original. Illustrated by Carole Humphries. *Breathmoss and Other Exhalations* by Ian R. MacLeod (Golden Gryphon) has seven stories, novelettes, and novellas including the World Fantasy Award–winning "The Chop Girl." *Darker Ages* by Paul Finch (Sarob Press) consists of two dark novellas about Vikings with an Introduction by Mike Ashley and cover art by Richard Gray. Neil Labute is an expert at depicting ugly, brutal (sometimes only psychologically brutal) sexual relationships in his movies and plays such as *In the Company of Men, Your Friends and Neighbors*, and *The Mercy Seat*. The twenty stories in *Seconds of Pleasure* (Grove Press) portray the ugliness in prose form. *Four Stories Till the End* by Zoran Zivkovic, translated from the Serbian by Alice Copple-Tošić (Polaris), has four surreal stories. *The Stranger at the Palazzo D'Oro and Other Stories* by Paul Theroux (Houghton Mifflin) includes the titular short novel, a story cycle, and two other stories. *Head Full of Traffic* by Brian Ames (Pocol Press) has nearly two dozen tales. *Brilliant Things* by Simon Morden (Subway) has thirteen

SF/F/H stories. *Satan's Daughter and Other Tales from the Pulps* by E. Hoffman Price (Wildside) has thirteen stories originally published in the '30s and '40s. The Library of America occasionally publishes material that's fantastic or horrific (2005's *Lovecraft*, but that will have to wait). In 2004 they brought out *Isaac Bashevis Singer: Collected Stories*. "A Friend of Kafka" to "Passions" collects sixty-five stories, "Gimpel the Fool" to "The Letter Writer" is drawn from Singer's first four English-language collections, published in the 1950s and '60s. "One Night in Brazil" to "The Death of Methuselah" contains stories from collections originally published between 1979 and 1988, which in turn mingles previously untranslated work with more recent stories. Also, in this volume are ten stories appearing in English translation for the first time. And to introduce the whole shebang is *Singer: An Album*, a photographic guide to the life and work of Isaac Bashevis Singer, with text by Joyce Carol Oates, Cynthia Ozick, Robert Giroux, Jonathan Safran Foer, and others. *Destination Morgue! L.A. Tales* by James Ellroy (Vintage) is a mixed fiction and non-fiction collection by a contemporary master of noir. About half of the fourteen pieces are in print for the first time. Included are three original novellas. *The Courage Consort* by Michael Faber (Harcourt) contains three dark novellas, two previously published as individual books in the U.K. in 2002.

Poetry

Dreams and Nightmares, edited by David C. Kopaska-Merkel, has been the premier magazine for dark poetry for almost twenty years and it's still publishing excellent work.

The Magazine of Speculative Poetry, edited by Roger Dutcher, published two issues and is a reliable mixed-genre venue. There was strong dark poetry by Morris Collins, r. kees, and Mario Milosevic.

Star*Line is the journal of the Science Fiction Poetry Association and is edited by Marge Simon. It publishes six issues a year, and although it specializes in SF and fantasy poetry, there are always at least a few darker poems lurking within.

Mythic Delirium, edited by Mike Allen, brought out two issues in 2004 and published good dark poetry by Sonya Taaffe, Bud Webster, Constance Cooper, and Gary Every.

Poe Little Thing: The Digest of Horrific Poetry, edited by Donna Taylor Burgess, published two issues by a variety of poets including Kurt Newton, Meg Smith, John Grey, Christina Sng, and others.

Death Poems by Thomas Ligotti (Durtro Press) is a limited hardcover of eighty pages. Despite the title, the brief poems are not only about death.

The Women at the Funeral by Corinne De Winter (Space and Time Press) is a very good collection of dark poetry with originals and reprints. Nice production values and beautiful, classic cover art by Rosetti.

Naked Snake Press published a few poetry collections: *PerVERSEities* and *PerVERSEities II* by Kurt Newton showcase the author's horror poetry, and most is published for the first time. Chris Friend illustrated them. From the same publisher comes *A Song of Bones* by Donna Taylor Burgess with twenty poems, about a third appearing for the first time. Illustrations are by the poet. Also, *Into the Beautiful Maze*, thirty-one very brief poems by Lida Broadhurst, with illustrations by Marge Simon. Almost half the poems are new.

Music of a Proto-Suicide by Catherynne M. Valente (J*A*M Pie Press) is a chap-book with some short-short stories and strong dark poetry, published in two very small editions. The cover art is by Poul A. Costinsky. One brief tale is reprinted herein.

Dark Regions Press published *The Desert* by Charlee Jacob, an excellent poetry collection with several new poems. The striking cover art is by Matt Taggart. Also, *Bone Sprockets*, collecting thirty poems by G. O. Clark. The cover art by Frank Wu is excellent.

Waiting My Turn to Go under the Knife by Tom Piccirilli (Darkwood Press) is a beautiful-looking hardcover collection with jacket art by Caniglia, and the work is sharp and very personal. However, I'm not sure I'd consider the sixty pieces poetry—more like poetic essays. Introduction by T. M. Wright.

The Devil's Wine, edited by Tom Piccirilli (Cemetery Dance Publications), is a terrific anthology of mostly dark poetry by many of the best poets in and out of the field such as Peter Straub, Peter Crowther, Melanie Tem, Michael Bishop, Joe Haldeman, Brian Hodge, Charles de Lint, Jack Cady, Elizabeth Massie, and others. The cover art and interior illustrations are by Caniglia. The only criticism one might make is the lack of individual copyright information which would enable the reader to differentiate between reprinted and original material.

Jolts by Aurelio Rico Lopez III (Sam's Dot Publishing) is a chapbook of horror haikus. Illustrated by Lette Teodosio.

Men Are from Hell, Women Are from the Galaxy of Death by Mark McLaughlin (Kelp Queen Press) is a mixed-genre collection of original and reprint poems, only a few of them horrific.

The 2004 Rhysling Anthology serves as the ballot for the Science Fiction Poetry Association's Rhysling Awards. It showcases SF/F/H poetry published in 2003.

Nonfiction

Plague: The Mysterious Past and Terrifying Future of the World's Most Dangerous Disease by Wendy Orent (Free Press) gives the background of the disease—also known as the Black Death—that killed millions over the centuries, and spotlights the possible dangers presented today and in the future; *Cave of a Thousand Tales: The Life and Times of Pulp Author Hugh B. Cave* by Milt Thomas (Arkham House) is a portrait of the personal and professional life of the late horror icon; *The Italian Boy: A Tale of Murder and Body Snatching in 1830s London* by Sarah Wise (Holt/Metropolitan) examines the trial of three body snatchers who were arrested in 1831 while trying to sell the cadaver of a teenage boy to a medical college; *My Life Among the Serial Killers: Inside the Minds of the World's Most Notorious Murderers* by Helen Morrison and Harold Goldberg (William Morrow) is a memoir by a foren-sic psychiatrist who keeps John Wayne Gacy's brain in her basement as a souvenir of her interviews with him; *Godzilla on My Mind: Fifty Years of the King of Monsters* (Palgrave Macmillan) is a short, lighthearted reflection that explores how the origi-nal *Godzilla* film was created and how it grew into a global phenomenon; *Witch Craze: Terror and Fantasy in Baroque Germany* by Lydal Roper (Yale University Press) draws on original trial transcripts from the witch trials in southern Germany, where most of the witches were executed. It paints a picture of their lives and fami-lies, explores the psychology of witch hunting, and explains why it was mostly older women who were the victims of witch crazes; *The Werewolf in Lore and Legend* by Montague Summers is an unabridged reprint and *The Vampire in Lore and Legend*, also by Summers, contains texts of *The Vampire: His Kith and Kin* and *The Vampire in Literature* (Dover); *Fear in a Handful of Dust: Horror as a Way of Life* by Gary A. Braunbeck (Betancourt & Company, 2003) is a heartfelt, personal series of essays about movies, books, and the author's fight against depression; *The Road to the Dark Tower: Exploring Stephen King's Magnum Opus* by Bev Vincent (New American Library) is an in-depth analysis of King's seven-volume Dark Tower series; *A Blazing World: The Unofficial Companion to the League of Extraordinary Gentlemen, Volume Two* by Jess Nevins (Monkeybrain Books) is a lovingly researched volume of panel-by-panel annotations of the second graphic novel series. There are also interviews with cocreator and author Alan Moore and cocreator and illustrator Kevin O'Neill; *A Vault of Horror* by Keith Topping (Telos) is a terrific compendium of eighty good and lousy British horror films from 1956–1974. Excellent for thumbing through. *Collected Essays, Volume 1: Amateur Journalism* by H. P. Lovecraft, edited by S. T. Joshi (Hippocampus Press), is a rich volume demonstrating Lovecraft's deep involvement in amateur criticism; *Collected Essays, Volume 2: Literary Criticism* by H. P. Lovecraft, edited by S. T. Joshi (Hippocampus Press), is the companion volume to the above and includes essays about Lord Dunsany, Frank Belknap Long, and Clark Ashton Smith, "Weird Story Plots," and the famous "Supernatural Horror in Literature"; *Primal Sources: Essays on H. P. Lovecraft* by S. T. Joshi (Hippocampus Press), the first major selection of Joshi's essays on the subject to be published, includes essays about Lovecraft's taste in films, the rationale for the author's use of pseudonyms, his involvement with *Weird Tales*, and twenty other topics, including close readings of some of Lovecraft's fiction. *True Vampires* by Sondra London (Feral House) is the newest entry in the annals of vampire lore. It's a detailed compendium of crimes committed by those who drink the blood of their victims; *Hanging Out with the Dream King: Conversations with Neil Gaiman and His Collaborators* by Joseph McCabe (Fantagraphics Books) is a well-produced, nicely illustrated, informative series of interviews with Gaiman and his graphic novel, prose, and film collaborators; *Stories from the Haunted South* by Alan Brown (University Press of Mississippi) collects supposedly true stories of hauntings around the American South; *Why Should I Cut Your Throat? Excursions into the Worlds of Science Fiction Fantasy and Horror* by Jeff VanderMeer (Monkeybrain Books) is an entertaining collection of personal reminiscences, critical essays, and reviews written over the past twenty years. VanderMeer often provides updates to the articles. Great cover art by Scott Eagle; *Conversations with Ray Bradbury*, edited by Steven L. Aggelis (University Press of Mississippi); *The Evolution of the Weird Tale* by S. T. Joshi (Hippocampus Press) collects eighteen critical and sometimes provocative essays about the work of F. Marion Crawford, Fritz Leiber, Les Daniels, David J. Schow, Poppy Z. Brite, and others; *Those Macabre Pulps* by Darrell C. Richardson (Adventure House) is a reference and art book that focuses on rare titles with short runs. It includes over one hundred full-color images, an essay on each title, an alphabetical listing of authors and stories in each issue, price, size, and frequency of publication; *Lord Ruthven the Vampire*, edited by Frank J. Morlock (Black Coat Press), includes the original story by Polidori, a fragment from Lord Byron showing his take on the character, two French plays, and a new story by the editor, pitting Ruthven, Dracula, Sherlock Holmes, and Father Brown; *The Return of Lord*

Ruthven, edited by Frank J. Morlock (Black Coat Press), includes Alexandre Dumas's sequel to Polidori's story plus an original by the editor; *Arkham House Books: A Collector's Guide* by Leon E. Nielsen (McFarland) is a guide to collecting, buying, and selling books from Arkham House, Mycroft & Moran, and Stanton & Lee. Foreword by Barry Abrahams; *Witches of Plymouth County and Other New England Sorceries*, compiled and edited by Edward Lodi (Rock Village Publishing), is an entertaining and attractive compendium of tales and historical facts about witchery; *The Horror Film* by Peter Hutchings (Pearson-Longman) considers the reasons for horror's disreputability and seeks to explain why horror movies have been so successful. Also discussed is the historical development of horror cinema, the relation of horror films to the national contexts of their production, and the critical methods developed to make sense of horror; *Ghouls, Gimmicks, and Gold: Horror Films and the American Movie Business 1953–1968* by Kevin Heffernan (Duke University Press) explores the economics of the horror film, arguing that major cultural and economic shifts in the production and reception of horror films began at the time of the 3-D film cycle of 1953–54 with *House of Wax* and *Creature from the Black Lagoon* and ending with the 1968 adoption of the MPAA ratings system; *The Cinema of John Carpenter: The Technique of Terror*, edited by Ian Conrich and David Woods (Wallflower Press), is a critical anthology of twelve essays by international film scholars covering such films as the *Halloween* series, *The Thing*, *The Fog*, and others; *The Complete Illustrated History of the Skywald Horror-Mood* by Alan Hewetson (Headpress) is the first book to chronicle the publishing house—active in the early to mid-'70s—that brought out such black-and-white horror comics as *Nightmare*, *Psycho*, and *Scream*; *Julia Pastrana: The Tragic Story of the Victorian Ape Woman* by Christopher Hals Gylseth and Lars O. Toverud, translated by Donald Tumasonis (Sutton Publishing), tells the tragic story of a woman born, in 1834 in rural Mexico, covered in hair and with apelike features who became a sideshow attraction and eventually married the owner, became pregnant, and died soon after the child she gave birth to. Then she and her son were stuffed and displayed. The authors take liberties with their extrapolation of Pastrana's thoughts and feelings and they often get sidetracked into discussions of other freaks, seemingly in order to take up space, as the actual story of poor Pastrana only takes up about half the book; *Horror Film: Creating and Marketing Fear*, edited by Steffen Hantke, has original essays that focus on how film technology, marketing, and distribution created the aesthetics and reception of horror films. The essays are by Michael Arnzen, Blair Davis, James Kendrick, Catherine Zimmer, and others; *Peter Jackson: From Prince of Splatter to Lord of the Rings* by Ian Pryor (Thomas Dunne Books/St. Martin's Press); *The Texas Chainsaw Companion* by Stefan Jaworzyn (Titan Books); *The Christopher Lee Filmography* by Tom Johnson and Mark A. Miller (McFarland & Co.); *They Came from Within: A History of Canadian Horror Cinema*, by Caelum Vatnsdal (Arbeter Ring Publishing); *Alternative Europe: Eurotrash and Exploitation Cinema Since 1945*, edited by Ernest Mathijs and Xavier Mendik (Wallflower Press). *Michael Marshall Smith: The Annotated Bibliography* by Lavie Tidhar (PS Publishing) has annotations by Smith. I caught several missing items so there are probably more, but all in all a useful work. *The Encyclopedia of Vampires, Werewolves, and Other Monsters* by Rosemary Ellen Guiley, Foreword by Jeanne Keyes Youngson, is a reference guide to supernatural monsters, with an emphasis on vampires in folklore, film, and literature. With Bibliography and Index; *Abel Ferrara: The Moral Vision* by Brad

Stevens (FAB Press); *Ray Bradbury: The Life of Fiction* by Jonathan R. Eller and William F. Toupance (Kent State University Press).

Chapbooks and Other Small-Press Items

Earthling Publications brought out *Game* by Conrad Williams, a powerful, weird, and violent novella that depicts the underbelly of London. Two women are forced to wreak terrible vengeance on three people whom a criminal holds responsible for his earlier incarceration. Earthling also published a fifteen-copy limited edition of the novelette "Mr. Dark's Carnival" by Glen Hirshberg, with art by Deena Warner and an Introduction by the author.

Telos Publishing Limited published *Breathe* by Christopher Fowler, a very funny/nasty satire about corporate greed represented by SymaxCorp, which pumps in some strangely enhanced air in order to keep its workers working at full throttle. Only the new hire, a temp, and a few others form a motley team to investigate the disappearance of the most recent corporate safety officer. Also *Houdini's Last Illusion* by Steven Savile, a clever variation of the great illusionist's legend wherein he is haunted by long-dead magicians he has known over his career.

Horror Express debuted a chapbook series with a reprint of Guy N. Smith's 1989 story "Come and Join Us," illustrated by Russell Dickerson. Second in the series was "The Forest," a story by editor Marc Shemmans. The illustrations are by Teresa Tunaley.

The Final Solution by Michael Chabon (HarperCollins/Fourth Estate) is a new hardcover edition of the author's Sherlock Holmes novella originally published 2003 in the *Paris Review*.

Wormhole Books published an attractive chapbook that excerpts a piece of Stewart O'Nan's 2003 novel *The Night Country*. The excerpt is entitled "Something Wicked." Edward Bryant has written an Introduction and the author provides an Afterword. Cover art and interior photography is by Thomas Meek.

Zoran Zivkovic's "Compartments" (also in the magazine *Postscripts*) is available in an attractive little paperback by Publishing Atelier Polaris, in English.

PS Publishing brought out several novellas in hardcover and trade paperback. There is a feeling of impending menace emanating throughout Lisa Tuttle's marvelous novella *My Death*, about a widowed writer whose interest in a dead artist and his mysterious model is piqued by a chance encounter with a painting. Cover art by Mark Harrison, Introduction by Thomas Tessier. Gary Greenwood's excellent *Jigsaw Men* is a complex alternative history that begins with a missing-person report. The British Empire is still going strong, thanks in part to the scientific techniques of Dr. Frankenstein, who has created a race of creatures cobbled together from the dead who make great soldiers. The hardcover limited has a ribbon book mark and gorgeous jacket art by Chris Nurse. Introduction by Mark Chadbourn. *Changing of Faces* by Tim Lebbon is about a young boy among a group of survivors threatened by not only zombies but by were creatures as well. Cover art is by Alan M. Clark. Introduction is by Simon Clark.

Subterranean Press published *Liar's House* by Lucius Shepard, a reprint of the Dragon Griaule novella that was originally published in 2003. The book has beautiful dragon-skin-looking endpapers and attractive, atypical nonphotographic jacket art by J. K. Potter. Also *Triads* by Poppy Z. Brite and Christa Faust expands their novella to seventy thousand words and the deluxe version adds two short stories related to the novel, one by Faust, published for the first time.

Pendragon Press published *The Ice Maiden*, a suspenseful novella by Steve Lockley and Paul Lewis about a divorced teacher who dreams about the future and her involvement in the disappearance of one of her students. Terry Cooper did the cover art.

Necessary Evil Press debuted its novella series with *Dead Man's Hand: Book 1 of the Assassin Series* by Tim Lebbon, a fast-moving, entertaining dark western about an unassuming storekeeper caught up in a fight between two godlike creatures, one who has become an assassin for hire and the other out to prevent the deed and destroy the perpetrator. Introduction by Tom Piccirilli and Afterword by the author. Also, *The Turtle Boy* by Kealan Patrick Burke is about a summer vacation gone bad as two adventurous eleven-year-old boys stumble upon a strange, oddly deformed boy. Introduction by Norman Partridge. The series of two novellas a year is available in two limited editions. Both of the first titles have cover art by Caniglia.

Delirium Press published Douglas Clegg's novella *The Attraction*, a well-told, chilling, and satisfying story about a group of college students off on a road trip and the roadside attraction they discover in the Arizona desert. The cover artwork is by Alan M. Clark. Clegg writes about the inspiration for the novella in an Afterword.

Scrybe Press published Eugie Foster's *Ascendancy of Blood*, a dark retelling of Sleeping Beauty, and *Camdigan* by C. Dennis Moore, a novella about a man who makes a wrong turn into a city of the dead and finds a little girl who might be the reincarnation of his dead wife. *Natalie's Grove* by Mikal Trimm is about a young man, the two women he's involved with, and the grove whose trees sing seductively. *Murdered by Human Wolves* by Steven E. Wedel is based on a true story of a young woman murdered in Oklahoma in 1915. In Wedel's well-told fictionalization, she encounters werewolves, and those who hunt them. Included is an interview with paranormal researcher Mary Franklin.

Dead Cat's Lick by Gerard Houarner (Bedlam Press) is a highly entertaining tale of the eponymous character's encounter with a monster at a jazz bar in Harlem. Nice use of hipster jargon and tone. Cover and interior illustrations are by GAK.

Night Shade Books published *Viator* by Lucius Shepard, a dark novella about a freighter grounded on the Alaskan coast. Five men are hired to live onboard, salvage the derelict, and regularly report back to their mysterious employer. The presumptive leader is torn between his lady friend in town and the pull of the ship, as his disturbing dreams start to become true. The language becomes increasingly exotic and transcendental as the ship drags its crew into another dimension. Also (a 2003 title not received until 2004), *Bubba Ho-Tep* presents the original story with an Introduction by Joe R. Lansdale and the screenplay with an introduction by Don Coscarelli. Included are a few stills from the movie.

Yard Dog Press published a two-story booklet by J. F. Gonzalez called *That's All Folks*. One story is about a serial killer and the other about biting cockroaches. Cover art is by Tim Chessmore. Also, *Shadows in Green* by Richard E. Dansky about a menacing forest of kudzu in South Carolina.

Biting Dog Publications brought out "A Question of Belief," an odd, unsatisfying zombie story by newcomer Brett McBean with very mixed production values: uneven inking of the copy right page but very fancy endpapers made of what looks like handmade paper. (This was the publisher that brought out such a nice limited edition of Neil Gaiman's "Snow Glass Apples" a few year's ago.)

Sarob Press published *Postcards from Terri*, a ghost-story novella by Tony Richards, as an attractive small-sized hardcover with cover art by Paul Lowe.

Endeavor Press published *The House of the Temple*, a chapbook with a novelette and a short story by Brian Lumley. Lumley provides brief Introductions to each piece, giving a bit of background on each. Cover art by Alan M. Clark and interior illustrations by Allen Koszowski.

Odds and Ends

Twelve Scary Guys is a calendar published by Borderlands Press, with black-and-white photos of Peter Straub, Douglas Winter, Stephen King, and new writers whose names would not be recognizable to the general public. Each responds to the same format: date and place of birth, first publication, favorite book, music, and movie. Each month has a few eerie noteworthy events.

Jabberwocky by Lewis Carroll, illustrated by Canadian Stéphane Jorisch (KCP Poetry), is one of my favorite nonsense verses so when it's used to create a political screed it burns me. The book is beautiful looking. The colorful images were created with pencil, pen and ink, watercolor, and Photoshop software. Although Carroll was a political artist he was far more subtle and I suspect he might be turning in his grave. Ignore the politics and just go for the beauty of the art and oddness of the text.

Tales of Mystery and Madness by Edgar Allan Poe, illustrated by Gris Grimly (Atheneum), relays four of Poe's tales with color illustrations that are an amusing combination of Ronald Searle and Edward Sorel with a lot of grotesquery thrown in.

Melinda by Neil Gaiman and Dagmara Matuszak (Hill House) is a dark tale about a lone girl who lives in a bleak decaying city. The text is poetic, as one would expect from Gaiman, and the artist's black-and-white and color work is quite impressive.

The Dark Horse Book of Witchcraft presents a graphic novel anthology of eight stories including a scene from Shakespeare, illustrated by Tony Millionaire, a Hellboy tale by Mike Mignola, an adaptation of a Clark Ashton Smith story, a disturbing tale of sibling rivalry, and a rousing drama about a pack of dogs and one cat striving to save the world, by Jill Thompson and Evan Dorking.

The Book of Ballads by Charles Vess (Tor) with a host of writers including Neil Gaiman, Sharyn McCrumb, Charles de Lint, and others. Several of the pieces are reprints from the *Books of Ballads and Sagas* published between 1995 and 1997 by Vess's Greenman Press. Great variety and wonderful, often dark, fun. The original ballads are provided at the end of each retold, illustrated version.

Spectrum 11: The Best in Contemporary Fantastic Art, edited by Cathy Fenner and Arnie Fenner (Underwood Books), juried by major fantasy artists, continues to be *the* showcase for the best in genre art—from fairies and half-metal warriors to monsters, femme fatales, and alien worlds. Michael Whelan was honored as Grand Master for his thirty-year, multiaward-winning career in book illustration. Although he mostly works in oil and acrylic, he also uses pencil and airbrush. Whelan's distinctive work helped bring narrative cover art back into style. There is also an overview of the field and a necrology. The jury—all artists themselves—convene

and decide on Gold and Silver Awards in several categories. This is a book for anyone interested in art of the fantastic, whether dark or light.

Lovecraft by Hans Rodionoff and Enrique Breccia, with Keith Giffen (Vertigo),
was inspired by a screenplay written by Rodionoff. The graphic novel combines biographical detail with Lovecraftian horrors from the author's imagination creating a
lurid, enjoyable, but mostly inaccurate story of Lovecraft's life.

Dr. Ikkaku Ochi Collection: Medical Photographs from Japan, edited by Akimitsu
Narayuma (Scalo), is a treasure trove of photographic portraits from 1895 docu-
menting horrible, deforming diseases, some of which no longer exist or are easily
curable with antibiotics. The photographic subjects are dignified and tragic. Hard
to look at but remarkable.

The Best of Gahan Wilson, edited by Cathy Fenner and Arnie Fenner (Underwood Press), is a selection of cartoons, comic strips, anecdotes, etc. from Wilson's
ongoing fifty-year career. Wilson's work is always entertaining and the color quality
is better than I've seen in most recent books of his work.

As Dead as Leaves by Caniglia (Shocklines Press) is a gorgeous book designed
and with text by the artist, showcasing his work. Many of the images are already familiar to horror readers: the walking phalanx of skeletons which is the Shocklines
Bookstore logo and the child with dragonflies on her face from Tom Piccirilli's novel
A Choir of Ill Children. Included are sketches and variations of images ranging from
delicately exquisite pencil and ink drawings of newborns to discordantly colorful oils
and gouaches of death-dealing skeletons.

The Paint in My Blood by Alan M. Clark (IFD Publications) is a wonderful sampling of the various types of art Clark creates, from science fiction through young-
adult art, and of course his best-known work—his grotesqueries. The one thing they
have in common is their imagination and artistry.

PUBLISHERS' ADDRESSES:

Ash-Tree Press: P.O. Box 1360, Ashcroft, BC V0K 1A0, Canada www.Ash-Tree
.bc.ca/ashtreecurrent.html

Babbage Press: 8740 Penfield Avenue, Northridge, CA 91324 www.babbagepress
.com/

Betancourt & Company: P.O. Box 301, Holicong, PA 18928-0301 www.wildside
press.com

Biting Dog Press: 2150 Northmont Pkwy, Suite H, Duluth, GA 30096 www.bit-
ingdogpress.com

Borderlands Press: P.O. Box 97, Fork, MD 21051 www.borderlandspress. com

Cemetery Dance Publications: 132-B Industry Lane, Unit #7, Forest Hill, MD
21050 www.cemeterydance.com

Charnel House: P.O. Box 633. Lynbrook, NY 11563 www.charnelhouse.com

Claw Foot Bath Dog: 1628 Bellevue Avenue, #103, Seattle, WA 98122 www
.clawfootbathdog.com

Dark Regions Press: P.O. Box 1558, Brentwood, CA 94513

Delirium Books: P.O. Box 338, N. Webster, IN 46555 www.deliriumbooks.com

Earthling Publications: 12 Pheasant Hill Drive, Shrewsbury, MA 01545 www
.earthlingpub.com

Elastic Press: 85 Gertrude Road, Norwich, Norfolk, NR3 4SG, U.K. www.elastic
press.com

Endeavor Press: 1515 Hickory Wood Drive, Annapolis, MD 21401 www .endeavorpress.net

Fairwood Press: 5203 Quincy Avenue S.E., Auburn, WA 98092 www.fairwood press.com

Five Star (an imprint of Gale): 295 Kennedy Memorial Drive, Waterville, ME 04901 www.galegroup.com/fivestar

Gauntlet Publications: 5307 Arroyo St., Colorado Springs, CO 80922 www.gauntlet press.com

Golden Gryphon: 3002 Perkins Road, Urbana, IL 61802 www.goldengryphon .com

Hippocampus Press: P.O. Box 641, New York, NY 10156 www.hippocampus-press .com

IFD Publishing: P.O. Box 40776, Eugene, OR 97404 www.ifdpublishing.com

Marietta Publishing: P.O. Box 3485, Marietta, GA 30061-3485 www.marietta publishing.com

McFarland & Company: Box 611, Jefferson, NC 28640 www.McFarlandpub .com

Midnight House and Darkside Press: 7713 Sunnyside North, Seattle, WA 98103 www.darksidepress.com

Naked Snake Press: 6 Rain Tree Lane, Pawleys Island, SC 29585 www.naked snakepress.com

Necro Publications: P.O. Box 540298, Orlando, FL 32854-0298 www.necropub-lications.com

Necessary Evil Press: 2722 South Hill Road, #31, Gladstone, MI 49837 www .necessaryevilpress.com

Night Shade Books: 1470 N.W. Saltzman Road, Portland, OR 97229 www.night-shadebooks.com

Overlook Connection Press: P.O. Box 526, Woodstock, GA 30188 www.overlook connection.com

Pendragon Press: P.O. Box 12, Maesteg, Mid Glamorgan, South Wales, CF34 0XG, U.K. www.pendragonpress.co.uk

Prime Books, Inc.: P.O. Box 301, Holicong, PA 18928-0301 www.primebooks.net

PS Publishing: Grosvenor House, 1 New Road, Hornsea, East Yorkshire HU18 1PG, U.K. www.pspublishing.co.uk

Sarob Press: Ty Newydd, Four Roads, Kidwelly, Carmarthenshire, SA17 4SF, Wales, U.K. http://home.freeuk.net/sarobpress

Scrybe Press: 15 Cook Street, Massena, NY 13662 www.scrybepress.com

Shocklines Press: www.shocklines.com

Short, Scary Tales Publications: Paul Fry, 15 North Roundhay, Stechford, Birm-ingham, B33 9PE, U.K. http://sstpublications.co.uk

Small Beer Press: 176 Prospect Avenue, Northampton, MA 01060 www.lcrw.net

Subterranean Press: P.O. Box 190106, Burton, MI 48519 www.subterranean-press. com

Tachyon Press: 1459 Eighteenth Street, #139, San Francisco, CA 94107 www .tachyonpublications.com

Tartarus Press: Coverley House, Carlton, Leyburn, North Yorkshire, DL8 4AY, U.K. http://homepages.pavilion.co.uk/users/tartarus/welcome.htm

Telos Publishing: 61 Elgar Avenue, Tolworth, Surrey KT5 9JP, U.K. www.telos .co.uk

Twilight Tales: 2339 N. Commonwealth #4C, Chicago, IL 60614 www.Twilight Tales.com

Undaunted Press: P.O. Box 70, St. Charles, MO 63302 www.undauntedpress.com

Underwood Books: P.O. Box 1609, Grass Valley, CA 95945 www.underwood-books .com

Wormhole Books: 7719 Stonewall Run, Fort Wayne, IN 46825 www.wormhole books.com

Yard Dog Press: 710 W. Redbud Lane, Alma, AR 72921-7247 www.yarddogpress .com

Fantasy and Horror in the Media: 2004

Edward Bryant

The Big Screen

THE HORROR, THE HORROR:
No question about it. The highlight of the horrific on the big screen in 2004 was the U.K. import hit, *Shaun of the Dead*. All too frequently, narrow-visioned directors focus on the utterly obvious, a practice that can lead to tedium, even crashing failure. Director Danny Boyle and writer Alex Garland avoided that with last year's zombie high point, *28 Days Later*. Ditto for director Edgar Wright and writer/actor Simon Pegg this year with *Shaun*. True, there's sufficient zombie depredation in the movie to ensure that no one will mistake it for a Disney holiday special, but the chomping and rending and general shambling about isn't the core of the movie. This is a sharp, funny, relationship-based tale that just happens to be catalyzed and accelerated by the happenstance that your neighbors have abruptly turned zombie and are starting to wander the countryside in search of gustatory fulfillment. In short, civilization is crumbling, but none of our slacker heroes notices for about half the picture. The only clues for the audience are the raggedy figures in the distance who stumble about like the terminally homeless, only gradually drawing nearer.

While this is going on, our characters are coping with the mundane terrors of everyday life: job insecurity, infidelity, crumbling relationships, parental disputes, and the like. Then the flesh-eating zombies become unignorable and start getting in the way of easy solutions. It's a terrific conceit, and it propels *Shaun of the Dead* to a masterful achievement in terms of melding compelling and all-too-human characters with a deadly escalation of black humor.

For big-budget horror, the year soon saw Stephen Sommers's *Van Helsing* with the eagerly awaited Hugh Jackman as a spiffed-up hunky version of Bram Stoker's implacable vampire hunter. The budget was $148 million, a horror in itself. Sommers's previous Universal blockbusters, *The Mummy* and *The Mummy Returns* had

kept us all suitably amused, particularly the latter. Even more air-puffed than its predecessors, *Van Helsing* was too dumb to succeed even as a guilty pleasure. There
were nice individual pieces. Broadway's Shuler Hensley played an engagingly klutzy
Frankenstein's Monster; Kate Beckinsale was lovely as ever, but sported a terrible
Transylvanian Gypsy accent; and Richard Rosburgh tried valiantly to keep Dracula
suave. Playing the melodrama with a straight face might have made all the difference in the world. But whether it was unfunny humor, tepid heroics, or the sexual
neutering of Dracula's undead brides, there was plenty to offend and disappoint anyone who simply wanted competent storytelling.

How the mighty have fallen. In the world of mix-and-match franchises, it probably sounded like a good idea in story meetings to cobble together *Alien vs. Predator*
as though it were a top-card match in a pro wrestling pay-per-view extravaganza. So
what did we get on the night of the big fight? An expedition goes to Antarctica to investigate a mysterious pyramid buried thousands of feet below the ice on which sits
an abandoned whaling station. Turns out the Predators have been coming to Earth
for millennia to enjoy the challenge of hunting and killing or being killed by Aliens
who have been bred here in haphazardly controlled environments akin to game
parks. As the movie starts, a new Predator hunting party is arriving and the current
Aliens are very, very hungry. This is pretty much a video game of a movie with little
attention paid to any sympathetic characters. Lance Henriksen is wasted in a perfunctory role. The only decent characters are a tough, take-charge sort of Ripley-
esque woman played by Sanaa Latham, and Sebastian de Rosa as the hunky Italian
scientist. Otherwise *AVP* is a weak confection that will only stale your popcorn.

Do effective horror films necessarily have to include demons, shape changers,
bloodsuckers and other appropriate metaphors? Nope. For example, as many viewers who wandered into *Jaws* early in its run fondly remember, mundane menaces
such as sharks can do the scary job with panache. Consider the low-budget hit *Open
Water*. Based on an actual incident in which a tourist couple out on a Caribbean
diving junket were accidentally left at sea by the tour company, *Open Water* features
Blanchard Ryan and Daniel Travis as a somewhat annoying yuppie couple who get
left behind. At first they naturally assume their absence from the party will be noticed and rescuers dispatched. But as time goes on, the reality of their peril starts to
sink in. Director-writer Chris Kentis shot this film primarily off the Bahamas on digital video for less than half a million dollars. Kentis has told the press that because
the budget didn't allow for special-effects sharks, the obvious answer was to bait real
sharks into participating. Like any true horror movie, *Open Water* goes beyond marine predators to batten on an even more basic human fear—a growing utter isola-
tion. This is a visually beautiful but ultimately chilling accomplishment. And like
Jack London's classic story "To Light a Fire," it doesn't impose a hokey happy out-
come. Nature offers many harsh realities we can't always ignore. I suspect *Open Water* will rarely be featured as the in-flight movie on tourist planes heading down to
any popular tropical paradise.

Please don't take offense, but I've got to list Mel Gibson's hotly debated *Passion
of the Christ* on my list of notable dark fantasies. Skeptics might maintain that it's
based on one of the greatest fantasy works of all time; I won't touch that. Rather I
will point out some significators that struck me when I joined a rather glum and
straitlaced audience seeing the film early in its run at a local multiplex. Whether
you've seen it or not, unless you're living under an isolated bridge, you know that the

level of violence and graphic brutality is fairly high. Jim Caviezel's Jesus really does go through a *lot* of physical anguish in the course of the film. But then, it *was* a rough era, and the accused of the time didn't have recourse to either the Geneva Conventions or the *Miranda* decision. You wouldn't think the lily of violence would need to be gilded, but frankly, I don't recall reading in my Bible about a raven plonking itself down on the shoulder of the surlier of the two thieves bracketing the crucified Christ and abruptly pecking out the miscreant's eyeball in a nifty splatter-flick gesture. A rather spookier touch is Italian actress Rosalinda Celentano's unnerving portrayal of an androgynous Satan who tends to drift bonelessly through the crowds of rubberneckers during Christ's trials. Her presence creates an eerie effect and lends a striking touch to the proceedings. Finally, I need to comment on one of the central disputes. Is *Passion of the Christ* itself a tool of the Devil in terms of anti-Semitism? I think it's pretty much of a filmic litmus test. If you're an anti-Semite when you enter the auditorium, nothing will happen that will change your mind. And if you're not an anti-Semite when you sit down for the screening, you're not going to exit the theater raving in Aramaic, frothing at the mouth, and cursing the Evil Zionist Conspiracy. But while the Aramaic (and Latin) dialogue is cool, and the political dilemmas of Pontius Pilate and the priests are fascinating insofar as they're treated, I think the film can hardly be lauded as an evenhanded work. Creative people unconsciously let their biases seep into their work. Director Gibson is undeniably creative. And *Passion of the Christ* is not exactly ideologically neutral.

For a film filtered through a rather different lens courtesy of Western Christianity, consider *Exorcist: The Beginning*. This prequel to the 1973 classic of head-spinning, pea-soup-spewing, Catholic terror seemed to possess its own cursed history. Announced for production in 1997, first-choice director John Frankenheimer died before shooting a single frame. Next director Paul Schrader completed a first cut, but the studio shelved it. Then Renny Harlin was hired. He rewrote the story, fired most of the cast, and reshot the whole movie. *That* is a troubled project. The version you can see first at the theater, now on video, isn't as unsuccessful as you might suspect. Stellan Skarsgard makes a pretty good younger Father Merrin in a story set a few decades before William Friedkin's initial version. The new priest goes to a creepy African archeological dig and encounters both a buried temple and, unsurprisingly, the demon Pazuzu hisownself. Pazuzu is only fearsome to the very impressionable, but the film's special-effects predatory hyenas are *definitely* unsettling.

Those darned vampires just never learn! You see the evidence in *Blade: Trinity*, Wesley Snipes's third outing as the human/vampire hybrid on an unholy mission to exterminate pesky bloodsuckers. If he could be half as effective with mosquitos, the West Nile virus would be stamped out. This is a seriously visual entertainment carrying so much flash and filigree it's hard to notice that the plot is mere gossamer. The cast appears to have a great time throughout, including Parker Posey and Ryan Reynolds as part of a brash, eager young team of ambitious vampire stalkers. Kris Kristofferson's character returns from apparent death to serve as Blade's cranky master weapons crafter, something of an M on a bad hair day. And Dominic Pursell provides a buffed avatar of Dracula himself.

Don Mancini's series of Chucky movies, beginning with *Child's Play* in 1988, has turned out to be a surprisingly durable franchise. Five movies later, the animate twenty-four-inch doll in red sneakers and Baby Gap–ish overalls, inhabited by the soul of executed serial killer Charles Lee Ray (voiced by Brad Dourif), is still as cranky and murderous as ever. In *Seed of Chucky*, aside from loving to commit violence, Chucky displays a soft spot for his bride, Tiffany (the funny and ever-adorable Jennifer Tilly). He also longs to recover their lost offspring, an androgynous and pacifistic young doll who calls himself Glen, and who has been exploited as a ventriloquist's dummy by a talentless hack in Europe. Whether it's *Pinocchio* or a variety of more contemporary pop-cultural references, *Seed* is jam-packed with sly jabs and in-jokes. The level of comedy is, in fact, quite high, giving this unlikely film a healthy amusement value. You certainly can, if you wish, think of this movie as a study of dysfunctional parents trying to communicate with their screwed-up kid. The fact that dolls, like clowns, are intrinsically disturbing icons only enhances the grotesque effect.

For an effective, moody exercise in house haunting, seek out the Korean production of *A Tale of Two Sisters*. There's always room for another exploration of a shattered family dwelling in a cursed house. Amityville doesn't have the monopoly on terribly troubled real estate, and *Two Sisters* is highly effective, part of that notorious modern movement in Asian horror filmmaking. And it's another good example of how mood and texture can trump splatter.

There's a reasonable argument that maybe Hollywood opportunists should resist the impulse to remake Asian horror hits with the intent of appealing to a huge American audience. Of course that's not going to happen. The prospect of big bucks is an irresistible lure to the big studios. It's true that last year's Hollywood remake of *The Ring* wasn't an utter botch. Naomi Watts held up her end of the script admirably. But it's also true that the Japanese original was discernibly chillier, an altogether nastier version of the material.

And so we come to *The Grudge*. In a gesture of experimental fairness, the director of the Japanese original, Takashi Shimizu, was given the opportunity to remake his own work. Still set in Japan, most of the cast were magically rationalized into Anglos with Sarah Michelle Gellar taking the lead as an American student working part-time as a social worker, and becoming ensnared by a house where an evil force created by past violence has taken up residence.

While the effects are slicker and the script restructured to make a bit more apparent sense, some of the thrill is gone. The remake just isn't as insidiously creepy as the original. It's that old devil, a tonal shift. The original *Grudge* is easily available for purchase or rental. Check it out

If you liked the puzzle approach to filmic storytelling à la *Identity* or *Memento*, then you'll get a kick out of *Saw*, though its success is a mixed blessing. Leigh Whannell (who also wrote the screenplay) and Cary Elwes play two characters who wake to find themselves chained in a grubby industrial cellar in the center of an elaborate scenario staged by an improbably clever and fiendish killer. Their challenge is to escape by using the tools they're given, including a hacksaw that just isn't sharp enough to cut through the chain links. In a parallel story, Danny Glover and Ken Leung play detectives racing to track down the criminal mastermind behind the series of "jigsaw killings." The sequential revelations come fast and furious and, if you pay attention, you may beat most of the rest of the audience in using deduction to figure out the identity of the hidden killer. *Saw* isn't nearly as bloody as you might have suspected. So far as it goes, it's an enjoyable exercise in gamesmanship.

Now I have to admit my own favorite guilty pleasure, one based on a video game, for God's sake. *Resident Evil: Apocalypse* again features Milla Jovovich as a renegade agent struggling to survive against impossible odds as the bungling and malign Umbrella Corporation manages to lose control (again! those people just don't learn) of the deadly T-virus, and that organism starts turning most of the population of Raccoon City into rampaging zombies. Honest, it's better than it sounds—at least visually. As an added attraction in this sequel, Jovovich's character is joined by another hard-nosed and competent agent played by Sienna Guillory. The pair could have matching "Chicks with Attitude" tees. The *Resident Evil* films are stylishly designed and filmed, and manage the clever achievement of pandering to your baser instincts without insulting your intelligence. Good work if you can get it.

CALL IT DARK FANTASY IF YOU WISH:
One of the happiest surprises of the year was the re-released expanded version of writer-director Richard Kelly's cult hit *Donnie Darko: The Director's Cut. Donnie Darko* originally played for about twelve days to indifferent reviews, and then faded, only to gain momentum as word of mouth spread that this was essential viewing for disaffected youth of all ages. Jake Gyllenhaal is terrific in the title role, perfectly cast as a moody young dreamer trying to figure out the Vonnegutian complexities of the Tangent Universe and how to survive in the arid, psychically toxic suburbs. Donnie's secret friend, a hideously anthropomorphic giant rabbitoid, looks something like *Harvey,* as experienced on a bad drug trip. Perfectly cast, the players include Katharine Ross as Donnie's therapist, Patrick Swayze dead-on as a self-help guru, and executive producer Drew Barrymore drawing dual duty as a teacher. This marks the welcome return of a movie that gives any audience plenty to talk about when they exit the theater.

It can be a very pleasant surprise to see a major studio entrust the third segment of a hugely profitable franchise to a clearly talented director of edgy independent pictures, and then see the potentially risky investment pay off. Director Alfonso Cuaron of the Mexican coming-of-age road flick *Y Tu Mamá También* took control of *Harry Potter and the Prisoner of Azkaban,* and came up with a winner. Tonally darker than its two predecessors, *Prisoner* finds Harry starting his third year at Hogwarts and beginning that scary transition into puberty. Daniel Radcliffe is still playing Harry, just as Rupert Grint and Emma Watson are still ably portraying his closest friends, Ron and Hermione. With Richard Harris's death, Michael Gambon ascends to the role of the new Professor Dumbledore. The ever-dangerous Gary Oldman catalyzes the plot as the eponymous prisoner, a renegade wizard who escapes his imprisonment for murder and is reported heading for Hogwarts on a mysterious mission involving Harry. In the meantime, the school has a new defense-against-the-dark-arts teacher, Professor Lupin (David Thewlis). Lupin has a dark secret, though one fairly transparent to any viewer who thinks twice about his name. Clue: the good professor is *not* a were-flower. At any rate, *Prisoner* marks perhaps the strongest chapter yet in Harry's filmed life.

Maybe it's not *that* dark, but it's still a fine bit of thoughtful fantasy. I'm referring to Marc Forster's imaginative film *Neverland* about English playwright J. M. Barrie (Johnny Depp), his friendship with the widowed Sylvia Llewellyn Davies (Kate Winslet) and her four boys, and the consequent inspiration for Peter Pan, the lost boys, and Neverland. Not really a biography, the film is more a meditation on loss, mortality, and the magic of the imaginative process. It deserves all the Oscar buzz it got.

MONSTERS IN TIGHTS:

The be-all and end-all of summer comic-book blockbusters was supposed to be *Spiderman II*, and indeed, Sam Raimi's paean to the conflicted Peter Parker (Tobey Maguire) and his ever-imperiled romance with the perky Mary Jane (Kirsten Dunst) was a big, slick, entertaining roller-coaster ride with Alfred Molina's steel-tentacled Doc Ock making for a spectacularly villainous foe. The characters were engaging, the effects and the action were nice, and Marvel's comic-book universe translated well. It was all smooth and fun and forgettable. There was no edge.

For edge, however, the summer's pleasant surprise was Guillermo del Toro's translation of Mike Mignola's graphic novel series, *Hellboy*. Ron Perlman was pretty wonderful as the big red galoot, originally a baby devil transplanted from hell to the human plane right at the end of World War II. In *Hellboy*'s alternate world, our eponymous hero is working on the front lines of the clandestine government agency dedicated to keeping us citizens free of pesky monsters and demons. To make things more complicated, neo-Nazis and even some aging *original* Nazis are lurking and plotting. Oh, and Rasputin's still around to raise a little hell. Part of what raised *Hellboy*'s index of fun to more than expectable levels is that the movie had attitude. A comic-book film with attitude is a mighty fine achievement. *Van Helsing* wouldn't have recognized attitude if it had bitten Hugh Jackman's throat. *Spiderman II* was just too good-hearted to have attitude. But *Hellboy*'s got Ron Perlman trying to blend his character's demonic personality and appearance in with humanity by grinding down his inhuman horns with a power buffer.

And then there was *Catwoman*. Oh my. Now, it's reasonable that some in the audience were satisfied just with the not-so-cheap thrill of watching Halle Berry in a tight greased-leather catsuit. How large is that demographic, anyway? Others might have been charmed if the script had done a better job showing our heroine crossing over to her true feline sensibility. Berry gingerly stalking along the top of her living room sofa was spot-on for evoking felinity, but most of the rest of the cat lore was pretty ham-handed. The script did diplomatically ignore the cat-box issue. In searching out any virtues lurking in *Catwoman*'s silliness, one should stop to appreciate Sharon Stone's energetic attempt to bring the villainous antagonist to life. Lambert Wilson and Benjamin Bratt, the second-banana villain and Kitty's love interest respectively, tackled their roles bravely.

Did anyone actually see *Thunderbirds*? This live-action version of the fondly recalled British TV marionette show from the '60s cost about $70 million and played in theaters for what seemed at the time to be a matter of hours. Actor Jonathan Frakes moved over from the *Star Trek* universe to direct, with a fine cast including Bill Paxton, Ben Kingsley, Anthony Edwards, and Sophia Myles. The trailers I caught featured really brightly colored superscience technology as the heroic Tracy family raced around the globe coping with all manner of natural and villainously induced disaster. I understand that after Universal execs saw the final cut, they decided to promote the movie as strictly a kiddy flick. It looks like only a successful DVD launch can save the world this time.

Those nostalgic for the original form of *Thunderbirds Are Go* theater technology might have ventured out to see the rambunctious and raunchy marionettes of Matt Stone and Trey Parker's *Team America: World Police*. The *South Park* boys didn't tap a large budget for good taste in their hyperkinetic, testosterone-driven tribute to the bad movies in which high-tech action teams take on ambitious villains who want to take over the White House, the whole world, or any combination of grandiose if megalomaniacal goals. Although the scattershot satiric jabs were as frequent as in the prior hit, *South Park: The Movie*, the range of targets was rather more circumscribed. *Team America* was primarily funny if you love shots at gays, Hollywood liberals, or a combination of those two groups. One can't fault the marionette work, though. The film got a lot of press for its puppet sex scenes. They weren't badly handled, but don't expect too much. No knot holes. But oh! the splinters. Truth to tell, my favorite scene was the intrusion of live actors when the maligned president of North Korea has his guards throw the hero and heroine into an arena where the big cats can be set loose upon them—big cats that turn out to be two personable live black American shorthairs! Now, *that's* inspired casting.

If you need a party tape to slap in the VCR when it's late and it's time to drive the laggards out of your home, you could do worse than to choose *Scooby-Doo 2: Monsters Unleashed*. The big, gallumphing dog of the title is animated; the human players apparently aren't supposed to be. Alas, the role of Daphne is one that Sarah Michelle Gellar took as a viable creative choice as she was leaving *Buffy*. Matthew Lillard, Freddy Prinze Jr., all the rest of the cast will probably choose not to endlessly replay this movie in the future, attempting to recapture their glory days. The misguided whimsy and the attempted humor is just painful to behold.

HITTING A HOMER OUT OF THE PARK:
The summer of 2004 saw a trio of big-budget would-be blockbusters, so close to fantasy they might as well be called slipstream, all stub a sandaled or booted toe. While the three were not without virtues, the sheer spectacle started to wear quickly.

Wolfgang Petersen is generally quite a good director. When his *Troy* took on Homer, the latter, while unbowed, ended up considerably bloodied. The writer just couldn't let the Trojan War go without a little historical rewriting to make the story arc meet traditional dramatic structure a bit more handily. The irony is, of course, that the Greeks *invented* the Hollywood story arc. While Brad Pitt makes a sulky Achilles and Orlando Bloom keeps Paris disappointingly fatuous, a surprising Eric Bana scores well, generating great presence as Troy's protector, Prince Hector. While not terribly compelling, it's still entertaining to see a bunch of guys in skirts with swords and spears, bashing one another around à la *Fight Club*. But $200 million worth? It should have bought a more impressive wooden horse. Or a great Trojan rabbit. Monty Python had it right.

We in the film audience are told that making *Alexander* was Oliver Stone's great dream for much of his life. I can't fault that. The life of Alexander the Great is a tremendously fascinating tale on which to ruminate and speculate. Unfortunately the film itself is a bit of a slog, even with Colin Farrell in the title role and Angelina Jolie playing his manipulative mum. With the peculiar continuity lapses of its uneven time scale, the movie might well have been more successful at even greater length, say, as a miniseries for cable. But the Indian elephant–based battle scenes are definitely spectacular. Skittish, trumpeting, rearing pachyderms can out-drama-queen a static wooden horse any day.

The underappreciated champ for fantastical history was *King Arthur*. No *Camelot* this time around. Director Antoine Fuqua (*Training Day*) brought in plenty of grit and frenetic action, not to mention a strong dash of *The Magnificent Seven* as Arthur and his remaining knights set off on a thankless trek through fifth-century England to rescue some laggardly Romans as the empire folds and pulls out of Britain while the nasty Saxons invade. The script by David Franzoni (*Gladiator*) and John Lee Hancock neatly lays in a background story for Arthur and his men's historical origin. Clive Owen is a convincingly weary but resolved Arthur, as are Ioan Gruffudd as Lancelot and the solid actors playing Bors and the rest of the Round Table guys. As Merlin, Stephen Dillane is a neatly fearsome indigenous rebel leader. And Keira Knightley's Guinevere turns out to be a highly competent Boadicea in disguise. The whole film's got a high fun quotient, with just enough character development and social/political/moral content to assuage viewer guilt. The high point's probably the nifty scene in which Arthur's rescue party and their charges must face off against the pursuing Saxon horde on a wintry frozen lake.

SCIENCE FICTION, THE FINAL FRONTIER:

The year began auspiciously with a terrific picture that played well with both genre and mainstream viewers. What less could you expect from *Eternal Sunshine of the Spotless Mind* with a script from Charlie Kaufman, the creative force behind such postmodern screwball successes as *Being John Malkovich*, and the sure direction of Michel Gondry? As with most of the best modern science fiction, the movie let speculative technology be the background motive force that sets into motion all manner of relationship and life complications for the characters. In this case, a dubiously matched couple played by Jim Carrey and Kate Winslet spirals into a chaotic scenario of fractured time when Winslet's character goes to the Lacuna Corporation, a company specializing in erasing bad memories from clients' minds. Trouble is, one of the company's employees decides to throw a spanner in the works by taking an all-too-unprofessional interest in Winslet, even as Carrey is grappling with partial memories of the relationship with Winslet and trying to reassemble the fragmentary clues. The result is provocative and affecting.

Far lower profile and much less endearing, the super-low-budget *Primer* is a small, personal film about techie sensibility and time travel. Writer-director-cinematographer Shane Carruth gives us a quartet of ambitious technogeeks looking for investment capital for a gadget they've cobbled together in the garage. As the story unwinds, it seems that their machine in some manner distorts time for whatever's inside. Curiosity leads to more experimentation, and the film's reality starts to get ever more complicated. What results is an intellectual puzzle bringing in all the variegated paradoxes, reality shifts, and unanticipated consequences that science fiction readers have always loved. *Primer* is a speculative think piece that doesn't star Steven Seagal or feature spectacular car chases. Take it for what it is, enjoy the challenges, and you'll be rewarded.

Being the smart-cookie film viewers you are, you probably had mixed expectations of the summer's big-budget *I, Robot*. A good adaptation of Isaac Asimov's classic fix-up novel? No, but for a variety of peculiar reasons. To some degree it's all a matter of creative thrift. Let's say the studio owns the rights to the Asimov book. Asimov and the title are marketable. Never mind the intriguing Harlan Ellison script of some years ago. Then the studio discovers they've got a sci-fi script called *Hardwired* on the shelf, a tale that involves the near future, robots, and murder. Voila! Smoosh everything together, add a few character names and Asimov's famed Three Laws of Robotics to the mix, and let highly visual director Alex Proyas (*Dark City* and *The Crow*) helm a really big-budget version of Jeff Vintar and Akiva Goldsman's script. This approach is not unique. The year also saw *Ocean's 12* developed by transplanting the characters from the original *Ocean's 11* remake into an existing caper-crime script, again from the shelf. At any rate, Will Smith added some charisma to his Chicago detective investigating a supposedly impossible murder by robot. Bridget Moynihan, as robot psychologist Susan Calvin, didn't really look like the character from Asimov's book, but she still did a good job with the role. The robots were properly flashy and fluid, with *I, Robot* being one of the increasing number of SF "green-screened" films with the human characters filmed all by their lonesome so that digital backgrounds can be added later.

Probably the most thoroughly greenscreened new science fiction feature was newcomer Kerry Conran's spectacularly retro *Sky Captain and the World of Tomorrow*. Talk about American success stories, no matter how unlikely. Novice Conran essentially got to direct his nostalgic paean to SF serials of the past on the basis of a demo reel thanks to a visionary imagination, some Mac programs, and a garage studio. Skip ahead beyond the unavoidable meetings and negotiations and suddenly there they are: Jude Law playing the classic pulp scientist-warrior (perhaps Howard Hughes on a slightly different career trajectory), Gwyneth Paltrow as a plucky journalist, Giovanni Ribisi as Sky Captain's almost equally brilliant but noncompetitive sidekick, and Angelina Jolie sadly underused as a tough-as-nails British sky admiral and Sky Captain's onetime love interest. Along with the digital backgrounds, the picture's technological innovations include a somewhat contentious appearance of the late Sir Laurence Olivier, thanks again to digital manipulation. To be fair, Olivier's character is *also* deceased in the context of the film. But it's still another portent of things to come when electronically resuscitated classic actors will play new roles in new movies. Certainly the best thing about *Sky Captain* is the visuals, ranging from the film's first spectacular shot of a zeppelin making a nighttime docking with the mooring mast at the top of the Empire State Building, to the giant robots stomping around on the streets of Manhattan. More problematic is the story. Deliberately pulpy, I suspect it appealed more to the older in the audience who remember the original tropes. Maybe if the script were just a little sharper, had a touch more wit . . . But then that could be said about most scripts these days.

When you saw the TV ads and trailers for M. Night Shyamalan's *The Village* you probably thought it was going to be some sort of dark fantasy horror/thriller. Those Hollywood flacks can be deceiving, can't they? I suspect quite a few viewers bought a ticket with unrealistic, though perfectly reasonable, expectations. Blame the marketing people. Well, surprise. *The Village* is inarguably science fiction, contemporary SF in a nineteenth-century Utopian mold at that. Imagine a zillionaire who wants to create an alternative to the evils of the out-of-control twentieth century. So he sets up a carefully guarded "game sanctuary" in rural Pennsylvania and creates an ideal colony cast in an early nineteenth-century mold. The adults know what's going on, but the children have no idea. They're simply told that the fearsome creatures in the woods will get 'em if they step out of line. Most of it all works save for the messy matter of how the adults deal with the reality of how to handle their kids' medical crises when the problem is beyond their meager homegrown abilities. Shyamalan's script does some fancy sidestepping, and not always successfully. The ensemble cast of Joaquin Phoenix, Adrien Brody, William Hurt, Bryce Dallas Howard, Sigourney Weaver, and others, does a good job with what they're handed, but that's ultimately not sufficient for a completely convincing and involving story. This was a brave try from the creator of *Sixth Sense* and *Signs*, but it just never quite jelled. It's reported that the cast spent weeks at a historical boot camp learning how to weave, dip candles, all that bucolic stuff that mostly only Jamestown reenactors do now. Little of that is displayed in the film.

The generally overlooked *The Forgotten* deserves a little more respect than it got during its brief run. Directed by Joseph Rubin and written by Gerald Di Pego, both of whom are old pros, *The Forgotten* doesn't go to great pains to define itself as the story unreels. Horror? Not likely. Hard-core science fiction? The clues seem to point that direction. Julianne Moore does her usual highly professional job, portraying a troubled mom whose child was lost the previous year in a tragic plane crash along with a handful of other kids, including the son of a retired professional hockey player a few doors down. Then Moore's shrink (Gary Sinise) tells her that she really had a miscarriage a year before and never had a son. Her memory is all a product of post-traumatic psychosis. Moore's resistant to the idea, particularly when a few strange things happen that convince her that her boy is alive and well. So is she crazy? Or is she the epicenter of some huge government conspiracy? Or maybe both? The apparent truth is admittedly presented in a fragmentary form that won't satisfy everyone. But if you pay attention in between the great special-effects scenes of human victims being jerked off the face of the earth by intangible forces and whipped up into swirling cloud pools, it's all there. If you're conversant with classic SF, think Eric Frank Russell's *Sinister Barrier* and repeat, "We are property."

Sergio Arau's *A Day without a Mexican* is something of a Latino variation rung on Philip Wylie's *The Disappearance* in which men and women suddenly find themselves literally living in different worlds. In Arau's pointed satire, the whole social fabric of California abruptly ravels one day when just about every Hispanic vanishes. Arau is a Mexican artist, musician, and political cartoonist who is the son of veteran director Alfonso Arau. Blood tells. His directorial debut shows great promise. Yareli Arizmendi, star of *Like Water for Chocolate*, plays a Latina TV reporter who apparently is about the only Mexican or Mexican-American not to vanish. It's all genuinely and uncomfortably funny.

While most people just talk about the weather, special-effects technicians can actually do something about it. In 2004 the viewer could spend hours watching fake weather in meteorological science fiction. The big-budget version was Roland Emmerich's summer feature, *The Day after Tomorrow*, with Dennis Quaid, Jake Gyllenhaal, Sela Ward, Ian Holm, Emmy Rossum, and a host of others trying to survive some huge storm fronts that do all manner of nasty things ranging from swamping Manhattan with a tidal wave to funneling instant-freeze temperatures down from the troposphere. The first half of the film demonstrates most of the nifty effects—I particularly liked the Russian freighter drifting up to the new island of the New York Public Library. The second half is a bit like the popular '50s British paperback novels about survival in a desperate future. You want a popcorn movie? This was it.

If you wished for a less intellectually challenging work, there was the CBS miniseries *Category 6: Day of Destruction*, which started promisingly enough with big tornadoes ripping up Las Vegas. This time it was *Randy* Quaid playing a storm chaser, along with the likes of Dianne Wiest, Thomas Gibson, and Brian Dennehy. You could go into the kitchen to microwave a new bowl of popcorn anytime you chose, without missing any dialogue you couldn't later instantly recreate in your head.

Writer-director David Twohy has done an admirable job for years now, creating low-to-medium-budget fantasy and science-fiction films, and getting them released.

I'm particularly fond of the Vin Diesel starship-crash-victims-stranded on-a-desert-planet-with-hungry-natives melodrama *Pitch Black,* and last year's haunted-submarine-*Twilight Zone*–ish supernatural fantasy *Below.* The summer of 2005 saw a bigger-budget sequel to *Pitch Black* called *The Chronicles of Riddick.* Vin Diesel returns as tough guy Riddick, accused murderer and fugitive, who has spooky eyes and a sense of rough honor. This time around he's up against the Necromongers, a rampaging interstellar cult led by Colm Feore with the obsessive-compulsive desire to convert everyone in the universe. Declining the invitation is not a safe option. Thandie Newton and Karl Urban have featured roles, but the real astonishment is Dame Judy Dench's intermittent presence as the ethereal (or perhaps hologrammatic) Aeron, a highly intangible observer who literally flits about. This beautifully designed and filmed adventure of escape and pursuit, battle and conquest, carries vivid resonances of classic SF, particularly notes struck in Jack Williamson and James Gunn's *Star Bridge.* Unfortunately the characters are never as involving as they were in *Pitch Black.* So you have to be satisfied mainly with going for the eye candy. Still, this was a sufficiently high-profile release to get its own set of action figures.

There are, sadly, no action figures for *Anacondas: the Hunt for the Blood Orchid,* sequel to the previous B-movie memorable primarily for Jon Voight being barfed up at the end by a huge serpent. Dwight Little directs a hapless crew of opportunists chugging up a river in Borneo in search of an invaluable pharmaceutical source, only to encounter rumors of headhunters and the actuality of really big digital snakes. A large part of the fun for the viewer would be to sit in front of the screen with a notebook and try for a world's-record list of all the goofs in the plot. After all, what can you say when a boatload of actors goes upstream and farther upstream — and then plunges over a huge waterfall? Think about it.

KING FOR A SEASON:
It's my hope that there will be some sort of DVD salvation waiting in the wings for *Stephen King's Kingdom Hospital.* You may recall this was a series based on Danish director Lars Von Trier's artfully spooky haunted hospital miniseries that played well in Europe, and seemed like a great idea for Stephen King to adapt for American television. Trouble is, ABC never seemed quite sure how to promote this effervescent mix of creepy horror (that little kid corpse riding on top of the elevator!), humor, sardonic commentary, and absurdism. And the audience seemed to have a difficult time figuring out how they were supposed to react. Or more precisely, it may be that the right appreciative audience never really found its way to the broadcast network where they could enjoy this weirdness. Or . . . perhaps the American audience needs a little more preparation to accept a big, shambling, supernatural anteater as a linking symbol for a complex cast and freewheeling plot. The show needed time to grow on the viewer; it didn't really get that. If there's ever a DVD version and you find yourself in fortunate possession of it, check out the baseball episode. Further the deponent sayeth not.

Over on the big-screen side of pop culture, the always interesting Johnny Depp starred in writer-director David Koepp's adaptation of the King novella, "Secret Window, Secret Garden." The truncated result, *Secret Window,* collapses in upon itself as Depp's character, increasingly disaffected writer Mort Rainey, flounders dismally about, attempting to figure out the real reason why John Turturro's over-the-top John Shooter is stalking him. Shooter claims to be a writer plagiarized by

Mort Rainey and he wants justice. The psychological surprises are just too few and too weak to juice up the picture's angst to a level of real suspense. Maybe good enough for the viewers who haven't read King, but not too successful, I suspect, for Stephen King's true fans.

For my money, the year's major success in adapting Stephen King material came with Mick Garris's low-budget version of "Riding the Bullet," the story that was King's first piece of fiction after his much-publicized, near-fatal, jogger-meets-van accident several years ago. Writer-director Garris expanded the story considerably, resetting it to the 1960s. The result originally played on USA, though shorter by fifteen minutes, and considerably edited by the network for time, language, and some content. *Riding the Bullet* has now been released as a DVD in restored form and that's the version you should see. Don't expect another *Stand* or *Shining*. This is very much a male coming-of-age, coming-to-terms story with fantastic elements but little gore. The director refers to it as a small film, a personal film, and it is definitely that, though Garris displays a fine and deft touch. I suspect the most sympathetic audience for *Riding the Bullet* will be the boomers, the children of the '60s who grooved to the tunes, were immersed in the politics, and who enjoyed the chords struck by *Stand by Me* and *Hearts in Atlantis*.

IN THE SLIPSTREAM:

If it walks like fantasy and talks like fantasy, and maybe looks like fantasy, but still doesn't have literal rocket ships, time machines, vampires, or rampaging demons, well, maybe it can find a comfortable berth in the slipstream.

Probably my favorite slipstream film for the year is Quentin Tarantino's *Kill Bill: Volume 2*, which more properly should be noted as the second half of the mega-movie started the year before with *Kill Bill: Volume 1*. Much as with Tarantino's *Pulp Fiction*, *Kill Bill* ditches a perfectly linear plot to fracture time lines and mix scenes in ways that ultimately all fit together with minimal fracture lines and make absolute sense. On the surface, the plot is all about vengeance as expert martial artist and assassin Beatrice (Uma Thurman) decides to give up her jet-setting life of murder and adventure and settle down to a chimerical domesticity. Her boss and erstwhile lover Bill (a superb David Carradine) takes umbrage and dispatches his other assassins to kill the bride and everyone else at her wedding rehearsal. The bride barely survives, eventually coming out of her coma to discover that her pregnancy came to term while she was unconscious, and her daughter is now in Bill's possession. Then things really switch into high gear. As writer-director and total film geek, Tarantino crafts a layered, seemingly effortless, homage to many of his favorite film forms: Hong Kong action flicks, '50s American drive-in exploitation pictures, Samurai movies, and on and on. But action isn't the only pertinent thing here. Tarantino uses the film to dig into the nature of love and commitment, violence and the people who practice it, honor and ethics. And it all works. Passionate conviction is usually a cardinal virtue for creative successes. I think that as a creator, Tarantino believes completely in everything he's done in *Kill Bill*. Love it or hate it, it's a triumph that stirs little ambivalence in anyone who views it.

A couple of years ago, the thriller *The Bourne Identity* was not only a smash at the theaters, it also became a major success when it hit the rental market. Not only did it showcase Matt Damon as a first-rate action-adventure hero but it also posed the unanswered question of whether the terribly capable protagonist was more than simply human. Was he a cyborg? A thoroughly brainwashed spy? A genetically modified *homo superior*? An alien supersoldier? No one knows yet. But now he's back with *The Bourne Supremacy*, again with Damon, and again with Franka Potente, although briefly, as Bourne's ill-fated lover. Really good directors from the independent arena keep getting tapped to try out as blockbuster helmers. In this case it's Paul Greengrass (*Bloody Sunday*) directing from a Tony Gilroy script. The eye candy's fine as the fugitive Bourne gets blamed for an assassination he had nothing to do with, and there are few new clues about who—and what—he really is.

For something completely different, check out Takeshi Kitano's off-the-wall entry in the canon of one of Japan's favorite characters: *The Blind Swordsman: Zatoichi*. Kitano himself plays the sightless itinerant killer who unluckily (particularly for the skyrocketing body count) wanders into gang war in an isolated Japanese mountain village. So do you like martial arts, sword battles, gambling, massage, Samurai honor, and tap dancing? *Zatoichi* might well be right up your alley.

Hero, from director Zhang Yimou (*Raise the Red Lantern* and *Ju Dou*) is generated from China's wealth of historical myth. Art and warfare, assassins and storytellers, all spin the complex web of loyalty, honor, and courage. But what the audience carries away most vividly is the visual look of the film. The swordswomen's duel in a swirling blizzard of autumn leaves is an image that will haunt the eye and memory forever. And as the protagonist, Jet Li is no slouch either.

For something considerably less romantic, search out Japanese director Takashi Miike's *Gozu*, a surreal carousel of weirdness, gangsters, disappearing corpses, guilt, violent revenge, and ghosts. It's a psychological amusement-park ride rather than a straightforward story, so just grip the sides of your seat and go along for the unpredictable ride. If *Gozu* (the name of a Japanese cow-headed demon) ultimately all makes complete sense to you, you're probably in deep, deep trouble.

Don't miss the dark, depressing, tragic gloom of *The Machinist*, ninety-seven minutes of affecting nightmare. Yes, I really *am* recommending this powerful psychodrama about a guy named Trevor Reznick (a dedicated Christian Bale who lost sixty-three pounds to play his deteriorating character), so haunted by his enigmatic past he cannot eat or sleep. Reznick's challenge, as he works in a Dante-esque machine shop, is to explore his own mind until he roots out the final mysteries. It's spellbinding.

WATCHING WITH ANIMATION:
DreamWorks released *Shrek II* in big-budget animation. It didn't have all the freshness of the original, but it still did the job. Certainly Eddie Murphy voicing the donkey was still as obnoxious as ever. In this episode ogre Shrek goes to visit his bride, Fiona's, parents, with predictably mixed and hilarious results. Midway through the picture there's a set piece that's worth the price of admission when ogre and donkey are confronted in the forest by a feline assassin dispatched by Fiona's curmudgeonly dad. Antonio Banderas boosts the whole picture with his silky interpretation of Puss-in-Boots. Any mass murder foiled by a sudden hairball attack is great by me.

Director Brad Bird made all U.S. animation fans sit up and cheer with *Iron Giant*, a nostalgic cold war mythic story about a lonely boy who befriends a huge extraterrestrial automaton that appears here on earth. Now Bird's got a huge hit on his hands with *The Incredibles*, a droll feature about what happens to superheroes after they retire and have families. The script is funny and intelligent, and the voices are cast well.

For the more doggedly conservative viewer, Disney gave us the perfectly competent but studiously unambitious *Home on the Range* with the admittedly attractive voices of Roseanne Barr, Dame Judi Dench, Cuba Gooding Jr., Randy Quaid, Jennifer Tilly, and other worthies. Writer-directors Will Finn and John Sanford are Disney veterans making their feature debut here with a film that probably made some respectable money. On the other hand, it stirred no ripples with its story of plucky ranch beasts thwarting a rapacious land baron. Where's *Animal Farm* when we need it?

While the shark content in *Shark Tale* isn't nearly so razor edged and funny as it was in *Finding Nemo*, this DreamWorks animation feature did accomplish one peculiar distinction: it was a big-budget, high-profile project that blended classic animation storytelling with an urban hip-hop–friendly ambiance. Rasta jellyfish (Ziggy Marley and Doug E. Doug)? Why not? Sharks as underwater urban mafia? Okay. Jack Black and Will Smith voicing characters who are unlikely pals (a young vegan shark and an upwardly mobile street hustler of a fish respectively)? Right. Competent it is. But another *Shrek*? Sadly not.

Director Robert Zemeckis and co-writer William Broyles Jr. gave their digitally animated version of *Polar Express* a distinctly new look in visual style. This was an expanded version of the story in Chris Van Allsburg's slender but lavishly illustrated book. Van Allsburg is one of the greatest modern illustrators of kids' books, and customarily lets the image do the bulk of communicating. This tale of a boy on the night before Christmas taking a magical train to the North Pole obliges him to learn important lessons about life and doubt and belief. It delivers its holiday message without becoming cloying. And yes, Virginia, there is a Tom Hanks here—in five different roles. *Polar Express* ended up being released first in standard theaters, then in IMAX houses all around the country. In the latter format, it looks like it's going to become a perennial holiday classic.

RETURN OF THE REMAKES:
Forget business economics. The only good reason to commit a remake is if you can genuinely bring something new to the film. The year 2004 brought us a good spectrum of examples: the good, the okay, and the ugly.

The surprisingly good example is the new version of George Romero's modern classic, *Day of the Dead*. People remember the 1978 version fondly for the central conceit: four survivors of a walking-dead holocaust barricade themselves in a shopping mall and attempt to hold out as the starving, walking—well, shambling—dead besiege the place. The point is that the zombies zero in on the mall because it was what they loved most when they were alive. A dead-on social observation like this carries a lot of power. The new writer and debut director Zach Snyder draws on this critique of consumer society to good effect in the remake. This time the setting's Milwaukee, right there in the center of Middle America, and a slightly larger enclave of mortal survivors gets trapped in the mall. But the zombies are still ubiquitous, and they're still not converting to vegan beliefs. There's plenty of blood and dismemberment for the hard core. And even more is effectively suggested. Sarah Polley plays to perfection a resilient zombie-widowed nurse. Ditto Ving Rhames as a tough cop. If you haven't yet seen this and plan to, be sure to hang in through the closing credit crawl for interpolated material that muddies the fictive waters troublingly. An added bonus is the great eclectic but absolutely appropriate music track for the film, opening with Johnny Cash's "The Man Comes Around" and ending with Jim Carroll's "People Who Died." So all in all, no injustice is done to George Romero. And for carnivore fans, watch for Romero's new *Land of the Dead* in 2005.

An even riskier gamble was Jonathan Demme's reworking of the 1962 techie political thriller *The Manchurian Candidate*. The first adaptation of Richard Condon's still-in-print novel gave us Lawrence Harvey as a Korean War hero who comes to suspect his memories of the past aren't as concrete as he would like to believe, and that, just maybe, he's being manipulated by malign forces. Angela Lansbury played his political-kingmaker mom with horrifying gusto. And Frank Sinatra starred as a fellow soldier and friend who finds himself unwillingly dissecting the mystery. Skip ahead to 2004 and the war in question is the Gulf War, Liev Schreiber is the vet tormented by unsettling flashes and dreams, Meryl Streep's his iron-willed mom, and Denzel Washington steps into the Sinatra role. Oh, and the malignly conspiring Korean Army is now the globe-spanning multinational conglomerate, Manchuria Corporation. Daniel Pyne's script is serviceable enough, and the realpolitik is still as chilly as it was forty years ago. Sadly, Condon's creation hasn't lost its relevance at all. But the new version's just not as crisp and disturbing, simply not as edgy and shocking as the '60s version. That might be due to a less adroit adaptation. Or, troublingly, it might be because we're now all too accustomed to the kind of nasty cynicism carried by the film's message.

For sheer waste of star power and budget, and for peculiar intentions, check out the new version of 1975's chilly film based on the Ira Levin bestseller *The Stepford Wives*. Whether it's director Frank Oz, writer Paul Rudnick, or the glittery cast of Nicole Kidman, Bette Midler, Matthew Broderick, Christopher Walken, Glenn Close, and the rest, no one seems to have a good public opinion of why anyone involved thought this particular remake was a good idea. Feminism, contemporary relationships—in particular, marriage—gender warfare paranoia, flight to the suburbs, all this and more were fairly sharply examined in the original. The new version seems to be a wildly—though not particularly telling and certainly not really amusing—scattershot comedy, full of froth and nonsense. Even the science-fiction element is bobbled. Were the rich, powerful, apparently sociopathic men of ideally suburban Stepford using technology to brainwash their independent-minded wives? Or were they replacing their spouses with actual replicants as in the original? The film as released can't seem to decide. In short, all the high-powered talent onboard can't relieve the atmosphere of escalating foolishness and tedium.

Finally, do we need yet another version of Jules Verne's *Around the World in Eighty Days*? Sadly, probably not. Director Frank Coraci's admirably independent production cost more than $100 million and looked like a sure bet for international profits with Jackie Chan top billed as Phileas Fogg's (British comic, Steve Coogan) dubious manservant, Passepartout. Jim Broadbent and John Cleese are present as well, along with an army of celebrity cameos ranging from Kathy Bates as Queen Victoria and Owen and Luke Wilson as the Wright brothers to Arnold Schwarzenegger as a Turkish prince. Released through Disney, was this amusing? Somewhat. A new classic? Eighty minutes after watching, you won't remember much about it.

The Small Screen

SCIFI FOREVER:
As the year started, brand-new from SciFi was *Code Name: Eternity*, in which an extraterrestrial bad guy holing up on contemporary Earth uses an amusing but not exceedingly competent robot named Mr. Dent, as well as red-shirt human minions, to defend himself against a home-world hit man sent to retrieve him by whatever means. Ethaniel, at first afflicted by traumatic amnesia, is befriended by a credulous human psychologist. I hope dumb and forgettable doesn't sound *too* harsh.

The SciFi Channel brought us another new season of *Stargate SG-1*. Starring Richard Dean Anderson, the series continued competent, lightweight, and *still* not MacGyver redux. Unfortunately.

But as the year continued, both the *Stargate* franchise and SciFi in general got more interesting, though not always through unequivocal triumph. The sophomoric reality series *Scare Tactics* lost Shannon Doherty as a host and gained a Baldwin brother. The cruel humor of friends colluding on spooky pranks to drive their buddies into underwear-changing paroxysms didn't really change. Then SciFi inaugurated another reality series called *Mad Mad House*, in which the contestants were closeted in a house with a voodoo priestess, a "vampire," a naturist, a witch, and a modern primitive. Dumb as it might sound, it was a surprisingly intelligent premise, prodding and testing a bunch of doofus straights to see if any of them could mature into a state of empathy for others unlike themselves. The ratings sucked sufficiently that this series will probably never return, but the effort was laudable. Another reality series with less ambition but better ratings is *Ghost Hunters*, which, alas, adds little new to our body of knowledge about the supernatural.

SciFi's original films were, by and large, about as ambitious as stacking rocks in a quarry. Saturday night movies featured endless variations on rampaging (and usually quite digitally large) crocs, spiders, snakes, and assorted parasites both alien and domestically raised through DNA engineering gone wacko.

Then there was *Five Days to Midnight*, a decent and diverting miniseries that essentially played off the central idea of the noir classic, *D.O.A.* Later in the year, Robert Halmi, plunderer (though usually in a benign way) of the classics, produced *The Legend of Earthsea*, based on two of Ursula K. Le Guin's Earthsea novels. The miniseries worked decently for those who had never read Le Guin and were coming to the work without expectations. They simply encountered a reasonably competent, if generic, fantasy. For Le Guin fans, the adaptation was atrocious and the author made her feelings publicly and eloquently known.

Farscape aficionados got a four-hour fix as Ben Browder and his merry crew of the alien and the alienated briefly returned from the death sentence of cancellation. It served as a reminder that things could always be worse. To wit, *Tripping the Rift*, a raunchy animated series that survived its first season and gained renewal for a second. The humor's pretty much on the level of the 1950s *Playboy* party jokes page, but it's interesting that the one character who's a touchstone for sense, intelligence, and ethics, is an alien female.

After years of development as a potential series, Eric Garcia's *Anonymous Rex* made it to the screen on SciFi. This first of three science-fiction mystery novels about a contemporary world in which the dinosaurs never actually went extinct but rather evolved into forms that allow them to live unsuspected among us homo saps, uses a wacky premise, but the result is enjoyable. Some of Garcia's humor made it intact to the screen, and having Faye Dunaway do a cameo as one the dinos' ruling council didn't hurt either.

By the end of 2004, SciFi turned its Friday nights into a showplace for effects-heavy science-fiction adventure. *Stargate SG-1* got something of a makeover, and then spawned *Stargate: Atlantis*, in which a Stargate team find themselves marooned far away from the here and now in a deserted Atlantean city and in a world beset by a vile, vampiric would-be master species.

Then the new series version of *Battlestar Galactica* roared onto the scene after its successful tryout a year before as a miniseries. Die-hard purists from the good old days of Lorne Green, Richard Hatch, and Dirk Benedict groused a bit, but simply found themselves obliged to accommodate to the new reality: that the character of Starbuck had changed genders, and the character of Boomer had switched both gender and ethnic extraction. The *real* change, however, is that *Galactica* is making a genuine effort to give what was originally a fairly perfunctory adventure series a real sense of cultural texture and social reality. Politics, economics, sociology are all coming into play even as the surviving humans of the Cylon genocide are battling their cybernetic enemies. This isn't so much ambitious SF as it is genuinely innovative *television* SF, and the team behind it should be commended. Anchor points for the series aren't so much the Viper pilots as the military leader (Edward James Olmos, with the same considerable presence he displayed in *Bladerunner*) and the political leader (Mary McDonnell, playing a bureaucrat kicked upstairs suddenly, and obliged to deal both with the survival of the small fleet of remaining humanity *and* her own personal cancer).

Finally, SciFi's Friday winds down with *Andromeda*, rescued from the shoals of syndication. The Kevin Sorbo space opera, now that *Star Trek: Enterprise* is breathing its presumed last, will be the only remaining Gene Roddenberry–connected ongoing project on TV.

WHAT TO WATCH WHEN YOU HAVE NO LIFE:
I can't help it. I'm biased. Am I a bad person just because whenever I see the WB's *Charmed* I think of *Buffy Lite*? The story of three young witch sisters living in a cool house in San Francisco and dealing with all manner of dark forces and working magically for good is, well, also a bit of Alice Hoffman Lite. Alyssa Milano, Holly Marie Combs, and Rose McGowan (who replaced Shannen Doherty a while back) do well at being pert and charming. There's a surefire story arc proceeding now that Combs's Piper has become a young mom. On the downside, of course, demon lover Julian McMahon left the show to become a more secular demon lover on *Nip/Tuck*.

Now, just to underscore the point that virtue does not always confer triumph, consider the case of Fox's *Wonderfalls*. This fantasy series about alienated drop-out Jaye Tyler (French Canadian actress Caroline Dhavernas) filling her empty days at a tourist-trap gift shop near Niagara Falls until the previously inanimate gewgaws around her start to talk, came to Fox's Friday night lineup, wowed the critics, and then was summarily executed after airing four episodes. Some good news is that the DVD with nine additional episodes, as well as the usual lot of extras, has been issued and can be found at your local video emporium. This series was a creation of *Dead Like Me*'s Bryan Fuller and *Malcolm in the Middle*'s Todd Holland, and it shows in

the askew humor and humanity of the scripts. Dhavernas's character is an often re-
sisting force for good, obliged to deal with the mysteries, those calculating forces of
the intangible and the wonderful. The whole cast of the ill-fated series is great, particularly William Sadler and Diana Scarwid as Jaye's parents. You should have
watched it when you had the chance; but there's still that DVD.

Speaking of great series parents, the couple played by Mary Steenburgen and Joe
Mantegna add considerably to the whole family of Amber Tamblyn's Joan in CBS's
Joan of Arcadia. Creator Barbara Hall's fantasy series about a young California teen
who has conversations with and gets orders from a variety of avatars of God, is customarily light and smart enough to afford genuine reward to even the nonbelievers
who might lurk in the audience. This past season, I particularly liked the episode
called "Queen of the Zombies," sort of a lightweight *Waiting for Guffman* treatment
of a hideous musical comedy, all-dancing, all-shambling, all-school play about the
undead. With, of course, a guest director.

And speaking of Christian-referenced series, the rather more adventurous, though
still warm and funny, *Dead Like Me* returned for another season on Showtime. The
hapless, ill-assorted crew of Grim Reapers who got sidelined after their mortal deaths
and are now stuck with the task of herding new souls in the Pacific Northwest are still
hanging out at the German pancake house and grousing about the lousy pay. The
great Mandy Patinkin continues to play Rube, the straw-boss father figure, and Ellen
Muth is still an endearingly acerbic and reluctant new Reaper recruit.

Over on the science-fiction side of the ledger, CBS gave *Century City* a brief run.
This attempt at using new technology as a plot basis for cases in a near-future L.A.
was an intriguing springboard for a new version of legal drama, but it just couldn't
seem to catch fire.

Whether you think of it as science fiction or dark fantasy, Anthony Michael
Hall's portrayal of the psychic Johnny Smith from Stephen King's *The Dead Zone* is
becoming a durable staple of USA, presenting another season as the Greg
Stilson/politician of the Apocalypse story arc plays out. After three years, the series is
still well executed and enjoyable.

TNT presented the world with a movie intended to lead to a series, if the ratings
were decent. All the returns aren't in yet for *The Librarian: Quest for the Spear*, starring Noah Wyle of *ER* as a bookish geek who applies for an advertised library job
only to find out that the library in question is far more than he bargained for. It turns
out to be one of those Borgesian repositories where just about all the neat stuff in
world mythology is piled around. In short, this is an Indiana Jones sort of tongue-in-
cheek, wildly careering adventure in which Wyle's character finds himself with a
tough blond assistant (Sonya Walger) trekking through jungles and up and down
mountains, duking it out with megalomaniacal (is there any other sort?) villain
(Kyle MacLachlan) for the occult spear that pierced Christ's side. It's all lightweight
but entertaining, and benefits from cameos by the likes of Bob Newhart, Jane
Curtin, and Olympia Dukakis. All told, it ranks well with the similarly toned *National Treasure*, the much higher-budgeted feature in which Nicholas Cage is trying
to locate a huge Knights Templar treasure hidden in the newly minted United States
two centuries ago, and which is accessible only by following an insanely complicated trail of clues that includes an invisible map on the back of the Declaration of
Independence. Oh, those wacky Masons!

For a genuine dark fantasy treat, check the Bravo channel late at night for its introduction to U.S. viewers of the British occult series *Strange*. It's about your basic defrocked Anglican priest enlisting help from one buddy who is apparently mentally challenged but keenly psychic, and from another who is a computer whiz, to fight demons in a drab contemporary English city after his wife is killed by the forces of darkness. Ian Richardson is on hand as an ambivalently sinister vicar, and guest stars such as Imelda Staunton (*Vera Drake*) stop by to great effect. This is another of those smart, snappy projects the British do so well.

THE FRESHMAN CLASS PRESIDENT:
In terms of television debuts, what many observers thought would be a long shot paid off big-time for ABC. *Lost* hit the ground running and has never looked back. Some commentators have suggested it's another *X-Files*, but that's a bit of a stretch. Creator J. J. Abrams and his confederates have set up a dramatic structure that drags in almost as many sudden plot elements as *24*, yet mostly avoids straining credulity. In the first episode, a passenger jet L.A.-bound from Sydney veers off course and crashes on an unknown Pacific island. The survivors try to make the best of things, though they soon begin to despair of quick rescue. Then the weird things start to ac-cumulate. Why are there polar bears on this tropical paradise? What's the giant, un-seen *thing* that rummages around in the jungle, occasionally darting out to gobble someone up? Why is the sea behaving strangely, from day to day gradually rising to swallow the plane wreckage? Who's the mysterious Frenchwoman, apparently the survivor of an earlier plane wreck sixteen years before, now living in a remote cave and broadcasting a continuous looped Mayday? What's the apparently impregnable metal hatch set in the ground out in the jungle? Who are the strangers on the island who attempt to kidnap the near-term pregnant Aussie girl and why do they want her baby? And so it goes, with plenty of mysteries and sparely doled out clues. By the end of the year viewers really had no firm idea whether they were watching fantasy or science fiction, horror or straightforward adventure. Is the island displaced in time? In something like the Bermuda Triangle? Is it purgatory or even hell? Is it an alien experiment? A government or corporate conspiracy? It's indisputably intrigu-ing, and for most, entertaining. Not only is there the appeal of the mystery but the show sets up a diverse microsociety of survivors and devises a credible device of flashbacks to give us an expanding number of background stories. Damned clever, these TV creators. Every once in a while, all stereotypes aside, they come through.

REQUIESCAT IN PACE:
As mentioned above, *Wonderfalls* came and departed in a virtual blink. *Farscape* limped a little further with a welcome respite before proceeding on into the pro-gramming darkness. *Angel* sadly came to the end of the line, but ended with a bang rather than a whimper. And the producers of *Star Trek: Enterprise* announced that it was entering its final season, heralding the first season in two decades that will not field a new show set in the *Star Trek* universe.

THINGS FROM ANOTHER WORLD:
There certainly are plenty of cool media-related things to buy if one simply has good charge cards. A prize for the avaricious collector of DVDs is the Monster Legacy line of Universal monster classics. Mother's Day last year saw the release of an elab-orate boxed set of *Dracula*, *Frankenstein*, and *The Wolfman*, along with all their as-

sorted sequels as well as a diverse set of critical commentaries. The bonus was a set of three cast resin busts of our three heroes. The package generally retailed for around eighty dollars. Also available as individual thirty-dollar sets were similar treatments of *The Mummy*, *The Invisible Man*, and *The Creature from the Black Lagoon*. It's a great chunk of film history to have on the shelf—and to watch. When's the last time you viewed *Dracula's Daughter*, *Son of Frankenstein*, or *The Creature Walks among Us?* Treat yourself.

On the toy side of the aisle, I particularly enjoyed Palisade's plush life-size version of the face hugger from *Alien*. It's the perfect gift for your kid's room, or for your sweetie on Valentine's Day. The critter's legs have wire armatures so that you can form-fit it around your face, or the face of any willing accomplice. Creep out your friends!

The toy company of the graphic-novel artist and creator of *Spawn*, Todd McFarlane, continues to boom with action figures from both the fantastical media and sports. The third series of McFarlane's Monsters is subtitled Six Faces of Madness, and delves into history with an infamous selection of real-life monsters ranging from Jack the Ripper to Attila the Hun. The morbid prize for most horrific goes to a tableau of Elizabeth Bathory, the Countess of Blood, lounging in her plasma-filled bathtub, sipping from a flagon filled with a ghastly cocktail, and surrounded by candles and the impaled heads of her child victims on spikes pressed into service as candelabra. Not a good Mother's Day gift for most. But it makes the plush face hugger look cuddly by comparison.

Clive Barker fans can buy from Reel Toys a third series of six action figures pulled from the later *Hellraiser* movies. Poor, misguided, flayed Frank is the most startling. Each figure includes one segment of a build-it-yourself Leviathan. And again from McFarlane, one can purchase Clive Barker's Infernal Parade, six elaborately designed wheeled carnival exhibit toys that will look great incorporated into your Barbie display. The added incentive to purchase a complete set is that each figure includes one section of a brand-new piece of Barker fiction.

ALL IN ALL?
A pretty good year.

Comics and Graphic Novels: 2004

2004

Charles Vess

In 2004 the graphic novel generated such an enormous amount of media attention that it might be safe to say that the form has well and truly established itself as a legitimate medium of artistic expression in the consciousness of the general public. This notice has come not just, as has been the case for so many years, from the few long-established critical voices within the comic-book marketplace such as *The Comics Journal*, but also, and perhaps more importantly, from mainstream literary critics. Substantial articles about the form have appeared in *The New York Times Magazine, Utne Reader, Time* magazine, *USA Today*, and a vast assortment of other newspapers and magazines across the country. Publishers Weekly continues to spotlight the genre and has reported on the continued upsurge in sales through the major bookstore chains and other sales venues throughout the year. Most of this sales upswing continues to belong to the subgenre of Japanese manga, though several books with a more general potential readership have done quite well, both critically and in sales.

Almost all of the major publishing houses have instigated their own graphic-novel lines or have announced their intention to do so. Of those, Pantheon has quickly risen to the top with the quality of their offerings, such as Chris Ware's *Jimmy Corrigan*, Dan Clowe's *David Boring*, and David B's *Epileptic*. All of these books are beautifully produced, highly personal statements by their respective authors, complemented by excellent artwork that is sensitive to the individual themes explored in each work. I was quite pleased to see that Pantheon had managed to succeed in getting the second volume of Marjane Satrapi's *Persepolis* racked right alongside the typical general-interest prose novels at bookstores everywhere. For once this lovely book was not relegated to the more typical graphic novel "ghetto" beside the newest gaming modules or *Star Trek* photo books. Indeed, in several newspaper headlines, Satrapi has been hailed as the new Art Spiegelman, which speaks volumes for the acceptance of this new medium. If the general public can be expected to be familiar enough with graphic novels to know who Art Spiegelman is, then this field truly seems to have come into its own.

All this is very exciting news, but to continue to grow and evolve the graphic novel medium needs an eager audience that is ready to purchase and read large quantities of the books that we have to offer. Where are the likes of John Grisham, Stephen King, or J. K. Rowling within our field? If we never produce even one mass-market popular author then the graphic novel eventually will be relegated to the dusty shelves of the equivalent of the lonely poetry section of your local bookstore. Publishers, after all, need to make a profit before they will seek to publish more of the same.

The typical critical writing on this medium seems to only spotlight either a trade-paperback collection featuring a superhero tie-in to the new would-be film block-buster or travel to the other end of the spectrum and focus on a "literary" work by a highly regarded alternative writer/artist. Of course, both of these areas of interest have produced brilliant, lasting work but where are the stories that speak to the more typical reading interests? And how can these same general-interest readers be expected to walk into a bookstore and know which graphic novels suit their reading taste?

Fortunately there is a large and growing selection of graphic novels that just such a reader might embrace. Jeff Smith's *Bone* is a prime example of this type of book. Smith's compelling plot and stylish art combine to tell a story that any typical main-stream reader could enjoy. There are others, of course, such as Bryan Talbot's *A Tale of One Bad Rat* or Jill Thompson's *Scary Godmother*, Linda Medley's *Castle Waiting* or Bill Willingham's marvelous *Fables* series, to name but a few examples. These are tales that could cross any border and please a wide range of readers. We simply need more books on this level in order to survive as an art form and an industry. So I offer this list as a guidepost to more works like this.

But before I begin my overview of the best fantasy and horror graphic novels of the year, there are a few books that don't fit within those categories but are of such quality that I would feel remiss if I didn't point them out to the readers of this survey. *Alia's Mission* (Knopf) is written and drawn by longtime *Village Voice* cartoonist Mark Alan Stamaty. This slight book tells a complex real-life story in simple terms. But it's a rather important story. In 2003, as the war in Iraq draws closer, Alia Muhammad Baker, the chief librarian of the Central Library in Basra, fears for the safety of the books under her charge. The government refuses to acknowledge her fears and so she enlists at first her husband and then all of her neighbors in smuggling more than thirty thousand volumes out of the library before it is bombed and burned to the ground. Countless volumes, the history of their entire culture, are all saved by the efforts of this one determined woman.

The literary magazine *McSweeney's* asked award-winning graphic novelist Chris Ware to guest edit and design a comics-themed issue, *McSweeney's Quarterly Concern*, issue 13. Ware produced a gorgeous volume packed to the brim with the top names in the alternative comics field. Here we have Robert Crumb rubbing shoulders with Chester Brown, Charles Burns, Ben Katchor, and a long list of other great talents. Noted scholars in the field cap the issue with several insightful essays concerning the medium.

And finally Craig Thompson, who gave us the phenomenal graphic novel *Blankets*, has returned with a slimmer but no less delightful offering, *Carnet de Voyage*.

More of a travel journal than a graphic narrative, it is nevertheless filled with Thompson's expressive drawings and clear-eyed observations on people, places, and the loneliness of travel on the road.

Here then, in no particular order, are my favorite graphic narratives of the past year.

One of the most significant events of the year was the completion of Jeff Smith's epic fantasy saga, *Bone* (Cartoon Books). Bringing this long-running series to a lovely but bittersweet conclusion has been a long journey for Smith and his multitude of patient readers, but worth the wait. To celebrate he published both the final, uncollected chapters in their own individual hardcover, *The Crown of Horns*, and then as a gift to all of his fans wrapped the complete *Bone* in a single volume. That's right: the entire story, over thirteen hundred pages of this delightful series, in one very thick volume. Reading the saga in its entirety serves to point out that Smith's assured mixture of comedy and drama in script and art adds up to a wholly satisfying high-fantasy epic. I, for one, will be sad to bid a final good-bye to all of those by now familiar and beloved characters.

The splendidly evocative and downright creepy painted art by Greg Ruth in his limited run series, *Freaks of the Heartland* (Dark Horse Comics), makes this one of the best horror titles of the year. Writer Steve Niles's moody tale is set in a remote valley in the rural heartland of America filled with dense shadows that conceal both monsters and madness. A band of children and their anything but ordinary playmates, a group of grotesque mutants, try to avoid the terrified adults that want to kill the "freaks." This miniseries is now available in trade paperback from the same publisher.

Kingdom of the Wicked (Dark Horse) is a horrific tale from writer Ian Edginton and artist D'Israeli. A hugely successful children's book writer suddenly finds himself transported to the beautiful, imaginary world that he had created as a young child, a world of soft whimsical fantasy that has been the wellspring for all his writing ever since. But now he finds only a dark landscape filled with terrifying creatures and continual bloody war. His journey to the heart of this transformation and the other self that he finds there makes for a hugely compelling tale.

Loki (Marvel Comics) is a beautifully painted (by Esad Ribic) miniseries that brings the arch trickster of Asgardian mythology to the fore as he assumes command over that fabled land and proceeds to enact a long-simmering vengeance against his half brother, Thor. Written by Robert Rodi, this tale is attuned to all of its inherent mythic resonances and is a delightful surprise, coming as it does from a publisher associated primarily with superheroes. By the time you read this summary it will be collected into lovely hardcover edition.

Age of Bronze: Sacrifice (Image) is the second collected edition of Eric Shanower's epic undertaking, a historically accurate rendering of the story of the Trojan War. This volume, a follow-up to his first collection, *A Thousand Ships*, weighs in at a little over two hundred pages of densely told and detailed black-and-white art. Shanower manages to give each character in his huge cast an individual look and personality, while deeply involving the reader with superb storytelling. A multitude of historical notes in the back of the book reveal much of the depth of research that Shanower has done for each of these volumes. This series continues to be a stunning achievement within the graphic-novel medium.

Soulwind (Oni Press) collects all five individual volumes of writer/artist Scott

Morse's invigorating epic tale of wonder and delight. Morse's surprising plot manages to transform many of the clichés of modern high fantasy, from the discovery of a magic sword to the revelation of a fairy world around us, and make them new again to the delight of every reader. The art begins rather crudely in the first several chapters but quickly gains assurance and strength and matures into a highly stylized but evocative shorthand for perfectly portraying the mythic icons that Morse increasingly turns to throughout the story's conclusion.

I was very pleased to see this new book, *Silk Tapestry and Other Chinese Folktales*, by writer/artist Patrick Atangan (NBM). This volume is a follow-up to his first beautiful collection of sensitively told Chinese folktales, *The Yellow Jar*. This time he has chosen to adapt three whimsical tales, each concerning a particular artist and the difficulties that his or her talent can bring with it. As Atangan says in his notes, "Folk tales are the bones of Society. From them the lessons of love, courage and maturity are told from an elderly generation to its children." I eagerly await new volumes by this wonderful talent.

Another delightful surprise is *It's a Bird* (DC/Vertigo), an original graphic novel written by Steven Seagle with stylized but extremely effective painted art by Teddy Kristiansen. The book, although nominally about the iconic superhero Superman, features a fascinating discussion of the power of stories, how they are able to heal and most importantly how they allow us to see inner truths. Kristiansen's art is less bound by physical reality than it is by a more psychological one that allows the reader to easily slip into and understand the mental outlook of the book's protagonist.

Regular readers of this column know that I have a special fondness for the work of Ted Naifeh and in particular his series of adventures featuring his adolescent protagonist Courtney Crumrin. In his latest collection, *Courtney Crumrin in the Twilight Kingdom* (Oni), Naifeh has once again spun a lovely, engrossing tale full of dark twisted forests, strange gothic mansions, and a fairy world rife with sharp, dangerous edges. Courtney and her companions set off through this tortured landscape to find and return a fairy changeling. In so doing, they encounter Titania and Oberon in their most threatening aspects.

Creatures of the Night (Dark Horse) is a solid adaptation by artist Michael Zuli of two of award-winning writer Neil Gaiman's short stories. The transformation from straight prose to panel-to-panel continuity flows smoothly and Zuli's heartfelt renderings of both "The Price" and "The Daughter of Owls" lend an appropriate air of moody horror to the collection. Zuli excels at drawing the animals that so densely populate these tales. His cats are as articulate as any of the human figures and his owls in the second story are particularly splendid, making the tale's horrific ending that much more satisfying. Talented author Neil Gaiman also produced the script for *1602* (Marvel Comics), wherein he transported most of the major players in the Marvel universe back to the era of Queen Elizabeth of England and the Spanish Inquisition. His subtle transformation of each of these well-known superheroes into an historically accurate representation of himself and his particular powers is pretty cool. The art by Andy Kubert carries this compelling story to its dramatic and satisfying conclusion.

The Dark Horse Book of Witchcraft (Dark Horse) is an anthology featuring work by a host of very talented writers and artists. Although most of the stories are excellent, the standout is the collaboration between writer Evan Dorkin and painter Jill Thompson, "Unfamiliar." This tale, at turns hilarious and horrific, features a cast of talking dogs and cats who must defend their turf from a coven of modern-day witches who have just moved into the animals' suburban neighborhood. Also included is a new, very short *Hellboy* story by Mike Mignola, and a lovely tale concerning the Salem witches by Scott Morse, all wrapped in a gorgeous cover by Gary Gianni.

Carla Speed McNeil continues to delight us with her latest collection *Finder, Mystery Date* (Light Speed Press). Her story revolves around a young woman, Vary, who is attending college to become a prostitute, a term which has very different connotations in McNeil's highly original science-fictional world. Using Vary as our guide through this strange world, McNeil employs elements of art, politics, and sex in developing her subtle story line, and uses her delicate rendering style to great effect.

To our delight the third volume of *The P. Craig Russell Library of Opera Adaptations* (NBM) was released in 2004. This new collection gathers adaptations of several operas, a longtime passion of the author/artist, which Russell originally published as separate books. Featuring *Pelleas and Melisande, Ein Heldentraum,* and *Cavalleria Rusticana,* all in full color and all elegantly drawn. I would single out the *Salome* as being the most effective of these adaptations, perhaps because of its rather dramatic story line. You do not need to be a fan of operas (I myself am not) to enjoy these superbly told and drawn adaptations. This year also saw the release of the fourth volume of the prolific Mr. Russell's adaptations of *Fairy Tales of Oscar Wilde* (NBM). Featured are lovingly drawn, sensitively told renditions of some of Wilde's more obscure fables, including "The Devoted Friend" and "The Nightingale and the Rose."

The second volume of writer Benoît Peeters and artist Francois Schuiten's *Cities of the Fantastic, The Invisible Frontier* (NBM) was published in the U.S. this year. As longtime collaborators, this pair of European creators have, for many years, been exploring surrealistic cityscapes within their stories. Now for the first time, one of their protagonists follows a map, tattooed on the back of a beautiful young girl, into the landscape outside those enigmatic cities. The rural landscapes quickly assume all the existential dread of those earlier twisted, closely packed city streets, echoing each protagonist's state of mind. Schuiten's lushly rendered painted art makes you feel as if you could walk right into the world depicted in one of his panels. Bravo!

Uncle Gabby (Dark Horse) is another off-kilter adventure featuring Tony Millionaire's surrealistic character Sock Monkey. The monkey and his best pal Mr. Crow follow a treasure map across a bizarre landscape rife with steam-powered dragons and monstrous rabbits, eventually reaching the literal edge of the world and the conclusion of this strange yet whimsical story. Millionaire's art style is a loving homage to the great pen-and-ink artistry from the golden age of book illustration but his manner of telling his stories makes them completely contemporary.

A trade-paperback collection of *The Hedge Knight* (Roaring Studios) is an adaptation of George R. R. Martin's novella of the same title. Writer Ben Avery and artists Mike Miller and Mike Crowell do a solid job of depicting the violent medieval-flavored fantasy world featured in Martin's enormously popular and acclaimed series of novels, *A Song of Ice and Fire.* A young squire assumes the mantle of his dead master, a wandering knight owing no allegiance to any particular lord or kingdom, In short order he must learn many lessons about truth, honor, loyalty, and the corruption of those in power.

Babel (Drawn & Quarterly) is a prequel of sorts to writer/artist David B.'s superb autobiographical tale, *Epileptic*, which was just released in a splendid hardcover format by Pantheon. Here David is given a larger magazine-sized format and a limited color palette, which he uses to full effect in exploring the dreams and conflicts of his very early years as he begins to grapple with the onset of his older brother's epilepsy. Not for the faint of heart, this harrowing journey rewards the reader with insights into a life that most will never personally experience.

The initial anthology collection of *The Matrix Comics* (Burlyman Entertainment) features short graphic narratives that first appeared online using the concepts popularized by the movie of the same name. The various stories are by Larry and Andy Wachowski, Geof Darrow, Bill Sienkiewicz, Neil Gaiman, Dave Gibbons, Paul Chadwick, David Lapham, and Peter Bagge, among others. While the individual pieces vary in quality, as in a prose anthology, each offers an interesting concept or a spectacular visual or two. The standouts here are a gentle story filled with subtle insights by Paul Chadwick, "The Miller's Tale," and Greg Ruth's lovely paintings in his tale, "Hunters (and) Collectors."

The Originals (DC/Vertigo) by writer/artist Dave Gibbons is a stylish take, with certain SF overtones, on bloody gang warfare and adolescent passions as seen through the eyes of two friends who follow very different paths to join those same gangs. Gibbon's lovely black-and-white art is awash in subtle tones of gray that lend this slight but compelling tale a unique and exciting visual aspect.

John Constantine, Hellblazer: Setting Sun (DC/Vertigo) collects some of the best received stories from this long-running series, just in time for the release of the motion picture based on this character. For years now John Constantine has been slogging through the worst black magic that all the denizens from hell are able to throw at him, keeping a grin on his face and a cigarette dangling from his lips on demon-haunted streets of modern London. In these eerie tales of dark magic artists Tim Bradstreet, Javier Pulido, James Romberger, and Marcelo Frusin join writer Warren Ellis in collaborating on the stories in this edgy collection.

Y, the Last Man: Safeword (DC/Vertigo) is the latest collection of this very entertaining series written by its creator, J. C. Vaughan, with solid art by Pia Guerra, et al. Yorick Brown, the last surviving human male on planet Earth, has managed to travel halfway across North America, through a postholocaust world awash with danger, in his continued efforts to reach a cloning lab on the West Coast. In the mythic heartland of America he faces his greatest obstacle. An absorbing, suspenseful plot keeps the reader wondering what will happen next and why.

Michael Morcock's Elric: The Making of a Sorcerer (DC) is an original prequel, in graphic narrative form, to the immensely popular series of novels featuring the albino Prince of Melnibone written by Moorcock himself. The extravagant and compelling art is by the great comic-book veteran Walter Simonson. We witness the transformation of Elric from callow young man into experienced warrior. The story plunges wildly through elaborate confrontations between men and otherworldly beings under skies that are thick with dragons and rife with untold dangers. This is a limited series that will, one hopes, soon be collected into a more easily accessible format.

Longtime writer/artist Mike Allred has chosen to adapt the entire Book of Mor-mon into graphic novel form. The first volume is *The Golden Plates: The Sword of Laban and the Tree of Life* (AAA Pop). His wife, Laura, overlays Allred's clear, concise line art with a subtle color palette. The combination makes for an elegant look. As the story unfolds it has much of the feeling of a typical high fantasy tale, what with a sword of power and prophetic visits by ghostly beings that inspire visions of a new land and a better future. Then too, the characters speak in language that has all the power and cadence of the Christian Bible. It will be interesting to follow Allred as he continues down this new path.

The strong, original graphic novel *The Life Eaters* (Wildstorm Comics) is written by noted SF author David Brin and painted with the customary elegance of Scott Hampton. Dark sorcery cast by the Nazis during the waning days of WWII resurrects the ancient Norse gods, who help bring defeat to the Allied armies in Europe. The war continues to ravage the globe for the next twenty years until a final confrontation between ancient gods and modern heroes who have risen to the challenge. A smooth blend of alternate history and SF and fantasy tropes makes for a dense story that is both texturally complex and dramatically exciting.

B.P.R.D.: Plague of Frogs (Dark Horse) is an offshoot of *Hellboy*. That acronym, in case you were wondering, stands for the Bureau for Paranormal Research and Defense, a secret government agency that deals with dark mysteries and monsters looming out of a Lovecraftian abyss of black horror. Four members of the organization must deal with a sky that, as the title suggests, rains frogs, with prophetic doom-laden dreams that continually assault one of their members, and with a mysterious decaying church that has become the breeding ground for creatures that seek to rip a hole in the very fabric of our existence. Mike Mignola keeps a firm hand on the proceedings and leavens the horrific tale with some much-needed humor. The loose but evocative art by Guy Davis ably supports this well-crafted story.

Fables: March of the Wooden Soldiers (DC/Vertigo) is the latest trade collection of this award-winning series written by Bill Willingham, with art by Mark Buckingham and Steve Leialoha. Willingham has developed a fascinating concept featuring the characters out of all the fairy tales and folklore that we grew up with. However in this world a mysterious Adversary has violently attached the lands of Fable, causing its inhabitants to flee to a new sanctuary, New York City, where they use their magic to produce a glamour that allows them to blend in with their mortal neighbors. In this collection the Adversary has begun to assault this latest refuge with hordes of wooden soldiers. Snow White and the Big Bad Wolf, in his more human form, attempt to coordinate a last-ditch defense of their new home. This collection includes "The Last Castle," also written by Willingham, but this time with lovely art by Craig Hamilton and P. Craig Russell. This is a prequel of sorts to the regular series, as here the remaining denizens of the legendary Fabled Lands are shown being either destroyed or forced to leave by the savage armies of the Adversary. Many subtle background details about the main characters here carry over into the current series and give a sense of a much larger thematic conflict still to come.

Writer/artist Batton Lash brings us a new collection of witty tales featuring his counselers of the Macabre, Alanna Wolf and Jeff Bird, in *Supernatural Law: Mister Negativity* (Exhibit A Press). Bizarre clients such as a muse who is suing the author she has inspired, a "born again" demon, and a gangster who is literally turned into an eight-hundred-pound gorilla, keep Wolf and Bird on their toes and up to their necks in laughs.

And I did want to at least mention my own graphic novel collection, *The Book of Ballads* (Tor). These adaptations of ancient Scottish and English ballads by writers such as Neil Gaiman, Charles de Lint, Jane Yolen, Sharyn McCrumb, Jeff Smith, and others are filled with all the horror, terror, and delight of these old songs. I especially want to mention the lovely and very informative Introduction by Terri Windling that gives these stories their historical context. Also included is a detailed discography of current recordings of these same songs, by noted music critic Ken Roseman.

The growing popularity and healthy sales of the graphic-novel form have resulted in the very deserving reissues of many long-unavailable titles. I wanted to mention a few of these before I close here. *Blood, A Tale* (DC/Vertigo) is a poetic, darkly evocative horror tale with lovely painted art by Kent Williams and script by J. M. DeMatteis. The horror anthology *Clive Barker's Hellraiser* (Checker Book Publishing) has stories based on Barker's popular series of the same name drawn and written by John Bolton, Larry Wachowski, Bernie Wrightson, Mike Mignola, and Bill Sienkiewcz among others. A significant event in the world of manga and comics in general was the seminal work by Mr. Katsuhiro Otomo, *Akira, Book One* (Dark Horse). Violent, explosive, and exquisitely drawn, this wild adventure is still extremely effective and should be read by all. Back in the late 1960s master artist Russ Manning brought us the SF/fantasy adventures of *Magnus, Robot Fighter* (Dark Horse). These tightly written, beautifully drawn tales of one genetically modified hero fighting against the tyranny of robotic overlords that now rule an indolent humankind in a far distant future are still a delight to read. Another futuristic SF/fantasy adventure, *Valerian* (I Books), brings us the long-running European graphic-novel series by artists Jean-Claude Mezieres and writer Pierre Christin. The heroes of these charming tales race through far-flung planets teeming with strange alien life forms on their way to a place in every reader's heart.

And I really don't want to leave before I at least mention the following worthwhile graphic narratives: *The Black Forest* (Image), written by Todd Livingston and Robert Tinnell, with art by Neil Vokes; *The White Lama, Book 1: Reincarnation* (Humanoids/DC) written by Jodorowsky, with art by Bess; the revival of Robert E. Howard's prototypical barbarian, *Conan* (Dark Horse), written by Kurt Busiek and drawn by various artists; *The Coffin* (Oni Press) written by Phil Hester, with art by Mike Huddleston. Lastly, I commend to you the continuing efforts by DC Comics to make the complete adventures of Richard and Wendy Pini's *Elfquest* available again.

And finally I wanted to mention two lovely art books that you might want to look out for. The first is *Dave McKean: Narcolepsy* (Allen Spiegel Fine Arts), a beautifully produced, hallucinatory walk through McKean's brain in full color, with commentary by various writers and Dave himself. Secondly a lavish art book was released this year by NBM featuring the absolutely gorgeous art of Francois Schuiten. Words fail me in trying to adequately describe *The Book of Schuiten*. It should be on everyone's bookshelf.

If you have any trouble locating any of these books through your local bookstore you might try calling the official Comic Shop Locator Service at 1-888-266-4226. Those fine folks will assist you in finding a full-service comic shop near you. Then too, many of these trade collections are carried by the friendly and well-stocked Bud Plant Comic Art (www.budplant.com).

Good luck and happy reading.

Anime and Manga: 2004

Joan D. Vinge

Getting What You Wished For

Welcome to this year's summation of the year's best fantasy and horror in the manga/anime genre.

Come on, do I have to say it again?

Apparently. Although it has been the most rapidly growing genre in the entertainment field for several years, most of the people I mention it to have never heard the terms; as with any entertainment, it always seems much larger when you're inside it looking out.

So: *Manga* is the Japanese term for graphic novels and/or comics—storytelling as serial art. *Anime* is animation—movies, TV series, or OVAs—"original video animation" movies or miniseries. This year's exploration of the genre is going to be different yet again, and probably briefer, since both the field and my eyesight are currently in a state of flux. I hope both will have stabilized (for the better) by next year.

What's News:

NEW YEAR'S PAST:
Four years ago, when I began this column, hoping to interest more F/SF&H readers/viewers in the genre of M&A, I wished in print that the genre would continue to increase. Well, so it has (for the most part), like a river rising after the spring melt.

This year the floodgates opened, and as I tried to surf the tide, I came close to premature burial beneath mounds of paper (and plastic cases). I felt like Yomiko Readman in the OVA of *Read or Die*. Furthermore, my debt by year's end looked like the national debt. I suspect a lot of *otaku* (fans) suffered budgetary wipeout this year, resulting in the genre market's "hesitation" in its forward momentum.

Am I tired of the stuff? M&A—never. I wouldn't mind spending most of my waking hours reading and watching just the F/SF&H–themed M&A—and there'd still be a lot I would miss. I did, however, find it nigh impossible to lay down the required fistfuls of dollars to pay for them.

Speaking of rivers, in the spring of 2004, heavy rains caved in the roof of Four Star Video, my favorite rental store. After they mopped up, they had to replace a lot of stock. Their anime section had been remarkably up to date before that; but with the number of new anime DVDs added to their other replacement costs, I can no longer count on them for help.

I am reminded of the old Chinese curse: "May you get everything you wish for, may you be noticed by people in high places, and may you live in interesting times. . . ."

STATE OF THE GENRE — QUEASY:

Why? Too full . . . for the same reason the stock market frequently has to "adjust" it-self: a hot genre market led too many companies to invest, often heavily, in the field all at once; not only new companies but also individual "old-timers" engaged in as much expansion as the field could manage: bringing out DVDs of anime that had previously only existed on tape, repackaging recent DVD series as boxed sets (usu-ally more compact, and cheaper) and importing more and more of the latest Japan-ese M&A.

The same goes for repackaging old manga series (some of them never before fin-ished) in "pocket" size, with flashier covers, as well as—maddeningly—doing the same with new unfinished series, plus licensing and releasing the first book or two of the latest new M&A series from Japan, Korea, and Hong Kong.

Unfortunately, it's much like a new TV season: series that perform well from the start continue on a regular schedule (sometimes for years—if it's that long, and that popular here, it was clearly that popular in Japan too). Because more of these stories have a clear beginning and end in mind than the typical American TV series, it comes as a surprise to realize how many twists and turns a popular series can take before it reaches that end. But then, certain creative American shows like *Buffy the Vampire Slayer* have "ended," only to return via a deus-ex-plot-machanism, when they are unexpectedly revived.

The rest of a publisher's or distributor's series may languish for months between volumes, or years, or forever, depending on the publisher's overall financial situa-tion—despite the work's quality, or readers' desire to find out what happens next. (If they have any fan base, you may find Web sites to help feed your addiction.)

The problem for both buyers and sellers is the same, a blessing and a curse, an embarrassment of riches. There is so much irresistible new M&A—books, DVDs, and related "swag"—coming out now that no one except Bill Gates could afford it all (and he's probably still into video games).

SIGNS AND PORTENTS:

Does this mean I think the M&A boom is over as abruptly as it happened, that its bubble popularity, now burst, will drop off the radar?

No. Of course not.

Elaborate on that? Sure. New publishers are still entering the field, if more cau-tiously; they include Del Rey, a U.S. publisher of F/SF, on tiptoe but with some promising series and striking cover art; Anime Works, a distributor of some really fine anime, which would like to do the same with manga; DC Comics, trying its hand at pocket-size paperbacks; and Seven Seas, a new Amerimanga publisher as of 2005, with some promising new series. Marvel and Devil's Due (a newer comics line, formerly part of Image) are also putting out pocket-size paperbacks of their Amerimanga-style series.

Synch-Point, the brilliant minds behind the translation of the *FLCL* DVD, are now venturing into print with Broccoli Books, as well as doing more anime. So far they have been conservative in their output, but the *Aquarian Age* combo of anime series, upcoming movie, and manga (aka *"Juvenile Orion"*) made a noticeable splash. Penguin Books, a British/American publisher, has made a deal with DMI (Digital Media Incorporated) to publish some of their eighteen-up–rated novels: *IGWP*, a mature drama series based on a popular television show, translated into an impressive manga, plus some *yaoi* ("boy's love," or gay romance titles, popular with women as well as gay men). They also have a good "How to Draw Manga" series.

DMI already has a distribution deal with Dark Horse, a graphic novel publisher that has been putting out some classic anime tie-in manga, including *Trigun* and *Hellsing*.

Longtime manga and anime company CPM seemingly has blossomed, with new releases and old favorites like the *Lodoss War* and *Slayers* (the latter is a comedy) series done in pocket-size smartly packaged new manga volumes, as well as boxed-set releases of their older anime titles. To sum up, many of the major companies suffered, unfairly, this year, but I believe that most will survive.

Re TV: There are more anime series being shown on TV than ever, it seems—cable channel Tech TV and a lot of other stations now run anime, not just the Cartoon Network, and M&A superpower ADV's Anime Network.

Important note of warning: Anime shown on television, especially during prime time, and even on Cartoon Network's "Adult Swim," is usually cut, sometimes for length, but more often for censorship reasons. If you like a series and want the real deal, seek it out elsewhere. I recently met someone who had no idea how the series *Trigun* actually ends, because Adult Swim cuts off the end credits—and during the final episode, the full, complete end of the show takes place during the credits. That's just wrong.

Also re TV, here's a culture note: *Buffy the Vampire Slayer* fits perfectly into the *maho shoujo*, or "magical girl," genre like *Sailor Moon*—one of the classic series in M&A. It even tosses in a couple of brooding *bishonen* (pretty-boy) bad boys, Angel and Spike (great anime names, when you think of it), the two vampires—literal lost souls—who develop self-destructive obsessions with the Slayer herself.

Since it is a mature "magical girl" tale we're dealing with, the heroine is in fact an archetypal priestess or shaman who gains her magical powers at puberty. Buffy's own deep conflicts and doubts about her fate lead her to embrace these tormented love/hate relationships until, like a priestess from *Inu-Yasha*, her power transforms the clouded violence in all their hearts, so that they are free to change their cursed destinies, and live their lives as true Heroes. The tradition descends, in Japan, from the pre-"Temple Shintoism" era, when priestesses were in charge of the Earth-reverent Shinto religion, serving as seers and healers—*miko*—the equivalent of the ancient proto-Wiccan healers of prehistoric Europe.

The comics field continues to be both up and down, achieving a kind of fluid equilibrium when it comes to manga—primarily Amerimanga. There were a couple of big losses in 2004, startling, if not downright shocking: CrossGen, a newish company that a couple of years ago was one of the major publishers in the field, apparently overextended itself, and went bankrupt. This was truly a loss, for lovers of their many, varied titles, and of top-notch serial art in general. They published only a handful of titles that could be called manga (*The Path, Way of the Rat*), but everything they did was first-class. Dreamwave, the first publisher dedicated to doing manga-style comics in full computerized color, has also gone under, possibly from overspecializing. They originally created independent titles, or settings like the *Warlands* fantasy world, in which they created various story arcs (my favorite are still the *DarkMinds* cyberpunk stories). They split off from Image Comics (which provides a variety of independent magazines with a united publishing/distribution "front" and logo, which some smaller publishers find too confining as they grow, taking with them the very successful *Transformers* franchise. That success seemed to elbow out all their other titles, and whatever happened after that, it proved a death sentence.

Before the demise of Dreamwave, another new company, Devil's Due, split off from them (this is beginning to sound like an anime movie). They took with them the big *GI Joe* franchise, and may wind up with *Transformers* too, as well as a number of other series reborn out of the 1980s nostalgia wave. *GI Joe*'s been undergoing "experimentation" lately, which may be a sign of flagging popularity; more changes to come. Hopefully it will survive, because the cast of characters is just real enough to care about and believe in. Other '80s series, such as *He-Man* (Image) and *Thundercats* (Wildstorm), have struggled with their updatings: the names in *He-Man*, for instance, just refuse to allow their characters to be taken seriously, and the overall trend seems to be fading. (*Battle of the Planets* still comes out in miniseries at Image.)

My personal favorite among all the retro-'80s comics has been *Voltron*, a genuine Japanese mecha tale, which came with a cast of humans and aliens that Devil's Due has been developing into intriguing, complex characters. The comics are collected in paperbacks, but I haven't seen a new original *Voltron* comic lately. I hope readers won't be left hanging from yet another cliff.

Devil's Due has been experimenting with several new series of its own, besides: the "Aftermath" near-future history, with four separate comics (not strictly speaking Amerimanga except one, but with a concept original enough to honor); and comics from the Korean CGI *manhwa* artists of Studio Ice, who did last year's stunning horror tale, *Defiance*, for Image.

Aftermath's story lines are miniseries with rather dark themes—risky business—but unlike the Big Picture that CrossGen never got to finish, they will come together in a resolution that will give birth to a new set of miniseries after only a few issues. The concept of changes that occur neither too fast (one issue) nor too slowly (CrossGen, alas) is, I think, unique, and I hope it works out for them.

Comics based on popular videogames are a natural—it happens in Japan all the time—but for some reason most seem to founder quickly here. Lack of sufficient backgrounding, and story lines that promise characterization and end up as empty-headed brawls, perhaps. But mega game-maker Capcom has already worked with Disney to make a surprisingly funky animelike videogame, *Kingdom Hearts*. U.S. comic companies seem determined to find the key to doing manga-like comics that have a heart as well as fists and large weapons.

Devil's Due now has a subsidiary line called Udon Comics. Studio Udon has been noted for its CGI coloring work for quite a while. Now they get their shot at glory, as the designated creators of Devil's Due's line of game-based comics; more books are coming in 2005, and it looks like they won't all be game based.

And—news flash for role-playing gamers and romantics everywhere—coming up in 2005, Devil's Due is going to be illustrating R. A. Salvatore's Dark Elf trilogy, based on the Forgotten Realms gaming world; it looks very promising.

DC and Marvel have been hiring actual manga writers as well as artists and new Amerimanga styling creators to do various runs on their regular titles, or create new ones. Wildstorm, a part of DC Comics, in particular focuses on experimenting with Amerimanga. There are seemingly a zillion indy publishers with promising titles that come and go, too. A constantly shifting equilibrium has been the norm for some time in the American comics field; you can bet they are not going to give up on Amerimanga anytime soon.

The biggest loss has been in the magazine/anthology field: *Animerica Extra*, Viz's *shoujo* (girls and young women) anthology companion to the successful *Shonen Jump*, its version of an original Japanese anthology magazine for boys and young men, is ceasing publication in mid-2005, and rumors have it that *Animerica*, the original American news magazine about M&A, will cease publication as well. That, in my opinion, may be the worst loss of the year.

Viz is planning to replace *Animerica Extra* with *Shoujo Beat*, an "authentic" Japanese *shoujo* anthology manga. I trust they'll continue reprinting the equally authentic manga stories from *Extra* in book form. But *Animerica* has always been my favorite M&A news magazine, with the most in-depth, varied, and balanced articles and reviews of the field.

Other M&A magazines have also been hard-hit. Gutsoon Publishing, whose *Raijin* magazine anthology and related paperback line went under last year, seems unlikely ever to revive either one, which is a real pity. Wizard's *Anime Insider*, and *AnimePlay*, each issue of which included a CD, are cutting back their pub schedules sharply, after increasing them last year.

On the other hand, Beckett, the publisher of card-collector's magazines, continues to put out a zine featuring popular anime and manga characters called *Beckett ANIME Unofficial Collector*. I surmise the name comes from the fact that it focuses on anime-related card games, as opposed to, say, Magic; but it also features articles about anime shows that don't even have card games, just attractive anime characters, usually with series currently on TV.

Beckett Anime, which seems to be directed at a preteen and 'tween audience, puts out occasional specials like one on *Inu Yasha* (superpopular anime and manga, which does have a game), and one titled *Anime for Girls*. It's a relief to see at least one magazine that keeps in mind its entire potential audience, and introduces both sexes to the appeal of anime-themed media, as well as games. I don't know if they put out Beckett Comics, an indy comic line with series like the crypto-western *Ballad of Sleeping Beauty*, which have a style reminiscent of certain stark, Goth Amerimanga.

Dark Horse's unassuming, reasonably priced, comiclike *Super Manga Blast* anthology continues its regular monthly appearance; paperbacks based on it often seem to be late in coming out, however. Dark Horse, like most American manga publishers, has all but ceased to do the monthly comics that were its original format, since the direct-to-paperback approach is more profitable, on a tight budget. But to their credit, they still put out *Blade of the Immortal* and *Usagi Yojimbo* (an Amerimanga title), both of which have striking covers, in completely different styles—in case you really thought all manga art looked the same—as well as great storytelling.

Antarctic Press, a longtime publisher of Amerimanga, still puts out its monthly *MangaZine*, and has also begun putting out competitively priced paperbacks of some of its series; it still publishes series in regular comic form, and seems to be thriving. It has even entered the "how to draw manga" field; unfortunately, its how-to books have an annoyingly adolescent "make the boobs bigger" style their comics generally lack (thank god).

The only new M&A magazine that has appeared here this past year is *Now*, a British import that covers not only M&A but a wide variety of Japan's popular culture. I recommend *Now* especially to those wanting to know more about the cultural context of anime and manga.

Which leaves us with *Newtype*, the big glitzy U.S. version of Japan's glitziest anime-and-manga news magazine, published here by ADV for the past few years. ADV is one of the two largest, most ubiquitous companies in the anime field; it has its own TV station on cable (the Anime Network), and a new line of manga. (Plus *blaring*, omnipresent ads for the Anime Network and *Newtype* at the beginning of their DVDs.)

In Japan, approximately 30 percent of the *otaku* are female—and *shoujo*-style art has influenced typically male stories to a degree I find striking. One Japanese character designer admitted in an interview that he deliberately made sure the men were as handsome as the women were pretty for an anime, because of the crossover market—girls and women enjoy adventure; boys and men enjoy romance. (You know you want it.) What's not to like?

GOOD SIGNS AND GOOD TIMES:
There are more and more conventions for M&A springing up; and *Comics Buyer's Guide*, a trade magazine in the field, seems only to have become aware of the whole M&A trend recently, since its spring 2005 issue features it on the cover (and the article inside discusses the genre as if it were a revelation about something utterly new). I think that's a healthy sign.

And there are indications that M&A fans are branching out, buying soundtrack music and collectables just as enthusiastically as do Japanese *otaku*.

POP GOES THE MUSIC, AND OTHER DISTRACTIONS:
More and more anime and game soundtrack CDs are being released here—at competitive prices *legally*, at last—as well as albums by J-pop groups (Japanese pop and rock groups whose music has become popular here from soundtracks) which are now releasing whole albums, under the new Tofu Records label.

More and more imported models, stuffed toys, clothes, posters, and other "swag" related to popular series are also becoming available at game stores and places like Suncoast video, as well as numerous online M&A specialty shops. (See Datafiles).

Ninja Screw Awards go to ADV and Pioneer/Geneon, however. ADV offered the year's most repulsive tie-in toy—the "Menchi on Barbecue" set (plush toy, real barbecue), based on the wacky *Excel Saga* anime and manga. Way to give sickos and drunken teens fresh inspiration when they decide to torment small animals. Runner-up Pioneer gets dishonorable mention for its badly-run "Buy four CDs, get one free" offer. Many music fans sent in coupons plus postage and received—nothing at all. Queries went unanswered. Worse yet, Pioneer tried the same thing again in late summer.

SO YOU WANNA BE AN M&A STAR?

At this point, there are a large number of aspiring artists and writers of manga graphic novels, home-computer illustration and animation auteurs, as well.

In Japan there are countless art books based on series or individual artists, for those who want more, or to create their own takes on favorite series, movies, and games; however very few, except Viz's Akira Miyazaki books (Disney has been releasing his movies) are available in stores, and in English. If a series haunts you, "Google" the Internet for fan sites, or go to some anime conventions to get a real idea of what's out there; check out online stores as well, and chances are you'll find what you seek sooner or later.

For those who are really serious about becoming an M&A star, creating "Amerimanga," for a living, there is currently a plethora of "How to Draw Manga (and/or Anime)" books, in English or translated from the Japanese, in the art sections of most large bookstores. As with other genres, new M&A creators usually spring from the ranks of fandom, simply because people who don't love the field don't understand it well enough to create convincing works. An addiction to videogames seems to be nearly universal among male *manga-ka* (manga creators) in Japan. There are plenty of well-known female *manga-ka* too. Interestingly, however, they seem to have actual lives, not just virtual ones.

GIRLS AND BOYS TOGETHER (?)

Also interesting is that at least half, if not a majority, of the fan artists featured in M&A magazines here seem to be female. Considering that fact, it is remarkable how few books there are on drawing the male figure (most of the fan-art pictures are of male characters that girls get crushes on), while there must be at least a dozen different books out there purporting to show "how to draw the female figure," in and out of clothes and fetishistic costumes. (And even Antarctic Press, an Amerimanga publisher, has how-to books loaded with sexist language. I spoke to one of their reps about it at Anime Central—a con—and as I did, I realized that Antarctic Press has only used *one* female artist/writer on a comic in recent memory. They usually feature a fair number of strong female characters, and that was a rude awakening, the female *manga-ka* also had to share equal cover billing with her male "assists" worker. "Dishonorable mention" duly noted here.) One is left to wonder how many guys buy how-to-draw books merely to look at the pictures.

In any case, as with F/SF&H, there is a far wider potential audience that M&A can reach, and the majority may never attend a convention. In Japan, it's perfectly acceptable for an adult on the way to work to read manga; it's time we got over the stigma inflicted on serial art here. Plus, both teen and adult women (30 to 50 percent of American M&A fans are female, according to one source), deserve more attention from M&A advertisers, as do adult males. All of these groups tend to be more sophisticated and open to the concept of "World Peace through Shared Culture" (motto of CPM, a longtime M&A company) than are adolescent boys, despite what M&A marketers seem to believe.

ADV's yin and yang have been particularly unbalanced, both in ads for Anime Network and in the tone of its *Newtype* magazine; the latter is particularly offensive, considering that someone in *Newtype*'s pages observed a couple of years ago, that "if the A&M market was to continue growing and thriving, it needed to attract more of a female audience."

This year ADV closed one of its anime dubbing studios and cut back its manga publishing schedule. Maybe they could mend those stress cracks if they hung that *Newtype* quote up in the front office, quit referring to girls and women as objectified "chicks" in their Anime Network ads, and balance the drooling fan-boy atmosphere at *Newtype* with some good female writers and reviewers. And, oh, let us not forget—more balanced "fan service," a promise they made to include more handsome-guy pictures that's been long unfulfilled. Because, let's face it, most people who say they "only buy *Newtype* for the informative articles" are lying.

GRACE NOTE:
I have finally made friends with a handful of other M&A fans around town, and we checked out a few nearby anime conventions this year. They are very much like SF cons—*otaku* means "fan" in every sense of the word—and yet different enough to seem fresh. There are also a fair number of F/SF&H fans who are already M&A converts, and vice versa.

AnimeIowa, my favorite M&A convention so far, was an easygoing, good-natured con (set unnervingly in the cornfed heart of the Bible Belt), where I got to know a group of talented aspiring artists (collectively known as Studio Antithesis), most of whom live here in Madison. In Chicago, I also spoke with the Artzilla crew, another immensely gifted group, whose new comic *Cannon Busters* will be out in 2005.

One difference between anime and SF conventions is the presence of Artists' Row, where you can meet artists and check out their work, and buy it: fertile ground for a writer who wants to try the graphic-novel field, and might find the illustrator he or she is looking for, who's also set to break new ground. It's also an excellent place for costumers and serious role players to show off their creativity—even more so than at SF conventions.

Chumming around with the Antithesis crew and their buddy Dirk Tiede (whose self-published Amerimanga *Paradigm Shift* is as entertaining as the pun hidden in its title; find it online), I met Amerimanga creator Lea Hernandez, whose work I knew and admired. She's the salt of the earth, and we bonded over "Oy, my kids—!" stories; but she has enough smarts, wry humor, and empathy for two writer/artists, plus a wicked grin that you'll only catch in the mirror's reflection of your own face as you read her books.

ORDER OF THE KITELea sets it all free in her graphic novels: her stories are full of strong, loving, funny, charming, unforgiving, unforgettable, and totally fascinating people, scattered from the 1800s badlands of Texas (in her Texas Steampunk trilogy (Image), to the addled hearts and tiara'd heads of the oddest trio of assassins ever to join the killer elite, in *Killer Princesses* (Oni) . . . and on into a bone-crunching, cyber-fantastic future in *Rumble Girls* (NBM). She's currently drawing a Hardy Boys comic for NBM, a change of pace that looks as if she's having fun with it; she's also done a how-to art book called *Manga Secrets* currently in book-stores.

I also had the pleasure of spending a half hour asking questions and talking about the good stuff with John Oppliger and his extremely good-natured friend. John answers fans' questions in his "Ask John" column at AnimeNation.com (See Datafile). To top it off, I got to talk swords with a member of the historic-recreation samurai swordfighting group Kamui (who played the Crazy 88 in *Kill Bill, Volume 1*), in the dealers' room. Altogether, these conventions are a highly recommended change from the every-day.

THE BOOK OF LISTS:

At last we get down to it. As you may have noticed, this year's essay is all news and no reviews, for which I applogize. Many of this year's best anime series did not finish coming out before year's end (and the manga series can run for literally years on end). But other circumstances beyond my control have made it more than difficult; so instead I offer you lists of the bests. There is so much variety now that you truly can do your own book and movie comparisons. (That's another thing I'd hoped to see, but hadn't expected this soon.)

By and large, the manga series tend to be more explicit (more blood, less clothing) than the anime, at least when the latter is a TV series. Keep that in mind.

Usually the manga comes first, though it may be an offshoot of a novel, and an anime may be inspired by a video game. The video game may be inspired by an anime or manga too; plus, some manga are novelizations of anime series or movies, while some short, and stand-alone anime may be pilot-film ads for a manga. It's an incestuous orgy of multimedia creativity, and with the online, video, and card games now available here, you can often live the experience in as many forms as you like, without ever leaving home.

Creators of manga inspired by anime have freedom to interpret, or reinterpret, the story line, just as anime frequently take big liberties with a manga story line. For example, the creator of the Chinese graphic novel (*manhua*) based on the film *Hero*, (ComicsOne), explained in a commentary at the end that by the time he'd reached the story's end, he disagreed with how the film ended. And so in his graphic novel, he created the ending he felt suited it better. The same thing often seems to happen with Japanese manga; yet on the other hand, some anime series, such as *Rurouni Kenshin*, follow the story line quite faithfully. (The anime's third season is a radical departure, because the manga wasn't yet finished.)

There is more and more good Amerimanga coming out, usually still in comic form, but also collected in paperback form. Many series or story arcs still appear in the full-size TPBs, but more are being put out in sizes closer to those of the (now traditional) pocket-size paperback of imported manga. Remember, too, that manga includes—*ore* and more *manhwa*,—Korean manga,—and *manhua*,—Chinese manga, generally created in Hong Kong, still the home of all those ass-kickin' movies.

Those are the rough facts, here are the lists. As a friend once said, "You may infer from them what you wish." Enjoy. These are in no particular order, even alphabetical; also please understand that this is only a fraction of what's out there. Feel free to look around.

Manga:

The majority of these are primarily fantasy, or F/SF combinations, with horror mixed in. Please check packaging for suggested age, and also read the descriptions, if you are especially sensitive, or have young eyes reading or watching with you.

SERIES, PLUS:
Major manga series not mentioned above that have associated anime series or movie, games, etc.

Rurouni Kenshin [***ORDER OF THE KITE***] because it's a great story
Trigun
Inu Yasha
Saiyuki
Hellsing
Samurai Deeper Kyo
Scryed
Rune Soldier Louie
Sailor Moon (now available uncut)
Card Capter Sakura
Mahoromatic
The Ring (based on original movie, plus more)
Nadesico (and other series by author Kia Asamiya)
Slayers (series, with novels as well)
Record of Lodoss War (series)
Gundam Seed (plus other Gundam series, both anime and manga, too many
    to list)
Revolutioinary Girl Utena
Flame of Recca
Candidate for Goddess (Pilot Candidate anime)
Basara
Fruits Basket
Fushigi Yugi
Ceres
Project Arms
Pretear
Descendants of Darkness
Hero
Crouching Tiger, Hidden Dragon
Rave Master
Yu Yu Hakusho
Naruto
One Piece
Five Star Stories
Shaman King
Knights of the Zodiac (Saint Seiya anime)
Ghost in the Shell (manga sequel plus two movies and TV series)
Hack/Legend of the Twilight

GetBackers
GTO
DNAngel
Jing, King of Bandits
Suikoden III (based on video game)
Berserk
Battle Royale

STAND-ALONE GRAPHIC NOVELS AND SERIES:
Rebirth
Banana Fish
Tuxedo Gin
Et Cetera
Battle Angel Alita (and sequel)
Demon Diary
Remote
The Kindaichi Case Files
Maniac Road
Peigenz
Dragon Hunter
Vampire Game
Dragon Knights
Five Star Stories
Blade of the Immortal
King of Hell
Tsubasa—Reservoir Chronicle
Firefighter! Daigo of Company M [***ORDER OF THE KITE***]
   (Overlooked gem about a firefighter with a "sixth sense" for finding victims
   missed by others. Terrific storytelling.)
Kwaidan
Doing Time [***ORDER OF THE KITE***] (Nonfiction: an autobiograph-
   ical graphic novel by a manga-ka sent to prison for creating work judged to
   be without redeeming social value; glimpse the "orderly" side of Japanese
   society, through the eyes of a creative rebel, and remember that when you
   read "fiction," it is exactly that. Be reminded, too, that however similar we
   humans are when stripped bare of our cultural heritages, and however similar our dreams may be, when in Rome (or Japan, or the U.S.), try not to
   stand out too much, unless you're ready for the consequences. . . .)

Amerimanga—Comics and Graphic Novels:

Usagi Yojimbo [***ORDER OF THE KITE***] (Always top-rate!)
Spyboy
Thor, Son of Asgard
The Couriers (3 GNs and prequel, Couscous Express)
Ninja High School
MegaTokyo

Twilight Storm
Hsu and Chan
Runaways
Sabrina the Teenage Witch (now in "manga-style")
Invincible
Mu
Megacity 909 (includes CG art lessons)
Victory
Misplaced
Battle of the Planets
Robotech (new version)
Voltron
Teen Titans (tie-in to successful Carton Network show)
Firebreather
Star Wars: Clone Wars Adventures (tie-in stories to the TV series)

Anime:

MOVIES:

Ghost in the Shell 2: Innocence [***ORDER OF THE KITE***] (Mind-boggling)
Dead Leaves
Rahephon, the Movie
Blue Gender, the Movie
Memories
Three Godfathers
Roujin Z (first DVD of satire on treatment of elderly)
R.O.D.—the OVA episodes.
Submarine 707-R (inspiration for Ganzo Studios' Blue Sub 6)

AMERICAN ANIMATION:

Samurai Jack
The Incredibles
Mulan II
Mulan (rerelease; special edition—at long last, respect!)
Star Wars: Clone Wars (a bona fide part of George Lucas's epic, done anime style.)

LIVE-ACTION MOVIES:

Onmyoji II
GoJoe
Twilight Samurai (aka Twilight Assassin)
Versus
Kill Bill, Volume 2
House of Flying Daggers (note: well-known Japanese actor Takeshi Kaneshiro, who starred, recently died; he will be missed all over the world)

ANIME SERIES: A YEAR FULL OF WONDERFUL, AND LESS WONDERFUL:

Inu-Yasha

Witch Hunter Robin [***ORDER OF THE KITE***] (a complex series that really gives you a lot to think about, regarding what a "normal" talent is, or isn't. A few holes in the plot, even after several viewings, but the characters stay with you.)

Heat Guy J

Neon Genesis Evangelion—Platinum (recut polished-up rerelease, with extensive notes to go with each DVD; a "definitive version" of possibly the most famous anime series ever)

Ninja Scroll—the series

Kiddy Grade

Captain Herlock (a.k.a. *Captain Harlock* in other series)

Final Fantasy Unlimited

Wolf's Rain

Magical Shopping Arcade Abenoyoshi

Haibane Renmai

Texhnolyze

Infinate Ryvius

Saiyuki

Aura Battler Dunbine

Bastof Syndrome (first Korean anime series released)

Zenki, part 4 (collected end of older series)

Hack//Sign

Gungrave (character designs by the creator of *Trigun*)

Nadesico (rereleased collection on three DVDs)

Patlabor series

Kaze no Yojimbo

Master Keaton

Big O II (first series to be continued due to U.S. popularity; result was mixed—too many cooks)

Geisters

Gad Guard

BoogiePop Phantom (rereleased in fancy boxed sets—see it before the new live version and compare)

Ghost in the Shell: Stand Alone Complex

Saint Seiya

Gundam Seed series

Gundam ZZ series

Twelve Kingdoms (a *lot* of buzz at conventions about this one)

R.O.D.—the series

Someday's Dreamers

Ushio and Tora (rereleased oldie series)

Orphen II

Yu Yu Hakusho

GetBackers

Kino's Journey

Last Exile [***ORDER OF THE KITE***] (Fascinating, moving and complex, with stunningly beautiful animation)

Cyber City Oedo—*don't miss*—(and *don't* watch dub, only sub!) Three stories about three very unusual individuals, cybercriminals forced to work for the law. A sleeper classic, at a bargain price.

Megazone 23

Zoids

Generator Gawl—*don't miss*—Excellent time-travel tale

Irresponsible Captain Tyler (watch it again before next year's new longer edition with bells and whistles!)

L/R—*Licensed by Royalty*

Project Arms II

Datafiles:

Where to find what you want, whether it's books about the field, or Asian culture, in your local bookstores (browse around), or online at venerable amazon.com, with its useful customer feedback.

For the actual M&A, there are more and more good sources. Support your local independent comic shop, if you have one; they change with the times, and most should now have a lot of TPBs including manga, plus other cool swag for the inner child in you, including M&A–related toys, T-shirts, etc. Also, you can get *Previews*—*the Comic Shop Catalog* there, see what's coming up, and discover gems you might overlook otherwise. It takes days to read; a ton of entertaining info at a bargain price. Make friends with the staff, and regular customers—people who share your enthusiasm; it's like *Cheers*, except you can still drive home.

The genre magazines mentioned above should be available in most comic shops and many bookstores.

Otherwise, bookstores now carry a lot of manga in new TPB sections; if there's a Suncoast store, they have a very well-stocked anime section, and now manga, CDs and . . . those other guilty pleasures, toys 'n' swag. Plus, once again, mostly very nice people behind the counter, who actually enjoy discussing their products (though they lack the autonomy of an independent store). Suncoast.com carries more of everything, but the personal touch is utterly lacking. Amazon.com carries manga and anime too, with reader reviews to help you make informed purchases. Their customer service is an AI; fine if you don't confuse it. I also highly recommend three real online specialty stores: rightstuf.com—a superstore with super customer service and some great sales; animecastle.com—an up-and-comer with some hard-to-find stock, and so far very good prices on things; and animenation.com, another big, well-stocked, customer-friendly store, with *lots* of links to enthrall Web surfers.

For hard-to-find, or gently used, back issues of manga or Amerimanga in all forms, try milehighcomics.com, a huge and well-stocked but very homey corner of cyberspace

You're not made of money? If you're lucky, a good independent video store exists near you; save by renting series first. Be nice to the staff, and you'll make more interesting friends. The Blockbuster chain carries more anime than it used to, and is a good place to find used DVDs at decent prices. Manga's harder to "borrow," but much easier to browse in a store, at least.

Domos:

To the Westfield Comics "*dojo*": Manager Bob-sensei, eternal and all-knowing; and the Three Samurai, Chad, Josh, and Nick. Overdue thanks this year to Nick Zinn, for proofing my first essay and also for a noble attempt to create a customer list that kept up with all the new manga products every week. Special *Domo arigato* to Kim Smuga-Otto for the anime analysis of *Buffy*; and to the Right Stuf customer service, especially Al Jones—the best online helpers in the world. They prove they have the "right stuff" every day. Thank you also to the good people in Right Stuf's DVD production wing, Devil's Due, Synch Point, the late Crossgen and Dreamwave companies, TokyoPop, generous enough to offer me some of their excellent products. Every bit helps this to be a better review. *Domo arigato!* And *heiwa* (peace), out.

Fantasy and Horror in Music: 2004

Charles de Lint

As I think back on the great music it's been my pleasure to listen to, both in concert and on disc, throughout this past year, I also find myself lamenting the fact that I've probably missed as much, if not more, simply because it didn't cross my radar. I mention this as a simple way of emphasizing that it's impossible for any overview such as this to be definitive. All I, or anyone, can ever offer is a glimpse of the fine recordings that did make it into our hands. Even then, there simply isn't room to cover them all. So with that caveat out of the way, here are a few of the highlights of 2004:

Celtic:

I could probably spend my whole word count for this piece talking about Christy Moore's *The Box Set 1964–2004* (Columbia). The importance of this six-CD collection to the Irish song tradition can't be stressed enough. Moore was a founding member of both Planxty and Moving Hearts, with a strong solo career both before and after his work with those bands, and his influence can be seen on pretty much every performer since, both in the field and beyond.

Though he's written some fine songs, Moore is best known as an interpreter, recasting both the big traditional ballads as well as songs by contemporary writers in a new light through his arrangements and heartfelt renditions. What's especially pleasing about this collection is that, while it does cover the scope of his career, he didn't simply pick previous versions of the songs and stick them in a new package. All the material here is taken from other alternate sources: outtakes, B sides, live and rehearsal recordings, with even a few intimate pieces recorded in his "shed." An accompanying booklet features his remarks on every song, though I'd recommend you also pick up a copy of *One Voice—My Life in Song* (Hodder & Stoughton, 2000) to read while you listen to the CDs. A comprehensive 280-some pages of song lyrics, anecdotes, and photographs, it makes a perfect companion to this remarkable collection.

Also released this year were CD and DVD versions of *Live 2004* (Sony), the Planxty reunion recorded live at Vicar Street, Dublin, in January and February. I'd recommend the DVD over the CD for the pleasure of actually getting to see the band playing. It also has three more songs plus some documentaries. However, no matter which version you get, the concert is brilliant.

All of which segues nicely into . . .

If you want to know if a band's the real deal, the only way you can do so is by seeing them live. There's simply too much tweaking that can be done in the studio—it's so prevalent now that I recently saw a disc with a notice on it reading "Made without the use of pitch correction software." Of course, we're not all lucky enough to be able to see all the acts we'd like to, which is where live recordings come in. But live records present their own problems, mostly featuring too much miking of the audience so that you might be listening to a quiet piece, but you can hear some wag out in the crowd whooping it up.

The best solution is what Lúnasa have done with their latest recording, *The Kinnitty Sessions* (Compass Records): invite a select audience into a studio environment, then make the record as if it were a concert: no overdubs, no tweaks, just the music standing on its own with that special buzz that comes from musicians playing live.

If you only buy one Celtic CD this year, make it *The Kinnitty Sessions*.

Which isn't to say there weren't some other great Irish CDs released this past year. The Sligo band Dervish's newest CD, *Spirit* (Compass Records), shows that the band is still at the top of its form. It's been years since Siobhán Peoples (daughter of esteemed fiddler Tommy Peoples) has released any recorded music, but *Time on Our Hands* (www.custysmusic.com), a fiddle/accordion duet CD with box player Murty Ryan, has made the wait worthwhile.

While the Donegal band Clannad hasn't broken up, they haven't released anything new in a while either, so fans of Moya Brennan's ethereal vocals will be happy to learn that she, at least, has a new recording with *Two Horizons* (Decca Records). And speaking of that whole Enya/Loreena McKennitt take on Celtic music, this is probably as good a time as any to also recommend *Beyond the Waves* (Festival Distribution) by harpist Sharlene Wallace.

Box player Sharon Shannon's newest CD is *Libertango* (Compass Records). I don't always see the necessity of loading up a recording with tons of guest vocalists (it's not like Shannon doesn't have the chops to carry an album on her own), but I do have to admit that in this case I wouldn't want to have missed Sinéad O'Connor's stunning rendition of the old ballad "Anachie Gordon."

London-born fiddler John Carty returns to the sound of his Connaught ancestral heritage with the laid-back sound found on *At It Again* (Shanachie); Solas accordionist Mick McAuley showcases his rich tenor voice on *At Ocean's Breadth* (Shanachie); and Dublin band Gráda returns with *The Landing Strip* (Compass Records), an outstanding follow-up to 2002's *Endeavour*.

With her Northumbrian piping (not to mention her fiddling) always such a treat, Kathryn Tickell's *Air Dancing* (Park Records) is easily one of my favorite CDs of the year: a rich and satisfying collection of dance tunes and airs. Luka Bloom's *Before*

Sleep Comes (Bar None Records) is a low-key but rewarding set of quiet songs that will undoubtedly have you trolling your local record store for more of his work.

And last, but certainly not least, we have a group of young musicians from British Columbia called the Coquitlam Celtic Ensemble with their debut release, *Dusty Windowsill* (www.coquitlamcelticensemble.com). For a touchstone, you might think of that big group feel that the Chieftains get sometimes, although there are also many pieces with smaller combinations of instruments.

British Folk:

First, a book rather than a recording. Shirley Collins doesn't have the best voice in British folk music, but she has that indefinable something that still makes a singer great and has shown that talent to fine effect in such classics as *Anthems in Eden* (1969, with her sister Dolly) and *No Roses* (1971, with the Albion Country Band). It turns out she's a fine writer, too.

America Over the Water (SAF Publishing) chronicles her involvement in the late '50s accompanying Alan Lomax in America's Deep South, collecting and taping songs, mixing those experiences with her memories of growing up in postwar Hastings, England. It's an utterly fascinating book, complete with many photographs, that should appeal to anyone with an interest in traditional music from either side of the water.

The one box set I really wanted to talk about in this section was Sandy Denny's *A Boxful of Treasures*, a five-CD set with booklet from Fledgling, one of the best reissue companies around, certainly rivaling Germany's Bear Family Records or Rhino in the States. Unfortunately, I never actually got my hands on a copy. But from the list of contents I've seen, and the reviews I've read, it appears that someone has finally put together the definitive collection by one of the greatest British singers ever. Especially intriguing is the fifth CD, a collection of home recordings. Hopefully, it'll show up in my local CD shop soon.

But there were other fine recordings this year, in particular the inimitable Kate Rusby, who graced us with *Underneath the Stars*, another lovely collection of mostly traditional material, and also her utterly charming concert DVD, *Live from Leeds* (Wea), that really makes you feel as though you were a part of the audience.

With her smoky voice and smart, melancholic songs, Polly Paulusma's *Scissors in My Pocket* (One Little Indian) showcases one of the finest singer-songwriters to emerge from Britain in a while. But I have to admit that my favorite is Thea Gilmore, and she had two releases this year: *Loft Music* (Hungry Dog), a collection of cover songs, and *Songs from the Gutter* (Hungry Dog), featuring her own material, songs of sharp social observation, delivered with heart and soul.

American Roots:

Sometimes all an old song needs is a new setting for us to see that it's still relevant. Or at least that seems to be the theory behind a couple of releases from the past year. On Tangle Eye's *Alan Lomax's Southern Journey Remixed* (Zoe Records), producers Scott Billington and Steve Reynolds take the original a cappella songs collected by Lomax and build backing tracks behind them, utilizing everything from acoustic instruments to programmed beats and loops. It sounds deliciously old and fresh at the same time.

On *Rock Island* (Little Monster), Bethany Yarrow (daughter of Peter Yarrow of Peter, Paul and Mary) opts to redo the lead vocal parts on the old ballads as well, singing them against a bed of instrumentation ranging from banjos and dulcimers to programmed beats and the sampled ghosts of some old trad singers. I don't know how it will sound in ten years' time, but right now it makes for a delightful mix of the contemporary and the traditional, and will no doubt draw some of its listeners back to the source material.

Of course, sometimes songs don't need anything more than straightforward renditions, as on much of Roger McGuinn's latest collection, *Limited Edition* (April First Productions), a mix of trad ballads, original songs, and covers, one highlight being his take on George Harrison's "If I Needed Someone." Greg Brown also takes a low-key approach, *Honey in the Lion's Head* (Trailer Records) with just the addition of a few tasteful backing instruments behind that rich voice of his.

Old-timey and string band music appears to be making a real comeback with young bands producing high-energy music that's faithful to the spirit of the old tunes, but played with a modern sensibility on their acoustic instruments. A couple of prime examples from the past year are *Rock That Babe* by Mammals (Signature Records), and *Livin' Reeltime, Thinkin' Old Time* by Reeltime Travelers (Sci Fidelity Records).

While you could never consider them even remotely a trad band, L.A.'s Concrete Blonde often has a mythic slant to their music, singing about ghosts and vampires and other things that go bump in the night. On *Mojave* (Eleven Thirty) the band leaves the city streets to wander in the desert badlands with songs of animal people and the spirits that inhabit the great open spaces. It's a perfect companion to their collaboration with Los Illegales a few years ago, featuring a looser sprawl of sound and a few spoken stories.

A Latin/Mariachi flavor often shows up in Calexico's recordings like this year's EP releases, *Convict Pool* (Quarter Stick) and *Black Heart* (EMI), a pair of excellent stopgaps until the next album. But the really good news is the release of a DVD concert, *World Drifts In* (Live at the Barbican London) (Wea) featuring the core group sharing the stage with a full mariachi band. The music is invigorating and magical, and I also recommend the bonus material with features on the origin of mariachi music and fascinating documentaries on the band's last tour.

If Calexico's story songs are a little oblique, that's not the case with this last handful of artists: on *Ashgrove* (Yep Roc Records), the Blasters's alumnus Dave Alvin returns to his roots, telling stories of his youth; Tom Russell explores the American West and Southwest on *Indians Cowboys Horses Dogs* (Hightone); Kevin Welch and Kieran Kane sing of monsters in the Jersey Pine Barrens, and small-town hustlers and lovers from everywhere, on *You Can't Save Everybody* (Compass Records); and Brock Zeman, a masterful new young songwriter whose songs range from contemporary Americana to stories that feel like old traditionals, debuted this year with not one but two excellent new CDs, *Cold Winter Comes Back* and *Songs from the Mud* (brockzeman.com).

Latin:

I'm not a Spanish speaker, but I love the sound of the language and get stories from the songs even when I don't know what they're actually talking about. A real Latin favorite that hasn't been off the stereo all year is *Alevosía* (Universal Latino) by Mexican rap artist Mala Rodríguez.

Two infectious recordings are Amparanoia's *Rebeldía con Alegría* (EMI), featuring frontwoman Amparo Sánchez's acoustic guitar and strong vocals played against a backdrop of urban beats and a mix of flamenco, Cuban salsa, and Brazilian tropicalia, and *Street Signs* (Concord Records), the latest from the L.A. music collective Ozomatli with its joyous mix of Latin rhythms, rap, and Bollywood strings.

A little quieter are *Una Sangre* (One Blood) (Narada) by Lila Downs, which has everything from inspired reworkings of "La Bamba" and "La Cucaracha" to songs reminiscent of her work on the *Frida* soundtrack, and *Verde* (Universal), on which Brazilian guitarist Badi Assad sings as much as she plays, and proves to be equally adept at both.

Fans of Robert Rodriguez's El Mariachi trilogy, or at least the music that plays backdrop to those films, will appreciate *Mexico and Mariachis* (Milan Records). But you don't have to be a movie buff to appreciate these songs, some from the soundtracks, some inspired by them, nor the DVD bonus disc that provides background and insight into the involvement of artists such as Los Lobos and Tito and Tarantula, as well as concert footage of Rodriguez playing onstage with the latter.

And speaking of Los Lobos, they released two new recordings this year: *The Ride* (Hollywood Records), on which they duet with everyone from Dave Alvin and Tom Waits to Elvis Costello and Mavis Staples, and somehow manage to never lose their own identity, and *Ride This: The Covers* EP (Hollywood Records) on which they cover a number of songs by those aforementioned collaborators. I've never gone wrong with a Los Lobos album and I doubt you will either.

Lastly, a quick mention of *President Alien* (Razor and Tie) by Yerba Buena, yet another successful mix of dance grooves, hip-hop, Afro-beat, and Latin salsa rhythms that makes for a compelling and addictive debut CD. And coming from a more commercial front, *Live and Off the Record* (Sony) is an entertaining CD/DVD combo chronicling Shakira's 2003 Tour of the Mongoose with live video footage from the tour as well as a documentary.

World:

Born in Algeria, raised in France, Rachid Taha has been delivering an intoxicating blend of punk rock and Algerian rai music since the early '90s. The stand-out track on *Tékitoi* (Wrasse), or at least the most immediately successful, is the Arab-language cover of the Clash hit, retitled "Rock El Casbah," but look a little deeper into the album and you'll find it's only the tip of the iceberg in terms of the man's charismatic talent.

The Traditional Crossroads label has come out with two welcome reissues from the '60s: *How to Make Your Husband a Sultan* and *Alla-Turca* by Özel Türkbas. Packaged with Türkbas's original belly-dance instructions, the music on these discs sounds as fresh and invigorating as anything being recorded today. With *Egypt*

(Nonesuch), Youssou N'Dour's voice soars on a CD dedicated to the Sufi brother-hoods of Senegal, with excellent backing by an Egyptian string orchestra and various Sengalese instrumentalists.

If you're looking for an introduction to the contribution of Gypsy musicians to jazz, you don't need to go further than the stunning *Mémoires: Memories of Django* (Le Chant du Monde) by Angelo Debarre and Tchavolo Schmitt. Meanwhile, Marie Daulne has taken Zap Mama from its roots as an a cappella women's group to a contemporary fusion of hip-hop, R&B, and African roots. The highly successful results can be found on *Ancestry in Progress* (Luaka Bop).

Afro-Celts founder Simon Emmerson has teamed up with DJ Phil Meadley to give us *The Outernationalists Present Ethnomixicology* (Six Degrees), a mix-CD of West African rhythms and contemporary beats. On a similar note, Thievery Corporation's *The Outernational Sound* (EsL Music), their follow-up to 2002's infectious *The Richest Man in Babylon*, has Rob Garza and Eric Hilton putting together a mash-up of everything from Kingston reggae sounds and Afro-beats to Brazilian jazz and funky rhythms. It gets a little busy, but it will keep the dance floor hopping.

On *Welcome to Haiti: Creole 101* (Koch Records), the Fugee's Wyclef Jean returns to his Haitian roots with a multilanguage discourse set against a musical background that's even more diverse, blending reggae and raga, South African township music and American R&B and blues. *True Love* (Mushroom) features Toots and the Metals playing their own brand of reggae with an all-star support cast (not that Toots needs them) of Ben Harper, Keith Richards, No Doubt, Ryan Adams, Bonnie Raitt, Willie Nelson, and others.

Tri Continental, made up of solo artists Madagascar Slim, Lester Quitzau, and Bill Bourne, return with a fourth album, *Drifting* (Tradition and Moderne). Like the Lúnasa CD mentioned above, this was recorded live in the studio in front of an invited audience, and the music—a mix of blues and world-beat—has that groove you can only get from a live recording. Madagascar Slim also shows up on *African Guitar Summit* (CBC Records) a collection by Canadian artists of African origin highlighting the give and take of musical traditions between Africa and the West, while Lester Quitzau lends his inspired guitar playing and voice to Mae Moore's *Oh, My!* (Poetical License), trading songs and guitar licks on some of the best music of her career.

Italian singer Pietra Montecorvino's latest is *Napoli Mediterranea* (L 'Empreinte Digitale), an album of Neapolitan music featuring her voice and the sound of the oud against a backing of Mediterranean-styled rhythmic percussion. On *Solen* (GO'??) the duo of Karen and Helene give us traditional Danish songs in new arrangements. *Selwa* (Six Degrees) features the chants and songs of Tibetan Buddhist nun Chöying Drolma and the guitar playing of Steve Tibbetts against a backdrop of acoustic percussion.

Led by sax and flute player Seta, *Introducing Vakoka: The Malagasy All-Stars* (World Music Network) brings together thirteen top musicians from Madagascar collaborating on songs featuring many of the island's unique instruments. From China, we have the Twelve Girls Band's *Eastern Energy* (Platia Entertainment) using Chinese versions of bamboo flutes, hammer dulcimers, and zithers to perform a selection of classical, pop, and traditional songs.

Solace (Independent Release) by Xavier Rudd is the new surf music, but it's about as far from the Beach Boys as you can imagine. For one thing, Rudd is a one-man band. When you see him in concert, the Australian native can be heard simultaneously playing a stomp box, lap slide guitar, and a didgeridoo. For another, the music, while certainly espousing a sense of goodwill and fun, has a strong focus on spiritual, environmental, and Aboriginal concerns.

Taima (Full Spin) is made up of Inuk singer Elisapie Isaac and Quebec guitarist Alain Auger. The group's name translates to "Enough! It's over . . . let's move on," and the band explores the relationship between Inuit people and whites. Lucie Idlout also explores race issues on *E5-770: My Mother's Name* (Arbor Records), but hers is a tougher approach, perhaps because the title of her latest album refers to the Canadian government's onetime practice of giving Inuit people a disc number to identify them, rather than using their names.

Lastly, while treading a little further off the track than might be my mandate with this wrap-up of the year's music, let me leave you with a recommendation for the recent reissue *The Complete Seven Steps* (Columbia) by Miles Davis. Everyone always seems to cite *A Kind of Blue* as *the* Miles Davis album, and it's certainly a wonderful recording, but the original *Seven Steps* is a personal favorite of mine, and this six-CD set collecting the whole recording session as well as a couple of live concerts from the same period is stellar jazz that will never get old. When you listen to the studio sessions, you wonder how they were ever able to edit them down to the length of one vinyl record all those years ago.

If you're looking for more than an annual fix of the sorts of music discussed above, I'd like to recommend a few Web sites that carry timely reviews and news:

www.frootsmag.com
www.endicott-studio.com
www.pastemusic.com
www.globalrhythm.net
www.greenmanreview.com
www.rambles.net

Or if you prefer the written page, check out your local newsstand for copies of *fRoots* (two issues per year carry fabulous CD samplers), *Global Rhythm* (each issue includes a sampler CD), *Songlines* (also has a CD sampler), *Paste* (with CD sampler; subscribers also get a DVD sampler), *Sing Out!* and *Dirty Linen*.

While I know there are lots of other great albums out there, I don't have the budget to try everything. But my ears are always open to new sounds. So if you'd like to bring something to my attention for next year's essay, you can send it to me c/o P.O. Box 9480, Ottawa, ON K1G 3V2 Canada.

Obituaries: 2004

James Frenkel

Inevitably, many talented and creative people died last year. Some of those whose names are reported below will be familiar to you; others may be either entirely unknown to you or merely vaguely familiar. All were people who helped create or nurture the imaginative arts in one way or another.

Joan Aiken, 79, was an extremely popular and highly acclaimed British young-adult fantasy author, with nearly one hundred books to her credit. She is best known to fantasy readers for her Dido Twite alternate-world series, perhaps most famously *The Wolves of Willoughby Chase*. Her other YA fantasies include, among others, *The Whispering Mountain* (1968); *Midnight Is a Place* (1974); *The Shadow Guests* (1980); *The Cockatrice Boys* (1996); and *The Scream* (2002). Winner of many awards, she was beloved around the world.

Julius Schwartz, 88, was a comic-book writer and editor who played a significant role in saving superhero comics in the 1950s by modernizing characters such as the Flash, Green Lantern, Justice League of America, Hawkman, and the Atom for comic book's oncoming silver age. In a long and productive career he also worked as a literary agent for such authors as Ray Bradbury and C. L. Moore, and continued to contribute to the field for six decades.

Jack Cady, 71, an author of lyrical, atmospheric horror, SF, and mainstream fiction, first gained recognition in the horror field with a pair of novellas, "By Reason of Darkness" and "The Night We Buried Road Dog" (both 1993), which won, respectively Nebula and Stoker Awards. He wrote eight novels under his own name, including *Inagehi* (1994). He also wrote horror thrillers under the name Pat Franklin, such as *Dark Dreaming* (1991) and *Embrace of the Wolf* (1993).

Hugh B. Cave, 93, was known best for his supernatural horror and weird fiction, but was also the author of hundreds of gothic, science fiction, hard-boiled detective, romance, western, and adventure tales. Cave's tales were published in magazines, hardcovers, and paperbacks. Cave was truly a prodigious author, writing more than a thousand works of fiction.

Janet Leigh, 77, will be remembered forever as Marion Crane, who was stabbed to death in the shower by Norman Bates in Alfred Hitchcock's film *Psycho*. She was a versatile actress who appeared in various other TV shows and films, including the horror film *The Fog*.

Christopher Reeve, 52, became famous for his role as the titular character in 1978's *Superman*, and two sequels. He acted in other films as well, continuing after a brutal spinal cord injury paralyzed him. The Christopher Reeve Paralysis Foundation has raised over $45 million for spinal cord research.

William Relling Jr., 49, was a horror writer best known for his novels *Brujo* (1986), *New Moon* (1988), and *Silent Moon* (1990). He also published several stories, essays, and reviews, with fiction appearing in *Omni*, *Cemetery Dance*, and various anthologies.

Patricia Mullen, 62, is remembered for her novel *The Stone Movers*. In addition to her novel, Ms. Mullen wrote several short stories for horror anthologies.

Robert Merle, 95, was an author who won France's highest literary honor, Le Prix Goncourt, for *Un Animal Doué de Raison*, which was the basis for the film *The Day of the Dolphin*. His other works include *Malevil* and *Les Hommes Protégés*.

Ray Stark, 88, was an influential Hollywood producer. His work included *On a Clear Day You Can See Forever*, among a number of hit films.

Jerry Goldsmith, 75, was a prodigiously productive and famous composer of film scores. Among scores to *Patton*, *Gunsmoke*, *Planet of the Apes*, *Basic Instinct*, and *L.A. Confidential*, Goldsmith particularly enjoyed composing for *The Twilight Zone*.

Elmer Bernstein, 82, was a famous film composer. His scores were heard in *The Man with the Golden Arm*, *To Kill a Mockingbird*, *The Great Escape*, *The Grifter*, and *Ghostbusters*. Bernstein was nominated for fourteen Academy Awards, winning one for *Thoroughly Modern Millie* in 1967.

M. M. Kaye, 95, a novelist and children's writer, is remembered for her children's fantasy, *The Ordinary Princess* (1980). Her other accomplishments include her best-selling historical novel *The Far Pavilions* (1978).

Pierre Pairault, 81, was better known by his pen name, **Stefan Wul**. Of the twelve novels published in his career, he is most remembered for *Le Temple du Passé*, translated as *The Temple of the Past* in 1973. His last novel, *Noo*, appeared in 1977.

Brian McNaughton, 68, was an American horror author. His collection *The Throne of Bones* won a World Fantasy Award in 1997.

Trina Schart Hyman, 65, was an influential book illustrator with a massive body of work. She won the Caldecott three times, and did the illustrations for versions of "Sleeping Beauty" and "Rapunzel," as well as "St. George and the Dragon: A Golden Legend Adapted from Edmund Spenser's 'Faerie Queen.'" **Syd Hoff**, 91, was a children's book author and illustrator most famous for the book *Danny and the Dinosaur*, which sold over 10 million copies and has been translated into a dozen languages.

Marlon Brando, 80, best known for his roles as Vito Corleone in *The Godfather* and Stanley Kowalski in *A Streetcar Named Desire*, was lured out of retirement in 1978 to play the role of Jor-El in the film *Superman*. Brando won two Oscars, for his work in *On the Waterfront* and *The Godfather*. **Mercedes McCambridge**, 86, was an actress. She did voice work in *The Exorcist* and *Amazing Stories* as well as guest appearances on *Lost in Space* and *Bewitched*. **Tony Randall**, 84, best known as one half of the Odd Couple, was a famous comedic actor who played roles in numerous films, including the *Seven Faces of Dr. Lao*. He also was a stage actor, founding the

National Actor's Theatre, and starring in numerous plays by Shakespeare, Shaw, and others. **Fay Wray**, 96, an actress appearing in over one hundred films, is best known for being the screaming damsel-in-distress in *King Kong*. She won Kong's giant heart, spending hours screaming and struggling in Kong's eight-foot hand.

Sir Peter Ustinov, 83, was best known for his nongenre work in such historical epics as *Quo Vadis* and *Spartacus*. He also appeared in such films as *Blackbeard's Ghost* and *Around the World in Eighty Days*. He provided the voice for Prince John and King Richard in Disney's animated *Robin Hood*.

Norman Talbot, 67, was the author of many SF/F stories, most recently "The Latest Dream I Ever Dreamed" in the anthology *Dreaming Down-Under* (1998). His work covered a broad range of genres and periods. The most recent of his numerous awards was the Broadway Poetry Prize at the 2002 Australian Poetry Festival.

Don Lawrence, 75, was a British science fiction illustrator and cartoonist. He has done graphics for the twenty-three-volume Dutch novel *Storm*, as well as Mike Butterworth's fantasy *The Rise and Fall of the Trigan Empire*, for which he drew nearly one thousand pages. He is also remembered for drawing Marvelman, considered Britain's first superhero. **Gil Fox**, 88, was a comic artist, editor, and writer who produced the covers for Police Comics in the 1940s that featured Plastic Man. Fox also wrote scripts for Will Eisner's *The Spirit*.

Irvin Yeaworth Jr., 78, was a film director best known for making the campy cult classic *The Blob* in 1958. He directed hundreds of other films outside the Sci-Fi genre. **Betty Miller**, 79, was a stage and screen actress. She played characters such as Gertrude in *Hamlet* and Lady Macduff in *Macbeth*. She also did film work including *Bringing Out the Dead* (1999) and *A League of Their Own* (1992). **Mary Selway**, 68, was a well-known British casting agent, responsible for assembling the casts of such films as *Harry Potter and the Goblet of Fire* and *Raiders of the Lost Ark*. **Neal Fredericks**, 35, was the cinematographer of the low-budget surprise hit *The Blair Witch Project*. **Max Rosenberg**, 89, produced horror films, most notably *Tales from the Crypt* and *The Curse of Frankenstein* (1957). He also edited horror anthologies, including *Dr. Terror's House of Horrors* and *The House That Dripped Blood*. **Pat Roach**, 61, is perhaps best known as the Nazi who was killed by a propeller in *Raiders of the Lost Ark*. He also appeared in *Conan the Destroyer* and *Indiana Jones and the Temple of Doom*. **Peter Diamond**, 74, was an actor, stuntman, and stunt arranger. He choreographed the light-saber duels in the original Star Wars trilogy, and participated in them as a stuntman. He also did work on *Raiders of the Lost Ark*, *The Princess Bride*, and *Highlander*. **Peter Woodthorpe**, 72, was a famous British character actor. Performed in the original *Waiting for Godot*, in 1955. Among his many accomplishments in the world of drama, he starred as Gollum in the 1978 animated film *The Lord of the Rings*. **David Hemmings**, 62, actor and director, died on December 4, 2003. Genre appearances included *Barbarella* (1968), *Dr. Jekyll and Mr. Hyde* (TV movie, 1981), *Equilibrium* (2002) and most recently *The League of Extraordinary Gentlemen* (2003). **Olga Druce**, 92, supplied radio voices for *House of Mystery* and *Superman*. **Nelson Gidding**, 84, wrote the screenplays for *The Haunting*, *The Andromeda Strain*, and *The Mummy Lives*. **Carl Anderson**, 58, was best known for his portrayal of Judas in the smash rock opera *Jesus Christ Superstar*. **Katherine Victor**, 81, appeared in many films, including *Teenage Zombies*, *The Cape Canaveral Monsters*, and *Superguy: Behind the Cape*. In addition to acting, she also worked as an animation checker for Filmation, Hanna-Barbera, Disney, and others.

Roger Straus, 87, was an editor and the cofounder of Farrar, Straus of Giroux. He worked with a number of Nobel Prize–winning authors during his career, including Isaac Bashevis Singer. **Jon White**, 58, was a longtime fan, book reviewer, and bookseller who was passionate about pulp magazines and vintage paperbacks. At one time he coedited the influential *Riverside Quarterly* with Leland Sapiro. **Judy Corman**, 66, was senior vice president of corporate communications at Scholastic Books. Her PR work for the Harry Potter series was instrumental in popularizing it in the U.S. **Nancy Larrick**, 93, wrote a comprehensive, widely used guide to children's literature. She also wrote some children's books herself.

Katherine Lawrence, 49, wrote SF stories, and teleplays for the television shows *Hypernauts, Conan the Adventurer*, the *Dungeons and Dragons* animated series, and many other series. Prior to 1990, Lawrence wrote under the name Kathy Selbert. **Rex Miller**, 65, began publishing in the 1980s with short stories and went on to write horror mysteries. His first novel, *Slob*, was a finalist for the Bram Stoker Award.

Artist **John Cullen Murphy**, 85, is best known as the illustrator of the Prince Valiant comic strip, which he began to illustrate in 1970. **Peter Baird**, 52, was a master puppeteer, in the tradition of his father, the trailblazer Bil Baird, and his family. His credits include marionette work in *The Muppets Take Manhattan, Pinocchio*, and *Team America: World Police*. **Harry Lampert**, 88, was an illustrator for DC Comics in the early 1940s. He was the first person to draw the popular superhero the Flash. **Elizabeth Chater**, 94, taught the first course in science fiction at San Diego State College. Chater wrote fantasies and romances. **Bob Haney**, 78, was a veteran comic-book writer from the silver age. Starting in 1948, he worked for a series of publishers, eventually tying in to DC Comics in 1956. Haney created the original Teen Titans, the Doom Patrol, and Metamorpho the Element Man and also wrote numerous scripts for *The Brave and the Bold*. **Kate Worley**, 46, wrote the comic book *Omaha: The Cat Dancer*.

Genia Melikova, 74, was a famed ballerina. She was Aurora and the Lilac Fairy in *Sleeping Beauty*, and Odette-Odile in *Swan Lake*. **Julia Trevelyan Oman**, 73, was a well-known and respected British theater designer. Her sets and costumes helped bring productions of *Swan Lake, Die Fledermaus*, and *The Nutcracker*, among others, to life.

Frank Thomas, 92, was a famous Disney animator and a member of Walt Disney's "nine old men." He animated the spaghetti-strand scene in *Lady and the Tramp*, the penguins in *Mary Poppins*, and Thumper teaching Bambi how to ice skate in *Bambi*. **J. P. Miller**, 91, was an animator for Disney who made major contributions to *Pinocchio, Fantasia*, and *Dumbo*. He also did illustrations for a number of best-selling children's books. **Harry Holt**, 90, designed scenes for the Disney films *Snow White and the Seven Dwarfs* and *Lady and the Tramp*. Holt also served as the principal designer of Disneyworld, with his sculptures used in the Pirates of the Caribbean and Haunted Mansion rides. Holt also did animation for the Hanna-Barbera cartoons and the Flintstones.

Danny Dark, 65, was the voice behind the scenes for various commercials including Budweiser, Starkist Tuna, and Raid. Not only did he intone cultural lines like "This Bud's for you" and voice "Charlie the Tuna," he also became the beloved voice to children of Superman on the cartoon series *Super Friends*.

The contributions these and others made to books, magazines, film, art, ballet, and opera fueled the imagination of millions. Though they are gone, their work survives them, and is an inspiration to those who may follow a career in the fantastic arts.

GREGORY MAGUIRE

The Oakthing

Gregory Maguire is the author of five acclaimed novels for adults, including the forthcoming Son of a Witch. *The hit Broadway musical* Wicked *is based on his novel of the same name. His books for children, the popular* Hamlet Chronicles *among them, include* Seven Spiders Spinning, Four Stupid Cupids, *and the charming and hilarious screwball collection* Leaping Beauty: Other Animal Fairy Tales. *He lives outside Boston.*

"The Oakthing" was first published in the anthology The Faery Reel. *In the author's note, Maguire says, "The inspiration for 'The Oakthing' is the drawings of Arthur Rackham, particularly those for* Peter Pan in Kensington Gardens. *They were very Edwardian creatures, those inventions of Rackham and J. M. Barrie. For my story, I transposed one of them to the Continent, at the very close of the Edwardian age, when the first of the century's terrible wars blasted modernity into our faces."*

—K.L. & G.G.

Though the sky was a peerless blue, there had been thunder since dawn. Low thunder, ground thunder, leaving an acrid odor in twists of gray gauze that the wind pushed across the fields. As if a hand had rubbed a rod of graphite against the horizon, sketching vertical shafts of ghost in the warming day. It was the foot soldiers pushing, though, pushing the line, and it was the artillery behind them and flanking them that made such persuasive thunder.

The farm was not quite in their way. Not yet; it was off to one side.

A family had lived there for many generations. The place was called—with a light mocking of the habits of gentlemen farmers to name their estates—Sous Vieux Chêne—under the old oak. To the villagers of Remigny, three miles east, it had been known only as the Gauthier place.

But at this point, there were few left in Remigny to call it anything. Most villagers, sensibly, had fled. The Gauthiers, capable farmers with farmers' stout common sense, were less practiced at dealing with invading armies. Though they did discuss the problem.

"We can't leave. There are the crops to bring in." The father was stubborn.

His wife more or less agreed, though pointed out, "Your main crop is not wheat." She'd glanced sideways at their lovely child, their slightly dim, affectionate Dominique. Quite old enough to attract the eye of war-maddened soldiers. "Might it be silly to risk her safety for the sake of our wheat?"

It was a topic of discussion they had played with all summer, as one by one their farmer neighbors and the villagers of Remigny had fled to points south. Surely the line would shift? The Huns would not dare to drive their war machine through Gauthier fields!

A certain sort of family insanity must obtain, surely, that they held to such convictions for so long. Neighbors had tried to reason with the Gauthiers, but the Gauthiers, back as far as any could remember, had not been a reasonable line. They had laughed and drunk their coffee with cow's milk and said, "But what means this *Schrecklichkeit*, this German frightfulness, to a Gauthier?" And said it over and over until there was no one left to hear it.

But with the dead and the starved animals all around, and the ruination of sugar-beet fields, and the 42-centimeter howitzers pounding the center of the market town eight miles further east . . . . It was hard to concentrate on wheat.

Finally the Great Panic came home to the current crop of Gauthiers. They were interrupted at their praying of the Angelus by a cloudburst of cannonfire nearer than ever. At last they came to their senses, or lost their nerve, or both at once.

They cobbled together what they could. An agricultural wagon suitable for the transport of hay, a smaller cart that a donkey could pull. They spent the morning piling what supplies were left, and a few pieces of the better furnishings, as if, meeting a caisson on the road, they could barter for safety with a choice armoire or a nice tureen boasting swan heads for handles.

In the end, the thunder leaning more heavily upon them, the artillery nearing, their exit was undignified, disorganized, and incomplete. Madame Marie-Laure Gauthier and docile, sentimental Dominique had hitched up the team and left with the wagon, toweringly overloaded. Around its bulk and over the noise of the invasion they shouted revised plans for their rendezvous.

Hector Gauthier followed a few minutes later in the cart, taking the last of the cheeses. The cow had been dead for a week, likely of terror, and so no milk to sprinkle on the doorstep, to sour and keep the little people out.

And thus good-bye to Sous Vieux Chêne, good-bye, good-bye. *Au revoir*, we hope! *À demain*, with luck. Good-bye. The German armies, which had romped through Belgium and showed every likelihood of tromping through the boulevards of Paris, had managed at last to scatter even the stubborn and mentally giddy Gauthiers. *Incroyable.*

All of them, that is, except Mme. Mémé Gauthier, the grandmother.

She had left her seat in the wagon because of an urge to use the outhouse. Her daughter-in-law had bawled around the edge of the sacks of bedding that Hector would need to take his own feeble mother, she could not wait any longer, Dominique would not be safe! But the thunder of cannon had smudged the sound of her voice. Hector Gauthier hadn't heard the full message, nor could he see around the worldly Gauthier goods heaped high in the wagon. When Mme. Marie-Laure Gauthier left, her husband assumed his mother was safely on board, cursing and praying the rosary simultaneously.

When Mémé Gauthier emerged refreshed, the wagon was gone. The cart was gone. Since the cow was still dead, Mémé Gauthier was glad her sense of smell was largely gone, too. And her hearing was not what it had once been, so the cannon noise wasn't objectionable.

She was well into her eighth decade, and frightened by little. She'd been born in the 1830s, when this was just the Gauthier place, not Sous Vieux Chêne. The old oak was old even in her childhood, and just a tree, just an oak, not the name of a headache or a property. Still, though, she'd cocked an eyebrow at news of uprisings in Paris, continental upheavals, even the invention of a steam engine to power a locomotive (she'd seen one once, too!), her life had been lived solely on the farm.

She was only mildly disappointed to have been forgotten by her son and his family. Indeed, she'd likely have forgotten herself, had she been in charge of the exodus.

Mémé Gauthier collected her walking stick—a nice bit of thorn with a smoothly knobbed head—and made her way through the forecourt of the barn buildings and around to the house's front door. Her son had locked it, but he'd likely have left the key in its usual place: a hollow in the eponymous oak. She had to think a bit about how to reach that high.

Finally she went and found a milking stool and dragged it from the barn where it was doing no one any good anyway. When she got to the oak, she saw that a number of its limbs had given up and fallen to the ground, like the spokes of a blown-out umbrella. What was left was a spiky pillar of old dead wood, knobbed with woody warts a century old.

But the hiding place was intact, and the stool afforded her enough height to grope in the hollow. Sure enough, she secured the key, an oversized iron thing from the days of her own father.

So she opened up the house that had just been closed against the invading armies. She invaded it herself. Well, why not, it was her own house. And she sat down on a chair with a rush bottom, to think about what to do next.

Likely she dozed. She napped a dozen times a day. Sometimes she thought she must doze even while she walked, for she didn't always remember where she was, when she came to think about it, nor where she was going.

When she opened her eyes, the trapezoids of sunlight had shifted across the terra-cotta tiles. Their lines were more acute, the patches of light more slanting.

She squinted and rubbed her eyes. Was that a house cat in the sun? Surely not. All the house cats had long ago run out and drowned themselves from terror, so far as anyone could tell. Even the mice had gone *en vacances*.

The thing made a kind of a curtsey. Or perhaps it was a rude gesture. At any rate, neither cats nor mice stood nine inches tall on hind legs. Unless some distant zoo in Louvain had been bombed and its monkey population scattered across the border into la belle France, this was a visitation by a little creature.

Where were her spectacles? She had given up needlework in her 70s, and the more ripely adolescent her granddaughter had become, the less often Mémé Gauthier had wanted to look closely at her. "You wait right here, you," she said, and went to look in the chiffonier. But the chiffonier was gone. What a *crétin* her son was! Fleeing from an invading army with a chiffonier! Anyway, her spectacles were gone with it.

When she came back, the creature was still there. Mémé Gauthier took considerable pains to get down on her knees, the better to see. While she was there she prayed for peace, and then she prayed she'd be able to get back up again. First, though, she looked to see what manner of mischief this thing might prove to be.

It was, she decided, a tree sprite of some sort. In sorry shape. Sorely in need of succor, or attention, or perhaps concealment; she couldn't tell. It seemed an angular knot of twigs, from one angle; and then again there were tines of thorn and froths of densely clumped root. Like pubic hair, or the hair in armpits, rangy, airy, and with a vegetable odor strong enough that even Mémé Gauthier could appreciate it. It was matted with mud that little by little was drying and falling in small clods on the floor.

But the thing—male, female, or neither, or both, or something else again, she couldn't tell—seemed to be, in the term used by those who practice the art of war, shell-shocked. It shook gently. If it had hands, it rubbed its elbows; if it had knees, or fetlocks, they knocked together. It did have something of a chin, and a yawp for a mouth, but its eyes were slitted closed like a newborn infant's, and its ears hung low, as if they'd died two separate deaths.

"And so a bit of company for Mme. Mémé Gauthier," she said courteously. "It's thoughtful of you to call, when my kin have seen fit to abandon me."

The creature's shoulders, or high-slung hips, or airy ribs, shook, perhaps not at the actual sentiment but at the sound of a voice sent so obviously its way.

"You're in need of some comfort, but of what sort?" she asked. "And whatever enticed you to come in?"

The house had been vacated for no more than an hour. But then, because the cow was dead, she'd been unable to splash on the doorstep the customary sour-milk prohibition against intruders.

"I suppose you're welcome," said Mémé Gauthier. "But I can't sit around and play a hand of cards with you. It may take a day or two for my feckless relatives to realize they've misplaced me. And the Lord alone knows whether one of them will be able to retrace their steps to collect me, considering the advancing armies. I'm on my own—present company excluded—and must fend for myself."

It had been some time since she'd been able to say that, and the prospect gave her some pleasure. Let's see, what was needed first? To lock the doors, to secure the valuables, to tend to the animals, to water the vegetables, to clean the baby, to bank the coals?

There was no need to lock the doors, as it turned out, as there were neither valuables, nor animals, nor babies, nor coals, nor much by way of vegetables, for that matter. The kitchen garden offered some carrots, some kale in the act of bolting, potatoes in their secret graves, no doubt, and various herbs for savor. Though herbs were a bit difficult to savor on their own.

Mémé Gauthier scraped together what she could. The farm had never been electrified and the portable oil lamps were gone. As the afternoon dragged on Mémé Gauthier's knees began to hurt, so she didn't trust herself to scale a chair and light the fancy ceiling lamp in the salon. She'd make just a small fire in the hearth, to lend some comfort and take the worst chill out of her fingers, and then she'd burrow under a blanket and wait till the gray dawn.

The creature's eyes hadn't yet opened, quite, but she thought it sensed her movements. When she went to the herb yard, it wandered toward that part of the property; when she went back to the pump, it retreated. But if she went farther—to the gate, to see if dim Hector or his Marie-Laure were hurrying back to save her—the oakthing was uncomfortable, and fidgeted like a dog or a worrying child. Having gained the house, it didn't want to leave, and it didn't want her to go either.

That's what it was, she decided, an oakthing. Evacuated from the battered tree that gave the farm its name.

"Scared out of your own home, you," she said to it, "just as Hector and Marie-Laure are scared out of theirs! Everyone packing up like tortoises and moving on. Well, I'm staying put, and let the Hun have it if he must. I'm too old to be of interest to a young soldier, in that certain way, I mean, and I'm too tedious and insignificant to detain an army in its mission. I've no food to steal and no virtue to protect, so I've nothing to lose. But what's your excuse?"

The oakthing collapsed into something resembling a sitting position, and put what it had of a face into what it had of hands.

"If it's the tree you're mourning," she said, "the old black umbrella that gives this farm its name, you're wasting your time. In its time it has sent out ten hundred thousand emissaries on its own behalf. Maybe more. Every spring, the seeds spiral and the wind catches at them, and the oak tree has ten thousand cousins across Normandy and Flanders alone. If your particular bedsit has collapsed, well, the bedsit doesn't care. Its roots are in the future."

She peered down at the oakthing. "Its roots are in the future. As are mine, you thing. Dominque has loins as ripe as any old oak tree in springtime, and she will litter the future with her issue, which will be mine, too, if you look at it a certain way."

But perhaps the oakthing had no issue.

What should she do for it? Given that she could do little for herself, had she an obligation to put out more effort for an ambulatory clot of vegetable matter? If it were a baby or a cat, she would give it milk.

"The cats are all gone," she told it.

And that, she saw, was part of its problem. It may have lived in a tree, but it lived near a farm, and all farms had mice so all farms had cats. And all cats drank milk.

In a desolate summer, even the mice were gone, and the cats were dead, and the cows were dry or dead or gone, and the farm's slender economy no longer afforded a saucer of milk at the door for the cat. And while milk souring would keep an oakthing and its cousins away, the fresh milk put out for a cat was probably the oakthing's primary diet.

She would think about it in her sleep, and dream up a solution if she could.

But Mémé Gauthier had no sleep that night, for the artificial thunder of the German advance and the scattershot pebble-rain of feeble French resistance punched holes in her efforts to doze. When there was enough light to rise safely, she did, and rinsed the chamber pot by the pump, and then brushed her hair and cleaned her teeth.

The oakthing, it seemed, was gone, and she felt a sort of pity for it. Had it dried up in the night, or maybe reclaimed what was left of its tree? Had it found her unsympathetic? Had it abandoned her? Had she anything more important to do, as the invasion swept field by field from the northeast, than to worry about a twiggy figment of rural superstition?

Perhaps not, which meant her life had shriveled down to very little, too.

So she was glad when she found it, huddled under the overturned bucket. The overturned milk bucket. It seemed to be shedding more of itself, in scraps of bark and trails of blond dust. "You're wanting me to find milk for the cat," said Mme. Gauthier. "As if I haven't anything better to do."

But, in fact, she hadn't. So she put on her rubber boots and took an umbrella, as if its flimsy ribs and taut cotton skin could protect her from shrapnel, and she clutched at her walking stick, and went off down the lane.

There were four farms this way, two the other, and across the ditch and two fields was a one-room schoolhouse that had once had a goat tethered in its yard. The farms were farther but the ditch was a problem; she wasn't sure she trusted herself to maneuver across a plank. Still, she remembered that the goat had had kids rather late in the season, and though they might have been slaughtered or stolen or died of fright, if the goat had been left behind she might still have milk. And Mémé Gauthier had not lived on a farm all her life without learning how to milk a goat if a goat had milk to give.

"Are you coming?" she asked the oakthing.

It didn't answer, but spat at her as a child might: wanting the fruits of her expedition but resenting her for leaving anyway.

"Thankless," she told it, with some satisfaction.

And as she left the yard, she looked again at the sundered trunk of the oak tree. Had one of yesterday's thunder blasts been real weather from God, accompanied by vengeful lightning? Or had a snippet of bomb gone awry and curled the old wood into lazy scrapes as if it were made of butter? The bushels of leaves still turning in the breeze—still attached to their twigs, poking from branches, dividing from the stems of thick split limbs. The leaves didn't know they were dead yet.

She closed up the umbrella, enjoying a spit of rain on her brow, and used it as a second cane. Her arthritic wrists ached by the time she was halfway across the plank, edging sideways inch by inch, but the strategy worked, and she didn't overbalance. The meadow was full of sumptuous hay ready for harvest. And no one to do it. It would die, too.

Swarms of summer bugs insensible of the military action made a second weather of droning commotion at her shoulder height. She thrashed her way through, keeping her eyes on the roof of the schoolhouse in its thicket of poplars.

These trees, it turned out, were also splintered, and the east-facing wall of the school, once a rosy pink stone, was scorched with explosives and had buckled into the yard. The shutters were blown off their hinges or straight through the shattered windows. A few sets of uncollected wooden shoes lay marvelously undisturbed beside what remained of the door. No children had been here for a week at least, maybe more. But the goat, crazed with grief and solitude, was still there, bucking against its tethers, its forehead scraped bloody raw in its efforts to escape.

She had a need. She had the goat. The goat had milk. She had fingers gnarled with arthritis. What she didn't have was a bucket. She'd forgotten that.

"You, stop your barracking," she told the goat. "I've got a little baby at home that needs what you give. I can't think with all your noise, though."

She hunted about in the debris, poking with her walking stick and her umbrella. There wasn't so much as a single tin cup to salvage.

So in the end, with blistered hands, she milked the goat into the largest of the pair of wooden shoes. Then she loosened the buttons on her farm-dress and sank the shoes as best as she could, toe-end down, between what remained of her breasts. She tied herself up as well as she could. The milk slopped as she moved, but she would go slowly, and not all of it would slop, she hoped. It was the best she could do. She was 86, or 84, or something: what could the oakthing expect?

After a few steps homeward, she turned back: why not bring the goat with her? Could she get it across the plank? If it overturned her into the ditch she'd die there, damply.

She never got the chance to try. The goat shied at the first opportunity and twisted its tether out of her feeble grasp. Into the overgrown fields it disappeared, bleating in hysterical joy, which she imagined would be short-lived, given the panic of the times.

The wind smelled as if it was burning. The sun had gotten high the meanwhile, and it winked brassily now and then, colored by the smoke of gunfire. More of the meadow was thrashed down than she had managed by herself. She imagined stalking ogres with breath like roasting gunpowder, and the stink of hot metal. Feet larger than human boots could hold were responsible for the wreckage. If not gathered immediately, mold would set in, and rot, and the hay go useless, and the animals go hungry.

Only there were no animals, she remembered, so let the hay be stomped upon by ogres.

The return trip took her longer than she'd imagined. Well, she was tired with her efforts. The sun was already weaseling down the western skies, shimmying between big bosomed clouds. One of the farms she'd thought about rooting around was, it seemed, on fire. The rutted track heading that way was muddy, torn up with iron-hooped wheels. Cannon had come through here, and horses, leaving their fresh stink.

But there was nothing at Sous Vieux Chêne for a scavenging corps, surely, nothing worth burning even?

And the oakthing—was it all right? Was it still there?

She couldn't go any faster than she could go. If the oakthing was going to die in the next four minutes for lack of fresh milk, it would just have to die. She had been inching forward in her life over all these decades at her own pace, and, as she well knew, things on farms died, in their time. Herself included, in her time, whenever that was.

But her breath came faster and, really, despite her farmer's philosophies, she *was* hurrying.

The door was kicked off one of its hinges and clods of mud were mulishly deposited on what had been a properly clean farmhouse floor. Beyond that, though, the house seemed intact. The advancing army had found nothing to steal, nothing to eat, and no one to rape, and perhaps the oakthing's need for milk had saved Mémé Gauthier herself. Taking her safely offstage at the right moment.

Not that she cared to be saved, particularly. Saved for what? To starve to death over the period of a week or two, watching the sun rise and fall, and hearing the crickets of late summer crisply gnaw through her last minutes, sounding like the merciless throb of a pendulum, until the pendulum finally wound down for good?

But she cared about the oakthing. After settling the shoes carefully in a dry sink, and propping them up with some towels so they couldn't slope over and the milk slop out, she went to hunt for it.

She found it clinging to the headboard of Dominique's low-slung bed. It looked more like a bug now, and its anxious movements were more twitchy than ever. It scrambled up and down the crudely carved post, inspecting the face of the man who lay with his head upon Dominique's thin pillow, adhering to it in a fracturing skin of dried blood and vomit.

"I *ought* to have managed that goat," said Mémé Gauthier. "But she managed me better than I could do her."

The man was a German soldier. A wound opened on the side of his neck like a red cabbage severed with a knife. For all her long life as a farmwife, Mémé Gauthier had never seen human anatomy laid quite this open to inspection. She was rather intrigued. The oakthing trembled in revulsion. It skittered down, looked at the wound, at the hideous mess of leakage, at the scorched brows and glossy burned temple, at the long elegant drawing-room nose and neat teeth, perfectly intact and as pearly as baby onions, not a brown one among them.

"It's the enemy," said Mémé Gauthier. "It's the German Army."

The German Army breathed in with long breaths, like a bellows with a leak, and when the German Army breathed out, flecks of dried blood danced with a copper brilliance in the slanting afternoon light.

The oakthing twisted its fingers and pointed. There was a rifle on the floor, and a leather satchel.

"I know rifles," she said to the oakthing. "I've shot mad dogs in my day, and a horse who had to be done in, too. And I've fired over the heads of brigands and priests who had too much interest in the affairs of the household."

But she didn't touch the rifle. She pawed through the satchel instead, hoping to find some dried bread, some rations, some identification. There were a few documents in German; she couldn't read them. Whoever had left the soldier here, however, had already done what foraging there was to be done. She found nothing useful but a long needle and a spool of thread.

She lit the kitchen fire with some kindling and she threw in some wooden spoons to build up the flame, for she couldn't take the time to hunt for anything else. She held the needle in the heat for as long as she could, to guard against contamination, and when it had cooled so that she could handle it, she settled herself on the edge of Dominique's bed. She stitched up the wound as well as she could. Without her spectacles, she couldn't scrutinize her work. The edges didn't quite match, and the blood began to flow again, but not torrentially. She had a sense, perhaps a false one, that she was doing some good.

She was pleased. She wanted him well enough to be able to sit up in bed and look at her in the face before she shot him between the eyes.

The oakthing came down and settled on his shoulder, for all the world like the parrot on the shoulder of a pirate. "You belong to the oak, and the oak belongs to the farm, and the German Army is a trespasser!" said Mémé Gauthier in disgust. "Get away from there, you. You traitor."

But the oakthing didn't attend to insults. It didn't care. It settled its twiggy apparatus of fingers against the fellow's wound as if, in the absence of milk, blood might substitute. Or maybe it liked invading armies who blasted its home, drove off the farmers it lived parasitically upon, turned the greens of the world into browns, and the late summer skies into boiling black hellfires.

There was still the matter of food, and Mémé Gauthier now had not eaten for more than a day. Though she was prepared to die of malnourishment, her fairly ample form would require her to starve for a while, first, and she wasn't eager for that experience. Furthermore she didn't want to nurse a marauder into some semblance of health and then herself pass away before she had a chance to kill him.

Perhaps she ought just pull the trigger, get it over with? Why exact the vengeance of terror upon him? He was a young thing, and hardly more than a flea on the flank of Kaiser Wilhelm's brute force. His was a tender and suffering face, in its way. But his was the face of war, his was the presence of the enemy: that was what the war had brought her. And war would be her death at last, at her ripe old age, so he was as good as the Angel of Death. So it gave her a cruel pleasure and a sense of final accomplishment to consider slaying the Angel of Death before he could, in his time, slay her. She hadn't asked for his company, after all. Who does?

She decided to sleep on the matter, for now she was certain she would sleep. "Come away from him, you," she said to the oakthing, who pulled a face and—perhaps—stuck out a flaking tongue at her. But obeyed. It scrabbled down. Mémé Gauthier covered the soldier as best she could with a mangy horse blanket found in the stable. Then she settled herself in a chair. She was afraid to sleep lying down for fear she wouldn't be able to get up.

She hadn't bothered to pull the shutters to. She'd always liked daylight, and there was precious little of it left for her. The oakthing sat upon the sill of the window. After a while her eyes became accustomed to the dark and she could see the oakthing quivering. She didn't know if it was sleeping, or keeping guard, or merely waiting for her to get up and do something else. It looked more like a homunculus at night, when the light was poor, more like a little human or a sprite of some sort. She closed her eyes, thinking: It probably hasn't the capacity to see its own death as well as I can see mine. One doesn't need spectacles to see *that*.

She slept better than usual. Well, all that effort expended yesterday, at getting the milk. The milk! It was her first thought upon awakening. She'd neglected to give the milk to the oakthing. By now it would have found the milk, and drunk it, surely?

A warm rain drummed and let up, drummed and let up, against the glass. The oakthing was back on the bedstead keeping watch over the hostage. The soldier seemed no better or worse, though his sleep was even and his smell more foul. The milk, it turned out, was still there in the shoes. She put a finger in it to check. Already beginning to sour slightly.

"If you're to have this, a little breakfast, come and have it," she said, and prepared to tip the milk into a shallow dish and set it upon the floor. "Here, thingy."

Before she could manage, though—complicated movements, to reach down that far without toppling over for good—there was a sound through the windy rain in the yard. It was common enough, a farm sound, no different than any she'd heard any day of her long life in this same home. Simply the sound of someone pushing through the gate of the kitchen garden and coming along the pebbled path. She put her hand to her chest and gasped. So war does this to us, that quickly: It makes the most common of experiences foreign. "Yes, what?" she hissed at the noise. Surely it was the comrades of the soldier come back to fetch him. She would kill them too, if she proved able to get to the chamber in time to get the gun. Damn, why had she left it on the floor by the bedside?

"Bring me the gun," she called to the oakthing, though she doubted it could understand her words, much less lift such a heavy thing and carry it.

The morning intruder paused on the doorstep. As if sensing the customs of the farm this century past, the intruder stopped and wiped the mud from boots against the granite stone set just so for that purpose. Then the door swung open and Mémé Gauthier stood up, reared her shoulders back, to face the next consequence of her fate and folly. "You!" she said, nearly spitting with irritation and, perhaps, relief. "You!" It was her granddaughter.

"I told them you'd be here," said Dominique in her airy way. She whipping a scarf from her head and sluicing the rain from her hair. "You old dog, giving them the slip like that."

"And they—they sent you back for me!" She trembled with rage at her son and daughter-in-law.

"They did not," said Dominique calmly, perhaps a bit proudly. "They didn't know I was leaving. If you could give them the slip, so could I."

"Girl, you're mad, madder than the rest of them. If they find out you've returned, they'll have to cross back through these treacherous reaches to rescue you! At least, when it was just me, they could shrug and say, *Alors*, it was her madness, God bless the bitch. But you have just consigned your parents to taking a terrible risk!"

"I left a note that I was going to Paris," she said calmly.

"Oh," said her grandmother. Maybe Dominique wasn't quite as slow as she always seemed. "Well, that was smart."

"And it wasn't all that hard to get through," said Dominique. "The roads were dry for half the night, and I kept to the shadows. I cut across the fields if I thought I heard the sound of boots thumping or horses. It was worse at the end, with the rain beating down, but that also kept early morning activity down, I think. So I had no trouble."

"You might have been raped, and beaten, and killed," said Mémé Gauthier. "Your parents struggle so hard to remove you from danger, and you thwart them. You taunt them. Why did you come back, *ma cherie*? And furthermore, did you bring any food?"

"You think I had time to market?" asked Dominique. "You think there is much more in the town than there is here? I came back because I didn't think you'd be able to manage alone, Grandmère. I couldn't see you foraging about the other farms for stores of dried food forgotten in corners of sheds, and the winter coming on."

"It's the highest of high summers!" said Mémé Gauthier. She had no intention of lasting into the early fall; the notion was laughable.

"I didn't come a moment too soon," said Dominique. "You've lost your mind even more than usual. I see you've got some milk from somewhere and stored it in your shoes?"

"I couldn't reach the pitcher on the high shelf. Don't be disrespectful." She was proud of having gotten that milk. "You'll have some for breakfast."

"I will, when I'm ready. First I need to lie down for an hour. It was an arduous walk, all the night long, and I'm exhausted from the excitement."

"No, don't settle in your room, come out here and lie on the floor, keep me company—"

"You want company, come sit in my room; I need to lie down," she said, and pushed through to the hall, and her voice went up and up.

Her scream woke the man.

"Now you've ruined everything," said Mémé Gauthier crossly. "He's not at all ready to kill. He wasn't even ready to get up yet."

The oakthing was sitting on the floor with its hands around the rifle trigger. It was unclear to Mémé Gauthier whether Dominique even noticed it. Perhaps it just looked like a scrap of broken branch to her; indeed, in the daylight, that's what it looked to the old woman.

"You've captured the German Army?" said Dominique in wonder. "Grandmère, how capable of you. Rude, though, to give him my bed. Why not yours?"

"He took your mattress for himself, without invitation, and my bedding is all gone to town or to hell or somewhere. Come away, girl."

"He's very weak," said Dominique, who had had a way with the sick ewe and the lamb that wouldn't suckle. "Some moron of a comrade sewed up his wound with a pretty poor eye for style, I'll tell you that."

"You try it, with no lamplight and a spot of arthritis in your wrists!"

"Oh, Grandmère," said Dominique, "you did it? I'm proud of you." She moved forward, nearly stepping on the oakthing, stepping over the rifle. The soldier looked neither startled nor even particularly interested, but he was awake enough to track her with his eyes as she crossed the room and sat right down on the bed. "He needs a good washing, first, and then that milk, I think."

"I haven't gotten the strength to prime the pump yet," said Mémé Gauthier. "I'm only just awake myself." She corrected her tone. "Dominique, the man is a soldier of the invading army that scared your family from our home. You can't wash his wounds and set him out in the sun to heal as if this were a pavilion for invalids. We have to kill him and get rid of the body. For all we know, his comrades will come back looking for him within the day or so."

"He has nice eyes," she said. "Good morning, you. Can you hear me? Can you understand me?"

"*Imbécile!*" Mémé Gauthier didn't have words ripe enough to express her degree of astonishment. "Dominique, come away from him! I forbid this! Don't even talk to him! That is aiding the enemy, a crime against your family, a crime against France!"

"He's a man who has been bleeding in my bed," said the girl. "I'm not proposing he be elevated to a Monsignor of the Church. Grandmère, please. *Guten Tag?*"

The soldier blinked at the German greeting. His head lurched a bit on his neck as if he was feeling a twinge of pain, and thereby remembering he was alive. "*Guten Tag?*" he mumbled back.

"Give me the milk," said the granddaughter. "Bring it here, Grandmère."

"I collected it for the tree sprite," said Mémé Gauthier, hopelessly.

"What tree sprite is that?"

Mémé Gauthier couldn't speak any more. She just pointed to the floor. But her granddaughter wasn't looking. The oakthing lay down against the rifle, lengthening, matching its thorny limbs to the long steel shaft and the scratched and polished wooden handle. "It needs the milk more than we do," said the grandmother, but she knew her voice was too frail, and that Dominique wouldn't listen.

The farm is dead, she said to the oakthing.

And so are you, it answered, or nearly. But you have a child here who will find a way to live and keep life going, cost what it will, and I have nothing.

I will get you the milk myself, she told it.

It is not for me. The milk was never for me, it answered. It was for the life around me, and I lived on its edges.

"It's cold in here; the rain makes everything raw," said Dominique decisively. "We'll build up a fire, Grandmère, and drag him into the kitchen for warmth. Don't worry," she added, at the grandmother's grieved expression. "I won't lose my head. I won't lose my heart to him, either. I'll keep my hands on the rifle." She swept the gun off the floor with one hand. With her other hand, she collected the litter of wood and leaves, for use as tinder.

Mémé Gauthier put her head in her hands and wished to die. But she was of strong country stock and, it seemed, life had not finished with her yet. So in time she straightened her shoulders and went to tend the fire, pour the milk, hector her granddaughter, confound the enemy, mop out the rain that seeped in under the door, and mourn, in a dry-eyed way, the living and the dead.

R. T. SMITH

Horton's Store

R.T. Smith edits Shenandoah: The Washington and Lee University Review. *His books include* Messenger (LSU, 2001), *which was awarded the Library of Virginia Prize, and* The Hollow Log Lounge (University of Illinois, 2003), *recipient of the Maurice English Poetry Prize in 2004. His first collection of stories is* Faith (Black Belt, 1995), *and he has almost completed a second collection,* Docent. *His short fiction has appeared in* Best American Short Stories, New Stories From the South, Southern Review, Virginia Quarterly Review, *and* Missouri Review. *He lives with his wife, the poet Sarah Kennedy, in Rockbridge County, Virginia.*

"Horton's Store" *was first published in* The Georgia Review.

—K.L. & G.G.

Over smashed beams, batten and soffet
the bent tin roofing was rusting in a sorghum
field gone to yellow dock, but I thought
I could raise it—woodstove, scarred counter,
one raconteur warming up to his story:
the man who never . . . the dwarf who nearly . . .
Where Trestle Road farmers gathered
for tobacco, Hadacol and yarns, the shack
was a haven, even if hog prices dropped.

Just learning the itch for fiction, I listened
to Newt Cooper blowing smoke and vowing
Muscogee ghosts ate a dozing plow horse
down to its bones. Ed Thaxton showing off
the banjo Old Scratch swapped for his soul
drove me under the counter with its jangle.
Cade Seeger whispered about a girl
who bathed in rose honey so she could fly.

Wanting every tale to have the gospel glow,
I was too amazed in the shadows to know
how every story cauled a grief, regrets,

cruel ruin and a world of the darkest scars.
In the lull after the last session's hum,
I dreamed of the long-buried and unspoken,
the way one glazed-over cracker would step up
and reach past facts as his neighbors' faces
strained to catch the tune of soothing untruth.

I wanted the knack, every bittersweet
technique that moved a tongue to utter *amen.*
I yearned to delight and bewilder and bind,
but looking back, I can't resurrect the hour
of cricket chirr and the lighted wicks.

Those evenings of cold Sun Drop, ambeer
and the odor of sweat seem half-hijacked
from Faulkner novels and country clichés.
The stuffed goshawk and knife-scarred floor?

Tainted myself, I'm just not sure. Licorice
whips and sen-sen drops? Yes, but what
of the Talmadge ham lynched from a rafter?
Was it Cy Whitfield or his brother Collis
killed later by a bucking baler who swore
a good story was the best part of being
a whole man? Did Hovis say then, "I swan,
it puts me in mind of the time my twill
trousers caught fire for no reason but spite"?

It's all a jigsaw now, a shambles asking
if I can't reach deeper than dock leaves
and rubble, to pull it up—threshold, joists
and ridgepole. To hear the floorboards
creak with human weight and catch Besom
Horton's sorghum voice and his hazel eyes,
I'll have to conjure that rapt Georgia boy
not quite baptized in the waters of story,
only half a man but already ready to lie.
Magic banjo? Rose honey? I'll have to fly.

MARGO LANAGAN

Rite of Spring

Margo Lanagan has published poetry, teenage romances, novels for children and young adults, and speculative fiction short stories, including the collection White Time. *Her most recent collection,* Black Juice, *is a remarkable, eclectic, and haunting selection of short stories.* Black Juice *was given a Victorian Premier's Literary Award, and the story "Singing My Sister Down" won an Aurealis Award for Best Young Adult Short Story, as well as the inaugural Golden Aurealis for Best Short Story. Lanagan was a tutor at Clarion South 2005. She lives in Sydney, Australia.*

"Rite of Spring" was first published in Black Juice.

—K.L. & G.G.

This wind doesn't shriek or moan—nothing so personal. When the river took Jinny Lempwick last spring and half-killed her while we watched, it was doing what the wind's doing now, racing so strongly that a little thing like a person was never going to matter. All I can do is keep myself out of the main force of it, because it doesn't know how to care.

It's madness to be here at all, up on Beard's Top in an end-of-winter blizzard— and I'm near mad. I'm past thinking about soup, about fire, about sleep; I can only gape at how dumb, what a stupid idea, who thought of this? My mitted hands grasp and fumble ice and rock in front of my eyes. How do they keep going? How do these legs keep pushing me up the mountain as if I believed, as if I were as mad as my mad mother, or my mad, holy brother? Don't they realize I'm not made of the same stuff?

I don't know how my scrawny brother managed last year, with this robe in his pack. I feel as if only my hunting, my built-up muscles and my good lungs, stop me toppling off into the darkness. Sappy little Florius is stronger than I thought. I knew Mum was strong; Mum's the kind of person, she can move a strapping great hunter like Stock Cherrymeadow aside with a word, with the force of a single lifted eyebrow. If she were in good health she'd be laughing now, thinking of me up here. Hellfire, she'd be here herself, not letting a big brawnhead like me go about her important business.

But she's not in good health. Felled to her bed, our mum, coughing, and raging at the cough. "Don't come near me, thick boy! Just stop still and listen for a change!" And between her instructions I could hear Florius trying to breathe, in the outer room by the fire. He sounded like a hog caught in a prickle bush. It hurt just to listen. Mark Langhorne's lost all his five daughters to this cough.

Here we are, the cairn. This is where it all starts to happen. "Don't get changed up top," Mum said, "or the wind'll snatch the robe away and we'll never afford another." *And I'll not forgive you, ever,* she may as well have said, *and neither will anyone else in the village. Anything that goes wrong from here until king's-turn will be your fault and no one else's. May as well throw yourself off after the robe, for your life won't be worth living if you come back without it.*

So I use what small shelter the cairn gives to wrestle the robe out of the pack. The cold has stiffened it into great gold-crusted boards—I'm afraid it'll crack apart in my hands.

It's a wondrous treasure. I've only seen it the once, when Parson Pinknose shuffled in with it, autumn before last. "It's all yours now, ma'am," he miseried. "They won't let me do the thing again, after three summers' drouth."

"Neither they should," crabbed my mum. "You Pinchnazes always do sloppy work, for all your prating about tradition. Next time *your* lot breeds a Deep One, do us all a favor and let its cord strangle it."

You could tell the parson was too low-feeling to fight her back as she liked. He sighed as he pulled open the cloth bag, and the robe—well, nothing like that had ever been in our house before. Like bagged-up dragon-fire, it was, all full of danger and brightness. It pulled me out of my corner as on a trap-loop.

"And you keep your mitts off," my mum said, smacking me away and pulling the drawstring tight. "What do you think you're up to, Parson, opening that here?" She glared at him.

"Just a last look, I thought," said Pinknose wetly.

"A look for every boy and his dog? You know that's only for the Deep to see." She shook her head and tut-tutted at the hopelessness of him and his ilk. "You!" she added, shouldering me backwards. "Stop gawping and bring some wood in."

And here I am wearing the thing, Mum, I say to her in my mind, *as neither you nor I would ever have imagined. Here's your thick boy, trying to keep side-on to a wind coming from every way, so that it doesn't catch the blessed robe like a sail and blow him off your holy mountain and splat into Beardy Vale.*

A terrible glumness settles on me. The thing is too big—not just the robe, which gets between my knees and presses on my shoulders like a pair of filled hods, but the whole damn weather and task and nonsense. *I'm* not Deep—everyone who knows me would laugh at the idea, loud and long.

"I can't do that sort of thing!" I whined in the sickroom. "I'm not like Flor . . . I can't even—"

" 'Can't' sets no blossom, boy!" Mum snarled, holding back a cough, looking all witchy with her slept-on hair and her bared teeth. " 'Can't' melts no snow. You get your boots on and take that pack out of my sight. And *now!*"

And I got out, thinking I'd just stay out overnight, go down the old Brimston mine and come back and say I'd done it.

"But she'll know," I said to myself, in the forest-green, in the mild and ferny places I can hardly remember now. And she will know, if I ever get back—ha!, it's a big *if*—she'll know if I haven't done it all, and done it exactly right. She'll see it in my eyes.

So I clump up, towards the top of the Top, wonky with the robe, drunk with cold and misery.

"Keep your thick head together," Mum said. "Say it back to me again." And she made me say it and say it, the whole long clanging unrhyming poem, tricky as a blade-fish playing the white-water, inning and outing and teasing you to beggary. And me realizing I'd have to remember it on the bawling Top, with a cowing blizzard at me, with a damn millstone on my shoulders: "Get off my back! I know it!" I shouted at her, and I slammed out of the house past wheezing Flor.

And now I'm not so sure. *Do* I know it? Do I know it *all*?

I've felt savage the whole way. "Not my job!" I've shouted at the trees, at the Top's foot, which pokes out low and flattish to lull you before you hit the hard stuff. "I do the hunting, remember? I just bring in the food! I'm just one of the dogs, going out to fetch!"

And speaking of dogs, I miss Cuff. I haven't been out without Cuff at my heel since I was tiny. "But there's no beasts on the Top, not for this," Mum said. "This is a human thing only."

"I'll tie her up to a tree down the bottom," I said.

"You'll box her up like I tell you," said Mum.

The look on Cuff's face when I put her in that box! Pull my heart into fish-bait, why don't you? So I was all aggrieved and misbalanced along the way. Cuff would have stopped me shouting, with her worry, with her wet nose at my hand.

And now I'm in such a rage with this bastard wind, that won't let me get to any kind of rhythm, that scours my face with coldness and bangs my nuisance hair in my eyes, and with the snow, that crusts up the gold on my shoulders and plasters itself to the front so that the mirrors won't shine anyway, awful wet snow that'll soak in and make the wretched burdensome thing even heavier, I tell you—

And all those years of Mum saying I was thick, and people looking on Flor, with his spindly legs and his moon eyes, as the one to treasure and to butter up and to bring soup and sweets to and little gewgaws from Gankly Market! All those years of jealousy—but of relief, too, for who wants to be carrying all these people's hope? Who wants to be Deep and different? Yet here I am *anyway*. All the years of putting up with being *not* the one and getting *nothing*, and yet it's me doing the grind, completely without anyone's thanks, only Mum yelling in my head: "Get a word wrong and you'll know about the flat of my hand, young fella."

So *many* words! I'm stuck somewhere in the first third of the thing, murmuring the wrong words over and over. I'm not a words person by any imagining—I like places where it's unwise to speak, in a hide beside the grazing field with the deer coming in from all around, among ferns watching a boudoir-bird darting and doubting at my snare. I like to walk in of an evening with a brace of cedar doves, lay them by the pot and go to wash. That way Mum keeps quiet; that's her thanks, her silence. Now there's a wordswoman. Talk you into a hole, my mum would. And she's always right, as well. Wears a person out.

So. I'm here at the summit. Not that it feels like I've arrived, when I have to stagger and throw myself against the ground to keep from blowing away. "You must stand for part of it," Mum said, "but you might have to start off sitting."

So I get seated, with the robe ends tucked under me, and my face into the wind, so I don't eat hair, and I start the gobbledygook.

I'm fine until I get to the first list. One Father's name dangles off my lips and I can't remember the next. Then comes the wind and smacks me over backwards with what feels like rocks in my face, a clump of snow-slop. "They won't want you to do this," Mum said. "Don't ever think things want to change. It's a battle to make it happen. Now start at the top again."

So I go back to the head of the Father list and I have another stab at it. Trouble is, our Fathers only had about three different names—then they'd add "the Seventh," or "the Strong" or "with the Askance Eye." It's a beggar to remember.

But, surprise, I do in the end. And then it's Beasts, which was a list I knew anyway; everyone gets taught the animals when they're little, just for fun. Then come the Mothers—another hard one, all those old witches with their sharp tongues coming out of their sharp brains. And then the Herbage—quite a lot of people know the plants, too, and I knew all of it except the herbs for beauty, which Mum taught me last night. There's only a few of them; I don't know why I didn't learn them before. "Useful to know for your wife," Mum grumped, "or for when you're going after a wife." Wife? I think of a wife, sometimes. A kind and quiet wife, not Deep, nothing fancy. A wife like me, except rather more beautiful, thanks.

I carve the words out of the icy air with my snow-blown lips. Amazing—I'm getting it all out! It's like Mum's here, coughing and scowling at me in the lamplight, propped up on one elbow. That look on her face stands for no carry-on, no wandering away. "Put your whole brain to it, boy!" she said, and now I see what she means. Even that part of my brain that's usually there at one side, knocking the rest into line and stopping me moaning against what I have to do, even that part's in on the job, passing me the words, worrying ahead for the next ones.

Now the lists are over and I'm into the wild stuff. *Get up, boy!* says my phantom mum. *You can't command the wind and weather when you're huddled on your bum, however fancy the robe you wear.* So I struggle up, shouting the words that I mumbled, so embarrassed, in front of Mum last night. They sounded powerfully pompous in our rough little home, but they suit this strong weather. They're something to throw at the wind; words seem like nothing, but they're tiny, fancy, *people's* things. Who cares whether they do anything? What else can we put up against the wind except our tininess and fanciness? What else can the wind put up against us but its big, dumb, howling brute-strength? *So there!* I tell it with my miniature mouth, my tiny frozen pipe of a throat, my stumbling tongue (and even the stumbling is good, for the wind never stumbles, never goes back and rights itself, don't you see?). *All you've got is your noise—and I've got noise, too! And mine's a thing of beauty!*

On through the verse I go. We're moving through all the world now, crop and town and ocean and sandhill, river and forest, rock and mist and tarn, describing the springtime we need for each. "Miss one and I'll lob you," said Mum. "Better to say some twice than miss one." I can't even hear the words, except in my head; my ears are full of the hooting and tearing of the wind. A gust nearly thumps me over the edge, and I fall to my hands and knees. The wind drags on the robe, grinding me backwards across the Top's top. I throw myself flat, still shouting; if I keep on, I might get through this alive. But the wind is trying to tell me otherwise: *Shut up and I'll stop*, it says, pounding me with hail-rocks. *Stop now and I'll let you go.*

The wind doesn't know my mother.

I'm glad of the words of that last verse; they save my life. They fill my mind and stop me thinking *How can a living soul get through this?* They give me a thread to cling to as the storm beats its sodden laundry on me. I get to the end and there is so much strife and thrashing weight against my back, I start the verse again, yelling it into the rock, wrapping my arms around my head against the beating.

Mindless minutes pass. I hang on, I shout, I wait for the wind's fingernail to lever me off the Top like a scaly-bug egg off a leaf. If I move, it'll only happen sooner: that sickening lift, that awful drop into nothing, that crash, those last seeping few seconds of smashed pain. I've seen a raddle-cat's face in between the two hard bashes it takes to stave in its skull; I think I have an idea; I think I know what's in store.

At least I got the thing done. And done right, hey.

Oof! *This* is the gust that will do it. No—this, *this* is the one. This one's got the lift, this one's got the fingernails—that's right, under the forearms, under the shoulders, flip me up, toss me in the boiling storm, then let me drop—

It's the robe that saves me. Saves my head being stove in like a cat's, anyway.

I wake up rather elegant, in a cradle of rock. The breeze taps my face with a robe corner. A lazy blueness, from a whole nother age, is spread all above me. A pair of keo-birds twindle slowly up into it, higher and higher to dots and then gone.

Lovely quiet. I don't want to move.

But things start moving without me. Feels like a new arm, stiff and not quite set in its glue. A lump of a leg, gone dead from lying so funny so long. And then very nervously my head, heavy as a river rock. Everything hurts, from skin through innards to my aching cold bones.

I'm sitting up, though I don't remember deciding to. The robe is soaked, heavy as plate-armor. I crawl out of it, and fold it after a fashion. The breeze, bright and brisk and icy, is trying to pretend it's not embarrassed about all that carry-on last night. If last night it was; I feel as if I lay there through a full round of seasons, and woke in a whole new life.

I glance down through the clouds and there's Gankly town, embroidered red on its green vale. Gankly's north of Beardy, and the cairn and our home are south. Clutching the lumpish robe to my chest, like an old madman all his worldly goods, I slide and scramble around the mountain.

Even weighted with all those stones, the pack has been dragged right across the cairn's clearing. I empty the stones, and stuff the robe in, and lift the whole soggy bundle onto my back.

It's a long, long way down—and quiet, the cautious, damaged quiet that comes after a big blow. I walk alone through the warming world; I step over wet black branches torn to the ground by the wind; I leap from side to side of the brook that yesterday was my dry path upward. All these months the Top's been without color, but now the winter grass is flushing greenish-gold before my eyes, the rocks are flecked violet and blood-red and patched with bronze lichen, and the sky is a deep, cloudless blue. I did it. I took hold of the mighty millstone of the seasons, and moved it, grinding and squeaking, onward in its circle. I hauled the words out of my memory one by one, and they stilled the winds, and brought this spring.

"Cuff?" I call, when I get home. In the shed her muffled bark is immediate and mad, and she throws herself about in her box. But no person comes to door or window of the house. Everything is too quiet.

I prepare myself to find Mum and Flor, calm as calm. Everything dies. Look at those Langhorne girls. Look at every deer and cat and bird and fish that ever I hooked or trapped. It's no big thing. I've been so alone these last hours, I can't imagine the aloneness ending, can't imagine other people, their speech, their eyes. That's marvelous stuff, lost to me.

On the driest grass I can find, I spread out the robe. It's still a feast for the eyes, even after all the feasting I've done on the way down. It's a different kind of feast, not grown by itself from seed or spore, but worked by people, for people's reasons, for people's use.

The house is dark, and smells of dead fire and the nettle-pulp for the coughs. Flor lies very still, his mouth open, his eyes slits of white. He's got the red quilt over him that we only use for guests; Mum must have struggled to get it onto him, being so sick herself. My little brother, always so thin and pale and smiley. He turned the seasons beautifully for us last year. He did what I did, and I don't know how. I remember it rained on and on, and Mum paced up and down and swore as she peered out the window waiting for him. I remember the little drowned rat that came home in the end, his eyes brilliant with what he'd done, all the fear and seriousness gone from his skinny, joyful frame.

I go over to him, for it's not often in your life you get a good close private look at a dead person; there are always funeral people about, making it rude to stare. I have a good long stare at Flor, long enough for Cuff to stop bothering to bark. Still as a log, still as a stone . . . and then there's a tremor of eyelashes, a glimmer of the eye-whites. I put my face closer and feel the warmth off him. A soft snore comes from the other room and I startle, and nearly laugh out loud. The two of them, both still here! Instead of struggling like before, Flor breathes deeply and silently—now I see the rise and fall of his chest under the motionless quilt.

"You great, soppy fool," I mutter to myself, sniffing back the sudden tears. "All they needed was bed rest, and a bit of nettle."

Mum is curled up like a possum, her face away from me. I go in, around the bed, with some half-baked notion in my head of waking her, of telling her, of claiming from her some kind of a blessing.

But then I go right off the idea. Her sleeping face is like punched-down bread dough; it's as creased as the rock of Beard's Top, and as polished, with the sweat of her broken fever. She's a sick little old lady—for now, at least. Before she wakes and starts pelting me with accusing questions and making me wish I'd never gone to all the bother. She needs sleep more than anything else. And the spring will come, whether she believes I brought it or not.

The shed smells of dog pee and wood-damp. It's dark, and I find Cuff's box by following her scratching and whining, the brush of her nose on the splintery wood.

"Cuff, Cuff, my girl!" I whisper.

She throws herself against my side of the box and barks twice.

"Shall we go up to Highfields, shall we?" I murmur, feeling along the bench for the jemmy I left there. "Shall we get ourselves a snow-hare, you and me, and put it in the pot for the invalids? I think we shall, girl. I think we shall."

And murmuring so, I ease up the box lid. Before the last nail's free, Cuff pours out the opening into my arms, all tongue and toenails. Then she's in the shed doorway, looking back, her raised paw saying, *When you're quite ready . . .* And beyond her is all the dampness and the dazzle of the first day of spring.

SIMON BESTWICK

A Hazy Shade of Winter

Simon Bestwick was born in 1974 and lives in the former Lancashire mining town of Swinton. He writes short stories, novels, and plays. He has been known to act now and again. He likes rock and folk music, good films, good food, real ale, and single malt whiskey. Dislikes intolerance, organized religion, and stupidity.

His work has appeared in numerous magazines, including Nasty Piece Of Work, Sackcloth and Ashes, Terror Tales, Scared To Death, Enigmatic Tales, Darkness Rising, Fusing Horizons, All Hallows, *and in the anthology* Beneath The Ground.

His story "A Hazy Shade of Winter" was first published as the title story of his first collection of stories.

—E.D.

Snow swirled down through the windy air of Christmas Day, plucked into spirals and mandalas as it fell. A soft white frosting covered the pavements and the roads like icing sugar, lightly dusted the hedges and the wall around the church, even the gravestones in the cemetery as we passed through the lychgate on our way up the path. A Victorian angel, bow-headed, was capped with snow.

In the day's chill gloom, church lights blazed. They lit up the stained glass from within, and more lights spilled over the surrounding grounds, the stones, and the graves—and on that odd little corner they had in the cemetery, a small, weed-grown patch, curiously unattended, unlike the rest of the well-verged churchyard, at the juncture of two of the walls. It was filled with lumpy, uneven ground, and small wooden crosses, often planted askew.

I'd forgotten my gloves, but so had Karen, so it wasn't so bad; our fingers warmed one another's on the way in. Her parents followed.

It was the first time I'd seen the inside of a church in more years than I cared to remember. I'd given up any belief in a God about the same time that I'd realized Santa Claus and the Tooth Fairy were likewise tales for children. But Karen's parents were both Christians, and she seemed to have inherited the faith. Still, we hadn't had any real arguments like that yet, so I was hoping that there was enough common ground between my principles and hers for things to work out. We'd only been together about three months, but it was already serious enough for me to be spending the season with her and her folks. Not that there was really anywhere else for me to spend it. . . .

The service was pretty much the usual. Various members of the church came up and told their little bit of the Nativity story; the focus seemed to be, as ever, on the birth of Christ, how he had come to unite all humankind in love, the Redeemer, the Messiah . . . you should know the drill by now. And nothing wrong with that, despite the really sharp-toothed atheist in me snarling: *Messiahs, Redeemers . . . people always too chicken to take responsibility for themselves, always wanting someone else to come along and take all the complicated stuff away. . . .*

Atheist or not, though, I do have a soft spot for Christmas carols. "Silent Night," "Hark, The Herald Angels Sing"—at times like that I really wish I could believe in God. And Santa Claus. And big floppy-eared rabbits called Harvey, if it comes to that.

Well, that night they played "God Rest Ye Merry, Gentlemen." The organ notes swelled and boomed inside the church, and the voices of choir and congregation rose in more or less tuneful harmony.

> God rest ye merry, gentlemen, let nothing you dismay
> For Jesus Christ our Savior was born upon this day
> To save us all from Satan's pow'r when we were gone astray . . .

Karen squeezed my hand throughout, but I couldn't help casting a jaundiced eye round the congregation to begin with. Wondering how Christian they were the rest of the year round, how much they loved their neighbors and all the rest.

But the mood gets to you. It was so much easier to go with the flow, accept and embrace the warmth and comradeship and love without inquiring too far into the depth of it. And before I knew it I was singing along with the rest.

> Now turn to one another, all you within this place
> And with true love and brotherhood each other now embrace

And I'm not (too) ashamed to admit that's exactly what Karen and I did.

> O, tidings of comfort and joy, comfort and joy,
> O, tidings of comfort and joy.

The only odd note was at the tail-end of the vicar's sermon.

Most of it was of a piece with all that had come before: platitudes and sentiments of love and peace and compassion and so forth. The vicar was a white-haired old fellow with blue eyes bright behind half-moon lenses, shooting grandfatherly smiles at the children throughout. Until the very last.

"We mustn't forget," he said, face suddenly stern, "that our lord Jesus came to us for a very good reason: to rescue us from a very real danger. That danger was from Satan, from the Devil. We mustn't forget that. We have to remember what He said to us and what that means, and keep that message alive in our hearts.

"But we also have to watch for the Devil and his servants. People who come to tempt us away from what's good. It isn't hard to see what good is, what the right way is. But the Devil will try and make us think that it *is* hard, that it's more complicated than it is. He'll try to confuse us, and—in our confusion—lead us astray.

"Let's not forget that even Jesus wasn't meek and gentle all of the time. He drove the moneylenders from the temple"—he wagged a finger at some of the children—"as I'm sure you'll remember from Sunday school." There was a ripple of laughter. Was it slightly nervous or was that just me? "When we see evil, when we witness it close to, we have to be strong and deal with it. Otherwise it will sneak and creep up on us, and corrupt those things we love and treasure."

He let that thought hang for a moment, and then smiled again. "But today, it's Christmas. Not just a time for presents and trees, but a time for remembering Jesus, who was born for our sakes over two thousand years ago. I want to thank you all for coming. For remembering that."

A moment later the organist started up with "O Come, All Ye Faithful."

"What was all that about?" I asked Karen as we walked back down the path, her parents once more trailing behind us. I'd shaken hands with the vicar as I went. It had been like clasping a dead mackerel. Half-frozen.

She cocked her head and frowned. Her hair was long and black, glossy as oil, falling over her collar, snaring snow from the wind. "What do you mean?"

Except for two pink flushes of color in her cheeks, her face was almost as white as the snow, the bones beneath fine as porcelain. I touched one pink cheek with my fingertips. "All that stuff about the Devil."

She shrugged. "You can't just keep the bits you like and chuck out the rest, you know."

With anyone else, I'd probably have said that was exactly what the church had been doing for the last two thousand years, but I bit my tongue and remembered that some of the good guys had played for this team too. "Just didn't seem the kind of thing you'd talk about at Christmas. Stuck out a bit from the rest, you know?"

Karen shrugged, embarrassed. I touched her chin and tilted up her face, leaning forward to kiss her. But the second our lips met, her mother coughed sharply behind me, and Karen pulled away, face flushing, her blue eyes down.

I was never too sure about her parents, for the simple reason that they never seemed too sure about me. It was Janice, Karen's mother, who was the driving force of the household. Her father Martin seemed almost like a ghost, watery-eyed and thin-haired; even his moustache seemed little more than stubble, however hard he tried to cultivate it. He'd taken retirement on medical grounds after some industrial accident or another, and there always seemed something tenuous about him, as if his substance might scatter on the first breeze or dissolve in the dawn's first rays.

Janice . . . well, there's an old proverb, isn't there, that if you're thinking of marrying a girl you should look at her mother, because that's what she'll become. I didn't know what to make of her. Janice was like a forty-something-year-old version of Karen, except with shorter hair and maybe a bit heavier in figure. She wore glasses, and her eyes were dark instead of blue, but otherwise there was a lot in common. But if Martin was just plain vague, Janice was anything but. There was an intensity in her, almost as if she'd plundered her husband for presence and vitality and stocked herself with it. Not that she was ever rude or cold; she was the soul of politeness and hospitality, as shown by her inviting me up for Christmas, and the rules of the house, such as they were, were pretty relaxed. But all the same there was a sense of reserve. As though, I think, she hadn't made up her mind about me, and wouldn't give anything of herself away, behind the mask of manners and formula goodwill, until she had. It was a little uncomfortable, because it made me feel as though I was under constant surveillance, every move, gesture, word, added up and dissected, scrutinized.

Privacy was hard to come by too. Everything was very much to be done as a family. It was frowned on to retire to your room for any real extended period, except at bedtime, and as for Karen and I *both* retiring together for any length of time . . . forget it.

On the other hand, we were able to get a bit of time to ourselves by volunteering to wash up while her parents watched whatever was on TV that day. I had no idea. I'd more or less given up watching TV since I thought most of the stuff on it was utter cobblers, which made for a further problem as, the dishes done, I was likely to be condemned to an evening of game shows and celebrity pantos.

"Fancy nipping out for a walk afterwards?" I asked Karen hopefully, drying a wineglass.

She gave a small, rueful smile and shook her head, soaping up a plate. "Better not."

"Why not?" I protested. "We can wrap up warm. Have a snowball fight if you want." And get away from the feeling of being under twenty-four-hour observation, I managed not to add, and having to watch all of the next several hours of TV crap.

Karen reached over and squeezed my hand; we both had to laugh when she did, as she was still wearing her rubber gloves. She flicked soap at me and I flicked some back at her. But even then I couldn't let it lie, could I? "Why not?" I asked again.

"Mum," she said at last, reluctantly. "She's just a bit funny like that on Christmas Day. Likes us all to stay in together as a family."

"You aren't five anymore," I said. I was irritated and trying not to show it. "You're grown up now. You've got a life of your own."

"I know. But it's Christmas. I know it's not all easy for you. I really appreciate you making the effort. It's important to me, Rog. That you get on with them as well as them with you. So just grin and bear it? Please?"

There was a slight edge to her voice too. I didn't know if she was annoyed at me or her parents or the situation of us both combined. I reached out and put an arm around her waist. "Okay. Sorry. I'll have my own place next month anyway."

"Oh yeah." She knocked her hip playfully against mine. At least, I reflected, she wasn't *that* much of a Christian. "That'll be fun, won't it?"

I took my chance to lean forward and kiss her properly. There'd been precious few opportunities over the past couple of days. Talk about gulping water after a drought; her arms went tightly round my neck and our bodies pressed firmly together.

The living room door opened and the handle of the kitchen door turned, the frosted glass filled with Janice's blurred shape. We sprang apart as she opened it, face unreadable, eyes like little black video cameras, flicking to and fro over us. "Karen, have you got a minute?" she asked.

Karen walked over to her and stepped out into the hall. The door swung closed and I shot glances at them, only catching odd words. ". . . cats and dogs . . . under my roof . . . remember . . . inside tonight . . . don't want him seeing anything if anything happens . . ."

Karen came back, head down, subdued. I touched her arm gently, but she didn't respond, and stayed quiet even after her mother had gone back into the living room. I clenched my teeth and seethed quietly, but there wasn't much I could do. Couldn't shout or scream with frustration and couldn't take it out on anything; I had to dry carefully, put things down carefully; breakages would only make it worse. Nothing must break the placid surface, crack the veneer of calm. Everything must be peaceful and happy and all right. Or at least it had to look and sound that way. It's the next best thing. No matter what's festering behind the mask.

Even so, I kept thinking about what I'd heard Janice saying. Most of it was pretty straightforward, the kind of thing you'd expect an over-protective—or just plain interfering, depending on how charitable or otherwise you were feeling, and I was starting to run a bit low on charity—mother to come out with. But the last bit was puzzling.

. . . *Don't want him seeing anything if anything happens* . . .

What the hell was *that* supposed to mean?

The rest of Christmas Day dragged agonizingly on. Janice made a few leftover-turkey sandwiches and passed them round. I suffered through variety shows involving the kind of bland and annoying pop bands that fourteen-year-olds like—the kind that, unfortunately, seem inexplicably popular with people who should have more sense. Karen seemed to like them—and so, oddly, did Janice. I had no idea about Martin. He just sat in his chair, sipping his tea and gazing rather blankly at the screen, occasionally letting out an insipid chuckle.

Now and again Karen and I managed to smile or wink at one another, and we were holding hands unobtrusively throughout. But I made damn sure I wasn't holding her hand with the one my watch was on. I kept glancing surreptitiously at it when I was as sure as I could be that no one was looking, trying to work out how soon I could decently excuse myself and get off to bed. Anything was better than this. Forget racks and red-hot pincers and flaming brimstone—Hell could quite satisfactorily be a Saturday night in with your girlfriend at her parents' house, watching TV. Where none of you ever goes to bed.

It was about nine-thirty. I'd decided that I could probably get away with hitting the sack at ten o'clock, so I was trying not to clock-watch any more than was strictly necessary. I squeezed Karen's hand gently and smiled into her eyes, badly wanting to kiss her.

Then there was noise outside. I could hear shouts and commotion, people running, even over the droning natter of the TV. Somebody banged hard on the front door. Janice jumped to her feet and went out into the hallway at a fast clip.

That was the first wrong note—well, the second, if you wanted to weave the end of the evening's sermon into the pattern. Janice was moving with urgency, and there was, I thought, a touch of nerves in her face. Fear. Not annoyance. If I heard that kind of racket and door banging on a Christmas Night, I'd assume drunken wallies before anything else, and probably wouldn't even bother answering the door.

I heard the front door open and a babble of excited voices. In under a minute, Janice came back through into the living room, pulling on her coat and throwing Karen's to her. "Come on."

Karen looked from me to her. "But Mum—"

"*Come on*. We've got Duties."

Something about the way she said that seemed to give it a capital D. Karen let go of my hand and pulled on her coat. I started to get up. "I'll—"

"No," said Janice, sharply. "No," she said again, more quietly. "It's just something we've got to do. Won't be a minute or two. You stay in with Martin and keep him company."

I opened my mouth to protest—what happened to everyone staying in on Christmas as a family?—but Karen came to me and hugged me tightly, kissing my cheek. "It's all right," she said. "It's all right, Rog. Do as she says. We'll be back in a mo."

She gripped my arms tightly, and I could feel the body language seeping through. *Don't rock the boat. Just do as you're told.*

And then they were down the hall and gone, the door slamming.

Trouble with me, though—it's always been the same. Just try asking *my* parents.

I've never been good at just doing as I'm told.

I turned to Martin. "Come on. What's all this about?"

"Oh . . ." He shrugged vaguely and settled back in his chair. "Just church stuff." He stared at the screen a few seconds more, then dimly registered that I hadn't meekly sat down again. He turned towards me and then started to push himself, stiffly, to his feet. "D'you want a cup of tea?"

"Um . . . no thanks," I said, moving easily round him and stepping out into the hall. There was a row of hooks near the foot of the stairs. My coat was hanging up on one of them. I picked it up and put it on.

"What're you doing?" Martin bleated—sorry, I know it sounds uncharitable, but it was the sound that best describes how he sounded.

"I'm going to see if they need a hand."

"Oh no! Don't do that. . . ." Martin trailed limply out into the hall after me and reached out ineffectual hands—he was more like a ghost than ever right then. "Don't . . ." He said that a lot, but it was about all he did; I think he'd been so passive so long that he hadn't the faintest clue of how to actually stop someone doing something. Plus which, he'd never been in great shape since his accident, which I sometimes suspected might have been caused by Janice kicking him down the stairs or something.

"Oh!" I heard him moan in distress as I opened the front door and stepped outside. Then the door shut and I couldn't hear him anymore.

The snow was falling even more heavily than before as I stepped out onto the pavement, thick white flakes caught in tubes and cones of light from streetlamps, and houses, and . . .

Torches?

Up the road, a knot of people had massed. Voices were shouting. Spines of torchlight punctured and cut the night. There were more shouts further up the road, where it bent round. More torch beams came from round the corner, more loud, urgent shouts. Suddenly the group of people surged forward, round the bend to meet the rest. I thought I glimpsed Karen's white sheepskin in the rush. I knew for sure, though, that I'd seen something else—several of them. I'd seen a baseball bat waved aloft in one hand, a hatchet in another, a sledgehammer in another still.

What the hell was going on? I ran up the road to the corner, just in time to see the two groups meet. For a moment I thought I was going to see a street battle, but there was none of that.

Instead the two groups were speaking to one another. Fingers pointed, and then a shout went up. Suddenly, the whole doubled mob surged down one of the narrow ginnels that ran between the back-to-back rows of terraced houses.

I broke into a run as well, trying to keep parallel to them. I heard another loud, savage shout flaring up from them, and heard something else scream. The shouts rose again, and then broke up into yelps and cursing. There was a crashing and a clattering, and I caught a hazy glimpse of something leaping a fence, scrambling through someone's backyard and then down their front drive—towards me.

I could only see it faintly at first, a shade. It looked half human and half animal. That is, it was shaped more or less like a man or woman, but loped on all fours the way a running dog might. It wove as it ran, looked back, tripped, rolled, and writhed feebly on the tarmac.

I ran towards it. There were shouts from the ginnel, much cursing and noise as the pursuers tried to get over the fence, falling off it and fighting among themselves as they jostled for position.

I reached the thing and turned it over. It was vaguely manlike, except—it wasn't.

Its skin was the color and texture of tree bark. Its hands and feet were bare and clawlike, tipped with talons, like a bird's or a lizard's. It was clad in torn, tattered rags that looked more like grave cerements than anything else, and although its face was humanlike—it looked something like the face of a young boy—its teeth were sharp, its ears pointed, and its eyes had a yellow glow.

But it was also in pain. It snarled in savage fright and whined in agony at the same time. Dark blood oozed through its pale, woolly hair from a gash on its leg. One arm hung limp and useless, probably broken. Dark patches on its barklike hide might have been bruises or natural coloring.

More shouts sounded as I took its uninjured arm and pulled it to its feet. The first of the pursuers was over the fence and coming down the drive. I'd seen him before, in the church. We'd been introduced, but I couldn't remember his name. He was a big red-headed man with a booming laugh and a merry red-flushed face. Now he was charging in with a pick-handle, bellowing like a maniac, and looking capable of anything.

I dragged the creature after me and ran. Don't ask me why I didn't just get the hell out of the way. It was ugly, it was weird-looking—the thing, not the man with the pick-handle, although he was the one who really scared the shit out of me—and I'm not a hero. I'm a certified physical coward. That night was the only time I ever got involved in someone else's fight. Why? Because I knew beyond doubt that they'd beat or hack the creature to death if I didn't help it, and because the state it was in . . . all I can say is, you should have heard the sounds it was making. Like a dog in pain. The snarls had given way almost entirely to whining and whimpers. No, I couldn't have left it. Nobody could. At least that's what I always think when I remember that night.

Except that then I always remember that there was a whole pack of people on the streets that night who could have just left it. In fact, who would have done a lot worse.

And did, in the end.

But not right then. Right then, I was running, supporting the wounded thing and legging it down the street as fast as I could, through the blinding fog of wind-driven snow. I didn't know where the hell I was supposed to be going; I didn't really know the area, unlike my pursuers, and, with the wind rising, even if I had, I couldn't see a bloody thing. I could only hope that would help me by hindering them. Because if they caught up with me in that mood, I doubted they'd distinguish much between me and the creature I was helping.

Snowblind, I blundered on down the street. The creature's legs collapsed under it and it almost slipped away from me. The mob was shouting behind us and my companion mewled piteously. I hauled it to its feet again and staggered.

An entrance loomed on our left; a narrow brick entrance to an alleyway. I ran into it, dragging the creature with me as I went.

The walls were high and there were trees beyond them on either side, screening out the worst of the snow. The bricks glistened on the walls. The creature clung to me, its claws digging in painfully, whimpering, stumbling on a paved floor slippery with ice and trampled slush.

The alley was dark, unlit except by stray light from the street. And then suddenly light flared: dozens of torches shone down the passageway, shining past us to illuminate—

A dead end.

I stumbled to a halt. The creature was hyperventilating now, letting out noises that sounded like sobs and low moans.

I turned around. The creature tried to wriggle behind me. Down the alley the pursuers came. Most of them were silhouettes behind the tiny burning suns of their torches, but I could see some faces. Some I knew. All were as hard as flint, and as ungiving.

"Out of the way," said a harsh voice.

"What are you going to do?" I asked. My voice only wavered once. I was quite proud of that. Still am.

"What do you think we're going to do with it?" said a woman's voice. I thought it might be Janice's. "We're going to send the thing back to where it came from."

"And where's that?" They'd started coming closer. Torchlight gleamed on aluminium baseball bats.

"Hell, you bloody idiot," someone else said.

"Roger, get away from it!" snapped one voice I knew too well.

"What's it done, Karen?" I asked.

"For the last time," someone else snapped, "get out of our bloody way."

"Not until—"

But I'd let myself get distracted and forgotten how close they were. And I'd made the mistake of assuming I might be able to reason with a lynch mob.

I saw the pick-handle swinging, and felt the explosion of pain in my shoulder that knocked me aside. I didn't see the next blow, only felt the eruption in my head, white stars dancing like snow behind my eyes, and then I was down on the alley floor, and the first kick hit me in the stomach, the second in the back. I tried to curl up into a ball, but everything was moving so slowly now, time slurred by the blow to my head, and a couple more kicks hit me before I could manage that.

Hands dragged the creature, squealing, cringing, and cowering, out into the street. Hands grabbed me too, dumped me on the pavement to watch. I was kicked again, and again, and again.

But most of them formed a loose circle round the creature, weapons held high. It crouched and held up its hands, letting out little noises. To this day, groggy as I was,

I couldn't tell you if they were just inarticulate animal sounds or some kind of speech. If it was, I don't think it was in any language I know of. Then again, I only really know English—and that none too well after the ninth pint of lager—and a bit of residual GCSE French.

Someone ventured forward and struck the first blow, landing it one with a baseball bat. It fell back howling. Someone else moved in and kicked it, and that was the signal for the rest. They moved in fast, boots kicking, clubs and axes rising and falling, rising and falling. And still the pitiful thing screamed, on and on.

Those who weren't mucking in with the primary bloodsport were getting stuck in on the second. I rolled from kick to kick. Every time I tried to curl up I was kicked in the back and my hair pulled, until I unfolded into a bigger, more vulnerable target.

A slim figure flailed in the heart of the mêlée, hitting and hitting at the thing on the ground. It was a feeding frenzy now, everyone jostling for position, trying to move in to unload their little portion of hate on the creature. The slim figure was thrown back, clear, half-turned so the streetlamp's glow fell on her face.

"Karen—" I shouted.

And then a kick caught me in the face. An explosion; white stars, blood, the taste of copper in my mouth. Red. Then black. Then nothing.

The snow on Boxing Day was heavier still. The churchyard was lost in whiteness, only tiny glimpses of the stones peeping out through the thick crust of snow. The Victorian angel was little more than a featureless column, some suggestion of a face, the crests of the wings, lifting free.

A foot crunched in snow nearby. I didn't look up. After a moment, she started speaking.

"Rog, I tried to warn you. You shouldn't have interfered."

I turned and looked across at her, to where she stood about ten feet away. My left arm was in a sling, and despite the numbing of the cold, my face still throbbed. "All my fault, is it?"

"You shouldn't monkey around with things you don't understand. So yes, if you want the truth, you brought it on yourself."

I looked back down. "It didn't try to hurt me, Karen. Christ, it was in pain. If you'd heard it—"

"It wasn't in pain, Roger. It couldn't feel pain. It wasn't human. It was a demon."

"It didn't do anything demonic."

"It was trying to trick you so you'd help it escape. That's what they do. You don't know them, Rog. You don't know what it was like around here and there was no time to explain. God knows what it would have done."

"But it didn't do anything, did it?" I asked. "Did it? Did it attack anyone? Harm anyone?"

"Roger—"

"Did it?"

"It would have—"

"Did it?" I shouted, and she didn't answer. Finally I turned and looked at her once again. "Did any of them?"

She didn't answer. The snow drifted down. Her face was red in places, from where she'd been crying. But it was still like stone. "Should we have waited for it to?"

"That's what your vicar was on about yesterday, wasn't it?"

"It was a devil," she insisted. "You only had to look at it to see."

"So if something looks different, it's from the devil and you kill it," I spat. "What do you do with left-handed people here? Or people with birthmarks, or club feet? Christ, you—"

"I saved your life!" she shouted.

"Yes. I know." After I'd been knocked out, it had been Karen who'd run in and stopped them kicking me to death. But that didn't change anything. "All so simple," I said bitterly. "Kill the outsider. The different one." I shook my head in disgust and looked away from her. "Well," I said. "I suppose I'll see you. Or rather that I won't."

Karen began crying again. "You don't have to do this. Mum says you can still stay with us. You didn't know what you were doing. She forgives you—"

"Forgives me." I spat. I seemed to be spitting a lot lately. "That's rich."

With an effort I tore my eyes away from the little plot of crosses squeezed into the churchyard's corner, and at the latest addition to their ranks, the still-raw earth already frozen solid but not yet covered with snow. "I'll go and pick my things up. Have a Happy New Year."

She wiped her eyes angrily. "We were just doing what we had to do. You think I liked doing it? But I told you, you can't just keep the bits you like and throw away the rest."

"Oh yeah," I said. "Nearly forgot. Duty. Always nice to have someone else telling you that you have to kill. Means you can just sit back and enjoy it because God or whoever's telling you to. And you liked it all right, Karen. Don't tell me you didn't enjoy it. Because I saw your face."

I walked past her without another word. As I did, I heard her laugh. For the last time, I turned back and looked at her. There was a bitter smile on her lips.

"Do you really think you're so different from us? Think you wouldn't enjoy destroying what you knew to be evil? That you wouldn't exult in it? We all would. That's why there's wars and cruelty in the world. It isn't the taking pleasure in it that's wrong, Roger. It's the confusion. People can't see it anymore, because the Devil's fogged their brains, just like the vicar said. But one day you'll understand. And you'll come back. And I'll forgive you. I love you, Rog." She kept her smile fixed there bravely and took a deep, painful, shuddering breath. "And I'll pray for you."

I couldn't answer her. I had no words left. I just turned my back on her, for good and all, walked down the path and out through the lychgate. I kept my head bowed, walking faster and faster down the street, as the snow swirled in the windy air.

DOUGLAS CLEGG

The Skin of the World

Douglas Clegg is the award-winning author of Goat Dance, Breeder, Afterlife, The Hour Before Dark, *and* The Priest of Blood, *among many other
books. His short stories have been published in the magazine* Cemetery
Dance, *and in the anthologies* Love in Vein, Little Deaths, Twists of the
Tale, *and* Lethal Kisses, *and reprinted in* Best New Horror *and earlier volumes of* The Year's Best Fantasy and Horror. *His website is www.DouglasC-
legg.com. He was born in Virginia and now lives in Connecticut with his
partner, Raul Silva, and a small menagerie of rescued animals.*

"The Skin of the World" was originally published in the collection
Machinery of the Night.

—E.D.

1

I gotta go, anyway," my brother Ray said.

He had a look on his face that I only now understand, a look of wanting to do
something without regard to consequences. He had a face like a raccoon, dark-
encircled eyes, and a need to get into things he wasn't supposed to. I remember
that face with fondness, not for his smile or his wildness, but for what came after.

It was 1969, and a man had landed on the moon the day before, which is why
we'd been staying at my uncle's. My uncle had a color television set and my father
didn't believe in them until the day a man walked on the moon. It had been an unpleasant family outing, and my brother was giving my father some lip. We drove past
the sign that said Vidal Junction, and my father turned to my older brother, Ray, and
told him to just keep it shut tight or he'd be walking from there back to Prewitt. As if
to show he meant it, my father slowed the car to ten miles an hour, and pulled off on
the shoulder. My mother was quiet. She kept facing forward, as she always did, and I
pretended I wasn't even there. Vidal Junction was just a sliver of a gas station and
maybe an old diner off the railroad tracks, but it had been abandoned back in the
thirties. When I was much younger my mother and I had stopped there to collect
some of the junk she took to her junk-shop dealers, like old telephone pole insula-
tors and bits from the gas pumps. It had looked the same since I was four, that junc-

tion, a ghost place, and that sign just sitting up there: VIDAL JUNCTION, as if it would continue, lifeless, into infinity.

"It's damn hot," my father said, parking the car so we could all look at Vidal Junction, and so my brother Ray could get good and mad about my father's threats to make him walk. "Look at that big heap behind that pumps."

My mother was trying to remain silent, I could tell. But she wanted to say something—she ground her teeth together so as not to let anything out.

"What do you boys think it is?"

"I don't know," I said. It looked like a piece of a car, but I didn't know cars too well, and it could've just as easily have been a piece of a rocket. I smelled something from my cracked window, something sweet like an early memory of candy or perfume.

"Maybe you can sell it to one of your junk shops," my father said to my mother.

"Antique stores," she said.

"This place is strange," my father said, "you'd think somebody would plow it over and put up some stores or maybe grow something. Maybe that thing's from outer space. Or Russia. Or maybe it's like space trash. Everything's space-something these days. Right, Ray? That's right, Ray? You think it's from Mars?"

I heard a click, and there was my brother Ray opening the door on his side of the car. "Maybe I will walk from here," he said, "just maybe."

"Just maybe my ass," my father said, "it's a sure thing."

Ray got full out of the car and left the door hanging open.

"Coop," my mother said. She reached over and touched my father gently on his shoulder. He shrugged. "Coop," she repeated, "it's twenty miles home."

"Only fifteen, by my estimate," my father said. "He's old enough. Or is sixteen still a baby?"

My mother was silent.

Ray walked across the steamy asphalt on the highway, over to Vidal Junction, and I wondered if he was going to burn to a crisp. As if he sensed this, he took his shirt off and rolled it up and stuck it under his right armpit. He was so bony that kids at school called him Scarecrow, and I swear you could read the bones of his back, line by line, and they all said *up yours*.

My father started up the station wagon.

"Coop," my mother said. Coop wasn't my father's name, but it's what Ray used to call him before I was born and my father was a corporal and wanted to be called Corporal but Ray could only say Coop. My mother had called him Coop since then. To my father it must have been the kind of endearment that reminded him that he was a father after all and no longer a corporal. My mother probably figured it would soften him, and it probably did.

"He wants to walk, let the boy walk," my father said. "I didn't make him walk. I didn't. His choice."

That was the end of that, and my father started up the car, and as we drove off toward Prewitt, I looked out the back window and saw Ray just sitting down by one of the old gas pumps and lighting up a cigarette because he knew he could get away with it.

We crossed the railroad track, and the road became bumpy again because nobody in the county much bothered to keep up this end of the highway, and it would stay bumpy until we got out of this side of the valley.

"Fifteen miles," my mother said. We were sitting on the front porch, just sweating and wondering when Ray would be home.

"Daddy said he used to run fifteen miles every Saturday."

My mother looked at me, and then back to the road.

"Used to," she said under her breath.

"Ray walked ten miles in the rain last March."

My mother stood up and said, "Oh." I thought at first it was because she saw Ray coming up the road, but there was nothing there. We had four neighbors, back then, before the development came through, and the nearest house was a half-mile down the road. Across the road was a pond and some woods, and beyond that the mountains and the Appalachian Trail. It was pretty in the summer, if the temperature dropped, to sit on the porch and watch the light fade by slow degrees until the sun was all but gone by nine-thirty and it was past my bedtime.

My father looked out through the screen door and said, "Well, you do a little math. They still teach math? At a slow pace, given the sun and other factors, you can figure on maybe three miles an hour, and that's only if he keeps a moderate pace. So he won't be home till eleven. Maybe midnight. Ray's stubborn, too. Got to factor that in. He may just sleep out back of Huron's, or by the river."

"Mosquitoes'll eat him alive if he does," I said.

"He's done this before," my mother said, more to herself than to anyone.

My father said, "Huron said he might carry some of your junk."

"Oh," she said. She walked out into the yard and called for the collie to come in for the night. I wondered what Ray was thinking right now, or if he was sneaking a beer at Huron's, or if he was just out of sight but almost home.

Seven days later, I was fairly sure we would never see Ray again, and we eventually moved, when I was twelve, to Richmond, where my father got a job that actually paid, and where I was sure we had arrived because it was so different from Prewitt. I thought of Ray often, and what our family would've been like if he had ever returned from his walk that day when I was ten and a half.

I have to admit that our family was the better for his loss. My father became a tolerable man, and the violence which I had known from early childhood transformed into a benevolent moodiness, an anger that took itself out on, not his family, but his employer, or the monthly bills, or the television set. No longer did he throw furniture against the wall when he and my mother argued, and never again did he raise his voice to me. I missed my brother somewhat, but he had never been kind to me, nor had he been my protector. Ray had always dominated things for me, and had even gone so far, once, to piss on my leg when I was five (and he was just about eleven) to prove that he was the brother with the power. Although my mother suffered greatly for a few years after Ray disappeared, I think even she finally blossomed, for Ray was a difficult child, who, according to her, since birth had been demanding and unreasonable and quick of temper. I think that Ray did a great service by walking the other way from Vidal Junction, or wherever I assumed he had marched off to, for my mother had the tragedy of loss, but over the years she drew strength from the thought that Ray was, perhaps, living in some rural Virginia town, and functioning better without the burden of his family. Perhaps he was even happy. Never once did it cross anyone's mind that Ray was dead. He was a cuss, and cusses don't die in the South. They become the spice of the land, and are revered in the smaller towns the way unusually beautiful women are, or three-legged dogs.

2

When I grew up, I moved around a bit, and raised a family, and then got divorced. When my own son was five, and we were going to drive to his grandma's for a belated visit—I had custody of Tommy for six whole days, which was generous of my ex-wife—I took the surface roads of the towns, and thought it would be nice to drive to Prewitt and show him the failed horse farm. But my memory of the area was bad, and I was too proud to stop at gas stations for directions, so we got a little lost. Tommy wanted lunch, and so we pulled off at a coffee shop that looked like it was made of tin and was shaped like an old-fashioned percolator. The waitress was cute and told Tommy that he was the red-headiest boy she had ever seen. The place smelled like rotting vegetables, but the ham biscuits were good, and I taught my son the lost art of see-food with the biscuits and some peanuts thrown in. His mother would hate it when he returned to Baltimore and kept opening his mouth when it was full of food.

"You know which way to Prewitt?" I asked the waitress.

She went and got a road map for me, and I moved over so she could scootch in next to me and show me the route down past Grand Island, and off to the south of Natural Bridge.

"All these new highways," I said, "got me confused."

"I know what you mean," she said. "They just keep tearing the hills up. Pretty soon it's gonna look like New York."

Because I wanted to keep flirting with her, I began the story of my missing brother, which never ceased to interest Tommy whenever I told him. While I spoke, I watched the girl's face, and she betrayed nothing other than interest. She was years younger than me, maybe only twenty, but it was nice that she enjoyed my attentions at least as much as I enjoyed hers. I ended, ". . . and to this day, we don't know where he went."

She looked thoughtful, and reached over, combing her fingers through Tommy's hair to keep it out of his eyes. "Well, I've heard about that place."

Tommy asked for more milk, and the girl got up to get him some. When she returned I asked her what she'd meant.

"Well," she said, her eyes squinting a bit as if trying to remember something clearly from the back of her mind, "they don't call it that, anymore, Vidal Junction, and the railroad tracks got all torn up or covered over. But it's still there, and people have disappeared there before."

"You talk like it's a news story," I said.

She laughed. "Well, it was one of those boogeyman kind of stories. When I was a kid."

You're still a kid, I thought. It struck me then that she reminded me in some way of Anne, my ex. Not her looks, but the girl in her.

"What's a boogeyman?" Tommy asked.

"Someone who picks his nose too much," I told him.

The waitress looked very serious, and she spoke in a whisper. "There was a girl in Covington who ran away from home. My cousin knew her. She got to that place and she didn't get further. My aunt said she was taken by her stepfather, but my cousin said that was just to keep us all from getting scared."

"It's one of those stories," I said, but then I started to feel uneasy, as if the child in me were threatening to come out. "You know, like you hear from a friend of a good friend about a dead dog in a shopping bag that these punks steal, or the hook in the back of the car."

"What's a hook in the back of the car?" Tommy asked.

"Fishing hook," I said by way of calming him. His mother had been telling me that he had severe nightmares and I didn't want to feed them.

But the girl went ahead and scared him anyway, by saying, "Well, folks around here I grew up with think it's something like the asshole of the universe."

I paid our bill, and I raced Tommy to the Mustang, because the girl had finally given me the creeps and convinced me that Tommy would have more nightmares — for which I would be rewarded with fewer and fewer weekends with him.

But, instead, Tommy said, "I want to go there."

"Where?"

"The asshole."

"Never say that word again as long as you live."

"Okay."

"She was weird, huh."

"Yeah," he said. "She was trying to scare you."

"I think she was trying to scare *you*."

He shrugged, preternaturally adult, "I don't scare."

I didn't hunt Vidal Junction down intentionally, but we happened to come upon it because of my superb driving which, at the rate we were going, would set us down at my mother's in Richmond at midnight. It was only five-thirty. I didn't recognize the Junction at once. It had changed. The sign was gone, and the old gas pumps, while they were still there, were surrounded and almost engulfed by abandoned couches and refrigerators, and the chassis of old rusted-out clunkers like trees growing along the roadside. The highway was itself worn down to a gravel groove, and I would've just driven by the place if it were not for the fact that Tommy told me that he had to pee. He could not wait, and what I had learned in my five years of fatherhood was that my son meant he had to go when he said it. So I pulled over and got out of the car with my son, and told him to pee behind one of the couches. I didn't stand near him just because I was afraid of the waitress's apocryphal warning, but because I worried about copperheads and perverts. I glanced around the Junction, and noticed that the girl in the coffee shop had lied: the railroad tracks were very much in evidence.

"Lookit," Tommy said, after he had zipped up. He grabbed my hand and pointed to the bottom of the torn-up old couch.

"It's asphalt," I said. *Or oil*, I thought.

Or something.

"Don't touch it," I told him, but I was too late. Tommy stooped over and put his fingers right into it. "I hope it's not doggie doo."

I pulled him up and away, but as I did he let out a squeal, and then I saw why.

The skin of his fingers, right where the pads were, appeared ragged and bleeding. The top layer of skin had been torn off.

"Owee," he said, immediately thrusting his fingers in his mouth.

The asshole of the universe is right, I thought.

"Hurts bad?" I asked.

He shook his head, withdrawing his fingers from between his lips. "Tastes funny."

"Don't eat it, Tom, for God's sakes."

He began crying as if I had slapped him (which I never did), and he got away from me and went running across the drying field of junk. I called to him, and jogged after him, but something made me move slowly, as if the earth were not dry at all but was made of mud. "Oh, Tommy, get back here right now."

But all I heard was a truck on some other highway, and then a screen door slamming. I went toward the sound, behind the old gas station, and there stood a man of about forty, with long hippie-style hair, and a white cotton T-shirt on and jeans, covered head to toe with dirt. "Tried to stop him," the man said. "He went in, and I tried to stop him."

"Tommy!" I called, and heard something that sounded like him from inside the gas station. The man blocked my way to the doorway, which had, in its last life, been the gas station restroom. It was odd that it had a screen door, and it seemed odder that this man standing there didn't move as I came rather threateningly towards him.

He had a puzzled look, and he nodded to me as if we knew each other. "It's a kind of attraction they smell. I don't smell it much now, but at first I did. The younger you are, the more you smell it."

From the restroom, I heard my son cry out, but not as if he'd been hurt.

"You don't want to go in there," the man said. He remained in front of me, and I felt adrenaline rush through my blood as I prepared for a fight. "I tried to stop the boy, but it's got that smell, and kids seem to respond to it best. I studied it for three years, and look," he said, pointing to his feet.

And then I understood why he stood so still.

The man had not feet, but where his legs stopped, his shins were splinted against blocks of wood. He squatted down, balancing himself against the wall of the building, and picked up a small kitchen knife and a flashlight, and then slid up again.

"Be prepared," he said, handing me the knife. "I was smart, buddy. I cut them off when it started to get me. Cauterized them later. It hurt like a son of a bitch, but it was a small sacrifice."

Then he moved out of the way, and I opened the screen door to the restroom, and was about to set foot inside when he shined a flashlight over my shoulder into the dark room. I saw the forms, and the beam of the light hit the strawberry-blond hair of my son, only it was not my son but something I can't even give a name to, unless it can be called skin, skin like silk and mud, moving slowly beneath the red-blond hair, and from it the sound of my boy as if he were retreating somewhere, not hurting, and not crying, but just like he was going somewhere beyond imagining, and was making noises that were incomprehensible. Skin like an undulating river of shiny eels, turning inward, inward.

Knife in my hand, I stood on the threshold, and the man behind me said, "They go in all the time. I can't stop them."

"What in God's name is it?"

"It's a rip in the skin of the world," he said. "Hell, I don't know. It's something living. Maybe anything."

I felt something against the toe of my shoe, and instinctively drew back, but not before the tip of my Nike was torn off by the skin. The toes of my left foot were bleeding.

"Living organism," he said. "I don't know how long it's been here, but it's been three years since I found it. Could've been here for at least a decade."

"Maybe more," I said, remembering my brother Ray and his cigarette in front of the gas station, and his words, "I gotta go, anyway." He would've gone around back to take a leak, maybe smelled whatever you were supposed to smell, and then just went in.

The skin of the world.

"Does it hurt them?" I asked.

The man looked at me, startled, and I wondered for a moment what I had said that could startle a man who had cut his own feet off. And it occured to me, too, what I had just asked. *Does it hurt them?* The man didn't have to say anything, because he knew then what I was made of. That I could even ask that question. And what that question meant.

He looked like he was about to tell me something, maybe advise me, but he knew and I knew that only a man who had given up would ask that question.

Does it hurt them?

Because, maybe if it doesn't hurt, maybe it's okay that my son went in there, and got pulled through the seam of the world, the asshole of the universe. That must be what a man like me means when he has to ask.

"How would I know?" the stranger said, and hobbled across the grass, moist with the sweat from the skin of the world.

3

I stood in that doorway, and could not bring myself to call to my son. I shined the flashlight around in that inner darkness, and saw forms rising and falling slowly, as if children played beneath a blanket after lights out. Soon, the evening came, and I was still there, and the man had gone off somewhere into the field of junk. I thought of Tommy's mother, Anne, and how worried she would be, and perhaps the need she would have that I could respond to. I began to smell the odor that the man had spoken of: it was gently sweet and also pungent, like a narcissus, and I remembered the day after my brother Ray had not come home, and how my mother and father held each other so close, closer than I had ever remembered them being before.

I remembered thinking then, as now, *It's a small sacrifice for happiness.*

ANDY DUNCAN

Zora and the Zombie

Andy Duncan has won two World Fantasy Awards and a Theodore Sturgeon Memorial Award. His books include Beluthahatchie and Other Stories, *and the coedited (with F. Brett Cox) anthology* Crossroads: Tales of the Southern Literary Fantastic. *His stories have appeared in* Asimov's, Conjunctions, Realms of Fantasy, *and in many anthologies, including* Mojo: Conjure Stories, Polyphony, *and* Starlight. *Duncan teaches at the University of Alabama. He lives in Alabama with his wife, poet Sydney Duncan.*

"Zora and the Zombie" was first published on SCI FICTION. Duncan says, "I've been inspired by the work of Zora Neale Hurston for years, as my stories 'Beluthahatchie' and others attest, but this is the only time I've attempted to write about her. Hurston really did meet the 'zombie' Felicia Felix-Mentor, and she writes about it in Tell My Horse, *her book on her Caribbean travels, which includes her photograph of the patient. My fascination with that photo, in particular, inspired this story. As I worked on it, I realized I partially was trying to recapture what zombies were like before George Romero poured salt on them. I marvel that many readers, judging from their comments, never heard of Hurston. Had I realized beforehand that this story would be many readers' introduction to her, I wouldn't have dared write it. I already felt foolhardy, trying to channel one of the twentieth century's great personalities and prose stylists, but you have to try foolhardy things. If this story inspires others to seek out her work, I'm happy."*

—K.L. & G.G.

"What is the truth?" the *houngan* shouted over the drums. The *mambo*, in response, flung open her white dress. She was naked beneath. The drummers quickened their tempo as the mambo danced among the columns in a frenzy. Her loose clothing could not keep pace with her kicks, swings, and swivels. Her belt, shawl, kerchief, dress floated free. The *mambo* flung herself writhing onto the ground. The first man in line shuffled forward on his knees to kiss the truth that glistened between the *mambo's* thighs.

Zora's pencil point snapped. Ah, shit. Sweat-damp and jostled on all sides by the crowd, she fumbled for her penknife and burned with futility. Zora had learned just

that morning that the Broadway hoofer and self-proclaimed anthropologist Katherine
Dunham, on her Rosenwald fellowship to Haiti—the one that rightfully should have
been Zora's—not only witnessed this very truth ceremony a year ago but for good
measure underwent the three-day initiation to become Mama Katherine, bride of the
serpent god Damballa—the heifer!

Three nights later, another *houngan* knelt at another altar with a platter full of
chicken. People in the back began to scream. A man with a terrible face flung himself through the crowd, careened against people, spread chaos. His eyes rolled. The
tongue between his teeth drooled blood. "He is mounted!" the people cried. "A loa
has made him his horse." The *houngan* began to turn. The horse crashed into him.
The *houngan* and the horse fell together, limbs entwined. The chicken was mashed
into the dirt. The people moaned and sobbed. Zora sighed. She had read this in
Herskovitz, and in Johnson too. Still, maybe poor fictional Tea Cake, rabid, would
act like this. In the pandemonium she silently leafed to the novel section of her
notebook. "Somethin' got after me in mah sleep, Janie," she had written. "Tried tuh
choke me tuh death."

Another night, another compound, another pencil. The dead man sat up, head nodding forward, jaw slack, eyes bulging. Women and men shrieked. The dead man lay
back down and was still. The *mambo* pulled the blanket back over him, tucked it in.
Perhaps tomorrow, Zora thought, I will go to Pont Beudet, or to Ville Bonheur. Perhaps something new is happening there.
      "Miss Hurston," a woman whispered, her heavy necklace clanking into Zora's
shoulder. "Miss Hurston. Have they shared with you what was found a month ago?
Walking by daylight in the Ennery road?"

Doctor Legros, chief of staff at the hospital at Gonaives, was a good-looking mulatto
of middle years with pomaded hair and a thin mustache. His three-piece suit was all
sharp creases and jutting angles, like that of a paper doll, and his handshake left
Zora's palm powder dry. He poured her a belt of raw white *clairin*, minus the nut-
meg and peppers that would make it palatable to Guede, the prancing black-clad
loa of derision, but breathtaking nonetheless, and as they took dutiful medicinal sips
his small talk was all big, all politics—whether Mr. Roosevelt would be true to his
word that the Marines would never be back; whether Haiti's good friend Senator
King of Utah had larger ambitions; whether America would support President Vincent if the grateful Haitians were to seek to extend his second term beyond the arbitrary date technically mandated by the Constitution—but his eyes, to Zora who was
older than she looked and much older than she claimed, posed an entirely different
set of questions. He seemed to view Zora as a sort of plenipotentiary from Washington, and only reluctantly allowed her to steer the conversation to the delicate subject
of his unusual patient.
      "It is important for your countrymen and your sponsors to understand, Miss
Hurston, that the beliefs of which you speak are not the beliefs of civilized men, in
Haiti or elsewhere. These are Negro beliefs, embarrassing to the rest of us, and confined to the *canaille*—to the, what is the phrase, the backwater areas, such as your
American South. These beliefs belong to Haiti's past, not her future."
      Zora mentally placed the good doctor waistcoat-deep in a backwater area of

Eatonville, Florida, and set gators upon him. "I understand, Doctor Legros, but I assure you I'm here for the full picture of your country, not just the Broadway version,
the tomtoms and the shouting. But in every ministry, veranda, and salon I visit, why,
even in the office of the director-general of the Health Service, what is all educated
Haiti talking about but your patient, this unfortunate woman Felicia Felix-Mentor?
Would you stuff my ears, shelter me from the topic of the day?"

He laughed, his teeth white and perfect and artificial. Zora, self-conscious of her
own teeth, smiled with her lips closed, chin down. This often passed for flirtation.
Zora wondered what the bright-eyed Doctor Legros thought of the seductive man-
eater Erzulie, the most "uncivilized" *loa* of all. As she slowly crossed her legs, she
thought: *Huh! What's Erzulie got on Zora, got on me?*

"Well, you are right to be interested in the poor creature," the doctor said, pinch-
ing a fresh cigarette into his holder while looking neither at it nor at Zora's eyes. "I
plan to write a monograph on the subject myself, when the press of duty allows me.
Perhaps I should apply for my own Guggenheim, eh? Clement!" He clapped his
hands. "Clement! More *clairin* for our guest, if you please, and mangoes when we
return from the yard."

As the doctor led her down the central corridor of the gingerbread Victorian
hospital, he steered her around patients in creeping wicker wheelchairs, spat vol-
leys of French at cowed black women in white, and told her the story she already
knew, raising his voice whenever passing a doorway through which moans were unusually loud.

"In 1907, a young wife and mother in Ennery town died after a brief illness. She
had a Christian burial. Her widower and son grieved for a time, then moved on with
their lives, as men must do. *Empty this basin immediately! Do you hear me, woman?
This is a hospital, not a chickenhouse!* My pardon. Now we come to a month ago.
The Haitian Guard received reports of a madwoman accosting travelers near Ennery. She made her way to a farm and refused to leave, became violently agitated by
all attempts to dislodge her. The owner of this family farm was summoned. He took
one look at this poor creature and said, 'My God, it is my sister, dead and buried
nearly thirty years.' Watch your step, please."

He held open a French door and ushered her onto a flagstone veranda, out of the
hot, close, blood-smelling hospital into the hot, close outdoors, scented with hibiscus, goats, charcoal, and tobacco in bloom. "And all the other family members, too,
including her husband and son, have identified her. And so one mystery was solved,
and in the process, another took its place."

In the far corner of the dusty, enclosed yard, in the sallow shade of an hourglass
grove, a sexless figure in a white hospital gown stood huddled against the wall,
shoulders hunched and back turned, like a child chosen It and counting.

"That's her," said the doctor.

As they approached, one of the hourglass fruits dropped onto the stony ground
and burst with a report like a pistol firing, not three feet behind the huddled figure.
She didn't budge.

"It is best not to surprise her," the doctor murmured, hot *clairin* breath in Zora's
ear, hand in the small of her back. "Her movements are . . . unpredictable." As yours
are not, Zora thought, stepping away.

The doctor began to hum a tune that sounded like

> Mama don't want no peas no rice
> She don't want no coconut oil
> All she wants is brandy
> Handy all the time

but wasn't. At the sound of his humming, the woman—for woman she was; Zora would resist labeling her as all Haiti had done—sprang forward into the wall with a fleshy smack, as if trying to fling herself face first through the stones, then sprang backward with a half-turn that set her arms to swinging without volition, like pendulums. Her eyes were beads of clouded glass. The broad lumpish face around them might have been attractive had its muscles displayed any of the tension common to animal life.

In her first brush with theater, years before, Zora had spent months scrubbing bustles and darning epaulets during a tour of that damned *Mikado*, may Gilbert and Sullivan both lose their heads, and there she learned that putty cheeks and false noses slide into grotesquerie by the final act. This woman's face likewise seemed to have been sweated beneath too long.

All this Zora registered in a second, as she would a face from an elevated train. The woman immediately turned away again, snatched down a slim hourglass branch and slashed the ground, back and forth, as a machete slashes through cane. The three attached fruits blew up, *bang bang bang*, seeds clouding outward, as she flailed the branch in the dirt.

"What is she doing?"

"She sweeps," the doctor said. "She fears being caught idle, for idle servants are beaten. In some quarters." He tried to reach around the suddenly nimble woman and take the branch.

"Nnnnn," she said, twisting away, still slashing the dirt.

"Behave yourself, Felicia. This visitor wants to speak with you."

"Please leave her be," Zora said, ashamed because the name Felicia jarred when applied to this wretch. "I didn't mean to disturb her."

Ignoring this, the doctor, eyes shining, stopped the slashing movements by seizing the woman's skinny wrist and holding it aloft. The patient froze, knees bent in a half-crouch, head averted as if awaiting a blow. With his free hand, the doctor, still humming, still watching the woman's face, pried her fingers from the branch one by one, then flung it aside, nearly swatting Zora. The patient continued saying "Nnnnn, nnnnn, nnnnn" at metronomic intervals. The sound lacked any note of panic or protest, any communicative tonality whatsoever, was instead a simple emission, like the whistle of a turpentine cooker.

"Felicia?" Zora asked.

"Nnnnn, nnnnn, nnnnn."

"My name is Zora, and I come from Florida, in the United States."

"Nnnnn, nnnnn, nnnnn."

"I have heard her make one other noise only," said the doctor, still holding up her arm as if she were Joe Louis, "and that is when she is bathed or touched with water—a sound like a mouse that is trod upon. I will demonstrate. Where is that hose?"

"No need for that!" Zora cried. "Release her, please."

The doctor did so. Felicia scuttled away, clutched and lifted the hem of her gown until her face was covered and her buttocks bared. Zora thought of her mother's wake, where her aunts and cousins had greeted each fresh burst of tears by flipping their aprons over their heads and rushing into the kitchen to mewl together like nestlings. Thank God for aprons, Zora thought. Felicia's legs, to Zora's surprise, were ropy with muscle.

"Such strength," the doctor murmured, "and so untamed. You realize, Miss Hurston, that when she was found squatting in the road, she was as naked as all mankind."

A horsefly droned past.

The doctor cleared his throat, clasped his hands behind his back, and began to orate, as if addressing a medical society at Columbia. "It is interesting to speculate on the drugs used to rob a sentient being of her reason, of her will. The ingredients, even the means of administration, are most jealously guarded secrets."

He paced toward the hospital, not looking at Zora, and did not raise his voice as he spoke of herbs and powders, salves and cucumbers, as if certain she walked alongside him, unbidden. Instead she stooped and hefted the branch Felicia had wielded. It was much heavier than she had assumed, so lightly had Felicia snatched it down. Zora tugged at one of its twigs and found the dense, rubbery wood quite resistant. Lucky for the doctor that anger seemed to be among the emotions cooked away. What emotions were left? Fear remained, certainly. And what else?

Zora dropped the branch next to a gouge in the dirt that, as she glanced at it, seemed to resolve itself into the letter M.

"Miss Hurston?" called the doctor from halfway across the yard. "I beg your pardon. You have seen enough, have you not?"

Zora knelt, her hands outstretched as if to encompass, to contain, the scratches that Felicia Felix-Mentor had slashed with the branch. Yes, that was definitely an M, and that vertical slash could be an I, and that next one—

MI HAUT MI BAS

Half high, half low?

Doctor Boas at Barnard liked to say that one began to understand a people only when one began to think in their language. Now, as she knelt in the hospital yard, staring at the words Felicia Felix-Mentor had left in the dirt, a phrase welled from her lips that she had heard often in Haiti but never felt before, a Creole phrase used to mean "So be it," to mean "Amen," to mean "There you have it," to mean whatever one chose it to mean but always conveying a more or less resigned acquiescence to the world and all its marvels.

"*Ah bo bo,*" Zora said.

"Miss Hurston?" The doctor's dusty wingtips entered her vision, stood on the delicate pattern Zora had teased from the dirt, a pattern that began to disintegrate outward from the shoes, as if they produced a breeze or tidal eddy. "Are you suffering perhaps the digestion? Often the peasant spices can disrupt refined systems. Might I have Clement bring you a soda? Or"—and here his voice took on new excitement— "could this be perhaps a feminine complaint?"

"No, thank you, doctor," Zora said as she stood, ignoring his outstretched hand. "May I please, do you think, return tomorrow with my camera?"

She intended the request to sound casual but failed. Not in *Dumballa Calls*, not in *The White King of La Gonave*, not in *The Magic Island*, not in any best-seller ever served up to the Haiti-loving American public had anyone ever included a photograph of a Zombie.

As she held her breath, the doctor squinted and glanced from Zora to the patient and back, as if suspecting the two women of collusion. He loudly sucked a tooth. "It is impossible, madame," he said. "Tomorrow I must away to Port-de-Paix, leaving at dawn and not returning for—"

"It must be tomorrow!" Zora blurted, hastily adding, "Because the next day I have an appointment in . . . Petionville." To obscure that slightest of pauses, she gushed, "Oh, Doctor Legros," and dimpled his tailored shoulder with her forefinger. "Until we have the pleasure of meeting again, surely you won't deny me this one small token of your regard?"

Since she was a sprat of thirteen sashaying around the gatepost in Eatonville, slowing Yankees aboil for Winter Park or Sunken Gardens or the Weeki Wachee with a wink and a wave, Zora had viewed sexuality, like other talents, as a bank of backstage switches to be flipped separately or together to achieve specific effects—a spotlight glare, a thunderstorm, the slow, seeping warmth of dawn. Few switches were needed for everyday use, and certainly not for Doctor Legros, who was the most everyday of men.

"But of course," the doctor said, his body ready and still. "Doctor Belfong will expect you, and I will ensure that he extend you every courtesy. And then, Miss Hurston, we will compare travel notes on another day, *n'est-ce pas?*"

As she stepped onto the veranda, Zora looked back. Felicia Felix-Mentor stood in the middle of the yard, arms wrapped across her torso as if chilled, rocking on the balls of her calloused feet. She was looking at Zora, if at anything. Behind her, a dusty flamingo high-stepped across the yard.

Zora found signboards in Haiti fairly easy to understand in French, but the English ones were a different story. As she wedged herself into a seat in the crowded tap-tap that rattled twice a day between Gonaives and Port-au-Prince, Felicia Felix-Mentor an hour planted and taking root in her mind, she found herself facing a stern injunction above the grimy, cracked windshield: "Passengers Are Not Permitted To Stand Forward While the Bus Is Either at a Standstill or Approaching in Motion."

As the bus lurched forward, tires spinning, gears grinding, the driver loudly recited: "Dear clients, let us pray to the Good God and to all the most merciful martyrs in heaven that we may be delivered safely unto our chosen destination. Amen."

Amen, Zora thought despite herself, already jotting in her notebook. The beautiful woman in the window seat beside her shifted sideways to give Zora's elbow more room, and Zora absently flashed her a smile. At the top of the page she wrote, "Felicia Felix-Mentor," the hyphen jagging upward from a pothole. Then she added a question mark and tapped the pencil against her teeth.

Who had Felicia been, and what life had she led? Where was her family? Of these matters, Doctor Legros refused to speak. Maybe the family had abandoned its feeble relative, or worse. The poor woman may have been brutalized into her present state. Such things happened at the hands of family members, Zora knew.

Zora found herself doodling a shambling figure, arms outstretched. Nothing like

Felicia, she conceded. More like Mr. Karloff's monster. Several years before, in New York to put together a Broadway production that came to nothing, Zora had wandered, depressed and whimsical, into a Times Square movie theater to see a foolish horror movie titled *White Zombie*. The swaying sugar cane on the poster ("She was not dead . . . She was not alive . . . WHAT WAS SHE?") suggested, however spuriously, Haiti, which even then Zora hoped to visit one day. Bela Lugosi in Mephistophelean whiskers proved about as Haitian as Fannie Hurst, and his Zombies, stalking bug-eyed and stiff-legged around the tatty sets, *all* looked white to Zora, so she couldn't grasp the urgency of the title, whatever Lugosi's designs on the heroine. Raising Zombies just to staff a sugar mill, moreover, struck her as wasted effort, since many a live Haitian (or Floridian) would work a full Depression day for as little pay as any Zombie and do a better job too. Still, she admired how the movie Zombies walked mindlessly to their doom off the parapet of Lugosi's castle, just as the fanatic soldiers of the mad Haitian King Henri Christophe were supposed to have done from the heights of the Citadel LaFerriere.

But suppose Felicia *were* a zombie—in Haitian terms, anyway? Not a supernaturally revived corpse, but a sort of combined kidnap and poisoning victim, released or abandoned by her captor, her *bocor*, after three decades.

Supposedly, the *bocor* stole a victim's soul by mounting a horse backward, facing the tail, and riding by night to her house. There he knelt on the doorstep, pressed his face against the crack beneath the door, bared his teeth, and *sssssssst!* He inhaled the soul of the sleeping woman, breathed her right into his lungs. And then the *bocor* would have marched Felicia (so the tales went) past her house the next night, her first night as a Zombie, to prevent her ever recognizing it or seeking it again.

Yet Felicia *had* sought out the family farm, however late. Maybe something had gone wrong with the spell. Maybe someone had fed her salt—the hair-of-the-dog remedy for years-long Zombie hangovers. Where, then, was Felicia's *bocor*? Why hold her prisoner all this time, but no longer? Had he died, setting his charge free to wander? Had he other charges, other Zombies? How had Felicia become both victim and escapee?

"And how do you like your Zombie, Miss Hurston?"

Zora started. The beautiful passenger beside her had spoken.

"I beg your pardon!" Zora instinctively shut her notebook. "I do not believe we have met, Miss . . . ?"

The wide-mouthed stranger laughed merrily, her opalescent earrings shimmering on her high cheekbones. One ringlet of brown hair spilled onto her forehead from beneath her kerchief, which like her tight-fitting, high-necked dress was an ever-swirling riot of color. Her heavy gold necklace was nearly lost in it. Her skin was two parts cream to one part coffee. Antebellum New Orleans would have been at this woman's feet, once the shutters were latched.

"Ah, I knew you did not recognize me, Miss Hurston." Her accent made the first syllable of "Hurston" a prolonged purr. "We met in Archahaie, in the *hounfort* of Dieu Donnez St. Leger, during the rite of the fishhook of the dead." She bulged her eyes and sat forward slack-jawed, then fell back, clapping her hands with delight, ruby ring flashing, at her passable imitation of a dead man.

"You may call me Freida. It is I, Miss Hurston, who first told you of the Zombie Felix-Mentor."

Their exchange in the sweltering crowd had been brief and confused, but

Zora could have sworn that her informant that night had been an older, plainer woman. Still, Zora probably hadn't looked her best, either. The deacons and mothers back home would deny it, but many a worshipper looked better outside church than in.

Zora apologized for her absent-mindedness, thanked this, Freida? for her tip, and told her some of her hospital visit. She left out the message in the dirt, if message it was, but mused aloud: "Today we lock the poor woman away, but who knows? Once she may have had a place of honor, as a messenger touched by the gods."

"No, no, no, no, no, no, no," said Freida in a forceful singsong. "No! The gods did not take her powers away." She leaned in, became conspiratorial. "Some *man*, and only a man, did that. You saw. You know."

Zora, teasing, said, "Ah, so you have experience with men."

"None more," Freida stated. Then she smiled. "*Ah bo bo*. That is night talk. Let us speak instead of daylight things."

The two women chatted happily for a bouncing half-hour, Freida questioning and Zora answering—talking about her Haiti book, turpentine camps, the sights of New York. It was good to be questioned herself for a change, after collecting from others all the time. The tap-tap jolted along, ladling dust equally onto all who shared the road: mounted columns of Haitian Guards, shelf-hipped laundresses, half-dead donkeys laden with guinea-grass. The day's shadows lengthened.

"This is my stop," said Freida at length, though the tap-tap showed no signs of slowing, and no stop was visible through the windows, just dense palm groves to either side. Where a less graceful creature would merely have stood, Freida rose, then turned and edged toward the aisle, facing not the front but, oddly, the back of the bus. Zora swiveled in her seat to give her more room, but Freida pressed against her anyway, thrust her pelvis forward against the older woman's bosom. Zora felt Freida's heat through the thin material. Above, Freida flashed a smile, nipped her own lower lip, and chuckled as the pluck of skin fell back into place.

"I look forward to our next visit, Miss Hurston."

"And where might I call on you?" Zora asked, determined to follow the conventions.

Freida edged past and swayed down the aisle, not reaching for the handgrips. "You'll find me," she said, over her shoulder.

Zora opened her mouth to say something but forgot what. Directly in front of the bus, visible through the windshield past Freida's shoulder, a charcoal truck roared into the roadway at right angles. Zora braced herself for the crash. The tap-tap driver screamed with everyone else, stamped the brakes and spun the wheel. With a hellish screech, the bus slewed about in a cloud of dirt and dust that darkened the sunlight, crusted Zora's tongue, and hid the charcoal truck from view. For one long, delirious, nearly sexual moment the bus tipped sideways. Then it righted itself with a tooth-loosening *slam* that shattered the windshield. In the silence, Zora heard someone sobbing, heard the engine's last faltering cough, heard the front door slide open with its usual clatter. She righted her hat in order to see. The tap-tap and the charcoal truck had come to rest a foot away from one another, side by side and facing opposite directions. Freida, smiling, unscathed, kerchief still angled just so, sauntered down the aisle between the vehicles, one finger trailing along the side of the truck, tracking the dust like a child. She passed Zora's window without looking up, and was gone.

"She pulled in her horizon like a great fishnet. Pulled it from around the waist of the world and draped it over her shoulder. So much of life in its meshes! She called in her soul to come and see."

Mouth dry, head aching from the heat and from the effort of reading her own chicken-scratch, Zora turned the last page of the manuscript, squared the stack, and looked up at her audience. Felicia sat on an hourglass root, a baked yam in each hand, gnawing first one, then the other.

"That's the end," Zora said, in the same soft, nonthreatening voice with which she had read her novel thus far. "I'm still unsure of the middle," she continued, setting down the manuscript and picking up the Brownie camera, "but I know this is the end, all right, and that's something."

As yam after yam disappeared, skins and all, Felicia's eyes registered nothing. No matter. Zora always liked to read her work aloud as she was writing, and Felicia was as good an audience as anybody. She was, in fact, the first audience this particular book had had.

While Zora had no concerns whatsoever about sharing her novel with Felicia, she was uncomfortably aware of the narrow Victorian casements above, and felt the attentive eyes of the dying and the mad. On the veranda, a bent old man in a wheelchair mumbled to himself, half-watched by a nurse with a magazine.

In a spasm of experiment, Zora had salted the yams, to no visible effect. This Zombie took salt like an editor took whiskey.

"I'm not in your country to write a novel," Zora told her chewing companion. "Not officially. I'm being paid just to do folklore on this trip. Why, this novel isn't even set in Haiti, ha! So I can't tell the foundation about this quite yet. It's our secret, right, Felicia?"

The hospital matron had refused Zora any of her good china, grudgingly piling bribe-yams onto a scarred gourd-plate instead. Now, only two were left. The plate sat on the ground, just inside Felicia's reach. Chapter by chapter, yam by yam, Zora had been reaching out and dragging the plate just a bit nearer herself, a bit farther away from Felicia. So far, Felicia had not seemed to mind.

Now Zora moved the plate again, just as Felicia was licking the previous two yams off her fingers. Felicia reached for the plate, then froze, when she registered that it was out of reach. She sat there, arm suspended in the air.

"Nnnnn, nnnnn, nnnnn," she said.

Zora sat motionless, cradling her Brownie camera in her lap.

Felicia slid forward on her buttocks and snatched up two yams—choosing to eat them where she now sat, as Zora had hoped, rather than slide backward into the shade once more. Zora took several pictures in the sunlight, though none of them, she later realized, managed to penetrate the shadows beneath Felicia's furrowed brow, where the patient's sightless eyes lurked.

"Zombies!" came an unearthly cry. The old man on the veranda was having a spasm, legs kicking, arms flailing. The nurse moved quickly, propelled his wheelchair toward the hospital door. "I made them all Zombies! Zombies!"

"Observe my powers," said the mad Zombie-maker King Henri Christophe, twirling his stage mustache and leering down at the beautiful young(ish) anthropologist who squirmed against her snakeskin bonds. The mad king's broad white face and syrupy accent suggested Budapest. At his languid gesture, black-and-white legions of Zombies both black and white shuffled into view around the papier-mâché cliff and marched single file up the steps of the balsa parapet, and over. None cried out as he fell. Flipping through his captive's notebook, the king laughed maniacally and said, "I never knew you wrote this! Why, this is *good!*" As Zombies toppled behind him like ninepins, their German Expressionist shadows scudding across his face, the mad king began hammily to read aloud the opening passage of *Imitation of Life*.

Zora woke in a sweat.

The rain still sheeted down, a ceremonial drumming on the slate roof. Her manuscript, a white blob in the darkness, was moving sideways along the desktop. She watched as it went over the edge and dashed itself across the floor with a sound like a gust of wind. So the iguana had gotten in again. It loved messing with her manuscript. She should take the iguana to New York, get it a job at Lippincott's. She isolated the iguana's crouching, bowlegged shape in the drumming darkness and lay still, never sure whether iguanas jumped and how far and why.

Gradually she became aware of another sound nearer than the rain: someone crying.

Zora switched on the bedside lamp, found her slippers with her feet, and reached for her robe. The top of her writing desk was empty. The manuscript must have been top-heavy, that's all. Shaking her head at her night fancies, cinching her belt, yawning, Zora walked into the corridor and nearly stepped on the damned iguana as it scuttled just ahead of her, claws *clack-clack-clacking* on the hardwood. Zora tugged off her left slipper and gripped it by the toe as an unlikely weapon as she followed the iguana into the great room. Her housekeeper, Lucille, lay on the sofa, crying two-handed into a handkerchief. The window above her was open, curtains billowing, and the iguana escaped as it had arrived, scrambling up the back of the sofa and out into the hissing rain. Lucille was oblivious until Zora closed the sash, when she sat up with a start.

"Oh, Miss! You frightened me! I thought the Sect Rouge had come."

Ah, yes, the Sect Rouge. That secret, invisible mountain-dwelling cannibal cult, their distant nocturnal drums audible only to the doomed, whose bloodthirst made the Klan look like the Bethune-Cookman board of visitors, was Lucille's most cherished night terror. Zora had never had a housekeeper before, never wanted one, but Lucille "came with the house," as the agent had put it. It was all a package: mountainside view, Sect Rouge paranoia, hot and cold running iguanas.

"Lucille, darling, whatever is the matter? Why are you crying?"

A fresh burst of tears. "It is my faithless husband, madame! My Etienne. He has forsaken me . . . for Erzulie!" She fairly spat the name, as a wronged woman in Eatonville would have spat the infamous name of Miss Delpheeny.

Zora had laid eyes on Etienne only once, when he came flushed and hatless to the back door to show off his prize catch, grinning as widely as the dead caiman he held up by the tail. For his giggling wife's benefit, he had tied a pink ribbon around the creature's neck, and Zora had decided then that Lucille was as lucky a woman as any.

"There, there. Come to Zora. Here, blow your nose. That's better. You needn't tell me any more, if you don't want to. Who is this Erzulie?"

Zora had heard much about Erzulie in Haiti, always from other women, in tones of resentment and admiration, but she was keen for more.

"Oh, madame, she is a terrible woman! She has every man she wants, all the men, and . . . and some of the women, too!" This last said in a hush of reverence. "No home in Haiti is safe from her. First she came to my Etienne in his dreams, teasing and tormenting his sleep until he cried out and spent himself in the sheets. Then she troubled his waking life, too, with frets and ill fortune, so that he was angry with himself and with me all the time. Finally I sent him to the *houngan*, and the *houngan* said, 'Why do you ask me what this is? Any child could say to you the truth: You have been chosen as a consort of Erzulie.' And then he embraced my Etienne, and said: 'My son, your bed above all beds is now the one for all men to envy.' Ah, madame, religion is a hard thing for women!"

Even as she tried to console the weeping woman, Zora felt a pang of writerly conscience. On the one hand, she genuinely wanted to help; on the other hand, everything was material.

"Whenever Erzulie pleases, she takes the form that a man most desires, to ride him as dry as a bean husk, and to rob his woman of comfort. Oh, madame! My Etienne has not come to my bed in . . . in . . . *twelve days*!" She collapsed into the sofa in a fresh spasm of grief, buried her head beneath a cushion and began to hiccup. Twelve whole days, Zora thought, my my, as she did dispiriting math, but she said nothing, only patted Lucille's shoulder and cooed.

Later, while frying an egg for her dejected, red-eyed housekeeper, Zora sought to change the subject. "Lucille. Didn't I hear you say the other day, when the postman ran over the rooster, something like, 'Ah, the Zombies eat well tonight!'"

"Yes, madame, I think I did say this thing."

"And last week, when you spotted that big spiderweb just after putting the ladder away, you said, 'Ah bo bo, the Zombies make extra work for me today.' When you say such things, Lucille, what do you mean? To what Zombies do you refer?"

"Oh, madame, it is just a thing to say when small things go wrong. Oh, the milk is sour, the Zombies have put their feet in it, and so on. My mother always says it, and her mother too."

Soon Lucille was chatting merrily away about the little coffee girls and the ritual baths at Saut d'Eau, and Zora took notes and drank coffee, and all was well. *Ah bo bo!*

The sun was still hours from rising when Lucille's chatter shut off mid-sentence. Zora looked up to see Lucille frozen in terror, eyes wide, face ashen.

"Madame . . . Listen!"

"Lucille, I hear nothing but the rain on the roof."

"Madame," Lucille whispered, "the rain has stopped."

Zora set down her pencil and went to the window. Only a few drops pattered from the eaves and the trees. In the distance, far up the mountain, someone was beating the drums—ten drums, a hundred, who could say? The sound was like thunder sustained, never coming closer but never fading either.

Zora closed and latched the shutters and turned back to Lucille with a smile. "Honey, that's just man-noise in the night, like the big-mouthing on the porch at Joe Clarke's store. You mean I never told you about all the lying that men do back home? Break us another egg, Cille honey, and I'll tell *you* some things."

Box 128-B
Port-au-Prince, Haiti
November 20, 1936

Dr. Henry Allen Moe, Sec.
John Simon Guggenheim Memorial Foundation
551 Fifth Avenue
New York, N.Y.

Dear Dr. Moe,

    I regret to report that for all my knocking and ringing and dust-raising, I have found no relatives of this unfortunate Felix-Mentor woman. She is both famous and unknown. All have heard of her and know, or think they know, the two-sentence outline of her "story," and have their own fantasies about her, but can go no further. She is the Garbo of Haiti. I would think her a made-up character had I not seen her myself, and taken her picture as . . . evidence? A photograph of the Empire State Building is evidence too, but of what? That is for the viewer to say.

    I am amused of course, as you were, to hear from some of our friends and colleagues on the Haiti beat their concerns that poor Zora has "gone native," has thrown away the WPA and Jesse Owens and the travel trailer and all the other achievements of the motherland to break chickens and become an initiate in the mysteries of the Sect Rouge. Lord knows, Dr. Moe, I spent twenty-plus years in the Southern U.S., beneath the constant gaze of every First Abyssinian Macedonian African Methodist Episcopal Presbyterian Pentecostal Free Will Baptist Assembly of God of Christ of Jesus with Signs Following minister mother and deacon, all so full of the spirit they look like death eating crackers, and in all that time I never once came down with even a mild case of Christianity. I certainly won't catch the local disease from only six months in Haiti . . .

Obligations, travel, and illness—"suffering perhaps the digestion," thank you, Doctor Legros—kept Zora away from the hospital at Gonaives for some weeks. When she finally did return, she walked onto the veranda to see Felicia, as before, standing all alone in the quiet yard, her face toward the high wall. Today Felicia had chosen to stand on the sole visible spot of green grass, a plot of soft imprisoned turf about the diameter of an Easter hat. Zora felt a deep satisfaction upon seeing her, this self-contained, fixed point in her traveler's life.

To reach the steps, she had to walk past the mad old man in the wheelchair, whose nurse was not in sight today. Despite his sunken cheeks, his matted eyelashes, his patchy tufts of white hair, Zora could see he must have been handsome in his day. She smiled as she approached.

He blinked and spoke in a thoughtful voice. "I will be a Zombie soon," he said.

That stopped her. "Excuse me?"

"Death came for me many years ago," said the old man, eyes bright, "and I said, No, not me, take my wife instead. And so I gave her up as a Zombie. That gained me five years, you see. A good bargain. And then, five years later, I gave our oldest son. Then our daughter. Then our youngest. And more loved ones, too, now all Zombies, all. There is no one left. No one but me." His hands plucked at the coverlet that draped his legs. He peered all around the yard. "I will be a Zombie soon," he said, and wept.

Shaking her head, Zora descended the steps. Approaching Felicia from behind, as Doctor Legros had said that first day, was always a delicate maneuver. One had to be loud enough to be heard but quiet enough not to panic her.

"Hello, Felicia," Zora said.

The huddled figure didn't turn, didn't budge, and Zora, emboldened by long absence, repeated the name, reached out, touched Felicia's shoulder with her fingertips. As she made contact, a tingling shiver ran up her arm and down her spine to her feet. Without turning, Felicia emerged from her crouch. She stood up straight, flexed her shoulders, stretched her neck, and spoke.

"Zora, my friend!"

Felicia turned and was not Felicia at all, but a tall, beautiful woman in a brief white gown. Freida registered the look on Zora's face and laughed.

"Did I not tell you that you would find me? Do you not even know your friend Freida?"

Zora's breath returned. "I know you," she retorted, "and I know that was a cruel trick. Where is Felicia? What have you done with her?"

"Whatever do you mean? Felicia was not mine to give you, and she is not mine to take away. No one is owned by anyone."

"Why is Felicia not in the yard? Is she ill? And why are you here? Are you ill as well?"

Freida sighed. "So many questions. Is this how a book gets written? If Felicia were not ill, silly, she would not have been here in the first place. Besides." She squared her shoulders. "Why do you care so about this . . . powerless woman? This woman who let some man lead her soul astray, like a starving cat behind an eel-barrel?" She stepped close, the heat of the day coalescing around. "Tell a woman of power your book. Tell *me* your book," she murmured. "Tell *me* of the mule's funeral, and the rising waters, and the buzzing pear-tree, and young Janie's secret sigh."

Zora had two simultaneous thoughts, like a moan and a breath interlaced: *Get out of my book!* and *My God, she's jealous!*

"Why bother?" Zora bit off, flush with anger. "You think you know it by heart already. And besides," Zora continued, stepping forward, nose to nose, "there are powers other than yours."

Freida hissed, stepped back as if pattered with stove grease.

Zora put her nose in the air and said airily, "I'll have you know that Felicia is a writer, too."

Her mouth a thin line, Freida turned and strode toward the hospital, thighs long and taut beneath her gown. Without thought, Zora walked, too, and kept pace.

"If you must know," Freida said, "your writer friend is now in the care of her family. Her son came for her. Do you find this so remarkable? Perhaps the son should have notified you, hmm?" She winked at Zora. "He is quite a muscular young man, with a taste for older women. Much, *much* older women. I could show you where he lives. I have been there often. I have been there more than he knows."

"How dependent you are," Zora said, "on men."

As Freida stepped onto the veranda, the old man in the wheelchair cringed and moaned. "Hush, child," Freida said. She pulled a nurse's cap from her pocket and tugged it on over her chestnut hair.

"Don't let her take me!" the old man howled. "She'll make me a Zombie! She will! A Zombie!"

"Oh, pish," Freida said. She raised one bare foot and used it to push the wheel-chair forward a foot or so, revealing a sensible pair of white shoes on the flagstones beneath. These she stepped into as she wheeled the chair around. "Here is your *bo-cor*, Miss Hurston. What use have I for a Zombie's cold hands? *Au revoir*, Miss Hurston. Zora. I hope you find much to write about in my country . . . however you limit your experiences."

Zora stood at the foot of the steps, watched her wheel the old man away over the uneven flagstones.

"Erzulie," Zora said.

The woman stopped. Without turning, she asked, "What name did you call me?"

"I called you a true name, and I'm telling you that if you don't leave Lucille's Etienne alone, so the two of them can go to hell in their own way, then I . . . well, then I will forget all about you, and you will never be in my book."

Freida pealed with laughter. The old man slumped in his chair. The laughter cut off like a radio, and Freida, suddenly grave, looked down. "They do not last any time, do they?" she murmured. With a forefinger, she poked the back of his head. "Poor pretty things." With a sigh, she faced Zora, gave her a look of frank appraisal, up and down. Then she shrugged. "You are mad," she said, "but you are fair." She backed into the door, shoved it open with her behind, and hauled the dead man in after her.

The tap-tap was running late as usual, so Zora, restless, started out on foot. As long as the road kept going downhill and the sun stayed over yonder, she reasoned, she was unlikely to get lost. As she walked through the countryside she sang and picked flow-ers and worked on her book in the best way she knew to work on a book, in her own head, with no paper and indeed no words, not yet. She enjoyed the caution signs on each curve—LA ROUTE TUE ET BLESSE, or, literally, "The Road Kills and Injures."

She wondered how it felt, to walk naked along a roadside like Felicia Felix-Mentor. She considered trying the experiment when she realized that night had fallen. (And where was the tap-tap, and all the other traffic, and why was the road so narrow?) But once shed, her dress, her shift, her shoes would be a terrible armful. The only efficient way to carry clothes, really, was to wear them. So thinking, she plodded, footsore, around a sharp curve and nearly ran into several dozen hooded figures in red, proceeding in the opposite direction. Several carried torches, all car-ried drums, and one had a large, mean-looking dog on a rope.

"Who comes?" asked a deep male voice. Zora couldn't tell which of the hooded figures had spoken, if any.

"Who wants to know?" she asked.

The hoods looked at one another. Without speaking, several reached into their robes. One drew a sword. One drew a machete. The one with the dog drew a pistol, then knelt to murmur into the dog's ear. With one hand he scratched the dog be-tween the shoulder blades, and with the other he gently stroked its head with the moon-gleaming barrel of the pistol. Zora could hear the thump and rustle of the dog's tail wagging in the leaves.

"Give us the words of passage," said the voice, presumably the sword-wielder's, as he was the one who pointed at Zora for emphasis. "Give them to us, woman, or you will die, and we will feast upon you."

"She cannot know the words," said a woman's voice, "unless she too has spoken with the dead. Let us eat her."

Suddenly, as well as she knew anything on the round old world, Zora knew exactly what the words of passage were. Felicia Felix-Mentor had given them to her. *Mi haut, mi bas*. Half high, half low. She could say them now. But she would not say them. She would believe in Zombies, a little, and in Erzulie, perhaps, a little more. But she would not believe in the Sect Rouge, in blood-oathed societies of men. She walked forward again, of her own free will, and the red-robed figures stood motionless as she passed among them. The dog whimpered. She walked down the hill, hearing nothing behind but a growing chorus of frogs. Around the next bend she saw the distant lights of Port-au-Prince and, much nearer, a tap-tap idling in front of a store. Zora laughed and hung her hat on a caution sign. Between her and the bus, the moonlit road was flecked with tiny frogs, distinguished from bits of gravel and bark only by their leaping, their errands of life. *Ah bo bo!* She called in her soul to come and see.

THEODORA GOSS

The Changeling

Theodora Goss's *poetry and short fiction have appeared in* Polyphony, Realms of Fantasy, Strange Horizons, *and* Lady Churchill's Rosebud Wristlet. *She is the editor of* Poems of the Fantastic and Macabre, *an online anthology of poetry from the middle ages to the modern era about supernatural creatures, imaginary places, and uncanny experiences. Some of her short stories and poetry were collected last year in the chapbook* The Rose in Twelve Petals. *Her first collection is forthcoming from Prime Books. Goss lives in Boston with her husband Kendrick, a scientist and artist, and their daughter, Ophelia, in an apartment filled with books and cats.*

"The Changeling" was first published in The Rose in Twelve Petals and Other Stories.

—K.L. & G.G.

What do you do? He wore his leather jacket to school,
Pulled the fire alarm, felt up one of the nuns.
Detention was a time to draw rocketships
Or racecars. He liked things that go fast (skateboards),
Things that were secret (cellars), things that squealed
(Mice mostly, but also hamsters). He never harmed them
But put them in desks, purses, girls' hair.
He read books on poisonous mushrooms and making bombs.

What do you do? Tell him, you are a doll,
Created from sticks and feathers? Go back where
You came from? He would grin, get your daughter pregnant,
Set your barn on fire.

STEPAN CHAPMAN

Revenge of the Calico Cat

Stepan Chapman's short fiction has been appearing in magazines and anthologies large and small for the last thirty years. A partial list of his publications includes Album Zutique, The Baffler, Chicago Review, Hawaii Review, Leviathan, McSweeney's, Orbit, The Thackery T. Lambshead Pocket Guide To Eccentric & Discredited Diseases, Wisconsin Review, and ZYZZYVA. He is the author of a short story collection, Dossier, and a novel, The Troika, which won the Philip K. Dick Award. Chapman lives with his wife Kia in Cottonwood, Arizona.

A surreal and surprisingly moving tale of balance and destruction, "The Revenge of the Calico Cat" was published in the cities-themed fourth volume of the World Fantasy Award–winning anthology series Leviathan.

—K.L. & G.G.

> I wasn't there; I simply state
> What was told to me by the Chinese plate.
> —Eugene Field

After Turtle got out of school, he and his pal Snake took a walk through the garment district. They got endless enjoyment just from watching the people go by. They marveled at all the different kinds of stuffies who lived here in Plush City. Snake made mental notes of everyone they passed.

A sock monkey in steel-toed boots. A fairy ballerina with cellophane wings and a bright pink tutu. A spider in a lacy white bonnet with a fly in velvet knee pants. A king in ermine cape and gold foil crown, pushing a toothless tiger in a wheelchair. A little green man with a propeller-headed whatsit on a leash. An Indian brave in a war bonnet with an eye-patched pirate on a peg leg. Plush City was like a Fourth of July parade every day of the year.

The sun sequin was still riding high in a cloudless sky. What a great place! Snake was so fucking glad she'd come here when she died.

Turtle and Snake wove their way through the sidewalk racks of the cut-rate doll clothing merchants. It was a sunny Friday afternoon in July of 1931. The pushcarts of the food vendors filled the air with the smells of roasted franks and hot pretzels. The kids passed the storefronts of the arm and leg sellers on Scrap Street between Rockabye and Velveteen, and all the little appliance repair shops and delicatessens and eye stores on the side streets.

They turned the corner at Nursery Avenue and Satin and walked east toward the three-story apartment block where Turtle lived with his mother. There was nothing much out front of the building—just some bare dirt and a sign that said NO LOADING. Turtle and Snake ducked down the alley where it was shady in the afternoon. Snake slapped an empty bottle around with the end of her green plush tail. Turtle tossed up bits of gravel and tried to hit them with a plank.

Up on the third floor, someone was playing a swing band record on a phono-graph. A female trio sang the lyric in close harmony: "The gingham dog said Bow Wow Wow! and the calico cat replied Meow! The air was littered in an hour or so with bits of gingham and calico."

"Is Plush City part of the United States?" asked Snake.

"Beats me," said Turtle.

"I been asking people where they come from. Everybody comes from America, it seems like."

"What about the Chinks?"

"I ain't talked to any Chinks," said Snake. Then she heard Mr. Brownbear shout-ing on the second floor. "Hey, that crazy bear is talking to himself again. You wanna go spy on him?"

Turtle and Snake scurried up the fire escape and crouched in gleeful silence out-side a kitchen window. If they peeked over the windowsill, they could see through a doorway into Teddy's den. Teddy was pacing up and down, flinging his arms around and ranting at the walls. The kids could only glimpse him, but they heard him loud and clear. "I bet you he breaks some furniture tonight," whispered Turtle.

"I bet you he breaks his old lady's head," said Snake. Everyone in the neighbor-hood knew about Teddy and Edna and their so-called fights.

Teddy Brownbear lived in a crummy sweltering apartment on the second floor. He was sitting in his armchair in his undershirt, boxer shorts, and socks and listening to a football game on his radio. He was also eating a bowl of popcorn and working on some cold bottles of brew. The wall clock said four.

Inside his fuzzy brown head, deep in his crushed velvet brain, Teddy was working up a grievance against his wife Edna Pinkbunny. Edna worked as a surgical nurse at the big uptown hospital. It wasn't right. She ought to be home taking care of her hus-band. Damned depression had everything turned around. On top of everything else, she'd be late getting home tonight. Teddy could sense it coming. A lot she cared, the bitch.

Teddy'd been out of work for more than a year, which gave him a lot of time to think about his ball and chain. He turned off his radio and paced around the den, kicking at the throw rugs and muttering to himself. He felt like kicking apart the furniture, but he couldn't afford that kind of indulgence. A man had to control him-self. Like when you slapped your old lady around, you didn't leave marks on her face. Unless of course you intended to.

He thought about Edna's face. That smug celluloid face of hers with the pert black nose and the wide acetate eyes with the little blue pupils inside that rattled when he shook her. Once he'd thrown hot coffee in that face, and she'd deserved it. Maybe tonight he'd mash her paw under that cut-glass ashtray. And if that whore upstairs called the police dogs again, he'd rearrange her face too.

Meanwhile, under the bathroom sink, Teddy's beloved hamster Fang was squeezing his fat mangy body through a gap in the wires of his cage. Fang was a vindictive wretch with bad breath and crooked teeth. He crept on the tips of his claws into the kitchen, staying under cover of furniture so as to sneak up on Cuddles. Cuddles was Edna's parrot, and a sickly specimen she was, living on her perch beside the Kelvinator. Her chief amusements were gnawing at her yellow plush claws with her yellow plush beak, pulling loose threads from her wings, and dry-humping her perch.

Cuddles caught sight of Fang and scolded, shuffling her claws from one end of the perch to the other and back again. Fang shinnied up the stand of the perch and snapped at her tail. Then he fell to the linoleum and landed on his head. Cuddles squawked feebly and groomed her tail.

Teddy threw a shoe into the kitchen. It hit the perch. Cuddles took flight and battered her head against the water-stained ceiling as she struggled to fly through it and escape. Fang raced madly to and fro along the baseboards, squeaking up at her. Teddy chuckled in his armchair. "Give her hell, Fang. It's good to have an interest in life." Fang scrambled up the grimy wallpaper and slid back down. He'd never learn.

Teddy turned to the kitchen. He thought he'd heard kids' voices. He threw down his bowl of popcorn, stormed into the kitchen, and thrust his head out the window. A couple of reptiles were hightailing it down the fire escape. "Get outa here!" Teddy shouted after them. "Ain't you got no better place to be?"

"Ah ya fadda's mustache!" Turtle yelled back.

"Go suck a lemon!" yelled Snake.

Teddy pitched a potted geranium after them. The pot exploded in the alley. Turtle and Snake ran west along Satin Street.

Teddy leaned on the windowsill. Above his head, music drifted from the open window of the dance instructor on the third floor. A phonograph was playing a record featuring the Lord Jellyfish Big Band and vocals by the Gopher Sisters. "The Chinese plate looked very blue and wailed, 'Oh dear, what shall we do?' But the gingham dog and the calico cat wallowed this way and tumbled that, employing every tooth and claw in the awfullest way you ever saw."

Teddy returned to his den and gave the ceiling a dirty look. Lazy slut, playing records all day and half the night. No consideration. He turned up his radio to drown out the music.

He eyed a kitchen chair with implacable hostility. He yearned to kick it to bits, just to relieve his aching heart. But Teddy was the kind of bear who kept control of himself. He would drink his beer and wait for Edna to get home.

A lavender plush octopus slithered past an out-of-business shoe store. He slid east on nervous tentacles, mumbling under his breath.

When T.B. was making a delivery or a pickup, he always walked. He never took buses, and he never even thought about a cab. Too easy to get jumped in a cab, and T.B. was a little guy, never much good with the rough stuff. He always walked, and he never took the same streets twice. Safer that way. He liked to play things safe.

T.B. wore his overcoat although it wasn't cold. He was carrying a briefcase full of play money to a Chinese laundry on the east side. The money wasn't T.B.'s money, and the laundry wasn't a laundry.

The money belonged to Little Vince the Ocelot. The laundry was a front for the Fighting Fish, a tough new organization that controlled various shady enterprises around the train yard. The Syndicate guys called them the Chinks.

T.B. Otherweiss was a very nervous octopus doing a nervous job for some extremely nervous stuffies. The job involved bundles of cash, balls of black opium, and other small packages, the contents of which he neither knew nor wished to know. T.B. was a regular one-mollusk messenger service for the Syndicate. But he'd never be a wise guy. Only mammals were eligible. No matter. The Syndicate gave him steady work and protection from the heat. Protection from everybody else in Plush City was his personal problem.

Two little kids followed T.B. for a couple of blocks. Frogs? Lizards? Something green. He ignored them, and they soon lost interest. He crossed under the elevated train tracks at Sleepytime Avenue and slid west along Button, a quiet industrial street of ice factories, ribbon dairies, and cotton packing plants. He made it to the laundry on Corduroy Street a little after five. There was no one inside but a small yellow shark behind a bare counter.

The shark led T.B. out the front door, in again at a side door, through a trap door, and down a narrow staircase into the bowels of an opium den. The air was thick, and the ceilings low. But the floors were clean and waxed, and the clientele were all discreetly screened from one another. The setup reminded T.B. of a sleeper coach in an interstate passenger train.

Just like every time before, the shark led him up a ladder to a well-lit room where sea bass in pigtails and coolie jackets sat at a long lacquered table counting play money and working abacus beads. Supervising the accountants and smoking a cigar was a shriveled old stingray with a Fu Manchu mustache, who wore an elegant high-collared tunic of dove-gray silk.

"Mr. Cho," said T.B. The stingray regarded him with a cold stare and a barely perceptible nod. T.B. slid the briefcase of money onto the table.

Normally at this point, one of the accountants would open the case and count the bills. Then a different accountant would replace the money with something the size of a grapefruit, tightly wrapped in butcher's paper. The oval bundles were presumably balls of opium. T.B. had never opened one.

Instead of the usual, no one moved. The abacus clicking trailed off. The stillness of the room grew eerie. "Mr. Cho?" said T.B. "Don't you want to count the money?"

"No good," said Mr. Cho. "This money no good. We no accept payment."

T.B. curled his tentacles a little tighter. "You think the money is counterfeit? Look at it."

"Money from you no good. You no good. Take money away."

"You don't have the merchandise ready? You want to reschedule? I hope you're not calling off the deal."

"Deal fine. Next week, same like always. This week, no good."

"Please talk to me, Mr. Cho. Or else please get on the phone and speak to Little Vince. He likes to know about this kind of stuff in advance."

"No talk Vince. No talk you. Go." A couple of big sharks had been standing against a wall in shadow. Now they advanced on T.B., who took a hint and grabbed his case in two tentacles.

"Little Vince ain't gonna like this," he said. Then he turned and climbed down the ladder through drifting layers of heavy smoke. He could hear the sea bass laughing at him.

T.B. left the laundry twice as nervous as when he'd arrived. Now he had to go back to the west side with the cash instead of the black stuff. And since the handoff was a wash, Vince might not even pay him this week, the little cheapskate. T.B. didn't do this for his health, damn it.

He paused at a newsstand beside the Playtime Avenue subway entrance. He suckered a dime from his pocket but dropped it trying to give it to the news vendor, a fat old walrus with a mustache. T.B. bent down to pick up the coin. His tentacles were shaking under him. Jesus, what a day. When he straightened up the walrus was holding his gut, and bright red ribbons were gushing through his ink-stained apron like party streamers. Jesus fuck! The poor guy was gut shot! T.B. whirled around, yanking his sweet little Derringer pistol from its holster.

T.B. spotted the moose with the Luger. The guy was right across the street. Wasn't even hiding. Hadn't expected any return fire. The moose got off another round before T.B. could draw a bead on him. The slug tore through T.B.'s overcoat and slashed his side. T.B. fired his pistol, missed the moose, and demolished the window of a jewelry store. A burglar alarm went off. The moose ran fast up the street. T.B. could have shot him in the back, but there were too many people around.

T.B. tucked his hardware back under his overcoat and staggered down the stairway to the subway station. As luck would have it, a westbound train was just loading. T.B. slid inside, and the train pulled out. The bullet wound still felt like a paper cut, but that wouldn't last. He had to return the cash to Vince while he could still get around. Then he'd get himself patched.

T.B. hung from a strap and puzzled over the moose. Why would a strange moose try to kill him in broad daylight? Presumably for the money. But who'd be dumb enough to snatch money that belonged to Vince the Ocelot? Vince was one of Boss Mandrill's top guys. Killing a nobody like T.B. was no big deal, but messing with the Syndicate's cash flow, that was serious. Unless it was somebody new in town who didn't know the score. But how would a new guy know about the briefcase? This was pointless. T.B.'s brain was spinning its wheels in the mud. First things first. Get the cash back to Vince before anything happened to it.

The train lights flickered. The train slowed and jolted to a stop between stations. What now? The giant monster thing again? Perfect timing. Now T.B.'s day was complete.

Turtle and Snake sat on the floor of the apartment block's vestibule with their backs against whitewashed cinderblock. Turtle sat under the mailboxes. Snake was curled up under the table where the postman dumped the circulars. Turtle stared at his feet. Snake stared at her tail. "You want to play Parcheesi?" asked Snake.

"Naw."

"You wanna watch those guys fix the street?"

Turtle picked his beak with his pinkie claw. "Naw."

"You wanna get your binoculars and go up on the roof? We might see a freighter dock at the pier. We might see the dog and the cat."

"Why would we see them? It ain't even dark yet."

"It's a full moon tonight."

"So?"

"They like to fight on the flatlands when the moon balloon is full."

"It ain't dark yet."

"But the moon is up."

"The hell it is."

"Go look at it. And the sky'll get dark soon."

"The hell it will."

"You wanna go get your binoculars? Huh, Turtle?"

"I got better things to do." Turtle stood up and sighed, making it clear that he was doing Snake a favor. "Okay. I'll get them." He went upstairs to his apartment. Snake stayed in the vestibule. Turtle's mother had a low opinion of Snake, so Snake stayed out of her way.

When Turtle got back, the binoculars were hung around his neck, and traces of powdered sugar clung to his green plush beak. "Maybe they'll fight near the city," he said hopefully. "You remember the time when they knocked over that silo at the train yard?"

"That was awesome," Snake had to agree. They started up the stairs to the roof. While they were climbing, the civil defense alarm bells went off. Turtle and Snake looked at one another. They couldn't believe their luck.

"The monsters are coming!" shouted Turtle. He took the rest of the stairs three at a leap, with Snake sidewinding breathlessly behind him. He ran to the eastern edge of the roof and trained his binoculars on the Dollhouse Mountains, where they sloped down into the badlands. But there were too many brown cardboard buildings blocking the view.

Snake was gaping at the sky. Cloud masses of cunningly tailored gray felt were moving west across the badlands. "Close your mouth," said Turtle. "You'll catch flies."

"I wouldn't mind eating a fly," said Snake with a grin. Turtle punched her playfully in the side of her neck. "Oww," she said. "That hurt." Turtle handed her the binoculars.

Snake looked out across a choppy sea of west-side roofs and water tanks and vent hoods. She focused the lenses on the landmarks of the city center. There was the observation deck of the Argyle Pleat Building. There was the spire of Crepe Cathedral. There were three lanes of outbound traffic being funneled onto Needle Overpass. There was the domed roof of Angora Stadium. There was the flag of the Stitch Museum. All bathing in a green twilight, as the sun sequin set into the skyline behind Snake's back.

Turtle snatched back the binoculars. "Where are they?" he asked crossly. "I don't see nothing."

Snake looked at the sky again. The faded blue silk of the daytime sky was peeling itself free from the ceiling of the world. It was beginning to creep west, wrinkling a little as it went, drawn toward the western horizon by unseen hands—the hard wrinkled hands of the Washerwoman Who Lives Beneath the Table Land. As the day sky was pulled down for a good scrubbing, the night sky was revealed, its star sequins glittering in all colors. Snake was struck by the strange and arbitrary nature of the world. Especially the parts that were beautiful. What a contrast the starlight made to the dingy yellow light that leaked from the city all night.

Forks of silvery tin lightning stabbed through the charcoal gray bellies of the darkening clouds. Unseen cymbals crashed behind the sky.

"I see them!" shouted Turtle. "I can see the dog and the cat!"

Drifting hazes of rainfall blurred the mountain slopes, and cloud shadows moved across the badlands. Two other huge forms were moving across the badlands as well—huge and slow as cloud shadows, but zigging and zagging or sometimes tracing a loop. The larger form was pursuing the smaller.

The pursuer was a stuffed hound done in orange-and-white checks—as long from nose to tail tip as a subway train. He grinned as he ran. His ivory shoe-button teeth gleamed in the green twilight and the drizzle. Silver saliva ribbons drooled from his muzzle, whipping in the wind. His long felt tongue licked strands of red ribbon from his gargantuan gingham-checked chops. His black glass eyes were wild and hungry. He'd been chasing the cat all day. Her blood ribbons tasted delicious. He couldn't wait for dinner.

Driving her out of the mountains was half the battle. Here on the badlands, the dog could outrun her. He'd bring her down easily now. Unless she made it to the cardboard city of the tiny folk. Cities had too many places where a cat could hide, even miniature cities.

The purple cat had put some distance between herself and the dog. Her mother-of-pearl claws gouged puncture wounds into the hardpan as she ran. The stitchings at the rims of her green glass eyes were bloodshot. She threw a glance behind her and sickened at the sight of her ripped hind leg. A triangle of white-dotted calico was detached from its canvas backing, flapping free. Another bite like that and she'd be leaking ribbons in piles. She yowled mournfully and ran a little faster. But she was only the size of a freight truck. She couldn't keep up this pace.

She let the dog catch up with her and wheeled on him, hissing. She raked her white claws across his black velvet nose. Goose down leaked from his snout and flurried around him like snow. He yelped and stumbled to a stop. He pawed glumly at the slash on his nose.

"You're such a pussy," said the cat.

The dog perked up. "That's very good."

"I thought you'd enjoy that."

"You're very clever," the dog said admiringly.

"I know it," said the cat.

"Well . . . shall we?"

"After you."

"But you should have a head start."

"Perhaps I should," said the cat.

Again the mad dash of the two behemoths exploded across the badlands. The cat made for the flatlands, galloping majestically westward. All along the eastern fringe of Plush City's industrial district, plaid watchmen in plaid watchtowers hit their red panic buttons and sounded the monster sirens. The sirens wailed away, soaring and dipping like banshees from another world. Searchlight beams stabbed out from the Argyle Pleat Building and swept the flatlands, casting strange shadows across the sagebrush and the stones.

Nurse Pinkbunny scrubbed in and pulled sterile latex gloves onto her paws. She was very adrenalinized. It wasn't every day that she assisted a prominent pediatric surgeon like Dr. Beaver. Besides which, today's procedure was very unusual. The patient was a newborn kangaroo with two heads. Dr. Beaver would attempt to normalize the infant without "sacrificing viability." In other words, he'd try to cut off one of its heads without killing it. Actually it was quite difficult to kill a stuffie, even an infant. Little things like lungs and kidneys grew back in a matter of days.

Edna backed into the O.R. through swinging doors, minding her gloves. She checked the instrument trays to make sure there'd be no surprises. Dr. Beaver was consulting with the anesthesiologist Dr. Grayclam. Though the air conditioner was humming, beads of moisture had already formed on Dr. Beaver's brow. A heavy perspirer. Edna unspooled some extra gauze and cut it into strips.

The newborn arrived on a gurney. Anesthesia was established. Dr. Beaver began the amputation with an incision to the deformed infant's left throat. The oxygen mask hissed at the edge of audibility. The lights were very bright.

"That artery," said Dr. Beaver to Nurse Peahen. "Is that silk or satin, would you say? I want the thread to match."

Nurse Peahen leaned in. "It looks rubberized."

"Radioactivity?" said Dr. Grayclam.

"Who knows," said Dr. Beaver. "People have no business having babies here in the first place. And these idiots were inhaling cleaning fluid."

Edna had to agree. Babies were supposed to arrive in Plush City from the material plane. A few new ones were found each morning, outside the hospital in wicker baskets. But strange medical conditions like pregnancy were growing more common since the giant monsters started battling so close to the city. There was talk that "monster radioactivity" had gotten into the water supply.

The baby was doing fine, but its neck anatomy seemed to have thrown Dr. Beaver. "*Suction*," he snapped at Nurse Peahen. "Over there by the . . . the . . . the . . . *That* thing. *There*. And get that kite string out of my way. And when I ask for suction, give me *suction*, God damn it!"

"Sorry, doctor." The nurse struggled to comply. But the more the surgeon snipped and sewed, the more tiny red ribbons spilled from the white cotton muscles.

Nurse Pinkbunny dabbed the sweat from Dr. Beaver's forehead. She could imagine the tense frown behind his white mask. "Thank you, Nurse Pinkbunny," he said. He'd remembered her name. Edna wondered whether he was attracted to her. Once in the cafeteria she'd caught him admiring her breasts.

The amputation went sour. The infant was fighting the ether, and if it woke up, it would go into shock. "I told you to have masks for both heads," Dr. Beaver harangued Dr. Grayclam. "But no. You had to do it *your* way." Meanwhile the nurses were having terrible problems with the jugular hemostats. The infant was losing a lot of ribbons.

Suddenly Nurse Peahen jumped back from the baby with an involuntary cry of disgust.

"What?" said Dr. Beaver. "What now?"

She pointed her index claw at the baby's furry beige belly. "Things are crawling on it."

Now the doctor jumped back. "We have bugs in here? *Bugs*?"

Edna leaned over the baby, peering down through her wire-rimmed glasses. "Tiny kangaroos," she said.

Dr. Beaver yanked off his mask. "*What?*"

"She's giving birth," said Edna. "She's having a litter. They're looking for her pouch."

Dr. Beaver flushed a darker brown, and his tail began to slap at the floor tiles. "The infant is giving birth to more infants?"

Edna nodded. "It must be a mutation."

"What shall we do with them?" Nurse Peahen asked querulously. "They seem to be viable."

"I give up!" said Dr. Beaver. He snapped off his gloves, hurled them to the floor, and marched out of the room. Dr. Grayclam looked at the nurses. The nurses looked at him.

"Who's going to finish the procedure?" asked Nurse Peahen.

"Hell," said Dr. Grayclam. "I'll do it. Anyone can do this stuff. It's just sewing."

At this point the voice of Miss Zebra made an announcement through a wall speaker. "Urgent phone call for Nurse Pinkbunny. Extension seventeen." Miss Zebra ran the hospital switchboard.

"I'll be right back," said Edna. She took off her gloves and walked slowly down a pale green corridor to a wall phone. It would be Teddy of course. Edna wondered what his idea of an emergency would turn out to be. Perhaps he'd run out of beer. She lifted the receiver.

"Teddy, why are you calling me at work? We've talked about this. I'll be home when I'm home. Have you been listening to the radio? The whole city is on monster alert. People are filling up the subway shelters. Just pull yourself together, Teddy. It's a dangerous world out here, and you aren't the only one in it."

Edna hung up. She felt calm and confident. Confident primarily that Teddy would beat the crap out of her tonight. Of course he would. As the night followed the day.

"Are you okay?" asked Nurse's Aide Sunflower, stopping in the corridor with her arms full of laundry.

"I'll live," said Edna.

T.B. struggled up the stairs of the Cookiemilk Avenue subway station. He had to fight his way through a steady stream of stuffies bound for the monster shelters. T.B. wasn't concerned about giant monsters. He was worried about getting the briefcase back to Vince before he passed out. When he emerged onto street level, Vince's bar was in sight, right up the block. He slid north, leaving a trail of red ribbons behind him on the sidewalk.

T.B. mopped his warty lavender head with his handkerchief and dried off the suckers of three or four of his arms. He hobbled past a pawn shop, a record store, and a bakery. There were signs in the windows. CLOSED FOR MONSTER ATTACK.

The bar was occupied by its normal clientele, a coven of sleazy mammals smoking cigarettes and guzzling dangerous rot-gut. Jerry Sloth and Ernie Koala were drinking whiskey sours at the bar. Rico the Mongoose and Yvette the Mink sat in a booth at a table crowded with ashtrays, dentures, empty shot glasses, and elbows. A couple of out-of-work elk were playing eight ball in the side room.

T.B. climbed onto a stool and leaned on the bar. Theresa the Sock Monkey approached him. "What's your poison, T.B.?"

"Not now, Monkey Face. I'm just resting my legs."

"You got a lot of legs to rest, T.B."

"I gotta talk to Vince."

"Back room. You know the way." He knew it well.

T.B. slid to the rear of the bar and limped up a hallway past a cigarette machine and the door to the lavatory. Harry the Mule stopped him for a frisk. Harry was Little Vince's personal bodyguard. He took T.B.'s Derringer but never touched the briefcase.

Vince's poker game was cranking along as usual, and as usual Vince wasn't playing. He was sitting at a circular table off to one side, going over some ledgers with his accountant Pokie the Stork. Sitting at a third table by herself and nursing a gin gimlet was Vince's bimbo, a doll that everybody called Ladybug for some reason. (She wasn't a ladybug, she was a doll.)

Ladybug was an eyeful. Her hair was fire-engine red, a bottle job but classy. She wore a sinuous ice blue evening gown, and her fishnet stockings stretched all the way down to a pair of stiletto heels.

No one in the room seemed overjoyed to see T.B. "You got the stuff from the Chinks?" said Vince. It wasn't really a question. Vince didn't ask people questions.

"No," said T.B. "There's a problem this week."

"What problem?"

"Mr. Cho wouldn't tell me. He sent me back here with your money. Said the money was no good, and I'm no good. Maybe he thinks it's counterfeit. I couldn't get a straight story out of him."

Vince scowled. "They didn't give you the stuff?" he snarled through his sharp little teeth.

"No, Sir." T.B. set the briefcase on the table next to the ledger. Déjà vu. At least the stork wasn't working an abacus.

Vince stroked his whiskers and smiled at T.B. This was something he'd never done before, and T.B. didn't enjoy the experience. "I don't want the money either," said Vince. "Take it with you when you go." The room fell silent. The poker game ground to a halt.

"It's not my money, Vince."

"It is now. I'm giving it to you. Hold onto it. Take a vacation." Vince was serious. What the hell was going on? And when the hell was someone going to let T.B. in on the gag?

"But Vince, it's your money. You want me to take it to the bank or something?"

"No, jerk-off. I want yer ugly face out of my bar. And don't bring it back. Take a hike."

T.B. was pleading now, wringing his tentacles distractedly. Sweat was trickling down his face and matting his plush. "Don't be like that, Vince. I'm not a bad guy. I don't mess with your money. I don't even nibble around the edges like some I could mention. It's your money. I'll just leave it here." T.B. started for the door.

Vince pulled a big black pistol from his coat. It wasn't the kind that shoots caps. The guys at the poker table sat up very straight. "Take the briefcase with you," said Vince.

"You're gonna shoot me if I leave it here? Well, I don't like getting shot, Vince. I've already been shot at once today. Maybe you know something about that."

"You're fired," said Vince. "Consider the briefcase your severance pay."

That raised a chuckle from the wise guys. Little Vince should be on the radio. He was a regular panic, this ocelot.

T.B. suckered one arm to the briefcase, snatched his gun from Harry the Mule, and limped down the hall. As he slid past the lavatory, he could hear the wise guys laughing at his expense. Déjà vu all over again. He sat down at the bar. Theresa nudged his arm. "Want a drink, Sailor?"

"No, Monkey Face. Gotta run. Which isn't easy with eight legs." The stupid gag bought him a smile. "Hey Theresa, can I leave something behind the bar?" Keep it light, T.B. Like an afterthought. Carton of eggs, quart of milk, a carton of Luckies, and leave the briefcase behind the bar.

Theresa gave him a look like a sock monkey who'd just been bitten by a snake. T.B. was a grifter and betrayed people as a matter of course, but he seldom came face to face with a look like this one. It was rapidly reducing him to a grease spot on the bar-room floor. "No, T.B, you *can't*," was all she said

He dragged the case off the bar. He was poison. He was wrong. He hit the street and slithered north. He knew a good greasy spoon about two blocks up the way at Cookiemilk and Pompom.

At the beanery, which was called Eat Here as far as anyone knew, T.B. took a corner booth at the back. The only other customer was a caveman in a leopard skin reading a racing form. He'd parked his club beside the coat tree. The waitress was a green plush dragon with buck teeth. She dropped a laminated menu to the table. T.B. ignored it. "Chili and a cup of mud, black."

"Wit' cheese?"

"Sure, with cheese. Cheese for the cheesy." She turned around without writing on her pad. A pro.

While T.B. nursed his coffee and waited for his chili, the beanery filled up a little. The caveman was joined by a pair of yellow sharks and a very familiar little sea bass. T.B. pegged the bass as one of the abacus pushers from the opium den. It was fairly obvious that the bass had T.B. pegged too.

Swell. The Fighting Fish were after him now. And knew exactly what was in the case. But why was Vince cooperating? Some kind of secret payoff? But why did T.B. have to die? What was Vince's angle? There had to be an angle. Things didn't just happen at random.

A stingray came in the door, jingling the bell. He sat down and studied the menu. It wasn't Mr. Cho, but so what? Asian faces didn't eat here. Certainly not four at the same time. These guys had AMBUSH stamped on their foreheads. What was T.B. supposed to do? Make a run for it? Draw his sidearm and mow them all down like in the cowboy movies?

T.B. sipped his coffee. A dagger whistled past his head and embedded its point in the wall plaster behind him. T.B. whipped his eyes back to the fish. All of them were smiling at him, but he couldn't tell who'd thrown the knife. Damn, these Chinks had fast fins. T.B. would probably get the wire-around-the-neck trick performed on him before he made the door.

Screw it. T.B. gulped the last of his coffee, slapped down a quarter, and scuttled for the door. He ran into the street and kept running, legs windmilling. The bell on the beanery door jangled behind him, and the rip in his side throbbed like a jellyfish in a bottle of Clorox. But hey! No one was coming after him. T.B. kept running anyway, for as long as he could manage. Then he leaned against a lamp-post on Comforter Boulevard, wheezing like an out-of-tune engine on a frosty morning.

What were the Fighting Fish playing at? Some kind of warning? Weren't bullets warning enough? He was caught in the middle of something, but what? The middle of *what*? It hardly mattered. T.B. had to blow Plush City fast and stay away until this whole mess blew over.

There were places he could disappear to. There was Puppetropolis. There was Lawn County where the tin toys lived. There was Ark where toys carved from wood went when they died. T.B. could buy a train ticket and ride. The money in the case made it simple. A bandage, a train ticket, maybe a change of clothes, and he'd be living it up in Candy Land on Vince's play money. He wouldn't go back to his rat-trap apartment though. That would be a sucker move after two slugs and a dagger in one afternoon.

Should he head for the train station? Maybe not. Get this rip mended first. T.B. buttoned his overcoat and moved on.

He thought of his girlfriend, Doris the Doll. Assuming she *was* his girlfriend after the blow-up last week. Maybe he should scout her hotel, see if she was home. Even if she wasn't, he could jimmy the lock and hide out for a couple of hours, pull himself together. But she'd probably be home. The daylight was still fading, and Doris was the kind of working girl who worked by dark of night.

Yeah, Doris's place was probably safe. If a giant monster didn't step on it.

Turtle and Snake cut north on Nursery, heading for the under-structure of Scissors Bridge. They figured their lookout fort on the bridge was the perfect vantage point for watching monsters wreck the place. Silk River made a cozy loop that encircled the whole west side, and from the middle of the bridge you could see half the city. You could look south and see Bastingstitch Bridge and the dockyards or look north and see Cutieface Bridge and the sewage plant. You could look west across the river and see Mildew Swamp or look east and see the lights of the Argyle Pleat Building.

Snake loved to see the lights of the city shimmer on the river water. Sometimes she rode the Velveteen Street bus for hours after dark, back and forth, just to look out her window while the bus crossed Scissors Bridge. At night the city was beautiful, because you couldn't really see it. You could make it something better in your mind. Then the sun sequin came up, newly polished by the Washerwoman, and its cold steely light made everything ugly again.

Turtle grabbed Snake by the neck. "Hide!" he whispered. "Beanbags!" The street ahead of them was blocked by a loitering gaggle of beanbags. The beanbags were the sumo wrestlers of the west-side gang scene. What they lacked in detail and personality, they made up for in sheer bulk.

A corduroy beanbag spotted the reptile kids and started jeering at them. "Hey, look at this. Here's a little fag that plays with *girls*. You like little girls, turtle? Maybe you *are* a little girl. You wanna bend over and find out?"

"Hey, Slobbo, would you fuck a snake?"

"I might fuck a *dead* snake, *haw haw haw*."

"Hey, Blobbo, what would you do with a snake?"

"I'd cut her head off and fuck her in the neck, *haw haw haw.*"

"Is that how you treat a little girl?"

"She *ain't* a little girl," Turtle called back, trying to sound defiant from behind a rain barrel.

The beanbags laughed and started to throw rocks. Turtle and Snake beat a hasty retreat. Their escape was facilitated by the passage of a flock of panic-stricken citizens with their red flannel mouths wide open and their arms in the air.

Turtle and Snake ducked into the doorway of a hardware shop and lay low. "Are you okay?" asked Turtle.

"I guess so," said Snake. "Nothing ripped."

"We can circle the block, cut north again on Porcelain."

"Yeah."

Turtle tied his tennis shoes, which were already tied. "You ain't really a girl, are ya? My mother said you was a tomboy."

Snake frowned. "It's a little hard to tell with snakes, but . . . Yeah, Turtle. I'm a girl. A tomboy is a girl that acts like a boy."

"*Uh,*" said Turtle. He couldn't quite wrap his tiny fabric brain around the concept. He took refuge in the familiar. "If I had a sulfuric acid cannon, I would dissolve those bastards."

"Yeah," said Snake. Then they heard the crash of giant monsters colliding with nearby buildings.

"We're missing the best part!" wailed Turtle.

They bolted south toward Silkfront Road. Turtle ran as fast as his plump little green plush legs would carry him, and Snake slithered loyally behind him.

The cat led the dog on a broken-field chase through the industrial district's steel foundries and chemical plants. As the monsters approached the city limit, the yellow plaid monster squads poured from their yellow plaid armory in their yellow plaid flatbeds with the swivel-action dart cannons.

The cat charged up the middle of Textile Street, three stories tall. Ahead of her swarmed a crush of shoving shouting stuffies, all trying like mad to get out of her way. They succeeded only in compacting each other into a solid mass. The cat stumbled through the screaming puddle of flesh, mashing flat no small number of them. The emergency rooms would be full tonight.

A monster squadsman fired his dart cannon at the cat. Unfortunately the rubber suction cup didn't stick, and the dart bounced off. The cat licked her side, looked around in confusion, and took her revenge on a florist's delivery truck. She rammed the truck through some plate glass into a penny arcade and crushed seven school children, whose pitiful burst bodies took weeks to heal. The cat was so distracted with pedestrians and trucks that she didn't hear the dog coming at her.

He pounced on her back, and instantly all hell broke loose. The two monsters seemed to levitate within an orange-and-purple tornado of slashing claws, snapping jaws, and flying bits of gingham and calico skin. They ricocheted off buildings like a madly spinning pool ball. Bricks flew like shrapnel, maiming the stuffies who cowered indoors. A movie marquee broke the back of a balding rag doll. Falling shards of glass cut dozens of unfortunates to ribbons. (And that can take *months* to heal.)

The cat looked west up Textile and saw the wide cardboard facade of the Piece-work Commerce Center. She made a sudden dash for the underpass where the street passed under the building, four lanes wide. She squeezed herself into the tunnel and out the other side, squashing the toy cars with the bad luck to be in her way. Several motorists suffered unscheduled amputations.

The dog tried to follow her through the tunnel, just as she'd hoped he would. He got stuck halfway through. He squirmed and growled and clawed at the commerce center, but still he couldn't budge. He bucked with the strength of desperation. The roof collapsed and buried him. He thrashed in the dusty dark and bucked some more. The building's cardboard shell split in two. The dog threw the two halves over on their sides and clawed his way clear of the wreckage. He shook the dust from his floppy checkered ears, slid down the mound of debris, and ran west again, sniffing for the scent of his dinner.

A yellow plaid monster squadsman positioned his flatbed for an artillery assault. His partner was manning the gunnery chair. They'd loaded their cannon with an experimental harpoon dart that had tacky glue all over the suction cup. They fired on the dog as he ran past, but he caught the dart in his teeth and kept running. Resultantly the flatbed was dragged three blocks on its side and wound up in the lobby of the Eyeglass Bank Building. So little was left of the two squadsmen that the surgeons uptown had to sew it all together just to keep any of it alive.

The cat was looking for a tree to climb. She settled for the el tracks. She scampered up the scaffolding and crouched on the tracks, spoiling for a fight. A toy train rounded a bend and came at her. She derailed it.

The dog was no climber, but he managed the el tracks and pounced on the cat again. The scaffolding crumpled beneath them. Some power lines came down as well, spitting blue sparks. The cat got a nasty electrical shock, which inspired her to a new burst of speed.

She careened south on Embroidery Boulevard and climbed the side of the Angora Stadium in one great scamper. The domed roof was too high for the dog to reach. He raced around and around the stadium, first clockwise then counterclockwise, trashing everything that got underfoot.

The cat was still nervous, looking around for higher ground. She crouched down on the stadium and launched a heart-stopping leap across the intersection of Flipflop and Suede. She landed on the northeast corner of the tenth story of the famous Argyle Pleat Building, Plush City's tallest skyscraper. While the dog yapped helplessly at street level, a million stuffies gaped up at the cat. She climbed the APB higher and higher.

Far above her, at the APB's cloud-capped summit, was the penthouse floor and the notorious Polar Club, the speakeasy where high-rolling Antarctic types came to blow their rolls in style. On the bandstand, a five-piece seal combo played hot jazz, while jitterbugging penguins covered every square inch of the open-air dance floor. Bootleg hooch, dizzy heights, and jitterbugging under the stars were all the rage with the well-connected penguin set this summer.

Besides the dance floor, the club provided a lounge, a skating rink, and a refrigerated pool. The rink was full of sea lions tonight, prosperous bulls in cravats and spats, with their flippers wrapped solicitously around the thick waists of their diamond-dripping cows.

The cat announced her arrival by darting onto the dance floor and devouring three penguins at one swallow. They really hit the spot too, after all that running around. The clientele evacuated the speakeasy with all due speed. Curious, the cat trotted around the facilities. She drank from the pool, sniffed at the ice rink, chewed on the bandstand. . . . Then she lay on her side on the dance floor and licked her calico flanks with her red velour tongue. First her flanks, then her forelegs, then her haunches. Then she tested her claws on a white shag carpet. She could hear the dog barking down below. Let him bark. The night was young.

The dog took a run at the skyscraper's base and slammed himself into it. It trembled. He rammed it again. It tipped. Again. It fell over like a tree and devastated seven city blocks. A fire broke out in the rubble. Red tin fire engines rushed to the scene, clanging their bells. Dalmatians in fireman's caps attached hoses to hydrants.

The cat leapt from the rapidly descending Polar Club to the pyramidal roof of the Stitch Museum. After that her bad leg was broken as well as ripped. She clung to the apex of the roof, leaking scarlet ribbons as if they grew on trees. Wads of her cotton stuffing tumbled down the roof and showered the tanbark paths of Tassel Park. Cotton floated on the ornamental pond. Then the cat herself skidded down the roof and fell like a sack of bricks to the pavement of Ping Pong Plaza.

At once the dog was on her, slavering and nipping. He sank his teeth into her broken hind leg. He shook her like a rat. The leg came clean off.

"Now you've done it," said the cat, lying woozily on her back.

"Oh there's worse to come," said the dog, whose mouth was full. "Shall we?"

"I really couldn't."

"I insist."

"But I can't even stand."

"Allow me." The dog clamped his jaws around her belly and carried her, dangling from his mouth, west up Suede Street to the bridge across Seam Expressway. He dropped her over a railing into the westbound traffic. An ambulance and four passenger cars piled up against her ribs with a squealing of toy tires and a crunching of painted tin.

The dog jumped down beside her, causing wrecks in the eastbound lanes. He heaved her into his jaws again and carried her along the expressway toward the river. He was tired from his long day of hunting. Now what he yearned for was a quiet place where he could eat his dinner in peace.

Police dogs arrived in their prowl cars and fired mortar shells after the monsters, who by then were out of range. The ambulance teams from Pattern General turned up next and began the work of removing crushed citizens from their cars. Minutes later the biplanes of the Civil Defense & Crop Dusting Corps arrived at the wreck of the Argyle Pleat Building with stink bombs and sneezing powder.

Edna had finally made it home from the hospital, hours late of course, thanks to the monsters. Now Teddy was slapping her around. He was bellowing. She was screeching. He'd been waiting all day for this.

He was working her over pretty good. He threw her into a wall, picked her up by her ears, dragged her into the kitchen, closed a drawer on her paw, and pushed her insipid pink face into the drawer knob for good measure. The noise from the neighborhood poured into the apartment—the screaming, the shattering of glass, the honking of toy auto horns, the endless rise and dip of the sirens. The noise level seemed to encourage Teddy.

He crumpled up an empty soup tin and used it for brass knuckles. The ragged metal edge opened up some nice deep cuts in Edna's face and tore loose tufts of pink fur when his blows struck her forearms. Afterwards he let her sit in the armchair and catch her breath. He even brought her a wet towel and let her wash her face. Then she said something that really pissed him off, and he was forced to go to the closet for his putting iron.

While Teddy had his fun in the den, Fang was amusing himself with Cuddles in the kitchen. The mischievous hamster was wearing his little chef's apron. He'd battered the parrot with egg whites and bread crumbs, trussed her up in aluminum foil, and arranged her on her back in a casserole dish, with some baby potatoes and parsley. He'd also preheated the oven. He tasted the marinade in the dish and applied it with a basting brush to Cuddles's exposed parts. She kicked feebly at the aluminum foil. Fang rummaged through a drawer and found the meat thermometer.

Back in the den, Teddy advanced on his wife with putting iron uplifted. You could break a little pink bunny's ankles with a putting iron. If the bunny had any bones, that is. No bones in Edna, sadly. But there were still things inside her that Teddy could break. And Teddy was ready to break them all tonight. He demonstrated his golf swing, whistling the putter's head through the air over Edna's head. She held her ears over her eyes and wailed in fear.

Just then the gingham dog came capering up Satin Street with the three-legged calico cat hanging from his mouth. The happy swinging of his tail knocked over lampposts on both sides of the street. He trotted right past the apartment block and veered left onto Fuzzy. As he passed, the cat's limply swinging head bashed one corner of the building.

In Teddy's den, a fat chunk of cement and rebar bashed through the ceiling and landed on his head. He crumpled to the carpet and lay where he fell—still breathing but knocked senseless. He was completely at Edna's mercy. With not a witness in sight.

Should she run away, she wondered. Talk to the police dogs? File charges?

Or should she simply take her revenge?

The phonograph needle in the room upstairs was skipping now, playing the same snatch of music over and over again. "Clock, it told me—clock, it told me—clock, it told me . . ."

T.B. was floating down a sidewalk in a strange city. All sorts of stuffies were swimming past him—stuffed cabbages, stuffed olives, stuffed salmon, stuffed turkeys . . . A sinister black limousine cruised past, wiggling its tail fins. A rear door flipped open. There was an eel in the back seat holding a machine gun.

All at once bullets were punching holes in innocent bystanders like they were cans of condensed soup. T.B. dove for the sidewalk and turned gray. Scraps of lead-riddled stuffies writhed like dying worms in the trash-strewn gutter. It was like some terrible dream.

T.B. woke up on a sofa in a furnished hotel room. Doris the Doll was wiping his face with a washcloth, sitting beside him in a black brocade robe. There was a bandage on his rip. Everything was Okay after all.

"You're awake," said Doris. "Is your head on straight?"

"Straight as it gets, Doll Face. Got any java?"

"You thumped on the door and passed out. You've lost a lot of ribbons."

"They grow back."

Doris nudged the bandage. "How'd you let a thing like this happen, T.B.? I thought you were smart."

"Where's my briefcase?"

"Under the sofa."

T.B. groped under the sofa with four of his arms. He retrieved the case, unsnapped the latches, and looked inside. The money was still there. "Where's my gun?"

"In a safe place. You can have it when you leave."

T.B. studied Doris's face. "Do you feel like a vacation, Doll Face? They say Candy Land is nice this time of year. I'm ready for something different."

"How different?" she asked, sliding onto his lap and twining her arms around his shoulders.

"Different enough, Sugar. What's the alternative? You gonna stay in this hellhole city until it kills you?"

There was a knock at the apartment door. T.B. shoved the briefcase back under the sofa. "Who would that be?"

"I dunno," said Doris. "It could be the lemur from next door. He pays me to loan him my clothes."

"Get rid of him."

Doris unbolted her door and opened it. Standing in the hallway were two Chinks. One was a yellow shark, big enough to be denting his fedora against the hall ceiling. The other was Mr. Cho. They strolled in like they owned the place and trained two big black guns on T.B.

T.B. stood up, not too steadily. "You sold me out," he said to Doris. "You called me in to the Fighting Fish."

Doris shrugged. "I called you in to Vince. I can't afford to cross Vince."

"You think I can?"

Doris touched his cheek. "Poor little mollusk," she said with sadness in her blue glass eyes. "You're poison now. You're wrong. And you're not going to talk your way out this time." Mr. Cho and the shark sat down on Doris's bed and made themselves at home.

"Why am I wrong? What have I done?"

Doris lit a cigarette. "You haven't done a thing. It's a deal that Boss Mandrill made with the triad. They're going to hunt you down like a dog, T.B. Which is just what Harry the Mule did to a triad kid last week, for no particular reason, just boredom. You heard about that kid they buried?"

"I heard about it."

"Well, the Fish didn't like it, and they complained to Boss Mandrill. So he cut them a deal. He offered them payback, and you're it. You and that cash in the briefcase. The cash is just to sweeten the deal. I don't know why Vince chose you for the patsy. I guess you're just the expendable type."

"So I'm tagged for the Big Burn Pile, and everybody's happy, huh?"

"I'm not happy at all, T.B."

"Well cheer up. Prohibition can't last forever."

Mr. Cho and the shark stood up and gestured with their guns, inviting T.B. to leave the hotel with them. Doubtless they'd throw him in the trunk of a car and drive him to a secluded spot, before or after they croaked him. They stood on either side of him, took a tight grip on two of his arms, and moved him toward the door.

"Can I at least have my overcoat?" he asked them. Mr. Cho nodded to Doris. She pulled T.B.'s coat off the back of the sofa and draped it around his shoulders.

"Doris," he said, "if you're planning to throw boiling water on these creeps, right now would be a good time." Doris laughed in spite of herself. T.B. could always make her laugh.

The fish and T.B. were tightly packed as they hustled him through the doorway. Tightly packed was exactly how T.B. wanted them. It was all so easy.

What happened next seemed to be over before it began. All at once the fish were flopping on the floorboards, grabbing at their necks while pink ribbons gushed out of them. They'd made sure that T.B. had no gun, and that had made them careless. They hadn't figured on the little concealed pockets in the hem of his overcoat. So they hadn't expected the straight razors. And best of all, they'd forgotten that an octopus has eight arms.

T.B. slid back into the apartment, heading straight for Doris. She was kneeling beside her phonograph, throwing records around and groping for something in a cabinet. At the last second she snatched the disk off the turntable and threw that at him. He knocked it aside and grabbed the collar of her robe. "Be careful with those things," he hissed into her pretty painted face. "Sharp edges." Her scream started strong then shrank into a gurgle. Half a minute later she was lying on the carpet with her throat slashed.

T.B. wiped his razors on the bedspread, retrieved his pistol from under the phonograph, and pulled his briefcase from under the sofa. Then he said goodbye to Doris. "Hugs and kisses, Sister. You've got some strange ideas about how to throw a party, but what the hell. See you in the funny papers."

T.B. slithered over the twitching heap of shark meat sprawled in the doorway. The stairs were just up the hall. He climbed to the roof and slid down a rear fire escape. Up the alley to Paisley Street, and he was free and clear. If any more sharks were waiting in front of the hotel, they'd be waiting there for a while. T.B. meandered north, comparing the various flops. Up the street a canvas sailor boy and a hula dancer in a grass skirt were leaning against a lamppost and fucking on their feet. Nice neighborhood.

T.B. was peering through a fly-specked window into a truly unsavory lobby when the moose with the Luger shot him in the back. This time the moose was standing up close and hit him dead center. The moose turned toward the sailor and the hula dancer in their pool of lamplight. They walked up the sidewalk at top speed and disappeared around a corner.

The street was deserted then. Just the moose and T.B. A light drizzle began to fall. T.B. could feel it wetting the back of his head. The moose knelt down beside him, rolled him over, and frisked him. T.B. thought of his gun and his razors, but putting up a struggle seemed too difficult suddenly. He just wanted to lie here on the sidewalk and go to sleep. But this moose. This crazy moose in the cheap green suit jacket. What was his angle?

The moose flipped open T.B.'s wallet and glared at the driver's license. "T.B. Otherweiss?" he said to himself aloud. "That ain't right. This ain't the guy. What kinda name is that for an octopus anyhow?"

"My name," T.B. croaked.

The moose jumped. "Christ. You scared me."

"So now we're even, huh?"

"Your name is Otherweiss? How come it ain't Octopus? You a *foreigner* or something?"

"I changed it."

"So you ain't Toby Octopus the insurance investigator?"

"Hell no. Do I look like an insurance investigator?"

"I feel real bad about this. It's all just a misunderstanding."

"So you're not with the Fighting Fish?"

"The who?"

T.B. started to laugh, which hurt so much he groaned. "You should ask a few questions before you go to the trouble of plugging a guy."

"It was no trouble."

"Still you coulda been more careful."

The moose smiled shyly. "Yeah, I coulda. But I'm not too bright. It's part of my colorful character."

"Would it have killed you to find the right octopus, you fucking dim bulb?"

The moose grinned. "I guess not. But for a dim bulb like me, that wouldn't really be in character, would it?" As if to demonstrate the subtlety of his point, he slugged T.B. in the head with his gun butt. The rest of the night got confused.

T.B. touched the tangle of rain-wet ribbons around his mouth. His tongue tasted like a wrought-iron railing. Some moose was carrying him over one shoulder. That explained it. All the ribbons were rushing to his head.

An hour later, and what a long hour it was, T.B. was hanging from the top of a flagpole above the courtyard of an elementary school. Eviscerated. Hung from a couple of flag hooks. Flapping in the cold wet wind. A lavender rag with eyes. Turned inside out. Staring at the streetlights through the back of his own translucent head. Hard to think in this condition.

The night was still. No more sirens. No more screaming. T.B. had reached a dead end, three stories off the pavement.

Down by the bank of Silk River, Turtle and Snake climbed the side of a concrete stanchion and ascended a steel web of pylons, girders, and bracing cables. Above them was their lookout fort.

"Hurry!" Turtle shouted. "They're coming closer! I can hear them!"

They reached the fort, a ramshackle wooden box that they'd cobbled together from discarded crates, rusty nails, and baling wire. There was just enough room inside for the two of them to sit together, play cards, and watch the world go by.

They soon saw the monsters. The dog walked wearily up the middle of Seam Expressway toward the bridge. The cat swung from his mouth. They were massive and slow and uncanny, like a dream spilling into the world. The dog knocked down a row of tollbooths and ventured out across the bridge's upper deck.

"They're right over us," marveled Snake.

"I can't see them!" wailed Turtle.

Perhaps the sound of running water roused the cat back to consciousness. Oh how she hated to get wet! Whatever the reason, she suddenly began to yowl and slash and struggle with her captor. The bridge shook like a three-legged card table. The dog lost his footing. The monsters fell from the bridge.

Their twin immensities smashed the pea green surface of the river. The lookout fort was suddenly awash in flying white water. The monsters surfaced and pounded the river with their paws, raising mammoth clouds of spray. The polka-dot cat paddled west across the river, spluttering in disgust. The dog swam after her, grinning from ear to ear, paddling efficiently and enjoying the exercise—a relentless gingham-checked torture machine.

A tugboat draped with truck tires chugged along the center of the channel. It was in the cat's path and had no time to maneuver. Her wake nearly capsized it. Then it got in the dog's way. He showed it all his teeth. It spun in his turbulence. He snatched it out of the water and tossed it over his head.

The tugboat tumbled end over end through the misty air. Ropes, floats, boat hooks, crewmen, everything not tied down hurtled in a loose cloud around the slowly revolving tugboat. Here it came. Snake could see the keel, then the deck, then the keel again. You could even see the white-haired tug captain—his skipper's cap, then his rubber boots, then his cap again. His flailing arms and legs couldn't alter his trajectory. Here he came.

The tugboat and its crew smacked headlong into the webwork of the bridge. Turtle took a blow to the head from a flying tin plate. He didn't quite pass out, but he lost track of things temporarily. Then it was like he woke up.

He looked around. He was drenched and dripping and sitting in the lookout fort, or what remained of it. A boat captain was pancaked against a nearby pylon.

Turtle looked down. Snake was draped across his lap. There was a plank fragment punched through her tail like a javelin, and half of her head was crushed. Turtle made a move to stand up.

"No," said Snake. "Leave me alone. I want to see this." Her good eye was still gazing across the water, watching the monsters as they swam toward the far bank of the river. "I want to see this," she repeated stubbornly.

Turtle sat and rocked his friend in his forelegs. He found himself singing a song he'd been hearing. "The gingham dog and the calico cat, side by side on the table sat. 'Twas half past twelve, and what do you think? Not one nor the other had slept a wink." He'd forgotten the rest of the words.

Turtle thought about the life Snake led. She didn't go to school. She had no home, no family. Turtle's mother didn't want her around. Turtle didn't even know where she slept or what she ate. She had nothing. He had everything. And now she was hurt, and he didn't know what to do.

Streams of river water cascaded through the bridge, and Turtle wept.

The three-legged cat dragged herself from the pea green river, trailing her pink satin intestines behind her in the mud. For a harrowing minute they snagged on a pile of logs. The cat had to backtrack and pull them loose with her mother-of-pearl teeth. She collapsed on the mud flat north of Cellophane Canal.

A rabble of filthy hobo rats crept from their burrows. They approached the fallen cat cautiously, wielding iron clubs and pointed sticks. They poked her, and she didn't move. The bravest rats among them tried to pry one of the green glass eyes from her head. Then the dog climbed from the river and shook himself. The rats took flight.

At last the dog ate his dinner. He ripped out her throat and pulled open her ribcage. He gnawed at leisure on the cotton muscles and packing twine sinews of her dear sweet legs. She was such a good cat.

After eating, the dog ran up and down the riverbank, guarding the corpse from the wild dog packs that haunted his dreams. He'd never actually seen another giant dog like himself. But he knew that they were out there, just waiting to steal his meat.

After patrolling the perimeter, he sat down beside the corpse and gazed at the fullness of the moon balloon and the beauty of the rainbow-spangled heavens. Then he rolled the cat over on her belly and stuck his stiff stuffed weenie into her slot. He raped the corpse with gusto. "Uk uk uk," he said.

"Ik ik ik," said the corpse.

The hands of the clock on the tower of the Eyeglass Bank Building inched toward midnight. The night sky looked down through her crinkled eye folds and winced in revulsion like a bedsheet on a clothesline when a gust of wind comes by. Beyond the badlands, the peaks of the Dollhouse Mountains cracked open their jagged mouths and moaned in pity for the cat. The city's poor few trees, filched from some model train set, wilted in shame. The bells of Crepe Cathedral rang the hour. The wind fell to nothing and held its breath. The colors drained from the stars.

A luminous form, hazy with distance, wavered in the moonlight over Mildew Swamp. It shone with a black light, like a midnight sun descended to the Table Land.

"Look," said Turtle, off across the water, on Scissors Bridge. "Something's coming."

"Turn my head," said Snake. "I can't move."

The form solidified into a figure that walked on legs, though its feet didn't touch the mud. It approached the city, striding across the swamp on legs like stone mesas.

"What?" said Turtle. "What did you say?"

Again Snake whispered the sacred name. "Ragged Anndy."

Anndy raised a foot like a swollen black planet at the end of a blue denim pants leg. The foot levitated across the mud flat and planted itself in the air. A second leg in a red-and-white striped stocking loomed forward. The first two legs were joined by a third, which came to rest between them. The third leg of the tripod was a doubled leg, two legs sewn together. For Ragged Anndy was Siamese twins.

The titanic stuffed goddess strode toward the riverbank. Her feet touched the mud now. Arabesques of frost formed in her footprints. Her heads were halfway to the sky.

Anndy's hair was giant loops of red yarn. Her eyes were four black buttons that glowed with compassion from the centers of radiating lash lines. Each face bore a triangular red nose and mouth of crimson embroidery thread. On the side where her right arm attached, Ann wore a frilly pink pinafore and a starched white apron with deep pockets. On the side where his left arm attached, Andy wore a light blue work shirt, bell-bottom trousers, and a navy blue pea jacket.

Anndy stood directly behind the dog. The dog went on raping the corpse. The water of Silk River squirmed like a flea-infested mattress. The moon balloon deflated herself slightly and crept down the ceiling of the world. Anndy's moon shadow fell across the dog's bent back. The little orange dog raped and raped and raped the little dead cat. "Ugh ugh ugh!" said the dog.

"Ik ik ik," said the corpse.

"Ugh ugh ugh!" said the dog.

"Jesus you're heavy," said the corpse.

Anndy shook her heads and rested her hands on her hips. Her arms bent like sausages, lacking bones. She waited to be noticed. She was fed up to here with these nightly visits to the Table Land, but what choice did she have? The curse lay on her heads just as much as it lay on theirs.

At last the dog noticed Anndy. He yanked his weenie free of the corpse and romped to and fro at the god's feet, yapping and slobbering blissfully. He ducked his head and wagged his gingham tail. Not a thought in his head that he'd misbehaved. Just the fervent undying hope that Anndy had come here to throw a stick for him.

Anndy knelt down and touched the cat's broken neck. She stirred and moaned and opened one swollen eye. She pushed aside the red ribbons that dripped from her brow, using a paw that was just a loop of wire with some cotton hanging off. She mewed piteously to Anndy.

Steam rose from her gaping belly. The air was filled with butcher shop smells, the smells of blood and meat. The smells made no sense in a world of stuffed toys, but the river rats could smell them just the same. Smelling them made the river rats feel very queer. They hadn't smelled meat since their half-remembered days on the ma-terial plane—that uncanny realm where all stuffies were forever mute and para-lyzed. The river rats scurried deeper into their burrows.

Anndy spoke to his pets, and his voice echoed across the swamp. "It is midnight," he said. The dog cocked his head. "Midnight by the old Dutch clock in the Parlor Behind the Sky," Anndy elaborated.

"Bow wow wow!" said the dog, trying to hold up his end of the conversation.

"Meow?" said the cat, trying to be helpful.

"Do you know why we have come here, little dog?"

"Haven't a clue," the dog answered.

"And you, little cat?"

"Good evening, Boss."

"Do you know why we are here, Ragged Ann and I?"

"Sorry," said the cat. "I just woke up."

Anndy sighed deeply. "So again you have remembered nothing. Again you know nothing of the curse which makes a hell of your lives."

"Now I'm completely lost," said the cat.

"A curse?" said the dog. "Gosh! You mean like an enchantment?"

Anndy spoke again, his voice a shade louder this time, so that it churned up the river water. "What do you think will happen tomorrow night at midnight, little dog, little cat?"

"Can you give us a hint?" asked the cat.

"Tomorrow night at midnight," said Anndy, "we will return to plead with you again."

"Is there something we can do for you?" the dog asked hopefully.

"Anything at all, Boss. You name it," said the cat.

"Again we will plead with you, just as we stand here pleading now. And all be-cause of your curse."

"There's that curse again," muttered the dog.

Anndy raised his voice, and windows broke all over the west side. The Dollhouse Mountains shivered and pulled their heads into their shoulders. "*Could you please just stop killing each other every night?! You're keeping the whole house awake! People are trying to sleep for Christ's sake! How can we sleep with the two of you tearing around like that?!*"

"We're keeping you awake?" said the dog in astonishment.

"We had no idea," said the cat.

"We'll be quiet as mice," the dog solemnly promised.

"You won't even know we're here," said the cat.

"No more crashing," said the dog.

"No more killing," said the cat.

Anndy rubbed his eyes and yawned. He sat down beside the monsters. "You could lift your curse tonight," he told them. "You could do it so easily. But you don't know how."

"So tell us!" said the dog.

Anndy hung his heads. "We can't. We're forbidden. It's part of the curse."

"How mysterious," mused the cat.

The dog whispered into the cat's tattered ear. "You talk to him. You're smarter than I am."

"Are we keeping you from something?" asked Anndy.

"Nothing important," said the dog. "I was raping her corpse, but we can do that after you leave."

"We won't make any noise," said the cat.

"I'll be in the parlor," said Anndy. "Playing solitaire and drinking warm milk."

"Sweet dreams."

"Nice seeing you."

"Drop in anytime."

"Don't be a stranger."

Ragged Anndy raised his colossal hand and touched the sequined sky. *Let all continue as before,* he said, and he sounded as if he meant it. The waterworks shriveled in terror, and fuel tanks hid their faces in their pipes.

Anndy turned and walked back across the swamp, but her feet no longer touched the mud. She parted the silken veil of the night sky, ducked her heads, and stepped through the parting into some larger world beyond.

Everyone in Plush City fell asleep, and I do mean everyone. For hours the place was as dead as a coffin nail. No one came, no one went, nothing moved. While the stuffies slept, the city's ruined buildings and damaged roads and burst pipes and severed power lines regrew themselves like weeds. The cardboard city had no eyes, no thoughts, words, no hands. Yet in the stillness of the night, while the stars twinkled solely for their own amusement, the city quietly rebuilt itself. It happened every night, while the stuffies slept.

The sun sequin rose into the pale blue sky of day and chased away the moon balloon. Certain details of the city had altered overnight, but none of the citizens seemed to notice.

Snake and Turtle went for a stroll in the early morning. There was no school on Saturday, and Snake felt like a walk. Naturally Turtle tagged along. It had rained in the night. The air was cool and clean for a change. Turtle was happy just to be walking beside his friend and talking note of all the different stuffies that they passed.

There went a masked hero in yellow leotards and a green cape. There went an eggplant and a pumpkin. A fox in a beaver coat escorting a headless chicken. A mermaid walking on her tail between a satyr and a sea serpent. And here was a mother kangaroo pushing a stroller with dozens of her cute little two-headed babies bouncing in and out of it.

Snake and Turtle passed a hospital. On a patio out in front, some fire-damaged Dalmatians were sunbathing in lounge chairs, regrowing their skins. A nurse in a white uniform was serving them glasses of lemonade. "Nurses are sexy," said Snake. "I like the little white caps."

"Yeah," said Turtle. Snake rumpled the plush on top of his head. He hated that.

Snake and Turtle passed their neighborhood movie palace, which was showing a Puppetropolitan remake of *The Lost World*. Turtle was crazy about the movies. He didn't care what was playing.

A porpoise in an eyeshade and sleeve garters was sweeping the sidewalk in front of a hole-in-the-wall tongue store. He looked like a foreigner. Snake wondered why so many foreigners looked so sad. Weren't they happy to be here?

Snake and Turtle walked past the apartment block where Snake lived. They ducked up an alley. Snake stopped under a fire escape. "You hear that?" she said. "That bunny is breaking dishes again. Working up a head of steam for when Teddy gets home, I bet you. That bitch sent Teddy to the hospital last month."

"I wonder why they got married," said Turtle. "They don't got no kids."

Snake and Turtle walked east. The parade of stuffies never ended. There went a llama in a priest's collar. There went a lantern fish and a twelve-legged cow. Part of a Humpty Dumpty. A swan and a vulture. A lion and a headless lion tamer. A punching bag and a little black Sambo. Plush City was like a masquerade ball that never ended.

Turtle wanted to stay here forever.

Edna Pinkbunny stood in her den and ironed her husband's shirts. A complaining electric fan provided a meager breeze while it drowned out Edna's radio. Perspiration dripped from her nose onto the steam iron. It was an ugly iron. The shirts were ugly shirts. Her doll furniture was ugly tasteless doll furniture, and the shoddy pasteboard walls of the apartment were ugly walls.

What killed Edna was that on Teddy's salary as an armed guard at the bank, they should've been able to afford a better place. The problem was Teddy's unfortunate habit of drinking half his paycheck every weekend. Edna imagined the look on Teddy's face if she accidentally dropped this iron on his big smelly foot. It would serve him right.

The radio was tuned to a morning soap opera about glamorous well-paid medical professionals who all worked at Pattern General Hospital. A nurse with a sexy voice was the ice princess of the nursing staff. All the doctors were hot for her, but she treated them like dirt. Edna wanted to be like that.

While Edna daydreamed in the den, Cuddles was in the bathroom, having her way with Fang. Edna ignored the torture chamber parrot laughter and the agonized rodent squeals. She had her own problems.

Cuddles was experimenting with a theory of hers that the sewer pipes beneath the toilet bowl were inhabited by little shit-eating sewer fish. Cuddles was convinced that if she fished in these sub-toilet waters with the proper bait, she could hook one of these sewer fish and capture it for science. She'd constructed a fishing pole from a curtain rod, some dental floss, and a paper clip. Her bait for today was none other than Fang.

Fang couldn't breathe underwater, but Cuddles took account for that. Every couple of minutes she hauled him to the surface. After he caught his breath, he usually started to squeal. But that was easily remedied. Cuddles simply flushed.

"Hamster want a cracker?" said Cuddles.

"Glub," said Fang.

Meanwhile Edna was collecting some cleaning supplies from a kitchen cupboard. She arranged the cans and bottles on the dinner table.

She glanced at the ceiling. The dance instructor upstairs had been playing the same record all morning. That Gopher Sisters number. The big band slid casually from chord to chord, while the trio sang sweet swing harmonies into the stale city air. "Next morning where the two had sat, they found no trace of dog or cat. And some folks think unto this day that burglars stole the pair away."

Edna sat down, put on her glasses, and studied the labels on the cleaning products. With particular attention to the instructions given in case of accidental poisoning.

Doris the Doll turned the corner of Storytime Avenue onto Taffeta. She wore a mauve cloche hat and a topcoat, although it wasn't raining. She clutched her beaded purse as she walked, and fussed nervously with the blonde curls of her wig.

Doris was on her way to Ladybug's bar on the other side of the elevated tracks. Her purse was full of play heroin. Her hair wasn't her hair, and the heroin wasn't her heroin. It belonged to Mama Sloth.

Fucking Syndicate bitches. Doris wanted to sink them all in the harbor in galoshes of cement. She also wanted to go to Candy Land and climb the Licorice Tower. Doris wanted to do a lot of things.

She paused at a newsstand run by a fat old sea cow with a mustache. She loitered on the sidewalk reading headlines. The wooden toys of Ark had invaded Lawn County and slagged hundreds of tin toys. The ceramic toys of Kiln were expected to mobilize before dark. Taxidermia, Inflatia, and the Baked Goods Section were expected to form an alliance for mutual protection. This would trigger a declaration of war from the mayor of Plush City. Fabulous. Giant monsters weren't enough for him. Now he needed a war. Meanwhile the paper dolls of Drawer were preparing to test their new super-bomb.

"This ain't a library," said the sea cow. Doris took off. She had places to go and people to see.

Doris didn't let the city drag her down. When she felt blue, she went to the movies. When she got home from the movies, she sat alone in her smoky apartment and played her records day and night, just to drown out her thoughts. Drinking coffee. Taking pills. Running errands for the scum of the west side. Some life for a nice little Kewpie doll from the Ohio State Fair.

What she really ought to do was slit her wrists. Do it up right. Get out while the going was good.

The sidewalk went on forever. An evangelist was preaching on the radio. Doris could follow the sermon through people's open windows. The priests said that the grown-ups of the material plane created dolls in their own image. But if that was true, then why did the grown-ups let dolls be used as the mute and paralyzed playthings of *children*. That seemed like truly demonic behavior to Doris.

The priests said that when a good little stuffed toy went to the Burn Pile down there, her soul ascended to the Table Land and was blessed with speech and mobility as a reward for her terrible sufferings down below. Did that make any sense?

What kind of an afterlife *was* this? People died here. What happened to your soul if you died here? Some *second* afterlife? To Doris the whole arrangement looked senseless. But very little made sense to Doris anymore. Except for one thing. One thing made lots and lots of sense.

She could end it all. She could go home right now and take all her pills at once. She could dispose of herself and do everybody a favor.

Unseen cymbals crashed behind the blue silk sky. Cold rain fell like funeral veils. The gingham dog was seen on the flatlands, running hard across the hard-pack. Shreds of ripped fabric hung loose from his shanks. Already he was leaking goose down and snow flurries of white pinfeather followed in his wake. He fled south from the Wiggly Mountains. He was making for the city. Already the calico predator of the mountains had chewed off his fine gingham tail. Now she was giving her prey a lead across the flatlands. That was how the cat operated. She was playful. She made a game of the thing. The dog would be just as gutted by sundown.

The dog's eye stitchings were red, and his ribs showed through his pelt. He'd been hiding in a cave for days, with nothing to eat but bats and centipedes. The cat had flushed him into the open perhaps an hour ago. He was far too exhausted to fight back. Perhaps he'd find a new hiding place in the cardboard city of the small folk.

A crowd of stuffies had gathered on Scissors Bridge. Their binoculars were trained on the Wiggly Mountains. The calico cat was tearing down a gully, covering ground at an incredible rate.

The dog didn't stand a chance. He was only the size of a freight truck, and the cat was bigger than a battleship. She'd run him down, humiliate him, tie him up like a steer in his own yanked-out packing twine, flay his skin, eat his tongue, and then hump his cadaver in the dead of night, while howling to wake the dead. And why not? The dog deserved it. The cat couldn't recall just what he'd *done*, but that wasn't important. He was guilty as sin, and he'd take what was coming to him.

That night the cat would cripple and devour her perpetual playmate, according to the ancient curse that neither monster could break, since neither could remember it. And at midnight Anndy would return to the Table Land with his questions and her impatience. And as usual the god's monstrous pets would try to follow their master's train of thought, as a dog might chase a car. But their answers to Anndy's questions would be stupid, as stupid as stupid could be, as stupid as the moronic celluloid smile on the face of a mute and paralyzed stuffed animal.

So things went in Plush City. On Monday, Wednesday, and Friday, the dog had hunted the cat. On Sunday, Tuesday, and Thursday, the cat had exacted her revenge. Next week the schedule would reverse itself, just as regular as a seesaw or a hobbyhorse or a metronome. Just as regular as the pendulum of the old Dutch clock in the Parlor Behind the Sky.

So nothing would ever change in Plush City, except in the way that a seesaw changes—back and forth, up and down. Which is really no change at all.

LUCY SUSSEX

Frozen Charlottes

Lucy Sussex was born in the South Island of New Zealand, and lives in Australia, where she works as a researcher and writer. She has published widely, with a particular interest in crime and Victoriana. Her fiction has won Ditmar and Aurealis awards.

Her short stories have been collected in My Lady Tongue *and* Sancta. *She has also written three books for younger readers, two for teenagers, and one adult novel,* The Scarlet Rider. *One of the four anthologies she has edited,* She's Fantastical, *was a nominee for the World Fantasy Award. She writes the "Covernotes" column for the* Age *and* West Australian *newspapers. Sussex is also completing a nonfiction book,* Cherchez les Femmes, *on early women crime and detective authors.*

"Frozen Charlottes" was originally published in the Australian anthology Forever Shores.

—E.D.

> We have long forgotten the ritual by which the
> house of our life was erected. But . . . when en-
> emy bombs are taking their toll, what enervated,
> perverse antiquities do they not lay bare in their
> foundations? What things were interred and sac-
> rificed amid magic incantations, what horrible
> cabinet of curiosities lies there below?
> —Walter Benjamin

That night, she thinks: never again. The woman to the left of her, a mere girl, has wept on and off, all afternoon; on the other side are a pair already into baby talk, and not even pregnant yet. She knows what the nurses say privately, to each other: raving bloody loonies, all of them, it's nature's way of preventing hereditary insanity. Sometimes she wonders if she is going mad herself, as the drug-induced depressions hit. No more, she thinks, this is it, now or never, even if that does mean *never* . . . And as the black tide of misery rises within her, squeezing out through her eyelids, she too weeps, but with an edge of relief.

Next day he visits. He takes her hand, doesn't squeeze it, just holds it, in silence, waiting for her to speak. In the end she whispers: "Get me out of here!"

Getting out of the hospital is easy. What is harder, though, is coming home to the big white outer suburban house, and looking out the window at the rows and rows of houses undulating away, their hills hoists blossoming with little white squares, little blue or pink clothes. Nappie Valley, the real estate agents call it. And the glances of fake sympathy hurt as much as the real sympathy, from relatives, and so-called friends. She can't bear, either, anyone so forward as to commiserate with her: leave me alone! In the end she doesn't go out much, creating a comfort zone around her: junk food, daytime TV. Until one day Jerry Springer's topic is *her* topic, too close to home, this home no longer, not to a nuclear family, two parents, one cat, one dog, a little boy and little girl. Not even one child lives here, despite the sunny room upstairs, all filled with nursery things, in their cardboard boxes, never unpacked. A monument to the what-might-have-beens . . .

He comes home to find her flipping through the real estate sections of the Internet. "I'm getting us out of here," she says.

He sits down, ready to listen. She moves from site to site, clicking on buttons.

"Remember when we were the renovators from hell?"

He chuckles, and she knows she is on the right track.

"And we'd talk about *Projects*, wrecker's delights really, but we'd find 'em, buy 'em, do them up, sell 'em . . ."

He says: "I remember: how we never wanted anything beyond six square meters of recycled Baltic Pine floorboards, or a match for the odd antique doorknob. Achievable things . . ."

Before, she thinks, before we decided we had to get real jobs, and with that everything that came with them: the suburban dream home, the pension plans, the desire to perpetuate ourselves . . .

She clicks again.

"So you're looking for a Project," he says.

She nods. "Just getting a feel for it. And then we can call up the old contacts, find which suburbs are about to boom, where you get good tools, or where the wrecking yards are these days."

"We can't go back in time, love," he says after a while.

"I know. But we have to move, move on, and this is one way. And it was fun, remember that? Despite the hammered fingers, the dust and dirt. You felt you were doing something creative, something positive."

He thinks. "I'm sick of driving a desk," he says finally. "You win. We'll give it a go."

Selling the big white house is easy. Selling his business, resigning from what she knows might be the last good job she'll ever have, is harder. But hardest of all is finding the Project, after they have narrowed down their hunt to a suburb where nobody knows them, a forgotten knot of old working-class inner city, stuck between industrial areas, and a rubbish dump about to be reclaimed.

It turns out to be one hell of a Project: a little two-room cottage of stone, with behind it shoddy addition after shoddy addition, on a block of land half solid concrete paving and half weed wilderness.

He says: "It's classified—oldest surviving building in the area. Which saved it from being flattened, at least."

She says nothing.

"I know it doesn't look like much, but you wanted a Project, love . . ."

She takes a deep breath: "It'll do . . ."

They buy a secondhand caravan, to live in during the worst of the renovations, and park it behind the house. The first night, they sit outside in the dark, balmy night, eating pizza and drinking beer. Around them is the concreted backyard, with fruit trees sticking out, above them the expanse of stars, dimmed by city lights.

"Tomorrow we start," he says, looking at the stars.

"Tomorrow," she says, and slips her arm around him. Later, they make love in the caravan, with no consideration for days of the month, charts and temperatures—just because they want to.

The old bluestone is sound on its stone foundations; the rest of the house is another matter, the stumps decaying, the floors pitched every which way. In the lean-to kitchen, water in the sink tilts at an uneasy angle. Each decade or so, something has been added to the house: an 1890s annex, a 1920s kitchen, 1950s bedroom, 1960s bathroom, 1970s brick patio.

"We'll have to demolish and start again," he says. "All except the bluestone."

"History," she says, stroking the blocks of stone. "I should go to the library, the local historical society, see what they know about it."

But in the morning, waking bright and early with the thumps as the skip is delivered, she forgets about research in the fun of getting dirty and sweaty again. In the garden they play tiger in the weed jungle, hunting rubbish for the skip: old tires, half a bicycle, broken bricks, a rusted old barbecue. In one corner, under the weeds, is buried treasure, an old claw-footed bath, which they manhandle out into the center of the backyard, for somewhere to put it. She is tipping a laden wheelbarrow into the skip when an old woman comes past, pushing a shopping trolley. She looks and bursts out laughing, a thin cackle, with little of fun about it.

"You won't catch me, you won't catch me . . . doin' that!"

Crash! The contents of the wheelbarrow hit the bottom of the skip, the noise relieving her feelings at the interjection. When she looks up, the old woman has gone.

The rest of the day passes in a blur of work. When they stop for coffee and sweet biscuits, their hands are so filthy they leave grimy marks on the mugs. Otherwise, though, they are happy as a sand boy and girl. Late in the day, they are ripping up onion skins of moldy carpet, then the lino beneath them, then old urine-yellow newspaper, so brittle with age it flakes in the fingers.

She stops, bending over the exposed floorboards.

"I can hear something. Hush!"

"What?" he says. "I don't hear anything."

"It's like a scratching, as if something's trying to get out." Cocking her head to one side she follows the thread of sound, her Blundstone boots echoing on the newly exposed boards. She tries to tiptoe, to minimize the sound, something hard to do in the boots.

"Watch that floor," he says, as she disappears through the doorway into the 1890s addition. "It's borer central in there."

A creak, a loud crunch, and then a shriek. He rushes in, to find her waist deep in rotten timber.

"Jeez! You all right?"

"Better than the floor," she says. She wrinkles her nose. "It smells like a stray cat lives down here. A tom, too. Maybe that was the sound I heard."

"Room enough for a wine cellar," he says, gauging the space between what is left of the flooring and the cracked, dry clay beneath. It forms a subterranean cave, littered with broken bricks, bottles and rusted cans. He tests a joist, finds it sound. "Here, I'll give you a hand up."

But she is looking at something small but shining whitely in the gloom. She crouches, brushing off a layer of powdered timber from it. Next moment she screams again, not the little bat-squeak of surprise, but the stuff of nightmare, and keeps on screaming.

He's run to the nearest off-license and bought a bottle of cheap brandy. Now he hands her an inch of the liquid in a hastily rinsed coffee mug. She drinks, chokes, drinks again.

"I'm sorry," she finally says. "Did you see it? A little white hand, it looked like, reaching up at me. The size of a fetus in a bottle."

She drains the rest of the cup, stands. "Well, they say you should face your fears." She is, though none too steady on her feet, as they near the gaping hole in the floor.

"Let me do it!" he says, and lowers himself to the ground. He bends down, then lifts his head, eyebrows raised.

"It's just a doll, love. See?"

"Leave it," she says. "Let's call it a day and go get a video."

But in the morning, though she is almost too stiff to move with the unaccustomed exertion, she pulls herself painfully through the house in her pajamas, and into the 1890s section again. Wincing, she lowers herself into the pit.

She hears his footsteps in the next room along.

"Hey! D'you think you could get me something to dig with? Please . . ."

The doll is china, and it has, quite definitely, been buried. The clay is hard as concrete, but she hesitates to use more than a trowel, lest she shatter the china. At the end, she has a blistered palm, but holds a baby doll, molded all in one piece: head, legs, arms and torso. In the bathroom, with its peeling op-art wallpaper, she washes off dirt from the doll in the basin.

"History," she murmurs. "Or herstory, given that a little girl must have played with this. I wonder how old it is."

That wonder sees her dry her hands, get dressed properly, and head off to the big city library. She comes back hours later with a sheaf of photocopies, so eager she starts talking the moment she sees him. Which is on the front doorstep, where he stands broom in hand, sweeping several years of accumulated leaf mold off the veranda.

"It's a type of doll made from 1850 to 1914—so it's the same era as the front sections of the house. They're called Frozen Charlottes, or Frozen Charlies. There was this popular song, called 'Fair Charlotte,' about a girl who went for a sleigh ride in the snow. She had a party dress she wanted to show off, so she refused to wear a blanket to keep herself warm. Nineteen verses later, she comes to a bad end:

"He took her hand into his own,
Oh God! It was cold as stone
He tore her mantle from her brow
On her face the cold stars shone

Then quickly to the lighted hall
Her lifeless form he bore,
Fair Charlotte was a frozen corpse
And her lips spake nevermore."

"Is that it?" he says.

"Yes."

"Charming," he says. "I'm not sure I could have sat still and listened to twenty-one verses of that."

From the street behind she hears the rattle of trolley wheels on pavement, a thin, cold laugh.

"You won't catch me, you won't catch me . . . doing that."

She turns, resolving to be neighborly.

"Surely *you* must sweep your veranda?"

The old woman continues on, not stopping. Over her shoulder she speaks, a parting shot, but a passing truck nearly obliterates the sound. Then she is past.

"Did you catch that?" he says.

"I'm not sure. Did she really say: catch me sweeping the house of horrors?"

"House of mumble was what I heard. Clearly the local weirdo. Okay, so you've been researching. I've been checking out the floors, and I think they'll all have to go. But that's not all: there's another of these freezing Charlies. I just found it, under the floor."

She kneels in front of the bathroom basin, a nail brush in hand, scrubbing dirt off the new doll.

"They're identical," she says.

"Like outa the same mold," he says, glancing over her shoulders.

"They *were* a popular, mass-produced doll. But why bury them?"

"Some little girl had a sadist for a brother, I'd guess."

She lay the dolls on the bath mat to dry.

"Oh, there's a foot missing. I'll see if I can find it."

He leaves her to it, starts taking a sledgehammer to the concrete footpath in the front yard. In the crunching of the hammer, his huffing and puffing, he forgets her, forgets the time. When he looks up it is sunset, and she is standing in the doorway. Even in the dim evening light he can see she is covered in dirt, and deathly white in the face.

"I found more than the missing foot. I found a whole army of dolls, all much the same, all buried. There's more to this than some poor little girl with a nasty older brother. It's like the day of judgment or something, the last trump, and up comes the dead . . ."

"Maybe the house was a doll factory once," he says. "And they had a lot of rejects."

Behind them, from the street, comes a now too-familiar sound, the sound of a shopping trolley. She crunches over the lumps of broken concrete, vaults the gate in her hurry.

"Hey you with the trolley! You know all about this house, you keep laughing at us! So tell us what the joke is, with all the dolls."

The old woman gapes and ducks past, breaking into a shaky run up the street. Her shoes flap, her knee stockings, neatly darned, slip down her skinny shanks. She thinks of tackling, if she knew how to do it, but instead uses her relative youth (elderly primagravida indeed!) to outpace, then confront the fugitive. It isn't hard—the old woman's trolley is laden, and she is panting hard enough to give herself a coronary.

"What is it about all the dolls buried under our house? You know, don't you?"

The old woman halts, slumps over the handles of the trolley and gasps for breath. Finally she speaks.

"I don't know 'bout any dolls. But I do know they dug up every inch of the land there was, and they found nuffin'. Like she said: 'you won't catch me.' And they didn't."

"Who said: 'you won't catch me'?" Apart from *you*, she thinks.

"Old Ma Wynne. Most famous person we ever had from round here. No footie player, no crook ever got her headlines. One of those series killers, they call 'em now. But they never found the bodies, and there must have been dozens of 'em."

Widow Wynne locked her front door and strode down the street, carpet bag in her hand, the cherries in her bonnet nodding with her passage, her long coat flapping in the cool breeze. The coat was black for widowhood, the cherries red, for merriment. Little enough of that around here, though. Three doors down, bailiffs at the door, loading furniture into the van. Empty house beside that, the tenants did a scarper, the rent well in arrears. Three children, their clothes clean even if they are coming out of their boots, dog her footsteps, keeping a safe distance. They're getting thinner, she thinks, their eyes hollow, their fingers like chicken bones in the old German story, Hansel and Gretel. Weren't those children abandoned in the forest by parents who couldn't feed them? Must have been a depression, whenever it was, just like now.

"Witch, witch," she hears behind her, a child's jeering whisper. She whirls round, clawing her hands, and they take to their heels. When she turns, back is the respectable widow and small businesswoman. Things get much worse around here, she thought, your mama and dadda, they'll abandon you . . .

At the train station she buys a return fare to the city, third class, and also a copy of the evening paper. In the classifieds there are her advertisements, each with a post office box number. Business is booming, about the only business that is, it seems. She glances through the rest of the news. "Legislature Debates Foundling Hospital Bill" is the headline. She skims the article quickly, pursing her lips at its conclusion: the bill was defeated "lest it encourage immorality." And whose immorality might that be, honorable sirs? Yours and the housemaid's? You're not the one who'll be sacked without references when you start to show. On the same page is the result of an inquest into a case of overlaying—a mother rolling on her baby when asleep, and smothering it. Third case this week. Drunk, was she? Husband out of work? How many children did she have? Not guilty . . . just like Hansel and Gretel's parents. At least they only abandoned their babes in the wood.

She folds the paper and devotes the rest of the ride to eyeing the scenery. The train passes through rows of mean little suburbs, their back lanes full of washing and brats. The pleasures of the poor, she thinks. Not a penny in the house but rich in children. We got steam trains, we got telegraph, but you'd think some know-it-all would come up with some way of giving the womenfolk a rest . . . and put me out of business, she thinks.

Several stops before the city, she alights, checking the address on an envelope before striding through sidestreets. She moves quickly, for this is slumland, dangerous for anyone who has the faintest whiff of prosperity. The single-fronted little terrace might have housed a small family once, but now it has been let, and sublet, to boarders. At the end of the passage is a room, and her client. Irish accent, hurt, bewildered eyes, pretty enough, if you liked carrot-tops.

She wastes no time. "You've got the money?"

The girl laboriously counts it out, as if expressing drops of her own blood, or milk. "All ready, then?"

The girl nods, her eyes filling. All in one movement she turns and bends, lifting from the mean little iron bed a limp bundle, in baby clothes. Mrs. Wynne bends over it, seeing the infant is clean, wrapped in a shawl, and on its lips the unmistakable smell, opiates and alcohol, laudanum, the mother's friend.

"Dear little thing," she says.

In a moment the transaction is over. Mrs. Wynne walks out the front door, leaving behind her weeping client, in her carpet bag the sleeping, drugged baby.

She doesn't look like a monster . . .

"She doesn't look like a monster," he says. They have spent all morning in the archival section of the library, reels of microfilm beside them, ancient newspaper history scrolling before their eyes. Now they sit at a communal table, in front of them microfilm photocopies.

The topmost is from a weekly paper of a century ago, showing a line engraving of their house, circa 1890s, the front yard full of policemen, digging. On the same page is another engraving, a middle-aged woman, in her black bonnet a nodding spray of cherries.

"'A kind face, seemed very fond of children,' that's what Witness A said. After handing over her baby and paying money to Mrs. Wynne's adoption agency. Which consisted of various P.O. boxes and one woman with a carpet bag."

"Who was a mass murderer. 'Massacre of the innocents' 'Out-heroding Herod,'" he says, reading from another photocopy. "And I thought media frenzy was a modern thing."

"If she was a mass murderer. Remember, she was acquitted for lack of evidence."

"Then what did she do with the babies?"

The question hangs in the air. He extracts a cartoon showing a witchlike crone, cherries in her hat, throwing an infant in the harbor.

"Look at these papers," she says. "Birth notices, welcoming fifth, sixth children. Overlaying, whatever that was. Babies found on church doorsteps. The past is a different country."

"I wouldn't like to have lived there," he says.

"Even though we could have adopted twelve kids or more if we wanted, nobody wanting illegitimate babies, especially with the over-supply?"

"Let's go," he said. "I'm not sure I can take much more of this."

Back at the house, she wanders through the 1890s rooms, trying to imagine a black coat, a hat with cherries. Finally she crawls under the house again, unearthing more dolls. He trundles in the wheelbarrow, and they fill it with the finds. When the barrow is laden, he takes it out to the yard. It seems a sacrilege, after what they know, to just dump the dolls on the brick or concrete, so he lines the claw-footed bath with an old blanket, and carefully lays the dolls on top. Then he returns to help her with the dig.

Hours later, utterly exhausted and filthy, they sit on the back doorstep, sharing sips from the bottle of brandy. Moonlight shines down on them, and on the bath, filled with little white forms, the heads turned towards them, the little dark painted eyes watchful. It is very still, hardly any traffic, but the empty air in front of them teems with movement, as if filled with moths glimpsed only from the corner of the eye, that slip out of sight if you try and look at them directly.

"Do you see?" she whispers.

"Not—see," he whispers back.

The contents of the bath seethe, sending dolls falling out onto the concrete. They break, a plaintive plink like drops of rain, then a shower, as they continue to tumble. The remaining dolls in the bath have transmogrified into chubby toddlers, who totter on the rim of the bath, fall to join their fellows. Child-dolls, taller and thinner, play in the bath, tussle, fight, and also topple. A group of boy dolls play soldiers, marching over their fellows, growing taller and thinner, into grown doll-men, short back and sides, painted moustaches. They form a battalion, then, as if to a "Hup, one, two, three!" march in formation over the side of the bath, crashing and breaking. A pause, then two doll-nurses appear over the side of the bath, carrying a stretcher, with a sick doll, its arms flopping helplessly. They toss it over the side, return to the writhing pile for another patient, then a third. Other nurses appear to help in the grisly task, with their own stretchers and sick. They finish, then throw themselves after their patients. A pause, then a doll dressed flapper-style appears over the side of the bath, sexily posing as she walks. Another doll approaches, pushes her off . . .

She closes her eyes, hides her head in his shoulder, unable to watch anymore. She hears, though, the continual crash of breaking china.

Finally the noise painfully stops. Around them it is still now, utterly quiet, even in the center of the city. She opens her eyes. Around the bath is a mass of broken china. They approach, stare into the depths, to see movement.

He gets the torch from the kitchen. They see one doll left, an old woman—except that nobody has ever made an old woman doll. She claws at the side of the bath, the wool of the blanket, trying to get out. Finally she collapses in a heap, stills. Before their eyes the doll breaks into pieces as if ground under a heel.

He turns off the torch. She reaches out to the pile of broken dolls, feels the china faintly warm and gritty under her fingers. Some of the dolls have been reduced to powder, their constituting earth.

" 'Dead and turned to clay,' " he says. "That's a line from somewhere."

"And I also remember from somewhere about bone china. That's china with bone ash mixed in with it."

She shivers.

He says: "I think it was the lives they would have led. Infant mortality was high at the time—that was the first wave. Childhood diseases, diphtheria, whooping cough, typhoid did the rest. Then we got 1914, followed by the influenza epidemic . . . and so on and so on. One made it to old age, it looks like."

"If they'd lived they'd all be dead by now."

"To this end we must all come, love, though we try and hide from it, by perpetuating ourselves, busying ourselves with Projects."

"Hush," she says, and takes his hand. Hand in hand they stand before the mass of china and clay dust, pondering their lives and those of these poor broken others, pondering the what-might-have-beens.

CHINA MIÉVILLE

Reports of Certain Events in London

China Miéville was born in 1972. His novels include Perdido Street Station, *winner of the Arthur C. Clarke and British Fantasy awards;* The Scar, *winner of the British Fantasy award; and* Iron Council. *His nonfiction includes* "Between Equal Rights," *a study of international law. He lives and works in London.*

"Reports of Certain Events in London," reprinted from Miéville's story collection Looking for Jake: Stories, *was first published in McSweeney's second literacy–fund-raising anthology,* McSweeney's Enchanted Chamber of Astonishing Stories.

—K.L. & G.G.

On the twenty-seventh of November 2000, a package was delivered to my house. This happens all the time—since becoming a professional writer the amount of mail I get has increased enormously. The flap of the envelope had been torn open a strip, allowing someone to look inside. This also isn't unusual: because, I think, of my political life (I am a varyingly active member of a left-wing group, and once stood in an election for the Socialist Alliance), I regularly find, to my continuing outrage, that my mail has been peered into.

I mention this to explain why it was that I opened something not addressed to me. I, China Miéville, live on ——ley Road. This package was addressed to a Charles Melville, of the same house number, ——ford Road. No postcode was given, and it had found its way, slowly, to me. Seeing a large packet torn half-open by some cavalier spy, I simply assumed it was mine and opened it.

It took me a good few minutes to realize my mistake: the covering note contained no greeting by name to alert me. I read it along with the first few of the enclosed papers with growing bewilderment, convinced (absurd as this must sound) that this was to do with some project or other I had got involved with and then forgotten. When finally I looked again at the name on the envelope, I was wholly surprised.

That was the point at which I was morally culpable, rather than simply foolish. By then I was too fascinated by what I had read to stop.

I've reproduced the content of the papers below, with explanatory notes. Unless otherwise stated they're photocopies, some stapled together, some attached with paper clips, many with pages missing. I've tried to keep them in the order they came in; they are not always chronological. Before I had a sense of what was in front of me, I was casual about how I put the papers down. I can't vouch that this was how they were originally organized.

{Cover note. This is written on a postcard, in a dark blue ink, a cursive hand. The photograph is of a wet kitten emerging from a sink full of water and suds. The kitten wears a comedic expression of anxiety.}

Where are you? Here as requested. What do you want this for anyway? I scribbled thoughts on some. Can't find half the stuff, I don't think anyone's noticed me rummaging through the archives, and I managed to get into your old place for the rest (thank God you file), but come to next meeting. You can get people on your side but box clever. In haste. Are you taking sides? Talk soon. Will you get this? *Come to next meeting.* More as I find it.

{This page was originally produced on an old manual typewriter.}

BWVF Meeting, 6 September 1976
Agenda.
    1. Minutes of the last meeting.
    2. Nomenclature.
    3. Funds.
    4. Research notes.
    5. Field reports.
    6. AOB.

1. Last minutes:
Motion to approve JH, Second FR. Vote: unanimous.

2. Nomenclature:
FR proposes namechange. "BWVF" dated. CT reminds FR of tradition. FR insists "BWVF" exclusive, proposes "S (Society) WVF" or "G (Gathering) WVF." CT remonstrates. EN suggests "C (Coven) WVF," to laughter. Meeting growing impatient. FR moves to vote on change, DY seconds. Vote: 4 for, 13 against. Motion denied.

{Someone has added by hand "Again! Silly Cow."*}*

3. Funds/Treasury report.
EN reports this quarter several payments made, totalling £—[*The sum is effaced with black ink.*]. Agreed to keep this up-to-date to avoid repeat of Gouldy-Statten debacle. Subscriptions are mostly current and with

{This is the end of a page and the last I have of these minutes.}

{The next piece is a single sheet that looks word-processed.}

1 September 1992
MEMO

Members are kindly asked to show more care when handling items in the collection. Standards have become unacceptably lax. Despite their vigilant presence, curators have reported various soilings, including: fingerprints on recovered wood and glass; ink spots on cornices; caliper marks on guttering and ironwork; waxy residue on keys.

Of course, research necessitates handling, but if members cannot respect these unique items conditions of access may have to become even more stringent.

Before entering, remember:

• Be careful with your instruments.
• Always wash your hands.

{The next page is numbered "2" and begins halfway through a paragraph. Luckily it contains a header.}

BWVF Papers, No. 223. July 1981.

uncertain, but there is little reason to doubt his veracity. Both specimens tested exactly as one would expect for VD, suggesting no difference between VD and VF at even a molecular level. Any distinction must presumably be at the level of gross morphology, which defies our attempts at comparison, or of a noncorporeal essence thus far beyond our capacity to measure.

Whatever the reality, the fact that the two specimens of VF mortar can be added to the BWVF collection is cause for celebration.

This research should be ready to present by the end of this year.

Report on Work in Progress: VF and Hermeneutics
by B. Bath

Problems of knowledge and the problematic of *knowing*. Considerations of VF as urban scripture. Kabbala considered as interpretive model. Investigation of VF as patterns of interference. Research currently ongoing, ETA of finished article uncertain.

Report on Work in Progress: Recent changes in VF Behavior
by E. Nugen

Tracking the movements of VF is notoriously difficult. [*Inserted here is a scrawl—"No bloody kidding. What do you think we're all bloody doing here?"*] Reconstructing these patterns over the *longue durée* [*the accent is added by hand*] is perforce a matter of plumbing a historical record that is, by its nature and definitionally, partial, anecdotal and uncertain. As most of my readers know, it has long been my aim to extract from the annals of our society evidence for long-term cycles (see Working Paper 19, "Once More on the Statten Curve"), an aim on which I have not been entirely unsuccessful.

I have collated the evidence from the major verified London sightings of the last three decades (two of those sightings my own) and can conclusively state that the time between VF arrival at and departure from a locus has decreased by a factor of 0.7. VF are moving more quickly.

In addition, tracking their movements after each appearance has become

more complicated and (even) less certain. In 1940, application of the De-
schaine Matrix with regard to a given VF's arrival time and duration on-site
would result in a 23 percent chance of predicting reappearance parameters
(within two months and two miles): today that same process nets only a 16 percent chance. VF are less predictable than they have ever been (barring, perhaps,
the Lost Decade of 1876–86).

The shift in this behavior is not linear but punctuated, sudden bursts of
change over the years: once between 1952 and '53, again in late 1961, again in
'72 and '76. The causes and consequences are not yet known. Each of these piv-
otal moments has resulted in an increased pace of change. The anecdotal evidence we have all heard, that VF have recently become more skittish and
agitated, appears to be correct.

I intend to present this work in full within eighteen months. I wish to thank
CM for help with the research. [*This CM is presumably Charles Melville, to
whom the package was addressed. Clipped to the BWVF papers is this handwritten note*: Yes, Edgar is a pompous arse but he is on to something big.]

{*What is it Edgar N. is on to? Of course I wondered, and still wonder, though now I
think perhaps I know.*}

{*Then there is a document unlike the others so far. It is a booklet a few pages long. It
was when I started to read this that I stopped, frowned, looked again at the envelope,
realized my inadvertent intrusion, and decided almost instantly that I would not stop
reading. "Decided" doesn't really get the sense of the urgency with which I continued,
as if I had no choice. But then if I say that, I absolve myself of wrongdoing, which I
won't do, so let's say I "decided," though I'm unsure that I did. In any case, I continued reading. This document is printed on both sides like a flyer. The first sentence below is in large red font, and constitutes the booklet's front cover.*}

Urgent: Report of a Sighting.
Principal witness: FR. Secondary: EN.
On Thursday, 11 February, 1988, so far as it is possible to tell between 3:00 A.M.
and 5:17 A.M., a little way south of Plumstead High Street SE18, Varmin Way occurred.

Even somewhat foreshortened from its last known appearance (Battersea
1983—see the VF Concordance), Varmin Way is in a buckled configuration due to
the constraints of space. One end adjoins Purrett Road between numbers 44 and
46, approximately forty feet north of Saunders Road: Varmin Way then appears to
describe a tight S-curve, emerging halfway up Rippolson Road between numbers
30 and 32 (see attached map). [*There is no map.*]

Two previously terraced dwellings on each of the intersected streets have now
been separated by Varmin Way. One on Rippolson is deserted: surreptitious en-
quiries have been made to inhabitants of each of the others, but none have remarked with anything other than indifference to the newcomer. Eg: In response to
FR's query of one man if he knew the name of "that alley," he glanced at the street
now abutting his house, shrugged and told her he was "buggered" if he knew. This
response is of course typical of VF occurrence environs (See B. Harman, "On the
Nonnoticing," BWVF Working Papers no. 5.)

A partial exception is one thirty-five-year-old Purrett Road man, resident in the brick dwelling newly on Varmin Way's north bank. Observed on his way toward Saunders Road, crossing Varmin Way he tripped on the new curb. He looked down at the asphalt and up at brick corners of the junction, paced back and forward five times with a quizzical expression, peering down the street's length, without entering it, before continuing on his journey, looking back twice.

{This is the end of the middle page of the leaflet. Folded and inserted inside is a hand-written letter. I have therefore decided to reproduce it here in the middle of the leaflet text. It reads:}

Charles,

In haste. So sorry I could not reach you sooner—obviously phone not an option. I told you I could work this out: Fiona was only on-site because of me, but I modestly listed her as principal for politics' sake. Charles, we're about to go in and I'm telling you even from where I'm standing I can see the evidence; this is the real thing. Next time, next time. Or get down here! I'm sending this first class (of course!) so when you get it rush down here. But you know Varmin Way's reputation—it's restless, will probably be gone. But come find me! I'll be here at least.

Edgar

{At the end of this note is appended, in the same handwriting as that of the package's introductory note: What a bastard! I take it this was when you and he stopped seeing eye-to-eye? Why did he cut you out like that, and why so coyly? *The leaflet then continues:}*

Initial investigation shows that the new Varmin Way–overlooking walls of the houses now separated on Purrett Road are flat concrete. Those of Rippolson Road, though, are of similar brick to their fronts, bearing the usual sigil of the VF's identity, and are broken by small windows at the very top, through the net curtains of which nothing can be seen. (See "On Neomural Variety," by H. Burke, WBVF Working Papers no. 8.)

Those innards of Varmin Way which can be seen from its adjoining streets bear all the usual signs of VF morphology (are, in other words, apparently unremarkable), and are in accordance with earlier documented descriptions of the subject. In this occurrence, it being short, FR and EN were able to conduct the Bowery Resonance Experiment, stationing themselves at either end of the VF and shouting to each other down its lengths (until forced to stop by externalities). [*Here in Edgar's hand has been inserted,* "Some local thuggee threatening to do me in if I didn't shut up!"] Each could clearly hear the other, past the kinks in this configuration of Varmin Way.

More experiments are to follow.

{When I reached this point I was trembling. I had to stop, leave the room, drink some water, force myself to breathe slowly. I'm tempted to add more about this, about the sudden and threatened speculations these documents raised in me, but I think I should stay out of it.

Immediately after the report of the sighting was another, similarly produced pamphlet.}

Urgent—Report of an Aborted Investigation.
Present: FR, EN, BH. [*Added here is another new comment in Charles's nameless contact's hand. It reads: "Dread to think how gutted you were to be replaced by Bryn as new favorite. What exactly did you do to get Edgar so pissed off?"*]

At 11:20 P.M. on Saturday, 13 February, 1988, from its end on Rippolson Road, an initial examination was made of Varmin Way. Photographs were taken establishing the VF's identity (figure 1). [*Figure 1 is a surprisingly good-quality reproduction of a shot showing a street sign by a wall, standing at leg height on two little metal or wooden posts. The image is at a peculiar angle, which I think is the result of the photograph not being taken straight on, but from Rippolson Road, beyond. In an unusual old serif font, the sign reads* varmin way.]

As the party prepared for the expedition, certain events took place or were insinuated which led to a postponement and quick regrouping at a late-night café on Plumstead High Street. [*What were those "certain events"? The pointed imprecision suggested to me something deliberately not committed to paper, something that the readers of this report, or perhaps a subgroup of them, would understand. These writings are a strange mix of the scientifically exact and the imprecise—even the failure to specify the café is surprising. But it is the baleful vagueness of the certain events that will not stop worrying at me.*] When the group returned to Rippolson Road at 11:53 P.M., to their great frustration, Varmin Way had unoccurred.

{Two monochrome pictures end the piece. They have no explanatory notes or legend. They are both taken in daylight. On the left is a photograph of two houses, on either side of a small street of low century-old houses which curves sharply to the right, it looks like, quickly unclear with distance. The right-hand picture is the two façades again, but this time the houses—recognizably the same from a window's crack, from a smear of paint below a sash, from the scrawny front gardens and the distinct unkempt buddleia bush—are closed up together. They are no longer semi-detached. There is no street between them.}

*{So.
I stopped for a bit. I had to stop. And then I had to read on again.}*

{A single sheet of paper. Typewritten again apart from the name, now on an electronic machine.}

Could you see it, Charles? The damage, halfway down Varmin Way? It's there; it's visible in the picture in that report. [*This must mean the picture on the left. I stared at it hard, with the naked eye and through a magnifying glass. I couldn't make out anything.*] It's like the slates from Scry Pass, the ones I showed you in the collection. You could see it in the striae and the marks, even if none of the bloody curators did. Varmin Way wasn't just passing through; it was *resting*, it was *recovering*, it had been attacked. I am right.

Edgar

{I kept reading.}

{Though it's not signed, judging by the font, what follows are a couple of pages of another typed letter from Edgar.}

earliest occurrence I can find of it is in the early 1700s (you'll hear 1790 or '91 or something—nonsense, that's just the official position based on the archives—this one isn't verified, but believe me, it's correct). Only a handful of years after the Glorious Revolution we find Antonia Chesterfield referring in her diaries to "a right rat of a street, ascamper betwixt Waterloo and the Mall, a veritable Vermin, in name as well as kind. Beware—Touch a rat and he will bite, as others have found, of our own and of the Vermin's vagrant tribe." That's a reference to Varmin Way— Mrs. Chesterfield was in the brotherhood's precursor (and you'd not have heard her complaining about that name either—Fiona, take note!).

You see what she's getting at, and I think she was the first. I don't know, Charles, correlation is so terribly hard, but look at some of the other candidates. Shuck Road; Caul Street; Stang Street; Teratologue Avenue (this last I think is fairly voracious); et al. So far as I can work it out, Varmin Way and Stang Street were highly antagonistic at that stage, but now they're almost certainly noncombative. No surprise: Sole Den Road is the big enemy these days—remember 1987?

Incidentally, talking of that first Varmin occurrence, did you ever read all the early cryptolit I sent you?)

> The Clerk entered into a Snickelway
> That then was gone again by close of day

Fourteenth century, imagine. I'll bet you a pound there are letters from disgruntled Britannic procurators complaining about errant alleyways around the Temple of Mithras. But there's not much discussion of the hostilities until Mrs. Chesterfield.

Anyway, you see my point. It's the only way one can make sense of it all, of all this that I've been going on about for so long. The Viae are fighting, and I think they always have.

And there's no idiot nationalism here either, as

{And here is the end of the page. And there is another message added, clearly referring to this letter, from CM's nameless interlocutor. "I believe it," he says, or she says, but I think of it as a man's handwriting, though that's a problematic assumption. "It took me a while, but I believe Edgar's bellum theory. But I know you, Charles, 'pure research' be buggered as far as you're concerned. I know what Edgar's doing, but I cannot see where you are going with this."}

Urgent—Report of a Traveler
Wednesday, 17 June, 1992

We are receiving repeated reports, which we are attempting to verify, of an international visit. Somewhere between Willesden Green and Dollis Hill (details are unclear), Ulica Nerwowosc has arrived. This visitor from Krakow has been characterized by our comrades in the Kolektyw as a mercurial mediaeval alleyway, very difficult to predict. Though it has proved impossible to photograph, initial reports correlate with the Kolektyw's description of the Via. Efforts are ongoing to capture an image of this elusive newcomer, and even to plan a Walk, if the risks are not too great.

No London street has sojourned elsewhere for some time (perhaps not unfortunate—a visit from Bunker Crescent was, notoriously, responsible for the schism in the BWVF Chicago Chapter in 1956), but the last ten years have seen six other documented visitations to London from foreign Viae Ferae. *See table.*

DATES	VISITOR	USUAL RESIDENCE	NOTES
6/9/82– 8/9/82	Rue de la Fascination	Paris	Spent three days in Neasden, motionless from arrival to departure, jutting south of Prout Grove NW10.
3/1/84– 4/1/84	West Fifth Street	New York	Appeared restless, settling for only up to two hours at a time, moving among various locations in Camberwell and Highgate.
11/2/84	Heulstrasse	Berlin	A relatively wide thoroughfare, the empty shopfronts of Heulstrasse cut north of the East London Crematorium in Bow for half a day, relocating late that night to Sydenham, and moving for three hours in backstreets, always just evading investigators.
22/10/87– 24/10/87	Unthinker Road	Glasgow	This tiny cobbled lane, seemingly only a chance gap between the backs of houses, occurred on the Thursday morning jutting off Old Compton Street W1, spent a day occurring with stealthy movements farther and farther into Soho, unoccurred on the Friday, recurring on Saturday,

			only to cut sharply south toward Piccadilly Circus and disappear.
15/4/90?	Boulevard de la Gare Intrinsèque	Paris	Uniquely, this Via Fera was not witnessed by an investigator, but by a rare noticing civilian whose enquiries about a French-named street of impressive dimensions and architecture in the heart of Catford came to the brotherhood's attention.
29/11/91– 1/12/91	Chup Shawpno Lane	Calcutta	The pale clay of C. S. Lane, its hard earth road cut by tram tracks, were exhaustively documented by TY and FD during its meanderings through Camden and Kentish Town.

{There is a thick card receipt, stamped with some obscure sign, its left-hand columns rendered in crude typeface, those on the right filled out in black ink.}

BWVF COLLECTION.

DATE: 7/8/1992
NAME: C. Melville
CURATOR PRESENT: G. Benedict
REQUESTED:
    Item 117: a half slate recovered from Scry Pass, 7/11/1958.
    Item 34: a splinter of glass recovered from Caul Street, 8/2/1986.
    Item 67: an iron ring and key recovered from Stang Street, 6/5/1936.

{This next letter is on headed paper, beautifully printed.}

Société pour l'étude des rues sauvages
20 June 1992

Dear Mr. Melville,

Thank you for your message and congratulations for have this visitor. We in Paris were fortunate to have this pretty Polish street rest with us in 1988 but I did not see it.

I confirm that you are correct. Boulevard de la Gare Intrinsèque and the Rue de la Fascination have both stories about them. We call him le jockey, a man who is supposed to live on streets like these and to make them move for him, but these are only stories for the children. There are no people on these *rues sauvages*, in Paris, and I think there are none in London that time, like no one knows why your Importune Avenue moved around the Arc de la Défence twelve years ago.

Yours truly,
Claudette Santier

{There is a handwritten letter.}

My Dear Charles,

I'm quite aware that you feel ill-used. I apologize for that. There is no point, I think, rehearsing our disagreements, let alone the unpleasant contretemps they have led to. I cannot see that you are going anywhere with these investigations, though, and I simply do not have enough years left to indulge your ideas, nor enough courage (were I younger . . . Ah, but were I younger what would I *not* do?).

I have performed three Walks in my time, and have seen the evidence of the wounds the Viae leave on each other. I have tracked the combatants and shifting loyalties. Where, in contrast, is the evidence behind your claims? Why, on the basis of your intuition, should anyone discard the cautions that may have kept us *alive*? It is not as if what we do is safe, Charles. There are reasons for the strictures you are so keen to overturn.

Of course, yes, I have heard all the stories that you have: of the streets that occur with lights ashine and men at home! of the antique costermongers' cries still heard over the walls of Dandle Way! of the street riders! I do not say I don't believe them, any more than I don't—or do—believe the stories that Potash Street and Luckless Road courted and mated and that that's how Varmin Way was born, or the stories of where the Viae Ferae go when they unoccur. I have no way of judging. This mythic company of inhabitants and street tamers may be true, but so long as it is also a myth, you have nothing. I am content to observe, Charles, not to become involved.

Good God, who knows what the agenda of the streets might be? Would you really, would you *really*, Charles, risk attempting ingress? Even if you could? After everything you've read and heard? Would you risk taking sides?

Regretfully and fondly,
Edgar

{This is another handwritten note. I think it is in Edgar's hand, but it is hard to be sure.}

Saturday, 27 November, 1999
Varmin Way's back.

{We are near the end of the papers now. What came out of the package next looks like one of the pamphlet-style reports of sightings. It is marked with a black band in one corner of the front cover.}

Urgent—Report of a Walk
Walkers: FR, EN, BH (author)

At 11:20 P.M. on Sunday, 28 November, 1999, a walk was made the length of Varmin Way. As well as its tragic conclusion, most members will be aware of the extraordinary circumstances surrounding this investigation—since records began, there is no evidence in the archives of a Via Fera returning to the site of an earlier occurrence. Varmin Way's reappearance, then, at precisely the same location in Plumstead, between Purrett and Rippolson roads, as that it inhabited in February 1988, was profoundly shocking, and necessitated this perhaps too quickly planned Walk.

FR operated as base, remaining stationed on Rippolson Road (the front yard of the still-deserted number 32 acting as camp). Carrying toolbags and wearing council overalls over their harnesses and belay kits, BH and EN set out. Their safety rope was attached to a fence post close to FR. The walkers remained in contact with FR throughout their three-hour journey, by radio.

In this occurrence of Varmin Way, the street is a little more than a hundred meters long. [*An amendment here: "Can you imagine Edgar going metric? What kind of a homage is this?"*] We proceeded slowly. [*Here another insertion: "Ugh. Change of person." By now I was increasingly irritated with these interruptions. I never felt I could ignore them, but they broke the flow of my reading. There was something vaguely passive-aggressive in their cheer, and I felt as if Charles Melville would have been similarly angered by them. In an effort to retain the flow I'll start this sentence again.*]

We proceeded slowly. We walked along the unpainted tar in the middle of Varmin Way, equidistant between the street lamps. These lamps are indistinguishable from those in the neighboring streets. There are houses to either side, all of them with all their windows unlit, looking like low workers' cottages of Victorian vintage (though the earliest documented reports of Varmin Way date from 1792—this apparent aging of form gives credence.

{*To my intense frustration, several pages are missing, and this is where the report therefore ends. There are, however, several photographs in an envelope, stuffed in among the pages. There are four. They are dreadful shots, taken with a flash too close or too far, so that their subject is either effaced by light or peering out from a cowl of dark. Nonetheless they can just be made out.*

The first is a wall of crumbling brick, the mortar fallen away in scabs. Askew across the print, taken from above, is a street sign. VARMIN WAY, it says, in an antiquated iron font. Written in Biro on the photograph's back is: "The Sigil."

The second is a shot along the length of the street. Almost nothing is visible in this, except perspective lines sketched in dark on dark. None of the houses has a front garden: their doors open directly onto the pavement. They are implacably closed, whether for centuries or only moments it is, of course, impossible to tell. The lack of a no-man's-land between house and walker makes the doors loom. Written on the back of this image is: "The Way."

The third is of the front of one of the houses. It is damaged. Its dark windows are broken, its brick stained, crumbling where the roof is fallen in. On the back is written: "The Wound."

The last picture is of an end of rope and a climbing buckle, held in a young man's hands. The rope is frayed and splayed: the metal clip bent in a strange corkscrew. On the back of the photograph is nothing.}

{*And then comes the last piece in the envelope. It is undated. It is in a different hand from the others.*}

What did you do? How did you do it? What did you do, you bastard?

I saw what happened. Edgar was right, I saw where Varmin Way had been hurt. But you know that, don't you?

What did you do to Varmin Way to make it do that? What did you do to Edgar?

Do you think you'll get away with it?

That was everything. When I'd finished, I was frantic to find Charles Melville.

I think the ban on telephone conversations must extend to e-mail and Web pages. I searched online, of course, for BWVF, "wild streets," "feral streets," "Viae Ferae," and so on. I got nothing. BWVF got references to cars or technical parts. I tried "Brotherhood of Witnesses to/Watchers of the Viae Ferae" without any luck. "Wild streets" of course got thousands: articles about New Orleans Mardi Gras, hard-boiled ramblings, references to an old computer game and an article about the Cold War. Nothing relevant.

I visited each of the sites described in the scraps of literature, the places where all the occurrences occurred. For several weekends I wandered in scraggy arse-end streets in north or south London, or sometimes in sedate avenues, even once (following Unthinker Road) walking through the centre of Soho. Inevitably, I suppose, I kept returning to Plumstead.

I would hold the before and after pictures up and look at the same houses of Rippolson Road, all closed up, an unbroken terrace.

Why did I not repackage all this stuff and send it on to Charles Melville, or take it to his house in person? The envelope wrongly sent to ——ley Road was addressed to ——ford Road. But there is no ——ford Road in London. I have no idea how to find Charles.

The other reason I hesitated was that Charles had begun to frighten me.

The first few times I went walking, took photos secretively, I still thought as if I were witnessing some Oedipal drama. Reading and rereading the material, though, I realized that what Charles had done to Edgar was not the most important thing here. What was important was how he had done it.

I have eaten and drunk at all the cafés on Plumstead High Street. Most are unremarkable, one or two are extremely bad, one or two very good. In each establishment I asked, after finishing my tea, whether the owner knew anyone called Charles Melville. I asked if they'd mind me putting up a little notice I'd written.

"Looking for CM," it read. "I've some documents you mislaid—maps of the area, etc. Complicated streets! Please contact:" and then an anonymous e-mail address I'd set up. I heard nothing.

I'm finding it hard to work. These days I am very conscious of corners. I fix my eyes on an edge of brick (or concrete or stone), where another road meets the one I'm walking, and I try to remember if I've ever noticed it before. I look up suddenly as I pass, to catch out anything hurriedly occurring. I keep seeing furtive motions and snapping up my head at only a tree in the wind or an opened window. My anxiety—perhaps I should honestly call it foreboding—remains.

And if I ever did see anything more, what could I do? Probably we're irrelevant to them. Most of us. Their motivations are unimaginable, as opaque as brickwork sphinxes'. If they consider us at all, I doubt they care what's in our interests: I think it's that indifference that breeds these fears I cannot calm, and makes me wonder what Charles has done.

I say I heard nothing, after I put up my posters. That's not quite accurate. In fact, on the fourth of April 2001, five months after that first package, a letter arrived for Charles Melville. Of course, I opened it immediately.

It was one page, handwritten, undated. I am looking at it now. It reads:

Dear Charles,
 Where are you, Charles?
 I don't know if you know by now—I suspect you do—that you've been excommunicated. No one's saying that you're responsible for what happened to Edgar—no one can say that; it would be to admit far too much about what you've been doing—so they've got you on nonpayment of subscriptions. Ridiculous, I know.
 I believe you've done it. I never thought you could—I never thought anyone could. Are there others there? Are you alone?
 Please, if ever you can, tell me. I want to know.
Your friend.

It was not the content of this letter but the envelope that so upset me. The letter, stamped and postmarked and delivered to my house, was addressed to "Charles Melville, Varmin Way."

This time, it's hard to pretend the delivery is coincidence. Either the Royal Mail is showing unprecedented consistency in misdirection, or I am being targeted. And if the latter, I do not know by whom or what: by pranksters, the witnesses, their renegade or their subjects. I am at the mercy of the senders, whether the letter came to me hand-delivered or by stranger ways.

That is why I have published this material. I have no idea what my correspondents want from me. Maybe this is a test, and I've failed: maybe I was about to get a tap on the shoulder and a whispered invitation to join, maybe all this is the newcomer's manual, but I don't think so. I don't know why I've been shown these things, what part I am of another's plan, and that makes me afraid. So as an unwilling party to secrets, I want to disseminate them as widely as I can. I want to protect myself, and this is the only way I can think to do so. (The other possibility, that this was what I was required to do, hasn't passed me by.)

I can't say he owes me an explanation for all this, but I'd like a chance to persuade Charles Melville that I deserve one. I have his documents—if there is anyone reading this who knows how I can reach him, to return them, please let me know. You can contact me through the publisher of this book.

As I say, there is no ——ford Road in London. I have visited all the other alternatives. I have knocked at the relevant number in ——fast and ——land and ——nail Streets, and ——ner and ——hold Roads, and ——den Close, and a few even less likely. No one has heard of Charles Melville. In fact, number such-and-such ——fast Street isn't there anymore: it's been demolished; the street is being reshaped. That got me thinking. You can believe that got me thinking.

"What's happening to ——fast Street?" I wondered. "Where's it going?"

I can't know whether Charles Melville has broken Varmin Way, has tamed it, is riding it like a bronco through the city and beyond. I can't know if he's taken sides, is intervening in the unending savage war between the wild streets of London. Perhaps he and Edgar were wrong, perhaps there's no such fight, and the Viae Ferae are peaceful nomads, and Charles has just got tired and gone away. Perhaps there are no such untamed roads.

There's no way of knowing. Nonetheless I find myself thinking, wondering what's happening round that corner, and that one. At the bottom of my street, of ——ley Road, there are some works going on. Men in hard hats and scaffolding are finishing the job time started of removing tumbledown walls, of sprucing up some little lane so small as to be nameless, nothing but a cat's run full of rubbish and the smell of piss. They're reshaping it, is what it looks like. I think they're going to demolish an abandoned house and widen the alleyway.

We are in new times. Perhaps the Viae Ferae have grown clever, and stealthy. Maybe this is how they will occur now, sneaking in plain sight, arriving not suddenly but so slowly, ushered in by us, armored in girders, pelted in new cement and paving. I think on the idea that Charles Melville is sending Varmin Way to come for me, and that it will creep up on me with a growl of mixers and drills. I think on another idea that this is not an occurrence but an unoccurrence, that Charles has woken ——ley Road, my home, out of its domesticity, and that it is yawning, and that soon it will shake itself off like a fox and sniff the air and go wherever the feral streets go when they are not resting, I and my neighbors tossed on its back like fleas, and that in some months' time the main street it abuts will suddenly be seamless between the Irish bookie and the funeral parlor, and that ——ley Road will be savaged by and savaging Sole Den Road, breaking its windows and walls and being broken in turn and coming back sometimes to rest.

JEAN ESTEVE

House of Ice

Jean Esteve, a poet and painter, lives on the Oregon Coast. Her poem "I Will Be Kind" appeared in Square Lake.
  The poem "House of Ice" was first published in The Harvard Review.
  —*K.L. & G.G.*

Although warned by the wolf as well as the goose
not to make my home in a house of ice,
I've settled in here and I find it nice.
So there! So there! Dick Andrew.

Its windows are clear and stay tight shut
to allay my fear of thieves and such.
Indeed I like it here very much.
So there! So there! Dick Andrew.

The stove-fire burns deep ice-blue
and casts blue shadows across the floor.
I could not ask for any more
but you, but you, Dick Andrew.

STEPHEN GALLAGHER

Restraint

Stephen Gallagher first made his mark as a Britpack horror and suspense novelist, and has been described by The Independent *as "the finest writer of British popular fiction since Le Carré."*

His work has been published in Weird Tales, The Magazine of Fantasy & Science Fiction, *the* Shadows *anthologies,* Best New Horror, The Year's Best Fantasy and Horror, *and* Best Short Stories; *he's been nominated for multiple genre awards, and twice voted "Scaremonger of the Year" in a readers' poll.*

His novels include Red, Red Robin, The Boat House, Valley of Lights, Rain, *and* Nightmare, with Angel. *His first major short story collection,* Out of His Mind, *came out in 2004, and a new novel,* The Spirit Box, *has just been published. He's currently working on* Eleventh Hour, *a series of four feature-length science-and-suspense thrillers starring Patrick Stewart for British TV.*

"Restraint" was originally published in the British magazine Postscripts.
—E.D.

Did you get a look at the driver who forced you off the road?"

The woman in uniform had pulled up a chair to put herself right alongside Holly's hospital trolley, so that she could speak close and keep her voice low.

Holly made the slightest movement of her head, not even a shake, and was instantly sorry.

The policewoman spoke again.

"Your son thinks it was your husband's car. Could that be right? We've called your house and there's nobody there."

Holly meant to speak, but it came out in an unrecognizable whisper.

"Where are the children?"

"Out in the waiting room. They've been checked over and neither of them's hurt. Your neighbors said you left after some kind of an argument."

"I'd like some water."

"I'll have to ask if that's all right."

Holly closed her eyes, and a moment later heard the sound of metal rings sliding as the policewoman stepped out of the cubicle. Only a curtain separated her from the Saturday night crowd out in Casualty, and a pretty lively crowd they sounded.

She lay with a thin blanket covering her. They'd brought her back here after the X-rays. It was a relief to hear that the children were unhurt, even though it was what she'd half-expected. That short trip down the embankment would have shaken them up, but it was only their stupid mother who'd neglected to put on her own seat belt after making sure of theirs.

That car. It had come out of nowhere. But if there was one thing that Holly knew for certain, it was that Frank couldn't have been at the wheel.

Why? Because she and Lizzie had struggled to lift him into the boot of their own car, not forty-five minutes before. And assuming he hadn't leaked too much and no one had lifted the lid for a look inside, he had to be lying there still.

He certainly wouldn't be going anywhere on his own.

The young policewoman was back.

"I'm sorry," she said. "I had to stop an argument. I forgot to ask about your water."

"Where's the car?" Holly croaked.

"Still in the ditch," the policewoman said. "The accident unit can get it towed away for you, but you'll have to sort out the rest with your insurers."

This was seductive. The linen smelled clean, and felt fresh. Holly was all but exhausted. She'd been lifted, laid down, tended to. It would be so easy to drift. The racket right outside was almost like a lullaby.

But her husband's dead body was in the boot of her car, and the police were all over it even as she lay there.

"Can I get that drink now?" she said.

As soon as the policewoman was gone, Holly tried to rise up on her elbows. The effort it called for surprised her at first, but she made it on the second attempt.

She was in her underwear, her outer clothing piled on a chair that stood against the wall. She started to climb off the trolley and it hurt, but it wasn't too bad; nothing grated and nothing refused to take her weight. Her head ached and she felt a great overall weariness, but there was no one part of her that screamed of special damage.

The floor was cold under her bare feet. She stood for a moment with her hand resting on the trolley, and then she straightened.

At least she could stand.

She tweaked open the side-curtain and put her face through the gap. In the next cubicle sat a young man on a chair, holding a spectacularly bloodstained dressing to the side of his head. He was in formal dress, with a carnation in his buttonhole and his tie all awry. He looked like the type who owned one suit and wore it for all his weddings, funerals, and court appearances.

"I wouldn't call you a shitsucker," Holly said.

He blinked at her, uncomprehending.

"The man you came in with just did," she said.

He was up on his feet in an instant, and as he flung back the outer curtain she got a glimpse of the scene beyond it. The rest of the wedding party was out there, arguing with the staff and with each other. The bride in her gown could be seen in their midst. They rose in a wave as the bloodied guest was spotted hurtling toward them, and then the curtain fell back as if on the world's most energetic Punch and Judy show.

That ought to keep her policewoman occupied for a while.

Holly could feel the adrenaline pumping now, flushing her of all weariness and pain, leaving her wired and edgy and ready to roll. She dressed as quickly as she could, and then instead of emerging into the open she started to make her way through one dividing curtain after another toward the end of the row. In the next occupied cubicle, an elderly West Indian man lay huddled under a red blanket. In the last sat a scared-looking woman with a small boy. They looked up apprehensively as she appeared out of nowhere.

"Sorry to disturb you," Holly said. "Where's the children's waiting room?"

It was around a corner and separated from the main area by a short passageway and a couple of vending machines. Under a mural of misshapen Disney characters stood a basket of wrecked toys, some coverless picture books, and some undersized chairs across which a sleeping form lay. She woke up Lizzie, and dragged Jack protesting out of the corner playhouse in which he'd made a den. He quietened suddenly when he looked at her face. She took them both by the hand and they followed a yellow line on the hospital floor toward the exit.

As they approached the automatic doors, Holly saw herself in the glass. But then the doors slid apart, and they sailed out into the night to look for a taxi.

In the presence of the driver they asked her no questions, and they gave her no trouble. Lizzie was twelve. She was dark, she was pretty, good at her lessons and no good at games. Jack was only six, a beefy little fair-haired Tonka truck of a boy.

The roads were quiet and the taxi got them to the place on the ring road in twenty minutes. It was a good half-mile on from where she'd expected it to be. The police were gone but the car was still there.

"Do you want me to wait?" the cab driver said, but Holly said no and paid him off.

She waited until the cab was out of sight before she descended to her vehicle.

The children hung back on the grass verge, by the deep earth-gouges that marked the spot where their car had left the carriageway. Spray-painted lines on the grass and on the tarmac showed where the accident unit had taken measurements. Down in the ditch, they'd left a big POLICE AWARE sticker on the back window of her Toyota.

The Toyota was old and it wasn't in the best of shape, but it was a runner. Usually. Right now it was stuck nose-first in the bushes along with all the windblown litter at the bottom of the embankment.

The keys had been taken, but Holly groped around in the wheel arch where she kept a secret spare. As she crouched there, she glanced up at the children. They were watching her, two shapes etched against the yellow sodium mist that hung over the road.

Her fingertips found the little magnetic box right up at the top of the arch, deep in the crusted road dirt.

"Got them," she said. "Come on."

Lizzie was nervously eyeing the Toyota as she and Jack came scrambling down.

"What are we going to do?" she said. "It's stuck here. We can't go anywhere."

"We don't know that for certain yet," Holly said, tearing off the police notice and then moving around to open the doors. She didn't know what the procedure was, but they couldn't have looked inside the boot. However quick the glance, Frank would have been hard to miss.

Jack climbed into the back, without an argument for once, and Lizzie got into the passenger seat.

Once she was behind the wheel, Holly checked herself in the rearview mirror. At least when she'd hit her head on the roof, her face had been spared. Her vision had been blurred in the ambulance, hence the need for an X-ray, but that had mostly cleared up now.

Still, she looked a sight. She ran her fingers through to straighten her hair and then she rubbed at her reddened eyes, but of course that only made them worse.

"Here goes," she said, and tried the engine.

It started on the second try. It was sluggish and it didn't sound at all right, but it caught just the same.

There was no point in trying to reverse up the banking, but she tried it anyway. The wheels spun and the car went nowhere. So instead she put it into first gear and tried going forward, squeezing on through the bushes.

For a moment it looked as if this wasn't going to work either, but with a jarring bump they lurched forward into the leaves. Switches bent and cracked as the Toyota forced its way through. She glanced in the mirror and saw Jack watching, fascinated, as foliage scraped and slid along the window only inches from his face. God alone knew what it was doing to her paintwork.

They came out onto what looked like a narrow limestone track, which was actually a soakaway at the bottom of the ditch. Staying in low gear, she began to follow its irregular line. After about a hundred yards she was able to transfer across to a dirt road, which led in turn to a lane. The lane took them under the ring road and then around and back onto it.

Once they were on hard tarmac again, Holly permitted herself to breathe. But not too much. There was the rest of the night still to be managed.

And then—perhaps even more of a challenge—the rest of their lives thereafter.

She hadn't seen it happen. She hadn't even been in the house. She'd come home to find Frank lying awkwardly at the bottom of the stairs and Lizzie sitting with her head in her hands at the top of them. It might have passed for an accident, but for the letter-opener stuck in Frank's neck.

He wasn't supposed to be in the house. The restraining order was meant to take care of that. He wasn't even supposed to come within a hundred yards of his daughter, regardless of where she might be.

So, technically speaking, by being in the boot of the car he was in breach of the order right now.

Holly's first thought had been to pick up the phone and call the police. Her second had been that perhaps she could first wipe off the handle and put her own prints onto it and take all the blame. Then a sudden rage had risen within her. She'd looked down on his twisted body and felt no horror, no awe. No anguish or dismay. Just cheated. Frank had contrived to poison their existence while he was around; was there to be no end to it even with him gone?

She'd made the decision right then. They would not enter that process. If they moved quickly enough, they could put him right out of their lives and make a clean beginning. It would be a credible move; Frank could make an enemy in the time it took him to buy a newspaper, and any suspicion would be dispersed among the many. She'd looked at Lizzie and told her exactly what she had in mind.

We can't, Lizzie had said.

So Holly had sat her down and for ten solid minutes had laid out the choices for her, making sure that she understood how much depended on the next few hours. What was done was done, she'd said to her, and there's no changing it now. Don't feel you're to blame. It isn't a matter of right or wrong. Your father made all the choices that caused this to happen.

It had worked. Kind of.

They couldn't use Frank's car. Being in the motor trade he'd use whatever vehicle was going spare on the lot, and of late he'd been favoring a red coupé that was hardly practical for the job in hand. So Holly had backed her Toyota into the garage on the side of the house, lined the boot with a plastic decorating sheet, and together they'd dragged Frank through the connecting door and manhandled his body into it. Handling him was less of a problem than Holly had expected. In the unpleasantness stakes, Frank dead was hard-pressed to match up to Frank in life.

Once he was safely stowed and covered in a couple of old towels, they'd driven out to collect Jack from school and then set off for the coast. Fish and chips on the pier, Jack. It's a surprise treat. We just have to make a call somewhere, first. Somewhere quiet. You'll stay in the car.

And then the accident, and the plan forced off-course.

But back on it, now.

From the ring road, they got onto the motorway. The traffic was heavier here, and it slowed when the carriageway narrowed to a single lane. For a long time there was no visible reason for it, and then suddenly they came upon a surfacing crew laying down new tarmac under bright worklights; a colossal rolling tar factory that belched and stank like a dragon as it excreted a lane-wide ribbon of hot road, men with shovels and brushes working furiously in its wake, supervisors in hard hats chatting by their vehicles.

"Look, Jack," Lizzie said. "Big trucks."

"Big, big trucks!" Jack said with awe, and turned in his seat to watch through the back window as they left the staged drama behind.

"You like the big trucks, don't you, Jack?" Holly said as the lanes cleared and the Toyota picked up speed again, but Jack didn't answer.

Holly couldn't put a finger on it, but the Toyota didn't feel quite right after the accident. She could only hope that it wouldn't let them down, and that the outside of the car wasn't messed up too much. A police stop was something that she didn't dare risk.

The next time she checked on Jack, he was asleep. His mouth was open and his head was rocking with the rhythm of the car. He slept the way he did everything else . . . wholeheartedly, and with a hundred per cent commitment.

For a moment, Holly experienced a sensation in her heart that was like a power surge. This was her family. Everything that mattered to her was here, in this car.

And then she remembered that Frank was in the car with them, too. Good old Frank. Consistent as ever. Bringing a little touch of dread into every family outing.

They left the motorway, took a back road, and drove through a couple of darkened villages. There was a place that she had in mind. Out to the north and west was a great bay whose inland fields and marshes were almost unknown beyond the region. At low tide, saltings and sand-flats extended the land almost to the horizon.

Much of what was now solid ground had once been part of the sea. In places the sea was claiming it back, pushing the coastline inland so that fields and even some roads were being lost forever. Hide something well enough in the part that was disappearing, and . . .

Well, she'd have to hope. It was the best she could come up with.

Somewhere along here there was a causeway road that had once led to a farm, long abandoned. People had trekked out to it for a picnic spot when there was something to see, but then the shell had become unsafe and it had all been pulled down. Now there was just rubble and the lines of a couple of walls, and that only visible at a low spring tide.

They crawled along, following the causeway with the Toyota's dipped beams. It didn't so much end as deteriorate steadily for the last couple of hundred yards. The concrete sections of the road had become tilted and skewed as the ground beneath them had given up any pretense of permanence. The sections had drifted, and in places they'd separated completely.

She had to stop the car and get out to locate the cesspit. When she turned back, Lizzie was out of the car and standing beside it.

She was looking around and she said, "Have I been here before?"

"Once," Holly said. "Before Jack was born. I brought you out here to show it to you, because it was a place my mother and father used to bring me. But it had all changed."

Lizzie tried to speak, but then she just nodded. And then her control went altogether, and her body was suddenly convulsed with an air-sucking sob that was shocking both in its violence, and in its unexpectedness.

Holly moved to her quickly and put her arms around her, holding her tightly until the worst of it passed. There in the darkness, out on the causeway, with the moon rising and this thing of such enormity to be dealt with. It would be no easy night, and no easy ride from here. Holly was only just beginning to appreciate how hard her daughter's journey would be.

"I can't do this," Lizzie whispered.

"Yes we can," Holly told her.

They got him out of the car into the pool and he floated, just under the surface, a hand drifting up into the pale shaft of dirtwater light from the Toyota's beams. The first stone sank him and then they added others, as many as they could lift. A sudden gout of bubbles gave them a fright. Holly was convinced that it caused her heart to stop beating for a moment.

They stood watching for a while to be sure of their work, and Holly sneaked a glance at Lizzie. Her face was in shadow and impossible to read.

"We should say a prayer," Lizzie said.

"Say one in the car," Holly said. "We need to get back and clean up the stairs."

Back on the motorway she watched for police cars, but she saw none. She *did* become aware of some lights that seemed to pace her for a while, but when she slowed a little the vehicle drew closer, and she was able to see that it lacked the telltale profile of roof bar and blue lights.

They had unmarked ones, of course. There was always that risk.

After a while, the headlamps in her mirror began to irritate her. She slowed even more to let the car pass, but it didn't. So then she picked up speed and tried to leave it behind; two minutes later and as many miles on, it was still there.

It surely meant nothing, but now it was making her nervous. Lizzie seemed to pick up on this. She saw Holly's frequent glances in the mirror and turned herself around in her seat, straining at her belt to look out of the back window.

"It's the same car," she said.

"What do you mean?"

"The one that pushed us off the road."

"It can't be," Holly said.

Lizzie clearly wasn't certain enough to argue the point.

"Well, it's similar," she said.

Holly increased her speed even further, up and over the limit, and the wheel began to vibrate in her hands as if the Toyota was beginning to shake itself apart. It couldn't be the same car. She couldn't imagine who'd want to follow her, or why.

It seemed to be working. They were leaving the other car behind, but then she saw something out of the corner of her eye. She looked down. The oil light was on, the brightest thing on the dash, and the one thing she knew about a car's oil light was that on a screaming engine it signaled imminent disaster.

She slowed, but it didn't go out. Other warning lights started to flicker on around it. So Holly quickly put the car out of gear and indicated to move off the motorway and onto the hard shoulder.

They coasted to a halt. The engine was already silent by the time they reached a stop. It had died somewhere during the deceleration, she couldn't be sure when. As they sat there, the cooling engine block ticked and clanked like coins dropping into a bucket.

In the back, Jack was stirring.

"Fish and chips on the pier," he said suddenly.

"I'm sorry, Jack," Holly said. "It's got too late. Another time."

The other car was pulling in behind them, hazard lights flashing. Right then a big bus passed them at speed in the inside lane, and its slipstream rocked the Toyota on its wheels.

"Who is it, then?" Lizzie said, peering back as the other car came to a halt about fifty or sixty yards back.

"I don't know," Holly said. "Nobody."

Jack said, "Is it Daddy?"

Holly looked at Lizzie, and Lizzie looked at her. There was a risk that Jack might have picked up on something then, but all his attention was on the road behind them. The following driver was getting out. Just as the car was an anonymous shape behind the glare of its own headlights, the driver's figure was a slip of shadow against the liquid stream of passing traffic.

"No, Jack," Holly said, an inexplicable anxiety rising up within her. "It can't be your daddy." She glanced down at the dash. All of the warning lights were on now, but that meant nothing. Everything always came on when the engine stalled.

"It *is*," Jack said.

Holly could tell him it wasn't. But she couldn't tell him why.

She heard Lizzie draw in a deep and shuddering breath, and let it out again. She found her daughter's hand in the dark and squeezed it once.

Traffic flew by, and the driver kept on coming. He was silhouetted against the flashing hazard lights of his own vehicle, pulsing like an amber heart.

Maybe he was your regular Good Samaritan, coming to offer them a hand.

Or maybe he was one of any number of things, as yet unrecognized and uncatalogued.

"He's been in the rain," said Jack.

Forget the oil pressure. Forget the ruinous cost of a thrown piston or a seized-up engine. Suddenly it was far more important to get herself and the children away from this spot.

But all the Toyota's power seemed to have gone. The engine turned over like an exhausted fighter trying to rise after a long count. She tried turning off the lights, and as their beams died the sound of the starter immediately improved.

It barked, it caught. All the warning lights on the dash went out, including the oil. She crashed the gears, checked her mirror once, and pulled out. Right now her only concern was to get moving again.

Jack was turned around in his seat, straining to see.

"Who is it, if it isn't Daddy?" he said.

"It's nobody," Holly said. "Face forward."

"He's running after us."

"Jack," she said sharply, "how many times have I got to tell you?"

She was expecting him to give her an argument. But something in her tone seemed to make him decide, and he complied without another word.

Nothing that she was supposed to hear, anyway.

"It *was* Daddy," she heard him mutter.

She knew it wasn't, but the thought was planted now and it spooked her. The sooner this was over with, the better. She wondered how they'd recall this night. Would it be etched in their minds so they'd relive it, moment by moment, or would it move to the distance of a remembered nightmare?

Jack must never know the truth. For him, the story would have to be that his daddy had gone away. He'd keep on looking forward to his father's return, but in time he'd grow and the hope would fade and become part of the background noise of his life.

For Lizzie it was going to be a lot trickier. But at least she was safe from her father now. Whatever problems she might have in dealing with the deed and its memory, that was the thing to keep in mind.

Over a wooded hill, down into a valley, heading for home. Out there in the darkness were the lights of all those small towns that didn't rate exits of their own, but were linked by the road that the motorway had replaced.

That following car was back in her mirror. Or perhaps it was some different car, it was impossible to say. All she could see was those anonymous lights. This time they were staying well back.

Here came the roadworks again. Same stretch, opposite direction. Again, one lane was coned off and the carriageway lights were out. A few moments after they'd crossed into this darker territory, the driver behind her switched on his beams. They were the pop-up kind. She saw them swivel into view like laser eyes.

Just like on Frank's coupé.

Jack said, "Can we have the radio?"

"Not right now," Holly said.

"It was working before."

"I'm trying to concentrate."

He was closing the distance between them. Holly knew she couldn't go any faster.

She looked down and saw that her ignition lights were flickering and that, once again, her oil warning light was full on.

They passed what remained of a demolished bridge, with new concrete piers ready to take its wider replacement. Beyond the bridge site, just off the road, stood a mass of caravans and portable buildings. It was a construction village, a shantytown of churned up mud and giant machines. A temporary sliproad had been bulldozed into the embankment to give access to works traffic.

Holly waited until it was almost too late. Then she swerved across the lanes and into the sliproad.

Something thumped against the car, and in the mirror she saw one of the cones go tumbling in her wake. The car behind her was swerving to avoid it. It made him overshoot the turnoff, so he couldn't follow her. Now he'd be stuck. The traffic wouldn't allow him to stop and back up again. He'd be heading in the same direction for miles and miles.

Good Samaritan? Good riddance.

All the lights in this temporary settlement were on, yet nothing moved. Jack was craning, eagerly looking around the various site office buildings as they entered the main area. But Holly got in first.

"Yes, Jack," she said. "They have big trucks here."

It was almost as bright as day, and completely deserted. The yard was floodlit and every portakabin office had its lights on. Holly could see through all the uncurtained windows that every one of the offices was empty.

She slowed, and stopped, and looked around.

A few vans, a couple of big diggers. Some concrete bridge sections waiting to be trucked out and assembled elsewhere. The site had the look of a frontier fort, obviously not intended to be here forever; but it was hard to believe that the scars it would leave on the land could ever easily heal.

They would, of course. The big machines would simply put it all back when they'd finished. It wouldn't quite be nature, but everybody would be going by too fast to notice.

She got out. There was the sound of a generator, banging away somewhere in the background.

"Hello?" she called out, and then glanced back at the car.

Jack and Lizzie were watching her through the side-windows. Pale children, out on the road past their bedtimes. They looked hollow-eyed and tired. Jack with his little round face, Lizzie like a stick-version of the teenager she'd soon be.

Holly gave them a brief smile, and then moved out to look for someone. She didn't want to get too far from the car. She didn't want to let them out of her sight.

She called again, and this time someone came out from behind one of the buildings.

He stood there, and she had to walk over to him. He looked like a toothless old shepherd in a flat cloth cap, knuckly hands hanging down by his sides. He could have been any age, from a well-preserved seventy down to a badly done-by fifty. Too old to be one of the road gang, he looked as if he'd been on road gangs all his life.

She said, "Is anyone in charge around here?"

"Never, love," the man said. "They all do what they sodding well like."

"Well . . . what do *you* do?"

"I'm just the brewman."

Holly looked around her at some of the heavy plant that stood under the lights, looking as if it had all been air-dropped in to remodel the face of Mars.

She said, "I've been having trouble with my car. Is there anyone who could have a look at it for me? I've got some money."

"Andy's the mechanic," he said.

"Is he here?"

"He's never here."

"Is it worth me waiting for him? Can I do that?"

"You can do whatever you want," and then added, as if it was his all-purpose charm to ward off evil, "I'm just the brewman." And then he trudged off.

She went back to the car.

"I'm fed up of this," Jack said.

"I can't help it, Jack," Holly said. "Try to understand."

"No," he said, barking it out like a little dog with all the passion and venom he could manage.

Rather than argue or get angry, Holly got out of the car again to watch for Andy the Mechanic.

The site wasn't quite as deserted as it looked, but it took a while to become attuned to it and to pick up the signals; the sound of a door opening and closing somewhere, a glimpse of a figure passing from one building to another.

She paced a little. She looked toward the motorway. For something to do, she raised the Toyota's bonnet and took a look at the engine in the vague hope that her car problems might have some blindingly obvious solution. But it looked like engines always did to her, grimy and complex and meaningless. There was a smell as if something had been burning, and when she held her hand out over the block she could feel the heat rising from it. She poked at a couple of the leads, to no effect other than to get her hands dirtier than they already were.

A voice called out, "Are you looking for someone?"

A man was walking across the open ground toward her. He was short, dark, powerfully built. He had at least six upper teeth missing on one side, but from the way that he grinned the loss didn't seem to trouble him.

"Would you be Andy?" she said.

"I might."

"Then I'm looking for you."

She quickly explained her problem in case he started to get the wrong idea, and he moved her out of the way so that he could take a look. It didn't take him long.

"Look at your fanbelt," he said. "If your drawers were that slack, they'd be down around your ankles. When that starts to slip, your battery runs down and you run out of power."

"Is it hard to fix?"

"If I said yes, you'd be more impressed," he said, and it was then that he noticed the two children inside the car. They were staring out at him.

"Yours?" he said.

"Yes," Holly said. "We've been to the seaside."

He looked at her, and then he looked at the car.

And then he said, "You take the kids and wait in the brew hut while I have a go at this. Tell Diesel to make you a cup of tea."

"Is Diesel the brewman's name?"

"It's what his tea tastes like, as well."

The brew hut was the oldest looking and most battered of the site buildings. It was up on blocks, and reached by three stairs. The floor sagged as they stepped inside. There were about a dozen folding card tables with chairs around them, and a sense of permanent grime everywhere; it was as if engine oil had been ground into the floor, rubbed into the walls, coated onto the windows.

The brewman was sitting by a plug-in radiator, reading a copy of *The Sun*. It wasn't a cold night, but the radiator was turned up high and the air inside the hut was stifling. He looked up as they entered.

Holly said, "Andy told us to wait in here. Is that all right with you?"

"Whatever you like," the brewman said. "I'm Matty."

"He said you were called Diesel."

Matty's face fell, and he looked out of the window.

"The bastard," he said, and he got up and stamped off.

Given his mood and the likely state of his crockery, Holly decided not to press him about the tea. She ushered the children onto grimy plastic seats that stood against the wall. On the wall itself was tacked a selection of yellowing newspaper cuttings, all of them showing the debris of spectacular motorway crashes.

Jack said, "It stinks in here."

"Shh," Holly said.

"It *does*."

She couldn't tell him it didn't, because it did. And she couldn't agree that it did in case Matty was listening. So she only said, "It won't be for long."

They waited. There was a clock on the wall, but it was wrong. Jack swung his feet, Lizzie stared at the floor. Outside, a massive engine began to rev up somewhere close behind the building, making their chairs vibrate.

Jack said, "I'm bored."

"Play I-spy," Holly suggested.

"I'm not playing with him," Lizzie said. "He can't spell."

Holly said, with an unexpected tightness in her tone, "Then why don't we all just sit here quietly?"

There was silence for a while and then Lizzie muttered, rebelliously, "It's true. He can't."

And Jack agreed with her. "I've got a giant brain," he said, "but I can't spell."

Holly covered her eyes. She wasn't sure whether she was laughing or crying and the two children, equally uncertain, were watching her closely for clues.

This night would pass. It would somehow all be fine.

Keep thinking that, she told herself, and it might even come true.

"Mum . . ." Lizzie said.

Holly looked at her and saw the unease and the apprehension in her eyes. She might be sharp, but she was still only twelve years old.

"When this part's over," she said, "what then?"

She was choosing her words carefully because of Jack, but Holly knew what Lizzie was trying to say.

"We'll carry on as normal," she said.

"Can we do that?"

"We'll have to," Holly said.

There was a tap on the window. Andy was standing there outside, raising himself up on tiptoe so that he could look in, and he beckoned to her.

She went out, and they walked over to the car together. He told her he'd left the keys inside it.

"Best I can do," he said. "I've tightened your fanbelt and cleaned off your plugs. They were blacker than Matty's fingernails."

"Thanks, Andy."

"You've got a lot of oil down there. I don't know where it's coming from. You might need a new gasket."

He showed her what he'd done and got her to feel the difference in the fanbelt, which she pretended to appreciate. She offered him twenty quid and he took it with no embarrassment. Then she went back for the children.

The brew hut door was open. Lizzie was alone inside.

Holly said, "Where's Jack?"

Lizzie had slumped down into her coat as if it was a nest, hands in her pockets and legs outstretched, looking at the toes of her shoes as she clacked them together. She said, "He followed you outside."

"I didn't see him."

"He wanted to look at the big trucks."

Holly went out. Jack hadn't gone over toward the car, or she'd have seen him. She stood in front of the brew hut and called out his name.

Nothing.

Lizzie was in the doorway behind her now.

"It's not my fault," she said defensively.

Holly went around by the side of the brew hut and found herself in an area lit by the most powerful of the overhead floodlights. Under the lights stood a few parked cars and a variety of dormant machines. She could hear the massive engine whose note had been shaking the brew hut's foundations, and could tell that it was somewhere close.

She looked back and saw that Lizzie had followed her some of the way.

"You look around the buildings," Holly said. "I'll look here."

She didn't wait to see how Lizzie responded, but started to make her way through the machine yard. It was like a giant's bazaar of heavy engineering, the night sun casting deep, dark shadows under the gear. These were machines for ripping up the land, and they had spikes and claws and teeth on a saurian scale. Encrusted with clay and battered by hard use, they stood like bombed-out tanks.

She hauled herself up and looked in the cab of a well-rusted bulldozer on tracks. Jack wasn't in it, but by hanging on she could look out over the yard. Down the next row, a wagon was being inched up onto a flatbed trailer by some driver she couldn't see. The tires on the wagon were enormous, and the ramps were bending under its weight.

She looked all around and called Jack's name, but she had little chance of being heard. The big engine roared and the great tonnage slowly rolled. In her mind's eye she saw Jack crushed or falling or struggling to get free of some unexpected snare. She saw gears turning, teeth meshing, pulling him in.

She called his name again, louder, and then hopped down to continue the search. She stumbled a little when she landed. The ground here was nothing more than churned-up dirt into which stones had been dumped to give it some firmness. It was no playground.

"Jack!" she called, moving forward.

As she came around by the bulldozer onto a firmer stretch of concrete road, she saw him. She could see all the way to the perimeter fence, where he was climbing.

Climbing? What was he *doing*?

And then she understood, and started to run.

It was a storm fence, about eight feet high. Jack was already over the top of it, and climbing down the other side. The fence rocked back and forth under his weight as the concrete posts shifted in their holes, but he clung to it like a bug; its close weave offered ideal purchase for his small feet and fingers.

Holly stumbled on the rough ground, but caught herself and went on. On the other side of the perimeter fence was an unlit country lane.

Out on the country lane stood the red coupé with the pop-up headlights.

"Hey," she shouted. "Hey, Jack, no!"

He was descending with his face set in a look of utter concentration. Behind him, the car was making a low purring sound with its engine off but its electric fan sucking in the cool night air. The driver hadn't stepped out, and she could barely see anything of him. She could only guess that he was watching her.

Holly reached the fence, looking through it and up at him. "Jack," she said. "Come down, Jack, please. You can't go over there. That's not your daddy. Believe me. There's no way it could be."

But Jack didn't look at her, and didn't even show any sign of having heard. He was moving like a monkey. He reached down with his foot, found another space in the diamond pattern, and hooked his scuffed trainer into it before lowering the rest of his weight.

She could touch his fingers as they hooked through, right in front of her eyes; her breath through the wire could fall onto his face. "Jack," she said, "no!"

But he wouldn't look at her, and although he was only inches away she couldn't reach him. She was powerless.

"Jack," she said. "Look at me, please. Don't do this. Don't go to him."

She made a move as if to try and catch his hands through the wire, but it was pointless. She couldn't hold him if she caught him. All she could do was risk hurting him.

"Lizzie's looking for you as well," she pleaded. "Oh, *Jack* . . ."

He jumped, and hit the dirt on the far side with a thump. Holly made a leap at the wire and felt the entire fence lean before her, but she didn't have his agility and couldn't begin to climb the way that he had.

He was running for the car, now, and the car's passenger door was opening to receive him.

Holly was screaming, although she didn't immediately realize it. The car door slammed and its laser eyes opened. The engine started, and its nose swung around as it began to turn in the narrow lane.

Her hands were up at the sides of her head. She'd heard of people tearing at their hair, but she'd always thought it was just an expression. She looked around wildly.

Then she started to run along the inside of the fence, ahead of the turning car.

The country lane ran close on the other side. If there was a gap anywhere, she'd get through it. The car wouldn't pass her. No way was she going to let that happen.

Here was a gate. It was a back way into the site, little used. A big double gate, wide enough for a lorry but chained and padlocked in the middle. There was enough play in the chain to make a gap of a foot or so.

It was a squeeze, but not an impossible one. She came out on the other side and all that she could see were the twin lights, the laser eyes of the beast that she had to impede.

She put on a burst and dived into its way, sliding to a halt in the middle of the lane and raising both of her hands. When it hit her, she felt nothing other than her own sudden acceleration; no impact, no pain, just the instantaneous switch from rest into motion as her legs were knocked from under her and she was spun down the side of the car.

Afterwards she'd never know whether she really saw it or only imagined the memory, but Holly went down hard in the wake of the moving car with a mental picture of her son's blank face only inches away on the other side of the glass.

She lay there.

She couldn't move. She could hear that the car had stopped and she wanted to lift her head to look, but nothing happened. Oh God, she was thinking, I'm paralyzed. But then when she made an enormous effort, her hand came up and braced itself against the ground. As she was doing it, she heard a car door opening.

She wasn't paralyzed, but she'd no strength. When she tried to push down with her hand to raise herself, her arm trembled and nothing happened.

Someone was walking up behind her.

Before she could muster the energy to turn and look, strong fingers gripped the back of her head and thrust her face down into the mud. In an instant, she was blinded and choking.

She found her strength now, all right, but it did her no good as a sudden knee in her back pinned her further to the ground. She struggled and flapped like a fish, but her face stayed under. The blood roared in her ears and lights exploded before her eyes.

Then in an instant, the pressure was off.

That first deep breath nearly drowned her on the spot, as she sucked in all the mud that had filled up her mouth. She retched and coughed, blowing it out of her nostrils and heaving up what she'd both swallowed and inhaled.

She felt a lighter touch on her shoulder and lashed out, only to hear a cry from Lizzie. She was there when Holly's vision cleared, keeping back and holding her arm where she'd been struck.

"I'm sorry, Mum," she said.

Holly stared dumbly for a moment before an understanding started to form. Lizzie was backing toward the waiting car.

"No, Lizzie!" she said. She tried to rise, but one of her legs wouldn't support her.

"I know how you want me to feel about it, but I can't. I wish I could. I'm sorry. It's never going to be right after tonight, whatever we do. Ever."

Holly made another massive effort and this time made it up and onto her feet, putting all of her weight onto the uninjured leg.

"Wait," she managed.

Lizzie had reached the car.

"I'm the one that he wants," she said. "But he'll take Jack if I don't go with him."

The passenger door popped open about an inch.

"I'm sorry," she said again, and she reached out and opened it all the way.

Holly wasn't close enough to see how it worked, but Jack popped out of the vehicle as if propelled on a spring. He landed on both feet, and Lizzie quickly slipped around behind him and into the car.

The door closed like the door on a well-fitting safe, and the car's engine started to rev. It was all as swift and as decisive as that.

Holly started toward them, half-hopping, half-limping, but the car was already moving off and starting to pick up speed.

"Frank!" she shouted. "You bastard! Give her back!" and at the sound of her voice, Jack seemed to wake as if from a daze.

He looked about, as if suddenly remembering something, and spotted those red tail lights receding off into the darkness.

He gave a strangled cry.

"Dad!" he called out, and started to run down the lane after the car, slapping down his feet so hard that the ground almost shook.

Holly hadn't yet reached him, and her cries couldn't stop him. Neither of them had any chance of catching the car. But both of them tried.

She caught up with him a full ten minutes later, still standing on the dark spot where his breath and his hopes had finally given out.

"He forgot me!" he wailed. Holly dropped to her knees and pulled him to her.

For once, he let her hold him.

JOHN KESSEL

The Baum Plan for Financial Independence

John Kessel is a professor of English at North Carolina State University. His fiction has won the Nebula, Theodore Sturgeon, Locus, and James Tiptree, Jr. awards, and he played a small role in the independent film The Delicate Art of the Rifle. *Kessel is the author of* Freedom Beach *(with James Patrick Kelly),* Good News From Outer Space, *and* Corrupting Dr. Nice, *as well as the collections* Meeting in Infinity *and* The Pure Product. *With Mark L. Van Name and Richard Butner, he has run the Sycamore Hill Writers' Conference, which produced the anthology* Intersections. *He lives with his wife and daughter in Raleigh, North Carolina. Kessel's fiction is ferocious, funny, sometimes joyful, and always deeply moving.*

"The Baum Plan for Financial Independence" appeared on Scifi.com's SCI FICTION *site on March 24.*

—K.L. & G.G.

When I picked her up at the Stop & Shop on Route 28, Dot was wearing a short black skirt and red sneakers just like the ones she had taken from the bargain rack the night we broke into the Sears in Hendersonville five years earlier. I couldn't help but notice the curve of her hip as she slid into the front seat of my old T-Bird. She leaned over and gave me a kiss, bright red lipstick and breath smelling of cigarettes. "Together again at last," she said.

The Sears had been my idea, but after we got into the store that night all the other ideas had been Dot's, including the game on the bed in the furniture department, and me clocking the night watchman with the anodized aluminum flashlight I took from hardware, sending him to the hospital with a concussion and me to three years in Central. When the cops showed up and hauled me off, Dot was nowhere to be found. That was all right. A man has to take responsibility for his own actions, at least that's what they told me in the group therapy sessions that the prison shrink ran on Thursday nights. But I never knew a woman who could make me do the things that Dot could make me do.

One of the guys at those sessions was Radioactive Roy Destry, who had a theory about how we were all living in a computer and none of this was real. Well if this isn't real, I told him, I don't know what real is. The softness of Dot's breast or the shit smell of the crapper in the Highway 28 Texaco, how can there be anything more real than that? Radioactive Roy and the people like him are just looking for an exit door. I can understand that. Everybody dreams of an exit door sometimes.

I slipped the car into gear and pulled out of the station onto the highway. The sky ahead was red above the Blue Ridge but the air blowing in the windows was dry and smoky with the ash of the forest fires burning a hundred miles to the northwest.

"Cat got your tongue, darlin'?" Dot said. I pushed the cassette into the deck and Willie Nelson was singing "Hello Walls."

"Where are we going, Dot?"

"Just point this thing west for twenty or so. When you come to a sign that says Potter's Glen, make a right on the next dirt road."

Dot pulled a pack of Kools out of her purse, stuck one in her mouth, and punched the car's cigarette lighter.

"Doesn't work," I said.

She pawed through her purse for thirty seconds, then clipped it shut. "Shit," she said. "You got a match, Sid?" Out of the corner of my eye I watched the cigarette bobble up and down as she spoke.

"Sorry, sweetheart, no."

She took the cigarette from her mouth, stared at it for a moment, and flipped it out her opened window.

Hello window. I actually had a box of Ohio Blue Tips in the glove compartment, but I didn't want Dot to smoke because it was going to kill her someday. My mother smoked, and I remember her wet cough and the skin stretched tight over her cheekbones as she lay in the upstairs bedroom of the big house in Lynchburg, puffing on a Winston between hacking up pieces of her cancerous lung. Whenever my old man came in to clear her untouched lunch dishes he asked her if he could have one, and Mother would smile at him, eyes big, and pull two more coffin nails out of the red-and-white pack with her nicotine-stained fingers.

One time after I saw this happen, I followed my father down to the kitchen. When he bent over to put the tray on the counter, I snatched the cigarettes from his breast pocket and crushed them into bits over the plate of pears and cottage cheese. I glared at him, daring him to get mad. After a few seconds he just pushed past me to the living room and turned on the TV.

That's the story of my life: me trying to save the rest of you—and the rest of you ignoring me.

On the other side of Almond it was all mountains. The road twisted and turned, the headlights flashing against the tops of trees on the downhill side and the cut earth on the uphill. I kept shifting and drifting over the double yellow line as we came in and out of turns, but the road was deserted. Occasionally we'd pass some broken-down house with a battered pickup in the dirt driveway and a rust-spotted propane tank outside in the yard.

The sign for Potter's Glen surged out of the darkness, and we turned off onto a rutted gravel track that was even more twisted than the paved road. The track rose steeply, the T-Bird's suspension was shot, and my rotten muffler scraped more than once when we bottomed out. If Dot's plan required us sneaking up on anybody, it was not going to work. But she had assured me that the house on the ridge was empty, and she knew where the money was hidden.

Occasionally the branch of a tree would scrape across the windshield or side mirror. The forest here was dry as tinder after the summer's drought, the worst on record, and in my rearview mirror I could see the dust we were raising vanish in the taillights. We had been fifteen minutes on this road when Dot said, "Okay, stop now."

The cloud of dust that had been following us caught up and billowed, settling slowly in the headlight beams. "Kill the engine and the lights," Dot said.

In the silence and darkness that came, the whine of cicadas moved closer. Dot fumbled with her purse, and when she opened the car door to get out, in the domelight I saw she had a map written on a piece of notebook paper. I opened the trunk and got out a pry bar and pair of bolt cutters. When I came around to her side of the car she was shining a flashlight on the map.

"It shouldn't be more than a quarter of a mile farther up this road," she said.

"Why can't we just drive right up there?"

"Someone might hear."

"But you said the place was deserted."

"It is. But there's no sense taking chances."

I laughed. Dot not taking chances? That was funny. She didn't think so, and punched me in the arm. "Stop it," she said, but then she giggled. I swept the arm holding the tools around her waist and kissed her. She pushed me away, but not roughly. "Let's go," she said.

We walked up the dirt road. When Dot shut off the flashlight, the only light was the faint moon coming through the trees, but after our eyes adjusted it was enough. The dark forest loomed over us. Walking through the woods at night always made me feel like I was in some teen horror movie. I expected a guy in a hockey mask to come shrieking from between the trees and cut us to ribbons with fingernails like straight razors.

Dot had heard about this summer cabin that was owned by the rich people she had worked for in Charlotte. They were Broyhills or related to the Broyhills, old money from the furniture business. Or maybe it was Dukes and tobacco. Anyway, they didn't use this house but a month or so out of the year. Some caretaker came by every so often, but he didn't live on the premises. Dot heard the daughter telling her friend that the family kept ten thousand dollars in cash up there in case another draft riot made it necessary for them to skip town for a while.

So we would just break in and find the money. That was the plan. It seemed a little dicey to me; I had grown up with money—my old man owned a car dealership, before he went bust. Leaving piles of cash lying around their vacation home did not seem like regular rich-people behavior to me. But Dot could be very convincing even when she wasn't convincing, and my father claimed I never had a lick of sense anyway. It took us twenty minutes to come up on the clearing, and there was the house. It was bigger than I imagined it. Rustic, flagstone chimney and entranceway, timbered walls and slate shingles. Moonlight glinted off the windows in the three dormers that faced front, but all the downstairs windows were shuttered.

I took the pry bar to the hinges on one of the shuttered windows, and after some struggle they gave. The window was dead bolted from the inside, but we knocked out one of the panes and unlatched it. I boosted Dot through the window and followed her in.

Dot used the flashlight to find the light switch. The furniture was large and heavy; there was a big oak coffee table that must have weighed two hundred pounds that we had to move in order to take up the rug and check to see whether there was a safe underneath. We pulled down all the pictures from the walls. One of them was a woodcut print of a Madonna and child, but instead of a child the woman was holding a fish; in the background of the picture, outside a window, a funnel cloud tore up a dirt road. The picture gave me the creeps. Behind it was nothing but plaster wall.

I heard the clink of glass behind me. Dot had opened the liquor cabinet and was pulling out bottles to see if there was a compartment hidden behind them. I went over, took down a glass, and poured myself a couple of fingers of Glenfiddich. I sat in a leather armchair and drank it, watching Dot search. She was getting frantic. When she came by the chair I grabbed her around the hips and pulled her into my lap.

"Hey! Lay off!" she squawked.

"Let's try the bedroom," I said.

She bounced off my lap. "Good idea." She left the room.

This was turning into a typical Dot odyssey, all tease and no tickle. I put down my glass and followed her.

I found her in the bedroom rifling through a chest of drawers, throwing clothes on the bed. I opened the closet. Inside hung a bunch of jackets and flannel shirts and blue jeans, with a pair of riding boots and some sandals lined up neatly on the floor. I pushed the hanging clothes apart, and there, set into the back wall, was a door. "Dot, bring that flashlight over here."

She came over and shined the flashlight into the closet. I ran my hand over the seam of the door. It was flush with the wall, the same off-white color, but was cool to the touch, made of metal. No visible hinges and no lock, just a flip up handle like on a tackle box.

"That's not a safe," Dot said.

"No shit, Sherlock."

She shouldered past me, crouched down, and flipped up the handle. The door pushed open onto darkness. She shined the flashlight ahead of her; I could not see past her. "Jesus Christ," she said.

"What?"

"Stairs." Dot moved forward, then stepped down. I pushed the clothes aside and followed her.

The carpet on the floor stopped at the doorjamb; inside was a concrete floor, and then a narrow flight of stairs leading down. A black metal handrail ran down the right side. The walls and ceiling were of roughed concrete, unpainted. Dot moved ahead of me down to the bottom, where she stopped.

When I got there I saw why. The stairs let out into a large, dark room. The floor ended halfway across it, and beyond that, at either side, to the left and right, under the arching roof, were open tunnels. From one tunnel opening to the other ran a pair of gleaming rails. We were standing on a subway platform.

Dot walked to the end of the platform and shined the flashlight up the tunnel. The rails gleamed away into the distance.

"This doesn't look like the safe," I said.

"Maybe it's a bomb shelter," Dot said.

Before I could figure out a polite way to laugh at her, I noticed a light growing from the tunnel to the right. A slight breeze kicked up. The light grew like an approaching headlight, and with it a hum in the air. I backed toward the stairs, but Dot just peered down the tunnel. "Dot!" I called. She waved a hand at me, and though she dropped back a step she kept watching. Out of the tunnel glided a car that slid to a stop in front of us. It was no bigger than a pickup. Teardrop shaped, made of gleaming silver metal, its bright single light glared down the track. The car had no windows, but as we stood gaping at it a door slid open in its side. The inside was dimly lit, with plush red seats.

Dot stepped forward and stuck her head inside.

"What are you doing?" I asked.

"It's empty," Dot said. "No driver. Come on."

"Get serious."

Dot crouched and got inside. She turned and ducked her head to look at me out of the low doorway. "Don't be a pussy, Sid."

"Don't be crazy, Dot. We don't even know what this thing is."

"Ain't you ever been out of Mayberry? It's a subway."

"But who built it? Where does it go? And what the hell is it doing in Jackson County?"

"How should I know? Maybe we can find out."

The car just sat there, silent. The air was still. The ruby light from behind her cast Dot's face in shadow. I followed her into the car. "I don't know about this."

"Relax."

There were two bench seats, each wide enough to hold two people, and just enough space on the door side to move from one to the other. Dot sat on one of the seats with her big purse in her lap, calm as a Christian holding four aces. I sat down next to her. As soon as I did the door slid shut and the car began to move, picking up speed smoothly, pushing us back into the firm upholstery. The only sound was a gradually increasing hum that reached a middle pitch and stayed there. I tried to breathe. There was no clack from the rails, no vibration. In front of us the car narrowed to a bullet nosed front, and in the heart of that nose was a circular window. Through the window I saw only blackness. After a while I wondered if we were still moving, until a light appeared ahead, first a small speck, then grew brighter and larger until it slipped off past us to the side at a speed that said the little car was moving faster than I cared to figure.

"These people who own the house—" I asked Dot, "—where on Mars did you say they came from?"

Dot reached in her purse and took out a pistol, set it down on her lap, and fumbled around in the bag until she pulled out a pack of Juicy Fruit. She pulled out a stick, then held the pack out to me. "Gum?"

"No thanks."

She put the pack back in the purse, and the pistol too. She slipped the yellow paper sleeve off her gum, unwrapped the foil and stuck the gum into her mouth. After folding the foil neatly, she slid it back into the gum sleeve and set the now-empty stick on the back of the seat in front of us.

I was about to scream. "Where the fuck are we going, Dot? What's going on here?"

"I don't have any idea where we're going, Sid. If I knew you were going to be such a wuss I would never of called you."

"Did you know about any of this?"

"Of course not. But we're going to be somewhere soon, I bet."

I got off the seat and sat down on the bench in front of her. That didn't set my nerves any easier. I could hear her chewing her gum, and felt her eyes on the back of my neck. The car sped into blackness, broken only by the occasional spear of light flashing past. As we did not seem to be getting anywhere real soon, I had some time to contemplate the ways in which I was a fool, number one being the way I let an ex–lap dancer from Mebane lead me around by my imagination for the last ten years.

Just when I thought I couldn't get any more pissed, Dot moved up from the back seat, sat down next to me, and took my hand. "I'm sorry, Sid. Someday I'll make it up to you."

"Yeah?" I said. "So give me some of that gum." She gave me a stick. Her tidy gum wrapper had fallen onto the seat between us; I crumpled the wrapper of my own next to hers.

I had not started in on chewing when the hum of the car lowered and I felt us slowing down. The front window got a little lighter, and the car came to a stop. The door slid open.

The platform it opened onto was better lit than the one under the house in the Blue Ridge. Standing on it waiting were three people, two men and a woman. The two men wore identical black suits of the kind bankers with too much money wore in downtown Charlotte: the suits hung the way no piece of clothing had ever hung on me—tailored closer than a mother's kiss. The woman, slender, with blonde hair done up tight as a librarian's—yet there was no touch of the librarian about her—wore a dark blue dress. They stood there for a moment, then one of the men said, "Excuse me? You're here. Are you getting out?"

Dot got up and nudged me, and I finally got my nerveless legs to work. We stepped out onto the platform, and the three well-dressed people got into the car, the door slid shut, and it glided off into the darkness.

It was cold on the platform, and a light breeze came from an archway across from us. Instead of rough stone like the tunnel under the house, here the ceiling and walls were smooth stucco. Carved above the arch was a crouching man wearing some kind of Roman or Greek toga, cradling a book under one arm and holding a torch in the other. He had a wide brow and a long straight nose, and looked like a guard in Central named Pisarkiewicz, only a lot smarter. Golden light filtered down from fixtures like frogs' eggs in the ceiling.

"What now?" I asked.

Dot headed for the archway. "What have we got to lose?"

Through the arch was a ramp that ran upward, switchbacking every forty feet or so. A couple of women, as well dressed as the one we'd seen on the platform, passed us going the other way. We tried to look like we belonged there, though Dot's hair was a greasy rat's nest, I was dressed in jeans and sneakers, I had not shaved since morning, and my breath smelled of scotch and Juicy Fruit.

At the top of the third switchback, the light brightened. From ahead of us came the sound of voices, echoing as if coming from a very large room. We reached the final archway, the floor leveled off, and we stepped into the hall.

I did not think there were so many shades of marble.

The place was as big as a train station, a great open room with polished stone floors, a domed ceiling a hundred feet above us, a dozen Greek half-columns set into the far wall. Bright sun shining through tall windows between them fell on baskets of flowers and huge potted palms. Around the hall stood a number of booths like information kiosks, and grilled counters like an old-fashioned bank at which polite workers in pale green shirts dealt with the customers. But it was not all business. Mixed among people carrying briefcases stood others in groups of three or four holding pale drinks in tall glasses, or leaning casually on some counter chatting one on one with those manning the booths. In one corner a man in a green suit played jazz on a grand piano.

It was a cross between Grand Central Station and the ballroom at the Biltmore House. Dot and I stood out like a pair of plow horses at a cotillion. The couple hundred people scattered through the great marble room were big-city well dressed. Even the people who dressed down wore hundred-dollar chinos with cashmere sweaters knotted casually around their necks. The place reeked of money.

Dot took my hand and pulled me into the room. She spotted a table with a fountain and a hundred wineglasses in rows on the starched white tablecloth. A pink marble cherub with pursed lips like a cupid's bow poured pale wine from a pitcher into the basin that surrounded his feet. Dot handed me one of the glasses and took one for herself, held it under the stream falling from the pitcher.

She took a sip. "Tastes good," she said. "Try it."

As we sipped wine and eyed the people, a man in a uniform shirt with a brass name pin that said "Brad" came up to us. "Would you like to wash and brush up? Wash and Brush Up is over there," he said, pointing across the hall to another marble archway. He had a British accent.

"Thanks," said Dot. "We just wanted to wet our whistles first."

The man winked at her. "Now that your whistle is wet, don't be afraid to use it any time I can be of service." He smirked at me. "That goes for you, too, sir."

"Fuck you," I said.

"It's been done already," the man said, and walked away.

I put down the wineglass. "Let's get out of here," I said.

"I want to go to see what's over there."

Wash and Brush Up turned out to be a suite of rooms where we were greeted by a young woman in green named Elizabeth and a young man named Martin. You need to clean up, they said, and separated us. I wasn't going to have any of it, but Dot seemed to have lost her mind—she went off with Martin. After grumbling for a while, I let Elizabeth take me to a small dressing room, where she made me strip and put on a robe. After that came the shower, the haircut, the steambath, the massage. Between the steambath and massage they brought me food, something like a cheese quesadilla only much better than anything like it I had ever tasted. While I ate, Elizabeth left me alone in a room with a curtained window. I pulled the curtain aside and looked out.

The window looked down from a great height on a city unlike any I had ever seen. It was like a picture out of a kid's book, something Persian about it, and something Japanese. Slender green towers, great domed buildings, long low structures like warehouses made of jade. The sun beat down pitilessly on citizens who went from street to street between the fine buildings with bowed heads and plodding steps. I saw a team of four men in purple shirts pulling a cart; I saw other men with sticks herd children down to a park; I saw vehicles rumble past tired street workers, kicking up clouds of yellow dust so thick that I could taste it.

The door behind me opened and Elizabeth stuck her head in. I dropped the curtain as if she had caught me whacking off. "Time for your massage," she said.

"Right," I said, and followed.

When I came out there was Dot, tiny in her big plush robe, her hair clean and combed out and her finger and toenails painted shell pink. She looked about fourteen.

"Nice haircut," she said to me.

"Where are our clothes?" I demanded of Martin.

"We'll get them for you," he said. He gestured to one of the boys. "But for now, come with me."

Then they sat us down in front of a large computer screen and showed us a catalog of clothes you could not find outside of a Neiman Marcus. They had images of us, like paper dolls, that they called up on the screen and that they could dress any way they liked so you could see how you would look. Dot was in hog heaven. "What's this going to cost us?" I said.

Martin laughed as if I had made a good joke. "How about some silk shirts?" he asked me. "You have a good build. I know you're going to like them."

By the time we were dressed, the boy had come back with two big green shopping bags with handles. "What's this?" Dot asked, taking hers.

"Your old clothes," Martin said.

I took mine. I looked at myself in the mirror. I wore a blue shirt, a gray tie with a skinny knot and a long, flowing tail, ebony cuff links, a gunmetal gray silk jacket, and black slacks with a crease that would cut ice. The shoes were of leather as soft as a baby's skin, and as comfortable as if I had broken them in for three months. I looked great.

Dot had settled on a champagne colored dress with a scoop neckline, pale pumps, a simple gold necklace, and earrings that set off her dark hair. She smelled faintly of violets and looked better than lunch break at a chocolate factory.

"We've got to get out of here," I whispered to her.

"Thanks for stopping by!" Elizabeth and Martin said in unison. They escorted us to the door. "Come again soon!"

The hall was only slightly less busy than it had been. "All right, Dot. We head right for the subway. This place gives me the creeps."

"No," said Dot. She grabbed me by the arm that wasn't carrying my old clothes, and dragged me across the floor toward one of the grilled windows. No one gave us a second glance. We were dressed the same as everyone else there, now, and fit right in.

At the window another young woman in green greeted us. "I am Miss Goode. How may I help you?"

"We came to get our money," said Dot.

"How much?" Miss Goode asked.

Dot turned to me. "What do you say, Sid? Would twenty million be enough?"

"We can do that," said Miss Goode. "Just come around behind the counter to my desk."

Dot started after her. I grabbed Dot's shoulder. "What the fuck are you talking about?" I whispered.

"Just go along and keep quiet."

Miss Goode led us to a large glass-topped desk. "We'll need a photograph, of course. And a number." She spoke into a phone: "Daniel, bring out two cases . . . That's right." She called up a page on her computer and examined it. "Your bank," she said to me, "is Banque Thaler, Geneva. Your number is PN68578443. You'll have to memorize it eventually. Here, write it on your palm for now." She handed me a very nice ballpoint pen. Then she gave another number to Dot.

While she was doing this, a man came out of a door in the marble wall behind her. He carried two silver metal briefcases, and set them on the edge of Miss Goode's desk in front of Dot and me.

"Thank you, Daniel," she said. She turned to us. "Go ahead. Open them!"

I pulled the briefcase toward me and snapped it open. It was filled with tight bundles of crisp new one-hundred-dollar bills. Thirty of them.

"This is wonderful," Dot said. "Thank you so much!"

I closed my case and stood up. "Time to go, Dot."

"Just a minute," said Miss Goode. "I'll need your full name."

"Full name? What for?"

"For the Swiss accounts. All you've got there is three hundred thousand. The rest will be in your bank account. We'll need your photograph, too."

Dot tugged my elegant sleeve. "Sid forgot about that," she explained to Miss Goode. "Always in such a hurry. His name is Sidney Xavier Dubose. D-U-B-O-S-E. I'm Dorothy Gale."

I had reached my breaking point. "Shut up, Dot."

"Now for the photographs . . ." Miss Goode began.

"You can't have my photograph." I pulled away from Dot. I had the briefcase in my right hand and shoved my bag of clothes under my left.

"That's all right," said Miss Goode. "We'll use your photographs from the tailor program. Just run along. But come again!"

I was already stalking across the floor, my new shoes clipping along like metronomes. People parted to let me by. I went right for the ramp that led to the subway. A thin man smoking a long cigarette watched me curiously as I passed one of the tables; I put my hand against his chest and knocked him down. He sprawled there in astonishment, but did nothing; nor did anyone else.

By the time I hit the ramp I was jogging. At the bottom the platform was deserted, the bubble lights still shone gold, and you could not tell whether it was night or day. Dot came up breathlessly behind me.

"What is wrong with you!" she shouted.

I felt exhausted. I could not tell how long it had been since we broke into the mountain house. "What's wrong with me? What's wrong with this whole setup? This is not sane. What are they going to do to us? This can't be real; it has to be some kind of scam."

"If you think it's a scam, just give me that briefcase. I'll take care of it for you, you stupid redneck bastard."

I stood there sullenly. I didn't know what to say. She turned from me and went to the other end of the platform, as far away as she could get.

After a few minutes the light grew in the tunnel and the car, or one just like it, slid to a stop before us. The door opened. I got in immediately, and Dot followed. We sat next to each other in silence. The door shut, and the vehicle picked up speed until it was racing along as insanely as it had so many hours ago.

Dot tried to talk to me, but I just looked at the floor. Under the seat I saw the two gum wrappers, one of them crumpled into a knot, the other neatly folded as if it were still full.

That was the last time I ever saw Dot. I live in France now, but I have a house in Mexico and one in Vancouver. In Canada I can still go to stock car races. Somehow that doesn't interest me as much as it used to. Instead I drink wine that comes in bottles that have corks. My vocabulary has improved. I read books. I listen to music that has no lyrics. All because, as it turned out, I did have a Swiss bank account totaling ten million dollars. The money has made a bigger difference than I could have imagined possible. It was like a sword hanging over my head, like a wall between me and who I used to be. Within a month I left North Carolina: it made me nervous to stay in the state knowing that the house in the Blue Ridge was still there.

Sometimes I'm tempted to go back and see whether there really is a door in the back of that closet.

When Dot and I climbed the concrete stairs and emerged into the house, it was still night. It might have been only a minute after we went down. I went out to the living room, sat in the rustic leather chair, picked up the glass I had left next to it, and filled it to the brim with scotch. My briefcase full of three hundred thousand dollars stood on the hardwood floor beside the chair. I was dressed in a couple of thousand dollars worth of casual clothes; my shoes alone probably cost more than a month's rent on any place that I had ever lived.

Dot sat on the sofa and poured herself a drink, too. After a while she said, "I told you I'd make it up to you someday."

"How did you know about this?" I asked. "What is it?"

"It's a dream come true," Dot said. "You don't look a dream come true in the mouth."

"One person's dream come true is somebody else's nightmare," I said. "Somebody always has to pay." I had never thought that before, but as I spoke it I realized it was true.

Dot finished her scotch, picked up her briefcase and the green bag with her old skirt, sweater, and shoes, and headed for the door. She paused there and turned to me. She looked like twenty million bucks. "Are you coming?"

I followed her out. There was enough light from the moon that we were able to make our way down the dirt road to my car. The crickets chirped in the darkness. Dot opened the passenger door and got in.

"Wait a minute," I said. "Give me your bag."

Dot handed me her green bag. I dumped it out on the ground next to the car, then dumped my own out on top of it. I crumpled the bags and shoved them under the clothes for kindling. On top lay the denim jacket I had been wearing the night I got arrested in the Sears, that the state had kept for me while I served my time, and that I had put back on the day I left stir.

"What are you doing?" Dot asked.

"Bonfire," I said. "Good-bye to the old Dot and Sid."

"But you don't have any matches."

"Reach in the glove compartment. There's a box of Blue Tips."

FRANCES OLIVER

Dancing on Air

*Frances Oliver was born in Vienna and brought up, educated, and married in the United States. Subsequently she lived in a number of countries with her husband, who wrote travel books and shared her passion for mountains and mountaineering. After her husband's death, she and her daughter moved to Cornwall. She has published three non-supernatural novels—*All Souls *and* The Peacock's Eye, *set in Austria, and* The Tourist Season, *set in Turkey—and two "occult" novels:* Xargos, *also set in Turkey, and* Children of Epiphany, *set in Greece. Besides writing, she devotes much time to environmental and animal welfare campaigns, and is a local group co-coordinator for Friends of the Earth. She also loves reading and writing ghost stories. Her work has appeared in* All Hallows *and the anthology* Shadows and Silence.*

"Dancing on Air" was originally published in her story collection of the same title.

—E.D.

W hen you are so late, you should telephone," the night clerk said.
"I couldn't phone. I had to rush to catch the last bus from the airport." The girl bent over the ornate ledger snapped out her answer, but a second later was close to tears. The whole first afternoon of the damned Congress missed, and now this bloody man being rude.

"You could telephone from plane."

"You're not allowed to use mobile phones on the plane. And anyhow I don't have one."

The night clerk, waking up a bit more, read her name and gave her a dismissive inspection; slight, uncharismatic Susan Faring, a person of no wealth or importance, who would rush for a last bus rather than take a taxi, and without even a mobile phone. Then his tired and somewhat drink-befogged brain registered that she was pretty, and he spoke more gently. "Anyway, you have a nice room, good view, right over the park to the Congress House. Gates right across the street. Tomorrow morning you are on time."

"Thank you," said Susan, unmollified. The clerk shrugged and handed her the key. He did not offer to help with the suitcase. She was not as pretty as all that, and almost certainly a low tipper. Anyway, all suitcases now had wheels. One of the wheels was jamming. The clerk, who came from a country where most suitcases did not in fact have wheels, watched through half-closed eyes as Susan struggled over the thick carpet, past cheese plants and stodgy modernist chairs, towards the lifts.

In her room Susan drew back the curtains and opened the window to a warm summer night. She *could* see right across the park, as the clerk had said, to a lighted cupola. That must be the top of the Congress House, Susan thought, remembering the picture in the brochure. The cupola held more than light; there was movement and color. Some kind of penthouse party? Susan was curious. She had brought binoculars, planning to go bird-watching on the Neusiedlersee when the Congress was over. Quickly, she unpacked the binoculars and trained them on the big dome shining above dark trees.

Yes, there was a party—there were people dancing. A ball, a very formal one—perhaps even a costume ball. Women in long dresses, men in suits as colorful as the dresses, wine red, emerald, icy blue. But focus as she would, she could not see them clearly. They seemed to whirl towards the glass walls and immediately away again. There was the flicker of a wide wheeling skirt, a toss of bright hair, the angle of a bent shoulder, clasped hands upraised—glimpses only, the briefest glimpses. As she watched, still trying to get the binoculars to focus better, thin strains of music reached her. A waltz—a Strauss waltz perhaps? Nothing she recognized, and too faint to tell. Certainly a very fast waltz. A truly frenetic waltz; these dancers moved at a dizzy, almost incredible speed. Of course, the Austrians were known for such waltzing. . . . Whatever this ball was, it was fantastic. She must get a closer look.

Forgetting her fatigue, Susan dabbed at her face, ran a comb through her hair, and rushed downstairs. The ball was surely nothing to do with the opening of her own boring Congress, rather the last fling of another; but with such a party on, the bar might still be open. She might get a drink, hear the music, maybe sneak up to the cupola and watch. "There's a ball," she said quite cheerfully to the night clerk. "I want to go and see."

The night clerk nodded, paying no attention. Susan hurried across the street to the gates. To her surprise they were closed and chained. There was a watchman in the kiosk at the entrance. Seeing Susan, he shook his head and motioned for her to go. "*Zugesperrt*," he said irritably. "Shut."

"But there's a party going on. There's a ball," Susan exclaimed, in her excellent German.

The watchman shook his head again. "*Zugesperrt*."

Puzzled, Susan walked slowly back across the deserted street. The night clerk was dozing now. Susan glanced at the clock above his head and was startled to see that it was even later than she'd thought. In her frustration at the plane's delay, she had forgotten to adjust her watch to the time change. It was already 2:00 A.M. The party must have ended.

Back at her window, she verified that the cupola was now dark and silent. But why were the gates already locked? The guests must have left by another exit, Susan decided. Perhaps for security reasons only one gate was used at night. Still, it was strange that the whole building should go dark all at once, that everything should end so abruptly, with no sounds of departure . . . but she was much too exhausted to puzzle over that now. She reset her watch and clocked her waking time into the phone. A few minutes later she was deeply, dreamlessly asleep.

Next morning, Susan walked up a long graveled drive lined with brutally pollarded plane trees. The building she approached was an awkward marriage of styles, a pseudo-Renaissance, pseudo-Classical, late nineteenth century (she guessed) "Palazzo," a massive square block with Doric columns and marble steps all around, various incongruous floral friezes, and the glass cupola as its crown. If taste had been sparing, expense had not. With the addition of some no-nonsense glass and concrete annexes which certainly added to the incongruity, this seat of a "timber-rich aristocrat," as the brochure described him, was quite big enough to house two or three small conferences or a single quite large one.

There were in fact two different congresses taking place. Concentrating on finding the right desk, Susan kept her eyes at ground floor level. It was not until she had finished her signing and pinned on her badge that she looked up—straight into the cupola of polished glass.

"But how—" Susan exclaimed out loud. Feeling suddenly dizzy, she took hold of the desk before her.

"I say—is something wrong? Are you feeling ill?"

"No, it's all right. Just giddy for a moment. Such a long trip yesterday. My plane was so late."

The stocky woman who had addressed her was peering at Susan's badge. "I see you're from Ellifont too. How do you do? I'm Muriel Staines." She waggled her lapel with the badge on it. "From the Weston branch," she added, noting that Susan was not concentrating on the introduction. "The other lot here is xenotransplantation. The policy here is to mix different groups—a scientific meeting, and some other lot the scientists would consider airy-fairy. They want bridges between science and culture. I think it's nonsense. Far more useful to have related disciplines, like urologists and bacteriologists; they'd have some worthwhile info to exchange. But this time they have got it spot on. With the latest merger—" She stopped, seeing that Susan's face was still blank and she was still leaning on the desk. "My dear, are you really okay?"

"Yes. Probably just jet-lagged. I'll be fine in a minute."

"Jet-lagged? Shouldn't think so, just flying from London. Do you want me to get you anything?"

"No, thank you." Susan stepped away from the desk. She could still not bring herself to look up again. "Was there a party here last night?"

"Party? Not that I heard of. Not unless the Xenos booked the restaurant after hours."

"Is there a restaurant upstairs?"

"Oh no. Just the smaller seminar rooms. You see how the place is built. Waste of space really. *Folly de granger*. Or however you pronounce it." Muriel herself gazed briefly upwards. "You'd think for a Congress Center they'd have filled in the floors. Still, I guess people find it impressive, this big hall going right up to the roof."

Susan was calmer now. It couldn't have been the cupola where she had seen dancers. There must be other rooms, and the light had somehow projected . . . but that made no sense. Ah—but there might have been some kind of *son et lumière*, some odd lighting which had projected images up into the glass. That was surely it. Some kind of demonstration—they had used the hall to show off some new virtual reality technique. But then the audience should have been outside in the park, looking across and up, as she had from her hotel window. Well, maybe they were. Maybe that was why the park was so dark. And if not—well, one could hallucinate when very tired, and groggy from hours of foul recycled air in an airport-confined plane. She determined to fix her attention on Muriel Staines, but Muriel Staines had fled, to badge-hole some other more responsive or important person across the hall.

During the first lecture, a sales talk trumpeting the wonders of Ellifont's new Biometristic Systems, Susan's mind continued to wander. *I wasn't that tired. I didn't imagine it. Some kind of demonstration—but what? Surely nothing to do with xenotransplantation. Then some new investment of Ellifont. Or just entertainment? And why then didn't Muriel know?*

"What was it they were demonstrating last night?" she said at lunch to the aging Ellifont executive—what branch was he from: Brussels? Hamburg?—seated beside her.

"Last night?" The grey man swallowed, nervous at being addressed, and peered at Susan's badge. *Running scared,* Susan thought. *Afraid he's missed something important.* "I didn't know there were any demonstrations. The bar closed at twelve and that was the last thing open. As far as I know. For some reason, they don't like late-night parties in this place."

"There couldn't have been a ball? Or some kind of *son et lumière?*"

"Son and who? Oh, oh yes, I get you. No ball with our crowd. And I don't see the xenotransplantation people doing the salsa." He was becoming more confident. "You're in the Barrymount branch. What do you do?"

"Translations from German. I work mostly at home."

"Translation, eh? Not very lively, I expect." Annoyed at this silly remark, Susan extolled the importance and interest of technical translation, though in fact most of what she did was boring, and she sometimes wondered if her previous job, editing a magazine for button collectors, had not been a far more rewarding one. Anyhow, her heart was not in the conversation. If there'd been no party and no demonstration, who or what could she have seen dancing in a floorless glass dome at half past one in the morning? That sweaty fat man next to her on the plane—a Russian Mafia type he seemed—could he have put something in her drink? *Don't be paranoid,* she told herself, and tried to keep her mind on her dull companion.

After dinner that evening, Susan hurried back to her room to put some notes in her laptop and get ready for an evening reception at the mayor's house. By the time she finished it was dark. With beating heart she looked across to the cupola. There was light, but only such as would come from below, not the glaring light of yesterday. No music, no dancers. *Thank God,* Susan thought, and drew the curtains. *That's it, I won't look out again.*

The reception was sensibly brief. Not being a Stockhausen fan, Susan had no interest in the concert which followed, and agreed to go to a nearby bar with some colleagues. Their table was drowned out by the next, which held a group of German-speaking xenotransplantationists being entertained by a hefty young Congress official with a shock of straw-blond hair, a drinker's nose and flush, and a resounding voice. He was telling jokes in local dialect. Then, in the abrupt way of the tipsy, he turned more serious, while his voice continued to boom.

"There are many local stories. Even about our wonderful Congress Center. The old place was a ruin before the town took it over, and someone had the brilliant idea to restore it for international meetings. Now it's one of the most popular in Europe and has lived down its bad reputation." He paused.

"What bad reputation? Tell us, Gottfried!" the audience urged. As if he needed encouragement, Susan thought. But she turned in her chair to hear him better.

"Well—do you know why they will not hold any dances here? That big hall—it is made for late parties, for dancing. Well, the original owner who built this pile, the Count of Tiefenwalden, was very extravagant. No money to keep up the place, but marvelous parties. When his daughter turned eighteen he invited all the aristocracy and the important people of the town—even some of the unimportant people—to a great ball. There was an orchestra in one of the balconies playing wild waltzes. The guests danced as if bewitched. But that night there was heavy snow and very strong winds. When he had that big dome made, Tiefenwalden did not think about our climate." He paused again, increasing the drama. His audience was appropriately hushed.

"Nobody knows if it was the snow, the heat from below, all those gas lamps and dancing people, the wind, the vibration of the music—or all of those together—but anyhow the dome broke and crashed down. That whole great bell of glass fell on the dancers. The one we have now, of course," he added, not too drunk to realize this story might have unwanted effects, "is an entirely modern one, very well designed and supported and perfectly safe in any weather.

"Many people were killed. It was carnage, terrible, like a bomb. When my mother was a child she had a friend whose great-grandmother was one of those who survived, but was scarred for the rest of her life. The Tiefenwaldens never lived it down. They sold their palazzo and moved away soon after. There were other strange stories about that family. Some said they were cursed. The daughter and her secret lover escaped; they had left the dance early to elope. But they were never heard from again.

"And this is not all; if you like ghost stories. But of course you are scientists, and you don't."

"Why should we not like ghost stories? Everyone can enjoy fantasy, you don't have to believe in it," a female Xeno said irritably, and others joined in, "Go on, tell us the ghost story, Gottfried."

"Well then. There is a local legend that sometimes those dancers, those dead dancers, reappear. Up in the dome itself, dancing on air, dancing in the dome that killed them. A kind of *Walpurgisnacht* scene, but much more colorful. No dancing skeletons, oh no, and the women in beautiful long dresses, just as they wore then. But if you look too close you might see some of them are covered in blood. But of course you can't look too close. You can only see them a distance away. When you come nearer they disappear. And when they are seen it can be before a catastrophic event. People claimed to have seen them before the two great wars began, and before the great flu epidemic. But people would say that. It can also be a more personal message, that if you and you alone see them, you or someone who lies very near to you is going to die."

"Now he's making a good story better," said one member of the audience to another.

"Or a banal story worse."

Gottfried overheard. "No, really. I am just reporting what the local people say. Of course it's all hysteria. When you have a horrible incident like that people will always start to see ghosts. And although of course all this is nonsense, there is a strong feeling among the local people that no dances and no big evening parties should ever be held in the place again. The hall could be hired for weddings, but no one has ever asked."

"What ridiculous superstition," said another of Gottfried's audience. "Don't you lose money by not holding dances in the great hall?"

"Oh no. After all, we hire to Congresses mostly, and since the famous Congress of Vienna, Congresses don't dance so much. And the place is actually a little grim at night. It's okay for lectures, but the acoustics are really terrible for music. We tried it once. It makes Mozart sound like Stockhausen. Also, we have so many other beautiful reception rooms in the town. When they've spent all day at the Center, people like a change of scene. Tonight you went to the Mayor's mansion—did you notice the inlaid Renaissance cupboards? Now there is another interesting story . . ."

". . . and there's a rumor that's what will happen if the next merger goes ahead. But I don't think we should worry. Not yet anyway. Susan?" Her neighbor leaned closer. "Really, Susan. You haven't listened to a word I said."

"Oh, I'm sorry. That man's voice is so loud. What was it—the next—the merger—" Susan trailed off.

"I'm not going to repeat it all," her neighbor said huffily. "Well. It is noisy in here. And hot. I think I've had about enough. Anyone walking back to the Park Hotel?"

Back in her room, Susan determined to keep away from the window. *Don't pull the curtains. Don't look.* She tried to concentrate on her detective story. "The vicar was late, thought Mary Byrne, coming in with her armful of wheat and flowers to arrange for the harvest festival. On the threshold she dropped her flowers and screamed. A trail of blood and broken glass led to the altar where . . ."

Susan put down the book and picked up her bird-watcher's manual. She had planned to tick all the birds you might see on the Neusiedlersee. Then, thinking she heard faint strains of music, she lay back and put her hands over her ears. What she could hear now was her heart thudding violently in her chest.

It's ridiculous. A ridiculous superstition. I don't even believe in ghosts, not even in ESP, all that rubbish. But I saw the dancers. There must be some rational explanation. It's a common sort of story, I could have read it before, seen it in a movie or something, and because I was tired and the bad air on the plane . . . But it was no use. The same sentence ran through her head, over and over. "*Du, oder jemand der dir nahe liegt wird sterben.*" You or someone who lies near to you is going to die.

Who then? In spite of herself, the morbid speculation took over Susan's mind. She was an only child and her parents were dead. She had parted from her last boyfriend a year ago, without much regret. She had friends but no best friends. No one in the category of very near. If someone was doomed it had to be herself. Better perhaps than a nearest and dearest, but a grim prospect; and no matter how often she told herself it was all absurd, her heart went on racing and the hands that still covered her ears were damp with sweat.

It was almost dawn before she slept, and it seemed she had slept only minutes when a loud commotion woke her. It sounded as if everyone was out in the corridor; she must have overslept. She struggled out of bed. Then she saw her alarm. It was only six. She felt another surge of fear. Was there a fire or something? Was this the catastrophe? She threw on her robe and quickly opened the door.

Muriel Staines, the bombastic Ellifont delegate, was out in the hall too, baggy and disheveled in yellow chenille and fuzzy mules. *Obviously not expecting night visits from colleagues* was the thought that came to Susan in spite of her fears.

"It's poor old Oscar," Muriel hissed. "Oscar Heard from our Personnel Department. Next door to you. He's had a heart attack. They're in there trying to get his heart going, but I think it's too late."

"Oh," said Susan. "How dreadful." Then, as Muriel was still hovering with her eyes trained on the closed door next to Susan's own, "I think we should go back inside then, don't you? Not stand about in the corridor like ghouls."

Muriel gave her a startled look. "I was hardly being that. I thought maybe they'd need help. Phone the family or something. My, but you are edgy."

"I'm sorry. I am edgy, I guess. I've had a bad night, don't mind me. I'll see you at breakfast."

They both went back into their rooms. Susan dressed rapidly and rehearsed a pretext for reappearing in the hall. Couldn't sleep any more, decided to have an early morning walk. Take binoculars, look for early birds. When she re-emerged with the binoculars round her neck, she was in time to see Oscar Heard carried out of his room on a stretcher, with a sheet over his face.

"Well, it can't have been as bad a night as all that, Susan," said Muriel at breakfast. "I haven't seen you smile so much since you arrived."

"Really? I suppose I'm just happy because I saw a crested lark this morning on my early walk. They're quite rare now."

"I suppose you record them all, and send the list to some bird preservation society."

"Yes, I do," Susan answered. She hadn't recorded it. She hadn't in fact seen it. She needed some excuse for the exaltation she could not hide. It was awful to be happy about someone else's death, and also awful to find oneself, a supposedly rational person, so affected by a silly superstition. One of the papers Susan had translated explained that according to statistical laws mere coincidence accounted quite easily for such things as the death of the man next door. And as for what she had seen—there still might be some logical explanation. Or there might be something to ESP after all, some form of electrical transmission by the brain we just haven't explored yet—why should it be any stranger than a mobile phone?

"Not listening," said Muriel. "Off with the birds again, she is. This isn't a twitchers' Congress, Susan, you know. We're here for Ellifont."

"Please pass the milk, would you?" Susan said, ignoring the sharpness of Muriel's tone. Big Sister, Big Brother types. Ellifont was full of them. Corporation loyalty was almost a religion, as well as a stick that employees like Muriel could use to beat anyone who offended them or threatened their jobs. When Susan began working for Ellifont she had once or twice made the obvious pun, "Elephantine multinationals," and learned quickly from the silence which followed that Ellifont was not to be joked about. She was glad she could work mostly at home, that her work was not in sales or research but only translation, something private and neutral. Anyway she needed her job.

"You'll be at the extra meeting tonight, will you Susan? Not off looking for owls. There's some new software that fits right into your line of work."

"Yes, of course I will." Damn the bitch. *It's almost as if she's deputized to test me, watch me.* A new anxiety surfaced. Why had she, obscure Susan Faring, been sent to the Congress anyway, most of which had nothing to do with her work; and why was Muriel playing Big Sister so determinedly? Susan wondered if she was under some kind of special scrutiny. Some of what she'd recently translated was marked confidential. Perhaps they were worried that she might give company secrets away. Put documents in a hollow tree for a fellow twitcher to pick up? Susan smiled again.

"Twitchers," said Muriel to the table at large after Susan had left. "If you ask me, they're all a bit barmy."

In spite of her new worry, Susan's buoyancy remained. Having a life, after all, was more important than having a job. Once more, she reprimanded herself. How stupid, how primitive to feel that because that poor man died she had actually been given her life back. But there must be something to account for such hallucinations—maybe something like whatever makes a big flock of birds with no leader all turn the same way at once. . . . She would find stuff to read about ESP when she got back. In the meantime, to hell with Muriel Staines and her meeting. Tonight she would celebrate what she could not help seeing as her reprieve.

"I wanted to talk to you," Susan accosted the official called Gottfried. She was emboldened by two quick glasses of wine, and Gottfried had obviously had more than that already. "That story you told last night. About the dancers in the glass dome. I've seen them. The night I arrived. And early this morning the man in the room next to mine died of a heart attack. I don't believe in things like this. I'm not—" Susan fished for a word and then fell back on the English. "I'm not psychic. I'm not superstitious. But I saw those dancers. Can you explain it?"

Gottfried's professional smile failed him for a moment. Then he laughed and patted her on the back. He answered in English, which Susan found a little insulting. Her German was as good as his English, or better. "My dear young lady, you cannot have seen anything because I made this story up. Even the scientists sometimes like a little frisson. Well—maybe I didn't make it up complete. I am not so creative. Ghostly dancers and so on—you know there are many legends like this. If you look you find the same stories all over the world."

"You mean there isn't any local legend? You mean there never were any dancers killed in this building?"

"Maybe. How do I know? I am not from here. I just make up this story. I am sorry if it upset you. Next time I make a happier story for our guests. Now excuse me. I have to meet some people. You look very good tonight. Maybe we have a drink later?" He patted her shoulder and moved off.

He's lying, Susan thought. *The story is true, but it's bad publicity and he wasn't supposed to tell it. Well, I'm going to tell it, even if people think I'm nuts.*

"Old Gottfried is circulating wildly tonight," said a tall man at her elbow. "What was it you said to him? He looked pretty worried."

"Oh. You're one of the xenotransplantationists? Do you speak German? Oh, you are German. Did you hear the story he told last night?"

"I think the explanation is quite simple," said Dr Hans Unruh, the xenotransplantationist, another drink later. "You were tired and nervous, so your brain played a trick on you, a little like a déjà vu, which is really, as you may know, like a very minor epileptic attack. You saw the dancers—a hallucination of course—after you heard the story, but your brain makes you remember it as something you saw before."

"That's complete nonsense," Susan answered, firmly but without rancor. She was aware that this man was quite attractive. "I haven't had a déjà vu since adolescence, and it was never like that."

"There you are—you are one of those who did have them. Sometimes in times of stress it comes back."

"And the man who died—that's pure coincidence?"

"Yes. And just what reinforced your false memory."

They went on arguing and drinking until the bar emptied for dinner and evening meetings. The argument was very convivial. Sometimes, making a point, Hans touched Susan's arm or hand, and once he let his hand stay on hers and she did not pull away. "We are missing dinner," Hans said finally, and later, "I'm late for my meeting."

Susan announced she was not going to her meeting, which would be a dead bore anyway. Hans said so would his. It was a paper on something called the Tafur virus that he'd already read and thought alarmist. If one paid attention to men like its author, Dr. Warheit, all their work would have to stop, science would never progress . . . really, he would prefer to ignore this paper, so why did they not go to a nice restaurant for dinner together? Which they did, still arguing a bit but concentrating less and less on the argument and more and more on each other. At last Susan said, "Look, I can prove it was the night I arrived. I said something to the night clerk about seeing a ball going on and wanting to go find out what it was. Maybe he'll remember. Oh, and also the porter at the gate. I thought the park would be open because of the ball and he kept saying it was shut. If we ask them and they confirm it, that will be proof."

By the time they reached Susan's hotel they were walking hand in hand and laughing a great deal. The night clerk said he could not remember. Afraid of deportation, he made it his business never to remember anything. The porter at the gate, annoyed by another drunken couple bothering him at his post, said there were always people asking to get into the park at night and he could not remember if Susan had been one.

"There you are," said Hans. They walked back to the hotel lobby and stood for a moment, a moment of awkwardness, of last hesitation. Then Hans said, "I know what we must do. Maybe I too am psychic. Maybe I too will see those dancers through your magic binoculars. Let's go up and try it. Do you mind?"

"No, I don't mind. Yes, let's go up."

In the lift, they gazed at each other and laughed again and then Hans leaned down and kissed Susan lightly on the mouth. In her room, given the binoculars, he made a great play of focusing them, and gave vent to a series of exclamations. "Amazing! Horrific! Truly out of this world!"

"The cupola is pitch dark. You haven't seen a thing." Susan was still laughing. What she was thinking was *It's been a year, a whole year. I need this man.*

"Oh yes. I do. A real *danse macabre*. All sorts of skeletons with floating chiffon. They are waving to me. Hello, skeletons." And he waved.

"Don't!" said Susan, to whom this was suddenly not so funny.

"What a nervous little mouse you are," said Hans affectionately. "I do see something. I see you." He put down the binoculars and took her in his arms.

Susan awoke to the sound of retching.

Her head was pounding from the amount she herself had drunk. Poor Hans; she hoped he wasn't embarrassed, though men usually seemed much less concerned about unappealing bodily functions. It was not very romantic to have made love half the night and wake to that sound, but you did not expect romance on a one-night stand. Her first and probably only. Had he even used a condom? She couldn't remember, she'd been so drunk. She couldn't remember much at all. In any case, a scientist, a biologist, would surely be healthy—and responsible. "Oh shit," murmured Susan, and buried her head in the pillow. In the light of this misty dawn the whole episode began to seem reckless and silly. Who was he, anyway, really—and what, if anything, had they in common? She didn't much like the idea of xenotransplantation, of whatever he did. And if he slept around at every Congress he might not be a very good risk.

What had made her do it, she realized, was not so much the frustration of a year's celibacy but the exaltation inspired by a stupid superstition. If she said that to him— "I slept with you because I was so jubilant that someone else had died and it did not have to be me"—then he would really have something to laugh at.

She heard a new sound, that of toothbrushing. He must certainly sleep around a lot if he carried a toothbrush in his pocket. Or was he using hers? Wide awake now, Susan sat up. She was very proprietary about things like her toothbrush. That a man slept with you did not give him the right . . . but she couldn't very well knock on the door and ask whose toothbrush it was. "Oh shit," she said to herself again, and lay back once more on the bed.

Hans emerged a few minutes later, smelling of toothpaste and soap. He sat down on the bed. "I woke you," he said. "Sorry. Mind if I switch on the light a minute? Well, we both had too much to drink."

He looked ashen. Still handsome but hollow-eyed and feverish, a different Hans. "It's okay," Susan said, conscious of her sweaty armpits and the sour taste in her own mouth. "I see you're all spruced up already. I think I need my turn in the bathroom."

When she came out he was fully dressed. "You're going," Susan said. There was no question, no complaint, no regret in her tone. He had used her toothbrush—and washcloth and towel and soap, all without asking, and she wanted him out.

"Yes. I should have been going over some notes last night. Better do it now before breakfast. There's just enough time. Well."

"Well," Susan echoed. Now he was dressed he looked better again and she almost asked that weak, fatal, and usually female question. No. Let him ask it. If anyone does, let him.

He did, but without conviction. "It's my last day. Will I see you again?"

"I'm going bird-watching when I leave here. On the Neusiedlersee. If you want to come. . . ." She knew he would not, and he said at once with visible relief, "Birdwatching? Not in my line. Sorry." He hesitated. "Well," he said once more. "Look— it was happy, wasn't it? It was a good night."

"Yes, it was." In fact it *had* been a good night. As much of it as she could remember.

"And I hope I have cured your fears about the *Walpurgisnacht* dancers."

"Uh, that. Yes, I suppose I was silly—but I *did* see them."

"Incorrigible," he said with last night's teasing smile, and took her hand. For a moment Susan thought he would shake it, like a good colleague, but he held it and then leaned over and kissed her lightly, as he had in the lift. She noticed that his hand was hot and his mouth dry. As he moved to the door, he lurched suddenly and leaned against the wall.

'Hans, are you all right?'

"Yes, I don't know what this is. Probably. I just don't take drink as well as I used to. Getting older. Good-bye, little mouse." And then he was gone.

Susan came back to London with her head full of birds. The Neusiedlersee had been marvelous. She had been so right to take a week of her holiday following the Congress, though she knew this was frowned upon. Ellifont expected you back from a Congress directly, fired up to advance their growth—that magic word—and of course your own career. At the moment, Susan didn't care. There was, however, a small cloud on the horizon, a strange nausea that had afflicted her the last two mornings. Too soon for pregnancy symptoms, and she'd taken a morning after pill just to be sure. Well, if it went on she would have a test.

She was not expected in the office till later that week, but two papers had already been faxed for her to translate, and an urgent message was on the machine. To phone a hospital, a hospital Susan had never heard of. Probably something to do with her work; the papers might be medical, though she didn't usually do medical papers. Glancing at the first page of the fax, her eye was caught by a phrase, and she remembered something that had escaped her at the Congress. *Jemand der dir nahe liegt* does not mean someone who lies near to you in space, like someone in an adjacent room. It means someone near and dear, someone you love. If there is no one like that it would have to be yourself. She told herself angrily not to be stupid and paranoid again. Then the phone rang.

It was the obscure hospital and whoever was calling, a Dr. Bermain, sounded both urgent and flustered. "Miss Faring? We've been trying to get hold of you. You were at the Ellifont Congress at Steinschlag—is that right?"

"Yes, I was. Why?"

"At the same time as a scientific group?"

"Xenotransplantation," said Susan, wondering why he himself had not used the word.

"Miss Faring—please bear with me. I must ask you a question. Did you have any—any close contact with anyone from that group?"

"Is that any of your business?"

"I'm afraid it is. And it is very important that you tell me."

"I met a man called Hans. I don't even remember his last name. I slept with him. Is that what you mean by close contact? And now please tell me what this is about. Is something wrong? Has something happened to Hans?"

The doctor cleared his throat. Susan found the conversation of that drunken night was now coming back with wonderful clarity. "Hans is dead, isn't he? Something called the Tafur virus. Was their research a little more dangerous than they thought?"

Dr. Bermain, caught off guard, sounded terrified. Far more terrified than Susan herself. "The Tafur virus! But how—" Then he checked himself. "Miss Faring, we really can't discuss this on the phone. It is most important that you come to see us right away."

Susan put her phone onto Record. "Yes, the Tafur virus," she said slowly and distinctly. "One of those transgenic ones, right? That come through gene splicing or xenotransplantation. Is it always lethal? How long do I have?"

"Miss Faring, I cannot—you must not assume—please do come to the hospital. We'll explain everything there."

"Shouldn't you send an ambulance? How contagious is it? How contagious am I?"

"The indications so far are for direct contact—but no, Miss Faring, it is simply imperative that you come. For your own sake and the sake of the wider community." That favorite phrase. The doctor was so frightened he was fairly spluttering. "We may have to impose a quarantine order. We prefer not to do that. Miss Faring, since you seem to know something about this, let me say one thing. When the first symptoms appear it may be too late."

The morning nausea, Susan thought. *Like Hans.* She still felt no fear. She felt rather a strange elation. There was a very sinister secret here and she was going to blow the lid off. Blow it sky-high. And that would indeed be something for Dr. Bermain's "wider community." She checked that the phone was recording. "Okay, I'll come. But first I want to hear more about this Tafur virus. For all I know this may be a hoax. Hans himself, you see, was given to joking. And I, Dr. Bermain, feel perfectly fine. You might say I feel as if I'm dancing on air."

M. RICKERT

Cold Fires

M. Rickert lives and works in upstate New York. Since the appearance of her first story in 1999, "The Girl Who Ate Butterflies," she has become a frequent and welcome contributor to The Magazine of Fantasy & Science Fiction. *Last year her story "Bread and Bombs" was reprinted in both* The Year's Best Fantasy and Horror *and* Year's Best SF 9. *Her work has been featured on the Webzine* Ideomancer *and in* Rabid Transit, *a curated chapbook series. Next year, Golden Gryphon Press will publish Rickert's debut short story collection,* Map of Dreams. *"Cold Fires," a haunting tale of love in winter, was published just in time for winter in F&SF's October/November double issue.*

—K.L. & G.G.

It was so cold that daggered ice hung from the eaves with dangerous points that broke off and speared the snow in the afternoon sun, only to be formed again the next morning. Snowmobile shops and ski rental stores, filled with brightly polished snowmobiles and helmets and skis and poles and wool knitted caps and mittens with stars stitched on them and down jackets and bright-colored boots stood frozen at the point of expectation when that first great snow fell on Christmas night and everyone thought that all that was needed for a good winter season was a good winter snow, until the cold reality set in and the employees munched popcorn or played cards in the back room because it was so cold that no one even wanted to go shopping, much less ride a snowmobile. Cars didn't start but heaved and ticked and remained solidly immobile, stalagmites of ice holding them firm. Motorists called Triple A and Triple A's phone lines became so crowded they routed the calls to a trucking company in Pennsylvania where a woman with a very stressed voice answered the calls with the curt suggestion that the caller hang up and dial again.

It was so cold dogs barked to go outside, and immediately barked to come back in, and then barked to go back out again; frustrated dog owners leashed their pets and stood shivering in the snow as shivering dogs lifted icy paws, walking in a kind of Irish dance, spinning in that dog circle thing, trying to find the perfect spot to relieve themselves while dancing high paws to keep from freezing to the ground.

It was so cold birds fell from the sky like tossed rocks, frozen except for their tiny eyes, which focused on the sun as if trying to understand its betrayal.

That night the ice hung so heavy from the power lines that they could no longer maintain the electric arc and the whole state went black, followed within the hour by the breakdown of the phone lines. Many people would have a miserable night but the couple had a wood-burning stove. It crackled with flame that bit the dry and brittle birch and consumed the chill air where even in the house they had been wearing coats and scarves that they removed as the hot aura expanded. It was a good night for soup, heated on the cast iron stove and scenting the whole house with rosemary and onion; a good night for wine, the bottle of red they bought on their honeymoon and had been saving for a special occasion, and it was a good night to sit by the stove on the floor, their backs resting against the couch pillows, watching the candles flicker in the waves of heat while the house cracked and heaved beneath its thick iced roof. They decided to tell stories, the sort of stories that only the cold and the fire, the wind and the silent dark combined could make them tell.

"I grew up on an island," she said. "Well, you know that. I've already told you about the smell of salt and how it still brings the sea to my breath, how the sound of bathwater can make me weep, how before the birds fell from the sky like thrown rocks, the dark arc of their wings, in certain light, turned white and how certain tones of metal, a chain being dragged by a car, a heavy pan that clangs against its lid become the sound of ships and boats leaving the harbor, I've already told you all that but I think you should know that my family is descended from pirates, we are not decent people, everything we own has been stolen, even who we are, my hair for instance, these blonde curls can be traced not to any relatives for they are all dark and swarthy but to the young woman my great-great-grandfather brought home to his wife, intended as a sort of helpmate but apparently quite worthless in the kitchen, though she displayed a certain fondness for anything to do with strawberries, you understand the same fruit I embrace for its short season, oh how they taste of summer, and my youth!

"Now that I have told you this, I may as well tell you the rest. This blonde maid of my great-great-grandfather's house, who could not sew, or cook, or even garden well but who loved strawberries as if they gave her life, became quite adept at rejecting any slightly imperfect fruit. She picked through the bowls that great-great-grandmother brought in from the garden and tossed those not perfectly swollen or those with seeds too coarse to the dogs who ate them greedily then panted at her feet and became worthless hunters, so enamored were they with the sweet. Only perfect berries remained in the white bowl and these she ate with such a manner of tongue and lips that great-great-grandfather who came upon her like that, once by chance and ever after by intention, sitting in the sun at the wooden kitchen table, the dogs slathering at her feet, sucking strawberries, ordered all the pirates to steal more of the red fruit which he traded unreasonably for until he became quite the laughingstock and the whole family was in ruin.

"But even this was not enough to bring great-great-grandfather to his senses and he did what just was not done in those days and certainly not by a pirate who could take whatever woman he desired—he divorced great-great-grandmother and married the strawberry girl who, it is said, came to her wedding in a wreath of strawberry ivy, and carried a bouquet of strawberries from which she plucked, even in the midst of the sacred ceremony, red bulbs of fruit which she ate so greedily that when it came time to offer her assent she could only nod and smile bright red lips the color of sin.

"The strawberry season is short and it is said she grew pale and weak in its waning. Great-great-grandfather took to the high seas and had many adventures, raiding boats where he passed the gold and coffers of jewels, glanced at the most beautiful women and glanced away (so that later, after the excitement had passed, these same women looked into mirrors to see what beauty had been lost) and went instead, quite eagerly, to the kitchen where he raided the fruit. He became known as a bit of a kook.

"In the meantime, the villagers began to suspect that the strawberry girl was a witch. She did not appreciate the gravity of her situation but continued to visit great-great-grandmother's house as if the other woman was her own mother and not the woman whose husband she had stolen. It is said that great-great-grandmother sicced the dogs on her but they saw the blonde curls and smelled her strawberry scent and licked her fingers and toes and came back to the house with her, tongues hanging out and grinning doggedly at great-great-grandmother who, it is said, then turned her back on the girl who was either so naïve or so cunning that she spoke in a rush about her husband's long departures, the lonely house on the hill, the dread of coming winter, a perfect babble of noise and nonsense that was not affected by great-great-grandmother's cold back until, the villagers said, the enchantment became perfect and she and great-great-grandmother were seen walking the cragged hills to market days as happy as if they were mother and daughter or two old friends and perhaps this is where it would have all ended, a confusion of rumor and memory were it not for the strange appearance of the rounded bellies of both women and the shocking news that they both carried great-great-grandfather's child which some said was a strange coincidence and others said was some kind of trick.

"Great-great-grandfather's ship did not return when the others did and the other pirate wives did not offer this strawberry one any condolences. He was a famous seaman, and it was generally agreed that he had not drowned, or crashed his ship at the lure of sirens, but had simply abandoned his witchy wife.

"All that winter great-great-grandfather's first and second wives grew suspiciously similar bellies, as if size were measured against size to keep an even girth. At long last the strawberry wife took some minor interest in hearth and home and learned to bake bread that great-great-grandfather's wife said would be more successfully called crackers, and soup that smelled a bit too ripe but which the dogs seemed to enjoy. During this time great-great-grandmother grew curls, and her lips, which had always seemed a mastless ship anchored to the plane of her face, became strawberry shaped. By spring when the two were seen together, stomachs returned to corset size, and carrying between them, a bald, blue-eyed baby, they were often mistaken for sisters. The villagers even became confused about which was the witch and which, the bewitched.

"About this time, in the midst of a hushed ongoing debate amongst the villagers regarding when to best proceed with the witch burning (after the baby, whose lineage was uncertain, had been weaned seemed the general consensus) great-great-grandfather returned and brought with him a shipload of strawberries. The heavy scent drove the dogs wild. Great-great-grandfather drove the villagers mad with strawberries and then, when the absolute height of their passion had been aroused, stopped giving them away and charged gold for them, a plan that was whispered in his ears by the two wives while he held his baby who sucked on strawberries the way other babies sucked on tits.

"In this way, great-great-grandfather grew quite rich and built a castle shaped like a ship covered in strawberry vines and with a room at the back, away from the sea, which was made entirely of glass and housed strawberries all year. He lived there with the two wives and the baby daughter and nobody is certain who is whose mother in our family line.

"Of course she did not stay but left one night, too cruel and heartless to even offer an explanation. Great-great-grandfather shouted her name for hours as if she was simply lost until, at last, he collapsed in the strawberry room, crushing the fruit with his large body and rolling in the juice until he was quite red with it and frightening as a wounded animal. His first wife found him there and steered him to a hot bath. They learned to live together again without the strawberry maid. Strangers who didn't know their story often commented on the love between them. The villagers insisted they were both bewitched, the lit candles in the window to guide her return given as evidence. Of course she never did come back."

Outside in the cold night, even the moon was frozen. It shed a white light of ice over their pale yard and cast a ghost glow into the living room that haunted her face. He studied her as if she were someone new in his life and not the woman he'd known for seven years. Something about that moon glow combined with the firelight made her look strange, like a statue at a revolt.

She smiled down at him and cocked her head. "I tell you this story," she said, "to explain if ever you should wake and find me gone, it is not an expression of lack of affection for you, but rather, her witchy blood that is to be blamed."

"What became of her?"

"Oh, no one knows. Some say she had a lover, a pirate from a nearby cove, and they left together, sailing the seas for strawberries. Some say she was an enchanted mermaid and returned to the sea. Some say she came to America and was burned at the stake."

"Which do you think is true?"

She leaned back and sighed, closing her eyes. "I think she's still alive," she whispered, "breaking men's hearts, because she is insatiable."

He studied her in repose, a toppled statue while everything burned.

"Now it's your turn," she said, not opening her eyes, and sounding strangely distant. Was that a tear at the corner of her eye? He turned away from her. He cleared his throat.

"All right then. For a while I had a job in Castor, near Rhome, in a small art museum there. I was not the most qualified for the work but apparently I was the most qualified who was willing to live in Castor, population 954, I kid you not. It was a nice little collection, actually. Most of the population of Castor had come through to view the paintings at least once but it was my experience they seemed just as interested in the carpeting, the light fixtures, and the quantity of fish in the river as they were in the work of the old masters. Certainly the museum never saw the kind of popular attention the baseball field hosted, or the bowling lanes just outside of town.

"What had happened was this. In the 1930s Emile Castor, who had made his fortune on sweet cough drops, had decided to build a fishing lodge. He purchased a beautiful piece of forested property at the edge of what was then a small community, and built his 'cabin,' a six-bedroom, three-bath house with four stone hearth fireplaces and large windows that overlooked the river in the backyard. Even though

Castor had blossomed to a population of nearly a thousand by the time I arrived, deer still came to drink from that river.

"When Emile Castor died in 1989 he stated in his will that the house be converted into a museum to display his private collection. He bequeathed all his estate to the support of this project. Of course, his relatives, a sister, a few old cousins, and several nieces and nephews contested this for years but Mr. Castor was a thorough man and the legalities were tight as a rock. What his family couldn't understand, other than, of course, what they believed was the sheer cruelty of his act, was where this love of art had come from. Mr. Castor, who fished and hunted and was known as something of a ladies' man (though he never married), smoked cigars (chased by lemon cough drops) and built his small fortune on his 'masculine attitude,' as his sister referred to it in an archived letter.

"The kitchen was subdivided. A wall was put up which cut an ugly line right down the middle of what had once been a large picture window that overlooked the river. Whoever made this decision and executed it so poorly was certainly no appreciator of architecture. It was ugly and distorted and an insult to the integrity of the place. What remained of the original room became the employee kitchen: a refrigerator, a stove, a large sink, marble countertops, and a tiled mosaic floor; a small stained-glass window by Chagall was set beside the remaining slice of larger window. It remained, in spite of the assault it suffered, a beautiful room, and an elaborate employee kitchen for our small staff.

"The other half of the kitchen was now completely blocked off and inaccessible other than by walking through the employee kitchen. That, combined with the large window which shed too much light to expose any works of art to, had caused this room to develop into a sort of oversized storage room. It was a real mess when I got there.

"The first thing I did was sort through all that junk, unearthing boxes of outdated pamphlets and old stationery, a box of old toilet paper and several boxes of old Castor photographs which I carried to my office to be catalogued and preserved. After a week or so of this I found the paintings, box after box of canvasses painted by an amateur hand, quite bad, almost at the level of a schoolchild, without a child's whimsy, and all of the same woman. I asked Darlene, who acted as bookkeeper, ticket taker, and town gossip what she thought of them.

"'That must be Mr. Castor's work,' she said.

"'I didn't know he painted.'

"'Well he did, you can see for yourself. Folks said he was nuts about painting out here. Are they all like these?'

"'More or less.'

"'Should have stuck to cough drops,' she pronounced. (This from a woman who once confided in me her absolute glee at seeing a famous jigsaw puzzle, glued and framed, hanging in some restaurant in a nearby town.)

"When all was said and done we had fifteen boxes of those paintings and I decided to hang them in the room that was half of what had once been a magnificent kitchen. Few people would see them there, and that seemed right; they really were quite horrid. The sunlight could cause no more damage than their very presence already exuded.

"When they were at last all hung, I counted a thousand various shapes and sizes of the same dark-haired, gray-eyed lady painted in various styles, the deep velvet colors of Renaissance, the soft pastel hues of Baroque, some frightening bright green reminiscent of Matisse, and strokes that swirled wildly from imitation of van Gogh to the thick direct lines of a grade schooler. I stood in the waning evening light staring at this grotesquerie, this man's art, his poor art, and I must admit I was moved by it. Was his love any less than that of the artist who painted well? Some people have talent. Some don't. Some people have a love that can move them like this. One thousand faces, all imperfectly rendered, but attempted nonetheless. Some of us can only imagine such devotion.

"I had a lot of free time in Castor. I don't like to bowl. I don't care for greasy hamburger. I have never been interested in stock car racing or farming. Let's just say I didn't really fit in. I spent my evenings cataloguing Emile Castor's photographs. Who doesn't like a mystery? I thought the photographic history of this man's life would yield some clues about the object of his affection. I was quite excited about it actually, until I became quite weary with it. You can't imagine what it's like to look through one man's life like that, family, friends, trips, beautiful women (though none were her). The more I looked at them, the more depressed I grew. It was clear Emile Castor had really lived his life and I, I felt, was wasting mine. Well, I am given to fits of melancholy, as you well know, and such a fit rooted inside me at this point. I could not forgive myself for being so ordinary. Night after night I stood in that room of the worst art ever assembled in one place and knew it was more than I had ever attempted, the ugliness of it all somehow more beautiful than anything I had ever done.

"I decided to take a break. I asked Darlene to come in, even though she usually took weekends off, to oversee our current high-school girl, Eileen something or other, who seemed to be working through some kind of teenage hormonal thing because every time I saw her she appeared to have just finished a good cry. She was a good kid I think, but at the time she depressed the hell out of me. 'She can't get over what happened between her and Randy,' Darlene told me, 'the abortion really shook her up. But don't say anything to her parents. They don't know.'

" 'Darlene, I don't want to know.'

"Eventually it was settled. I was getting away from Castor and all things Castor-related. I'd booked a room in a B&B in Sundale, on the shore. My duffel bag was packed with two novels, plenty of sunscreen, shorts and swimwear and flip-flops. I would sit in the sun. Walk along the shore. Swim. Read. Eat. I would not think about Emile Castor or the gray-eyed woman. Maybe I would meet somebody. Somebody real. Hey, anything was possible now that I was getting away from Castor.

"Of course it rained. It started almost as soon as I left town and at times the rain became so heavy that I had to pull over on the side of the road. When I finally got to the small town on the shore I was pretty wiped out. I drove in circles looking for the ironically named 'Sunshine Bed and Breakfast' until in frustration at the eccentricity of small towns, I decided that the pleasant-looking house with the simple sign 'B&B' must be it. I sat in the car for a moment hoping the rain would give me a break, and craned my neck at the distant looming steeple of a small chapel on the cliff above the roiling waters.

"It was clear the rain would continue its steady torrent so I grabbed my duffel bag and slopped through the puddles in a sort of half-trot, and entered a pleasant foyer of classical music, overstuffed chairs, a wide-eyed calico asleep in a basket on a table and a large painting of, you probably already guessed, Emile Castor's gray-eyed beauty. Only in this rendition she really was. Beautiful. This artist had captured what Emile had not. It wasn't just a portrait, a photograph with paint if you will, no this painting went beyond its subject's beauty into the realm of what is beautiful in art. I heard footsteps, deep breathing, a cough. I turned with reluctance and beheld the oldest man I'd ever seen. He was a lace of wrinkles and skin that sagged from his bones like an ill-fitting suit. He leaned on a walking stick and appraised me with gray eyes almost lost in the fold of wrinkles.

"'A beautiful piece of work,' I said.

"He nodded.

"I introduced myself and after a few confused minutes discovered that I was neither in Sunnydale nor the Sunshine B&B. But I could not have been more pleased on any sunny day, in any location, than I was there, especially when I found out I could stay the night. When I asked about the painting and its subject, Ed, as he told me to call him, invited me to join him in the parlor for tea after I had 'settled in.'

"My room was pleasant, cozy and clean without the creepy assortment of teddy bears too often assembled in B&Bs. From the window I had a view of the roiling sea, gray waves, the mournful swoop of seagulls and the cliff with the white chapel, its tall steeple tipped, not with a cross, but a ship, its great sails unfurled.

"When I found him in the parlor, Ed had a tray of tea and cookies set out on a low table before the fireplace which was nicely ablaze. The room was pleasant and inviting. The cold rain pounded the windows but inside it was warm and dry, the faint scent of lavender in the air.

"'Come, come join us.' Ed waved his hand, as arthritic as any I've ever seen, gnarled to almost a paw. I sat in the green wing chair across from him. An over-stuffed rocking chair made a triangle of our seating arrangement but it was empty, not even the cat sat there.

"'Theresa!' he shouted, and he shouted again in a loud voice that reminded me of the young Marlon Brando calling for Stella.

"It occurred to me he might not be completely sane. But at the same moment I thought this I heard a woman's voice and the sound of footsteps approaching from the other end of the house. I confess that for a moment I entertained the notion that it would be the gray-eyed woman, as if I had fallen into a Brigadoon of sorts, a magical place time could not reach, all time-ravaged evidence on Ed's face to the contrary.

"Just then that old face temporarily lost its wrinkled look and took on a divine expression. I followed the course of his gaze and saw the oldest woman in the world entering the room. I rose from my seat.

"'Theresa,' Ed said, "'Mr. Delano of Castor.'

"I strode across the room and offered my hand. She slid into it a small soft glove of a hand and smiled at me with green eyes. She walked smoothly and with grace but her steps were excruciatingly small and slow. To walk beside her was a lesson in patience, as we traversed the distance to Ed who had taken to pouring the tea with hands that quivered so badly the china sounded like wind chimes. How had these two survived so long? In the distance, a cuckoo sang and I almost expected I would hear it again before we reached our destination.

"'Goodness,' she said, when I finally stood beside the rocking chair, 'I've never known a young man to walk so slowly.' She sat in the chair swiftly, and without any assistance on my part. I realized she'd been keeping her pace to mine as I thought I was keeping mine to hers. I turned to take my own seat and Ed grinned up at me, offering in his quivering hand a chiming tea and saucer, which I quickly took.

"'Mr. Delano is interested in Elizabeth,' Ed said as he extended another jangling cup and saucer to her. She reached across and took it, leaning out of the chair in a manner I thought unwise.

"'What do you know about her?' she asked.

"'Mr. Emile Castor has made several, many, at least a thousand of the same woman but nothing near to the quality of this one. That's all I know. I don't know what she was to him. I don't know anything.'

"Ed and Theresa both sipped their tea. A look passed between them. Theresa sighed. 'You tell him Ed.'

"'It begins with Emile Castor arriving in town, a city man clear enough in his red roadster and with a moustache.'

"'But pleasant.'

"'He knew his manners.'

"'He was a sincerely pleasant man.'

"'He drove up to the chapel and like the idiot he mostly was, turns his back on it and sets up his easel and begins to try to paint the water down below.'

"'He wasn't an idiot. He was a decent man, and a good businessman. He just wasn't an artist.'

"'He couldn't paint water either.'

"'Well, water's difficult.'

"'Then it started to rain.'

"'You seem to get a lot.'

"'So finally he realizes there's a church right behind him and he packs up his puddle of paints and goes inside.'

"'That's when he sees her.'

"'Elizabeth?'

"'No. Our Lady. Oh, Mr. Delano, you really must see it.'

"'Maybe he shouldn't.'

"'Oh, Edward, why shouldn't he?'

"Edward shrugs. 'He was a rich man so he couldn't simply admire her without deciding that he must possess her as well. That's how the rich are.'

"'Edward, we don't know Mr. Delano's circumstances.'

"'He ain't rich.'

"'Well, we don't really—'

"'All you gotta do is look at his shoes. You ain't, are you?'

"'No.'

"'Can you imagine being so foolish you don't think nothing of trying to buy a miracle?'

"'A miracle? No.'

"'Well, that's how rich he was.'

"'He stayed on while he tried to convince the church to sell it to him.'

"'Idiot.'

"'They fell in love.'

"Ed grunted.

"'They did. They both did.'

"'He offered a couple a barrels full of money.'

" 'For the painting.'

" 'I gotta say I do believe some on the church board wavered a bit but the women wouldn't hear of it.'

" 'She is a miracle.'

" 'Yep, that's what all the womenfolk said.'

" 'Edward, you know it's true. More tea, Mr. Delano?'

" 'Yes. Thank you. I'm not sure I'm following. . . .'

" 'You haven't seen it yet, have you?'

" 'Theresa, he just arrived.'

" 'We saw some of those other paintings he did of Elizabeth.'

"Ed snorts.

" 'Well, he wasn't a quitter, you have to give him that.'

"Ed bites into a cookie and glares at the teapot.

" 'What inspired him, well, what inspired him was Elizabeth but what kept him at it was Our Lady.'

" 'So are you saying, do you mean to imply that this painting, this Our Lady is magical?'

" 'Not magic, a miracle.'

" 'I'm not sure I understand.'

" 'It's an icon, Mr. Delano, surely you've heard of them?'

" 'Well, supposedly an icon is not just a painting, it is the holy manifested in the painting, basically.'

" 'You must see it. Tomorrow. After the rain stops.'

" 'Maybe he shouldn't.'

" 'Why do you keep saying that, Edward? Of course he should see it.'

"Ed just shrugged.

" 'Of course we didn't sell it to him and over time he stopped asking. They fell in love.'

" 'He wanted her instead.'

" 'Don't make it sound like that. He made her happy during what, none of us knew, were the last days of her life.'

" 'After she died, he started the paintings.'

" 'He wanted to keep her alive.'

" 'He wanted to paint an icon.'

" 'He never gave up until he succeeded. Finally, he painted our Elizabeth.'

" 'Are you saying Emile Castor painted that, in the foyer?'

" 'It took years.'

" 'He wanted to keep her alive somehow.'

" 'But that painting, it's quite spectacular and his other work is so—'

" 'Lousy.'

" 'Anyone who enters this house wants to know about her.'

" 'I don't mean to be rude but how did she, I'm sorry, please excuse me.'

" 'Die?'

" 'It doesn't matter.'

" 'Of course it does. She fell from the church cliff. She'd gone up there to light a candle for Our Lady, a flame of gratitude. Emile had proposed and she had accepted. She went up there and it started raining while she was inside. She slipped and fell on her way home.'

"'How terrible.'

"'Oh yes, but there are really so few pleasant ways to die.'

"Our own rain still lashed the windows. The fat calico came into the room and stopped to lick her paws. We just sat there, listening to the rain and the clink of china cup set neatly in saucer. The tea was good and hot. The fire smelled strangely of chocolate. I looked at their two old faces in profile, wrinkled as poorly folded maps. Then I proceeded to make a fool of myself by explaining to them my position as curator of the Castor museum. I described the collection, the beautiful house and location by a stream visited by deer (but I did not describe the dismal town) and ended with a description of Emile's horrible work, the room filled with poor paintings of their daughter, surely, I told them, Elizabeth belonged there, redeemed against the vast assortment of clowns, for the angel she was. When I was finished the silence was sharp. Neither spoke or looked at me but even so, as though possessed by some horrible tic, I continued. 'Of course we'd pay you handsomely.' Theresa bowed her head and I thought that perhaps this was the posture she took for important decisions until I realized she was crying.

"Ed turned slowly, his old head like a marionette's on an uncertain string, he fixed me with a look that told me what a fool I was and will always be.

"'Please accept my apology for being so . . .' I said, finding myself speaking and rising as though driven by the same puppeteer's hand. 'I can't tell you how . . . Thank you.' I turned abruptly and walked out of the room, angry at my clumsy social skills, in despair actually, that I had made a mess of such a pleasant afternoon. I intended to hurry to my room and read my book until dinner when I would skulk down the stairs and try to find a decent place to eat.

"That I could insult and hurt two such kind people was unforgivable. I was actually almost blind with self-loathing until I entered the foyer and saw her out of the corner of my eye.

"It is really quite impossible to describe that other thing that brings a painting beyond competent, even beyond beauty into the realm of great art. Of course she was a beautiful woman, of course the lighting, colors, composition, brushstroke, all of these elements could be separated and described but this still did not account for that ethereal feeling, the sense one gets standing next to a masterpiece, the need to take a deep breath as if suddenly the air consumed by one is needed for two.

"Instead of going upstairs I went out the front door. If this other painting was anything like the one of Elizabeth then I must see it.

"It was dark, the rain only a drizzle now, the town a slick black oil, maybe something by Dalí with disappearing ink. I had, out of habit, pocketed my car keys. I had to circle the town a few times, make a few false starts, once finding myself in someone's driveway, before I selected the road that arched above the town to the white chapel, which even in the rain glowed as though lit from within. The road was winding but not treacherous. When I got to the top and stood on that cliff the wind whipped me, the town below was lost in a haze of fog that only a few yellow lights shone through. I had the sensation of looking down on the heavens from above. The waves crashed and I felt the salt on my face, tasted it on my lips. Up close the chapel was much larger than it looked from below, the steeple that narrowed to a needle point on which its ship balanced into the dark sky, quite imposing. As I walked up those stone steps I thought again of Edward saying he wasn't sure I should see it. I reached for the hammered iron handle and pulled. For a moment I thought it was locked but it was just incredibly heavy. I pulled the door open and entered the darkness of the church. Behind me, the door heaved shut. I smelled a flowery smoky scent, the oily odor of wood, and heard from somewhere, a faint drip of water as though there was a leak. I was in the church foyer, there was another door before me, marked in the darkness by the thin line of light that shone beneath it. I walked gingerly, uncertain in the dark. It too was extremely heavy. I pulled it open."

He coughed and cleared his throat as though suddenly suffering a cold. She opened her eyes just a slit. The heat from the wood stove must have been the reason for the red in his cheeks, how strange he looked, as though in pain or fever! She let her eyes droop shut and it seemed a long time before he continued, his voice raspy.

"All I can say is, I never should have looked. I wish I'd never seen either of those paintings. It was there that I made myself the promise I would never settle for a love any less than spectacular, a love so great that it would take me past my limitations, the way Emile's love for Elizabeth had taken him past his, that somehow such a love would leave an imprint on the world, the way great art does, that all who saw it would be changed by it, as I was.

"So you see, when you find me sad and ask what's on my mind, or when I am quiet and cannot explain to you the reason, there it is. If I had never seen the paintings, maybe I would be a happy man. But always, now, I wonder."

She waited but he said no more. After a long time, she whispered his name. But he did not answer and when she peeked at him from the squint of her eyes, he appeared to be asleep. Eventually, she fell asleep too.

All that night, as they told their stories, the flames burned heat onto that icy roof which melted down the sides of the house and over the windows so that in the cold morning when they woke up, the fire gone to ash and cinder, the house was encased in a sort of skin of ice which they tried to alleviate by burning another fire, not realizing they were only sealing themselves in more firmly. They spent the rest of that whole winter in their ice house. By burning all the wood and most of the furniture and eating canned food even if it was out of date, they survived, thinner and less certain of fate, into a spring morning thaw, though they never could forget those winter stories, not all that spring or summer and especially not that autumn, when the winds began to carry that chill in the leaves, that odd combination of sun and decay, about which they did not speak, but which they knew would exist between them forever.

RICHARD MUELLER

And the Sea Shall Give Up
Its Dead

Richard Mueller was conceived on V.J. Day in 1945, making him the last act of World War II, and he's been fascinated with it ever since. After a career as an actor, he turned to writing science fiction in the 1980s, and drifted, as did many Los Angeles SF writers, into writing for television animation.

Several years ago he began to exhume his prose roots, and after an absence of eighteen-odd years, broke back into The Magazine of Fantasy & Science Fiction *with "And the Sea Shall Give Up Its Dead." He is currently working on a series of historical pulp action romance novels set in the 1930s.*
— E.D.

I found Broussart huddled over the farthest table, where the crooked stone wall makes a turn and seabirds sometimes perch to watch for opportunities among the diners. He had placed his *Capitaine's* coat on the wall to keep the gulls at bay and was mulling over a disreputable stack of papers held down against the breeze by a heavy piece of dark metal, a fist-sized gear of polished steel. "Souvenir?" I asked.

"Yes," he grunted. "A remembrance of *de Brazza.*"

The colonial sloop *Savorgnan de Brazza* had been Broussart's last ship. When the Free French Navy had run out of steam and shut down, Broussart was promoted to *Capitaine,* beached, and given the choice of release in Mauritius or transportation back to metropolitan France. Since the only ships going to France these days were German or Vichy, Broussart decided to become a Mauritian. The last I had heard he was working with the British as a liaison officer but, being French, he seldom spoke of such things. ("Liaison to what exactly?" I asked. "Ah ha, yes, you see perfectly," he replied.) Liaison, of course, meaning intelligence. As I opened the chessboard, Broussart shuffled the papers together and jammed them into a patch pocket on his coat. His "reports." I thought this was pretty shabby for an intelligence officer.

"You've never heard of a briefcase?" I asked, turning the gear over in my hands. It was very dense, solid, as if it were responsible for controlling and moving many other gears. A Chief Engineer of gears. Broussart sniffed.

"Briefcases cost money."

"A paper bag then."

"Undignified."

"Suit yourself." I laid out the pieces on the board: black for Broussart, white for me. Broussart always played black, claiming that he was part Negro. He also claimed to be part Jew, part Gypsy, part Slav, part anything else that the Germans hated. "I won last time," I said, "so first move to the French."

"I am only part French."

"Yeah, I know."

We played five or six desultory moves, unsettled and tentative, as the fishing boats moved in and out of Port Louis and patrolling Warwicks watched the sea. It was only 130 miles to Reunion where the swastika-tricolor flew. The peace that kept the intervening waters quiet was little more than a pause, a breathless truce that flickered uneasily like a guttering candle.

"Your mind is elsewhere."

"Always," he said.

"Must be nice." I took a knight. Broussart shrugged, sniffed, and turned his eyes seaward. A whiff of diesel smoke. I caught it too.

"One of yours?" I followed his gaze. A submarine was blowing its tanks near the outer buoy. As the water streamed from her conning tower, a helicopter swooped low over the deck. A pilot boat and a Fairmile launch were also racing to meet it.

"Australian, I think. An A-class. I didn't know that any of the big ones were out here." Mauritius was the last westward dot of the British Pacific Empire, existing only by dint of the truce. If Germany decided she had built up enough venom for another strike, this island would be the first to go, and an American base here wouldn't stop it.

We played a few more rounds.

The world had been at a general peace for eight months. Uneasy peace, like a poor man's sleep: never at rest, a rat's nest of interlocking treaties and truces. Undeclared peace and dormant war. As executive officer of the *U.S.S. Unicorn*, I spent most of my time patrolling the waters between Cape Agulhas and Dondra Head. We were supposed to be a deterrent to the Germans and their territorial ambition, not that there was that much territory in the Indian Ocean left to protect. South Afrika and India had each declared their independence and everything in the vast arc between them was either Pan-Arab, Deutsch-Afrikan, Vichy French, or seething in some complicated tribal anarchy. Only Mauritius and Ceylon were still held by the British, and though President Dewey had sworn to continue the Grand Alliance and back the British defense of the remaining free world, Americans had grown tired of the war. Treaties sworn, promised, and whispered were bound to disappear, but until they did we were still here.

The breeze turned round from the south, picked up a knot or two of strength, and brought a chill. I pulled my coat tighter about me but Broussart seemed oblivious to the cold. He was probably part Eskimo as well. He studied the pieces, smoking continuously and humming under his breath.

"Have you been to Madagascar, Andre?"

"Yes. Many times."

"What's it like?"

"Big, hot, nasty. Full of monkeys and Jews."

The Germans had been resettling the Jews there since shortly after the fall of France. Two million at last count, if you believed the statements of Herr Doktor Goebbels, which most of us did not. "You believe about the Jews?"

"Yes, as you know—"

"You're part Jewish, yeah," I said. "But you haven't been there since the *Boche* arrived."

"But I have."

I looked at Broussart. He seemed entirely serious, yet he did not appear to be the sort of agent who would be landed from a submarine in the dead of night. More like a railway station agent. "When?"

"About a month after the cease fire when you were still based in Australia. There was a Truce Commission for the Indian Ocean area. It met at Diego Suarez. The British put a Royal Navy uniform on me and took me along as interpreter to deal with the Vichy. The Germans were very proper; stiff. You know what they're like. They confined us to the port district but the town was busy, productive, and full of Jews."

"You could tell?"

Broussart shrugged. "They looked Jewish, I think. Shabby, downcast, yet defiant in that way they have. They wore the yellow star. Their relations with the Germans were . . ."

"Friendly?"

"Hardly. Proper and correct. I saw no brutality or even coercion. More like the British here; pleasant, prewar colonial style. A caste system."

"Did you see SS?"

"Yes."

"Gestapo?"

"Who can say?"

"And it was peaceful?"

"Peaceful enough."

The Germans claimed to have resettled Jews in Russia, Algeria, Madagascar, even Finland, but there was a lot of debate on the question. Most of the peace parties back in the States were willing to believe it and back off, while the Warhawk Democrats claimed it was all eyewash. I didn't know what to think. My job was to watch their ships and go where the Navy sent us. If it came to it, I'd sink them, or they'd sink me. From what I knew of their new Type XXV boats, I wouldn't give our *TENCH* class much of an edge, but no one was paying me to live forever.

Broussart pointed across the patio. "Is he for you?"

Ensign Crockett, our lanky young Gunnery Officer, was snaking between the tables, heading our way. He saluted.

"Sir, we have a four-hour recall to sail, but you're to report to the squadron commander on the double."

"Me?"

Crockett smiled. "Seems like you're in command, Skipper."

I heard the noon gun from the harbor battery just as I tapped on Captain Carpenter's door. "Come."

I saluted.

"At ease, Andrews." He waved me to a chair. "You heard about Commander Picerni?"

"Yessir. Just now. A heart attack?"

Carpenter scratched his bluish stubble. "I guess it got past the physical. He's out of submarines now and I don't have a replacement—so you're it, Lieutenant." He handed me a manila folder. "Look at these."

I did. They were line drawings of what appeared at first to be a rather pedestrian-looking ocean liner. The legend named it the *Peter Strasser*. "What is she, sir?"

"Intelligence says it's a repatriation transport and they're not sure what that means, but there's at least one of them in the Indian Ocean. It could be a supply ship, a U-boat mother ship, an attack transport, even a missile carrier. ComSubWest wants us to find it and find out."

How, I thought? Ask to go aboard for a tour? But I replied, "Aye, aye, sir. Just *Unicorn*?"

"*Roncador* will run from south of Rodrigues to the Mozambique Channel. *Guavina* will cover a line from here to the Persian Gulf. They'll be patrolling with orders to watch for the *Strasser* but they are mostly cover. You will take *Unicorn* up the east coast of Madagascar to Socotra and then run box patrols in the Gulf of Aden."

I studied the large map on the wall, marked with colliding jurisdictions and intersecting arcs. "Sir, we'll be well within the Aden patrol circle."

"Yes."

"I understand that the krauts are pretty touchy about anyone getting close to the Red Sea. Suez . . ."

Carpenter regarded me with a long, silent question, probably trying to decide whether he'd made a mistake, if he should give the job to someone else, but when he spoke he surprised me by echoing my thoughts. "You're wondering why I didn't pick a more senior man for this job. Someone with more experience of command."

I nodded, trying to look as if I fully understood, because the only ship I'd ever commanded was a training sub in Puget Sound and Carpenter knew it.

"Relax, Lieutenant."

I tried, suddenly conscious of the background sounds of Mauritius. Seabirds called over the anchorage, the ceiling fans whirred and thumped, and the breeze brought the faint sound of native music. Carpenter leaned forward. It was not a gesture of conspiracy or comradeship. He did it to take a kink out of his back, injured last year when his sub had hit a mine off Honshu.

"You'll get a set of orders for a routine patrol. You'll exceed those orders in the manner I've described. An older, more seasoned officer wouldn't do that; at least not the captains under my command. It wouldn't be plausible."

"Yessir." He had meant that they wouldn't risk their careers or their ships.

"You'll find the *Strasser*, find out what you can about her, then come home."

"And if we're attacked?"

"You may take any measures you deem appropriate to defend yourselves, but try not to restart the war."

We were quite happy to sail in a ship called the *Unicorn*, though initially few of us were aware of the symbolism. Like all American submarines, *Unicorn* was named for a fish, another name for *Monodon monoceros*, the narwhal. Up until modern times, horns of the seagoing unicorn often turned up in antiquarian hordes and were thought to be from the hoofed unicorns, the mythical horse variety, a creature that never existed except in folklore. It was Greiner who told us what unicorns signified.

Moe Greiner was our Radioman's Mate, our RM2. He had a Masters in European history with a minor in English Literature. He spoke at least four languages (English, German, Latin, and Yiddish) with enough linguistic backwash to get along in French, Italian, and Hebrew. He was our all-purpose intellectual and well respected, the moreso that he hailed from Brooklyn and had once played shortstop for a Dodgers farm club.

"They're a symbol of purity," Moe had told us early in our commission. "They may only be approached by the purest of maidens." He smiled. "Which means the sort of women of which none of you are familiar."

There was a ripple of laughter. "I hope not," someone muttered.

"They are also a symbol of purity of purpose, of the essential innocence of decency, of the quest for the right, of honor—"

"Right up there with the Holy Grail," Chief Perry said. Like Moe, our Chief Engineer was a reader. "All of the Arthurian stuff."

Moe nodded. "The roots are in chivalry, at a time when people, some people, believed in the idea of a just war, fought cleanly, with rules."

A just war, fought cleanly with rules. Some journalist had dubbed it "the American way of war—fought hard and relentlessly, yet with kindness and decency to the defeated foe." That was before Kyushu and Honshu, where they just kept killing us, whatever the toll in blood. Where they refused to give up until we were napalming anything that moved. MacArthur's draconian methods had finally ended the Japanese resistance but at such a cost that the survivors would hate us for a thousand years.

As *Unicorn* worked her way north through the Seychelles, running surfaced at night, our lookouts and Sugar William radar kept us on edge, ready to dive at any provocation. I tried to relax into the mission but it was my first command; the greatest responsibility I could carry for a ship and the lives of eighty men, and I could never fully rest. I haunted the bridge, the conn, the wardroom, saying little and probably driving the crew crazy, though no one mentioned it. They gave me a good deal of leeway, which was understandable since I had their lives in my hands. Old lives, of old, young men. There's something about trying to establish routine in the Valley of the Shadow of Death that darkens men's souls and makes them old before their time.

It was more or less routine, as we worked our way northward. During the day we ran submerged, avoiding known minefields and taking periscope photos of every island, port, and ship we encountered. At night we made better time on the surface, recharging our batteries. We saw a few freighters, a German destroyer, fishing boats, and aircraft, though the Kriegsmarine had not yet developed much of a night ASW capability. As we had a trained and seasoned crew, I primarily supervised the ship's routine, filled out the log pages, and played chess with our supercargo.

Andre Broussart had been just as surprised as I, not that he'd admitted it. He'd arrived on the dock clad in British submarine kit and carrying a duffle. His grumbled, "I had a date," gave away any later attempt to convince me that he had known about this (and every other movement in the Indian Ocean) all along.

"Yes," I chuckled. "After all, you're part American." He just scowled.

After ten days I was beating him evenly at chess and we were both beginning to believe that the hunt for the *Peter Strasser* was a wild goose chase. Broussart was along ostensibly as liaison, but he quickly confided in me that his family business back in France had been concerned with shipyards.

"Freighters, coasters, fishing boats," he said one evening as we pored over the drawing of the *Strasser*. "Not little ones; the big South Atlantic whalers. Our yard built the *Jacques Cartier*."

"Which is . . . ?"

"Was," he grumped. "A giant whale factory ship. She was sunk off South Georgia in '42. What do you make of this?"

"This" was three rows of windows along the upper decks of the *Strasser*, each row bordered by rectangular lines. The rows were of identical size and ran three-quarters of the ship's length. There was no reason to have them. "Decoration?" I asked.

"I doubt it," Andre replied. "Windows like this aren't practical. On a ship in wartime—"

"Not windows then, but a gallery framing some sort of promenade deck. Where did this drawing originate?"

Andre shrugged and puffed, his cigarette smoke leaving a blue mist in the air of my cabin. "Some agent with an artistic bent in Aden or Suez. It's a very good line drawing but it is not a blueprint. It says that the thing is five hundred and fifty feet long."

"Big. But why build this in wartime? Germany and Italy have liners, theirs and yours, Dutch, Swedish. This is new."

"These galleries could hide guns."

I shook my head. "No one would build a merchant cruiser from scratch. Besides, there are too many warships and aircraft and not enough neutral flags left to hide behind."

"Missiles? Aircraft? Mines?"

"There's no point," I said firmly. "They're either something else or nothing at all." And so they remained as we ran north.

Then we found him.

We were two days south of Socotra. That night we'd avoided an Italian squadron comprising a *Littorio*-class battleship, two cruisers, and four destroyers, sailing around in that corner of the Indian Ocean that the Germans had let them keep. As we surfaced in their wake, the night moonless but spread brightly with equatorial stars, we almost ran over him. Seaman Bone, our best lookout, spotted him before anyone.

"Object on the port bow, sir."

Through the glasses it looked at first like a log. "Skipper," said Tompkinson, our First Lieutenant, "I think there's a man on that thing."

"All stop. Pick him up."

He was alive. We carried him below to Doc Gordon. Broussart and I waited in the passageway until the Doc came out.

"How is he, Leo?"

Leo Gordon spread his broad flat hands and passed me the clipboard. "Better than he has any right to be. These are shark waters and my guess is he's been on that log for days. And, I think he's a Jew."

"That would explain why he'd risk the sharks," Broussart said. "Better company than the *Boche*, for a Jew."

"His clothes are European. Shabby. No identification but a number tattooed on his arm."

"He say anything?"

"Yeah, but I can't make it out," Gordon said. "It sounds German."

"Get Greiner."

We waited while Moe went in to talk to the man, who appeared debilitated but calm, lying flat on his back, blinking at the bright lights of our makeshift dispensary. After a few minutes Greiner stepped out into the passageway.

"The language you heard was Polish," he said, rubbing his bearded chin, a prognathous jaw that went well with his blocky frame. "I don't speaka da Polack, but he also speaks Yiddish, which I do know. His name is Herschel Dubrovski, he's starving, exhausted, and I think something really horrible happened to him."

Broussart snorted. "Of course it did. He's a Jew."

Two days later we lay on the ocean floor off Cape Ras Aser and heard a recovering though still weak Herschel Dubrovski tell his story. There were three of us; Broussart, Greiner, and I. Greiner also ran the wire recorder. What follows is an edited transcript of Herschel Dubrovski's story as translated by RM2 Moe Greiner.

"I grew up in southern Poland and was in Krakow when the war began. I knew that I should have left; run, run anywhere, but I was part of a large family. There were parents, grandparents, aunts and uncles, brothers, sisters, nephews and nieces and cousins in great profusion. Four generations. As far as I know, I am the only survivor.

"We were scattered to the winds. Before the war I had been a hydraulic engineer for the city government of Krakow, but the Nazis made me a farm laborer and sent me first to East Prussia and later to the Ukraine.

"After the Fall of France, and then the British Isles, the Germans turned on Russia. We heard about Turkey and the British having to give up Africa. We worked and we died, but as long as we grew crops they did not often kill us.

"Always we heard of resettlement. In the north, east in Siberia, in Africa and Madagascar. Special ships were being built. There would be subservient Jewish states but we would be allowed to live. Then, last winter, we were told that our farms were going to be resettled with ethnic Germans. We were to make ready to go to Madagascar. Germans from the SS came to our farms and lectured us about Madagascar: about the forests, the animals, the climate, the work we would have. They explained that we would be autonomous. We would have our own culture and, so long as we remained peaceful and productive, we would be protected. Some of us believed all of it, some believed none of it. Most of us expected some amount of sorrow, perhaps with a silver lining. We Jews have made our way for centuries. We survived Babylon and Rome. We would survive the Nazis.

"Ten, maybe twelve weeks ago we were marched to the trains. As always, they sealed us in freight cars but the ride was short. A day and a night brought us to Sevastopol, which the Germans have made into a resort. We were allowed to clean up at the station and then we were marched to the docks. There were few guards. We were going to our own land. We were happy. Besides, there was nowhere to run.

"There were three ships, all the same, and clean and new as these things go. Ours was named the *Gorch Fock* and she looked like the picture you showed me. We were to be carried on three decks on each side, and when I saw the accommodation I was puzzled. There were fifteen hundred of us in our compartment. It was very long, with doors on each end that we were not allowed to pass through. On the inner wall there were painted murals of pastoral scenes but no doors or windows. There were tracks or grooves in the steel decking, perhaps every twenty feet apart, running from the inner wall to the outer and in the outer wall were open gallery windows where we could stand and watch the sights passing: the Black Sea, the Bosphorus, Egypt, and the Suez Canal. Most of us had never even seen the ocean before. We felt exhilarated and alive for perhaps the first time in years.

"The accommodations consisted of screens and simple furniture, which we could arrange as we saw fit. Soon we had apartments and rooms in place, with lavatories built over holes in the deck designed for that purpose. Food was delivered. It was very basic and prepared in advance, but it was plentiful. There were two SS officials, a man and a woman, assigned to answer our questions and requests and they seemed solicitous and kind. A shipboard society quickly grew up. We were required to do no work. We were on holiday.

"I knew about a score of people who had come from my farm and we held long discussions about what was awaiting us. Most of us were cheerful and optimistic. I had my doubts. The ship seemed strange, and from my background as a hydraulic engineer it seemed that much of it did not make sense. I could not imagine that anyone would design a ship like this but then, the Germans had won the war. Perhaps this was based on new mechanical discoveries of which I had no knowledge.

"It was after we entered the Indian Ocean that we discovered what all of this meant.

"The night was moonlit and the wind was out of the east. I am not sure, but I think that those conditions had something to do with the fact that I am still alive.

"I was standing at the gallery windows with my friend Moshe Morser. We were watching the sea. We knew that we were close to Madagascar and we would be there in less than a week. Moshe was a printer and looked forward to finding work in his field. The colony must have a newspaper, perhaps several. Even the Germans must need things printed. Then we smelled it.

"At first we thought that the ship must be flushing its sanitary tanks, but I had worked in the farm's butcher shop and I knew that smell for what it was. Blood and offal. They were pumping quantities of it into the sea, but for what purpose I could not guess. Until we saw the sharks.

"They were drawn by the blood and came in ones and twos and tens until there were a hundred or more following the ship. Of course the same thing had to have been happening on the other side. At that point I had a terrible feeling that I knew what must come next, though I did not know how. Then the sound began.

"It was like a great dam opening its floodgates—huge motors, gigantic grinding gears, and then a terrible vibration in the deck. The night lighting went out and people began to scream. And then I saw that the inner wall was beginning to move outward, pushing everything before it: furniture, belongings, and people. The wall was compressing us all toward the gallery windows. At first we thought it was a mistake and we beat on the doors but they were not opened as the wall rolled on the tracks set into the floor, squeezing fifteen hundred of us together. Then the gallery walls began to lift, opening the side of the ship, and the first people began to fall out.

"We fought, we prayed, we pleaded, we tried to stop the wall with our bodies, but we fell into the sea all the same, splashing down among the trunks and suitcases and furniture. Some hit the lifted gallery walls below us but there was no place to hang on. Some who knew that I had been an engineer begged me to find a way to stop it but of course there was nothing I could do. I beat on the walls until I, too, was pushed over.

"The fact that I hit the water and nothing else, that I didn't pass out, that I was able to climb aboard a trunk and hang on is the only proof I have that God was watching. Why he saw fit to save me while nine thousand others perished that night I do not know. I do not have to tell you what I saw and heard that night and the next day and night as the sharks came and killed everyone and turned the sea red.

"By the second morning it was over and I was still alive. The sharks were gone and the seabirds were finishing the job. I managed to stay alive for three more days until I reached an uninhabited island where I remained for six weeks. Then, two days ago, a German patrol ship arrived and put a landing party ashore. I knew they were looking for people like me, so I took to the sea. I was trying to reach another is-land when you found me."

We left Greiner and Dubrovski conversing quietly in Yiddish. Later Greiner pulled the curtains on the Radio Room and got quickly, quietly, and illegally drunk. Instead of preferring charges, I had Chief Perry put him to bed.

I attended to the changing of the watch and told Tompkinson to surface the boat an hour after sunset and set a course for Costivy Island in the Seychelles. Then I went to my cabin and began to study the charts.

It was reasonably easy, if you knew the winds and ocean currents, to backtrack Dubrovski to his island. And from there I could estimate where the *Gorch Fock* had dumped its human cargo.

The German racial planners were clever. They would have researched water depth and shark activity and timed the drops for nights when wind and weather conditions were right. They could hold a ship at Aden until a storm had passed and thus insure that their disposal system worked perfectly. And they were methodical. They would return to the same spot again and again with hundreds of thousands of victims until such time as the sea would give up her dead in the light of the world to come. Leave it to them to design such a solution.

There was a tap on the door. Broussart looked pale and I could tell that he, too, had been drinking. We had done our best to keep the crew from finding out about Dubrovski's story, but submarines are like small towns, and the word had passed swiftly. The men were, by degrees, depressed, fearful, or quietly angry. War was one thing, but this—

"I know," Broussart said, offering me his flask. I waved it away. "Trust the Germans to come up with something so monstrous. Sharks. My God!"

Broussart had sailed these waters far longer than I had. "Andre, could that happen? Could sharks kill so many? Might there be other survivors?"

"I do not know, Gregory, but these Jews came from Poland, Slovakia, the Baltic States, the Ukraine. Farmers and townsmen. I'd bet that few could swim and the ones who could were probably pulled under by those panicking around them. You wouldn't even need sharks, except to clean up the evidence."

Trust the Germans. My mother was second generation German, her family from the east bank of the Rhein. America was full of Germans, most of whom would be sick with fury if they knew. I couldn't believe that the average German in Germany could condone this either. "Andre, how big do you think this is?"

"God help me, I do not know. Dubrovski saw three identical ships. They have been building them for the purpose. How many? Dozens? A hundred, a thousand, like your Liberty ships? Sailing out of every port in Europe, loaded with Jews going to their new homeland, then coming back empty to pick up more while the sharks feed. And when they run out of Jews? Blacks and Arabs perhaps. Slavs and Poles, Balkans, Balts, then finally even the French and Spanish until the entire German world is populated solely with Aryans. Tell me, *Capitaine*, is that possible?"

I said nothing. After a long moment I pushed the map over to him. "I think," I said at last, "that we had better find out."

We lay quietly on the surface, in and out of drifting patches of fog, waiting. There was a full complement of lookouts and gunners topside and others lurked in the hatches, listening, waiting to know and act. The American need to achieve justice through action. These men were not war-weary. They were skilled, motivated, and dangerous, and I was in command.

I knew about regulations, that I had been verbally ordered to exceed my written orders. But how far? Not enough, or too much, and it became the old service trap: investigation, court martial, and sentence.

I stood on the bridge with Broussart, Greiner, and Herschel Dubrovski. The lookouts' binoculars were useless in the fog but above us the radar scoop was turning smoothly, probing the darkness. "You know that whatever happens we cannot prevent it," said Broussart.

"I know."

"We're here only to witness."

"Yes."

"Jew if by sea," Greiner muttered. I looked at him.

"What?"

He blinked at me but did not back away. "One if by land, Jew if by sea," he said softly. "And I on the opposite shore will be."

"That's enough, Greiner."

"Yessir."

The intercom buzzed. It was Tompkinson. "Skipper, we've got a good-sized target bearing Starboard Six-Oh at eight thousand yards."

"Steer to intercept. Take us in at eight knots." Greiner was nodding, his head moving in little bobs, his lips moving silently. I grabbed his arm and pushed him toward the hatch.

We closed on the target at periscope depth. She was running with lights, indicating a merchantman, but her boxy silhouette soon revealed her for what she was. As she bore down on us we ducked into a patch of fog. "Take her up," I said quietly. "Decks awash."

With just the top half of our conning tower above the water we presented a difficult target for the German radar, but at any rate they were busy with other things. The ship came on slowly. At first the smell was faint but the damp fogs carried it to us. I looked at Dubrovski, who touched his nose and nodded. As he did, I saw the fin of a large shark sweep by us in the mist. I touched the intercom button. "Ready, Mr. Tompkinson?"

"Aye, aye, sir."

The German ship had slowed to a few knots of headway. It couldn't be more than a thousand yards away. Dubrovski and I and the lookouts waited. Below, standing at the base of the ladder, Broussart was watching me through the open hatch. I glanced at Dubrovski again. His eyes were closed and his lips were moving, his head bobbing like Greiner's. He was praying.

We heard it all from where we were. First the grinding mechanical sounds of the moving walls, then the cries of the people betrayed, the splashes, and finally the terrible screams from the water. The lookouts swore and Dubrovski tried to shut it out as I focused in on the ship with my glasses.

"What are you doing, *Capitaine?*" Broussart had climbed up far enough to stick his head through the hatch. I continued to watch the ship, waiting.

"Exceeding my orders."

"Yes, but—"

Then I saw it. The gallery walls were closing. The murderers were finished, their cargo unloaded, and ready to sail for home. Below in the water, their victims were dying. "Ready, Mr. Tompkinson?"

"Yessir."

"Fire Tubes One and Two."

The boat gave a lurch as the two torpedoes left their tubes, curved, and streaked toward the ship. "What have you done?" Broussart wailed. I kept my eyes on the ship.

Both fish hit amidships almost simultaneously with a terrific roar and a submerged detonation that must have killed some of those in the water. There was no cheering aboard our sub. I watched the death ship heel rapidly over, too quickly for her crew to lower the boats. They would go into the water with the Jews and take their chances with the sharks.

Broussart pounded on the deck. "Do you know what you've done? You've started the war all over again!"

"What makes you think it ever stopped?" I replied.

We surfaced and moved into the wreckage, distributing all of our rafts and covering our deck with terrified, bewildered survivors. Our marksmen did their best to keep the sharks away but when we left a half hour later they were still running wild among the screaming survivors. There was nothing more that we could do.

We could not stay on the surface and we could not submerge with people on deck, so we sailed for the island that Dubrovski had reached and just before dawn we landed over three hundred survivors. Dubrovski went with them, to show them the way, to try to give them a fighting chance. Some of our rifles and pistols went with them. It wasn't much, but it was something. Twelve women and children we kept aboard to take back to Mauritius.

Later that day, as we were heading due east away from the sinking, Greiner came by my cabin. "Sir?"

"Come in," I said. "Coffee?"

"No thank you, sir. There's a lot of German radio traffic. It seems they've got a ship missing. No details. I guess those bastards we sank didn't get a radio signal off. High Command doesn't know it was torpedoed."

"They will soon enough," I said. "Anything else?"

Greiner obviously wanted to say something comforting, but all he could come up with was, "I hope they give you a medal, sir."

Not much chance of that, I thought. Not for restarting the war. But I smiled. "Thanks, Moe. You go back to your radio."

Then I lay back, content to await events as we shaped our course for Mauritius.

For Marc Wedner

TINA RATH

A Trick of the Dark

Tina Rath lives in London with her husband and several cats. She earned a Ph.D. from the University of London for her thesis on The Vampire in Popular Fiction. *She has had numerous short stories published both in the small and mainstream press, some cowritten with her husband, Tony, and several novels looking for publication. She also works as an actress, model, and occasional debt collector.*

The author says about her story: "'A Trick of the Dark' was sparked by a postcard showing an early Dracula *cover: the contrast between the cozy furnishings of Lucy's bedroom—the eiderdown, the lamp, so very un-Gothic—and the looming vampire was irresistible."*

The story was originally published in The Mammoth Book of Vampires.

—E. D.

W hat job finishes just at sunset?"

Margaret jumped slightly. "What a weird question, darling. Park keeper, I suppose." Something made her turn to look at her daughter. She was propped up against her pillows, looking, Margaret thought guiltily, about ten years old. She must keep remembering, she told herself fiercely, that Maddie was nineteen. This silly heart-thing, as she called it, was keeping her in bed for much longer than they'd ever thought it would, but it couldn't stop her growing up . . . she must listen to her, and talk to her like a grown-up.

Intending to do just that, she went to sit on the edge of the bed. It was covered with a glossy pink eiderdown, embroidered with fat pink and mauve peonies. The lamp on Maddie's bedside table had a rosy shade. Maddie was wearing a pink bedjacket, lovingly crocheted by her grandmother, and Maddie's pale blonde hair was tied back with a pink ribbon . . . but in the midst of this plethora of pink Maddie's face looked pale and peaky. The words of a story that Margaret had read to Maddie once—how many years ago?—came back to her: "Peak and pine, peak and pine." It was about a changeling child who never thrived, but lay in the cradle, crying and fretting, peaking and pining . . . in the end the creature had gone back to its own people, and she supposed that the healthy child had somehow got back to his mother, but she couldn't remember. Margaret shivered, wondering why people thought such horrid stories were suitable for children.

"What made you wonder who finishes work at sunset?" she asked.

"Oh—nothing." Maddie looked oddly shy, as she might have done if her mother had asked her about a boy who had partnered her at tennis, or asked her to a dance. If such a thing could ever have happened. She played with the pink ribbons at her neck and a little, a very little color crept into that pale face. "It's just—well—I can't read all day, or—" She hesitated and Margaret mentally filled in the gap. She had her embroidery, her knitting, those huge complicated jigsaws that her friends were so good about finding for her, a notebook for jotting down those funny little verses that someone was going to ask someone's uncle about publishing . . . but all that couldn't keep her occupied all day.

"Sometimes I just look out of the window," Maddie said.

"Oh, darling . . ." Margaret couldn't bear to think of her daughter just lying there—just looking out of the window. "Why don't you call me when you get bored? We could have some lovely talks. Or I could telephone Bunty or Cissie or—"

It's getting quite autumnal after all, she thought, and Maddie's friends won't be out so much, playing tennis, or swimming or . . . You couldn't expect them to sit for hours in a sickroom. They dashed in, tanned and breathless from their games and bicycle rides, or windblown and glowing from a winter walk, and dropped off a jigsaw or a new novel . . . and went away.

"I don't mind, Mummy," Maddie was saying. "It's amazing what you can see, even in a quiet street like this. I mean, that's why I like this room. Because you can see out."

Margaret looked out of the window. Yes. You could see a stretch of pavement, a bit of Mrs. Creswell's hedge, a lamppost, the postbox and Mrs. Monkton's gate. It was not precisely an enticing view, and she exclaimed, "Oh, darling!" again.

"You'd be amazed who visits Mrs. Monkton in the afternoons," Maddie said demurely.

"Good heavens, who—" Margaret exclaimed, but Maddie gave a reassuringly naughty giggle.

"That would be telling! You'll have to sit up here one afternoon and watch for yourself."

"I might," Margaret said. But how could she? There was always so much to do downstairs, letters to write, shopping to do, and cook to deal with. (Life to get on with?) She too, she realized, dropped in on Maddie, left her with things to sustain or amuse her. And went away.

"Perhaps we could move you downstairs, darling," she said. But that would be so difficult. The doctor had absolutely forbidden Maddie to use the stairs, so how on earth could they manage what Margaret could only, even in the privacy of her thoughts, call "the bathroom problem"? Too shame-making for Maddie to have to ask to be carried up the stairs every time she needed—and who was there to do it during the day? Maddie was very light—much too light—but her mother knew that she could not lift her, let alone carry her, by herself.

"But you can't see anything from the sitting room," Maddie said.

"Oh darling—" Margaret realized she was going to have to leave Maddie alone again. Her husband would be home soon and she was beginning to have serious doubts about the advisability of reheating the fish pie . . . She must have a quick word with cook about cheese omelettes. If only cook wasn't so bad with eggs . . . "What's this about sunset anyway?" she said briskly.

"Sunset comes a bit earlier every day," Maddie said. "And just at sunset a man walks down the street."

"The same man, every night?" Margaret asked.

"The same man, always just after sunset," Maddie confirmed.

"Perhaps he's a postman?" Margaret suggested.

"Then he'd wear a uniform," Maddie said patiently. "And the same if he was a park keeper I suppose—they wear uniforms too, don't they? Besides, he doesn't look like a postman."

"So—what does he look like?"

"It's hard to explain." Maddie struggled for the right words. "But—can you imagine a beautiful skull?"

"What! What a horrible idea!" Margaret stood up, clutching the grey foulard at her bosom. "Maddie, if you begin talking like this I shall call Dr. Whiston. I don't care if he doesn't like coming out after dinner. Skull-headed men walking past the house every night indeed!"

Maddie pouted. "I didn't say that. It's just that his face is very—sculptured. You can see the bones under the skin, especially the cheekbones. It just made me think—he must even have a beautiful skull."

"And how is he dressed?" Margaret asked faintly.

"A white shirt and a sort of loose black coat," Maddie said. "And he has quite long curly black hair. I think he might be a student."

"No hat?" her mother asked, scandalized. "He sounds more like an anarchist! Really, Maddie, I wonder if I should go and have a word with the policeman on the corner and tell him that a suspicious character has been hanging about outside the house."

"No, Mother!" Maddie sounded so anguished that her mother hastily laid a calming hand on her forehead.

"Now, darling, don't upset yourself. You must remember what the doctor said. Of course I won't call him if you don't want me to, or the policeman. That was a joke, darling! But you mustn't get yourself upset like this . . . Oh dear, your forehead feels quite clammy. Here, take one of your tablets. I'll get you a glass of water."

And in her very real anxiety for her daughter, worries about the fish pie and well-founded doubts about the substitute omelettes, Margaret almost forgot about the stranger. Almost, but not quite. A meeting with Mrs. Monkton one evening when they had both hurried out to catch the last post and met in front of the postbox reminded her and she found herself asking if Mrs. Monkton had noticed anyone "hanging about."

"A young man?" that lady exclaimed with a flash of what Margaret decided was rather indecent excitement. "But darling, there are no young men left." Margaret raised a hand in mute protest only to have it brushed aside by Mrs. Monkton. "Well, not nearly enough to go round, anyway. I expect this one was waiting for Elsie."

Elsie worked for both Mrs. Monkton and Margaret, coming in several times a week to do "the rough," the cleaning that was beneath Margaret's cook and Mrs. Monkton's extremely superior maid. She was a handsome girl with, it was rumored, an obliging disposition, the sort who would never have been allowed across the threshold of a respectable household when Margaret was young. But nowadays . . . Mrs. Monkton's suggestion did set Margaret's mind at rest. A hatless young man— yes, he must be waiting for Elsie. She might "have a word" with the girl about the propriety of encouraging young men to hang about the street for her; but, on the other hand, she might not . . . She hurried back home.

Bunty's mother came to tea, full of news. Bunty's elder sister was getting engaged to someone her mother described as "a bit n.q.o.s., but what can you do . . ." "N.q.o.s." was a rather transparent code for "not quite our sort." The young man's father was, it appeared, very, very rich, though no one was quite sure where he had made his money. He was going to give—to give outright—(Bunty's mother had gasped) a big house in Surrey to the young couple. And he was going to furnish it too, unfortunately, according to his own somewhat . . . individual . . . taste.

"Chrome, my dear, chrome from floor to ceiling. The dining room looks like a milk bar. And as for the bedroom—Jack says"—she lowered her voice—"he says it looks like an avant-garde brothel in Berlin. Although how he knows anything about them I'm sure I'm not going to ask. But he's having nothing to do with the wedding," she added, sipping her tea as if it were hemlock. "I wonder my dear—would dear little Maddie be well enough to be a bridesmaid? It won't be until next June. I want to keep Pammy to myself for as long as I can . . ." She dabbed at her eyes.

"Of course," Margaret murmured doubtfully. And then, with more determination, "I'll ask the doctor."

And, rather surprising herself, she did. On Dr. Whiston's next visit to Maddie, Margaret lured him into the sitting room with the offer of a glass of sherry and let him boom on for a while on how well Maddie was responding to his treatment. Then she asked the Question, the one she had, until that moment, not dared to ask.

"But when will Maddie be—quite well? Could she be a bridesmaid, say, in June next year?"

The doctor paused, sherry halfway to his lips. He was not used to being questioned. Margaret realized that he thought she had been intolerably frivolous. "Bridesmaid?" the doctor boomed. And then thawed, visibly. Women, he knew, cared about such things. "Bridesmaid! Well, why not? Provided she goes on as well as she has been. And you don't let her get too excited. Not too many dress fittings, you know, and see you get her home early after the wedding. No dancing and only a tiny glass of champagne . . ."

"And will she ever be well enough . . . to . . . to . . . marry herself and to . . ." But Margaret could not bring herself to finish that sentence to a man, not even a medical man.

"Marry—well, I wouldn't advise it. And babies? No. No. Still, that's the modern girl, isn't it? No use for husbands and children these days—" and he boomed himself out of the house.

Margaret remembered that the doctor had married a much younger woman. Presumably the marriage was not a success . . . then she let herself think of Maddie. She wondered if Bunty's mother would like to exchange places with her. Margaret would never have to lose her daughter to the son of a nouveau riche war profiteer. Never . . . and she sat down in her pretty chintz-covered armchair and cried as quietly as she could, in case Maddie heard her. For some reason she never asked herself how far the doctor's confident boom might carry. Later she went up to her daughter, smiling gallantly.

"The doctor's so pleased with you, Maddie," she said. "He thinks you'll be well enough to be Pammy's bridesmaid! You'll have to be sure you finish her present in good time."

Margaret had bought a tray cloth and six place mats stamped with the design of a figure in a poke bonnet and a crinoline, surrounded by flowers. Maddie was supposed to be embroidering them in tasteful naturalistic shades of pink, mauve, and green, as a wedding gift for Pammy, but she seemed to have little enthusiasm for the task. Her mother stared at her, lying back in her nest of pillows. "Peak and pine! Peak and pine!" said the voice in her head.

"Do you ever see your young man anymore?" she asked, more to distract herself than because she was really concerned.

"Oh, no," Maddie said, raising her shadowed eyes to her mother. "I don't think he was ever there at all. It was a trick of the dark."

"Trick of the light, surely," Margaret said. And then, almost against her will, "Do you remember that story I used to read you? About the changeling child?"

"What, the one that lay in the cradle saying 'I'm old, I'm old, I'm ever so old'?" Maddie said. "Whatever made you think of that?"

"I don't know," Margaret gasped. "But you know how you sometimes get silly words going round and round your head—it's as if I can't stop repeating those words from the story. 'Peak and pine!' to myself over and over again." There, she had said it aloud. That must exorcize them, surely.

"But that's not from the changeling story," Maddie said. "It's from 'Christabel',— you know, Coleridge's poem about the weird Lady Geraldine. She says it to the mother's ghost: 'Off wandering mother! Peak and pine!' We read it at school, but Miss Brownrigg made us miss out all that bit about Geraldine's breasts."

"I should think so, too," Margaret said weakly.

Autumn became winter, although few people noticed by what tiny degrees the days grew shorter and shorter until sunset came at around four o'clock. Except perhaps Maddie, sitting propped up on her pillows, and watching every day for the young man who still walked down the street every evening, in spite of what she had told her mother. And even she could not have said just when he stopped walking directly past the window, and took to standing in that dark spot just between the lamppost and the postbox, looking up at her . . .

"Where's your little silver cross, darling?" Margaret said suddenly, wondering vaguely when she had last seen Maddie wearing it.

"Oh, I don't know," Maddie said, too casually. "I think the clasp must have broken and it slipped off."

"Oh, but—" Margaret looked helplessly at her daughter. "I do hope Elsie hasn't picked it up. I sometimes think . . ."

"I expect it'll turn up," Maddie said. Her gaze slid away from her mother's face and returned to the window.

"How's Pammy's present coming along?" Margaret asked, speaking to that white reflection in the dark glass, trying to make her daughter turn back to her. She picked up Maddie's work-bag. And stared. One of the place mats had been completed. But the figure of the lady had been embroidered in shades of black and it was standing in the midst of scarlet roses and tall purple lilies. It was cleverly done: every fold and flounce was picked out . . . but Margaret found it rather disturbing. She was glad that the poke bonnet hid the figure's face . . . She looked up to realize that Maddie was looking at her almost slyly.

"Don't you like it?" her daughter asked.

"It's—it's quite modern isn't it?"

"What, lazy daisies and crinoline ladies, modern?" How long had Maddie's voice had that lazy mocking tone? She sounded like a world-weary adult talking to a very young and silly child.

Margaret put the work down.

"You will be all right, darling, won't you?" Margaret said, rushing into her daughter's room one cold December afternoon. "Only I must do some Christmas shopping, I really must . . ."

"Of course you must, Mummy," Maddie said. "You've got my list, haven't you? Do try to find something really nice for Bunty, she's been so kind . . ."

And what I would really like to give her, Maddie thought, is a whole parcel of jig-saws . . . and all the time in the world to see how *she* likes them . . . She leaned against her pillows, watching her mother scurry down the street. Margaret would catch a bus at the corner by the church, and then an Underground train, and then face the crowded streets and shops of a near-Christmas West End London. Maddie would have plenty of time to herself. She knew (although her mother did not) that cook would be going out to have tea with her friend at Mrs. Cresswell's at half-past three, and for at least one blessed hour Maddie would be entirely alone in the house.

She pulled herself further up in the bed, and fumbled in the drawer of her bed-side table to find the contraband she had managed to persuade Elsie to bring in for her. Elsie had proved much more useful than Bunty or Cissie or any of her kind friends. She sorted through the scarlet lipstick, the eyeblack, the facepowder, and began to draw the kind of face she knew she had always wanted on the blank canvas of her pale skin. After twenty minutes of careful work she felt that she had succeeded rather well.

"I'm old, I'm old, I'm ever so old," Maddie crooned to herself. She freed her hair from its inevitable pink ribbon, and brushed it sleekly over her shoulders. Then she took off her lacy bed-jacket and the white winceyette nightie beneath it. Finally she slid into the garment that the invaluable Elsie had found for her (Heaven knew where, although Maddie had a shrewd suspicion it might have been stolen from an-other of Elsie's clients—perhaps the naughty Mrs. Monkton). It was a nightdress made of layers of black and red chiffon, just a little too large for Maddie, but the way it tended to slide from her shoulders could have, she felt, its own attraction.

All these preparations had taken quite a long time, especially as Maddie had had to stop every so often to catch her breath and once to take one of her tablets . . . but she was ready just before sunset. She slipped out of bed, crossed the room, and sat in a chair beside the window. So. The trap was almost set. (But was she the trap or only the bait . . . ?) Only one thing remained to be done.

Maddie took out her embroidery scissors, and, clenching her teeth, ran the tiny sharp points into her wrist . . .

The bus was late and crowded. Margaret struggled off, trying to balance her load of packages and parcels and hurried down the road, past the churchyard wall, past

Mrs. Monkton's red-brick villa, past the postbox—and hesitated. For a moment she thought she had seen something—Maddie's strange man with the beautiful skull-like face? But no, there were two white faces there in the shadows—no . . . there was nothing. A trick of the dark . . . She dropped her parcels in the hall and hurried up the stairs.

"Here I am, darling! I'm so sorry I'm late . . . Oh, Maddie . . . Maddie darling—whatever are you doing in the dark?"

She switched on the light.

"Maddie. Maddie, where are you?" she whispered. "What have you done?"

PHILIP RAINES and
HARVEY WELLES

The Bad Magician

Philip Raines and Harvey Welles have had stories published in Albedo One, Aurealis, Lady Churchill's Rosebud Wristlet, New Genre, *and* On Spec. *Their story "The Fishie" was reprinted in* The Year's Best Fantasy and Horror: Seventeenth Annual Collection *and was an honorable mention in the 2004 Fountain Awards. Raines lives in Glasgow and is a member of the Glasgow Science Fiction Writers Circle. Welles lives in Milwaukee.*

"The Bad Magician" was first published in the Irish magazine Albedo One.

—E.D.

I'm not good with tricks.

For the past two hours, sitting at the kitchen table in my Hounslow bedsit, I've been practicing the card trick that Selim taught me. But my hands are too thick and clumsy, they slip. The secret card never stays hidden, it jumps between my fingers, as if the surfaces of the world have been coated with grease to stop me gripping anything. Yet I keep trying to get it right, not because I know I can eventually, but because if I concentrate hard enough, I won't think about my half-packed holdall on the bed or the awful noise that fills this room like a storm screaming through the forest. Or Leslie and why it all went badly wrong.

Cleveland. I don't have to return to Croatia, I can go to my cousin Mirko in America. There's always somewhere I can run. I put down the cards and look at the bag, neither spilling my life out nor trying to swallow it, but frozen in a moment of indecision. What can I take with me? What will I be allowed to leave behind?

These are the same questions that Leslie asked eight days ago. And as the wailing rises again to deafen me, I think, Tell yourself the story, forget the noise, try to understand what happened.

Tell the story of the Good Luck Suitcase.

The Saturday before last, we were working the early shift in Heathrow. For the other baggage handlers, this was the worst shift with overnight transcontinental flights coming into Terminals 3 and 4, heavy with Americans and their luggage. I didn't mind so much, I'd always been used to rising early. As the sky lightened above the distant trees at the airport's perimeter, I often thought of all the other places I'd seen the dawn: glorifying the plastered concrete side of my hospital in Vukovar, silvering the birches in the Dinara mountains where we camped, brushing the tops of sky-scrapers in Zagreb, Paris, finally London. As a young man, I used to enjoy coming out onto the hospital roof for a cigarette break and see the sky above and the Danube below swell with morning, making me feel like a king of the world.

In the ten years since the war, my feelings about this time of day had changed. I'd lived in towns where the sky had been cramped, squeezed out of streets behind warehouses and restaurant kitchens. Heathrow was the first place in a long time where I could look at a sky that stretched beyond what I could see. But it wasn't the same anymore. I didn't mind the morning chill, the grumbles of the other handlers, but I felt different about the sky now. I felt exposed beneath it.

Like me, Leslie didn't complain about the shifts, something that brought us to-gether when I first got the job with the airport. But unlike me, Leslie volunteered for these shifts. He cherished them. People are groggy off the morning flights, he said—what better time to go through their things?

Leslie had timed the gap between the baggage cart trips and knew he had six minutes at the conveyor belts to open a suitcase and rummage (as he called it). I didn't approve of this, but I'd learnt to keep quiet about the other handlers' actions. Besides, Leslie was my friend, one of the few I knew who wasn't afraid to ask me about life in Croatia. We'd talk about the war crimes trials in the Hague, and if sometimes he confused the war in Bosnia with our war of independence, I wasn't insulted—at least he'd understood that something terrible had happened and couldn't be ignored.

But that morning, I wasn't happy with him. A crowded BA flight had landed from Miami and I was working hard to separate transfer bags from bags going into the ter-minal while Leslie was wasting time with his little games. "How can Americans have so many things?" he said, pulling first one, two, then three electric toothbrushes from the case he had opened on the tarmac.

Normally, I might have smiled, remembering how we used to say the same thing about the Americans in UNPROFOR, but my shoulders were starting to ache. "Leslie, shift your ass."

"Arse, Goran. Only Yanks have asses. Here in England we talk through our arse." Carefully, he replaced the toothbrushes and started flipping through what looked like a diary, stopping occasionally to read pages. "I keep telling you, why take a job like this if you don't peek. It's all harmless."

"Until you are caught."

"I won't get caught."

"You always are caught."

This was true, and Leslie wasn't going to deny it. Guilt stuck to Leslie, even when it wasn't his. A few months ago, there'd been a police crackdown on a drug-running ring of customs officers and airport workers. I knew who was involved, but it wasn't my business, so I kept my head down until the police had eventually given up in frustration. No one was arrested. No one lost their job. But Leslie, one of the few handlers not smuggling something or getting a little extra for looking the other way from time to time, was the one brought in and interviewed by detectives and airport services. Twice. My friend didn't have everyone else's knack of avoiding culpability. He was a magnet for trouble.

Most other handlers thought so. While none of them disliked Leslie, his hands were too fidgety for them and he was always asking questions. Rajeesh said you couldn't trust someone who'd grown and shaved off a moustache three times over the past year, as if he couldn't settle on a disguise. He'd changed his accent so often that Billy had a small pool on how many he'd try before the Christmas night out (so new to this country, I couldn't tell the difference between them). So for the most part, they left Leslie alone.

To me, Leslie did hint at his background. When we took our lunch breaks out by the crash barrier and watched the planes wheel into position for take-off, he'd tell me stories about people he knew during his time inside and criminals he'd run with in Leeds and Nottingham. Every time he repeated these stories, Leslie never changed names or held back facts. They always involved some crime where no one had been caught, an injustice still left hanging, and I was amazed at how openly, how innocently, Leslie could talk about such things. He once admitted that there were some people from the North still looking for him. A part of Leslie believed they'd find him, and some nights after we'd been to the pub, he'd ask me to wait with him at the stop until the bus arrived. He was scared, but it didn't stop him talking.

By the time the next cart came around the corner of the tunnel, Leslie was making a show of helping me load bags onto the belt, but as soon as he saw it was Gareth, he relaxed and went over to talk. "Thought I was Merc, didn't you, Les?" Gareth joked. "Thought I'd catch you sniffing some knickers, didn't you?"

People avoided Leslie, but a few of us looked out for him. Gareth was one. I liked Gareth. The two of us had got off to a bad start when I mistook his Newcastle accent for Scottish, but when he realized it was only because I was foreign, we became good friends. We both enjoyed wrestling—not watching the stupid clowning they call wrestling on TV, but real wrestling—and shifts permitting, I looked forward to Monday evenings in our gym in Hounslow.

"I'm not a perv, you Geordie dick," Leslie growled, while Gareth laughed and pumped the air above Leslie's head with soft punches. "I just like to know what people get up to."

"That makes you the dick, Les. The private dick." Gareth jumped down from the truck, felt the pockets of his plastic orange jacket and reached back inside the cabin of the vehicle. I thought he was looking for his cigarettes.

He wasn't. He brought out a suitcase he'd stashed away. "Les—found it."

Leslie wasn't a young man—a good ten years on me, and I've not seen youth myself for a decade—but standing there, his face draining of the usual anxiety and filling up with hope, he almost looked a different person.

"You—sure?" he asked nervously.

"Black Samsonite, silver handle, broken wheels, right?"

"And the mark?"

"And a mark right in the center of it." With his foot, Gareth tipped the case over. It fell with a heavy boom. "That weird squiggle you drew for me. Burned right into the plastic."

All of us stared at the strange symbol branded into the side of the cheap, medium-sized, matte-black case, barely distinctive from the other scrapes and scratches, like an old scar that would never fully heal. "What is this about, Leslie?" I asked quietly.

"The Good Luck Suitcase," Leslie whispered, not for me, but for awe. He traced the mark with his finger, not touching it. In his face, there was no doubt of it.

Gareth got back in the cart. "Look, finish unloading. We've taken too much time already. This Monday, Goran?"

I waved to him and quickly, silently, Leslie and I got the bags off the trolley, sifting out the transfers and loading the conveyor. The Samsonite had a LHR final tag, but when I moved to put it with the others, Leslie was faster, hauling the bag out of sight under the lip of the belt's machinery.

"This is wrong," I told him, but Leslie smiled, nodded as if there was suddenly no time to speak and we had to get back to work.

When we were done, Leslie dragged the case out of its hiding place. "We've got twenty minutes until Vancouver's due."

I hesitated. "Do you want me with you?" I asked, wanting to know what was going on, but at the same time, hoping he didn't want to involve me.

"I've got no secrets from you, Goran," he lied. "Come on." He said this casually, but his eyes were pleading, and shivering, I realized I couldn't turn a friend down.

As the airport began to stir with morning traffic, there were not many quiet places we could go and remain undisturbed. Leslie was having trouble with the case, so I carried it for him. It felt like it had been filled with bricks, and as we struggled along the terminal's service tunnels, greeted by other drivers and maintenance crews I knew, I began to sweat with its weight and the thought of being caught. But Leslie had planned this, and took us somewhere nearby, the locker room where we kept our street clothes. We were lucky, and found ourselves alone with the case.

Seeing my face, Leslie said, "Jesus, I'm only borrowing it—do you know what this is?"

"The Good Luck Suitcase," I repeated back to him.

Leslie heaved the case onto the bench in front of him, lowered it gently. No locks, just two sets of snaps. He opened it slowly. "Yes, but do you know what this is?"

The case looked empty. How could it be so heavy? "But I thought you were talking piss then."

One night at the pub, the day our wages had been paid, we'd gotten very drunk together. Over vodkas, Leslie and I talked. I told him how it felt to be crouching in the hospital corridors, too terrified to go outside because of the shells raining down from the sky, knowing the Chetnik troops would soon be entering the outskirts of my city. And Leslie told me about a special suitcase he'd heard of.

At the time, I was sure this was another joke at the expense of the credulous foreigner, but as I now watched Leslie take a duffel bag out of his locker and start to stuff his own clothes into the Good Luck Suitcase, I realized he'd been looking for this for a long time. It was probably the reason why he'd kept a spare set of clothes in the locker, and thinking about it, very likely why he was working here at the airport. A lot of suitcases passed through Heathrow.

Leslie was doing such a bad job of packing that I took over from him. If there was one thing you learn in the army, it was how to fit a lot of things into small spaces.

"I don't know where I first heard about it," he told me. "Maybe Maggie in Nottingham, or that Albanian pimp. But when I did, Goran, I just knew. I could see what I needed to do. And I've always been good at finding things out. You know, patient. They used to call me 'ferret' at school, you know that? I knew I just had to wait here long enough."

I wanted to ask him what ferret was but I knew that Leslie was going away and there were some things he had to say first. "I can't wait anymore," he continued. "They'd catch me. Macpherson, Beck—one day, they'd find me, wherever I went. I'm not very good at hiding, Goran."

When I was done, everything just about fitted into the case except Leslie's leather jacket. But that wasn't all Leslie wanted to put in. Without saying a word, Leslie stripped off his overalls, breathing hard as he pulled off his boots and socks, his vest. I watched, frightened that maybe this was something else, my friend having a nervous breakdown. Last, he took off his pants, and then without looking at me, packed these into the Samsonite as well. Grunting as he pushed the top down, he shut the case.

"Leslie—" I began, not sure what to say, praying desperately that no one would walk in right now.

"Everything I own has to go in there," Leslie said, shaking in the cold of the locker room. "This is all I've left myself now, Goran, it's all got to go in the case. It's the—rules. Magic rules. You know about magic, Goran?"

Magic. I knew magic.

Before the war, my grandmother collected herbs down by the river in the late summer and used to make pastes that builders put into their bricks for strength and luck. The village where I grew up—before my family moved to Vukovar—had a church containing a fingerbone of Saint Stephen. Every Lent, the bishop came to the village and heard confessions with the jewelled reliquary in his lap, touching the heads of the faithful with it once they'd finished—as if the finger could wipe away their sins and guilt, as if forgiveness could be given away, the past forgotten and everything put right that easily.

I knew magic, and hated it.

"What about your jacket?" I asked him.

Leslie looked at the jacket—his favorite, I knew—as if it was an oversight. But he surprised me. "Wanted you to have it, Goran."

I was nearly two feet taller than Leslie, broad in the shoulders where he was fat at the waist. The jacket could never fit me, but I accepted the gift. My friend stood there, sad in his nakedness, his hairless body tensing from imaginary blows, until I hugged him.

"I've got to do the next bit myself," Leslie said, so we didn't say good-bye. I just left him in the locker room and went to find the Vancouver flight. As I jogged back to Terminal 3, I remembered what Leslie had said that night in the pub about the Good Luck Suitcase. You put your whole life into the case, but when you took it out again, you left behind all the bad luck. I hoped that Leslie would leave behind his.

I hoped that I'd never see him again and put him from my mind.

After Vancouver, I had to work another three flights before my lunch break. But I'd only finished the Rio flight when Paula told me that Merc was looking for me and would I go immediately to lost luggage in Terminal 4.

Coming through a service door, I felt shock at seeing the activity in the terminal. You forgot sometimes the difference between what passengers saw of airports and the huge invisible world behind that supported it. Out here, bags disappeared and reappeared from the terminal—like magic, I reluctantly admitted to myself—and no one thought about the complex machinery and procedures that were necessary to get luggage smoothly from the terminal buildings to the planes and back again. Probably no one thought at all about what went on outside the terminals. That English expression—out of sight, out of mind—was so true, as the people hurried from check-in to their gates, without pausing to glance in my direction, or wonder why I was here in the airport.

Merc was waiting at the lost luggage desk with a representative from the airline and someone I guessed was a passenger. I knew what this was about even before Merc—a nasty little man with too many rings in his ear—began to ask me if I could remember any bags that might have slipped off the cart, maybe a case damaged by accident and I hadn't got around to saying something. Gareth would have called his tone snide, but I didn't show any anger, I played dumb. No, I didn't know of any missing bags. None had fallen off the cart as far as I knew. No, I hadn't seen Leslie since he complained about pains in his back and had gone to find the doctor.

Both Merc and I knew this was all show for the airline rep and the passenger. Bags could go missing in a hundred ways at an airport. The black Samsonite could turn up in the rubbish bins outside of a Burger King, and someone would just wipe it down, bring it out front and come up with a story about how it had been put into the transfer stream accidentally. As long as nothing was damaged or missing, there'd be no complaints, and since I knew there was nothing in this case to break or steal, they couldn't touch me—or Leslie. What they would say if the case or Leslie didn't turn up, I didn't think about—I could be very good at putting things out of my head when I wanted to.

Merc nodded, making sarcastic remarks, but not really listening. My being here was unorthodox, just to appease an angry passenger, so it didn't matter what I said. When he and the airline rep conferred, I took the time to study the passenger, the man who owned the Good Luck Suitcase.

He was a young man, Gareth's age, wearing a mustard-colored linen jacket and a collarless, black silk shirt. To me, he looked like a Muslim, but when I heard him exchange words with the rep, knew he must be American. A wealthy one. Black hair neatly trimmed and greased back, his dark skin smooth, he was well-groomed, streamlined, nothing excessive about him, no space to hide anything. He didn't look like someone who'd just got off a seven-hour overnight flight from America. He reminded me of the medicine smugglers I'd once worked for, urbane, understanding, and—I somehow knew instantly—ruthless at a moment's notice.

Nothing more could be done and I was late to help with a Bombay flight, so Merc let me go. Gratefully I left the overlit, exposed terminal building for the darker passages that lay beyond. I served out the rest of my shift, ate my lunch alone and didn't think about the suitcase or Leslie. Mid-afternoon, my shift was over. I avoided the locker room, and carrying the leather jacket Leslie had given me, went to the carpark, ready to drive to Slough for my English class.

The American was waiting for me, leaning against the locked gate that led to the main road.

So surprised was I that the first thing I said was, "How did you get in here?" For all the petty crime that went on here, security wasn't taken lightly in Heathrow, and people couldn't just wander into this carpark.

But the man grinned, a big, disarming smile that he did with his eyes as well as his mouth, and put out a hand to shake. "Selim Bass."

"Goran," I said back. No reason to give him more. "How did you get in?"

"A trick," he said, amused at my tenacity.

A trick? That made me realize that I had seen him before. "You are—the magician? I've seen you on—the Channel Four."

"I prefer illusionist," he said, bowing slightly.

"I saw you do tricks. With the cards. It was—" I couldn't find the right words to tell him. "Very good. Can you do one now?"

I didn't know why I asked him that. Perhaps I was so unnerved by his appearance that I wanted to do the same to him, and it worked. "I'm not David fucking Blaine," he spat at me, his skin going darker with a fury that must have never been far below the surface. "You want a show, you pay and see me in Drury Lane."

"Who is David Blaine?"

Selim Bass hid his hands in his jacket pockets, maybe his way of keeping me off-balance. "Where's your friend?"

"This about your case?" I bluffed, allowing my English to slip. "Authorities find it. Two days most."

"Your friend doesn't know what he's doing. He'll fuck it up."

"Two days," I repeated. I knew how to do that smile as well, I'd had to do it through four years of abuse from French and English bastards who didn't know the difference between a Russian and someone from the Balkans, let alone between a Serb and a Croat.

For a moment, I thought the anger in his face was going to explode and he'd try and throw a punch. But he saw my size, he could see I could handle myself, and any shout from me would bring over a security guard before he could run. So he let his body relax, made the smile return and stood back.

"If you were a card, Goran," he said, "what card would you be?"

"Card?"

"Which one?"

I was confused, so I said, "The Fool?"

"Not the fucking tarot. Normal cards."

My gaze hardened. "Ace."

"Interesting. You choose the tricky card, my friend. The one that's both high and low. I'd say you were an Ace of Spades."

"I'm not your friend."

"You'll want to be soon," he said and turned to go. "Check your pocket."

The card was in Leslie's jacket: on one side, the Ace of Spades, the other, Selim Bass's mobile phone number.

The Ace of Spades stayed with me, because I wanted to prove Selim Bass wrong. I wanted to be Hearts, though there hadn't been anyone—not anyone of the heart—since Maria was killed by a sniper in Vukovar. I could be Diamonds, like those who'd also fled Croatia, who'd lost so much that it was easy to steal from others. Even Clubs, the man of action, who'd fought to liberate his country. But the Ace of Spades made me think of the Motorhead tape we listened to on sentry duty in the Dinaras.

And an Ace of Spades was a man who dug graves.

Had Selim Bass known? Had he unearthed my life? That frightened me. Maybe he could read the guilt in my face. That frightened me even more, so I carried the card with me as I worked, touching its edge, fraying it. Then sometimes I'd roll up my trouser leg, and touch the edge of the scar, a white line running from kneecap to calf, given to me during one of my beatings after Vukovar fell. In the winter of 1991, I'd been marched out of the town with the wound, the blood leaving boot prints on the light snow, and it was still seeping a week later when they made the dozen of us that were still fit dig a long trench outside of Ovcara. By the time I'd escaped our captors, stealing through the forest alone because Mato and Ivica were too tired to run, it was starting to heal. The pain was something I couldn't remember now, but as I fingered the card, I could still feel the spade in my hand, and above all, the terrible shame as I left behind my friends.

In the English papers, I read about the tribunal in the Hague. The media celebrated the few Serbs who'd been caught and punished, and wrung its hands at the failure to capture those still at large, Mladic, Karadzic, even the beast Milosevic himself, the ones responsible for Sarajevo, Srebrenica, all the atrocities of the Bosnian war. But did they remember what happened to my people? Did they try to bring to justice the butchers of Vukovar? No—there were no witnesses, so nothing happened. People wanted to forget the bad things, but I knew they'd bubble up again. The world wouldn't let them put this aside.

But people could be so good at forgetting. For the next few days, no one mentioned Leslie, not even Merc, who'd normally have skinned anyone for dropping shifts without warning. Even I found myself thinking less and less of my friend, and when I did, and realized how easily he'd slipped away, I was glad. His luck had truly changed.

But maybe it was because there were other things distracting people. I didn't notice for the first two days, but Leslie wasn't the only one not turning up to work. Handlers, engineers, reps, dozens of people were calling in sick, as if a wave of flu had suddenly passed through the airport. Those of us who were still healthy had to cover with overtime. I had to cancel my Monday night at the gym with Gareth, but it wasn't until Tuesday that I took in what was going on.

By then the stories were passing around. That people weren't really sick. Rajeesh told me about an incident involving one of the women working in the BA ticket office in Terminal 2, how her ex-husband turned up and started yelling abuse and they had to call security to escort him out. Shaken, she'd gone home and took the rest of the week as holiday. Then there was Doreen, a lovely woman working in the BAA payroll department, who always asked when I'd find myself a good woman. On Monday, a small boy of about four was found wandering in Terminal 1, crying and calling out her name. When the police brought him to Doreen, she'd gone white as frost, said she didn't know who the boy was and ran to the toilet. One of her colleagues said she left the airport straight afterwards, calling in her resignation before the end of the afternoon.

I didn't make the connection, not until Wednesday afternoon, when Gareth came to me. Then I understood that this was something else.

Billy and I had finished loading a Birmingham flight when Gareth found us repairing broken tags on bags that had gone astray. Looking at him, I remembered how Samantha had described Doreen's face when the police brought her lost son. "Gareth, what is it?"

"You know about this sort of thing, Goran."

Billy shrugged, so I took Gareth into the bus waiting room for passengers in transit to other terminals, empty at the moment. "This sort of thing?"

"You can help, right? You know about shit like this?"

"Gareth, what?"

"Vampires." By now, he was gripping my shoulder, twisting it as if we were wrestling. "The undead. They know about things like that where you're from, right? Transylvania shit."

He was so rattled that I didn't correct him. "It wasn't my fault, right? I was in a hurry, and it was night, but I wasn't drunk, or asleep, or anything like that. It just wasn't my fault. Understood, right?"

As soon as I'd agreed, Gareth released my shoulder and sat down. A few passengers showed up for the bus, but seeing Gareth distraught, sat in the far corner. "Five years ago, I used to have a courier job for a big property firm. There used to be a lot of overnight packages between London and Bristol, so I drove the M4 three, four times a week."

He raised a hand to do something to his face, but seemed to forget halfway, and let it hang there for a moment. "She must have been wandering along the road, looking for an emergency phone. I don't know. She was just, all of a sudden, there, in the middle of the road. The bloody motorway, right? I couldn't do anything. No braking distance, nothing. She was some old woman, like she'd escaped from a hospital. Christ. She had this green dress, something your granny kept at the back of a wardrobe from a wedding fifty years ago. And she's wearing the same bloody dress."

"You've—seen her?"

"She was dead. I wouldn't have driven away if she was injured, right?" The passengers looked over in our direction, then picked up their bags and went outside the building to wait for the bus. "Christ, Goran. When she saw me, she screamed. The police are going to find her, and—you'll tell them, Goran? Please. It wasn't my fault!"

"Where you see her?"

She wasn't outside where he told me, the depot where the baggage carts were brought for maintenance. I looked along the service road running up the side of Terminal 3, then the bus station platforms, even down the tunnel leading to the Underground, but I didn't see her. Maybe she was a ghost, I thought, the strain of these strange days making Gareth hallucinate. There wasn't enough time for me to look everywhere, I had to be back for the incoming Lyon flight. I had just about given up.

Then I saw her.

There, under a pedestrian bridge joining two buildings, by some large metal bins. Arms holding her thin dress close for warmth, looking confused. Sitting with her back to the bushes, her legs kicking as she rocked forward and back. Hair falling around her shoulders, but leaving her neck bare. The dead woman.

I tried to hide, behind a pillar. But it was too late, she'd seen me. And started—screaming. The way Gareth had said.

I fled, the terrible sound chasing after me.

"I'll see you after the show."

I didn't have to tell Selim Bass anything on the phone. All I had to do was tell him where we could meet in the airport.

That night, we sat in a bar in Terminal 3's shopping area, watching businessmen drink too many whiskies before their transatlantic flights. Bass stared into his glass sourly. "They water the beer. Can't anyone else here taste it?"

That didn't stop him from draining his glass, hungrily gulping it all down. "Of course not," he answered himself. "People don't want to know."

He was still in his stage costume: a dark blue jacket that was so loose that it looked like a kimono, a white turtleneck, black leather trousers. He hadn't said anything since I explained it all to him. "This strange shit, it's because Leslie took the case? Magic. Your business."

"I don't do magic," he snapped at me. "Illusions, I told you. Real magic's for the weak, like your friend."

Bass began folding his paper beermat into quarters. "Illusion's what we all do. Most of us can do sleight of hand, whether it's to get laid, or find a job, or tell a story to hide behind. But there's always the few who can't. The clumsy ones. And 'cause they can't, they got to cheat, find some way of twisting the rules of the world to cover the fact they're crap at tricks. Only losers use magic."

"Like the bag," I said. "The Good Luck Suitcase."

Bass looked at me, bemused. "Good luck? First time I've heard it called that, but that kind of makes sense. Yeah, like the bag."

Finishing my vodka, I waved to the waitress, held up a finger for another. Slow down, I told myself, but I couldn't stop myself drinking today. "So why keep it? Why take it around if such trouble?"

"Well, wouldn't have been any trouble at all if the fucking bubblehead at the gate in Miami hadn't decided it was too big for hand luggage," he snarled. "Had to go into the hold. Couldn't believe it—they've never pulled that shit on me before."

Selim shrugged, taking out an elegant silver cigarette case. He didn't offer me a smoke. "It was always an easy risk. Take the case out of the vault, give it a little air, make a little money between shows. A couple of English losers I knew were interested, losers who didn't like the normal rules of the world. The kind who left unsupervised with the bag would fuck up everything. Losers like your friend."

He lit his cigarette and blew smoke across the table. "Okay. You're going to help me get it back."

"Tell me first what it does."

When we were done, Bass let me pay the drinks bill. As he stood to go, I told him, "That card trick the other day, you planted the card in my jacket earlier."

For the first time that night, Bass smiled, not one of his show-business smiles, but genuine admiration. "Couldn't help it. I found you during the afternoon, and while you weren't looking, I slipped you the card. The Ace was just a lucky guess. You didn't look a King or Jack man to me. As for the rest, that's just simple misdirection."

"You're very good."

Again, Bass shrugged. "Not really. Everyone wants to be fooled. It's why we're so good at illusion—we don't like to look too carefully. Trouble is, you can't keep people fooled for long, even if they want to be. The world won't allow it. We make a line between what we want to know and what we don't, but the world doesn't respect those kinds of boundaries. There's always something out there that'll trip you up, expose what you're doing. Take my trick—you worked it out. You could see it was a trick 'cause you knew I was trying to fool you, and you thought, he's pulling something on me, so how's he doing it. No, the best tricks are the ones where even the magician fools himself."

Bass took a puff on his cigarette, and winked at me. "And unlike some people, I just can't fool myself."

On Thursday morning, police detectives were swarming around the airport. Billy said someone had dropped some photos with customs and now Rajeesh and several airport workers were being questioned about drug smuggling. Then Billy disappeared for the rest of the afternoon. A skeleton staff was keeping the airport going as best they could, but flights were being delayed. After seven straight days on, I needed to talk to Merc about the shifts, but Merc wasn't at work either. His secretary Lillian gleefully told me the rumor that he was being investigated for tax fraud. Outside the airport, journalists were already asking questions as people came off work.

I had to find Leslie. My friends were suffering and I had to do something. How did I know that he wasn't already gone? Small signs that he'd never left were there if you knew how to see them. Everything was so chaotic that no one would notice if I was gone for a few hours, so I waited by the crash barriers where I'd seen new Kit Kat wrappers lying in the grass.

Towards sunset, he joined me to watch the huge 747s rise, flashing briefly before they vanished into the western sky like a coin in Selim's hand. "Oh Leslie—why didn't you go?"

"It's such a mess, Goran." The man beside me seemed to shrink, and for a moment, the light bleached him so he was indistinguishable from the chipped white paint of the barrier's concrete surface. "I didn't want all this."

When I tried looking directly at the man, I thought, This couldn't be Leslie eating chocolate. The clothes were slightly different, his features caught the light in a way that made him look like someone else. Even when I closed my eyes and listened to him talk about the suitcase, his voice sounded like it had been treated. If I'd spoken with him on the phone, I'd have sworn it wasn't my old friend.

"When you'd gone, I opened the case, took out my stuff," he explained. "That's how it's supposed to work, kind of like a washing machine. That's what the Albanian told me. Dry-cleans the soul, he promised me."

Only it doesn't, I thought, but kept that to myself as Leslie continued. "Once I put my clothes on, I knew I'd be Okay. I just knew immediately. Macpherson wasn't going to find me now. All I had to do was shut the case, lose it on one of the baggage routes. I could go anywhere. I could even go back to Leeds, and nobody would ever know who I'd been."

He started shaking, and I wanted to put my hand on his arm, comfort him, but I was scared my hand would pass through the apparition. "So what did you do?"

"It's a mess," he sobbed. "It's my fault, isn't it? I had all my stuff and I should've shut the case. But there was something else there. I thought it was empty, but there was this—bulge. Under the lining. I'm so sorry. I couldn't help myself, Goran."

"What happened?"

He blew his nose messily onto a candy wrapper. "Show you."

To complete his transformation, Leslie had taken the case to the pound for unclaimed baggage, a temporary storage area until construction had finished on a proper facility. It was a yard closed off with chain-link fencing and protected from the rain by corrugated plastic sheeting, a place where hardly anyone came. All the cases and boxes left unaccounted for after a month's chasing by the airlines went into this limbo, abandoned in stacks until someone could be bothered to clear everything out for charity auctions.

There was no mistaking the Good Luck Suitcase. It was the only one with the lid open.

"I was too scared to close it," Leslie confessed, insisting that we both crouch behind the fence and a tower of undelivered cardboard boxes. I was going to ask what were we waiting for when a gust must have torn something from inside the Good Luck Suitcase—it looked like a huge black and white photograph—and shimmied it along the ground. Watching the picture made me feel uneasy. It dragged along the ground with bizarre purpose, moving in sudden jerks that carried it around the other bags, under the fence and along the road that curled away from us and towards the terminal buildings, reeled in by an invisible fishing line.

"The first thing I pulled out were these papers," Leslie whispered to me, as if the suitcase could hear us. "Tax records, something like that. They had Merc's name on them, but before I could do anything, they were—snatched from me. I don't know how else to describe it. Like a wind. And then I—I don't know what else I expected to find. But I reached back into the case, under the pocket and—oh God. Oh God."

We were looking at the case sideways on, and I could tell that something else was being pulled out. Something larger, like a sweater at first. But then the hand gripped the side of the case, and I could see the fingers whiten with the strain. I looked down at my own hands, which were just as pale. Then back at the man's head, rising slowly over the edge of the lid.

"Leslie? What is—"

But he couldn't look and stared in the direction the photograph had gone. "The first one, the boy, let go of my hand, ran away. The next one, all the others, didn't need my help. They just poured out. I wanted to close the lid but I was scared to. I thought about them, banging inside the case. Shouting. Accusing me."

The young man didn't look anything like them, but I suddenly thought of my friends, Mato and Ivica, shaking the soil from their clothes. I pushed myself farther back into hiding. He looked dazed, not sure about these clothes, why he was here, but something seemed to know what to do with him. With faltering steps, he followed the fence around to the open gate, then up the road with the same determination as the picture before him.

Whose secret was he? I thought.

"What did I do wrong?" Leslie moaned. "Is it my fault?"

I should have told him what Selim had told me: that the case was a portal between this world and the invisible one, the place where we tried to banish our secrets. You could slip some things, some lives, from this world into that dark place, but you had to be careful. The barrier wasn't stable. The world didn't like to stay hidden, it was always trying to find a way back into the light, and if you started to pull things back across, it was like chipping a hole in a dam. The pressure of all those secrets couldn't be held back.

"I'm so sorry. Goran—you've got to help me." He grabbed my arm, the touch of a ghost. "Please."

Reaching up to pat his head, I said, "I help my friends."

Within two days, the secrets vanished, as if they'd never been there. No charges were pressed against Rajeesh and Doreen was persuaded to return to work when she was reassured the boy hadn't been seen since. Even Merc came in, chastened as he walked into the office, not meeting anyone's gaze. Everyone in the airport went back to forgetting, and because the case only seemed to affect the lives of the people in its vicinity, everything was quickly normal again. No—almost everything. Gareth avoided me—but after confessing so much weakness to me, I knew we couldn't continue wrestling every Monday as if nothing had happened.

Coming off work Sunday evening, I saw Selim pulling cards out of the cameras of the photographers seeing him off to America. When he saw me, he wheeled over a trolley with his luggage. The Samsonite was there on top.

"No one has said about Leslie," I had to say to him, the reason I'd sought him out this one last time.

He petted my arm, as if I was a small child who was too young to understand yet. "They won't. They've forgotten already."

"I will not forget."

How could I? I didn't like to use my strength, but I had to hit Leslie several times before he stopped struggling. How could I forget hurting him? And emptying his duffel bag, still full of everything he owned in the world, and undressing him as he moaned and Selim did something with his hands to hush the spirits in the Samsonite long enough to put all Leslie's things back into the case. I couldn't keep any of this out of my head. Not how Leslie looked when we emptied the case and put his clothes back on, more exposed and vulnerable than I'd ever seen him.

You can shut the lid of the case, Selim had told me in the bar. But you can't close the portal. There's only one way to do that. Your friend's got to pass back through. Right through. Sorry, but it's the rules of the world.

Only passing Leslie back through the boundary made him more visible than before, a siren drawing every secret he'd ever tried to hide from. There was no point trying to hide him, Selim argued, but I had to try. I didn't take him home but to one of the airport hotels. I took out three hundred pounds from a cashpoint and left the money in an envelope in his pocket. And still, when I came by the next morning, the ambulance was there, and the police were asking questions about a shooting, and already no one knew anything.

So tonight I've stayed here in the bedsit, with this pack of cards Selim gave me, knowing I can't forget. Telling myself the story of this last week hasn't worked. I can't forget what I did.

For she is still here, crouched in the corner, screaming silently at me.

She's not like the other secrets. She was when I first saw her, sitting in those bushes under the terminal bridge, but she hasn't gone, has she. I try to give her Leslie's jacket, but she isn't really there and the jacket falls through to the floor. See, this is only a hallucination now, just a prank played on your mind by the stress. But she won't go, not until I can work out the magic words to banish her, find a story that can obliterate the guilt, stop the screaming.

She didn't scream the first time, not when our unit came howling down from the Dinara forests, liberating Krajina, finally driving the Serbs out of Croatia in 1995, like the terrible storm wind they called the *Kosava*. She said nothing when we gathered up the menfolk who'd not fled the village and gave them spades. She only watched as Mladen took her father away, and because of that look in her face, that conviction that having witnessed it all herself, the world itself would never forget, I pushed her back into her kitchen.

Gareth says I have strong hands, but her neck was so small, it didn't take much strength.

Now my hands are thick and clumsy, and the cards won't stay still. Selim showed me the trick before the final departure call was announced. And don't let this haunt you, Goran. Remember—guilt's a trick of the world. Innocence is the trick we play on it.

I will never learn how to do this, I told him. I will never forget.

Yes, you will, he said to me. We always do.

Speir-Bhan

Tanith Lee has published over seventy-five novels and short story collections.
Her most recent books include Metallic Love (a sequel to The Silver Metal
Lover) and a young adult novel, Piratica: Being a Daring Tale of a Singular
Girl's Adventure Upon the High Seas. Lee, who is Irish on her mother's side,
lives in England with her partner, writer and artist John Kaiine.

"Speir-Bhan," which is based on the twelfth-century legend of Aeritech's
daughters and the heroes with the harp and spear, was published in the
wide-ranging anthology Emerald Magic: Great Tales of Irish Fantasy edited
by Andrew M. Greeley.

—K.L. & G.G.

This I offer to the memory of my mother,
my unmet grandfather and great-grandfather—who never,
so far as I ever heard, reneged on any bargain.

This story, if that's what it is, is written in two voices. Both are mine. My blood
is mixed, fire with water, earth with air.

I was never in Ireland, though from there I came.
The answer to this riddle is simple enough. I am mostly Irish, genetically and in
my blood, but was born in another country.

My mother it was who had the Irish strand. Her eyes were dark green—I have
never seen elsewhere eyes so dark and so green, save sometimes now, with those who
wear colored contact lenses.

She it was who told me of that land where, too, she'd never gone. O'Moore was
her maiden name. She said the weather there was "soft"—which meant it rained,
but a rain so fine and often warm, a sort of mist, accustomed as the air. They came
from the Ghost Coast, the O'Moores of my mother's tribe, the haunted west of Ireland, where the rocks steep into the sea, harder than hearts. My mother's father had
a Spanish name, Ricardo. She used to speak of him lovingly. His father, her grandfather, was a gallant man called Colum. He lived to be over a hundred, and died in
his hundred and first year from a chill, caught while escorting his new wife, a

young lady of forty-five, to the theatre in Dublin. Ah the soft weather then wasn't always kind.

Ireland is the land of green—emerald as her eyes, my mother. She has gone now, to other greener golden lands under the hollow hills. But one day, searching through her things some years after her death, I found my great-grandfather Colum's book. It wasn't any diary, or perhaps it was. It seemed the book of a practical man who is a poet, and cares for a drink, the book of a canny liar who will tell stories, or it is the book of one who speaks the truth. All of which, with arrogant pride and some reticence, I might say also of myself, saving the book and my gender.

There arrived a night when, having found his book, I met my great-grandfather Colum, for the first, in a dream. He was a tall, thin man, who seemed in his sixties, so probably he was about eighty, for at ninety-nine I had heard, he had looked ten years his younger.

"So you found it then," he said.

"So I did."

"Where was that?"

"In a box that had my mother's letters and some of *her* mother's things."

"Tucked up among the girls," he said. "Why should I complain."

I didn't mention my grandmother's fox-fur cape, also in the box—I had been afraid of this cape when a child, and last week, locating it again, had sent it to a charity.

In the dream, Colum told me of his house that was of stone, and had a narrow stone stair. The windows looked across the valley to the sea, where the sun went down at night. It was not the Dublin big house of later years, this, but where he had been a boy.

In the dream, we walked, he and I, through that valley of velvet green. We climbed up inside the house and watched the sunset. Birds cooed, settling on the roof, and in the yard was an old well, full of good water.

Nearby—that was, maybe, seven miles along the shore—stood ruinous and supernatural Castle *Seanaibh*, or Castle Sanvy as the tourist guide has it.

In his book, Colum says that he was there all one night. In the dream he told me that, too.

We drank whisky, the color of two garnets in amber, and the red sun set, and a magpie flew over the stone house in the valley, chattering its advice.

But all this I dreamed had been written in Colum's book anyway. Along with a story, between two lists of things, one of which is a list of fish caught from a boat, and the second a list of likely girls he had seen in town.

In those days, Colum was twenty, tall and slender and strong, with hair that was black, and eyes that were grey, with the smoky ring around the iris no one, who does not have it—they say—can ever resist.

He worked at a desk in the family business, which was to do with leather goods, nor did he like it much, but it left him time and gave him money to go to the dances, and once a week to drink until he could call to stars, and they would fly down like bees. It was on a night just like that, having danced for five hours and drunk for two, that Colum set off along the road to get home. It was about a mile along that road, to the house. On either side the land ran up and down, and trees stood waning in the last wealth of their summer leaves. The full moon was coming up from her own boozy party, fat and flushed and not quite herself. So Colum sang to her as he walked, but she only pulled a cloud across her face, petulant thing. Oh, there were girls like that, too.

A quarter way along the road, Colum stopped.

It felt, he said, as if he had never been on that road, not once, in all his days, when in fact he had traveled it twice a week for many years, and often more than twice. Since he was an infant he had known it, carried along it even, in his mother's belly.

Boulders lay at the roadside, pale, like sheep that dozed. That night he felt he had never seen one of them, though he had carved his name in several.

It was not, he reckoned, a special night, not a night sacred to any saint that he could think of, or to any fey thing, not Samhain, nor Lug's night either. He stood and blamed the pub whisky, or the fiddler in the hall, for the way the road had altered.

And then there they were. Those Others.

He said, in the dream, "It wasn't like the magical effects they do now, with their computer-machines for the films." He said, one minute there was just the empty road under the cloudy moon, and then there was something, as if vapor had got into your face. And then you saw them.

They were of all kinds. Tall as a tall man, or a tall house, or little as a rabbit, or a pin. They trotted along the road, or walked, or pranced, or rolled. There were horses, with flying manes, but they were not horses, you could see that plainly enough; they had human eyes, and human feet.

None of them had any colors to them, though they looked solid. They were like the stones at the roadside, only they moved, and all of them in front of him, and none of them looking back.

Another man would have dropped down by the boulders. Another again would have run off back to the dance hall and the public house.

Colum fell in behind the travelers, at a mild, respectful distance.

He had learned two things in his young life. First, he could not always get or have everything he would like. Second, he could have and get quite a lot.

He thought anyway, none of *them* would turn to see him. They were the Royal Folk, some band of them, and what they were doing out he didn't know, for they had no business to be. He was not afraid. As he told me, if he had danced and drunk less, he might have been—but that was to come.

So he followed them up the road, and soon enough it turned in at a wood. There was no similar wood in the area that he recalled. The trees were great in girth, and thick and rich with leaves, and moon-washed. The road was now a track. They and he ambled along, and presently the track curved, as the road never had, and then they were climbing up and up, and where the tree line broke, Colum saw the fish-silver ocean fluting down below. They must all have covered seven miles by then, and done it in record time, for next up ahead he beheld the castle called Sanvy. But it was not a ruin that night, it was whole and huge, and pierced with golden lights like spears.

It was haunted, naturally, this castle. Every castle, crag, cot, and byre is haunted, it seems, along the Ghost Coast of Ireland. So Colum thought it was the ghosts who had tidied up and lit all the lamps, and he waited for some coach with headless horses, or running fellow with hell's fire all over him, to come pelting down the track. But instead there came a walking woman, with a burning taper held high in her hand.

Ah, she was lovely. Slim and white, but *colored in*, not like the others, for her hair, which was yards long, was like combed barley, with stars in it and her eyes, he said, like the gas flame, blue and saffron together.

She let the Host pass her, bowing to some, and some in turn nodded to her. Then, when they had gone by and on toward the castle gate, her gas-flame eyes alighted on Colum.

Colum, well he bowed to the ground. He was limber enough and drunk enough to manage it.

She watched him. Then she spoke.

"Do you know me, Colum?"

"No, fair miss. But I see you know me."

"I've known you, Colum, since you were in your cradle, kicking up your feet and sicking up your milk."

Colum frowned. You did not like a pretty girl to remind you of that sort of thing. But at his frowning, she laughed.

She came down the track and touched him on the neck. When she did so, it was the coldest—or hottest—as ice will burn and fire seem icy—touch he had ever felt. He paused, wondering if she'd killed him, but after a moment, he felt a strange sensation in his neck.

"It was as if an eye opened up there—as if something looked out of me, out of my throat."

After that, he found he could speak to the woman on the track in another language, that he had never known, though perhaps he might dimly have heard it sometimes, among the tangle of the hills and valleys.

"What night is this, fair miss," he said, "when the Folk are on the road?"

"Your night, Colum," she said.

Then she turned and moved back toward the castle of *Seanaibh*-Sanvy. And he realized, in that instant, what and who she was. She was a Speir-Bhan, his muse. So he ran after her as fast as he could. But, just before he raced in at the gate, he threw a coin away down the rocks into the sea, for luck, and since no others were left now save that water, and the moon, to watch his back.

Then he was in the gate, across a wide yard, and up among the lights.

Well, he wrote this in his book—wrote it in years later, obviously, in another ink. It says: "I have seen a motion picture in color. An American gentleman showed me. It was like that, when I went in there."

He said, coming in from the yard to the castle's hall, it was as if a rainbow had exploded, and the sun come up out of the night without warning.

If there were a hundred candles burning, there were a thousand, nor did they resemble any candles he had ever seen before, but were stout, and tall like a child of three years. In color they were like lemon curd. And behind, torches blazed on the walls, and showed tapestries hanging down, scarlet, blue, and green, and thick with gold. The Royal Folk had taken on color too. He could see the milk-whiteness of their skins and the berry-red of their women's lips, and how their hair shone like gold or copper. Their clothes were the green of water or the purple of lilac, as the trees are, half of them, they say, in the Lands beneath the hills. But that was not all, for all around, in the body of the castle, which had suddenly gone back in time and back to life, sat the human persons who had once dwelled there, kings and princes from countless centuries, in their finest finery. And the fey horses with human feet walked couthly up and down, white as snow, with silver manes, and the tiny little creatures bounced and rang against the walls like bells, and white dogs with crimson eyes and collars of gold lay still as statues. Yet one thing now was all the same with them. Every eye in that great place was fixed on Colum.

Colum was a handsome man, and used quite often to being made much of. He was accustomed to going into a room, or a dance hall, to a crowd of eyes that turned and whispers behind hands.

But never from such as these.

He turned to stone himself, stood there growing sober as a pain.

However, she, his Speir-Bhan, she turned and took both his hands in her cold-fire fingers.

"Now, Colum, it's your night. Haven't I told you. What is that you're carrying?"

And looking down, Colum saw that now in his left hand, which she no longer held, was a small curved harp of smoothest brown wood, with silver pegs and strings the light had gilded.

"Fair miss," said Colum, "if I'm here as the harper, you'd better know, I can play 'Chopsticks' on my granny's piano, and that's the sum of my parts."

But she only shook her head. And by then, somehow, they had got to the center of the room.

Directly before Colum on four great chairs knuckled with gold, sat two kings and two queens. No mistaking them, their heads were crowned. "I have never known enough of the history to describe those clothes they wore," said Colum, "but I thought they were from the far-off past, before even the castle had come up there out of the rock. And one of the queens, too, she that had the creamy golden hair falling down to her little white shoes, I think she was not only earthly royal, but of the Royal Folk, too."

"Well, Colum," said the king to the right, "will you be after playing us anything, then?"

Colum swallowed.

Then he found his hands—the hands the Speir-Bhan had held—had each opened, like his neck, an eye—not visible, but to be felt. And he put both hands on the harp and a rill of music burst glittering into the many-colored room, and every-where around was silence, as *they* listened.

This was the song that Colum sang, written as it is in his book:

> Woman veiled with hair, shaming the gold of princes,
> In your sun-bright tresses dwells
> A flock of sun-bright cuckoos,
> That will madden with jealous unease
> Any man yearning to possess you.
> So long and fair your streaming crown,
> It is a golden ring,
> And your face set in there like a pearl,
> And your eyes like sapphires from a lake.
> This is your finest jewelry,
> These yellowest ringlets,
> Which have caught me now in their chains,

Shackled, your thrall indeed.
No wonder then the cuckoo
Winters in the Underlands,
To sleep in the heaven
Of your veil of hair.

Colum struck the last chord. The silence stayed like deafness. And in the quiet, he heard over in his mind what he had sung—the musicality of his voice and art of his own playing—and the unwiseness of his words that none could doubt he had addressed to a woman of Faerie, sitting by her lord.

Now is the time, thought Colum, *to take my leave.*

He had forgotten the right of harpers to praise the beauty of any woman, royal or not.

Then the applause came, hands that smote on tables, feet that stamped, and voices that called. He saw the Royal Ones were amused, not angry.

The king to the left got up. His tunic was the red of blood, and his cloak was made of gold squares stitched by scarlet thread to yellow. He was, Colum thought, a human king, and from long, long ago.

"You are the one to do it, Colum," said this king, "as heroes have before you."

Colum, who had blushed with relief, and pride, changed over again in his mood.

"What would that be, that you want doing by me, your honor?"

"Why, that you rid the land of the threefold bane that's on it. For only through a song can it be done."

Colum gazed round wildly.

The Speir-Bhan poised at his elbow, cool as Sunday lettuce.

"What do I say now?" he asked her. "Tell me, quick."

"Say yes."

Colum cleared his throat. She was his muse, but he knew some of the old tales, in one of which he seemed presently to be snared. A "bane" could only be something bad, some fiendly thing, and it was "threefold" as well. And he was to tackle it?

Before he could speak, either way, the noise in the hall, which was still coming and going like waves, died again in an instant. The hall doors shot open, and in trudged a group of men, and they too were patched in bloodred, but now it was not any dye, and it was wet.

"They are out again!" cried one.

Another shouted, "My wife they have killed! My lovely wife, and my child in her body!"

"And my living son!" cried another.

Then all the group roared out examples of death, even of whole villages laid waste, doors and roofs torn away, and babies dragged out on the track, rent and devoured.

"No pity, they have none."

Shadow fell in the gleaming hall of *Seanaibh*. The candles faded. Colum stood in the dimness, and the fey woman he had sung to, she with the hair of golden shackles, she stood there before him, one last torch that blazed.

"Those they speak of are three uncanny women, Colum, that with every full moon become three black foxes, each large as a boar. They roam the hills and do as you have heard, killing and eating humankind. The one geas on them they must obey, makes them love the music and song. If any goes where they are that has great skill in these things, he will live. Oh, warriors have gone out against them, with swords, and been brought home in joints, what was left. But you are the harper. Once they were slain before, in this way, this *sort* of way. Listen, Colum, if you will do this, I will gift you a sip of Immortality from under the hills. You shall live a happy hundred full years in the world of men, and die soft and peaceful in your bed."

It was at this point in my great-grandfather's story that I had to turn a page of his book. What should I find on the other side, but this:

"I woke at the roadside in the dusk before the dawn. My head was sore and the road looked as you would expect. So I knew I had dreamed it."

And then: "Next week, in the town, I noted a very taking girl. Her name is Mairi O'Connell."

There follows the list of young women I mentioned before.

When I read this, over the page, I thought at first other pages had been torn out. But there was no evidence of that.

Then I thought, *Well, he spun his tale but had no idea of how to go on with it. So he leaves it in this unsatisfying way—as if someone had set a rare old meal in front of you, with meat and fruit and cakes and cream, tea in the pot, wine in the glass, and a little something stronger on the side, but as you pull up your chair, the feast is carried off, a door closes on it, and there you are, hungry and thirsty, the wrong side.*

Madly I thought, *If it was a dream, still he* did *it.*

For she promised him a hundred years of life, and he wrote of that in the faded ink of his youth, as of the promise of a soft death—and both of them he had.

Then, that night when I had my own dream that I met Colum in Ireland, in the stone house, he told me this, the very matters that should have been there on the following pages.

He said, once the fey woman had spoken, the castle faded like its light, and all the people with it, human and un, and there instead he was, on the savage hills that ran behind the cliff. The moon had put off her handkerchief, and was round, and pale as a dollar.

Up from the ancient woods of oak and thorn there ran three shapes, which cast their shadows before them.

He thought them dogs, then wolves, then giant cats. Then he saw they were three black foxes, black as the night, with white tips to their tails and eyes that smoked like sulfur.

And he struck the harp in a panic, and all that would come out of it was a scream, the very one you can hear a fox give out in the country on a frosty autumn night, the cry that makes the hair stand up on your head.

No one else was there with Colum. His muse, he noted, had deserted him, as sometimes, in the worst extremity, they do.

It seemed to him that after all the royal lord in the castle had sent him here to punish him for his impertinent song, and Goldenhair herself, she had been glad enough to see him off. And all the while, those three black, long-furred *things* ran nearer and nearer up the hill, and they screeched as the harp had done, a cry like the Devil himself, and Colum's hands were made of wood, and his throat shut.

"It was plain fear woke me up," he said, as we drank the dreamwhisky in his house, "So I believe. I could no more have stayed there in that mystic horror—be it sleep or truth—than held myself down in a pool to drown."

"Yet," I said, "she gave you your hundred years."

"I'll tell you," he said, "I was no harper, no poet. Speir-Bhan though that one was, she went to the wrong fellow, so she did. And for that, I think, they let me wake, and gave me a present for my trouble. But you," he added to me, "now you have the means."

"What means?" I said.

"Is it not," said Colum, sad and resigned, "that you can play and sing a little?"

I scoffed. I said, pointedly, "But the Speir-Bhan is the muse of *male* poets and bards. And all the heroes are men."

"There is Maeve," said my great-grandfather, "riding on her raids in her chariot. There is the nun, Cair, who sang like the angels on her isle."

In *my* dream, the magpie was on the roof again. I heard what it said now. "Give it up! Give it up!"

So giving up, as Colum did, I woke.

The flat is in Branch Road, ten minutes walk from the last stop of the underground train at Russell Park Station.

I work in English London four days a week, a dull job to do with filing papers, making and taking calls, and preparing coffee for my betters. It pays enough to keep the flat, and leaves me free on Thursday night till Monday morning. Those between-times then, I go to play in the clubs and pubs—by which I mean play music. It isn't a harp I carry, but my guitar, shiny brown as a new-baked bun. The name I use for myself on these occasions, is Neeve, which should be spelled *Niamh*, nor is it my given name. But there we are.

This life of mine is curious. It feels like a stopgap, a bridge. As if one day something will change. But I've passed my thirty-ninth birthday, and nothing has, so perhaps it never will.

It was Thursday night, and I was coming home on the tube from London, deep in the hollow underground that catacombs below all the city and half its suburbs.

I was sitting there with my bag of groceries, reading my paper and thinking how the world was going to hell in a hurry, just as it always has, since the Year 0. Then the lights flickered, as they do, and there in the tunnel, also as they do, the train halted. As I say, that happens. There was a small crowd left on the train, for we were still five stops from the end of the line. The visiting tourists take a stalling tube in their stride, used to the efficiencies of the New York subway and the Paris Metro, but we locals look about, uneasy, distrusting what is indigenously ours.

After a moment, the train started up again with a cranking hiss. That was when the old woman came staggering between the seats and sat herself down beside me. I thought she was drunk, she smelled of liquor, I thought. I had some sympathy. In my bag there waited for me, with the bread, cheese, and fruit, a green bottle of gin. On the other hand, when she turned her face to me and spoke, I deeply regretted she was there, let alone *drunk* and there, and myself her chosen victim.

"It's cleaner they are now, the filthy worms."

I smiled, and turned away.

Insistently the old woman put her claws on my arm. "The trains it is, I'm meaning. Like worms, like snakes, running through the bowels of the earth. Look there, a paper on the ground—" And leaning over she scooped it up. It was the wrapper from a chocolate bar. She read the logo ponderingly. "Mars," she breathed. Not for the first, I confess, I, too, considered the notion of a chocolate named for a planet or god of war. A delicious smell rose from the wrapper—but died in the wall of alcohol that hung about the old woman and now me. Everyone else, of course, stayed deep in their books, papers, thoughts. They weren't going to see the old woman. She was my problem.

For a moment I wondered where she had come from. Had she been on the tube all this while, and just got up and come staggering along to me on a whim? She spoke in the musical lilt of the green land, but I do not, for I'm only an Irish Londoner.

Then off she goes again.

"What's there in your bag? Is it of use? Sure, it looks nice to me. A rosy apple and a bottle of green glass. Well, we'll be dancing, then."

We?

I read my paper, the same paragraph, over and over. And she kept up her monologue. It was all about me, and the bottle, and what the train was like, and how it was a snake, and that *we* would soon be home, so we would.

Well, I thought of calling the police on my mobile when I stepped off the train at Russell Park, and she came lurching off with me, clutching my free arm to steady herself. Should I ease away? Should I push her, shout at her—or for help? No. Nobody would pay attention, besides she was a poor old inebriated woman, in quite a good, clean, well-made, long coat, and boots of battered leather. And her long grey hair was a marvel, thick as wool and hanging to her waist; and if it was all knotted and tangled, no surprise, she would need to groom such a mane every day, like a Persian cat, to keep it tidy, and obviously she'd had other things on her mind.

Before I could think, we were on the escalator, riding up toward the street, and her still on my arm as if we were close friends, going to the cinema in 1947.

Embarrassed, I looked around and noticed two or three Goth girls were on the escalator behind us. They had the ferocious, look-at-me beauty of the very young, all in their black, and liquid ink of hair. They wore sunglasses, too, the blackest kind— all the better not to see us with. I only gave them a glance, relieved really they'd have no interest in me or my companion.

"Where is it you need to get to?" I asked her, politely, as we arrived in the ticket-hall.

"Here I am," she said.

"No, I mean which station do you need? Or is it a particular road here you want?"

"Branch Road," said she, in a stinging puff of whisky.

Oh my Lord, I thought, oh my Lord.

But it wasn't until I went through the mechanical barrier with my ticket, and she somehow slipped through *exactly* with me, which is impossible, emerging the other side—not till then that I began to see. But *even* then, I didn't. I just concluded she was criminally adept, though drunk as a barrel.

So out we go on the street. And the dusty summer traffic roars by, and she clicks her tongue in fascinated disapproval.

"Well, now," she says, "well, now, *cailín*, let's be going where we're to go."

Then she winked. Her eyes were blue, but as she closed one in the wink, they gave off a flash of daffodil yellow. So then, I had to know, didn't I. It was only seven days before, mind you, I had found and read Colum's book and talked to him in my dream.

Outside the flat, the trees in the street were a green bloomed by dust and pollution, but they filled the front windows like flags of jade. All was as I had left it, messy, cleaned four weeks ago and not since, the washing machine full of washed and dried washing, the cupboards fairly bare.

I put my bag down and watched the Speir-Bhan as she pottered around, peering into this and that, craning into the tiny bathroom, lifting the lid of a pan of baked beans left on the stove. When she managed to undo the washing machine and most of the load fell out on the floor, I made no move. I couldn't have kept her out of the flat. I couldn't stop her now.

"What do you want?"

I knew. But there.

She was at the fridge by then, cooling herself with sticking her head, tortoiselike, forward in among the salad.

"Well now, look at this, they keep winter in a box. That's clever," she congratulated me. Then she shut the fridge door and turned and looked at me with her blue-saffron eyes. "Ah, *cailín*," she said. She, too, knew I knew what she was there for.

"Calling me 'colleen' isn't enough," I said. I added, "Your Highness—" It's as well to be courteous. "I've never been over the sea to the Isle. Colum made a bargain, or you did. It isn't mine."

"Yes," she said. "How else did you get your talent? Oh, it was there in him, but he wouldn't work for it. He preferred the desk behind the leather shop and then the boss's desk at the factory in Dublin. Oh, the shame and waste of it, when he might have made his way through his voice, and by learning a bit of piano in his grandlady's parlor. He kept his music for talk, to woo the women. Well and good. He was not the one. But it's owed, my girl, for that night."

I hovered in the kitchenette. I said, "And when he was on the savage hill, and *they* came running, where were you?"

"Where should I be and all? Up in his fine skull, waiting for him to hear me inspire him."

"There's the gin," I said. "Have a drink."

I went and ran a bath. I knew she would never come in to plague me there, nor did she. She was from a forthright yet modest age. But when I was out and anywhere else in the flat, there she was.

She sat, like my own geas, across from me at supper, eating apples. She sat by me on the couch as I watched TV, drinking gin. She lay down at my side—somehow, for the bed was narrow—when I tried to go to sleep. And all night long as I stretched rigid like a marble figure on a tomb, she chattered and chanted on and on to me, telling me things that filled my head so full, I myself couldn't move about there. Near dawn after all I slept, hoping to find my great-grandfather again and have a word. But if I dreamed, I didn't recall.

The next night I was to go to sing and play at a pub in Kentish Town. Waking up, my throat was as sore and hoarse as if she, the old hag, had been strangling me in my sleep. Yet no sooner had I croaked into the phone and canceled my gig, than my throat was well, as if from the strongest antibiotic known to man.

"I won't," I said.

But she only opened the fridge door again, and spoke to the winter within, of ice and snows and berries and belling stags, and low sun and the lawless winds of the *Cailleach Bheare*, the winter goddess from the blue hills.

I must pay her no heed. There was nothing to fear. Ignored, in the end she would leave me alone.

All Friday, all Saturday, there we were, we twain.

Saturday afternoon I went out to the shops, and she went with me, hooking her loathsome, withered, iron-tough arm in mine. A tourist herself from another time, another country, another dimension, oh such pleasure she had among the market stalls, and in the supermarket. No one else either saw or heard her, but once or twice, when I forgot and spoke to her, as when I told her to leave the cabbages alone, then I got the funny looks the crazed receive.

Perhaps that was it. Had I gone crazy?

"Hoosh," said she, "that is not your fate, my soul."

When we were coming back from the shopping, she dragging on my arm like a bundle of whisky-damp laundry, the next thing happened. In fact, it had happened before, and I knew it had and that it must, if not quite yet what it was.

"Who are they?"

"Who do you think, my soul?" said she.

"The Faerie Folk?"

"Hush, never call the Gentry that, keep a wise tongue in your head, so you must. But no, nor they are."

At which I *must* know, for what and who else was left then that they could be?

They darted through the crowds, the three of them, silken-lithe and gorgeous. I recollected I had seen them before on the escalator, and today in the market, and taken them, as you would, for three Goth girls of unusual beauty. They were clothed in fringed black down to their ankles and to their little black boots, and on their hands were black gloves and bracelets of gold that might be Indian, and off their milk-pale faces, the black hair poured like three black rivers to black seas, and to the backs of their very knees. Unlike my old woman, these were not truly invisible. Some people did see them, and turn and look admiringly at them, but I doubt in that case anyone noted their sunglassless, kohl-ringed eyes, just as I never did till we were nearly at my door. For if any had—

"Run—run, old lady—"

So we ran, and she, bounding along at my side, the eldritch wretch, as if she staggered *now* on the limber springs of a kangaroo. Up the steps, in the door, away and away into the upper rooms of the flat. Door slammed and locked. From the window I squinted down. There they were still, out on the hot summer pavement of London's Russell Park. Three beautiful young girls, loitering.

Irish eyes—I said: Who, that doesn't have them, can resist. *Put in by a smutty finger*, they call that smoky ring around the iris. Colum had it, and my mother did, and her father, too, and I. *She* had it, the Speir-Bhan—And *they* did, down there, the trio of Goth girls in black, who were not. For inside the smoky rings, the irises of *their* eyes were sulfur-smoking-red—the fleer-fire optics of foxes in a nightmare I had once as a child, about that fox-fur cape of my grandmother's.

Scathing eyes, cruel eyes, *heartless, mindless, soulless* eyes—no-pity eyes that would tear you up in joints and eat you blood-gravy hot—if they had no teeth to do the service for them instead. But they had teeth. They smiled them up at me from below.

The Speir-Bhan brought me a cup of tea, strong, with gin in it. I'd never known a poet's muse could make tea. I suppose they can, if they can haunt you to claim back a family bargain for the Fair Fey Folk, do anything they please.

"What are they?" I whispered. "*What—what*? Do you know?"

City dusk had come down. The moon was up. It was one night off the full, and never till now had I remembered.

I was lying down with my head in her lap, the Speir-Bhan. It was as if I had my mother with me again, and my grandmother as well. Though they had not been so exacting.

She told me the story, and I listened, for outside on the pavement, under the rustling dusty English trees, they still idled, the three fox-vixens, with their rows of glinting teeth.

The Speir-Bhan told me of two heroes, sons of the gods or the Fey Folk, and of how one sat harping on a hill, and the three devilish women came to hear. They were, by birth, the daughters of some sort of demon in a cave, but in those days, their shapeshifting was to a kind of wolf—a werewolf, no doubt—human, or passing for it all month, but not on the night of the full moon, when they would change their skins and prey on everything they could find that lived. It occurs to me now, that by Colum's day, no wolves were left in Ireland, only foxes. And maybe the foxkind was angry with mankind, as wolfkind had been, seeing as how foxes were hunted by then instead, and made into coats and capes.

Whatever it was, one hero harped, and he persuaded the demon-girls to put off their wolf-skins. And then they sat as human to hear him, one beside another, elbow to elbow, the story said.

"No doubt they were fair to see," sang my muse to me, "fair as three dark lilies on a stem. But no doubt of it either, between the long teeth of them was the rose-red blood of what they had slaughtered, and matted in their sloughen skins and raven locks, the bones of babies."

So while the women were tranced by the music, and songs that were so flattering to them, the second hero, standing below the hill, took his longest, sharpest spear, and slung it, as only heroes can. Up it flew, and passed in at the arm and shoulder of one girl, straight through her heart to the body and heart of the second, and through her into the third, body and heart, and came out at her neck. Then all three were there, spitted on the spear like three beads on a thread.

Did I ask her why that had needed to be done while they were in human form? Was that the only sorcerously potent method to be sure of them—or had it been easier to kill a woman than a beast? I think I never asked. I have no answer.

All I have is the story, which she then concluded. "After which, he took off their heads with his sword, he did." So crooned my Speir-Bhan. She was uncivilized and cruel, too, of course—what could you expect of a muse? Yet not so bad as young girls who rip lambs and children apart with their fangs. The heroes had only done as they'd had to.

"Then it's a job for two strong men," I said.

"It's a job for one that's cunning," said the Speir-Bhan. "But first there must be the song, or they will never stay."

"They're out there on the *street*," I snapped. "They've *stayed*."

"Sing to them, and you live. Without a song, they'll tear you up the first."

"Or, I could stay in. Bolt the door. Wait till Monday—the waning moon. What then?"

"They'll always be there, patient. Till *next* full moon," the old horror murmured, in that honey brogue I can't speak at all. "And next after that next, and next for ever." Not whisky on her breath—*uisege beatha* and flowering heather.

"Why?"

"You found Colum's book."

"Hasn't anyone ever read his bloody book before?"

"You have," said she, "eyes in your eyes. You see what others don't. The curse of your kind it is. And your blessing."

We remained as we were, and the fat moon came up. It glided over the window. That was Saturday. Tomorrow the fat moon would be full.

That Saturday night I slept, but had no dreams. I had other experiences. The Speir-Bhan did me the great kindness of sleeping on the couch. Twice I got up. The first time it was about 4 A.M. Outside, down on the pavement, I couldn't tell if *they* were there or not, among the tree shadows and the orange bluster of the streetlamp.

Then, near sunrise, a noise—something—in the garden-yard behind the flats— and I got up again. I went to the back windows now to see, and saw. Shapes . . . shapes in long sombre gowns, circling the single tree that grows there among the rough grass. A glimmer of bangles, spangle of eyes—oh as if their bracelets and their eyes together sprang right at me so I started back. The eyes were red, redder than the lamps over the wall. For a moment as I stood there on the floor, the memory of their red gaze locked with mine—it seemed to me *my* eyes were just the same, bloodred, like *theirs*.

Minutes passed. I made myself creep back and look again. The dancing figures by the tree were merely someone's washing, hanging on the makeshift line that now and then appears there, and the gleam of gold and red—some trick of my vision in the fugitive dark.

It was like the dentist's. You can only put up with it, put it off so long. Something has to be done once the thing's gone wrong.

When I was a kid, I used to travel on the tube with my mother. She would hold my hand as I climbed laboriously on. I recollect journeys, and her wearing the French perfume she wore then, called *Emeraude*—Emerald. She told me stories on trains. They're gone; she told me so many, just wisps and drifts of fantasy and idea left behind, which mold quite often the things that I create. In her teenage years, before there were teenagers, she'd written songs and sung them. She had a wonderful singing voice, I've heard, but I never heard it, for by the time I was born, somehow it had left her.

To my embarrassment, I don't even know if they have an underground system in Ireland. Surely they must? Lord help them if they do. Because it will pass, won't it, through all the hollow hills, through all the supernatural caves—in and out of the Many-Colored Land, which is the Hereafter, or Faerie—or both.

This time, the Speir-Bhan did not hang heavy on my arm. She walked unaided with a steadier and more sprightly middle-aged tread. She had become, too, more assimilated. Her hair was less knotted, and shiny. Like me, she had on jeans and a

T-shirt, though she'd kept to her old boots and her long coat. There were earrings in her ears. They looked to me like polished diamonds, or, more likely, stars. Maybe, maybe. Her wardrobe was psychic, of course, and she could put on what she wanted.

I carried my guitar in its case. I'm used to taking it on the tube. It's alive, but I never need to buy a ticket for it, because no one else *sees* it's alive—and so with the Speir-Bhan. We slipped through the robot barrier on my ticket like melted butter out of a crock. Then down the escalator, she and it and I, into the hollows under London.

Under the tube, *around* the tube, are Roman remains, ancient banqueting halls, plague-pits. I've never heard of fey things there, but naturally there are ghost stories. Like the castle then, Castle Sanvy, where Colum went that night, among the ghosts and Lordly Ones.

We sat facing forward.

After four or five stops—I wasn't counting or looking—the lights flickered. The train halted. I glanced about. The carriage, apart from ourselves, was vacant. Then it was full of something else—clouds, I'd say, clouds on the underground. They tell you, she comes from the sky, *a* Speir-Bhan, Speir Bhean, *Shpervan* . . . her name means something like that, to do with beauty and the firmament—she is Heaven Sent.

We three, she, it, I, were out in the tunnel next, soot-black and echoing with trains. And then the tunnel, too, was no more.

I have said, I've never been in Ireland. I meant, never in the flesh, to visit the actual place. Where now I went, I believe, was the genetic Ireland in my blood and physical soul. *There.*

Whether at sun's rise or evening, by land or water, though I know I must die, thank God, I know not when . . .

It was night.

I was on a hill. The Speir-Bhan had vanished. She had said she would sit in the brain to inspire, as she must. So perhaps she did.

This then must be how I *imagine* Ireland, or so I suppose. That is, the Ireland not only of its own past, but of its own eternity, behind the cities and the accumulating modern ways, the trains and graves and Euro currency.

Over there, the cliff edge, not even a castle on it now, but the late-summer dash of the sea over and beyond. The sun was sinking to the ocean. The water was like wine. The land was green and everywhere rolled the woods of yew and oak and rowan and thorn. Hawks sailed away down the air inland. Bear moved like brown nuns through the thickets. It was very quiet. I could smell wild garlic, flowers, and apples.

For myself, my clothes had altered in some incoherent way, but my guitar had not become a harp. I tuned it as I waited for the dark to begin, and the round moon to rise above the woods. As I waited for *them* to come running, with their barking shadows before them. I was lonely, but no longer afraid. Can I tell you why? No, I don't know why it was.

After the moon came up, I waited still. Then I began to play, just some chords and showy skitters over the strings. I knew they were coming when the guitar itself barked out in their vixen scream, the sound that puts the hair up on your head. Colum hadn't known what it was, how the harp had done that. But I had guessed. It was calling them in, that was all. The way you sometimes say to the crowd, what tune will you have?

I watched them run out of the woods. Not girls now, but three black beasts, too big for foxes, far too big, thick-furred, and neon-eyed.

My hands played and the guitar played, and up the hill they sped.

I could smell them. They didn't smell of animals, even the feral sort, but of summer night, like grass and garlic and blooms, but also they reeked of uncooked meat and blood.

They circled me, panting a little, their long, black tongues lying out, so the spit sometimes sparkled off them to the ground.

Part of me thought, *They are weighing it up, to see if they like the music well enough to sit down, or if they'll prefer to kill me and have dinner.*

But the other part of me started my voice. I began to sing to them a melody I had made for them in my head.

I'm used to awkward audiences. Noisy ones and restless ones, the chime of glasses and raucous laughter, to keeping on, weaving the spell if I can, and making the best of it if I can't. But these creatures, they, too, in their own perverse way, had the blood of the green land. Presently they gave over their circling. They sat down before me in a row, closed their jaws, and watched, with their ears raised like radar bowls. What I sang them was this:

> Women veiled with hair, shaming the black of the raven's wing,
> In your night-deep tresses dwell
> A murder of crows,
> That will madden with delight or envy
> Any, be they woman or man,
> Seeing you go by.
> So long and be-glamoring your streaming crowns,
> That glow like the blue-burning coals,
> And your faces set there like three white flames,
> And your eyes like sparks from the fire.
> This is your finest jewelry,
> These midnight ringlets,
> Which catch the moon herself in their chains,
> So she must serve you, shackled,
> Your slave indeed.
>
> No wonder then the crow
> Can prophesy to men.
> Since he lives in the starry heaven
> Of your veils of hair.

It was Colum's song, of course, or the song he had been given to please the Faerie woman at Sanvy, and which I had adapted for these three daughters of the dark, to flatter and cajole. As it seemed it did.

When I ended the song, and only went on lightly playing little riffs and wanderings, they were still there on the hillside before me. But they were not elbow to elbow, nor human.

Then I did what the first hero did. Over the music, I said to them softly, winningly, "Oh, how beautiful you are as foxes, my highnesses. But I know that, as human women, your beauty is beyond the beauty of the moon herself. Never forget, I saw you, even in your female mortal shape." Then I paused, playing on, and said, musingly, "It occurs to me, as you exist mostly in your human form, you'd hear my songs to you better with your human ears." Did I speak the Gaelic to them? I shall never know.

The guitar certainly would do anything I wanted. I could fashion things with it, things of light and air, that I had never been able to call up before, and never would again. My voice, too, which is good enough, was that night on the hill of Other-Ireland, the voice you hear sing only in your own head.

Presently, as in the legend, they removed their skins.

I have seen films, movies with computer effects that are miracles, but never did I see anything like that disrobing. Each of them, one by one, rose up on her hind limbs and drew off her fox-body, as a woman pulls off her dress. Off over their heads they drew the fox-skins, and laid them on the ground. Then they shook themselves and sat down once more, in their white complexions and mantles of ebony hair.

Their eyes, I've said, were awful either way, but now I got used to their eyes, as you can, to anything, yes, if you must, and even quite rapidly. And then, once I was used to their eyes, I learned the real atrocity of them. For these three were the most beautiful beings of any sex I have ever seen, yet there they sat, and I could clearly make out the piles of gnawed bones and the gouting blood, not caught in their hair or teeth, but snarled up in those eyes, mired and stuck deep, like poison, in their ruined astral insides. They were like lovely women riddled with some wasting death for which there is no cure. Except, they never could really die, they must, as now, always somehow eventually come back, and besides, who could, even for a century or so, kill them? They would never be done with this. And, just as I'd become accustomed to them, so *they* had become accustomed to themselves.

Did that mean they liked it? No, for you do not have to learn to accept that which you love. It is a part of you, from the start.

All these facts were there in their sulfurous eyes, like rot in apples. And like the apple skin, they mostly hid it, but only from *themselves*.

I'd sung to flatter them, aiding and abetting their self-deceiving. To flatter them stupid, for perhaps that way, I'd thought, I might be able to strike some new bargain. I hoped some inspiration would come to me, trusting the music, and the muse in my head.

But now I found I sang no more of that. I had begun instead to sing of what I saw lying there, putrid, in their eyes.

Colum had taken his chance, praising the golden-haired woman. Now I took mine. We neither of us had a choice. The poet's right—and curse.

Over and over. Not able to stop. I sang about those dreadful things within them. Till the beauty was all mingled with the stench and terror, and the filth hammered down into the beauty. And there they were, those hellgirls, with their fox-skins lying on the ground, sitting elbow to elbow, listening in a trance.

Now was the hour, like the last time in the legend, for my best friend, or my brother, to stand below us on the slope and cast the spear. Up through arms and hearts and breasts and necks. After which he must come striding with the beheading sword to finish our task. But I have no one like that. All my lovers and kin are under the hollow hills. All I keep is the past, and a Speir-Bhan up in the gallery of my mind. Plus my guitar, which is not a harp.

Yet, singing the horror to them, I saw them change, those three on the hill. Not from fox to girl, but from *beast* to human. I saw their eyes sink like six red suns covered by white skies of lids and thunder-burning clouds of lashes. Then they got up. They stared at me, but now *with their closed eyes*.

I could never have stopped what I was at. The music and the voice came out of me, and I hung up in the air and watched it all.

In that manner, I saw how they began, the tears that slipped out under their lids. They were ghastly tears, as the eyes were ghastly, the color of old, sick blood. Yet tears they were. I heard them, too, maidens whispering, but like dead leaves on a dying tree. They spoke of their father, some demon-lord, I didn't properly catch his name—Artach, or something like that—they spoke of a childhood they had never had, of a mother they had never seen, of wicked things done to them, of misery, and a life like night without stars or a lamp. There was nothing in their voices to match the tears. No sorrow. They had no self-pity, being pitiless, but even so, most evils spring from other evils done, and they were no different in that.

Down their faces fled the soiled tears, then the talk stopped, and in unhuman screams they began their emotionless lament. They rushed about the hill, snatching and scratching at each other, yet avoiding the spot where I sat as if it would scald them. They shrieked now like foxes, now like owls—and now, worst of all—like children in fear, perhaps the very ones they had preyed on. But they were not afraid, not unhappy—it, too, was worse, they were *damned*, and they knew it.

I couldn't end my song. On and on it went. It made me ache, my hands bleed, throat all gravel, and it broke me down. I could do no other than play and sing, and witness them as they screamed and ran in circles, weeping.

Then, oh then, I understood. *I* had done the work of two. I had tranced them with music, and with music also I had pierced their hearts of steel, and now, by music, too, I took their reason, and they lost their heads.

If there had ever been a bargain at the whim of the Fair Folk, or if demons had only got the scent of Colum, and so of me, these three had no further use for it. They did not care now that they were alive, or what they were. Did not even care to be girls, or foxes that slaughtered.

The wind came up the hill. It smelled of wheat and moonlight, and furled them up like the dead leaves they were. They blew away with it, down the slopes, over the tree-hung heights and valleys of my imagined Ireland. And on the ground they left the fox-skins lying.

Only when their three figures were gone from my sight into unmeasured distance, did the song leave me. I'm glad to say I remember not a word of it. If I did I would, trust me, never write it down.

My numb hands fell off the guitar, which they had covered with my blood.

At last, in the silence under the sinking moon, I dared to pick them up, those flaccid, forgotten skins. They were, all three, briefly like that cape of my grandmother's, which had so scared me in my fourth year, and with the same demonic, frightened eyes of leaden glass. And then, they fell apart to nothing.

The moon though, as she set, blinked, yellow-blue.

I was on the tube, of course. It was very crowded for a Thursday night. My hands were clean and healed, my throat not raw. The Speir-Bhan was shambling down the carriage, an unsober old hag with dirty hair. She plumped herself beside me and said, in ringing tones that made most of the carriage look up at her, "'Ere, luv, tell us when we gets up Holland Park."

She smelled of port. I explained she was on the wrong tube line.

Philosophically if copiously she swore, and at the next stop, hiccuping, she left the train.

Months later, not even on a night of full moon, I dreamed I put on the skin of a black fox, and ran over the hills of a vague, perhaps-Ireland. And though I avoided killing anything be it a sheep or a man, a rabbit or a baby, with my teeth, yet I learned from this dream the lesson of my success, why Colum had *not* succeeded, maybe why the heroes had. It wasn't only music, but also the spear and the sword. Not only courage, or honor, but unkindness. Not only talent, but the *emptiness* with which talent pays for itself. It is, you see, the mirror that reflects best the flaws it is shown in another.

For them, they never came near me again. Nor she, the Speir-Bhan, though I will suppose she's there, up there in my brain, where they generally sit.

As for Colum's book, I never read another sentence, not even his leather accounts. I burned it that autumn on a handy neighborhood bonfire. A shame, but there.

For the mortal foxes that steal now and then into the gardens at the back of the flats in Branch Road, I remain one of those that feeds them, dog food and brown bread. Their coats are russet, their eyes the color of whisky, the *uisge bheatha*, Water of Life.

Acknowledgments

The legend of Aeritech's Daughters and the heroes with harp and spear is to be found in Irish myth of the twelfth century and earlier; Colum's song, and many other references, are based on Irish sources, poetry and prose, between the ninth and sixteenth centuries. The idea of a Speir Bhean, or Aisling, is still current.

I would like to thank Beryl Alltimes for helping to clear the way to this, and the *Wolf's Head and Vixen Morris* for undoubted inspiration, for invaluable guidance, Barbara Levick of St. Hilda's College, Oxford, and especially, for his insights on the Gaelic, Professor Thomas Charles-Edwards of Jesus College, Oxford. However, all errors, liberties taken, and flights of fancy are mine.

As is obvious from the dedication of this tale, I do indeed have Irish blood (though less than that of the narratrix, just as I am quite a few years older), and am very proud of my Irish connection. That side of the family hails from what I call the Ghost Coast—the west of Ireland—County Clare. After this, of course, fiction parts from fact, but not entirely. You must judge what is true and what fantasy—as so must I.

JOHN FARRIS

Hunting Meth Zombies in the Great Nebraskan Wasteland

John Farris was born in Jefferson City, Missouri and currently resides near Atlanta, Georgia.

He sold his first novel in 1955, the summer after he graduated from Central High School in Memphis. He had his first million-seller, Harrison High, *at twenty-three. He is also the author of* The Fury, Sharp Practice, *the classic* All Heads Turn When the Hunt Goes By, *and other novels. Apart from his vast body of fiction, his work on motion picture screenplays includes adaptations of his own books (*The Fury*), original scripts, and adaptations of the works of others (such as Alfred Bester's* The Demolished Man*). He wrote and directed the film* Dear Dead Delilah *in 1973. He has had several plays produced off-Broadway, and also paints and writes poetry.*

"Hunting Meth Zombies in the Great Nebraskan Wasteland" was originally published in Elvisland, *his second collection of short stories.*

—E.D.

Term paper
Sheffield Hardesty III
English 12A/ Mr. Coombs
The Roycedon School

I. Purpose

The purpose of my term paper is to show how the supervised hunting and culling of "Meth Zombies" aids in balancing "an anomaly of nature run amuck"[1] that became an unintended consequence of efforts to deal with the millions of methamphetamine addicts created by circumstances of the Second Great Depression.[2]

II. Source Material

In addition to cybernet archives, my research also consisted of personal experiences and observations in the Nebraskan Wasteland, with anecdotal material provided by professional tracker-hunters.

III.

Two-thirds of what is now the unsettled territory of Nebraska was once largely a desert, part of the so-called "Great American Desert." But as a result of the westward migrations that began in the early 1860's, what had been considered land unfit for settlement became prosperous farms and ranchland due to the tireless efforts of homesteaders lured west from ever-more-crowded places by the Federal Government's promise of free land grants. During the Twentieth Century, except for the hard times of the First Great Depression, those Nebraskans willing to work hard and endure extremes of climate, often causing havoc to man and beast (the brutal winter of 1886–87), became prosperous from their labors. Even so, in times of plenty the western half of the state was sparsely populated, with fewer than five persons per square mile.

The onset of the Second Great Depression, with the ending of Federal Government subsidies and the beginning of seven years of drought, made worse an exodus from the land that had begun slowly in the 1980's as small farmers called it quits and migrated to the cities in search of their livelihood. Only the biggest ranchers were able to stick it out.

Small towns became ghost towns. The grasslands of the Sand Hills returned to desert as the Second Great Depression continued. Rivers shrank to mere trickles between their banks. A pall of dust blew this way and that way across the barren landscape.

Only the improvident, the uneducated or those with no will to leave stayed on. Living as best they could off the land. But "Nature abhors a vacuum."[3] First the rogue bikers, driven by militia from their usual haunts in the TransMojave or New Carolina, arrived and claimed abandoned settlements as their own. Then others, seeking places to hide: "persons of interest," criminals let out of prisons where there was no money to keep them.[4] And the indolent or unproductive members of society in our new city-states became drifters again: east to west, west to east. In the Great Nebraskan Wasteland some of the drifters were enslaved by the biker gangs, whose methamphetamine labs were scattered by the hundreds throughout. In their labs they manufactured the product most in demand by a demoralized public during "The Dark Age of the American Addict."[5]

Methamphetamine was a drug that was simple and cheap to manufacture in all of its varieties. Addiction to "meth" or "crank" became a scourge second only to the ravages caused by AIDS in more primitive places of the world. In extreme stages of physical and mental deterioration due to malnutrition and disease or the terrifying "herd tramples" such as killed more than two thousand addicts in Metro-Chesapeake in 2010, the addicts lost every vestige of their humanity.[6] Also some addicts had become plague carriers.

The Federal Government in its last days was unable or unwilling to cope with the huge amphetamine trade operating from the Nebraskan Wasteland (the Congressional black bag scandals of '07). Once centralized governments, including our own, had become impractical due to the proliferation and popularity of one-to-two kiloton portable nuclear weapons among religious and tribal zealots, the Republican city-states that formed to replace the "Eternal Glowpit"[7] of Washington, D.C. acted swiftly to snuff out the menace of addiction that was destroying the fabric of our new society.

The wealthier city-states, which had no cumbersome and ineffective legislative machinery to deal with, responded to the menace by acquiring the bankrupt state of Nebraska, then banishing those citizens who still clung to decaying urban centers such as Omaha. Mercenary troops were hired to drive the drug cartels into a relatively small (5000 square miles) "Ring of Fire" zone within the War Cry Badlands. Once this had been accomplished, the city-states rounded up and transported to the Wasteland those addicts that the biker cartels had created. It was a cost-effective means to preserve the health and integrity of all city-states. Top ecologists and other social scientists, including experienced penologists, agreed that within a relatively short time the overwhelming number of "Addict Transportees" would succeed in destroying the gangs in order to obtain plentiful supplies of the drug that, inevitably, would seal the addicts' doom. Leaving the matter of ultimate extinction to the forces of human nature and the Malthusian parameter.[8]

But the Unintended Consequence of this "Final Solution"[9] to our Republic's problem was the mutation of some addicts into a superdrug species that became known as "Meth Zombies." These are, as everyone has heard, soulless creatures whose biological responses to the drug that should destroy them instead enables them to maintain a state of being that is closer to death than life. Science remains puzzled by this phenomenon, and by the fact that in their "Twilight Life"[10], the zombies continue to mate with each other. Because of the existence of "meth caches" estimated to be in the millions of pounds within the Ring of Fire Zone, ecologists have postulated that the population of Meth Zombies could increase from an estimated two thousand we now know of to many thousands in only a few years.

Scientific analyses of zombies captured for research purposes all show that, while they have a low order of intelligence and most have the lost the power of speech except for certain communicative babbling sounds, they retain a high order of brute cunning. They exist in quasi-family groups that rarely exceed ten members, and these groups do not interact. When they travel it is usually at night or in the early light of dawn. Two attempts by Merc troops to eradicate them proved to be costly failures. The city-states had no further interest, as of 2014, in sponsoring more attempts, rationalizing that the Meth Zombie population in remote Nebraska was of no concern to them.

Unfortunately within the past few years there have been cases of Meth Zombies somehow making their way through the minefields and wandering into rural townships many miles away. On the night of July 7, 2015, a Meth Zombie suddenly appeared on the front porch of the Lewis R. Wilkens home in Lairwulf, Iowa, where he dismembered a border Collie and those family members who were too young or too enfeebled to run away before a neighbor, responding to desperate screams, killed the zombie with his shotgun.[11] Another zombie, thought to have stowed away on an 18-wheeler passing through the Wasteland, subsequently turned up in a schoolyard in Big Rock, Montana, with horrific results.

As a barrier to Meth Zombie migration, the Ring of Fire Zone with its anti-personnel mines appeared to be flawed. For every hundred wandering zombies blown to smithereens, because they lacked an awareness of danger, one or two might make it through. "It is not beyond the realm of possibility," says Dr. Ely Romero, an authority on Meth Zombies and the Willis Hockney Professor of Ecology at Tulane University in New Orleans, "that small family groups could escape to proliferate in hiding near large urban areas, with potential appalling consequences to human life."[12]

Because the Great Nebraskan Wasteland was an "Unclaimed Jurisdiction," no city-state wished to have the responsibility for cleaning up the zombie problem that arose as a consequence of their "Final Solution." In other words, if no problem was acknowledged by a legal authority, no problem existed. Meanwhile, as Dr. Romero feared, zombies continued to roam freely. (One somehow managed to board a cruise ship sailing to the Caribbean and remains aboard to this day, although those passengers who survived this intrusion were evacuated last year.) At the annual meeting of the International Federation of Sportsmen in Upsala, Sweden, in 2017, the President of the Federation, Dr. Franz E.H. Rodecke, proposed that the IFS establish jurisdiction over the Ring of Fire Zone, then dedicate it as a members-only hunting preserve.

"I have concluded after long study and prayerful contemplation of the brief submitted by our Committee for Responsible Hunting Practices that we must accept their recommendations," Dr. Rodecke said. "We, the members of the IFS, have both a moral and societal obligation to fulfill. Only well-trained and dedicated hunters such as ourselves have the skill, experience and, yes: the courage to deal with this Meth Zombie thing. Wholesale slaughter of any creature the Almighty has put on this earth (however inscrutably) we can never condone. The matter of whether Meth Zombies have souls is best left to theological debate. In the words of one of our truly great hunters, 'I think they were made to shoot, and some of us were made to shoot them.' Ethically and humanely, depending on the circumstances. A limited number of licenses will be made available on a seasonal basis. Our standards of sound hunting practice on every continent have always been above reproach. These standards will not be compromised as we fulfill our solemn trust for the benefit of mankind. Good shooting, gentlemen."[13]

My father, Dr. S.M. Hardesty II, Lifetime Member of the IFS, was one of the fortunate few to obtain a five-day license in the first lottery conducted in March of this year. On June 28th my father and I and my brother Blair, who is fourteen, flew to the Wasteland. At the airstrip near the Visitors' Center on the southwest boundary of the Ring of Fire we were met by our expedition guides, Wichita Dan Meskill and his wife Truly, both experienced tracker-hunters in the Wasteland. They each had several Meth Zombie kills to their credit. They were friendly and modest about their accomplishments.

Mrs. Meskill wore a black eye patch (left eye). She was partially blind in that eye from sun and dust. She and Blair hit it off right away. Most women single him out at first sight for some mothering. Dad and I are pretty tough on him, I guess. Blair is the best natural shot I've ever seen, but not a natural hunter. He's an experienced wing-shooter but the largest game he'd hunted before the Ring of Fire is Rocky Mountain Bighorns. He was nervous getting on the plane at Santa Monica Airport and more nervous getting off. We almost got into a fight en route over something I said. I'm still learning when it's time to back off and give Blair room to work out whatever's bothering him. Also he's already taller than I am and he'll swing his fists. Last year I shot a wild boar in the Pyrenees and I was still feeling pretty good about that. Cocky, my father said, when he wanted to tone me down some, but always with a little smile that meant he saw a lot of himself in me. Any kid can play football, but not many have crossed paths with a wild boar. Their tusks can grow to half a foot in length, and they're as sharp as a chert knife. If a boar gets a man down, he's a goner. I broke the neck of my boar at less than thirty yards with a 220-grain .30-06 solid. Everybody hunting with us said it was a terrific shot. My hands were steady afterward but I sweated so much I became dehydrated and had a sore throat for two days.

The camp crew who worked for the Meskills unloaded our gear into Hummers and we were driven to the War Cry Lodge. There were clouds on the horizon but the sun was really beating down. This part of Nebraska is a barren brown plain rising toward the still snow-dusted Wyoming mountains in the distance. Part of it has already returned to desert. There were sand drifts on the crumbly blacktop road.

On the way to the Lodge, by a spring that supported a few twisted trees, we passed a trailer park that looked as if it had been dumped there by a windstorm. Some men were tinkering with a couple of ultralight airplanes, and they had a small helicopter. We heard Gospel music over loudspeakers. There were stickers on pickup trucks and ramshackle old rubber-tire Winnies: Cowboys for Christ and Stop the Slaughter of Innocents and Peace to All God's Children.

"Our job would be a sight easier without all this going on," Truly said with a scowl.

"Who are they?" I asked.

"I'm as good a Christian as anybody else, but if it's the Lord's business leave it to the Lord. Now these people, who I am dead for certain ain't never seen a zombie up close, who if they should run across one unexpected they'd diddy in their britches, these people fly into the Zone with thur dink aircraft and drop Bible tracts and food parcels for the Zombs. Which all that does is complicate our business. Feed 'em, and they just might get stronger."

"But there's no evidence they actually eat anything," Dan said. "Pica, prairie dogs, seeds, snake. It's likely that thur entire metabolic systems is meth-based now."

"Has the cult back there tried to establish contact with the zombie population?" my father asked.

"Bring the good news of the Gospel?" Dan said. He ran a thumb over his short salt-and-pepper beard. "So far I allow they ain't been foolish enough to try. Anyways they ain't been holding no funerals we heard about."

Blair was looking out the window with the lip-biting serious expression that told me he wished he was a thousand miles from there. I figured I had to talk to him when we were alone that night, and if our noses got bloody at least I might be able to straighten him out before he spoiled the hunt for Dad and me. I was so pumped being there, finally, I hadn't thought about much else for a couple of weeks. The new patch I was going to get for my hunting vest.

"Maybe somebody should try to talk to them," Blair said, but his voice was so low I could barely make out what he was saying. Mom died when Blair was four and he wore the silver cross she'd left him but he wasn't all that religious as far as we knew. But he was sounding like "The Scientist" in all of those old movies about alien invaders. *We must make an effort to communicate with them.*

When we got to the Lodge and were getting out of our Hummer I pinned him to the side for a few seconds and said, "Hey, Blair. Those aren't people we're hunting. They're freaks of nature."

He shook his head. "What if some of them are still—human? And trapped out there by the minefields?"

"You're the biggest damn what-iffer I ever met. Can't you take it easy for once?"

He shook me off and looked at the setting sun. "No."

I knew he was going to be trouble, sooner or later. I'd have to make it my responsibility that he didn't get dad's temper going. And his drinking, which always followed. But before I could say anything else Truly Meskill came over, looked at my face, and put an arm around Blair's shoulders. She looked at me again.

"Okay, let's check out what you guys brought to shoot with."

One of my rifles was a Steyr Mannlicher Scout, chambered for the .308 Winchester and topped with a Leupold 2.5X scope. I'd also brought my short-action Savage, same caliber but with a Burris scope, as my backup if the terrain was bad and the distances under a hundred yards. On the lodge range before dusk I hammered home two groups within seven-tenths of an inch on silhouettes, two hundred yards with the Scout.

Blair, as usual, was at his best on the range where he didn't have to worry about drilling meat. He shot the Harris Gunworks Custom titanium mountain rifle in .30-06 Dad had ordered for his birthday in May.

We had rainbow trout simmered in butter and elk steak for dinner. After that we relaxed in the lounge and looked at videos of several expeditions inside the Ring of Fire. Wichita Dan delivered what amounted to a lecture about the zombie habitat and how good they were at making themselves scarce when hunters were near. They could hide where it didn't look as if the terrain afforded many hiding places.

"What's that?" I said. We were looking at an aerial view of some buildings, one of them a huge flat-topped structure like Mayan pyramids we had seen in the Yucatan last year while hunting alligators. But this pyramid had been mostly glass before it was half-destroyed.

"Brig Sparr's folly," Dan said, referring to the once-upon-a-time media king and bison fancier who had owned millions of acres of western graze land. "It were called the Sparr Biosphere. Designed for study of the earth's environment in a sealed ecosystem. Cost ol' Brig upwards of two hundred million before the economy and his bankroll went bust. Inside those buildings thur was something like four thousand different animal and plant species. And eight human beings. They had a rain forest, marshes, desert, even a scale-model Pacific Ocean."

"Why do you call it a folly?" I asked Dan.

"Well, they had problems inside thur with a buildup of natural gasses from the substrata. But mostly I reckon it was because eight scientific researchers couldn't manage to get along with one 'nuther. How about that? What my ol' Pap used to say, before government bureaucrats in the old days run him off his range and into his grave, 'Man is the one disease of nature for which there ain't never gonna be a cure.' So there the biosphere sits, and maybe it were a noble ideal, but all it's fit'n for today is shelter for Zombs."

"How many?" my father said, rolling ice cubes around in his glass. He'd poured himself two whiskeys already.

"Wouldn't want to try a head count. The biosphere is off limits to hunters anyhow. After what happened to that big-shot actor and his friends inside."

"TV said they were killed in a WinneGlide accident," I reflected.

Dan shook his head. "Tore to pieces. Men and horses both. Takes something powerful inhuman to do that."

When the video got to closeups of Zombs in body bags, Blair left the lounge without a word to anybody. Dad was so annoyed he fixed himself a third Scotch.

I helped myself to ginger ale and said to him, "Look, I'll take care of this." He just shook his head and grumbled something.

Truly Meskill said, "Well, if we're going to get us an early start..."

Blair was in bed when I got to our room. Eyes closed but I was pretty sure he wasn't sleeping. I stripped and laid down with an Indian blanket over me and listened to the coyotes for a few minutes, listened to him breathe.

I said, "In 1894 Bubonic Plague killed thirteen million people in Asia."

He stirred under his own blanket.

"In April 1991, a cyclone drowned 138,000 people in Bangladesh."

Blair moved again, turning his back to me.

"So what?"

"In 1976 in Tangshen Province, China, an earthquake killed 750,000 people."[14]

He squirmed. He hated it because he had to dig for grades and I have a photographic memory. (Oops. Maybe I shouldn't have said that, Mr. Coombs.)

"I said, so what?"

"Probably none of them ever did anything to deserve their fate. Just minding their own business. But Meth Zombies made themselves what they are. Call them "people" if you want to, but Jesus, Blair—there are so many people."[15]

Blair still wasn't talking to me when we left the next morning at a quarter to five. The moon big and full, the wind out of the northwest. Dan looked a little bothered because there was enough wind at this hour to kick up some dust. The last thing we wanted was to be out there in the Zone during a big blow. A sandstorm would keep the hovercraft on the ground, and it could reduce visibility to ten or twelve feet for half a day. If a blow caught us away from camp we could lose track of where we were even with our GPS homers, which usually don't work in a bad storm.

We traveled a couple of feet above the minefields in three 'Glides toward Biosphere country. One 'Glide for us, one for the camp crew and armorers, and the third, largest 'Glide for the horses and wranglers.

Blair might not have been happy about the hunt but he lived for horses and long trail rides. His mount was a big three-year-old left-handed bay (horses, like people, are either right- or left-handed) named Hoedown. It was love at first sight for Blair and maybe for Hoedown too. Blair talked to his horse in a low voice and ignored me when I made a point of riding up alongside him. I was on a piebald gray called Shuteye, not because he was partly blind but because (Dan claimed) he liked his sleep and could snooze up to half a mile through a rocking-chair canter.

I was wide-awake, for sure. Both of my rifles were in saddle boots. We had covered about ten miles of broken upland country toward the Biosphere with sunrise at our backs and the wind still blowing when Dan signaled a halt. We all dismounted while he and Dad scouted the terrain with the Meskills' chief tracker, an old Indian named Claude Catwin. Blair, Truly, and I followed on foot with the horses through a coulee with tufts of grass and rabbitbush clinging to the crumbling sides. I couldn't see much on the hardpan of the coulee floor.

"What are they looking for, scrape?" I asked Truly.

"Never seen any Zomb scrape," Truly said. " 'Nother reason we believe they don't eat. But they'll drink blood and they need water so they piss a lot. That's the meth. They're always thirsty, so they dig for water in coulees like this one in dry times."

Above us the wind was blowing sand into the snaking coulee. Up ahead Claude Catwin had paused, sniffing. We could smell it too. A rancid odor like unwashed hair, greasy skin.

Truly said, "Been some here recent, Danny boy. Since moonrise, I reckon." She looked around the coulee walls. There were shallow craters in the dirt, but nothing big enough to hide in. We caught up with the others who were standing around a muddy place, dirt and scree piled up around pits in the track.

"Bore holes," Wichita Dan said. "They'll dig down eight, ten feet to find water."

From the litter on the mudpiles, it looked as if the Zombies had been digging with flint and bones. But not animal bones. I knew a humerus when I saw one.

"Family group," Truly said.

"Eight of 'em," Dan agreed, studying footprints. "Now they're carrying water. Probably on their way back to the Biosphere. We'll leave the horses here." He pointed out a trail up one side of the coulee. "Shooting will be better from the ridgeline."

It was full light when we emerged from the coulee, within sight of but a couple of miles from the Sparr Biosphere, where shards of what had been thousands of panes of glass in the pyramid and surrounding buildings glistened like bees around a broken honeycomb. We topped a ridge and on the valley floor between us and the Biosphere we saw figures headed that way, carrying buckets on yokes across their shoulders. Except for the Biosphere we might have been in a dry part of Kenya. The figures were dark, from sun and grime.

They were about three hundred yards from the ridge. A sporting distance, and with wind to consider. I could easily tell, through my scope, that two of the Zombs were females.

Wichita Dan said to my father, "Your shot, Dr. Hardesty." Dad was already making adjustments to the scope on his .30 caliber, long-range Sporter. He dropped his safari glasses down over his eyes and shot standing up. He went for the smallest of the targets. Base of the skull, from the way she sprawled and didn't move again. Water had splashed high from the buckets she was carrying, and there was a quick rainbow in the air.

The other Zombs looked slowly around. One of them tried to save some of the water that was in a galvanized bucket lying on its side. None of them paid much attention to the dead Zomb.

Dan said, "Damn fine shot, sir," and Truly whistled in appreciation. Dad nodded, then said to Blair and me, "Let's give the boys a crack at them."

My mouth was drying up but I smiled back at him and stepped forward, looking over the small herd of Zombs again. You might have expected them to scatter at the crack of the first shot, but they just stood around until, at a signal of some kind, or by herd consent, they resumed plodding toward the Biosphere.

I felt more comfortable taking my shot sitting cross-legged for stability. I wasn't all that nervous: afraid only of wounding but not missing my target. I sighted in on one of those swinging buckets, then moved the crosshairs to the center of the back between my buck Zomb's shoulder blades.

I must have heard the helicopter coming behind us but I was totally focused on the kill, taking my time. I wasn't aware of the helo until it flew over us on the ridge, raising so much dust with the rotors I lost sight of my target.

A loudspeaker was blasting. I heard a woman's shrill voice. Quoting from the Bible, so it was the religious zealots we'd noticed yesterday by the spring. I jumped to my feet so mad I was ready to fire on the helicopter, but Truly Meskill pulled the barrel of my rifle down. The helo circled and came nose-down from a different direction, kicking up more dirt. Something bigger than a clod of dirt glanced off my forehead. We all crouched down and I'd bet there was a lot of swearing going on, but the helo and that damn loudspeaker was making so much noise I couldn't hear my own voice.

"AND THE LORD WENT BEFORE THEM DAY BY DAY IN A PILLAR OF CLOUD, TO LEAD THEM THE WAY."[16]

That was one of the biblical quotations I remember hearing, as the helicopter left us and went down into the valley toward the Zombie herd that was now moving out of range while the dust settled on the ridge and fouled our rifles.

Truly put a hand to my forehead; her fingers came away bloody. The blood was beginning to run down my face. She took a first-aid kit from her backpack.

Dad said, "Where's Blair?"

Little brother's mountain rifle was lying on the ground gray with dust and grit but Blair was missing. Dad didn't know whether to be angry or upset. He started calling. I was sure that Blair had ducked out on us. I was mad because I was hurt and mad at the zealots and mad because I hadn't got my shot off.

Everybody but Truly was calling for Blair; the expression in her good eye told me she knew where he had gone.

"You can't make him into what he's not," she said, clamping the cut on my forehead and taping a bandage over it.

"But you don't know Blair. He'll try to—" I wiped at some blood on my eyelashes, I wasn't mad any more, I was scared. "He can be as big a fool as those people in the helicopter." I got to my feet then, both hands on my rifle. Truly had to steady me for a second. "He's gone to the horses," I said. I pulled away from her and ran down the ridge toward the coulee. Everybody was calling *me* now.

I'd backtracked a couple of hundred yards in the coulee when Blair came riding at me on Hoedown, full gallop. He was looking right at me but his eyes were red and wet and I don't know if he saw me at all. He sure didn't try to rein in his horse and there was no room to go around me. I scrambled up against the coulee wall and hung there by my fingertips as they galloped past. He was headed for the mouth of the coulee and the plain and that herd of Zombies. I knew that all he had on his mind was to try to make it right somehow, the killing of the female. That was Blair's strength but also his "emotional blind spot." Not thinking that they would destroy him if he rode into their midst. Even the zealots, from all accounts, weren't that reckless.

Running hard the rest of the way to where the horses were, I slid my rifle into the scabbard behind Shuteye's saddle and mounted. Flailed his ribs with my heels and wheeled him around. He was in no mood to run but I yelled in his ear a few times until he reluctantly began to gallop after Blair's horse.

I was eating their dust as we came out of the coulee and plunged down a short but steep slope to the plain. Looking up at the ridge, I saw my father trying to wave me off. Truly seemed to be tracking Blair through binoculars and I don't know where Wichita Dan and Claude Catwin were. Maybe they had gone down into the coulee after the other horses. I hoped so.

I wiped my eyes and made out Blair about half a mile to the north of me, distance I wasn't going to make up easily because old Shuteye was winded already. I had to let him slow down or risk a stumble. The plain wasn't perfectly flat: there were gopher holes and diagonal cuts in hardpan and rocky washes, none of them more than five feet deep but plenty dangerous. Shuteye was no fool and got even slower, as if he felt another nap coming on. No matter how much I yelled and pounded him in the ribs he made his way across the plain in fits and starts.

Unexpectedly we came to the helicopter, forced down I guess, and smoking. When I was close enough I could see what a pile of junk it had been to start with. Two men were trying to make repairs. I rode past them at a good distance downwind. A woman with a bullhorn was yelling something about my being chastised by scorpions. The men turned to look at Shuteye and me. I thought about giving them the finger but I'd been raised better than that.

Dust was swirling in the wind, and through the dust cloud in front of me the Biosphere glittered. I was riding closer to it than I wanted to and not seeing Blair or Hoedown anywhere.

Shuteye made a shying move to his left that almost unseated me. Tossed his head back as if he smelled trouble. Then I saw what it was: a Zombie twenty feet away rising up from the plain in swirling dust as if he'd climbed out of a hole in the ground. He was a big one. I drew my rifle from the scabbard while I was trying to calm Shuteye down with my other hand. The buck Zomb came right at us and he wasn't plodding like the others we'd seen.

I snapped a shot at him and dropped him in mid-stride. It was only the second time I'd shot at anything from horseback so I was probably just lucky to hit him square enough to put him down. Shuteye wasn't cooperative, dancing around, squirrely as they come. When I looked around there were two more Zombies in the blowing dust, both male and coming closer. I'd ridden into the midst of the herd.

"Blair!" I screamed. Heard him answer but couldn't see a thing; no matter which way we turned the wind seemed to be hitting me in the face. Without my shooting glasses that dust probably would've blinded me.

I was worried about Shuteye throwing me, and losing my rifle. I had lost all sense of direction, but eventually Shuteye decided on a way to go.

And he found Blair for me, too: in a wash a few yards from where Hoedown was lying on his side, kicking feebly with the foreleg that wasn't broken. Blair was on his hands and knees and eye to eye with a female Zomb.

I yelled at him not to move, reined Shuteye in, raised up in the stirrups and took my shot. It went wild. Then Blair was on his feet, nearly blocking the target. Gesturing frantically for me to go away.

"No, Sheff, don't! She's—"

But the Zomb had turned to stare at me and gave me the best target I could've hoped for, the whites of her eyes. I let go of the reins, steadied my aim and shot her. The bullet snapped her head back and that was that.

I sheathed my rifle and rode closer, offered my hand to Blair to lift him up behind me. But he was only interested in the female Zombie sprawled near him. He went down on one knee and touched her as if she was one of our Yorkies run over in the street.

"You dumb son of a bitch," I said, "we've got to get out of here, now!"

I heard three shots, close together, behind us, and my father calling. It was probably the greatest feeling of relief I'd had since waking from bad dreams when I was four or five, seeing his face in the lamplight, feeling his hand covering my forehead. Knowing from his smile that everything would be all right, and the sleep-terrors wouldn't be back.

"Don't touch her!" I shouted at Blair.

But he was sitting now. He had pulled the dead Zomb's body half into his lap. As I circled him on Shuteye he stared up at me with a face from a nightmare of his own.

"Look at what you did!" He sobbed. Then he wiped blood and brain tissue away from the hole in her forehead.

I heard horses behind us in the rocky wash. "Over here! Blair's okay!"

"Look," Blair said, still sobbing. "Look at her, Sheff."

He was getting up again, pulling and tugging at my kill, lifting her in his arms like a limp dance partner. I saw it then, lying on a naked breast, winking in the dust-shrouded sunlight as Blair wrestled with her dead weight. It was a cross that the Zomb wore on a chain around her neck. Smaller than Blair's own crucifix, but they're all the same, mean the same thing.

"She was trying to protect me after Hoedown broke his leg!"

Oh, sure.

I could tell, although the female was very dirty, that she was young. Not a lot older than me. I didn't feel anything about that, but I may have wondered what she would've looked like cleaned up, or before she found her way to the Wasteland.

Farther off I heard the bullhorn again, that echoing, metallic voice against the wind, and I remembered the zealots in their dark shabby clothes who went out a couple of times a week in a crummy helicopter to drop food packages and little bundles of religious articles. Religion was their meth.

But, as my father said later, the world would be a less interesting place without its fools, its villains and clowns. Shakespeare wouldn't have had anything to write about.

Even so it made me a little sad to realize that the way Blair was shaping up, my brother would be spending his life in the ranks of the fools.

IV. Conclusion

Hunting Meth Zombies is exciting but dangerous work, and the sportsmen of the IFS are performing a needed and valuable service in their efforts to eradicate what otherwise might become a serious threat to mankind.

Sheffield Hardesty III

FOOTNOTES:

[1] Taylor, Carvelle. "Meth Zombies: Evolution or Devolution?" *Scientific American*, July, 2009.

[2] Blish, Webster, *The Second Great Depression*. New York, Doubleday/Scribners/Penguin. 2012.

[3] Spinoza, Benedict. *Ethics*, Part I, proposition 16. Place and publisher unknown. 1677.

[4] Fletcher, Demario P. *American Journal of Penology*. Winter, 2008.

[5] Thompson, Hunter S. *Death Throes of American Culture & Other Diversions*. New York, Forge/Tom Doherty/Random House. 2006.

[6] *The Jerry Springer Show*, Syndicated. April 14, 2010.

[7] Dickinson, Emily. Poem # 1,879 (Untitled).

[8] Woodward, Bob. "The Badlands Alternative." *Global Times Sunday Magazine*. October 14, 2012.

[9] First attributed to Adolph Hitler (1889–1945). German dictator and advocate of genocide.

[10] Attributed to Oprah Winfrey (1953?-). Talk show hostess.

[11] Archives, SAT 24 news report. July 8, 2015.

[12] Romero, Ely. *Syndetic Enthalpy in Modern Eugenics*. Cambridge, Massachusetts, Harvard University Press.

[13] Rodecke, Franz E.H. Address to the general assembly of the International Federation of Sportsmen, March 18, 2017.

[14] *Consumer Reports*, February, 2011.

[15] Attributed to Ted Bundy, American serial killer.

[16] *Holy Bible* (King James Version). Exodus 13:21.

(A-)

Excellent paper, Sheff! Watch where you put those commas and be careful about run-on sentences.

CHUCK PALAHNIUK

Guts

Chuck Palahniuk is of French and Russian descent but his last name is from the Ukraine. He gained recognition with his first book Fight Club *which was made into a film. He went on to gain popularity with the subsequent books* Survivor, Invisible Monsters, Choke, Lullaby, Diary, *and most recently* Haunted: A Novel.

He has also written a travel book about his hometown, Portland, Oregon, entitled Fugitives & Refugees *and a collection called* Stranger Than Fiction: True Stories. *He lives in Washington State.*

"Guts" was originally published in Playboy. *This story, which contains some rather graphic elements, is not for the faint of heart.*

—E.D.

Inhale.

Take in as much air as you can. This story should last about as long as you can hold your breath, and then just a little bit longer. So listen as fast as you can.

A friend of mine, when he was thirteen years old he heard about "pegging." This is when a guy gets banged up the butt with a dildo. Stimulate the prostate gland hard enough, and the rumor is you can have explosive hands-free orgasms. At that age, this friend's a little sex maniac. He's always jonesing for a better way to get his rocks off. He goes out to buy a carrot and some petroleum jelly. To conduct a little private research. Then he pictures how it's going to look at the supermarket checkout counter, the lonely carrot and petroleum jelly rolling down the conveyer belt toward the grocery store cashier. All the shoppers waiting in line, watching. Everyone seeing the big evening he has planned.

So my friend, he buys milk and eggs and sugar and a carrot, all the ingredients for a carrot cake. And Vaseline.

Like he's going home to stick a carrot cake up his butt.

At home, he whittles the carrot into a blunt tool. He slathers it with grease and grinds his ass down on it. Then, nothing. No orgasm. Nothing happens except it hurts.

Then, this kid, his mom yells it's supper time. She says to come down, right now.

He works the carrot out and stashes the slippery, filthy thing in the dirty clothes under his bed.

After dinner, he goes to find the carrot, and it's gone. All his dirty clothes, while he ate dinner, his mom grabbed them all to do laundry. No way could she not find the carrot, carefully shaped with a paring knife from her kitchen, still shiny with lube and stinky.

This friend of mine, he waits months under a black cloud, waiting for his folks to confront him. And they never do. Ever. Even now that he's grown up, that invisible carrot hangs over every Christmas dinner, every birthday party. Every Easter egg hunt with his kids, his parents' grandkids, that ghost carrot is hovering over all of them. That something too awful to name.

People in France have a phrase: "staircase wit." In French: *esprit de l'escalier*. It means that moment when you find the answer, but it's too late. Say you're at a party and someone insults you. You have to say something. So under pressure, with every-body watching, you say something lame. But the moment you leave the party . . .

As you start down the stairway, then—magic. You come up with the perfect thing you should've said. The perfect crippling put-down.

That's the spirit of the stairway.

The trouble is, even the French don't have a phrase for the stupid things you ac-tually do say under pressure. Those stupid, desperate things you actually think or do.

Some deeds are too low to even get a name. Too low to even get talked about.

Looking back, kid-psych experts, school counselors, now say that most of the last peak in teen suicide was kids trying to choke while they beat off. Their folks would find them, a towel twisted around their kid's neck, the towel tied to the rod in their bedroom closet, the kid dead. Dead sperm everywhere. Of course the folks cleaned up. They put some pants on their kid. They made it look . . . better. Intentional at least. The regular kind of sad teen suicide.

Another friend of mine, a kid from school, his older brother in the Navy said how guys in the Middle East jack off different than we do here. This brother was stationed in some camel country where the public market sells what could be fancy letter openers. Each fancy tool is just a thin rod of polished brass or silver, maybe as long as your hand, with a big tip at one end, either a big metal ball or the kind of fancy carved handle you'd see on a sword. This Navy brother says how Arab guys get their dick hard and then insert this metal rod inside the whole length of their boner. They jack off with the rod inside, and it makes getting off so much better. More intense.

It's this big brother who travels around the world, sending back French phrases. Russian phrases. Helpful jack-off tips.

After this, the little brother, one day he doesn't show up at school. That night, he calls to ask if I'll pick up his homework for the next couple weeks. Because he's in the hospital.

He's got to share a room with old people getting their guts worked on. He says how they all have to share the same television. All he's got for privacy is a curtain. His folks don't come and visit. On the phone, he says how right now his folks could just kill his big brother in the Navy.

On the phone, the kid says how—the day before—he was just a little stoned. At home in his bedroom, he was flopped on the bed. He was lighting a candle and flip-ping through some old porno magazines, getting ready to beat off. This is after he's heard from his Navy brother. That helpful hint about how Arabs beat off. The kid looks around for something that might do the job. A ballpoint pen's too big. A pencil's too big and rough. But dripped down the side of the candle, there's a thin, smooth ridge of wax that just might work. With just the tip of one finger, this kid snaps the long ridge of wax off the candle. He rolls it smooth between the palms of his hands. Long and smooth and thin.

Stoned and horny, he slips it down inside, deeper and deeper into the piss slit of his boner. With a good hank of the wax still poking out the top, he gets to work.

Even now, he says those Arab guys are pretty damn smart. They've totally reinvented jacking off. Flat on his back in bed, things are getting so good, this kid can't keep track of the wax. He's one good squeeze from shooting his wad when the wax isn't sticking out anymore.

The thin wax rod, it's slipped inside. All the way inside. So deep inside he can't even feel the lump of it inside his piss tube.

From downstairs, his mom shouts it's supper time. She says to come down, right now. This wax kid and the carrot kid are different people, but we all live pretty much the same life.

It's after dinner when the kid's guts start to hurt. It's wax, so he figured it would just melt inside him and he'd pee it out. Now his back hurts. His kidneys. He can't stand straight.

This kid talking on the phone from his hospital bed, in the background you can hear bells ding, people screaming. Game shows.

The X-rays show the truth, something long and thin, bent double inside his bladder. This long, thin V inside him, it's collecting all the minerals in his piss. It's getting bigger and rougher, coated with crystals of calcium, it's bumping around, ripping up the soft lining of his bladder, blocking his piss from getting out. His kidneys are backed up. What little that leaks out his dick is red with blood.

This kid and his folks, his whole family, them looking at the black X-ray with the doctor and the nurses standing there, the big V of wax glowing white for everybody to see, he has to tell the truth. The way Arabs get off. What his big brother wrote him from the Navy.

On the phone, right now, he starts to cry.

They paid for the bladder operation with his college fund. One stupid mistake, and now he'll never be a lawyer.

Sticking stuff inside yourself. Sticking yourself inside stuff. A candle in your dick or your head in a noose, we knew it was going to be big trouble.

What got me in trouble, I called it Pearl Diving. This meant whacking off underwater, sitting on the bottom at the deep end of my parents' swimming pool. With one deep breath, I'd kick my way to the bottom and slip off my swim trucks. I'd sit down there for two, three, four minutes.

Just from jacking off I had huge lung capacity. If I had the house to myself, I'd do this all afternoon. After I'd finally pump out my stuff, my sperm, it would hang there in big, fat, milky gobs.

After that was more diving, to catch it all. To collect it and wipe each handful in a towel. That's why it was called Pearl Diving. Even with chlorine, there was my sister to worry about. Or, Christ almighty, my mom.

That used to be my worst fear in the world: my teenage virgin sister, thinking she's just getting fat, then giving birth to a two-headed, retard baby. Both heads looking just like me. Me, the father and the uncle. In the end, it's never what you worry about that gets you.

The best part of Pearl Diving was the inlet port for the swimming pool filter and the circulation pump. The best part was getting naked and sitting on it.

As the French would say, Who doesn't like getting their butt sucked? Still, one minute you're just a kid getting off, and the next minute you'll never be a lawyer.

One minute I'm settling on the pool bottom and the sky is wavy, light blue through eight feet of water above my head. The world is silent except for the heartbeat in my ears. My yellow-striped swim trunks are looped around my neck for safekeeping, just in case a friend, a neighbor, anybody shows up to ask why I skipped football practice. The steady suck of the pool inlet hole is lapping at me and I'm grinding my skinny white ass around on that feeling.

One minute I've got enough air and my dick's in my hand. My folks are gone at their work and my sister's got ballet. Nobody's supposed to be home for hours.

My hand brings me right to getting off, and I stop. I swim up to catch another big breath. I dive down and settle on the bottom.

I do this again and again.

This must be why girls want to sit on your face. The suction is like taking a dump that never ends. My dick hard and getting my butt eaten out, I do not need air. My heartbeat in my ears, I stay under until bright stars of light start worming around in my eyes. My legs straight out, the back of each knee rubbed raw against the concrete bottom. My toes are turning blue, my toes and fingers wrinkled from being so long in the water.

And then I let it happen. The big white gobs start spouting. The pearls. It's then I need some air. But when I go to kick off against the bottom, I can't. I can't get my feet under me. My ass is stuck.

Emergency paramedics will tell you that every year about 150 people get stuck this way, sucked by a circulation pump. Get your long hair caught, or your ass, and you're going to drown. Every year, tons of people do. Most of them in Florida.

People just don't talk about it. Not even French people talk about everything. Getting one knee up, getting one foot tucked under me, I get to half standing when I feel the tug against my butt. Getting my other foot under me, I kick off against the bottom. I'm kicking free, not touching the concrete, but not getting to the air, either.

Still kicking water, thrashing with both arms, I'm maybe halfway to the surface but not going higher. The heartbeat inside my head getting loud and fast.

The bright sparks of light crossing and crisscrossing my eyes, I turn and look back . . . but it doesn't make sense. This thick rope, some kind of snake, blue-white and braided with veins, has come up out of the pool drain and it's holding on to my butt. Some of the veins are leaking blood, red blood that looks black underwater and drifts away from little rips in the pale skin of the snake. The blood trails away, disappearing in the water, and inside the snake's thin, blue-white skin you can see lumps of some half-digested meal.

That's the only way this makes sense. Some horrible sea monster, a sea serpent, something that's never seen the light of day, it's been hiding in the dark bottom of the pool drain, waiting to eat me.

So . . . I kick at it, at the slippery, rubbery knotted skin and veins of it, and more of it seems to pull out of the pool drain. It's maybe as long as my leg now, but still holding tight around my butthole. With another kick, I'm an inch closer to getting another breath. Still feeling the snake tug at my ass, I'm an inch closer to my escape.

Knotted inside the snake, you can see corn and peanuts. You can see a long bright-orange ball. It's the kind of horse-pill vitamin my dad makes me take, to help put on weight. To get a football scholarship. With extra iron and omega-three fatty acids.

It's seeing that vitamin pill that saves my life.

It's not a snake. It's my large intestine, my colon pulled out of me. What doctors call prolapsed. It's my guts sucked into the drain.

Paramedics will tell you a swimming pool pump pulls eighty gallons of water every minute. That's about four hundred pounds of pressure. The big problem is we're all connected together inside. Your ass is just the far end of your mouth. If I let go, the pump keeps working—unraveling my insides—until it's got my tongue. Imagine taking a four hundred-pound shit and you can see how this might turn you inside out.

What I can tell you is your guts don't feel much pain. Not the way your skin feels pain. The stuff you're digesting, doctors call it fecal matter. Higher up is chyme, pockets of a thin, runny mess studded with corn and peanuts and round green peas.

That's all this soup of blood and corn, shit and sperm and peanuts floating around me. Even with my guts unraveling out my ass, me holding on to what's left, even then my first want is to somehow get my swimsuit back on.

God forbid my folks see my dick.

My one hand holding a fist around my ass, my other hand snags my yellow-striped swim trunks and pulls them from around my neck. Still, getting into them is impossible.

You want to feel your intestines, go buy a pack of those lambskin condoms. Take one out and unroll it. Pack it with peanut butter. Smear it with petroleum jelly and hold it under water. Then try to tear it. Try to pull it in half. It's too tough and rubbery. It's so slimy you can't hold on.

A lambskin condom, that's just plain old intestine.

You can see what I'm up against.

You let go for a second and you're gutted.

You swim for the surface, for a breath, and you're gutted.

You don't swim and you drown.

It's a choice between being dead right now or a minute from right now.

What my folks will find after work is a big naked fetus, curled in on itself. Floating in the cloudy water of their backyard pool. Tethered to the bottom by a thick rope of veins and twisted guts. The opposite of a kid hanging himself to death while he jacks off. This is the baby they brought home from the hospital thirteen years ago. Here's the kid they hoped would snag a football scholarship and get an MBA. Who'd care for them in their old age. Here's all their hopes and dreams. Floating here, naked and dead. All around him, big milky pearls of wasted sperm.

Either that or my folks will find me wrapped in a bloody towel, collapsed halfway from the pool to the kitchen telephone, the ragged, torn scrap of my guts still hanging out the leg of my yellow-striped swim trunks.

What even the French won't talk about.

That big brother in the Navy, he taught us one other good phrase. A Russian phrase. The way we say, "I need that like I need a hole in my head," Russian people say, "I need that like I need teeth in my asshole . . ."

Mne eto nado kak zuby v zadnitse.

Those stories about how animals caught in a trap will chew off their leg, well, any coyote would tell you a couple bites beats the hell out of being dead.

Hell . . . even if you're Russian, someday you just might want those teeth.

Otherwise, what you have to do is you have to twist around. You hook one elbow behind your knee and pull that leg up into your face. You bite and snap at your own ass. You run out of air and you will chew through anything to get that next breath.

It's not something you want to tell a girl on the first date. Not if you expect a kiss good night. If I told you how it tasted, you would never, ever again eat calamari.

It's hard to say what my parents were more disgusted by: how I'd got in trouble or how I'd saved myself. After the hospital, my mom said, "You didn't know what you were doing, honey. You were in shock." And she learned how to cook poached eggs.

All those people grossed out or feeling sorry for me . . .

I need that like I need teeth in my asshole.

Nowadays, people always tell me I look too skinny. People at dinner parties get all quiet and pissed off when I don't eat the pot roast they cooked. Pot roast kills me. Baked ham. Anything that hangs around inside my guts for longer than a couple of hours, it comes out still food. Home-cooked lima beans or chunk light tuna fish, I'll stand up and find it still sitting there in the toilet.

After you have a radical bowel resectioning, you don't digest meat so great. Most people, you have five feet of large intestine. I'm lucky to have my six inches. So I never got a football scholarship. Never got an MBA. Both my friends, the wax kid and the carrot kid, they grew up, got big, but I've never weighed a pound more than I did that day when I was thirteen.

Another big problem was my folks paid a lot of good money for that swimming pool. In the end my dad just told the pool guy it was a dog. The family dog fell in and drowned. The dead body got pulled into the pump. Even when the pool guy cracked open the filter casing and fished out a rubbery tube, a watery hank of intestine with a big orange vitamin pill still inside, even then my dad just said, "That dog was fucking nuts."

Even from my upstairs bedroom window, you could hear my dad say, "We couldn't trust that dog alone for a second . . ."

Then my sister missed her period.

Even after they changed the pool water, after they sold the house and we moved to another state, after my sister's abortion, even then my folks never mentioned it again.

Ever.

That is our invisible carrot.

You. Now you can take a good, deep breath.

I still have not.

SIMON BROWN

Water Babies

Simon Brown lives with his wife Alison and two children—Edlyn and
Fynn—in Mollymook, New South Wales, Australia.

Brown's fantasy trilogy, the Keys of Power, has recently been published by
DAW Books. A new trilogy, the Chronicles of Kydan, starts in 2005 with
Empire's Daughter, also from DAW. He's won the Aurealis Award twice for
his short fiction and has had a short story, co-written with Sean Williams,
reprinted in The Year's Best Science Fiction, and another short story, co-
written with his wife, Alison, in David G. Hartwell's Year's Best Fantasy. He
has appeared in both volumes of the Year's Best Australian Science Fiction
and Fantasy.

Twelve of his stories have been collected in Cannibals of the Fine Light
issued by Ticonderoga Publications in Australia.

"Water Babies" was originally published in the anthology Agog! Smashing Stories.

—E.D.

Detective Sergeant Joanne Walsh parked behind the white police van. A
narrow trail wound its way through tall grass from the roadside to the bank
of the Nepean River. The ground was wet, and Walsh groaned as mud
oozed up over her leather shoes.

From the edge of the bank she looked down; a woman was kneeling over the
body and a young constable was standing nearby. Walsh started making her way
down the slope when the constable called out: "Watch your footing, Sergeant!"
Walsh bit back a reply. Odds were if she said anything she'd cap it off by falling arse
over tit into the river, which would be a grand way to start her new promotion.

"Who dragged the body up the bank?" she demanded angrily.

The woman bent over the corpse looked up at her calmly. "Who are you?"

"Detective Sergeant Walsh. And who the hell are you?"

The woman returned her attention to the body. "Dr. Louise Pelham. I live just up
the road."

"Who dragged it up the bank?"

"Corbett, Detective Sergeant Walsh. *Its* name was Warren Corbett."

Walsh blinked. "You knew him?"

"By sight. His family's lived in the region for a century. He was seventeen years old."

Walsh nudged past the constable and took a closer look at the body. Judging by the color and looseness of his skin, she guessed he had been in the water for less than a day, but reminded herself that all her previous drownings had come from the sea; maybe fresh water worked differently.

"How long?"

Pelham shook her head. "My first impression was that he must have drowned less than twelve hours ago. But look at this." The doctor turned the corpse toward her slightly, allowing Walsh a glimpse underneath.

"Jesus! What did that?"

"Carp?" the constable suggested helpfully, his face paling.

Pelham looked up at him. "Carp are mud filterers. Yabbies, perhaps. But to do that much damage they'd have to have been at it for longer than twelve hours."

"Eels?" Walsh asked.

"Possibly. Anyway, we'll know after an autopsy." Pelham stood up, a little unsteadily. Walsh watched, enviously, as the doctor stretched to her full height, at least twenty centimeters taller than Walsh herself.

"And to answer your first question," Pelham continued, looking down at the policeman, "the schoolboys who found the body brought it up the bank. They didn't know if he was alive or dead."

Walsh nodded, turned to the constable. "Have the boys been interviewed yet?"

"Senior Constable Biggins is doing that now, Sergeant, at Dr. Pelham's surgery."

"Where exactly was the corpse found?"

The constable pointed to a clump of tangled branches and weeds in the river about two meters from the bank.

Walsh looked up and down the river, blooming with green algae from too much fertilizer washing in after the last heavy rain. To the northwest, the Nepean was swallowed by woods that bordered the lowlands around Camden airport; upriver, eastwards, it curved through fields to Camden itself, disappearing under Cowpasture Bridge; from there, Walsh knew, it swung southeast, the town growing beside it like a misshapen twin.

"Do we know where Corbett fell in?"

The constable nodded. "We think so. He was often seen fishing off the footbridge connecting the reserves on Chellaston Street and River Road."

"Do we know if he was with anyone?"

"No, but Senior Constable Biggins has people carrying out a routine search around the footbridge."

"Do many people fall from the footbridge and drown?" Walsh asked Pelham.

"I've never heard of a drowning around here before, and I've been practicing in Camden for ten years."

"I don't mean to tell you your job, Sergeant, but until the autopsy is finished, I wouldn't assume this was an accidental death."

Walsh threw cutlery into the sink with gusto.

"I don't mean to tell you your job, Sergeant . . ." she mimed, then followed the cutlery with an old saucepan. ". . . I wouldn't assume this was an accidental death . . ."

"Mum?"

"What?"

Fourteen-year-old Celia was looking at her with an expression of feigned anger, which Walsh knew meant Celia was going to ask for something she knew mother wouldn't surrender without a fight.

"Kylie and Laura are going into the city on Thursday night—"

"Who are Kylie and Laura?"

"From school, and they're going with Laura's sister who's seventeen—"

"No."

"But, Mum—"

"Forget it. I don't care if you're going with an armed escort. You're too young to go into the city at night."

"Laura's mum says—"

"Screw Laura's mum."

Celia's mouth shut like a trap.

Walsh closed her eyes for a moment. *Damn.*

"Celia, I'm sorry. I shouldn't have said that."

"But Laura's sister—"

"Is seventeen, I know." She remembered that Warren Corbett had been seventeen. "But believe me, honey, seventeen is nothing."

Celia looked at her blankly.

"We'll all go into the city together on Saturday," Walsh offered. "You and me and Rowena and Miriam."

"Dad's picking us up Saturday," Cecilia said glumly.

"God, you're right. I forgot. Next Saturday, then."

"You're just upset because that boy drowned."

Walsh's two younger daughters, who'd been happily watching television in the family room, turned around to pay more attention to the goings-on in the kitchen.

You're right. And I'm worried about our move here to Camden, and my new job, and your new schools, and Rowena sucking her thumb . . .

"Rowena, take it out before you bite it off!" Rowena took it out. "Celia, start the washing up." Celia made a face like she'd just sucked on a lemon, but she moved towards the sink. "Miriam, haven't you any homework?"

"No," Miriam said definitely. "Did you see the drowned boy? Was it like the others?"

"Who told you about the drowning?"

"The boys who found the body come from our school," Celia explained.

"I see. And what's this rubbish about the others?"

"She means the other children who drowned before this one," Celia said.

"I was told no one else had ever drowned here."

"Years ago. Two children, Laura told me. In the 70s."

Walsh felt suddenly uneasy, and changed the subject. "Miriam, are you sure you haven't got any homework?"

The telephone rang before Miriam could answer. Walsh picked it up and snapped: "Yes?"

"Umm, Detective Sergeant Walsh?"

"Who's this?"

"Senior Constable Biggins, ma'am. Just thought you'd like to know that the Corbett boy was last seen fishing off the bridge in the Chellaston Street Reserve only four hours before his body was found."

The next morning, after dropping off her children at school, Walsh drove to the footbridge on which Warren Corbett had last been sighted. She found it some fifty meters from the end of Chellaston Street, a cul-de-sac lined with pretty weatherboard houses and jacarandas.

The footbridge spanned thirty meters across the Nepean, connecting the reserve with a turf farm that even from this distance smelled faintly of blood and bone. The bridge looked in danger of collapsing at any moment; it swerved erratically halfway along its course and the hand-railing twisted like a swimming snake. Many of the bridge's timber beams and supports were splitting and warping.

She walked to the start of the bridge, stepping over a battered sign that read NO CROSSING—BRIDGE UNDER REPAIR, and looked up and down the river. A few ripples marking where logs or stones lay just under the surface. Running west along the bank was the reserve proper, a confusion of tall native trees and tangled clumps of privet. The beginnings of a dirt trail was swallowed by the darkness.

"Kids are always throwing fishing lines off the bridge," said a voice. Walsh turned, saw a tall man in a constable's uniform; he wasn't wearing his cap, and a lick of dark hair fell across his forehead like a signature. He approached her, held out his hand.

"Constable Ewan Davies," he said. "I've been assigned to work with you while you settle in."

Walsh shook the hand. "How did you know I'd be here?"

"I didn't," Davies replied. "I thought I'd come here and check out the site before going to work."

"Good thinking," she said evenly. Then, in case the compliment went to his head: "Where's your cap?"

The faintest of smiles crossed his face. "Back in the car. I didn't know anyone else would be here."

Walsh nodded. "What happened to the bridge?"

"Floods. Every couple of years the waters rise high enough and fast enough to wash tree trunks into the river; they collide against the bridge's supports. Every time the council fixes the bridge, it seems there's another flood." Davies leaned over the railing and pointed to a jumble of logs and detritus caught beneath the bridge. "The kids' fishing lines snag down there and they go down to untangle them."

"That's what happened to Corbett?"

Davies shrugged. "There was a message for you back at the station. Corbett's autopsy was finished last night, and the report will be couriered to us later today—"

"I want it now," Walsh said curtly.

"—or I could go directly to the morgue and pick it up myself."

Detective Inspector Crozzi was waiting for Walsh at Camden Police Station; he was perched on her desk, sitting between her two large cardboard boxes, still unpacked.

"Hello there, Joanne," Crozzi said cheerfully. He patted one of the boxes. "Still moving in, I see?"

"I've been busy," Walsh said shortly.

"Oh, the Corbett case. We've heard about that way over in our province."

"In what capacity are you here, Eduard? Ex-husband or ex-boss?"

"How are the kids?" he asked, smiling.

"Surviving. You can ask them yourself on Saturday."

Crozzi nodded. "I've been asked by God to pay you a visit. He's concerned about the Corbett case. He was wondering if maybe it should be given to us in Homicide."

"Tell Chief Inspector McDermott that there is no evidence of foul play. It is a drowning, pure and simple."

Crozzi pursed his lips. "The marks on the boy's chest suggest there could be more to it than that."

Walsh knew what he meant was that McDermott thought her judgment might be affected by a need to validate her move to Camden.

"You can tell McDermott that I know my job. I'll call in Homicide if the Corbett case should prove suspicious. Until then, it is strictly a local matter, and you and your fellow thugs can butt out."

Crozzi started at the vehemence of her tone. "I'm not questioning your competence, Joanne. I know you can handle this new position."

That isn't what you said in the Family Law Court, she thought. "Of course not, Eduard. You're just the messenger boy."

Crozzi stood up. "Alright, Joanne. It was just a friendly visit. I'll let God know you're handling everything. I'll see you on Saturday."

After he was gone, Walsh cursed herself for losing her temper. *He does this to me all the time. Why did I ever think a divorce would change things?*

Walsh dropped her copy of the autopsy report on her desk. "I wanted some clues as to what caused the marks to Corbett's chest and stomach."

"The report suggests they may have been made by the body being dragged along the branches of sunken trees—"

"The river's too slow to have caused that much damage. And anyway, why aren't there marks on his head or neck? Dead bodies hang upside down in water; anything catching on his torso would have marked his face and scalp. All this tells me is that he died in the water. Sand and algae were found in his lungs. If he'd died on the surface, neither would be present there."

"You thought he might have been dead before entering the water?"

"It was a possibility."

"So you're saying he drowned."

"No autopsy can prove death by drowning," Walsh said flatly. "What we can say is that he died while under water, that's all."

"So what's next?"

"I want you to find the reports on two drownings in this area back in the 70s. Apparently both involved children."

Davies nodded and left.

Walsh unpacked her boxes, organized her desk, then studied the autopsy report again. The report dismissed the possibility of the damage being caused by a knife or other sharp tool, or by some animal because there were no bites on the extremities and the eyes were still intact.

As far as the pathologist was concerned, the only remaining possibility was the one described, a conclusion supported by the traces of wood fiber found under the damaged skin.

Walsh considered ordering a search of the river and the surrounding terrain, but dismissed the idea. It would give Homicide the excuse they needed to take over the case; besides, she had no *real* reason to suspect foul play.

She left the station, leaving a message for Constable Davies that she could be found at Chellaston Street Reserve.

Walsh returned to the bridge and looked down into the river. The water gurgled under her, taking its time on its journey west. Water skates pranced on the surface and above them hovered dragonflies; sunlight reflected back into her eyes, making her squint. The river rippled gently, like muscles under skin. The softest of breezes brushed against her cheeks.

She shook her head to clear it, crossed the bridge, and made for the trail leading into the reserve. She ducked under arching branches and stopped to allow her eyes to adapt to the dim light. She could smell damp humus under her feet and the wet bark of a nearby melaleuca. As her eyes adjusted, she saw that the trail meandered for several meters before losing itself between privet and a storm of tangled vines and runners. Sunlight filtered down, splattering on leaves that glided with the faintest touch of wind.

As she walked along the trail, hearing her feet crunch on leaves and twigs, she realized there was no sound from civilization. Even on the footbridge there was the drone of distant traffic and the regular thumping of the irrigation pumps feeding river water to the turf farm. But here she could hear only the occasional buzz of an insect and her own breathing. Even when a breeze moved the tops of trees far above, the canopy filtered out any sound.

Walsh followed the trail and soon found herself on the lip of a steep bank covered in grass and moss. The trail continued along the lip for a few meters before petering out amid the drooping branches of a willow. She was about to turn back when the sun glittered off something near the water's edge. She carefully climbed down the bank and found a key, half-covered in silt and algae. She picked it up and used a fistful of grass to wipe away the grunge. It looked like a key to a small padlock, the kind her children used to chain their bikes. Judging from its appearance, it had not been in the water for long. She squatted on her heels and carefully sifted the water's edge with her hands for anything else that may have washed up, but only succeeded in muddying the water.

She heard someone walking along the trail, coming in her direction. She looked over her shoulder but could see no one. As she stood up to get a better view, something touched her ankle. Startled, she cried out.

There was a splash of water that doused her pants and Walsh cried out a second time. She jumped back from the river and slipped, landing on her backside. She looked up in time to see a wide V-shaped ripple moving away from the bank and towards the middle of the river. There was an explosion of bubbles and the ripple disappeared, its wash slowly echoing against the reeds and mud near her feet.

"Sergeant?" Davies voice. "Are you all right?" He appeared at the top of the bank, and looked down at her with obvious concern.

"I . . . I slipped, that's all," Walsh said.

"You should be more careful, Sergeant," he said while scrabbling down the bank. "The river's depth drops off real sharp there." He held a hand out to her, which she took begrudgingly.

"I know how to swim," she said angrily. He mumbled an apology, and she immediately felt guilty.

"I'm sorry," she said gruffly, wiping slime off the bottom of her pants. "Hurt pride, that's all."

They helped each other climb back to the trail.

"I got your message at the station, thought I'd better come out."

"What's the hurry?" she asked, looking back over the river. It looked as peaceful as ever.

"I got the files on those two drownings back in the 70s. Thought you'd better see them for yourself."

"Interesting reading?"

"Depends on your definition of interesting," he said grimly.

Davies retrieved the files from his car and brought them to her, then returned to the station with the key she had found. Walsh went home. She needed to change her clothes and wanted to read the files away from any distraction.

Bedraggled, still unsure about what exactly had happened to her at the river's edge, she entered her home depressed and tired. Her shoes squelched on the front hall carpet; she glanced over her shoulder and saw black footprints following her on the new nylon pile.

"Fucking great," she said aloud.

A sudden scuffle came from the lounge room. Walsh put down the files she was carrying and slipped the automatic out from its holster on her belt. She hid the gun in her jacket pocket, her hand around the grip. She heard more sounds, panicky and desperate. Holding her breath, she sidestepped in front of the lounge room entrance.

"*Hold it!*" she ordered.

Her daughter Celia froze, her shorts halfway up her bottom, her bra hanging on by one strap and the grace of God. At her feet, struggling to pull on a pair of black jeans, was a boy about Celia's age. Walsh noted that his underpants had a spider motif.

"What are you doing here?" Celia demanded.

"What am *I* doing here? Why aren't you in school?"

The boy moaned. He tried standing up, but the jeans tripped him up and he landed on his knees. He looked up pleadingly at Walsh. "Hello, Mrs. Walsh. I'm—"

"*Detective Sergeant* Walsh," she replied tartly. "Get your bloody pants on and get out."

"Mum!" Celia cried, embarrassed now.

"Shut up, Celia. I'll talk to you in a minute."

The boy scrabbled desperately, eventually managing to zip up his jeans and pull on a T-shirt. He sat down to put on his shoes and socks, thought better of it and tucked them under one arm. He backed out of the lounge room to the hallway. He mumbled something to Celia about seeing her later.

"Over my dead body," Walsh growled.

The boy turned quickly, one foot landing on the files Walsh had put there a moment before. He yelped as his foot flew out from beneath him and he landed, hard, on his back. He waved his arms and legs like a stranded turtle before finally getting back to his feet. Papers and photographs from the files were scattered everywhere.

"Christ, sorry, Mrs.—Sergeant—Walsh . . ." His voice faltered when he saw the photographs. His mind registered small bodies, swollen and mutilated.

"Oh, God," he wheezed, flung open the front door, and fled from the house.

Walsh faced her daughter and asked, in her most imperious voice: "And who was that dignified young gentleman?"

In retrospect, Walsh knew she had taken the wrong approach with her daughter. Celia told her to mind her own business and refused to answer any questions. Walsh lost her temper, demanded answers. Exit Celia, in a rage, declaring she would never return.

Angry at Celia for growing up too quickly, and angry at herself for not knowing better, Walsh sat at the dining-room table and studied the files on the two earlier drownings. The photographs, all in black and white, were some of the most gruesome she had ever seen, made worse by the ages of the victims: a boy of seven and a girl of nine.

The boy's body had been discovered on a cold Saturday morning in 1974, not far from where Warren Corbett had been dragged out of the Nepean; he had been missing for three days. The girl's body had been discovered closer to town, near Cowpasture Bridge, in 1978, only a few hours after her parents had reported her missing.

The coroner's verdict on both counts had been accidental drowning, but for Walsh there was no mistaking the marks on their torsos. The only difference was that the markings on the boy's chest led to noticeable holes where his heart, kidneys, and intestines should have been; the coroner decided, on the pathologist's advice, that eels or yabbies had caused the damage.

Then why did he still have eyes, ears, and fingers? she asked herself. *And how could the holes be so specific?*

There was a hand-written note at the very end of the girl's file, signed by someone named P. Fielding.

"Met Ben Older on 5 Sept. No Darug story explains this. Shot in the dark, anyway. So why the marks? Cf File 54/74."

Walsh checked the cover of the earlier file: 54/74. So someone, twenty years before, had wondered about the similarity of the marks in the two cases. But without success, apparently. And why had the writer of the note consulted the Darug, the local Aboriginal people?

And who, exactly, were P. Fielding and Ben Older?

Walsh checked her watch. It was nearly three in the afternoon. She would have to pick up Miriam and Rowena in a few minutes, but she could drop them off home and then dash back to the station to ask Davies to do some more scrounging for her.

You idiot, she told herself. *Celia won't be here to look after the kids.*

Thinking of her oldest daughter made her heart heavy. How long would Celia stay angry with her? Where could she go, anyway?

Walsh shook her head. Celia had pulled this sort of stunt before, especially during the divorce, and had always turned up before dark.

Walsh rushed in to the station to ask Davies to find out about Fielding and Older, then picked up Miriam and Rowena. Before returning home, they shopped for groceries and Walsh bought a bucket of Celia's favorite ice cream to serve as a peace offering.

It had been dark for over an hour and Celia still had not come home. Walsh put the two smaller children to bed and sat down in front of the television without really watching it.

The phone rang and she leapt up to get it.

"It's Davies, Sergeant."

Walsh's heart sank. "What is it?"

"Fielding was a Senior Constable posted to Camden during the time of the earlier drownings. He raised questions about the coroner's decision in the second case, but no one listened to him. He was transferred soon after to Goulburn. He retired from the force about fifteen years ago and died last year; cancer, I'm told."

"And what about Older?"

"A local Aborigine. A carpenter. Fielding and Older were friends. Older had a heart attack and died soon after the second drowning."

"Two dead ends," Walsh said, and laughed humorlessly at her unintended pun.

"Not quite," Davies continued, his voice somber, which made Walsh feel foolish. "Older's daughter Katherine is still alive and living in the area. I've got her address." Walsh wrote down the address as he read it out. "And one more thing. That key you found on the river bank belonged to Corbett. Some kind of bicycle lock."

"Thanks for your work, Constable. I'll see you tomorrow." She hung up, swallowed the lump in her throat.

The phone rang again almost immediately.

"Detective Sergeant Walsh?" A vaguely familiar voice, but Walsh couldn't put a name to it.

"Who's this?"

"Dr. Louise Pelham."

This is all I need, Walsh thought.

"It's late, Doctor—"

"I'm Rob's mother."

"Rob?"

"The boy you chased out of your house this afternoon."

Walsh closed her eyes, tried to control her temper, but knew it was a losing battle. "Your son, Doctor, was—"

"Yes, I know, Sergeant. That's why I'm ringing. First, to apologize for my son's behavior, and second, to let you know that Celia's at our place."

The relief was so great Walsh felt the blood rush from her face. "Oh, God . . ."

"I knew you'd be worried, Sergeant—"

"Yes," Walsh said faintly.

"Would you object if she stayed with us tonight? Celia's exhausted. I don't know how long she's been walking. We have a spare room, and I promise to surround her with barbed wire. Both Rob and Celia are very sorry for what they've done."

Walsh surprised herself by laughing. "That's fine, Doctor. Thank you. Thank you for letting me know."

"Good night, Sergeant."

Walsh ordered herself not to cry, but the tears came anyway.

It was an embarrassing few moments. Celia mumbled an apology, followed by Rob who stood in the background, looking more sheepish than Walsh would have believed possible. She waved the teenagers through, telling them to make themselves scarce while their mothers talked.

Now it was Walsh's turn to feel sheepish. "I'm sorry if I seemed rude last night—"

Pelham laughed. "*I'm* sorry Rob's put you through all this trouble."

"Celia's running away was all my own fault. I'm still shell-shocked from owning a pubescent daughter. I don't suppose it was right of me to stop them."

"Of course, you were right. For one thing, they're both too young—and I'm speaking as a doctor. But I don't think we can stop them seeing each other, or for that matter stop them having sex if their hormones are set on it."

Walsh nodded. Her watch beeped at her. "I have to get to work, Doctor. I'm sorry to cut this short."

Pelham nodded in the direction of the kitchen. Walsh heard Celia laughing. "We'll have other opportunities to talk, I think."

Katherine Older stayed behind the front door, peering around it like a shy child.

"Police? I don't know anything you'd be interested in." Her large brown eyes studied Walsh carefully, without welcome or hostility.

"I wanted to talk to you about your father."

"My father's dead. Been dead for nearly twenty years."

"He was a friend of a policeman called Fielding."

"Peter Fielding? He's dead, too. You're out of luck on both counts."

Older seemed suddenly sad.

"I need to talk to you about a conversation they had."

Older laughed. "Oh, crikey! You expect me to remember what they said to each other? They talked *all* the time!"

"One conversation in particular, Ms. Older. Please, it won't take long."

The old woman sighed, opened the door wider, and let Walsh in. The place was clean and well kept, but there wasn't much furniture. In fact, Walsh noticed, there wasn't much of anything. She heard a dog barking half-heartedly in the backyard.

Older led the way into the kitchen, and she and Walsh stood on a linoleum floor that undulated with rising damp. Older put on a kettle.

"There were two drownings about twenty years ago, both involving children."

"Oh, yeah. I remember that, all right. Been another, I hear."

"Constable Fielding talked to your father about the two drownings. Were you present at the conversation?"

"Sure. You don't forget that sort of talk, no matter how old you get."

"What did Fielding want to know?"

Older looked aside, pretended to check on the kettle.

"Ms. Older?"

"It's kinda hard to explain. It's not something you discuss in normal conversation, or with strangers."

"This is a formal investigation," Walsh said.

"Oh, yeah, I know all about those." Older laughed, but didn't elaborate. The kettle started whistling and she poured hot water into a tea pot, then said quietly: "Fielding wanted to know if the Darug had any myths about creatures living in the river that took children."

Walsh blinked. This is not what she'd expected to hear. She felt foolish. "You mean monsters?"

Older still refused to look at Walsh. "If you want."

Walsh didn't know what to say. Older poured two cups and handed her one. "I got some sugar somewhere . . ."

Walsh shook her head. "What did your father say?"

Older turned back to Walsh, stared her straight in the eye. "My dad was frightened. He said, 'You whites don't have to look to us for answers.'"

"What did he mean by that?"

Older sipped carefully on her tea. She seemed even more reluctant to speak, but after a moment she said: "My dad meant there was no point looking at us Darug for an answer to the drownings. He said the whites had brought their own demons with them." Her brown eyes seemed to lose their focus, and Walsh got the feeling she was looking back on all her people's history. "And damn if he didn't mean it."

The rain started that afternoon. A furious southerly, bringing half the Pacific Ocean with it, swept over the coast for a hundred kilometers either side of Sydney. The sky turned leaden, and the clouds roiled as they raced over Camden, shutting out the light before releasing their burden. The rain fell so heavily on the corrugated roof of the police station it was almost impossible to hold a conversation.

Frustrated by her lack of progress on the Corbett case, disappointed and strangely unsettled by her conversation with Katherine Older, Walsh was almost relieved when a report about an armed robbery at a local petrol station landed on her desk. She collected Davies and went to interview the station's manager, a young man called Stuart still suffering from the aftereffects of shock. Davies knew him casually, so Walsh let him carry out the interview while she walked around the main building and the tarmac looking for anything that might present itself as a clue. Unfortunately the rain was washing everything into the stormwater drains. She inspected each of the drains in case something had been caught in their cement grills, but found nothing. Davies joined her.

"What do you think?" she asked him.

Davies shrugged. "Not much chance of catching the offender. Stuart didn't recognize him. Probably an addict from Sydney looking for cash. Stuart said he ran away on foot, but most likely there was a car nearby."

"He might be back, then."

"Sure. We'll get him in the end, but probably won't be able to pin this job on him."

They started walking back to the car when Walsh stopped.

"What's the matter?" Davies asked.

Walsh cocked her head to one side. "That sound." She could hear a dull roaring, like the breathing of a sleeping giant.

Davies looked puzzled for a moment, and then realized what Walsh was hearing. "That's the river. See those hills over there?" He pointed south and east. "That's where the Nepean starts. Most of the run-off this side of the highlands feeds into it. If it rains like this for more than a couple of days, the river will overflow into the flood plains around Camden. That's something you'll never forget."

Walsh straightened, her skin prickling. Davies looked at her curiously. "My grave's being walked on," she said vaguely, still looking towards the hills.

On Saturday the rain was still falling. Walsh's ex-husband arrived to pick up the children for the weekend, driving up in his shiny new Subaru with the rear spoiler, which Walsh thought made the car look like an overgrown potato peeler.

The kids greeted him enthusiastically and Walsh felt a pang of jealousy. He came through her front door like a knight to the rescue, sweeping up in his arms each of the children in turn and sending them on to the car. He offered Walsh a peck which she deflected from her lips to her cheek.

"So, how's the new job going?" he asked innocently.

"Oh, fine."

"Any more leads on the drowning?" He asked the question too casually for it to have been simple curiosity on his part.

"Looks like just a simple drowning. The autopsy says so, anyway."

Crozzi nodded. "Jeez, with all this rain, I hope you don't get another one. Have you seen the river?" Walsh shook her head. "Water's up to the banks. You'll need Noah's Ark by tomorrow." He laughed at his own joke.

"Where are you taking the kids?"

"Celia phoned me during the week. She wants to go in to the city. Maybe we'll catch a film, do some shopping. Give them a break from country life, you know."

Walsh felt a lump in her throat. "Hope you have a nice time." He waved and left. She shut the door and rested her back against it, wishing to God she didn't hurt so much inside.

She spent the morning cleaning the house, then doing the week's washing and draping most of the furniture with uniforms, bras and nickers, socks and pantyhose. The air was so moist she didn't think any of it would be ready in time for Monday. There was a laundromat in town she could use if she had to, but the thought of spending a couple of hours sitting on a plastic chair watching a barrel load of washing spin around in a dryer made her feel even more depressed.

Around mid-morning she made herself a cup of coffee and a ham sandwich, plopped down in a seat to watch the cricket replay. Australia had gone up against Pakistan the night before, and lost as usual. When the phone rang she answered it almost with a feeling of relief.

"It's Davies. I think we've found the robber."

"Which one?" she asked absently, still chewing some of her sandwich. The ham tasted funny.

"The one who held up the petrol station."

"Hey, good work! Where did you pick him up?"

"I didn't. An emergency crew from Prospect Electricity did. From the river."

Walsh swallowed hard. "Where are you?"

"About fifty meters upstream from Cowpasture Bridge."

"I'll be there in ten minutes."

She was there in five, dressed in tracksuit pants, T-shirt, runners, and raincoat. She didn't have to slide down the bank this time—the river was so full, it met her almost at ground level. Davies and two other police were setting up a cordon. The body was hidden under a plastic sheet. Standing nearby were two electricity workers, wearing hardhats, yellow jackets, and serious looking tool belts. Walsh went straight to Davies. He nodded to the sheet and handed her a sodden wallet. Walsh opened it up and checked the name on the driver's licence showing under a warped plastic window. "Thurmon, James," she said quietly. "Twenty-one." She pointed to the electricity workers.

"What were they doing here?"

"Following a landline route the Council wants put in. They were ordered to see how the rain had affected the ground."

"Have they been interviewed yet?"

"Not in detail," Davies said. "I got in touch with you as soon as I saw the body." Walsh studied Davies' face, but couldn't read his expression.

"Tell them to go to the station. They can wait for us there out of the rain."

Davies went to talk to the workers. Walsh lifted one corner of the plastic sheet. She saw a small man, lank dark hair, a hint of blue skin. She lifted the sheet further. Sweatshirt, probably originally orange in color. Jeans. One sandshoe on one foot, the other foot a crimpled, folded piece of flesh and bone, as pale as ivory. She moved around, letting the sheet run through her fingers. When she saw the face she exhaled sharply. Davies joined her.

"Is it just the face?"

He shook his head. "Chest, stomach, and groin as well."

"Has the pathologist been called?"

"Not yet. I wanted you to see the body first."

"Who's on roster this weekend?"

"Taylor, from Campbelltown."

"I know him. Call Dr. Pelham instead. She saw the Corbett boy. I want to see what her reaction is." Davies went to his car to make the call.

Walsh dropped the sheet and stepped away from the river.

Pelham spent nearly half an hour looking at the body. When she had finished she joined Walsh in her car. Their breathing misted the windows, and their hair stank of sweat and rain.

"How long since death?" Walsh asked.

"At least two days."

Walsh sighed deeply, not wanting to ask the next question. Pelham double-guessed her.

"It won't be easy to determine the cause of death. His body's been in the river for too long, and the current has been tremendous since the rain started. Almost anything could have caused those injuries. The surface tissue is so badly damaged it may not even be possible to determine what injuries were inflicted before death, and which after. There's definite signs of something having chewed on his face and fingers, but whatever caused it was small, like an eel or a turtle."

"But the chest injuries—"

"Bear a superficial resemblance to those we found on Warren Corbett."

Walsh snorted. "Superficial!"

Pelham pointed to the surging Nepean. "This bloke has been churning around inside that river for fifty hours or more, banging up against submerged tree branches, rocks, bits of glass, and aluminium cans." The doctor saw Walsh's expression and shook her head. "I'm sorry, I wish I could tell you more."

Walsh left Davies to finish off at the river while she returned to the station to interview the two electricity workers; they provided no new information, and after getting them to check and sign their statements she let them go.

She tried to write up her own report, but was unable to concentrate enough to complete it; her mind always drifted back to the mutilated remains of a small-time villain who had, somehow, fallen into the river. By itself, of course, it would not have affected her so much, but on top of the Corbett drowning and the files of the drownings twenty years before, she couldn't help feeling she was missing something vitally important and it frustrated her that she didn't know what it was.

And constantly lurking in the back of her memory was her interview with Katherine Older. She had tried dismissing the woman's words, but they kept turning up like a bad penny, detouring Walsh's mental processes into areas where she didn't want them to go. She kept on telling herself she was, at best, looking at four drownings with superficial similarities, and at worst the beginnings of a pattern that pointed to a serial murderer, and even the latter made her curse her overactive imagination.

No, Joanne, she told herself, *not demons. Not here, not now, not ever.*

She stood up angrily, ignored the surprised look a nearby constable threw her, and walked out of the station. She would go home, fix herself some lunch and not worry about the report until Monday. Then she noticed the library across the road.

She found the book she wanted in the children's section. Big format, lots of gruesome color illustrations, big text, and some names to follow up. She wrote them down and went home. She made herself a big mug of extra strong coffee and sat down in front of Celia's computer. It took a few minutes fumbling before she remembered how to open up a line to the 'net and start a search program. She entered the names she had written down at the library, then followed through with as many of the links as she could. Slowly, and with growing unease, she learned about the water demons that had haunted her British and Irish ancestors.

Their names were like cruel schoolyard monikers: Black Kate, Peg Powler, Straywater Bess, Annie-in-the-marsh, Jenny Greenteeth, and a dozen others. All working-class and female names. Women gone bad: women that hated, slew, and devoured children. It occurred to her that many, maybe most, of the monsters used to scare children *were* female. She remembered the villains in the Disney films she had seen as a kid, and in almost every case they were female, too.

It made her angry that myth and legend made women the destroyers of lost and disobedient children. If Eduard was here they'd have an argument about it. He would say she was taking it too seriously, and she would resort to terms that infuriated him—patriarchy, sexism, prejudice—partly because it did infuriate him, but mostly because she had always hoped that if she said the words often enough something of their meaning would get through his own patriarchal, sexist prejudice.

All of the demons had other things in common, she noted. They infested rivers and ponds and streams; none was from the sea. All freshwater bogies. They all lay in wait for stray children who wandered too close to a river or a fen or a bog. Walsh wanted to laugh, feeling foolish having spent so much time investigating a crazy whim. But her unease never left her.

"Our demons," she said to herself quietly, remembering again Kath Older's words.

As the day waned Walsh started feeling depressed; she could not shake the dark mood that slowly enveloped her. She tried to read a book, but found herself scanning the same page again and again. Eventually she gathered the necessary energy to make herself some dinner. She caught herself looking at the telephone. Sometimes the kids rang when they were with their father, more out of courtesy than any real understanding of how much she missed them even after a few hours. But sometimes they just forgot.

I want to hear your voices. I want to know you're okay. Walsh shook her head. Of course they were okay.

The house filled with the sound of rain, falling steadily, flooding the gutters and drowning the barely established garden outside. She imagined the Nepean swelling like something alive, filled with dark water and pale, wrinkled bodies . . .

Oh, for Christ's sake, Joanne!

She got ready for bed and lay there for hours trying to find sleep, and when eventually it came it brought with it dreams of shadowy children walking by a wide brown river, their flesh as white as chalk, calling for their mothers and unaware of the creature in the water that glided alongside of them, waiting.

Walsh woke with a start, sitting up straight, her eyes wide, her mouth opened to scream—and stopped. She gulped in air, looked at the rain splattering against the window.

She had a long shower, washing away the remnants of her nightmare. Afterwards, she didn't feel like eating anything, but drank two mugs of strong, black coffee. The house was silent around her and she hated it. She did not want to be here by herself. She decided to go to the station.

Davies was there, almost as if he had been expecting her to come in.

"I want you to do some research for me," Walsh told him. "Anything to do with kids drowning in this part of the river. No—wait! Anywhere along the Nepean-Hawkesbury system."

Davies sighed. "I'll do what I can, but that covers twenty-four districts . . ."

"And I want you to go as far back as possible."

"That's nearly two hundred years!"

"Then the sooner you start . . ."

He shook his head and left for registry.

Walsh sat behind her desk and retrieved from her computer the report she had started the day before on the latest drowning. Keeping her mind on the facts only, she finished it in under an hour. She printed it off, and held the three pages in her hands. It wasn't the whole story, she knew, but how could she place her suspicions and fears in an official report?

Davies appeared with an armful of old files. Walsh felt sick inside; she had hoped he would find nothing.

"Look at these," the constable said excitedly. "I searched the registry database, and found seventeen drownings just along this stretch of the river between 1825 and now. They occur in batches, twenty to thirty years apart. Most of the reports are from this century, but a hundred years ago a lot of people went missing and were never chased up, or their bodies were found and simply buried without anyone informing the authorities. Furthermore, all the drowning seemed to have occurred between Cowpasture Bridge and a point about half a klick upriver from Chellaston Street Reserve."

He placed the stack on Walsh's desk. "And from what I can see, at least two thirds of the victims have marks similar to those we found on Corbett and Thurmon."

He rested back on his heels and stretched his spine, looking very satisfied with himself.

"What about the rest of the river?" she asked sullenly.

Davies looked hurt. "I'll get back and start on it now."

"What's the significance of the gaps between the drownings?" she asked aloud.

Davies shrugged, then half-jokingly said: "Maybe we're looking at a family of serial murderers. Some bad gene passed down generation after generation . . ." His voice trailed off when he saw Walsh's expression. He pulled on an earlobe and started moving away.

"Or something that needs to feed only every twenty or thirty years," Walsh said quietly.

Davies stopped, looked curiously at his superior. "What?"

Walsh shook her head as if to clear it. "Grab your raincoat. We're going for a walk."

"Where?"

"Along the river from the Reserve to Cowpasture Bridge."

"But the waters—"

"Are over the banks, I know."

Davies seemed despondent. "I'll get my coat."

Walsh stood up and regarded him carefully. "By the way, that was fast work with the files. Well done."

Davies smiled half-heartedly. "Thanks. I think."

The Nepean was alive. It made its hurried way in broad sweeping curves that cared little for the works of humans. Fields were flooded, fences drowned, homes threatened. Its ally, the rain, continued to fall steadily, turning the ground into a sodden, squelching morass. Walsh parked her car near the bridge at the reserve and she and Davies began their cautious, solemn parade on the south side, walking as close to the river as they could without slipping into it.

"What did you mean back at the station?" Davies asked after a few minutes.

"I interviewed Katherine Older, did I tell you?"

Davies shook his head, and Walsh recounted their conversation.

"You can't be serious," he said.

"Probably not. But do you have an explanation?"

Davies thought for a few moments. "There's something else."

"Something else?"

"All those drownings I've dug up in the files. In every case except three, they involved children."

Walsh stopped, held Davies by the arm. "Except three?"

Davies nodded. "Two of them were average-sized women. Average-sized for the first half of last century, which means around five feet. The third was Thurmon, and as you saw he was a small man, no bigger than yourself." Walsh grimaced. "Which fits in rather too nicely with your story about some creature who kills and eats children."

"Oh, Christ," Walsh said hollowly.

They resumed their walk.

"Are we looking for anything in particular?" Davies asked.

Walsh shook her head. "Anything that might help. Anything that will . . ." Her voice trailed off.

"Take us back to a more rational explanation?" Davies finished for her.

"You got it."

They found nothing. Davies returned to the station to finish his research while Walsh continued on home. Her raincoat hadn't made much difference: her clothes were soaked, her hair matted to her skull, her nose dripped like a buggered tap. She parked in the driveway, tired and feeling sorry for herself, not noticing the Subaru holding station on the street outside her house. She trudged to the front door and pulled out her key, only to find it opening before her. Eduard stood there like an impatient parent.

"Where the hell have you been?" he demanded. "I told you I had to drop off the kids right after lunch."

Walsh stood there, the key held out in anticipation. *This is how Celia must feel when I rail at her.*

"Sorry, Eduard. I forgot." She pushed her way past him and made for the laundry, where she ditched her shoes and dripping pants and sweatshirt. Eduard followed her and hovered in the laundry doorway.

"You forgot? Well, when it comes to our children, dammit, I don't think that's good enough—"

"Eduard, I'm in my undies. I'm cold. I'm wet. Get the fuck out of my way or I'll kick you in the balls."

Eduard's mouth opened in surprise. Walsh then noticed Miriam lurking behind her father. The twelve-year-old put her hand to her mouth and backed away.

Oh, God. Why me? "Miriam, come here, honey . . ."

But it was too late. Her daughter was retreating from her, tears springing into her eyes.

"Daddy and I are just talking, Miriam . . ."

"Let the kid go, Joanne," Eduard said fiercely, and she knew what he really meant. She grabbed his shirt collar in both hands and pulled his head down to her level so quickly he had no time to react.

"You can see the kids anytime you want, you shit, but you will never *never* get custody of *my* child." She heaved him back, stormed past him to her bedroom. She pulled off her bra and panties, scrounged in her drawers for fresh underclothes, then put on another tracksuit. Eduard appeared again, shouting at her, but all she could hear was Miriam and Rowena crying together in the lounge room. By the time she got there, Eduard in tow and still shouting at her, the two girls were squatting together on the sofa and holding each other tightly. Celia stood behind the sofa, looking accusingly at both her parents. Walsh stood in front of her children, trying desperately to calm her anger, but it boiled inside her. She turned on Eduard and hit him in the chest with the side of her fist.

"Get out!" she screamed. "Get out of my house!"

Eduard went white. He barely felt the blow under his jacket, but she had never struck him before. He stared at her incredulously.

"Mum!" Celia cried out, frightened and pleading. Miriam and Rowena cried even more piteously.

Eduard cleared his throat. "Celia, get the children and take them to my car. I'll take you to Grandma's. You can stay there tonight."

Walsh froze as soon as she struck Eduard, aware of what she had done but hardly believing it had happened. She bowed her head, stared at the floor, barely breathing. She wanted to run to her children, to hold them close to herself, but she knew they were frightened. If they cringed away from her it would be too much for her to bear. So she let them go. She heard them walk softly past her, heard Eduard say something to her. She turned in time to see Celia pause at the front door with her overnight bag in one hand, looking at her strangely, and then she was alone again.

For a minute Walsh remained where she was, still in shock at how quickly everything had happened, and then the tears came, ceaseless and burning.

She woke from a fitful sleep, deluded for a moment by the welcoming light of a cloudless day. Then she remembered it was a Monday, and the house was not filled with the sound of her children getting ready for school. She got out of bed and dressed for work.

The sun was making up for lost time. When Walsh got to work the temperature was already over thirty degrees Celsius, and the humidity was suffocating. Steam rose off the road and the roofs of buildings, rising into the sky like the smoke from a hundred offerings. Still, she thought, it was definitely an improvement.

Davies was waiting for her at her desk, waving a piece of paper.

"What's that?" she asked testily. "Your birthday wish list?"

"Message from a Detective Inspector Crozzi. Something about meeting for lunch."

"Detective Inspector Crozzi can fuck off," she said.

Davies read the paper. "His number's here. Want me to phone him and pass on your message?"

Walsh ignored him and looked over his shoulder to glance through a window at the outside world. She saw blue sky, people passing by with their heads held up for the first time in days. At that moment she felt foolish for ever thinking about Kath Older's demons. The world was nasty enough without her delusions adding to it. She thought then of her children, and in her mind she replayed her actions last night and shuddered involuntarily. *Plenty of demons already inside each of us.*

She noticed that the street outside was suddenly crowded with schoolchildren. "What's going on?" she asked of no one in particular.

"Probably another biology expedition," Davies said.

"A what?"

"Now that the rain's stopped the schools are sending out students to collect the detritus thrown up by the flood," Davies explained. "They'll come back with a few hundred specimens of dead fish and frogs crammed into glass jars. There's going to be a lot of pissed-off parents tonight when they find their kids using the best cutlery to dissect a carp that's been dead for a few days."

Walsh stared hard at Davies. The hair stood on her arms. "They're going down by the river?"

Davies nodded amiably, then stopped himself. He returned Walsh's stare, then shook his head. "Oh, come on, Sergeant. They're being supervised by teachers—"

But Walsh wasn't listening. "Down by the *river*?" she demanded, and grabbed her jacket. "Come on."

Davies sighed deeply and followed Walsh out to her car.

The waters of the Nepean had receded, but were still well above the banks. There were at least three different groups of schoolchildren wandering along the reserve, carrying nets, prongs, and specimen jars, and being shepherded by teachers.

Walsh and Davies swapped their shoes for gumboots, put on polarized sunglasses and made their way down to the river.

The students and teachers ignored them, intent on their own explorations. One boy had found a dead eel and was holding it up by the tail while two friends poked at it with sticks. A teacher barked at them to put it down. There were hundreds of birds around, pecking and grubbing for stranded snails and fish. The Nepean had deposited huge layers of river silt that sucked at shoes and boots and gave off a noisome smell. Flies and mosquitoes skimmed along the surface in their millions.

Walsh went right to the water's edge and followed its course westwards, maneuvering between willow and privet as best she could. The heat and humidity made her sweat profusely, and she was continuously swatting at insects that wanted to colonize her eyes and mouth. She stopped every few minutes to gaze into the river itself. The polaroids helped get rid of most of the reflected glare, but all she could see were drowned roots and the silver bellies of dead fish. Davies kept to higher ground, watching the students, trying not to appear as bored as he felt.

An hour later they had moved beyond the reserve and were in sight of Cowpasture Bridge. Most of the students had left by now, hugging their jars, their uniforms splattered in mud. "Looks like the great hunt's over," Davies observed, watching them tramp their way back to their schools.

Walsh nodded, feeling relieved and disappointed. She joined Davies on higher ground and they started back to the car. They were overtaken by one of the teachers, who smiled at them and said: "Lost a couple of my kids!" He hurried past, moving at a jog and calling out "Celia! Rob!"

At first the names did not register with Walsh; her mind was on another track. And then she realized what the teacher had said. She stopped so quickly Davies bumped into her.

"Oh, no . . ."

"What's wrong?" Davies prompted.

"Get back to the car and start at the eastern end of the reserve. I want those kids found."

Davies nodded, catching the urgency in her voice, and raced off after the teacher.

Walsh ran down to the edge of the river and was soon among the trees and bushes that marked the reserve's western border. She moved as quickly as she could among the confusion of branches and twisted roots. The air was still and it was difficult to breathe. She took off her jacket and hung it from a grey and dying melaleuca. The water, brown and sluggish, lapped gently against the land like a caressing hand.

"Celia!" Walsh shouted. "Celia!" There was no response. She moved on, and a minute later again called out. She heard laughter not far ahead. She broke past a privet bush and slipped, sliding into the river. The land dipped to her right and was under water; on the other side of the hollow, standing behind the bushes so no one above them could see them, she saw her daughter and Rob holding hands, laughing still.

"Hello, you two," she said, placing her fists on her hips, looking as stern as she could in her relief at finding them.

The pair looked at her, and Celia pulled her hand away from his. "Mum," she said, her voice neutral. Rob simply nodded, his face showing he was still afraid of Celia's mother.

"Your teacher's looking for you," Walsh told them. "Why didn't you stay with the others?"

"We got lost," Celia said, grinning, and Rob jabbed her; he wasn't finding this anywhere near as amusing as Celia.

Walsh sighed. She wanted to speak to Celia privately, but her daughter looked at her with an expression that warned her off. A soft pain gnawed inside her. "Well, you're found now. Get back to school. I'll let your teacher know you're okay."

Rob started moving up to drier land. He put out a hand to help Celia, but as she reached for it she slid back. She let out a small squeal, started laughing again, and splashed into the river. Rob bent down and offered his hand again, but suddenly she was pulled away from the bank. She fell face down into the water. Her head came up briefly, gasping for air, and then she was jerked back again and she was under. There was an explosion of bubbles. Her hands grabbed at the muddy bank as she was pulled down.

"Celia!" Rob cried, and slid down the bank after her.

"Stay there!" Walsh shouted at him, and ran toward him, lifting her feet clear of the water and mud.

Rob ignored her and jumped in after Celia. He stopped then, turned desperately to Walsh. "She's gone!" he wailed.

She reached him and grabbed his arm, turning him away from the river. "Get out of the water!" she ordered. "There's another policeman at the other end of the reserve. Tell him to come here." She searched for any sign of her daughter. Rob still hadn't moved. "Quickly!" she screamed, and he bolted.

"Celia!" she called out. "Celia!" She saw ripples moving near the edge of the water ten meters upstream. She got out of the river, ran to the spot, and jumped in again. The ripples were another three meters along by then, but she saw one of Celia's shoes just beneath the surface of the water and she reached for it, just missing. She lunged forward, grabbed the shoe and heaved back with all her strength. Celia resurfaced, snorting and gulping for air. Walsh lifted her upright, holding her tightly, almost crying in relief. Blood was streaming down her daughter's chest. Walsh cursed and pushed her out of the water, getting one hand under her bottom and heaving as hard as she could. Celia collapsed onto the muddy ground, coughing up water and moaning in pain. Walsh put her right foot on land to follow, then felt something hard and painfully sharp grasp her by the left knee. She was pulled down into the river.

Walsh twisted, lashing out with her free leg. She connected with something hard and unyielding. She kicked again. The water erupted around her and she was forced under. She wanted to scream, but managed to hold it in. The water was green and turgid, filled with algae and suspended silt. She bent over to reach whatever it was that held her knee, felt something like a hand and pulled at its fingers. Walsh was weakening quickly, and needed air. She was dragged into deeper water, and she kicked out again with her right foot. Water forced its way up her nose as she was turned around and she gagged involuntarily, forcing water into her mouth. Frantic now, panicking, she flexed her whole body, doubling up and straightening as violently as she could with the little strength remaining. The water swirled around her. She saw a long shape move above, something vaguely seal-like, spindled and brown, but the skin was furrowed and wrinkled like tree bark. Two luminous yellow orbs blinked at her and she saw a serrated maw, wide as her own head, gape open.

This time Walsh did scream, and all her horror, all her anger and hate, exploded in her. She desperately lashed out at the thing, using her fingers to gouge at one of the eyes. And she was free. She kicked down, found the bottom, lifted her head above water, spluttering, gasping for air. She searched frantically for any sign of the thing that attacked her. There was a surge in the water to her right. Before she could react two sets of needle-like claws grasped her on both hips and she was pulled under again. Water filled her lungs. One of the claws scraped along her hip and up towards her stomach. Walsh punched with both hands, but her blows only glanced off the tough hide of her attacker.

Walsh knew she was going to die, but she didn't care anymore. She just wanted to kill this thing that was attacking her, had attacked her daughter. She kept on punching, tried to lift her knees up to protect her abdomen. Then suddenly she was released. She was caught in a maelstrom of water and mud. Her feet found bottom once more and she kicked up, falling back. Her arms flayed like windmill blades and she managed to keep upright. She gagged, dragged in lungfuls of air, gagged again. She heard a pistol shot, flinched involuntarily. There was a swirl of red blood all around her, so dark it was almost black, and so pungent she could smell the iron in it.

The river in front of her seemed to bulge, and the creature's head reared up almost to her own level, its arms reaching out for her. There was another shot and an explosion of gore whipped Walsh's face. The creature's mouth gaped, the top of its head completely gone, and it slid back into the river and disappeared in a froth of blood.

Walsh wanted to scream, but her lungs wouldn't work.

"Sergeant! Hold on!" It was Davies' voice. She heard someone splash into the water, and a moment later a man's arms were around her waist and she was dragged back to land.

She turned to thank her rescuer, saw that it was the teacher. Davies was still on the river's edge, his pistol held in both hands, his eyes searching the water for any further sign of the creature that had attacked her.

"You got it," she said numbly.

Davies kept his aim on the river. "Are you sure?"

Walsh wiped her face, held up her bloody hand. "This isn't mine." She turned to the teacher. "Did you see it?"

"I saw something," the teacher said shakily.

She tried to stand, but the pain in her sides and in her knee was too much. She sat there for a moment, looking out over the Nepean, and then she saw it—a V-shaped wave, a stream of blood in its wake. When it reached the middle of the river it stopped, its wash widening in a dying ripple. The water became calm and flat, as if nothing had ever disturbed its passage.

"I don't believe it," she murmured.

She looked around and saw Celia nearby, still groaning in pain, Rob's arms around her. She pulled herself across to them, the teacher helping her, and inspected her daughter's wounds.

"Not deep," she said to no one in particular. "You'll live," she told Celia gently, and kissed her.

Davies came to the teacher, held out his gun. "Know how to use one of these?"

The teacher shook his head.

"Just hold it tight, point it at anything that comes out of the water and blast the fuck out of it." The teacher nodded, took the gun. "Good. I'm going back to the car to call for an ambulance."

Walsh held Celia tightly against her for a long while, and then cupped her face in her hands and kissed her again. "Everything's going to be okay," she said, surprised by the waver in her voice. "You know that, don't you?"

Celia regarded her with eyes too wise for her fourteen years, and nodded.

PETER STRAUB

Mr. Aickman's Air Rifle

Peter Straub is the author of seventeen novels, which have been translated into more than twenty languages. They include Ghost Story, Koko, Mr. X, *two collaborations with Stephen King,* The Talisman *and* Black House, *and his most recent* In the Night Room.

He has also written two volumes of poetry and two collections of short fiction. He edited Conjunctions 39: The New Wave Fabulists *and Library of America's* H.P. Lovecraft: Tales. *He has won the British Fantasy Award, four Bram Stoker Awards, two International Horror Guild Awards, and two World Fantasy Awards. In 1998, he was named Grand Master at the World Horror Convention.*

"Mr. Aickman's Air Rifle" was first published in McSweeney's Enchanted Chamber of Astonishing Stories.

—E. D.

1

On the twenty-first, or "Concierge," floor of New York's Governor General Hospital, located just south of midtown on Seventh Avenue, a glow of recessed lighting and a rank of framed, eye-level graphics (Twombly, Shapiro, Marden, Warhol) escort visitors from a brace of express elevators to the reassuring spectacle of a graceful cherry wood desk occupied by a red-jacketed gatekeeper named Mr. Singh. Like a hand cupped beneath a waiting elbow, this gentleman's inquiring yet deferential appraisal and his stupendous display of fresh flowers nudge the visitor over hushed beige carpeting and into the wood-paneled realm of Floor 21 itself.

First to appear is the nursing station, where in a flattering chiaroscuro efficient women occupy themselves with charts, telephones, and the ever-changing patterns traversing their computer monitors; directly ahead lies the first of the great, half-open doors of the residents' rooms or suites, each with its brass numeral and discreet nameplate. The great hallway extends some sixty yards, passing seven named and numbered doors on its way to a bright window with an uptown view. To the left, the hallway passes the front of the nurses' station and the four doors directly opposite, then divides. The shorter portion continues on to a large, south-facing window with a good prospect of the Hudson River, the longer defines the southern boundary of the station. Hung with an Elizabeth Murray lithograph and a Robert Mapplethorpe calla lily, an ocher wall then rises up to guide the hallway over another carpeted fifty feet to a long, narrow room. The small brass sign beside its wide, pebble-glass doors reads SALON.

The Salon is not a salon but a lounge, and a rather makeshift lounge at that. At one end sits a good-sized television set; at the other, a green fabric sofa with two matching chairs. Midpoint in the room, which was intended for the comfort of stricken relatives and other visitors but has always been patronized chiefly by Floor 21's more ambulatory patients, stands a white-draped table equipped with coffee dispensers, stacks of cups and saucers, and cut-glass containers for sugar and artificial sweeteners. In the hours from four to six in the afternoon, platters laden with pastries and chocolates from the neighborhood's gourmet specialty shops appear, as if delivered by unseen hands, upon the table.

On an afternoon early in April, when during the hours in question the long window behind the table of goodies registered swift, unpredictable alternations of light and dark, the male patients who constituted four-fifths of the residents of Floor 21, all of them recent victims of atrial fibrillation or atrial flutter, which is to say sufferers from that dire annoyance in the life of a busy American male, nonfatal heart failure, the youngest a man of fifty-eight and the most senior twenty-two years older, found themselves once again partaking of the cream cakes and petit fours and reminding themselves that they had not, after all, undergone heart attacks. Their recent adventures had aroused in them an indulgent fatalism. After all, should the worst happen, which of course it would not, they were already at the epicenter of a swarm of cardiologists!

To varying degrees, these were men of accomplishment and achievement in their common profession, that of letters.

In descending order of age, the four men enjoying the amenities of the Salon were Max Baccarat, the much-respected former president of Gladstone Books, the acquisition of which by a German conglomerate had lately precipitated his retirement; Anthony Flax, a self-described "critic" who had spent the past twenty years as a full-time book reviewer for a variety of periodicals and journals, a leisurely occupation he could afford due to his having been the husband, now for three years the widower, of a sugar-substitute heiress; William Messinger, a writer whose lengthy backlist of horror/mystery/suspense novels had been kept continuously in print for twenty-five years by the biannual appearance of yet another new astonishment; and Charles Chipp Traynor, child of a wealthy New England family, Harvard graduate, self-declared veteran of the Vietnam conflict, and author of four non-fiction books, also (alas) a notorious plagiarist.

The connections between these four men, no less complex and multilayered than one would gather from their professional circumstances, had inspired some initial awkwardness on their first few encounters in the Salon, but a shared desire for the treats on offer had encouraged these gentlemen to reach the accommodation displayed on the afternoon in question. By silent agreement, Max Baccarat arrived first, a few minutes after opening, to avail himself of the greatest possible range of selection and the most comfortable seating position, which was on that end side of the sofa nearest the pebble-glass doors, where the cushion was a touch more yielding than its mate. Once the great publisher had installed himself to his satisfaction, Bill

Messinger and Tony Flax happened in to browse over the day's bounty before seating themselves at a comfortable distance from each other. Invariably the last to arrive, Traynor edged around the door sometime around 4:15, his manner suggesting that he had wandered in by accident, probably in search of another room altogether. The loose, patterned hospital gown he wore fastened at neck and backside added to his air of inoffensiveness, and his round glasses and stooped shoulders gave him a generic resemblance to a creature from *The Wind in the Willows*.

Of the four, the plagiarist alone had surrendered to the hospital's tacit wishes concerning patients' in-house mode of dress. Over silk pajamas of a glaring, Greek-village white, Max Baccarat wore a dark, dashing navy-blue dressing gown, reputedly a Christmas present from Graham Greene, which fell nearly to the tops of his velvet fox-head slippers. Over his own pajamas, of fine-combed baby-blue cotton instead of white silk, Tony Flax had buttoned a lightweight tan trench coat, complete with epaulettes and grenade rings. With his extra chins and florid complexion, it made him look like a correspondent from a war conducted well within striking distance of hotel bars. Bill Messinger had taken one look at the flimsy shift offered him by the hospital staff and decided to stick, for as long as he could get away with it, to the pin-striped Armani suit and black loafers he had worn into the ER. His favorite men's stores delivered fresh shirts, socks, and underwear.

When Messinger's early, less successful books had been published by Max's firm, Tony Flax had given him consistently positive reviews; after Bill's defection to a better house and larger advances for more ambitious books, Tony's increasingly bored and dismissive reviews accused him of hubris, then ceased altogether. Messinger's last three novels had not been reviewed anywhere in the *Times*, an insult he attributed to Tony's malign influence over its current editors. Likewise, Max had published Chippie Traynor's first two anecdotal histories of World War I, the second of which had been considered for a Pulitzer prize, then lost him to a more prominent publisher whose shrewd publicists had placed him on NPR, the *Today* show, and—after the film deal for his third book—*Charlie Rose*. Bill had given blurbs to Traynor's first two books, and Tony Flax had hailed him as a great vernacular historian. Then, two decades later, a stunned graduate student in Texas discovered lengthy, painstakingly altered parallels between Traynor's books and the contents of several Ph.D. dissertations containing oral histories taken in the 1930s. Beyond that, the student found that perhaps a third of the personal histories had been invented, simply made up, like fiction.

Within days, the graduate student had detonated Chippie's reputation. One week after the detonation, his university placed him "on leave," a status assumed to be permanent. He had vanished into a his family's Lincoln Log compound in Maine, not to be seen or heard from until the moment when Bill Messinger and Tony Flax, who had left open the Salon's doors the better to avoid conversation, had witnessed his sorry, supine figure being wheeled past. Max Baccarat was immediately informed of the scoundrel's arrival, and before the end of the day the legendary dressing gown, the trench coat, and the pin-striped suit had overcome their mutual resentments to form an alliance against the disgraced newcomer. There was nothing, they found, like a common enemy to smooth over complicated, even difficult relationships.

Chippie Traynor had not found his way to the lounge until the following day, and he had been accompanied by a tremulous elderly woman who with equal plausibility could have passed for either his mother or his wife. Sidling around the door at 4:15, he had taken in the trio watching him from the green sofa and chairs, blinked in disbelief and recognition, ducked his head even closer to his chest, and permitted his companion to lead him to a chair located a few feet from the television set. It was clear that he was struggling with the impulse to scuttle out of the room, never to reappear. Once deposited in the chair, he tilted his head upward and whispered a few words into the woman's ear. She moved toward the pastries, and at last he eyed his former compatriots.

"Well, well," he said. "Max, Tony, and Bill. What are you in for, anyway? Me, I passed out on the street in Boothbay Harbor and had to be airlifted in. Medevaced, like back in the day."

"These days, a lot of things must remind you of Vietnam, Chippie," Max said. "We're heart failure. You?"

"Atrial fib. Shortness of breath. Weaker than a baby. Fell down right in the street, boom. As soon as I get regulated, I'm supposed to have some sort of echo scan."

"Heart failure, all right," Max said. "Go ahead, have a cream cake. You're among friends."

"Somehow, I doubt that," Traynor said. He was breathing hard, and he gulped air as he waved the old woman farther down the table, toward the chocolate slabs and puffs. He watched carefully as she selected a number of the little cakes. "Don't forget the decaf, will you, sweetie?"

The others waited for him to introduce his companion, but he sat in silence as she placed a plate of cakes and a cup of coffee on a stand next to the television set, then faded backward into a chair that seemed to have materialized, just for her, from the ether. Traynor lifted a forkful of shiny brown goo to his mouth, sucked it off the fork, and gulped coffee. Because of his long, thick nose and recessed chin, first the fork, then the cup seemed to disappear into the lower half of his face. He twisted his head in the general direction of his companion and said, "Health food, yum, yum."

She smiled vaguely at the ceiling. Traynor turned back to face the other three men, who were staring open-eyed, as if at a performance of some kind.

"Thanks for all the cards and letters, guys. I loved getting your phone calls, too. Really meant a lot to me. Oh, sorry, I'm not being very polite, am I?"

"There's no need to be sarcastic," Max said.

"I suppose not. We were never friends, were we?"

"You were looking for a publisher, not a friend," Max said. "And we did quite well together, or so I thought, before you decided you needed greener pastures. Bill did the same thing to me, come to think of it. Of course, Bill actually wrote the books that came out under his name. For a publisher, that's quite a significant difference." (Several descendants of the Ph.D.s from whom Traynor had stolen material had initiated suits against his publishing houses, Gladstone Books among them.)

"Do we have to talk about this?' asked Tony Flax. He rammed his hands into the pockets of his trench coat and glanced from side to side. "Ancient history, hmmm?"

"You're just embarrassed by the reviews you gave him," Bill said. "But everybody did the same thing, including me. What did I say about *The Middle of the Trenches*? 'The . . .' The what? 'The most truthful, in a way the most visionary book ever written about trench warfare.'"

"Jesus, you remember your *blurbs*?" Tony asked. He laughed and tried to draw the others in.

"I remember everything," said Bill Messinger. "Curse of being a novelist—great memory, lousy sense of direction."

"You always remembered how to get to the bank," Tony said.

"Lucky me, I didn't have to marry it," Bill said.

"Are you accusing me of marrying for money?" Tony said, defending himself by the usual tactic of pretending that what was commonly accepted was altogether unthinkable. "Not that I have any reason to defend myself against you, Messinger. As that famous memory of yours should recall, I was one of the first people to support your work."

From nowhere, a reedy English female voice said, "I did enjoy reading your reviews of Mr. Messinger's early novels, Mr. Flax. I'm sure that's why I went 'round to our little bookshop and purchased them. They weren't at all my usual sort of *thing*, you know, but you made them sound . . . I think the word would be *imperative*."

Max, Tony, and Bill peered past Charles Chipp Traynor to get a good look at his companion. For the first time, they took in that she was wearing a long, loose collection of elements that suggested feminine literary garb of the nineteen twenties: a hazy, rather shimmery woolen cardigan over a white, high-buttoned blouse, pearls, an ankle-length heather skirt, and low-heeled black shoes with laces. Her long, sensitive nose pointed up, exposing the clean line of her jaw; her lips twitched in what might have been amusement. Two things struck the men staring at her: that this woman looked a bit familiar, and that in spite of her age and general oddness, she would have to be described as beautiful.

"Well, yes," Tony said. "Thank you. I believe I was trying to express something of the sort. They were books . . . well. Bill, you never understood this, I think, but I felt they were books that deserved to be read. For their workmanship, their modesty, what I thought was their actual decency."

"You mean they did what you expected them to do," Bill said.

"Decency is an uncommon literary virtue," said Traynor's companion.

"Thank you, yes," Tony said.

"But not a very interesting one, really," Bill said. "Which probably explains why it isn't all that common."

"I think you are correct, Mr. Messinger, to imply that decency is more valuable in the realm of personal relations. And for the record, I do feel your work since then has undergone a general improvement. Perhaps Mr. Flax's limitations perhaps do not permit him to appreciate your progress." She paused. There was a dangerous smile on her face. "Of course, you can hardly be said to have improved to the extent claimed in your latest round of interviews."

In the moment of silence that followed, Max Baccarat looked from one of his new allies to the other and found them in a state too reflective for commentary. He cleared his throat. "Might we have the honor of an introduction, madam? Chippie seems to have forgotten his manners."

"My name is of no importance," she said, only barely favoring him with the flicker of a glance. "And Mr. Traynor has a thorough knowledge of my feelings on the matter."

"There's two sides to every story," Chippie said. "It may not be grammar, but it's the truth."

"Oh, there are many more than that," said his companion, smiling again.

"Darling, would you help me return to my room?"

Chippie extended an arm, and the Englishwoman floated to her feet, cradled his rootlike fist against the side of her chest, nodded to the gaping men, and gracefully conducted her charge from the room.

"So who the fuck was *that*?" said Max Baccarat.

2

Certain rituals structured the nighttime hours on Floor 21. At 8:30 P.M., blood pressure was taken and evening medications administered by Tess Corrigan, an Irish softie with a saggy gut, an alcoholic, angina-ridden husband, and an understandable tolerance for misbehavior. Tess herself sometimes appeared to be mildly intoxicated. Class resentment caused her to treat Max a touch brusquely, but Tony's trench coat amused her to wheezy laughter. After Bill Messinger had signed two books for her niece, a devoted fan, Tess had allowed him to do anything he cared to, including taking illicit journeys downstairs to the gift shop. "Oh, Mr. Messinger," she had said, "a fella with your gifts, the books you could write about this place." Three hours after Tess's departure, a big, heavily dreadlocked nurse with an island accent surged into the patients' rooms to awaken them for the purpose of distributing tranquilizers and knockout pills. Because she resembled a greatly inflated, ever-simmering Whoopi Goldberg, Max, Tony, and Bill referred to this terrifying and implacable figure as "Molly." (Molly's real name, printed on the ID card attached to a sash used as a waistband, was permanently concealed behind beaded swags and little hanging pouches.) At six in the morning, Molly swept in again, wielding the blood-pressure mechanism like an angry deity maintaining a good grip on a sinner. At the end of her shift, she came wrapped in a strong, dark scent, suggestive of forest fires in underground crypts. The three literary gentlemen found this aroma disturbingly erotic.

On the morning after the appearance within the Salon of Charles Chipp Traynor and his disconcerting muse, Molly raked Bill with a look of pity and scorn as she trussed his upper arm and strangled it by pumping a rubber bulb. Her crypt-fire odor seemed particularly smoky.

"What?" he asked.

Molly shook her massive head. "Toddle, toddle, toddle, you must believe you're the new postman in this beautiful neighborhood of ours."

Terror seized his gut. "I don't think I know what you're talking about."

Molly chuckled and gave the bulb a final squeeze, causing his arm to go numb from bicep to his fingertips. "Of course not. But you do know that we have no limitations on visiting hours up here in our paradise, don't you?"

"Um," he said.

"Then let me tell you something you do not know, Mr. Postman. Miz La Valley in 21R-12 passed away last night. I do not imagine you ever took it upon yourself to pay the poor woman a social call. And *that*, Mr. Postman, means that you, Mr. Baccarat, Mr. Flax, and our new addition, Mr. Traynor, are now the only patients on Floor 21."

"Ah," he said.

As soon as she left his room, he showered and dressed in the previous day's clothing, eager to get out into the corridor and check on the conditions in 21R-14, Chippie Traynor's room, for it was what he had seen there in the hours between Tess

Corrigan's florid departure and Molly Goldberg's first drive-by shooting that had led to his becoming the floor's postman.

It had been just before nine in the evening, and something had urged him to take a final turn around the floor before surrendering himself to the hateful "gown" and turning off his lights. His route took him past the command center, where the Night Visitor, scowling over a desk too small for her, made grim notations on a chart, and down the corridor toward the window looking out toward the Hudson River and the great harbor. Along the way he passed 21R-14, where muffled noises had caused him to look in. From the corridor, he could see the bottom third of the plagiarist's bed, on which the sheets and blanket appeared to be writhing, or at least shifting about in a conspicuous manner. Messinger noticed a pair of black, lace-up women's shoes on the floor near the bottom of the bed. An untidy heap of clothing lay beside the in-turned shoes. For a few seconds, ripe with shock and envy, he had listened to the soft noises coming from the room. Then he whirled around and rushed toward his allies' chambers.

"Who *is* that dame?" Max Baccarat had asked, essentially repeating the question he had asked earlier that day. "*What* is she? That miserable Traynor, God damn him to hell, may he have a heart attack and die. A woman like that, who cares how old she is?"

Tony Flax had groaned in disbelief and said, "I swear, that woman is either the ghost of Virginia Woolf or her direct descendant. All my life, I had the hots for Virginia Woolf, and now she turns up with that ugly crook, Chippie Traynor? Get out of here, Bill; I have to strategize."

3

At 4:15, the three conspirators pretended not to notice the plagiarist's furtive, animal-like entrance to the Salon. Max Baccarat's silvery hair, cleansed, stroked, clipped, buffed, and shaped during an emergency session with a hair therapist named Mr. Keith, seemed to glow with a virile inner light as he settled into the comfortable part of the sofa and organized his decaf cup and plate of chocolates and little cakes as if preparing soldiers for battle. Tony Flax's rubber chins shone a twice-shaved red, and his glasses sparkled. Beneath the hem of the trench coat, which appeared to have been ironed, colorful argyle socks descended from just below his lumpy knees to what seemed to be a pair of nifty two-tone shoes. Beneath the jacket of his pin-striped suit, Bill Messinger sported a brand-new, high-collared black silk T-shirt delivered by courier that morning from Sixty-fifth and Madison. Thus attired, the longer-term residents of Floor 21 seemed lost as much in self-admiration as in the political discussion under way when at last they allowed themselves to acknowledge Chippie's presence. Max's eye skipped over Traynor and wandered toward the door.

"Will your lady friend be joining us?" he asked. "I thought she made some really very valid points yesterday, and I'd enjoy hearing what she has to say about our situation in Iraq. My two friends here are simpleminded liberals; you can never get anything sensible out of them."

"You wouldn't like what she'd have to say about Iraq," Traynor said. "And neither would they."

"Know her well, do you?" Tony asked.

"You could say that." Traynor's gown slipped as he bent over the table to pump coffee into his cup from the dispenser, and the three other men hastily turned their glances elsewhere.

"Tie that up, Chippie, would you?" Bill asked. "It's like a view of the Euganean Hills."

"Then look somewhere else. I'm getting some coffee, and then I have to pick out a couple of these yum-yums."

"You're alone today, then?" Tony asked.

"Looks like it."

"By the way," Bill said, "you were entirely right to point out that nothing is really as simple as it seems. There *are* more than two sides to every issue. I mean, wasn't that the point of what we were saying about Iraq?"

"To you, maybe," Max said. "You'd accept two sides as long as they were both printed in *The Nation*."

"Anyhow," Bill said, "please tell your friend that the next time she cares to visit this hospital, we'll try to remember what she said about decency."

"What makes you think she's going to come here again?"

"She seemed very fond of you," Tony said.

"The lady mentioned your limitations." Chippie finished assembling his assortment of treats and at last refastened his gaping robe. "I'm surprised you have any interest in seeing her again."

Tony's cheeks turned a deeper red. "All of us have limitations, I'm sure. In fact, I was just remembering . . ."

"Oh?" Chippie lifted his snout and peered through his little lenses. "Were you? What, specifically?"

"Nothing," said Tony. "I shouldn't have said anything. Sorry."

"Did any of you know Mrs. LaValley, the lady in 21R-12?" Bill asked. "She died last night. Apart from us, she was the only other person on the floor."

"I knew Edie LaValley," Chippie said. "In fact, my friend and I dropped in and had a nice little chat with her just before dinnertime last night. I'm glad I had a chance to say good-bye to the old girl."

"Edie LaValley?" Max said. "Hold on. I seem to remember . . ."

"Wait, I do, too," Bill said. "Only . . ."

"I know, she was that girl who worked for Nick Wheadle over at Viking, thirty years ago, back when Wheadle was everybody's golden boy," Tony said. "Stupendous girl. She got married to him and was Edith Wheadle for a while, but after the divorce she went back to her old name. We went out for a couple of months in 1983, '84. What happened to her after that?"

"She spent six years doing research for me," Traynor said. "She wasn't my *only* researcher, because I generally had three of them on the payroll, not to mention a couple of graduate students. Edie was very good at the job, though. Extremely conscientious."

"And knockout, drop-dead gorgeous," Tony said. "At least before she fell into Nick Wheadle's clutches."

"I didn't know you used so many researchers," Max said. "Could that be how you wound up quoting all those . . . ?"

"Deliberately misquoting, I suppose you mean," Chippie said. "But the answer is no." A fat, sugar-coated square of sponge cake disappeared beneath his nose.

"But Edie Wheadle," Max said in a reflective voice. "By God, I think I—"

"Think nothing of it," Traynor said. "That's what she did."

"Edie must have looked very different toward the end," said Tony. He sounded almost hopeful. "Twenty years, illness, all of that."

"My friend and I thought she looked much the same." Chippie's mild, creaturely face swung toward Tony Flax. "Weren't you about to tell us something?"

Tony flushed again. "No, not really."

"Perhaps an old memory resurfaced. That often happens on a night when someone in the vicinity dies—the death seems to awaken something."

"Edie's death certainly seemed to have awakened you," Bill said. "Didn't you ever hear of closing your door?"

"The nurses waltz right in anyhow, and there are no locks," Traynor said. "Better to be frank about matters, especially on Floor 21. It looks as though Max has something on his mind."

"Yes," Max said. "If Tony doesn't feel like talking, I will. Last night, an old memory of mine resurfaced, as Chippie puts it, and I'd like to get it off my chest, if that's the appropriate term."

"Good man," Traynor said. "Have another of those delicious little yummies and tell us all about it."

"This happened back when I was a little boy," Max said, wiping his lips with a crisp linen handkerchief.

Bill Messinger and Tony Flax seemed to go very still.

"I was raised in Pennsylvania, up in the Susquehanna Valley area. It's strange country, a little wilder and more backward than you'd expect, a little hillbillyish, especially once you get back in the Endless Mountains. My folks had a little store that sold everything under the sun, it seemed to me, and we lived in the building next door, close to the edge of town. Our town was called Manship, not that you can find it on any map. We had a one-room schoolhouse, an Episcopalian church and a Unitarian church, a feed and grain store, a place called the Lunch Counter, a tract house, and a tavern called the Rusty Dusty, where, I'm sad to say, my father spent far too much of his time.

"When he came home loaded, as happened just about every other night, he was in a foul mood. It was mainly guilt, d'you see, because my mother had been slaving away in the store for hours, plus making dinner, and she was in a rage, which only made him feel worse. All he really wanted to do was to beat himself up, but I was an easy target, so he beat me up instead. Nowadays, we'd call it child abuse, but back then, in a place like Manship, it was just normal parenting, at least for a drunk. I wish I could tell you fellows that everything turned out well, and that my father sobered up, and we reconciled, and I forgave him, but none of that happened. Instead, he got meaner and meaner, and we got poorer and poorer. I learned to hate to the old bastard, and I still hated him when a traveling junk wagon ran over him, right there in front of the Rusty Dusty, when I was eleven years old. 1935, the height of the Great Depression. He was lying passed out in the street, and the junkman never saw him.

"Now, I was determined to get out of that godforsaken little town, and out of the

Susquehanna Valley and the Endless Mountains, and obviously I did, because here
I am today, with an excellent place in the world, if I might pat myself on the back a
little bit. What I did was, I managed to keep the store going even while I went to the
high school in the next town, and then I got a scholarship to U. Penn., where I
waited on tables and tended bar and sent money back to my mother. Two days after
I graduated, she died of a heart attack. That was her reward.

"I bought a bus ticket to New York. Even though I was never a great reader, I
liked the idea of getting into the book business. Everything that happened after that
you could read about in old copies of *Publishers Weekly*. Maybe one day I'll write a
book about it all.

"If I do, I'll never put in what I'm about to tell you now. It slipped my mind
completely—the whole thing. You'll realize how bizarre that is after I'm done. I forgot all about it! Until about three this morning, that is, when I woke up too scared to
breathe, my heart going *bump, bump,* and the sweat pouring out of me. Every little
bit of this business just came *back* to me, I mean everything, every goddamned little
tiny detail. . . ."

He looked at Bill and Tony. "What? You two guys look like you should be back in
the ER."

"Every detail?" Tony said. "It's . . ."

"You woke up then, too?" Bill asked him.

"Are you two knotheads going to let me talk, or do you intend to keep interrupting?"

"I just wanted to ask this one thing, but I changed my mind," Tony said. "Sorry,
Max. I shouldn't have said anything. It was a crazy idea. Sorry."

"Was your dad an alcoholic, too?" Bill asked Tony Flax.

Tony squeezed up his face, said, "Aaaah," and waggled one hand in the air. "I
don't like the word 'alcoholic.'"

"Yeah," Bill said. "All right."

"I guess the answer is, you're going to keep interrupting."

"No, please, Max, go on," Bill said.

Max frowned at both of them, then gave a dubious glance to Chippie Traynor,
who stuffed another tiny cream cake into his maw and smiled around it.

"Fine. I don't know why I want to tell you about this anyhow. It's not like I actually *understand* it, as you'll see, and it's kind of ugly and kind of scary—I guess what
amazes me is that I just remembered it all, or that I managed to put it out of my
mind for nearly seventy years, one or the other. But you know? It's like, it's real even
if it never happened, or even if I dreamed the whole thing."

"This story wouldn't happen to involve a house, would it?" Tony asked.

"Most goddamned stories involve houses," Max said. "Even a lousy book critic
ought to know that."

"Tony knows that," Chippie said. "See his ridiculous coat? That's a house. Isn't it,
Tony?"

"You know what this is," Tony said. "It's a *trench coat,* a real one. Only from World
War II, not World War I. It used to belong to my father. He was a hero in the war."

"As I was about to say," Max said, looking around and continuing only when the
other three were paying attention, "when I woke up in the middle of the night I
could remember the feel of the old blanket on my bed, the feel of pebbles and earth
on my bare feet when I ran to the outhouse, I could remember the way my mother's

scrambled eggs tasted. The whole anxious thing I had going on inside me while my mother was making breakfast.

"I was going to go off by myself in the woods. That was all right with my mother. At least it got rid of me for the day. But she didn't know was that I had decided to steal one of the guns in the case at the back of the store.

"And you know what? She didn't pay any attention to the guns. About half of them belonged to people who swapped them for food because guns were all they had left to barter with. My mother hated the whole idea. And my father was in a fog until he could get to the tavern, and after that he couldn't think straight enough to remember how many guns were supposed to be back in that case. Anyhow, for the past few days, I'd had my eye on an over-under shotgun that used to belong to a farmer called Hakewell, and while my mother wasn't watching I nipped in back and took it out of the case. Then I stuffed my pockets with shells, ten of them. There was something going on way back in the woods, and while I wanted to keep my eye on it, I wanted to be able to protect myself, too, in case anything got out of hand."

Bill Messinger jumped to his feet and for a moment seemed preoccupied with brushing what might have been pastry crumbs off the bottom of his suit jacket. Max Baccarat frowned at him, then glanced down at the skirts of his dressing gown in a brief inspection. Bill continued to brush off imaginary particles of food, slowly turning in a circle as he did so.

"There is something you wish to communicate," Max said. "The odd thing, you know, is that for the moment, you see, I thought communication was in my hands."

Bill stopped fiddling with his jacket and regarded the old publisher with his eyebrows tugged toward the bridge of his nose and his mouth a thin, downturned line. He placed his hands on his hips. "I don't know what you're doing, Max, and I don't know where you're getting this. But I certainly wish you'd stop."

"What are you talking about?"

"He's right, Max," said Tony Flax.

"You jumped-up little fop," Max said, ignoring Tony. "You damned little show pony. What's your problem? You haven't told a good story in the past ten years, so listen to mine, you might learn something."

"You know what you are?" Bill asked him. "Twenty years ago, you used to be a decent second-rate publisher. Unfortunately, it's been all downhill from there. Now you're not even a third-rate publisher, you're a sellout. You took the money and went on the lam. Morally, you don't exist at all. You're a fancy dressing gown. And by the way, Graham Greene didn't give it to you, because Graham Greene wouldn't have given you a glass of water on a hot day."

Both of them were panting a bit and trying not to show it. Like a dog trying to choose between masters, Tony Flax swung his head from one to the other. In the end, he settled on Max Baccarat. "I don't really get it either, you know, but I think you should stop, too."

"Nobody cares what you think," Max told him. "Your brain dropped dead the day you swapped your integrity for a mountain of coffee sweetener."

"You did marry for money, Flax," Bill Messinger said. "Let's try being honest, all right? You sure as hell didn't fall in love with her beautiful face."

"And how about you, Traynor?" Max shouted. "I suppose you think I should stop, too."

"Nobody cares what I think," Chippie said. "I'm the lowest of the low. People despise me."

"First of all," Bill said, "if you want to talk about details, Max, you ought to get them *right*. It wasn't an 'over-under shotgun,' whatever the hell that is; it was a—"

"His name wasn't Hakewell," Tony said. "It was Hackman, like the actor."

"It wasn't Hakewell or Hackman," Bill said. "It started with an A."

"But there was a *house*," Tony said. "You know, I think my father probably was an alcoholic. His personality never changed, though. He was always a mean son of a bitch, drunk or sober."

"Mine, too," said Bill. "Where are you from, anyhow, Tony?"

"A little town in Oregon, called Milton. How about you?"

"Rhinelander, Wisconsin. My dad was the chief of police. I suppose there were lots of woods around Milton."

"We might as well have been in a forest. You?"

"The same."

"I'm from Boston, but we spent the summers in Maine," Chippie said. "You know what Maine is? Eighty percent woods. There are places in Maine, the roads don't even have names."

"There was a *house*," Tony Flax insisted. "Back in the woods, and it didn't belong there. Nobody builds houses in the middle of the woods, miles away from everything, without even a road to use, not even a road without a name."

"This can't be real," Bill said. "I had a house, you had a house, and I bet Max had a house, even though he's so long-winded he hasn't gotten to it yet. I had an air rifle, Max had a shotgun, what did you have?"

"My Dad's .22," Tony said. "Just a little thing—around us, nobody took a .22 all that seriously."

Max was looking seriously disgruntled. "What, we all had the same *dream?*"

"You said it wasn't a dream," said Chippie Traynor. "You said it was a memory."

"It felt like a memory, all right," Tony said. "Just the way Max described it—the way the ground felt under my feet, the smell of my mother's cooking."

"I wish your lady friend were here now, Traynor," Max said. "She'd be able to explain what's going on, wouldn't she?"

"I have a number of lady friends," Chippie said, calmly stuffing a little glazed cake into his mouth.

"All right, Max," Bill said. "Let's explore this. You come across this big house, right? And there's someone in it?"

"Eventually, there is," Max said, and Tony Flax nodded.

"Right. And you can't even tell what age he is—or even if it *is* a he, right?"

"It was hiding in the back of a room," Tony says. "When I thought it was a girl, it really scared me. I didn't want it to be a girl."

"I didn't, either," Max said. "Oh—imagine how that would feel, a girl hiding in the shadows at the back of a room."

"Only this never happened," Bill said. "If we all seem to remember this bizarre story, then none of us is really remembering it."

"Okay, but it was a boy," Tony said. "And he got older."

"Right there in that house," said Max. "I thought it was like watching my damnable father grow up right in front of my eyes. In what, six weeks?"

"About that," Tony said.

"And him in there all alone," said Bill. "Without so much as a stick of furniture. I thought that was one of the things that made it so frightening."

"Scared the shit out of me," Tony said. "When my dad came back from the war, sometimes he put on his uniform and tied us to the chairs. Tied us to the chairs!"

"I didn't think it was really going to injure him," Bill said.

"I didn't even think I'd hit him," Tony said.

"I knew damn well I'd hit him," Max said. "I wanted to blow his head off. But my dad lived another three years, and then the junkman finally ran him over."

"Max," Tony said, "you mentioned there was a tract house in Manship. What's a tract house?"

"It was where they printed the religious tracts, you ignoramus. You could go in there and pick them up for free. All of this was like child abuse, I'm telling you. Spare-the-rod stuff."

"It was like his eye exploded," Bill said. Absentmindedly, he took one of the untouched pastries from Max's plate and bit into it.

Max stared at him.

"They didn't change the goodies this morning," Bill said. "This thing is a little stale."

"I prefer my pastries stale," said Chippie Traynor.

"I prefer to keep mine for myself, and not have them lifted off my plate," said Max, sounding as though something were caught in his throat.

"The bullet went straight through the left lens of his glasses and right into his head," said Tony. "And when he raised his head, his eye was full of blood."

"Would you look out that window?" Max said in a loud voice.

Bill Messinger and Tony Flax turned to the window, saw nothing special—perhaps a bit more haze in the air than they expected—and looked back at the old publisher.

"Sorry," Max said. He passed a trembling hand over his face. "I think I'll go back to my room."

4

"Nobody visits me," Bill Messinger said to Tess Corrigan. She was taking his blood pressure, and appeared to be having a little trouble getting accurate numbers. "I don't even really remember how long I've been here, but I haven't had a single visitor."

"Haven't you now?" Tess squinted at the blood-pressure tube, sighed, and once again pumped the ball and tightened the band around his arm. Her breath contained a pure, razor-sharp whiff of alcohol.

"It makes me wonder, do I have any friends?"

Tess grunted with satisfaction and scribbled numbers on his chart. "Writers lead lonely lives," she told him. "Most of them aren't fit for human company, anyhow." She patted his wrist. "You're a lovely specimen, though."

"Tess, how long have I been here?"

"Oh, it was only a little while ago," she said. "And I believe it was raining at the time."

After she left, Bill watched television for a little while, but television, a frequent and dependable companion in his earlier life, seemed to have become intolerably stupid. He turned it off and for a time flipped through the pages of the latest book by a highly regarded contemporary novelist several decades younger than himself. He had bought the book before going into the hospital, thinking that during his stay he would have enough uninterrupted time to dig into the experience so many others had described as rich, complex, and marvelously nuanced, but he was having problems getting through it. The book bored him. The people were loathsome and the style was gelid. He kept wishing he had brought along some uncomplicated and professional trash he could use as a palate cleanser. By 10:00, he was asleep.

At 11:30, a figure wrapped in cold air appeared in his room, and he woke up as she approached. The woman coming nearer in the darkness must have been Molly, the Jamaican nurse who always charged in at this hour, but she did not give off Molly's arousing scent of fires in underground crypts. She smelled of damp weeds and muddy riverbanks. Bill did not want this version of Molly to get any closer to him than the end of his bed, and with his heart beating so violently that he could feel the limping rhythm of his heart, he commanded her to stop. She instantly obeyed.

He pushed the button to raise the head of his bed and tried to make her out as his body folded upright. The river-smell had intensified, and cold air streamed toward him. He had no desire at all to turn on any of the three lights at his disposal. Dimly, he could make out a thin, tallish figure with dead hair plastered to her face, wearing what seemed to be a long cardigan sweater, soaked through and (he thought) dripping onto the floor. In this figure's hands was a fat, unjacketed book stained dark by her wet fingers.

"I don't want you here," he said. "And I don't want to read that book, either. I've already read everything you ever wrote, but that was a long time ago."

The drenched figure glided forward and deposited the book between his feet. Terrified that he might recognize her face, Bill clamped his eyes shut and kept them shut until the odors of river water and mud had vanished from the air.

When Molly burst into the room to gather the new day's information the next morning, Bill Messinger realized that his night's visitation could have occurred only in a dream. Here was the well-known, predictable world around him, and every inch of it was a profound relief to him. Bill took in his bed, the little nest of monitors ready to be called upon should an emergency take place, his television and its remote-control device, the door to his spacious bathroom, the door to the hallway, as ever half-open. On the other side of his room lay the long window, now curtained for the sake of the night's sleep. And here, above all, was Molly, a one-woman Reality Principle, exuding the rich odor of burning graves as she tried to cut off his circulation with a blood-pressure machine. The bulk and massivity of her upper arms suggested that Molly's own blood pressure would have to be read by means of some other technology, perhaps steam gauge. The whites of her eyes shone with a faint trace of pink, leading Bill to speculate for a moment of wild improbability whether the ferocious night nurse indulged in marijuana.

"You're doing well, Mr. Postman," she said. "Making good progress."

"I'm glad to hear it," he said. "When do you think I'll be able to go home?"

"That is for the doctors to decide, not me. You'll have to bring it up with them." From a pocket hidden beneath her swags and pouches, she produced a white paper cup half-filled with pills and capsules of varying sizes and colors. She thrust it at him. "Morning meds. Gulp them down like a good boy, now." Her other hand held out a small plastic bottle of Poland Spring water, the provenance of which reminded Messinger of what Chippie Traynor had said about Maine. Deep woods, roads without names . . .

He upended the cup over his mouth, opened the bottle of water, and managed to get all his pills down at the first try.

Molly whirled around to leave with her usual sense of having had more than enough of her time wasted by the likes of him, and was halfway to the door before he remembered something that had been on his mind for the past few days.

"I haven't seen the *Times* since I don't remember when," he said. "Could you please get me a copy? I wouldn't even mind one that's a couple of days old."

Molly gave him a long, measuring look, then nodded her head. "Because many of our people find them so upsetting, we tend not to get the newspapers up here. But I'll see if I can locate one for you." She moved ponderously to the door and paused to look back at him again just before she walked out. "By the way, from now on you and your friends will have to get along without Mr. Traynor's company."

"Why?" Bill asked. "What happened to him?"

"Mr. Traynor is . . . gone, sir."

"Chippie died, you mean? When did that happen?" With a shudder, he remembered the figure from his dream. The smell of rotting weeds and wet riverbank awakened within him, and he felt as if she were once again standing before him.

"Did I say he was dead? What I said was, he is . . . *gone.*"

For reasons he could not identify, Bill Messinger did not go through the morning's rituals with his usual impatience. He felt slow-moving, reluctant to engage the day. In the shower, he seemed barely able to raise his arms. The water seemed brackish, and his soap all but refused to lather. The towels were stiff and thin, like the cheap towels he remembered from his youth. After he had succeeded in drying off at least most of the easily reachable parts of his body, he sat on his bed and listened to the breath laboring in and out of his body. Without his noticing, the handsome pin-striped suit had become as wrinkled and tired as he felt himself to be, and besides that he seemed to be out of clean shirts. He pulled a dirty one from the closet. His swollen feet took some time to ram into his black loafers.

Armored at last in the costume of great worldly success, Bill stepped out into the great corridor with a good measure of his old dispatch. He wished Max Baccarat had not called him a "jumped-up little fop" and a "damned little show pony" the other day, for he genuinely enjoyed good clothing, and it hurt him to think that others might take this simple pleasure, which after all did contain a moral element, as a sign of vanity. On the other hand, he should have thought twice before telling Max that he was a third-rate publisher and a sellout. Everybody knew that robe hadn't been a gift from Graham Greene, though. That myth represented nothing more than Max Baccarat's habit of portraying and presenting himself as an old-line publishing grandee, like Alfred Knopf.

The nursing station—what he liked to think of as "the command center"—was oddly understaffed this morning. In a landscape of empty desks and unattended computer monitors, Molly sat on a pair of stools she had placed side by side, frowning as ever down at some form she was obliged to work through. Bill nodded at her and received the nonresponse he had anticipated. Instead of turning left toward the Salon as he usually did, Bill decided to stroll over to the elevators and the cherrywood desk where diplomatic, red-jacketed Mr. Singh guided newcomers past his display of Casablanca lilies, tea roses, and lupines. On his perambulations through the halls, he often passed through Mr. Singh's tiny realm, and he found the man a kindly, reassuring presence.

Today, though, Mr. Singh seemed not to be on duty, and the great glass vase had been removed from his desk. OUT OF ORDER signs had been taped to the elevators.

Feeling a vague sense of disquiet, Bill retraced his steps and walked past the side of the nursing station to embark upon the long corridor that led to the north-facing window. Max Baccarat's room lay down this corridor, and Bill thought he might pay a call on the old gent. He could apologize for the insults he had given him, and perhaps receive an apology in return. Twice, Baccarat had thrown the word "little" at him, and Bill's cheeks stung as if he had been slapped. About the story, or the memory, or whatever it had been, however, Bill intended to say nothing. He did not believe that he, Max, and Tony Flax had dreamed of the same bizarre set of events, nor that they had experienced these decidedly dreamlike events in youth. The illusion that they had done so had been inspired by proximity and daily contact. The world of Floor 21 was as hermetic as a prison.

He came to Max's room and knocked at the half-open door. There was no reply. "Max?" he called out. "Feel like having a visitor?"

In the absence of a reply, he thought that Max might be asleep. It would do no harm to check on his old acquaintance. How odd, it occurred to him, to think that he and Max had both had relations with little Edie Wheadle. And Tony Flax, too. And that she should have died on this floor, unknown to them! *There* was someone to whom he rightly could have apologized—at the end, he had treated her quite badly. She had been the sort of girl, he thought, who almost expected to be treated badly. But far from being an excuse, that was the opposite, an indictment.

Putting inconvenient Edie Wheadle out of his mind, Bill moved past the bathroom and the "reception" area into the room proper, there to find Max Baccarat not in bed as he had expected, but beyond it and seated in one of the low, slightly cantilevered chairs, which he had turned to face the window.

"Max?"

The old man did not acknowledge his presence in any way. Bill noticed that he was not wearing the splendid blue robe, only his white pajamas, and his feet were bare. Unless he had fallen asleep, he was staring at the window and appeared to have been doing so for some time. His silvery hair was mussed and stringy. As Bill approached, he took in the rigidity of Max's head and neck, the stiff tension in his shoulders. He came around the foot of the bed and at last saw the whole of the old man's body, stationed sideways to him as it faced the window. Max was gripping the arms of the chair and leaning forward. His mouth hung open, and his lips had been drawn back. His eyes, too, were open, hugely, as they stared straight ahead.

With a little thrill of anticipatory fear, Bill glanced at the window. What he saw, haze shot through with streaks of light, could hardly have brought Max Baccarat to this pitch. His face seemed rigid with terror. Then Bill realized that this had nothing to do with terror, and Max had suffered a great, paralyzing stroke. That was the explanation for the pathetic scene before him. He jumped to the side of the bed and pushed the call button for the nurse. When he did not get an immediate response, he pushed it again, twice, and held the button down for several seconds. Still no soft footsteps came from the corridor.

A folded copy of the *Times* lay on Max's bed, and with a sharp, almost painful sense of hunger for the million vast and minuscule dramas taking place outside Governor General, he realized that what he had said to Molly was no more than the literal truth: it seemed weeks since he had seen a newspaper. With the justification that Max would have no use for it, Bill snatched up the paper and felt, deep in the core of his being, a real greed for its contents—devouring the columns of print would be akin to gobbling up great bits of the world. He tucked the neat, folded package of the *Times* under his arm and left the room.

"Nurse," he called. It came to him that he had never learned the real name of the woman they called Molly Goldberg. "Hello? There's a man in trouble down here!"

He walked quickly down the hallway in what he perceived as a deep, unsettling silence. "Hello, nurse!" he called, at least in part to hear at least the sound of his own voice.

When Bill reached the deserted nurses' station, he rejected the impulse to say, "Where is everybody?" The Night Visitor no longer occupied her pair of stools, and the usual chiaroscuro had deepened into a murky darkness. It was though they had pulled the plugs and stolen away.

"I don't get this," Bill said. "*Doctors* might bail, but nurses don't."

He looked up and down the corridor and saw only a gray carpet and a row of half-open doors. Behind one of those doors sat Max Baccarat, who had once been something of a friend. Max was destroyed, Bill thought; damage so severe could not be repaired. Like a film of greasy dust, the sense descended upon him that he was wasting his time. If the doctors and nurses were elsewhere, as seemed the case, nothing could be done for Max until their return. Even after that, in all likelihood very little could be done for poor old Max. His heart failure had been a symptom of a wider systemic problem.

But still. He could not just walk away and ignore Max's plight. Messinger turned around and paced down the corridor to the door where the nameplate read Anthony Flax. "Tony," he said. "Are you in there? I think Max had a stroke."

He rapped on the door and pushed it all the way open. Dreading what he might find, he walked into the room. "Tony?" He already knew the room was empty, and when he was able to see the bed, all was as he had expected: an empty bed, an empty chair, a blank television screen, and blinds pulled down to keep the day from entering.

Bill left Tony's room, turned left, then took the hallway that led past the Salon. A man in an unclean janitor's uniform, his back to Bill, was removing the Mapplethorpe photographs from the wall and loading them facedown onto a wheeled cart.

"What are you doing?" he asked.

The man in the janitor uniform looked over his shoulder and said, "I'm doing my job, that's what I'm doing." He had greasy hair, a low forehead, and an acne-scarred face with deep furrows in the cheeks.

"But why are you taking down those pictures?"

The man turned around to face him. He was strikingly ugly, and his ugliness seemed part of his intention, as if he had chosen it. "Gee, buddy, why do you suppose I'd do something like that? To upset *you?* Well, I'm sorry if you're upset, but you had nothing to do with this. They tell me to do stuff like this, I do it. End of story." He pushed his face forward, ready for the next step.

"Sorry," Bill said. "I understand completely. Have you seen a doctor or a nurse up here in the past few minutes? A man on the other side of the floor just had a stroke. He needs medical attention."

"Too bad, but I don't have anything to do with doctors. The man I deal with is my supervisor, and supervisors don't wear white coats, and they don't carry stethoscopes. Now if you'll excuse me, I'll be on my way."

"But I need a doctor!"

"You look okay to me," the man said, turning away. He took the last photograph from the wall and pushed his cart through the metal doors that marked the boundary of the realm ruled by Tess Corrigan, Molly Goldberg, and their colleagues. Bill followed him through, and instantly found himself in a functional, green-painted corridor lit by fluorescent lighting and lined with locked doors. The janitor pushed his trolley around a corner and disappeared.

"Is anybody here?" Bill's voice carried through the empty hallways. "A man here needs a doctor!"

The corridor he was in led to another, which led to another, which went past a small, deserted nurses' station and ended at a huge, flat door with a sign that said MEDICAL PERSONNEL ONLY. Bill pushed at the door, but it was locked. He had the feeling that he could wander through these corridors for hours and find nothing but blank walls and locked doors. When he returned to the metal doors and pushed through to the private wing, relief flooded through him, making him feel light-headed.

The Salon invited him in—he wanted to sit down, he wanted to catch his breath and see if any of the little cakes had been set out yet. He had forgotten to order breakfast, and hunger was making him weak. Bill put his hand on one of the pebble-glass doors and saw an indistinct figure seated near the table. For a moment, his heart felt cold, and he hesitated before he opened the door.

Tony Flax was bent over in his chair, and what Bill Messinger noticed first was that the critic was wearing one of the thin hospital gowns that tied at the neck and the back. His trench coat lay puddled on the floor. Then he saw that Flax appeared to be weeping. His hands were clasped to his face, and his back rose and fell with jerky, uncontrolled movements.

"Tony?" he said. "What happened to you?"

Flax continued to weep silently, with the concentration and selfishness of a small child.

"Can I help you, Tony?" Bill asked.

When Flax did not respond, Bill looked around the room for the source of his distress. Half-filled coffee cups stood on the little tables, and petits fours lay jumbled and scattered over the plates and the white table. As he watched, a cockroach nearly two inches long burrowed out of a little square of white chocolate and disappeared around the back of a Battenburg cake. The cockroach looked as shiny and polished as a new pair of black shoes.

Something was moving on the other side of the window, but Bill Messinger wanted nothing to do with it. "Tony," he said, "I'll be in my room."

Down the corridor he went, the tails of his suit jacket flapping behind him. A heavy, liquid pressure built up in his chest, and the lights seemed to darken, then grow brighter again. He remembered Max, his mind gone, staring openmouthed at his window: what had he seen?

Bill thought of Chippie Traynor, one of his molelike eyes bloodied behind the shattered lens of his glasses.

At the entrance to his room, he hesitated once again as he had outside the Salon, fearing that if he went in, he might not be alone. But of course he would be alone, for apart from the janitor no one else on Floor 21 was capable of movement. Slowly, making as little noise as possible, he slipped around his door and entered his room. It looked exactly as it had when he had awakened that morning. The younger author's book lay discarded on his bed, the monitors awaited an emergency, the blinds covered the long window. Bill thought the wildly alternating pattern of light and dark that moved across the blinds proved nothing. Freaky New York weather, you never knew what it was going to do. He did not hear odd noises, like half-remembered voices, calling to him from the other side of the glass.

As he moved nearer to the foot of the bed, he saw on the floor the bright jacket of the book he had decided not to read, and knew that in the night it had fallen from his movable tray. The book on his bed had no jacket, and at first he had no idea where it came from. When he remembered the circumstances under which he had seen this book—or one a great deal like it—he felt revulsion, as though it were a great slug.

Bill turned his back on the bed, swung his chair around, and plucked the newspaper from under his arm. After he had scanned the headlines without making much effort to take them in, habit led him to the obituaries on the last two pages of the financial section. As soon as he had folded the pages back, a photograph of a sly, mild face with a recessed chin and tiny spectacles lurking above an overgrown nose levitated up from the columns of newsprint. The header announced CHARLES CHIPP TRAYNOR, POPULAR WAR HISTORIAN, TARRED BY SCANDAL.

Helplessly, Bill read the first paragraph of Chippie's obituary. Four days past, this once-renowned historian whose career had been destroyed by charges of plagiarism and fraud had committed suicide by leaping from the window of his fifteenth-story apartment on the Upper West Side.

Four days ago? Bill thought. It seemed to him that was when Chippie Traynor had first appeared in the Salon. He dropped the paper, with the effect that Traynor's fleshy nose and mild eyes peered up at him from the floor. The terrible little man seemed to be everywhere, despite having *gone*. He could sense Chippie Traynor floating outside his window like a small, inoffensive balloon from Macy's Thanksgiving Day Parade. Children would say, "Who's that?" and their parents would look up, shield their eyes, shrug, and say, "I don't know, hon. Wasn't he in a Disney cartoon?" Only he was not in a Disney cartoon, and the children and their parents could not see him, and he wasn't at all cute. One of his eyes had been injured. This Chippie Traynor, not the one that had given them a view of his backside in the Salon, hovered outside Bill Messinger's window, whispering the wretched and insinuating secrets of the despised, the contemptible, the rejected and fallen from grace.

Bill turned from the window and took a single step into the nowhere that awaited him. He had nowhere to go, he knew, so nowhere had to be where he was going. It was probably going to be a lot like this place, only less comfortable. Much, *much* less comfortable. With nowhere to go, he reached out his hand and picked up the dull brown book lying at the foot of his bed. Bringing it toward his body felt like reeling in some monstrous fish that struggled against the line. There were faint watermarks on the front cover, and it bore a faint, familiar smell. When he had it within reading distance, Bill turned the spine up and read the title and author's name: *In the Middle of the Trenches*, by Charles Chipp Traynor. It was the book he had blurbed. Max Baccarat had published it, and Tony Flax had rhapsodized over it in the Sunday *Times* book review section. About a hundred pages from the end, a bookmark in the shape of a thin silver cord with a hook at one end protruded from the top of the book.

Bill opened the book at the place indicated, and the slender bookmark slithered downward like a living thing. Then the hook caught the top of the pages, and its length hung shining and swaying over the bottom edge. No longer able to resist, Bill read some random sentences, then two long paragraphs. This section undoubtedly had been lifted from the oral histories, and it recounted an odd event in the life of a young man who, years before his induction into the armed forces, had come upon a strange house deep in the piney woods of East Texas and been so unsettled by what he had seen through its windows that he brought a rifle with him on his next visit. Bill realized that he had never read this part of the book. In fact, he had written his blurb after merely skimming through the first two chapters. He thought Max had read even less of the book than he had. In a hurry to meet his deadline, Tony Flax had probably read the first half.

At the end of his account, the former soldier said, "In the many times over the years when I thought about this incident, it always seemed to me that the man I shot was myself. It seemed my own eye I had destroyed, my own socket that bled."

BENTLEY LITTLE

We Find Things Old

We Find Things Old.

It is the name of our company and a fair description of what we do. We are paid scavengers, tracking down toys from childhood, finding particular decorating items to complete a thematic motif, scouring junk yards and thrift stores and garage sales for the castoff item of one person's life that is the missing jigsaw piece to another's happiness. It's a good job, an interesting job, a challenging job. A fun job.

Or at least, it started out that way.

Our clientele has always been rather exclusive due to the triviality of our profession, running primarily to hip members of the idle rich, and to the major movie studios. It's from the studios that we get most of our business, obtaining period pieces for set designers and prop departments, locating the idiosyncratic items that directors feel necessary to fulfill their visual vision, and it was with a movie studio that the trouble started.

We were under deadline, scouting for freestanding 50s lamps and art studio equipment to fill out one scene of a serious multi-decade love story set in the trendy and ever-changing world of New York bohemianism. Everything else had been found by Tim Hendricks, the film's art director, but the director of the movie, a bad-tempered Brit with an oversized ego, vowed that there would be no fudging with the reality of even the most minor detail on this picture, and instead of allowing the prop department to dummy up some retro lamps and easels, he called us in.

We were given a deadline of a week by the director, but the executive producer told us with a nudge-nudge wink-wink that our stock would not go down with the studio if we failed to find the items at all. I think he wanted to teach the director a lesson and use us as the instrument, but it's always been a matter of personal pride with us to provide the goods as contracted, and though the deadline was more than a little unreasonable, we were determined to meet it.

We had a meeting to discuss strategy, and Tony said he remembered seeing a slew of kitsch items in a Bargain Land in the desert outside Lancaster a few months back, so on the day after we were given the assignment, he and I drove out to the Mojave, leaving Carole and Sims to hold down the fort and make scouting calls to our usual L.A. sources.

The Bargain Land was an empty furniture store in an undeveloped section outside of town, and we found it with no problem, letting a series of paint-peeled billboards and their arrows guide us. We found a lamp all right, and an easel, but the store's stock of artist studio equipment was pitiful, to say the least. The owner, a bearded desert rat who looked like Gabby Hayes and cultivated that resemblance by dressing the part, told us that there was an empty house a few miles down the road that used to be home to a commune. "There was lots of artists there," he said, "but when the leader got busted for pot, the rest of 'em all went their separate ways. They left most everything. The house itself's been pretty much looted, but there's a lot of stuff still rotting in the sand outside, shit that no one else wanted. I think most of the art stuff's still there."

We got directions, thanked him by slipping him an extra five, and walked back out to the van.

"We going to check it out?" Tony asked.

"Sounds like late sixties, early seventies," I said.

"Yeah, but they were poor hippies. If they did have art supplies they were probably secondhand. I bet we could salvage something."

I nodded. "Let's do it."

At the time of its last paint job, obviously several decades back, the small brick house had been coated in shocking pink, with a bright yellow, smiling wavy-ray sun painted on the garage door. The color had faded and chipped in the face of the desert heat and wind, giving it an almost hip, almost current look, but the inside of the building could make no such claims. The multicolored walls were filled with punched holes and flaked peeling plaster, the few items left in the rooms smashed and broken and thrown into piles. Everything was covered with a surprisingly thick layer of sand.

I looked at Tony, sighed. "Why don't you go through the rooms, see what you can find. I'll check outside, in the back."

He nodded and headed immediately toward a pile of what appeared to be bedsprings and blocks of wood in the corner of the room. I walked through the beer-can-littered kitchen and out the back door. Before me, the skeleton of a motorcycle was sticking out of a small hill of sand next to an empty picture frame and a barrel stove. I walked over and pulled the frame out of the sand, but one of the sides was broken and it was too damaged to be of any use. I scanned the area, saw old oil drums, a barbecue, and the cross-post of a downed clothesline. Where were the art supplies?

My eye was caught by a flash of light, a reflection of sun near a patch of brown weeds, and I made my way through the detritus toward it. The reflection was probably coming from a broken mirror or glass shard, but it couldn't hurt to look. Maybe it was part of a sheet metal sculpture or something.

I reached the weeds and stopped.

An object was lying half-buried in the sand before me.

A humanoid figure the size of a small dog.

I stared at the—thing—in front of me, feeling suddenly chilled. I was not quite sure what it was, but I did not like it and there were goosebumps on my arms as I gazed upon its form. The object looked almost like a doll, but something about it bespoke organic origins. The face was monkey brown and made of a wrinkled shiny material, although its features did not resemble anything I'd ever seen. The eyes were missing, their empty-holed sockets proportionately too small for the rest of the face. There was no nose, no nostrils of any kind, and the mouth was a strangely curved slit which followed the form of a smile but did not give the appearance of mirth. On top of the head was a floppy red clown's hat, and the rest of the body was covered in a garish mummy wrap made from the same material. Elf shoes with bells covered the foot that was not buried under sand, white gloves were on the hands.

Despite having lain in the desert for who-knew-how-many years, the figure was not rotted or at all decrepit. The colors of its clothes were not even faded. Yet, somehow, the object gave the appearance of great age, and in my mind I saw dinosaurs trampling through a primeval forest—while the figure in its gaudy clothes lay unmoving at the foot of a prehistoric tree, looking exactly as it did right now.

That scared me, somehow.

"Anything there?"

I jumped at the sound of Tony's voice.

I wanted to move away from the figure, to steer him toward a different area of the yard so that he wouldn't see it, but before I could even make a move in that direction he was at my side.

He whistled appreciatively. "That's a find," he said, looking down.

I shook my head. "I don't think it's right for this project."

"Are you kidding? Strip off the clown duds and we got ourselves a clay sculpture."

"It's not clay."

"It'll look like it on film."

He was right. We were under deadline, and this was free and it fit the bill. But I still didn't like it. There was something about the figure that bothered me, though I couldn't quite put my finger on the reason. "Maybe Carole and Sims have found something," I said.

"And maybe not. I say we snag it."

He bent down and reached for it, but I was quicker than he was, and I grabbed one of the figure's arms, yanking it out of the sand. I didn't want Tony to touch it. Even through the material, the form felt uncomfortably alien to my touch, and I had to resist the urge to drop it and step on it.

"We'd better get going," Tony said. "It's at least an hour ride, and we still have some more scouting to do this afternoon."

"Okay," I agreed.

I tried not to let the disgust show on my face as I carried the thing back to the van.

On the freeway on the way back, the bells on the figure's feet jingled as we bounced over the bumps in the road.

It stayed in my mind, that thing we found in the desert, and though we soon moved on to another job, trying to find a mint '56 Wurlitzer pipe organ for a super-agent who was turning the barn on his canyon property into a rec-room replica of the pizza palace owned by his father, the figure still haunted me.

I dreamed of it at night, and in my dreams it had claws.

We were, of course, invited to the movie's premiere nine months later. The stars of the film and their friends in the industry paraded in front of the paparazzi on their way into the theater, and a host of wannabes and has-beens arrived as well, hoping to get their faces on *Entertainment Tonight*, or at least on one of the local L.A. newscasts.

We sat in the back row, and I don't know about Carole, Sims, or Tony, but I paid more attention to the sets and art direction than I did the acting and the plot. That's always true for me. Even with a great movie, it isn't until my second viewing that I can enjoy the totality of a film. This, however, was not, by any stretch of the imagination, a great movie, and it was clear long before the end credits that the studio had a dog on its hands.

The stars and starlets who'd been so happily and prominently on display going into the theater avoided the *Entertainment Tonight* cameras on the way out, not wanting to badmouth their friends who were involved with the picture or go on record endorsing an obvious loser.

I still could not get the figure out of my mind. It had been positioned far in the background of an artist's studio, as a failed sculpture or an aborted attempt at something or other, and had been onscreen for a total of no more than a minute, half of that out of focus, yet it had leaped out at me and had so dominated the scene in which it had been featured that I had not been able to look at or concentrate on anything else.

I wondered if anyone else had had the same reaction, but I was afraid to ask.

The strange thing was that the director had not stripped off the clown hat and clothes. That disconcerted me. After all the effort that had gone into making even the most minor detail absolutely authentic, the director had decided to leave in the artist's garish doll. Stripped, it could have passed for a work-in-progress or a failed experiment, but as it was, it seemed jarringly out of place.

I said nothing to anyone, though. Not to Tony or Carole or Sims. Not even to Val, my wife.

We all went together to the post-premiere party.

The next morning, I read in the *Times* that Susan Bellamy, the female star of the movie, had died of a drug overdose.

Val and I read the article together, me looking over her shoulder. She folded the paper when she was through and sat there for a moment, staring silently out the window of the breakfast nook at the other homes on the hill. "It had to be an accident," she said finally. "Susan was fine last night."

An accident.

Logically, it made sense. The movie had been a dud, but the general consensus had been that Susan's star power remained undiminished, and she alone had emerged from the film unscathed. There was no way she could have been depressed enough over first-night reaction to the movie to do something this drastic. Besides, it was well known that she often celebrated to excess, that she liked to party a little too hard. An accident was likely. Probable, even.

But I did not believe it.

I don't know why. And I don't know why I was so certain. Intuition, I guess. Or maybe it was because I had come into contact with that—thing—myself. But no matter what the paper said, no matter what anyone else thought, I knew what had really happened. In my heart, in my gut, I knew.

She had died because she'd been filmed in a scene with the doll.

It made no sense on any sort of rational level, but with unshakable certainty I knew it to be true, and when I called Tony an hour or so later and learned that Robert Finch had died as well, had committed suicide this morning by slitting his wrists in his Beverly Hills bathtub, I could not say that I was completely surprised.

Finch had played the artist and had been in the scene with Susan.

And the doll.

I told Tony that I'd be late today, if I showed up at all. I asked him to go ahead with the indie project we were supposed to be working on, and after giving Val the bare facts of Finch's death, telling her nothing, I headed over to the studio.

The place was in an uproar. Both stars dying on the same morning had put people into a panic; and mourning, damage control, and hype were being conducted simultaneously in the suites of offices that served as the studio's nerve center. I bypassed the hurricane's eye, got myself a pass from Security and, alone and ignored, made my way to the props building. I knew Tim Hendricks would be around somewhere, since he was working on a low-budget horror flick with a scheduled release date four months from now, and after following a trail of grunts and nodded heads, I finally found him dummying up a breakaway staircase on one of the soundstages.

I cleared my throat to get his attention and he looked up from his work.

"You heard?" I asked.

He straightened, nodded. "Who hasn't?" He walked toward me.

"I need to ask you a question," I said. I wasn't sure how to bring it up, but I plunged right in. "What did you do with the props from that movie? The sculptures and things in the background of the art studio?"

He frowned. "Why?"

"I want to buy one of the pieces back."

"Which one?"

"It's a figure about a foot high. With a clown suit. Looks like it was made out of—"

"That." His eyes widened in recognition and an involuntary look of revulsion passed over his features. "You don't want that."

"Yes, I do."

"No, you don't. It's . . ." He glanced down. "It's unclean."

I stared at Hendricks. He was probably the most rational, practical, and least superstitious man I'd ever met. Even in an industry crawling with cynics, with men and women who would break all of the Ten Commandments and then some if it would mean a bigger opening weekend, Hendricks stood out. He scoffed at all actors' superstitions, scorned all religious conversations, and matter-of-factly admitted his disbelief in God or anything other than the material world around him.

Yet he was afraid of the doll.

I shivered, remembering the chill I'd felt in the desert that first day.

"I know why you want it," he said.

I looked at him, not challenging him, not explaining, not saying anything.

He met my gaze. "I know what's going through your mind, and maybe you're right. Maybe it did have something to do with Sue and Rob. Then again, maybe it didn't. Either way, I don't think you should be fooling with it."

"I don't want to fool with it," I said.

"You're going to do what, then? Harness it? Try to use it on someone you don't like?"

"I'm going to put it back where I found it."

He was silent after that, staring down at his feet, wiping his hands nervously on his jeans. "I believe you," he said finally. "And I'd give it to you if I could. But it's gone. I looked for it myself this morning. I don't know if it was farmed out by Taylor or . . ." He left the sentence unfinished, and I had a sudden mental picture of the figure crawling out of the building on its own, that mirthless half-smile frozen on its thin mouth as it made its way through the darkened studio at night.

"What were you going to do with it?" I asked.

"Torch it," he said. "Acetylene."

I nodded. "If you find it," I said, "go ahead. But I want you to let me know."

"Yeah." He turned away, obviously not wanting to talk, and I watched him return to his staircase.

I went out the way I'd come in, troubled.

I told Tony about the figure and my suspicions, since he'd been with me when we found it, but I made him promise not to say anything to Sims or Carole aside from asking them to keep an eye out for it. He did not believe me, but he humored me, and under the circumstances I knew that was probably the best I could hope for.

I did not talk to Val about it at all.

It was nearly a year before I saw it again, lying amidst a bed full of dolls and stuffed animals in the room of a pampered little rich girl in a heartwarming comedy.

The girl died immediately after the film's premiere, supposedly a victim of an undetected congenital heart defect.

No one at that studio, from the set designer to the props men, could tell me what had happened to the figure.

A month later, three elderly stars from Hollywood's golden age who had banded together to do a TV caper about a gang of over-the-hill bank robbers died in a plane crash.

The movie had been broadcast the day before.

The doll had been in the window of a pawnshop the three thieves had comically robbed in order to obtain handguns.

Outwardly, my life continued on as normal. At least I think it did. I took jobs and performed them. I was a friend to my friends, a husband to my wife, an employer to my employees. But inside, I felt as though I were a murderer. I knew that I had caused the death of six people, six actors.

At least six.

Maybe there were others.

I had never thought of that before, and I went to the library and looked up all of the movie people, all of the actors, directors, writers, or producers who had died within the past year. Some of them, I knew, had had films released shortly before their deaths, and I went to a video store and rented those films.

I was prepared for the worst, but, to my surprise, I did not see the figure in any of the movies.

Thank God.

I began thinking about the doll more and more, trying to figure out what it was, where it had come from. I had surreptitiously kept tabs on most of the major players connected with Susan and Finch's film, but there had been no other deaths, and my theory that those two had died because they'd been *filmed* with the doll was reinforced.

My mind kept returning to that first day in the desert, and more than once I wondered what would have happened had I not seen that flash of reflected sunlight in the patch of weeds, if I had not walked into the backyard of the commune house. Most likely, the thing would still be lying half-buried in the sand. It would probably have lain there for years, perhaps decades, the desert covering it up before it was discovered by anyone.

Tony had a part in this, too, I realized. It was he who had convinced me, against my better judgment, to take the doll home. Part of this was on his head. But, ultimately, the blame rested with me. I was the boss. I could have said no, I could have made the decision not to take the figure with us.

But I had not done so.

We Find Things Old.

The name of our company seemed almost prophetic now.

Life went on. I was no longer as excited or as stimulated by my job as I had been, but I had house payments to make and car payments to make and Val was talking about starting a family, and, truth be told, I could not think of anything else that interested me at all. I kept on keeping on, as the song said, but the shine had definitely gone out of Tinseltown for me, and each time I did a studio job, I kept wondering if the people on this project would stumble across the figure some place, if the stars I met would die.

I ran into Hendricks periodically. I even worked with him on a nostalgic coming-of-age film. But we did not speak of the doll.

I finally saw it again two days ago.

On my birthday.

It was one of my presents.

At least I think it was.

Already the memory is fuzzy, the facts jumbled. Val had taken me to Musso and Frank's, where I was supposed to be surprised by a party. The place was packed with friends, acquaintances, clients, and there was a mountain of presents, both real and joke, piled high on two pushed-together tables. We mingled, drank, danced, drank, ate, and drank some more, and by the time I got around to the presents in the wee hours of the morning, I was not sure which were from whom. Nor did I care. The house photographer was recording this for posterity on 35 millimeter, one of Val's friends was videotaping it, and I was nearly through opening presents when I happened to glance next to me and saw, on top of the boxes and wrapping paper, the doll.

It looked just as I remembered it—same shiny brown face and ancient alien features, same brightly colored clown garb—and I did not realize until that moment how clearly and permanently its appearance had been etched upon my mind.

There was a flash as the photographer took my picture, and I suddenly understood that my image and *its* image were being recorded on film.

And videotape.

I leaped up and over the table, knocking down most of my presents. Everyone must have thought I'd gone crazy. I grabbed the camera from the photographer's hand and smashed it against the tabletop before throwing it onto the floor and stomping on it. I looked around for Val's friend with the camcorder, but she was obviously aware of my intentions and was already beating a hasty retreat toward the women's room. I shoved my friends aside, ran through the crowd, caught the woman just inside the lounge, and yanked the camcorder from her hands, using all of my strength to throw it on the floor. The machine was tough and didn't break, but I bent down, popped out the videocassette, and smashed it beneath the heel of my shoe.

I apologized profusely, but everyone was nervous and unsure of how to react, and several people were already making for the exit. I heard the muttered phrase "too much to drink" and the words "nose candy," but I ignored them and shrugged off Val's and Tony's worried inquires as I made my way back to the table.

The figure was still lying on top of the boxes.

"I have to go," I said. "There's something I have to do." I grabbed the thing's arm, and felt again that repulsive unnaturalness beneath the material.

"Wait," Tony said. "I don't think you're—"

Across the room, I saw Hendricks. He met my gaze and nodded grimly. He understood.

"I have to go!" I said.

Holding tightly to the figure's long thin arm, I ran out of the restaurant and jumped into my car.

I drove.

It was dawn by the time I reached the hippie house, sunrise a pink glow on the flat eastern edge of the desert. I parked, pulled a flashlight out of the glove compartment, and grabbed the doll. I had thrown it in the back seat for the trip, and more than once I had worried that it would begin moving back there, trying to get me, to strangle me from behind, but I had resisted the urge to turn around and look, and it lay now in the same position into which it had been thrown.

I hurried around the side of the house.

Though there'd obviously been wind and rain in the two intervening years, though entire drifts had grown, shrunk, or moved, the small niche in the sand where I had found the figure remained undisturbed by nature. Sand had not filled in the small hole, rain had not eroded the contours of its outline. It lay at the foot of the weed patch, vaguely humanoid in shape, a miniature grave.

Gingerly, I took the figure and, using only my fingers to hold the tip of its clown hat, dropped it into the hole. The small bells on its feet tinkled once as the figure fell perfectly into the opening, and then sand settled around the figure, covering the bottom half and the upper left side until it looked exactly the same as it had the day I found it.

I walked to the car without looking up.

I drove home to L.A.

It has been two days now, and I don't know what is going to happen to me. Susan didn't last two days. Neither did Finch. Neither did the others. I see this as a good sign.

I think the fact that I destroyed both the film and the videotape before they could be seen or shown might have saved my life. I am not sure. But I think so. I hope so.

Val still doesn't understand.

Tony does a little.

I'm not sure why I didn't torch the figure as Hendricks planned to do, or why I didn't destroy it in some other way. I was acting on instinct that night, not thinking clearly, and my instincts told me to return it to the desert, to its home. That is what I did. It felt right then, and it feels right now, and I think that perhaps all is as it should be.

We'll see.

All I can do now is wait.

And pray that no one else in the restaurant had a camera that night.

ELIZABETH HAND

Wonderwall

Elizabeth Hand is the author of seven novels, including Winterlong, Waking the Moon, *and* Mortal Love, *a luminous and bewitching fantasy which weaves together pre-Raphaelite painters, rock stars, and the mysterious, recurring figure of a female muse. Hand has published two short story collections,* Last Summer at Mars Hill *and* Bibliomancy, *which won the World Fantasy Award in 2004. Her short fiction has appeared in* The Magazine of Fantasy & Science Fiction, Asimov's Science Fiction, Best New Horror, *and* Conjunctions. *She won both the World Fantasy and Nebula Award for her novella "Last Summer at Mars Hill." Hand lives on the coast of Maine, where she is currently working on a novel called* Generation Loss.

"Wonderwall" appeared in the anthology Flights. *Hand says, "Nearly everything in this story pretty much happened exactly as it's written here, including the parts about me seeing things. I changed the names of my friends; they know who they are. For the record, drinking cough syrup is a really bad idea."*

—K.L. & G.G

A long time ago, nearly thirty years now, I had a friend who was waiting to be discovered. His name was David Baldanders; we lived with two other friends in one of the most disgusting places I've ever seen, and certainly the worst that involved me signing a lease.

Our apartment was a two-bedroom third-floor walkup in Queenstown, a grim brick enclave just over the District line in Hyattsville, Maryland. Queenstown Apartments were inhabited mostly by drug dealers and bikers who met their two-hundred-dollars-a-month leases by processing speed and bad acid in their basement rooms; the upper floors were given over to wasted welfare mothers from P. G. County and students from the University of Maryland, Howard, and the University of the Archangels and Saint John the Divine.

The Divine, as students called it, was where I'd come three years earlier to study acting. I wasn't actually expelled until the end of my junior year, but midway through that term, my roommate, Marcella, and I were kicked out of our campus dormitory, precipitating the move to Queenstown. Even for the mid-1970s, our behavior was excessive; I was only surprised the university officials waited so long before getting rid of us. Our parents were assessed for damages to our dorm room, which were extensive; among other things, I'd painted one wall floor-to-ceiling with the image from the cover of *Transformer*, surmounted by *JE SUIS DAMNE PAR L'ARC-EN-CIEL* scrawled in foot-high letters. Decades later, someone who'd lived in the room after I left told me that, year after year, Rimbaud's words would bleed through each successive layer of new paint. No one ever understood what they meant.

Our new apartment was at first an improvement on the dorm room, and Queenstown itself was an efficient example of a closed ecosystem. The bikers manufactured Black Beauties, which they sold to the students and welfare mothers upstairs, who would zigzag a few hundred feet across a wasteland of shattered glass and broken concrete to the Queenstown Restaurant, where I worked making pizzas that they would then cart back to their apartments. The pizza boxes piled up in the halls, drawing armies of roaches. My friend Oscar lived in the next building; whenever he visited our flat, he'd push open the door, pause, and then look over his shoulder dramatically.

"Listen—!" he'd whisper.

He'd stamp his foot, just once, and hold up his hand to command silence. Immediately we heard what sounded like surf washing over a gravel beach. In fact, it was the susurrus of hundreds of cockroaches clittering across the warped parquet floors in retreat.

There were better places to await discovery.

David Baldanders was my age, nineteen. He wasn't much taller than me, with long thick black hair and a soft-featured face: round cheeks, full red lips between a downy black beard and mustache, slightly crooked teeth much yellowed from nicotine, small well-shaped hands. He wore an earring and a bandanna that he tied, pirate-style, over his head; filthy jeans, flannel shirts, filthy black Converse high-tops that flapped when he walked. His eyes were beautiful—indigo, black-lashed, soulful. When he laughed, people stopped in their tracks—he sounded like Herman Munster, that deep, goofy, foghorn voice at odds with his fey appearance.

We met in the Divine's Drama Department and immediately recognized each other as kindred spirits. Neither attractive nor talented enough to be in the center of the golden circle of aspiring actors that included most of our friends, we made ourselves indispensable by virtue of being flamboyant, unapologetic fuckups. People laughed when they saw us coming. They laughed even louder when we left. But David and I always made a point of laughing loudest of all.

"Can you fucking believe that?" A morning, it could have been any morning: I stood in the hall and stared in disbelief at the Department's sitting area. White walls, a few plastic chairs and tables overseen by the glass windows of the secretarial office. This was where the other students chain-smoked and waited, day after day, for news: casting announcements for Department plays; cattle calls for commercials, trade shows, summer reps. Above all else, the Department prided itself on graduating Working Actors—a really successful student might get called back for a walk-on in *Days of Our Lives*. My voice rose loud enough that heads turned. "It looks like a fucking *dentist's* office."

"Yeah, well, Roddy just got cast in a Trident commercial," David said, and we both fell against the wall, howling.

Rejection fed our disdain, but it was more than that. Within weeks of arriving at the Divine, I felt betrayed. I wanted—hungered for, thirsted for, craved like drink or drugs—High Art. So did David. We'd come to the Divine expecting Paris in the 1920s, Swinging London, Summer of Love in the Haight.

We were misinformed.

What we got was elocution taught by the department head's wife; tryouts where tone-deaf students warbled numbers from *The Magic Show*; Advanced Speech classes where, week after week, the beefy department head would declaim Macduff's speech—*All my pretty ones? Did you say all?*—never failing to move himself to tears.

And there was that sitting area. Just looking at it made me want to take a sledgehammer to the walls: all those smug faces above issues of *Variety* and *Theatre Arts*; all those sheets of white paper neatly taped to white cinder block with lists of names beneath: callbacks, cast lists, passing exam results. My name was never there. Nor was David's.

We never had a chance. We had no choice.

We took the sledgehammer to our heads.

Weekends my suitemate visited her parents, and while she was gone, David and I would break into her dorm room. We drank her vodka and listened to her copy of *David Live*, playing "Diamond Dogs" over and over as we clung to each other, smoking, dancing cheek to cheek. After midnight we'd cadge a ride down to Southwest, where abandoned warehouses had been turned into gay discos—the Lost and Found, Grand Central Station, Washington Square, Half Street. A solitary neon pentacle glowed atop the old *Washington Star* printing plant; we heard gunshots, sirens, the faint bass throb from funk bands at the Washington Coliseum, ceaseless boom and echo of trains uncoupling in the rail yards that extended from Union Station.

I wasn't a looker. My scalp was covered with henna-stiffened orange stubble that had been cut over three successive nights by a dozen friends. Marcella had pierced my ear with a cork and a needle and a bottle of Gordon's gin. David usually favored one long drop earring, and sometimes I'd wear its mate. Other times I'd shove a safety pin through my ear, then run a dog leash from the safety pin around my neck. I had two-inch-long black-varnished fingernails that caught fire when I lit my cigarettes from a Bic lighter. I kohled my eyes and lips, used Marcella's Chloé perfume, shoved myself into Marcella's expensive jeans even though they were too small for me.

But mostly I wore a white poet's blouse or frayed striped boatneck shirt, droopy black wool trousers, red sneakers, a red velvet beret my mother had given me for Christmas when I was seventeen. I chain-smoked Marlboros, three packs a day when I could afford them. For a while I smoked clay pipes and Borkum Riff tobacco. The pipes cost a dollar apiece at the tobacconist's in Georgetown. They broke easily, and club owners invariably hassled me, thinking I was getting high right under their noses. I was, but not from Borkum Riff. Occasionally I'd forgo makeup and wear army khakis and a boiled wool navy shirt I'd fished from a Dumpster. I used a mascara wand on my upper lip and wore my bashed-up old cowboy boots to make me look taller.

This fooled no one, but that didn't matter. In Southeast, I was invisible—or nearly so. I was a girl, white, not pretty enough to be either desirable or threatening. The burly leather-clad guys who stood guard over the entrances to the L & F were always nice to me, though there was a scary dyke bouncer whom I had to bribe, sometimes with cash, sometimes with rough foreplay behind the door.

Once inside, all that fell away. David and I stumbled to the bar and traded our drink tickets for vodka and orange juice. We drank fast, pushing upstairs through the crowd until we reached a vantage point above the dance floor. David would look around for someone he knew, someone he fancied, someone who might discover him. He'd give me a wet kiss, then stagger off; and I would stand, and drink, and watch.

The first time it happened, David and I were tripping. We were at the L & F, or maybe Washington Square. He'd gone into the men's room. I sat slumped just outside the door, trying to bore a hole through my hand with my eyes. A few people stepped on me; no one apologized, but no one swore at me, either. After a while I stumbled to my feet, lurched a few feet down the hallway, and turned.

The door to the men's room was painted gold. A shining film covered it, glistening with smeared rainbows like oil-scummed tarmac. The door opened with difficulty because of the number of people crammed inside. I had to keep moving so they could pass in and out. I leaned against the wall and stared at the floor for a few more minutes, then looked up again.

Across from me, the wall was gone. I could see men, pissing, talking, kneeling, crowding stalls, humping over urinals, cupping brown glass vials beneath their faces. I could see David in a crowd of men by the sinks. He stood with his back to me, in front of a long mirror framed with small round lightbulbs. His head was bowed. He was scooping water from the faucet and drinking it, so that his beard glittered red and silver. As I watched, he slowly lifted his face, until he was staring into the mirror. His reflected image stared back at me. I could see his pupils expand like drops of black ink in a glass of water, and his mouth fall open in pure panic.

"David," I murmured.

Beside him, a lanky boy with dirty-blond hair turned. He, too, was staring at me, but not with fear. His mouth split into a grin. He raised his hand and pointed at me, laughing.

"*Poseur!*"

"Shit—shit . . ." I looked up, and David stood there in the hall. He fumbled for a cigarette, his hand shaking, then sank onto the floor beside me. "Shit, you, you saw—you—"

I started to laugh. In a moment David did, too. We fell into each other's arms, shrieking, our faces slick with tears and dirt. I didn't even notice that his cigarette scorched a hole in my favorite shirt till later, or felt where it burned into my right palm, a penny-size wound that got infected and took weeks to heal. I bear the scar even now, the shape of an eye, shiny white tissue with a crimson pupil that seems to wink when I crease my hand.

It was about a month after this happened that we moved to Queenstown. Me, David, Marcy, a sweet spacy girl named Bunny Flitchins, all signed the lease. Two hundred bucks a month gave us a small living room, a bathroom, two small bedrooms, a kitchen squeezed into a corner overlooking a parking lot filled with busted Buicks and shockshot Impalas. The place smelled of new paint and dry-cleaning fluid. The first time we opened the freezer, we found several plastic Ziploc bags filled with sheets of white paper. When we removed the paper and held it up to the light, we saw where rows of droplets had dried to faint grey smudges.

"Blotter acid," I said.

We discussed taking a hit. Marcy demurred. Bunny giggled, shaking her head. She didn't do drugs, and I would never have allowed her to: it would be like giving acid to your puppy.

"Give it to me," said David. He sat on the windowsill, smoking and dropping his ashes to the dirt three floors below. "I'll try it. Then we can cut them into tabs and sell them."

"That would be a *lot* of money," said Bunny delightedly. A tab of blotter went for a dollar back then, but you could sell them for a lot more at concerts, up to ten bucks a hit. She fanned out the sheets from one of the plastic bags. "We could make thousands and thousands of dollars."

"Millions," said Marcy.

I shook my head. "It could be poison. Strychnine. *I* wouldn't do it."

"Why not?" David scowled. "You do all kinds of shit."

"I wouldn't do it 'cause it's from *here.*"

"Good point," said Bunny.

I grabbed the rest of the sheets from her, lit one of her gas jets on the stove, and held the paper above it. David cursed and yanked the bandanna from his head.

"What are you *doing?*"

But he quickly moved aside as I lunged to the window and tossed out the flaming pages. We watched them fall, delicate spirals of red and orange like tiger lilies corroding into black ash then grey then smoke.

"All gone," cried Bunny, and clapped.

We had hardly any furniture. Marcy had a bed and a desk in her room, nice Danish Modern stuff. I had a mattress on the other bedroom floor that I shared with David. Bunny slept in the living room. Every few days she'd drag a broken box spring up from the curb. After the fifth one appeared, the living room began to look like the interior of one of those pawnshops down on F Street that sold you an entire roomful of aluminum-tube furniture for fifty bucks, and we yelled at her to stop. Bunny slept on the box springs, a different one every night, but after a while she didn't stay over much. Her family lived in Northwest, but her father, a professor at the Divine, also had an apartment in Turkey Thicket, and Bunny started staying with him.

Marcy's family lived nearby, as well, in Alexandria. She was a slender, Slavic beauty with a waterfall of ice-blond hair and eyes like aqua headlamps, and the only one of us with a glamorous job—she worked as a model and receptionist at the most expensive beauty salon in Georgetown. But by early spring, she had pretty much moved back in with her parents, too.

This left me and David. He was still taking classes at the Divine, getting a ride with one of the other students who lived at Queenstown, or else catching a bus in front of Giant Food on Queens Chapel Road. Early in the semester he had switched his coursework: instead of theater, he now immersed himself in French language and literature.

I gave up all pretense of studying or attending classes. I worked a few shifts behind the counter at the Queenstown Restaurant, making pizzas and ringing up beer.

I got most of my meals there, and when my friends came in to buy cases of Heineken, I never charged them. I made about sixty dollars a week, barely enough to pay the rent and keep me in cigarettes, but I got by. Bus fare was eighty cents to cross the District line; the newly opened subway was another fifty cents. I didn't eat much. I lived on popcorn and Reuben sandwiches from the restaurant, and there was a sympathetic waiter at the American Café in Georgetown who fed me ice cream sundaes when I was bumming around in the city. I saved enough for my cover at the discos and for the Atlantis, a club in the basement of a fleabag hotel at 930 F Street that had just started booking punk bands. The rest I spent on booze and Marlboros. Even if I was broke, someone would always spring me a drink and a smoke; if I had a full pack of cigarettes, I was ahead of the game. I stayed out all night, finally staggering out into some of the District's worst neighborhoods with a couple of bucks in my sneaker, if I was lucky. Usually I was broke.

Yet I really *was* lucky. Somehow I always managed to find my way home. At two or three or four A.M., I'd crash into my apartment, alone except for the cockroaches— David would have gone home with a pickup from the bars, and Marcy and Bunny had decamped to the suburbs. I'd be so drunk, I stuck to the mattress like a fly mashed against a window. Sometimes I'd sit cross-legged with the typewriter in front of me and write, naked because of the appalling heat, my damp skin grey with cigarette ash. I read *Tropic of Cancer*, reread *Dhalgren* and *A Fan's Notes* and a copy of *Illuminations* held together by a rubber band. I played Pere Ubu and Wire at the wrong speed, because I was too wasted to notice, and would finally pass out only to be ripped awake by the apocalyptic scream of the firehouse siren next door—I'd be standing in the middle of the room, screaming at the top of my lungs, before I realized I was no longer asleep. I saw people in my room, a lanky boy with dark-blond hair and clogs who pointed his finger at me and shouted *Poseur!* I heard voices. My dreams were of flames, of the walls around me exploding outward so that I could see the ruined city like a freshly tilled garden extending for miles and miles, burning cranes and skeletal buildings rising from the smoke to bloom, black and gold and red, against a topaz sky. I wanted to burn, too, tear through the wall that separated me from that other world, the *real* world, the one I glimpsed in books and music, the world I wanted to claim for myself.

But I didn't burn. I was just a fucked-up college student, and pretty soon I wasn't even that. That spring I flunked out of the Divine. All my other friends were still in school, getting boyfriends and girlfriends, getting cast in university productions of *An Inspector Calls* and *Arturo Roi*. Even David Baldanders managed to get good grades for his paper on Verlaine. Meanwhile I leaned out my third-floor window and smoked and watched the speed freaks stagger across the parking lot below. If I jumped, I could be with them: that was all it would take.

It was too beautiful for words, too terrifying to think this was what my life had shrunk to. In the mornings I made instant coffee and tried to read what I'd written the night before. Nice words but they made absolutely no sense. I cranked up Marcy's expensive stereo and played my records, compulsively transcribing song lyrics as though they might somehow bleed into something else, breed with my words and create a coherent storyline. I scrawled more words on the bedroom wall:

I HAVE BEEN DAMNED BY THE RAINBOW
I AM AN AMERICAN ARTIST, AND I HAVE NO CHAIRS

It had all started as an experiment. I held the blunt, unarticulated belief that meaning and transcendence could be shaken from the world, like unripe fruit from a tree; then consumed.

So I'd thrown my brain into the Waring blender along with vials of cheap acid and hashish, tobacco and speed and whatever alcohol was at hand. Now I wondered: Did I have the stomach to toss down the end result?

Whenever David showed up it was a huge relief.

"Come on," he said one afternoon. "Let's go to the movies."

We saw a double bill at the Biograph, *The Story of Adele H* and *Jules et Jim*. Torturously uncomfortable chairs, but only four bucks for four hours of air-conditioned bliss. David had seen *Adele H* six times already; he sat beside me, rapt, whispering the words to himself. I struggled with the French and mostly read the subtitles. Afterwards we stumbled blinking into the long ultraviolet D.C. twilight, the smell of honeysuckle and diesel, coke and lactic acid, our clothes crackling with heat like lightning and our skin electrified as the sugared air seeped into it like poison. We ran arm-in-arm up to the Café de Paris, sharing one of David's Gitanes. We had enough money for a bottle of red wine and a baguette. After a few hours, the waiter kicked us out, but we gave him a dollar anyway. That left us just enough for the Metro and the bus home.

It took us hours to get back. By the time we ran up the steps to our apartment, we'd sobered up again. It was not quite nine o'clock on a Friday night.

"Fuck!" said David. "What are we going to do now?"

No one was around. We got on the phone, but there were no parties, no one with a car to take us somewhere else. We riffled the apartment for a forgotten stash of beer or dope or money, turned our pockets inside out looking for stray seeds, Black Beauties, fragments of green dust.

Nada.

In Marcy's room we found about three dollars in change in one of her jeans pockets. Not enough to get drunk, not enough to get us back into the city.

"Damn," I said. "Not enough for shit."

From the parking lot came the low thunder of motorcycles, a baby crying, someone shouting.

"You fucking motherfucking fucker."

"That's a lot of fuckers," said David.

Then we heard a gunshot.

"Jesus!" yelled David, and yanked me to the floor. From the neighboring apartment echoed the *crack* of glass shattering. "They shot out a window!"

"I said, not enough money for *anything.*" I pushed him away and sat up. "I'm not staying here all night."

"Okay, okay, wait . . ."

He crawled to the kitchen window, pulled himself onto the sill to peer out. "They *did* shoot out a window," he said admiringly. "Wow."

"Did they leave us any beer?"

David looked over his shoulder at me. "No. But I have an idea."

He crept back into the living room and emptied out his pockets beside me. "I think we have enough," he said after he counted his change for the third time. "Yeah. But we have to get there now—they close at nine."

"Who does?"

I followed him back downstairs and outside.

"Peoples Drug," said David. "Come on."

We crossed Queens Chapel Road, dodging Mustangs and blasted pickups. I watched wistfully as the 80 bus passed, heading back into the city. It was almost nine o'clock. Overhead the sky had that dusty gold-violet bloom it got in late spring. Cars raced by, music blaring; I could smell charcoal burning somewhere, hamburgers on a grill and the sweet far-off scent of apple blossom.

"Wait," I said.

I stopped in the middle of the road, arms spread, staring straight up into the sky and feeling what I imagined David must have felt when he leaned against the walls of Mr. P's and Grand Central Station: I was waiting, waiting, waiting for the world to fall on me like a hunting hawk.

"What the fuck are you *doing*?" shouted David as a car bore down and he dragged me to the far curb. "Come *on*."

"What are we getting?" I yelled as he dragged me into the drugstore.

"Triaminic."

I had thought there might be a law against selling four bottles of cough syrup to two messed-up looking kids. Apparently there wasn't, though I was embarrassed enough to stand back as David shamelessly counted pennies and nickels and quarters out onto the counter.

We went back to Queenstown. I had never done cough syrup before; not unless I had a cough. I thought we would dole it out a spoonful at a time, over the course of the evening. Instead David unscrewed the first bottle and knocked it back in one long swallow. I watched in amazed disgust, then shrugged and did the same.

"Aw, *fuck*."

I gagged and almost threw up, somehow kept it down. When I looked up, David was finishing off a second bottle, and I could see him eyeing the remaining one in front of me. I grabbed it and drank it, as well, then sprawled against the box spring. Someone lit a candle. David? Me? Someone put on a record, one of those Eno albums, *Another Green World*. Someone stared at me, a boy with long black hair unbound and eyes that blinked from blue to black and then shut down for the night.

"Wait," I said, trying to remember the words. "I. Want. You. To—"

Too late: David was out. My hand scrabbled across the floor, searching for the book I'd left there, a used New Directions paperback of Rimbaud's work. Even pages were in French; odd pages held their English translation.

I wanted David to read me "*Le lettre du voyant*," Rimbaud's letter to his friend Paul Demeny; the letter of the seer. I knew it by heart in English and on the page but spoken French eluded me and always would. I opened the book, struggling to see through the scrim of cheap narcotic and nausea until at last I found it.

Je dis qu'il faut être voyant, se faire voyant.

Le Poète se fait voyant par un long, immense et raisonné dérèglement de tous les sens. Toutes les formes d'amour, de souffrance, de folie; il cherche lui-même . . .

I say one must be a visionary, one must become a seer.

The poet becomes a seer through a long, boundless and systematic derange-
ment of all the senses. All forms of love, of suffering, of madness; he seeks them
within himself . . .

As I read I began to laugh, then suddenly doubled over. My mouth tasted sick, a
second sweet skin sheathing my tongue. I retched, and a bright-red clot exploded
onto the floor in front of me; I dipped my finger into it then wrote across the warped
parquet.

    Dear Dav

I looked up. There was no light save the wavering flame of a candle in a jar. Many
candles, I saw now; many flames. I blinked and ran my hand across my forehead. It
felt damp. When I brought my finger to my lips, I tasted sugar and blood. On the
floor David sprawled, snoring softly, his bandanna clenched in one hand. Behind
him the walls reflected candles, endless candles; though as I stared I saw they were
not reflected light after all but a line of flames, upright, swaying like figures dancing.
I rubbed my eyes, a wave cresting inside my head then breaking even as I felt something splinter in my eye. I started to cry out but could not: I was frozen, freezing.
Someone had left the door open.
"Who's there?" I said thickly, and crawled across the room. My foot nudged the
candle; the jar toppled and the flame went out.
But it wasn't dark. In the corridor outside our apartment door, a hundred-watt
bulb dangled from a wire. Beneath it, on the top step, sat the boy I'd seen in the uri-
nal beside David. His hair was the color of dirty straw, his face sullen. He had
muddy green-blue eyes, bad teeth, fingernails bitten down to the skin; skeins of
dried blood covered his fingertips like webbing. A filthy bandanna was knotted
tightly around his throat.
"Hey," I said. I couldn't stand very well, so slumped against the wall, slid until I
was sitting almost beside him. I fumbled in my pocket and found one of David's
crumpled Gitanes, fumbled some more until I found a book of matches. I tried to
light one, but it was damp; tried a second time and failed again.
Beside me, the blond boy swore. He grabbed the matches from me and lit one,
turned to hold it cupped before my face. I brought the cigarette close and breathed
in, watched the fingertip flare of crimson then blue as the match went out.
But the cigarette was lit. I took a drag, passed it to the boy. He smoked in silence,
after a minute handed it back to me. The acrid smoke couldn't mask his oily smell,
sweat and shit and urine; but also a faint odor of green hay and sunlight. When he
turned his face to me, I saw that he was older than I had first thought, his skin dark-
seamed by sun and exposure.
"Here," he said. His voice was harsh and difficult to understand. He held his
hand out. I opened mine expectantly, but as he spread his fingers only a stream of
sand fell onto my palm, gritty and stinking of piss. I drew back, cursing. As I did, he
leaned forward and spat in my face.
"*Poseur.*"
"You *fuck*," I yelled. I tried to get up, but he was already on his feet. His hand was
tearing at his neck; an instant later something lashed across my face, slicing upward
from cheek to brow. I shouted in pain and fell back, clutching my cheek. There was

a red veil between me and the world; I blinked and for an instant saw through it. I glimpsed the young man running down the steps, his hoarse laughter echoing through the stairwell; heard the clang of the fire door swinging open then crashing shut; then silence.

"Shit," I groaned, and sank back to the floor. I tried to staunch the blood with my hand. My other hand rested on the floor. Something warm brushed against my fingers: I grabbed it and held it before me: a filthy bandanna, twisted tight as a noose, one whip-end black and wet with blood.

I saw him one more time. It was high summer by then, the school year over. Marcy and Bunny were gone till the fall, Marcy to Europe with her parents, Bunny to a private hospital in Kentucky. David would be leaving soon, to return to his family in Philadelphia. I had found another job in the city, a real job, a GS-1 position with the Smithsonian; the lowest-level job one could have in the government, but it was a paycheck. I worked three twelve-hour shifts in a row, three days a week, and wore a mustard-yellow polyester uniform with a photo ID that opened doors to all the museums on the Mall. Nights I sweated away with David at the bars or the Atlantis; days I spent at the newly opened East Wing of the National Gallery of Art, its vast open white-marble space an air-conditioned vivarium where I wandered stoned, struck senseless by huge moving shapes like sharks spun of metal and canvas: Calder's great mobile, Miro's tapestry, a line of somber Rothko's, darkly shimmering waterfalls in an upstairs gallery. Breakfast was a Black Beauty and a Snickers bar; dinner whatever I could find to drink.

We were at the Lost and Found, late night early August. David as usual had gone off on his own. I was, for once, relatively sober: I was in the middle of my three-day workweek—normally I wouldn't have gone out, but David was leaving the next morning. I was on the club's upper level, an area like the deck of an ocean liner, where you could lean on the rails and look down onto the dance floor below. The club was crowded, the music deafening. I was watching the men dance with each other, hundreds of them, maybe thousands, strobe-lit beneath mirrorballs and shifting layers of blue and grey smoke that would ignite suddenly with white blades of laser light, strafing the writhing forms below so they let out a sudden single-voiced shriek, punching the air with their fists and blasting at whistles. I rested my arms on the rounded metal rail and smoked, thinking how beautiful it all was, how strange, how alive. It was like watching the sea.

And as I gazed, slowly it changed; slowly something changed. One song bled into another, arms waved like tendrils, a shadow moved through the air above them. I looked up, startled, glanced aside and saw the blond young man standing there a few feet from me. His fingers grasped the railing; he stared at the dance floor with an expression at once hungry and disdainful and disbelieving. After a moment, he slowly lifted his head, turned and stared at me.

I said nothing. I touched my hand to my throat, where his bandanna was knotted there, loosely. It was stiff as rope beneath my fingers: I hadn't washed it. I stared back at him, his green-blue eyes hard and somehow dull—not stupid, but with the obdurate matte gleam of unpolished agate. I wanted to say something, but I was afraid of him; and before I could speak, he turned his head to stare back down at the floor below us.

"*Cela c'est passé*," he said, and shook his head.

I looked to where he was gazing. I saw that the dance floor was endless, eternal: the cinder-block warehouse walls had disappeared. Instead, the moving waves of bodies extended for miles and miles until they melted into the horizon. They were no longer bodies but flames, countless flickering lights like the candles I had seen in my apartment, flames like men dancing; and then they were not even flames but bodies consumed by flame, flesh and cloth burned away until only the bones remained and then not even bone but only the memory of motion, a shimmer of wind on the water then the water gone and only a vast and empty room, littered with refuse: glass vials, broken plastic whistles, plastic cups, dog collars, ash.

I blinked. A siren wailed. I began to scream, standing in the middle of my room, alone, clutching at a bandanna tied loosely around my neck. On the mattress on the floor David turned, groaning, and stared up at me with one bright blue eye.

"It's just the firehouse," he said, and reached to pull me back beside him. It was five A.M. He was still wearing the clothes he'd worn to the Lost and Found. So was I: I touched the bandanna at my throat and thought of the young man at the railing beside me. "C'mon, you've hardly slept yet," urged David. "You have to get a little sleep."

He left the next day. I never saw him again.

A few weeks later my mother came, ostensibly to visit her cousin in Chevy Chase, but really to check on me. She found me spread-eagled on my bare mattress, screenless windows open to let the summer's furnace heat pour like molten iron into the room. Around me were the posters I'd shredded and torn from the walls; on the walls were meaningless phrases, crushed remains of cockroaches and waterbugs, countless rust-colored handprints, bullet-shaped gouges where I'd dug my fingernails into the drywall.

"I think you should come home," my mother said gently. She stared at my hands, fingertips netted with dried blood, my knuckles raw and seeping red. "I don't think you really want to stay here. Do you? I think you should come home."

I was too exhausted to argue. I threw what remained of my belongings into a few cardboard boxes, gave notice at the Smithsonian, and went home.

It's thought that Rimbaud completed his entire body of work before his nineteenth birthday; the last prose poems, *Illuminations*, indicate he may have been profoundly moved by the time he spent in London in 1874. After that came journey and exile, years spent as an arms trader in Abyssinia until he came home to France to die, slowly and painfully, losing his right leg to syphilis, electrodes fastened to his nerveless arm in an attempt to regenerate life and motion. He died on the morning of November 10, 1891, at ten o'clock. In his delirium, he believed that he was back in Abyssinia, readying himself to depart upon a ship called *Aphinar*. He was thirty-seven years old.

I didn't live at home for long—about ten months. I got a job at a bookstore; my mother drove me there each day on her way to work and picked me up on her way home. Evenings I ate dinner with her and my two younger sisters. Weekends I went out with friends I'd gone to high school with. I picked up the threads of a few relationships begun and abandoned years earlier. I drank too much but not as much as before. I quit smoking.

I was nineteen. When Rimbaud was my age, he had already finished his life work. I hadn't even started yet. He had changed the world; I could barely change my socks. He had walked through the wall, but I had only smashed my head against it, fruitlessly, in anguish and despair. It had defeated me, and I hadn't even left a mark.

Eventually I returned to D.C. I got my old job back at the Smithsonian, squatted for a while with friends in Northeast, got an apartment, a boyfriend, a promotion. By the time I returned to the city, David had graduated from the Divine. We spoke on the phone a few times: he had a steady boyfriend now, an older man, a businessman from France. David was going to Paris with him to live. Marcy married well and moved to Aspen. Bunny got out of the hospital and was doing much better; over the next few decades, she would be my only real contact with that other life, the only one of us who kept in touch with everyone.

Slowly, slowly, I began to see things differently. Slowly I began to see that there were other ways to bring down a wall: that you could dismantle it, brick by brick, stone by stone, over years and years and years. The wall would always be there—at least for me it is—but sometimes I can see where I've made a mark in it, a chink where I can put my eye and look through to the other side. Only for a moment; but I know better now than to expect more than that.

I spoke to David only a few times over the years, and finally not at all. When we last spoke, maybe fifteen years ago, he told me that he was HIV positive. A few years after that, Bunny told me that the virus had gone into full-blown AIDS, and that he had gone home to live with his father in Pennsylvania. Then a few years after that she told me no, he was living in France again, she had heard from him and he seemed to be better.

Cela C'est passé, the young man had told me as we watched the men dancing in the L & F twenty-six years ago. *That is over.*

Yesterday I was at Waterloo Station, hurrying to catch the train to Basingstoke. I walked past the new Eurostar terminal, the sleek Paris-bound bullet trains like marine animals waiting to churn their way back through the Chunnel to the sea. Curved glass walls separated me from them; armed security patrols and British soldiers strode watchfully along the platform, checking passenger IDs and waving people towards the trains.

I was just turning towards the old station when I saw them. They were standing in front of a glass wall like an aquarium's: a middle-aged man in an expensive-looking dark blue overcoat, his black hair still thick though greying at the temples, his hand resting on the shoulders of his companion. A slightly younger man, very thin, his face gaunt and ravaged, burned the color of new brick by the sun, his fair hair gone to grey. He was leaning on a cane; when the older man gestured he turned and began to walk, slowly, painstakingly down the platform. I stopped and watched: I wanted to call out, to see if they would turn and answer, but the blue-washed glass barrier would have muted any sound I made.

I turned, blinking in the light of midday, touched the bandanna at my throat and the notebook in my pocket, and hurried on. They would not have seen me anyway. They were already boarding the train. They were on their way to Paris.

D. ELLIS DICKERSON

Postcretaceous Era

David Ellis Dickerson's work has appeared in The Atlantic Monthly, *the* Gettysburg Review, *and* StoryQuarterly. *He is single and lives in Tallahassee, Florida, where he is finishing up a Ph.D. in American Literature and (coincidentally) finishing his first novel, a "Monty-Pythonesque literary fantasy" based on the voyages of St. Brendan. He used to write greeting cards for Hallmark, has written crosswords for the* New York Times *and* Games Magazine, *and one day hopes to get a job people will actually pay good money for.*

"Postcretaceous Era," a deft and comic story of romance among the carnivorous and herbivorous almost-extinct, was first published in StoryQuarterly.

—K.L. & G.G.

Phil stood alone in his loft apartment at nine o'clock on New Year's Eve, staring at his scaly face in the mirror, blinking his reptilian eyes. *Christ, I look old,* he said and pulled his facial hide taut with his weak foreclaws, released and it sprung back, more wrinkled than ever. He sighed. Sighing was a habit he'd gotten into since Peggy moved out.

"You need to get a nice car," said Peggy the first time. "That's what makes people promotable. You *look* the part first."

"I'm too big for a car. Where would my tail go?"

"There are surgeons," Peggy had suggested, more brazenly as time went on. "Get a tailectomy. They can improve your posture, strengthen your puny arms—"

"They're forelimbs."

"But they could be arms. Exfoliate your hide and make it smooth, like skin."

"You liked my hide!"

"I liked what was inside the hide. You, being sweet. But you aren't going anywhere," she said finally. "You have the same job you had the first year I met you. You're no closer to being manager now than you were then. I had bigger dreams."

"I can't change that much!"

Remembering, Phil wailed into the night. Peggy was dating a normal-sized accountant now.

It's not my fault. He looked in the mirror again. *Everything moved too fast for me. I'm doing all I can.* There in his bare apartment, with just one bed, one closet, and one sturdy old *chaise longue*—no table, not even a refrigerator—doing all he could wasn't leaving him very much. It was pathetic.

Tonight was New Year's Eve. Phil squinted at the yellow legal pad in his claw.

RESOLUTIONS:

1. Get out more
2. Fin. . . .
3.
4.

He couldn't think of anything else. After a long time, he started to write #2, Find more resolutions, but it seemed silly. He pitched the pen.

It was going on nine-thirty now. This would be the time to get out, onto the street, meet tiny short-lived people. He thought of his face again, thought of being old, then realized he was stalling. *What the hell. If I'm uncomfortable, I'll just write it off as a bad resolution and never worry about it.* He put on an evening suit—with tails—and a natty red tie. Good old dependable red. He inhaled nervously with a sound like bus brakes: *fooosh.*

Phil tromped through the city, careful not to step on cars and people, skill born of experience. No one looked up because it was a big city, with lots to do. Even if someone had looked up, no one would have panicked, because this was an old, old city. People had seen everything by now. He tried to get into the rhythm of the city, *bup! bup! bup! bup!*—a snatch of conversation, a chorus of horns, a push, a shove— all one steady, chorused pulse three times as fast as his massive heartbeat. It made him short of breath.

Phil tromped this street and that, wondering how many people, with differently shaped feet, had walked this place before. The footprints of his ancestors, those of ones his ancestors had eaten, any of them might be fossilized beneath him, where people were stepping. How much tromping could the ground take, so stiff and cold it made his knees hurt. And then all that tar. Even the gravel had been trapped and smothered.

None of the clubs looked interesting. The noise and smoke that these little people endured baffled him. None of the clubs were going to get any better either, and with his legs sore he might as well go somewhere nearby and relax. He ducked down low to read the sign—THE AUTOMATIC GROOVE. Why not?

The club had less noise and fewer lights, but lots more smoke. Phil slunk in, the hard scales on his neck scraping the ceiling. He looked for a corner where he wouldn't be conspicuous. He shouldered over and stood in a room by the pool tables. The building creaked and fluorescent lights hung from the ceiling, swaying like traffic signals. Everyone ignored him. Fifteen seconds and he started to wonder why he was there, why he bothered. He decided to go back home, as soon as his eyes adjusted enough to make out the exit.

Several tables distant and facing away from him, there was a female ankylosaurus sitting at the bar, staring morosely into the mirror. She was wearing a dapper evening suit, also topped off with a red tie—in this case, a foulard that looked a little desperate, like a gout of blood spurting from under her chin. His jaw dropped, issuing an accidental spurt of saliva (an old habit from more carnivorous days). Looking at her in the mirror, Phil felt suddenly self-conscious about his own red tie. *Don't tell me I look like a survivor.* He'd wanted to seem up and peppy.

He started to go over, but stopped. *You're a carnivore! She's an herbivore!* He swallowed uncomfortably. He might have killed her relatives. How would she react? Just looking at her, Phil could smell again open air, huge plants, warmth in the earth and a Cretaceous breeze—remembering when he felt like a mosquito on an artery, the whole world alive beneath him. She turned her head, and he could picture her in a fern grove. The entrance squeaked open, and it reminded Phil of a pterodactyl's screech on a scenic twilight, sun dangling, huge and languid, over a hot tar pit. A strange timelessness descended. He would rather die than pass up this chance. He thought up an opening line as he made his way over to her.

"Hi!" he said, settling on a stool next to her. "You're an ankylosaurus!"

She turned her head and her eyes widened, instinctive fear, and then she looked around. "You wouldn't attack me here, in front of all these people."

"I didn't come here for meat. I wanted to talk."

"I've heard that one before." But she smiled. The armor plates over her eyebrows crinkled. "I'm Ruby, and I'm not an ankylosaur. I'm a polacanthus. See?" she said, looking over her shoulder and twitching her tail. "No club on the end, just spikes down my lower back."

"Oh, Christ," said Phil. "I'm so sorry! I—"

"That's okay," said Ruby. "It was confusing even then. When the mammals started showing up, a glyptodon tried to mate with me. With that rodentlike face and those hairy legs—*ugh!* He had nice armor, though. I could understand the confusion."

"It's been so long." Phil nodded.

"And frankly, I was never good at carnosaurs," said Ruby. "I just ran without learning their names. Are you a T. rex?"

"Nope. A deinonychus. Close, though. I'm a lot smaller—thirteen feet tall—and I have a bone spur I use for attack, or defense. See?" He pointed to a forelimb.

"I was way off," said Ruby. "You're too kind."

"No, no. I get the tyrannosaurus thing all the time."

"God!" said Ruby, with a sudden grinder-exposing smile. "It feels like it's been millions of years since I've seen another dinosaur!"

Phil smiled back, and they sat there smiling, Phil a little giddy. He hadn't felt giddy for centuries. "I'm Phil!"

"I'm still Ruby. Buy me a salad?"

"So how did you survive?" Phil asked, after a few drinks and several salad bowls.

"Seclusion. I'm from the La Brea area, and I knew some places to go. It wasn't developed then, of course. That's why I think it was disease that did it. I stayed alone, nobody touched me, so here I am." She swirled her Manhattan. "I was lonely, but I told myself it didn't matter. I survived. What about you?"

"Oh, I was originally from Europe, and just outran everything. I saw my friends and family die, kicking and howling all around me. I ran and ran, looking for the meteor that brought the death—to rip out its throat. I never did find it, but when the dust settled, my head cleared and I was still alive."

"How did you get to America?"

"There was a land bridge. I couldn't do it now."

"Europe," said Ruby. "I thought I recognized an accent."

More drinks. Another salad.

"We weren't too big to survive," said Phil. "The world just got too small. Now it doesn't have the same grandeur, the scope it used to, back when creatures weren't afraid to be sizable. Everything starts really swell and then deteriorates. That's entropy for you."

"Actually, I think the world got too large," said Ruby. "All these people crammed into all these buildings, which get taller every year, like tree-mountains. All the newspapers filled with so much information no one can keep up with it. Face it, Phil, we didn't die out because of entropy. We just came around too early. There's too much to keep track of now. We're gone because humans forgot us, just like kids forget their parents when they learn new things at college. They'll never be ignorant enough to be impressed by mere size, not ever again."

"Well, we can always hope for another meteor shower," said Phil, raising his Harvey Wallbanger. "To meteors!"

"To meteors!"

Clink.

Whiskey and sours. No pretense of salad.

"You know what's nice about being a dinosaur?" said Ruby.

"In today's world? I hate it. There's nothing nice about it. People ignore you. You can't take cabs. Rooms are too small. There's no raw food around. If you're a carnivore, good luck hunting. They fine you or just kill you outright. And let's talk some time about shoddy indoor plumbing."

"What's nice about being a dinosaur is that no one knows you except yourself. No one expects anything of you. You can make your own rules."

She shifted on her stool, fixing Phil with a slightly dazed eye. "For example, in the old days, you would have been trying to eat me. I would have been trying to hide or, failing that, hoping to rip your mouth with my spikes. Now we can talk like this. It's fun." She looked at Phil's reflection in the mirror. "I wonder how many of your old friends I would've gotten along with. I bet you would've liked my mother. She was a fighter like you."

"Remember pterodactyls?" said Phil. "Remember the fern groves? Remember the way the sunsets used to look, when the sun was bigger and redder and the world was filled with swampy air? I remember rainbows ten times a day. Ten times a day!" He started nodding vigorously. "Ten times! Great fucking rainbows!"

"Those were the days all right," said Ruby. "Haven't you had a little much to drink? You're big, but we have slow metabolisms."

We. Meaning us dinosaurs. The word affected Phil strangely. He froze and tears plopped to the bartop, like dew on an arthropleura.

"What's wrong?"

"I . . . I'm sorry!" he managed, with a throaty wheeze. "I'm sorry about your sisters, your brothers, your mother, your aunt . . . I'm a stupid fucking carnivore. I didn't know . . ."

"You were just doing your job," said Ruby. "You didn't kill *me.*"

Phil calmed down, still snuffling. He looked at her, his eyes still blurry with tears.

"You, Ruby, if I may say it . . . you're the first herbivore that I . . . well, you seem damn near *unkillable*." He frowned and added, "And I mean that as a compliment."

"Funny. I feel that way too. Now that you're here." She grinned.

Phil didn't know what to say. His mouth dropped open.

"My big cute carnivore," said Ruby. Then, "What are you looking at? I'm an adult, I can say what I want."

The whole place smelled like champagne. The crowd got noisy.

"How long have we been talking?" asked Phil.

"I just heard someone say *Happy New Year.*"

"Another one of those." He shrugged. "Anyway, tell me more about your family."

"Where's your place?"

"Not far."

They tromped to Phil's flat along newspaper-strewn paths, through tenuous night beginning to desert the sky.

"Here we are."

A click in the lock. Shuffling. The elevator. More shuffling. They kept bumping into each other as they shambled down the halls, and Phil noticed that her spines felt warm.

"Here it is," he said. "Welcome."

"It's nice."

Phil started to say it was pathetic, but shrugged. "Maybe it is. And here's the bed."

Creaking, along with a few small ripping sounds. The mattress took spikes poorly. Shuffling. More creaking and ripping. "Hello there!"

"Hello."

They stared at each other, and Phil noticed how short she was. She had to throw her neck back to look up at him. It was almost a posture of surrender. She had a beautiful neck that made his own begin to pulse.

"So what now?" said Ruby

Phil waved his forelimbs helplessly. "Where do I begin?"

"You know what you could do," she said, and she leaned in close so Phil had to bend over and cock his head to hear. "You could bite me. Just a little."

Phil's heart hammered and he struggled to breathe. Bending over made his eyes mist red. "I've . . . I've wanted to, but I'm afraid I might . . ."

"Just on the shoulder, near the heavier plating. It's what I'm built for. Let's see how long we can hold it."

Phil opened his jaws wide for what seemed the first time in forever, loving the ache it caused his cheeks. Gingerly he moved his mouth over her shoulder.

"Phil!" whispered Ruby, her hot breath spouting into his ear. "I have strong armor. And very sharp spikes."

"I think I remember," Phil murmured.

He clamped his mouth hard against her shoulder. She stiffened as his teeth closed softly, pierced her hide, and then clamped down until he felt her bony plate an inch beneath the skin. Then he froze, his mouth still, teeth just deep enough to bury his shorter incisors. Blood trailed down along her foreleg, her smell filling the room. He heard her sniffing the air, and suddenly he was back in Cretaceous—as if humans never happened. He lapped up her blood; but her spines pricked his tongue. They both poised, unmoving—eater and eaten—their blood pooled together and dribbled *pat-pat-pat* on Phil's sheets. They breathed together, hissing through their teeth, Phil wondering if he could bear to open his mouth. He imagined the entire city crumbling, other cities being built, those cities falling in turn. He knew that however long the world might last, it would never produce anything so painful, so sweet.

M.T. ANDERSON

Watch and Wake

M.T. Anderson's novels include Burger Wuss, Feed (a National Book Award Finalist and winner of the Los Angeles Times Book Award), and Thirsty, a wonderful and very dark coming-of-age tale. He is the author of children's picture books on Eric Satie, Handel, and the Gloucester sea serpent, and his extremely funny novel, The Game of Sunken Places, should appeal to both young adult and adult fans of Edward Gorey, John Bellairs, and Joan Aiken. Anderson teaches in Vermont College's MFA in Writing for Children Program, lives in Boston, Massachusetts, and is fiction editor of 3rd bed, a journal of absurdist literature. "Watch and Wake" is darker than our usual selections, but it was inspired by Lucius Apuleius's "Tale of The Golden Ass." "Watch and Wake" appeared in Deborah Noyes's delightfully scary young adult anthology Gothic!

—K.L. & G.G.

At around eight o'clock in the evening, I finally got off the bus at some town. It was the first town in many miles where there were not lines of people waiting around the demon-towers. Throughout the afternoon, I had watched town after town pass, and in each one, there were the gantries, the pits, the symbols drawn by schoolchildren in crayon stapled to the struts. My head bobbed against the bus window. Villages passed, mini-malls, car lots, grocery stores. I drew on the back of my hand with a pen. The people on the bus stopped talking while we went through the places between towns, the dark places marked by forest, broken tarmac, Ski-Doo rentals, and auto-body repair.

I was nearly out of money, and it was going to be another three days' drive home. I did not know what my parents would say when I got there.

The town where I stepped off was small and without much interest. The streets were pretty empty. They had two stoplights. There was a pizza place and a hair place and an old, rusted demon-tower hung with knives; there was a general store that sold big-headed dolls in the window.

I dragged my duffel bag behind me down the steps of the bus. I thanked the driver. He closed the door and drove away.

I needed a B & B. There were some old houses that I could picture being a B & B. I didn't have any money, but I figured, at a B & B, I might be able to talk them into calling my parents and getting my parents to pay for a night somehow over the phone.

My parents would be surprised. It would be nice, maybe. They would find out I was coming home. I had not heard from them for some time.

I stood with my bag in my hand. Some kids were standing outside the pizza place. They didn't look nice, and they didn't look mean. The boys had more acne than I did, and the girls looked like they were going out dancing.

I walked past them. I went in and sat down at a booth. The two guys behind the counter were talking about their home phones. One had a home phone with lots of noise on the line.

"It's like it's fizzing," he said. "Always. It really bugs me."

The other one said, "I bet. That could really get on your nerves."

I left my bag on the seat and went up to talk to them. I asked them about places to stay in town.

One said, "Oh, yeah, sure!"

The other guy said, "Good one!"

I stood there, with my arm on the counter. I guess I looked confused or uncomfortable.

"No place," one explained.

"There was one place," said the other, "but it closed. The dish reception there sucked."

"They got nothing," said the other guy.

I did not know what to do.

I ordered an Italian sub with olive oil. Sometimes when they put olive oil on it, it really hits the spot. The guys looked at me. I patted my belly.

Later, my sub came, and I ate it at the table, reading a book for school. I underlined the important passages. I had a highlighter pen.

At around ten, a man came into the pizza place and asked the guys some questions. They yelled over to me that I was in luck.

"Why?" I said. I stood up.

The man looked at me. He walked over. He said, "I'll pay you to watch a corpse for the night."

I half shrugged. I said, "Why?"

He said, "Come with me." He pointed toward the door. I threw away my paper plate and foil, and closed my book and put it in my pack. I followed him outside.

The kids were gone. The night was cold.

"You on your way home?" the man asked. He was striding.

I nodded.

"That's nice," he said.

I said, "I'd like to know where we're walking."

For a while we walked. He asked me, "Do you know what it's like to feel a grief so deep it's like someone is shouting?"

I waited. He waited. Finally, he said, "My best friend's wife asked me to find someone to sit with his corpse through the night. He's . . ." The man clapped once, loud. Then he put his knuckles together as we walked. He asked, "What's your name?"

"My name is Jim," I said.

"Jim. Ha. You have a last name?"

I looked at him. Then I shook my head.

"It's nice to meet you," he said. He shook my hand. We were walking down the street. There were streetlights. In their light, we could see some old oaks and some rubble and Dumpsters.

He said, "We have a problem with witches. It's witches, here. Nothing is growing anymore. Cooked meat always shivers like it's cold now. It shivers right on your plate, and it bleeds when you poke it. Cars don't run well. The sky stinks. All because of them. Here's the thing. The witches eat the faces of the dead. They can take any form. A mouse, a sparrow, an insect, the lowly roach. This wife, my friend's wife, she needs someone to keep watch."

"How do I keep watch?"

"Just sit up," he said. "They won't approach if someone's awake. They come in through dreams."

We were at a low house on a lawn. The motion light came on near the driveway. We went up to the front door. The man knocked.

The dead man's wife answered. She was beautiful, not much older than me. She had on a T-shirt, and had been rubbing her wet eyes with it. Mascara was smeared across her belly.

"Charlie," she said, "you found someone."

"He'll do it," said the man. "He agreed."

"I didn't agree yet," I said.

"Have a good night, Jenn," said Charlie. "You going to be okay?"

"I'll be okay," said Jenn. "My mom is here."

I went into the house. There were people there in the shadows. They fingered key chains. They were spaced around the living room. The television said, "How can you hold me back? This dog is America's heartthrob!"

"Jenn," said a woman. "Jenn, I called the professional mourners. They're going to call back. They want to know how many people for wailing."

"Okay."

"And the loudness."

"Thanks." The wife led me toward the kitchen. She stopped and looked around the living room. "Who has the baby?" she asked, squinting. "Do you have him?"

"Marty has him," said the woman, nodding her head.

A man had the baby, and was whispering to it.

The wife led me through a door.

The husband was on the kitchen table. They had laid out a nice tablecloth under him, and candles at his head and hands and feet. There was a ring of salt around him to stop death from spreading. He was naked, and all of him was pale. His mouth was open, and his tongue was rich and black.

The wife couldn't look at her husband. She kept her face turned in a different way, like against a garbage wind.

I wondered if she had been in high school when they were married.

"I'm sorry," I said.

She scrunched her neck up. She nodded into the garbage wind.

I leaned against the counter. She went to the cupboard and got out some Triscuits.

She said, "We're going to bed soon. We've been up for two days."

"What am I doing?"

"We'll pay you a hundred dollars."

"Do I just sit here?"

"Just, on the chair. Make sure nothing comes in and calls to him or attacks the face."

"What do I do if something comes?"

She shrugged. "Frighten it." She walked over to the door. "The lights are here. They're on a dimmer." She swiveled the dimmer.

"I think I'll leave them full-strength," I said. I could not stand near the body. His eyes were closed, each one covered with a plastic decal of archangels, but I could not stop myself from believing that his hand would move and grab my leg.

"Don't worry," she said. "Just keep watch."

She left.

I pulled out a chair. It was ten-thirty. Eight hours until dawn.

I sat down. I took out my book. I was about to start reading again, when I thought about the placement of the chair. I wanted to see the door and the corpse at once. I did not want a window at my back.

I stood up and looked at the window. There were no blinds or shades. Outside, it was pitch black. There were shells lined up on the windowsill. They were from a fine day at the beach.

I moved the chair so it was against a closet door. I sat down again and watched the corpse.

My book was open on my lap.

The door slammed open. I jumped.

It was Jenn, in a different T-shirt and some plaid boxers. "Do you know what helps me sleep?" she asked. "Celery." She went and got some out of the fridge. When she stood up with the bag of celery, I tried to look in the vent of her boxers to see if she had anything on underneath. I couldn't tell. She washed the celery.

"We had the necromancer come earlier today," she said. "He told us we should take off the head before nightfall." She rubbed the groove of the celery with her thumb. She said, "I just couldn't do that. There's no way. No way in hell." She shut off the water by knocking the faucet with her wrist.

She told me good night again and left.

I was alone with the corpse.

The kitchen clock ticked.

I looked down toward my book.

Eight hours.

I took out my highlighter pen. I read several pages, underlining important passages. I looked up every so often to make sure the candles were still burning. I was at the foot of the body. Its gray flab was foreshortened.

In the dead, all muscle is flab.

I looked up after a while. There was a light I hadn't noticed earlier.

The refrigerator door was open a little bit. The light was on. The bag of celery was out on the counter.

I couldn't remember whether I had seen Jenn put it away.

I stood up and went to pick up the bag. It hung from my hand. There was a picture of a farmer turkey on it.

The corpse still had its face. The eyes were closed. The mouth was open.

I put the celery back in the crisper.

While I squatted there, rattling the crisper into place, I thought I heard some-thing behind me.

I did not want to turn around. I wanted to remain facing into the fridge.

I forced myself to look over my shoulder.

The corpse lay motionless on the table. Nothing else moved in the kitchen.

I closed the refrigerator door.

Then I opened it, and took out a Coke, and closed it again.

Caffeine.

I drank the Coke leaning against the counter. I calculated whether I was in grab-bing distance of the corpse. The question was whether it would lunge before it grabbed.

The man's hair grew in irregular patches. It was uneven across his chest.

To pass the time, I raised up my shirt and looked at my chest in the window, for comparison. I used the window as a mirror. Outside, through my mirror, it was dark. I reached up and touched my own chest. My hair was straggly, but symmetrical. My nipples tickled.

I tucked in my shirt and sat down.

I read several more pages of the book and outlined important passages. I tried to memorize a few. I could not remember them. I tried to say them out loud, softly. They would not stay in my memory, so I stopped.

There was a weasel in the window.

I dropped the book. It fell between my knees. I looked up at the weasel. On the wall clock, I saw it was three.

The weasel looked in at the body. Its eyes were small and black.

I stood up and went to the window. There was nothing to be afraid of. There was glass between me and the weasel. The weasel showed its teeth. I reached out to-ward it.

It stared just at me, now.

I knocked on the window, and it crouched. It ran.

I was left, looking out the window at the night.

I turned and went back to my seat.

I sat and picked up my book where it had fallen.

I looked for my page. I couldn't find it.

I couldn't remember what I had been reading about.

I fumbled for my highlighter pen.

I turned the book over. It was warm from my flesh.

I was asleep and knew it. Asleep in my seat near the corpse. Hours passed, and I dreamed of something.

I slept.

Something slapped something else, and I was awake.

I grabbed the book. It almost fell on the floor. There was light.

I stood.

"Morning," said Jenn, coming backward into the kitchen with a tray.

I felt a panic. My skin was numb. I looked at the corpse. I wanted it to still have a face.

She took the tray to the sink and put it down.

"How are you?" she said.

The face was fine. Nothing had happened. The sun was out.

"Anything?" she said.

"There was—it was a weasel," I said. "It came to the window."

Jenn nodded. "A witch," she said. "They can be weasels." She turned around and went to the fridge. "I'd like some orange juice," she said. "You want some orange juice?"

"Yeah," I whispered. My throat was dry. There was a bad taste in my mouth.

"You headed somewhere?" she asked.

"My parents'."

"Nice. There wasn't anything beside the weasel, was there?"

"No. Nope."

"Because sometimes they can be a bear. It takes two of them. They're different paws."

"No."

"You don't mess with that. Bears."

She gave me orange juice and made a big omelet. She put some on a plate for me and some on other plates for members of her family. I stayed in the kitchen and ate. The rest ate in the dining room. Her mother and aunt came in and washed the plates. I still sat there. They told me she would be right down with my money. While they washed, they talked quietly about the arrangements for the funeral.

I stood next to the corpse and looked at it carefully. It was fine. Just fine. It was a narrow escape. I wanted to get away from there. I didn't know if they had some way of telling about my sleep.

When Jenn came back, she was dressed. She had a hundred dollars in cash.

"Thanks," she said. "I was worried you'd fall asleep."

I nodded. I folded up the cash.

She looked at me. "But you didn't fall asleep," she said. It was a question.

I shook my head.

She reached out and took my chin in her hand. She stared at me. She took in my features. I blinked. I tried not to react. "You're a good-looking kid," she said. "Don't make the same mistakes I made."

She dropped her hand. I nodded.

"Good luck getting home," she said. "You have to go far?"

"I'm going by bus."

"Which way?"

"West."

"Sucks," she said. "They've seen huge footsteps in the corn."

I left the mourning household. I could not get away fast enough.

I went down the drive and turned left, to go into town.

The buses were not running on their regular schedule. I waited for some hours in the center of town. People went into the market to use the ATM.

At around eleven, I heard noise from up the street. It was the professional mourners walking in front of the corpse. They were dressed for business and hitting themselves in the chest with stones. They were not supposed to see the things of this world anymore, so their eyes were X'ed out with short strips of electrical tape. They walked the road by memory, as do all who mourn for someone dead.

They yowled and screamed.

Behind them was the corpse, carried on a white sheet that had been filled with flowers by relatives in black.

In front of them all was Jenn, her head down, her hands behind her back. She wore a matching skirt and jacket. She looked like a little girl.

The family followed behind. Tiny boys were in tiny suits. One of the grandmothers carried an antipasto in plastic wrap.

They were headed to the church just up the street. People came out of businesses to watch them pass.

They were almost past us when a car drove up from behind and began honking.

I was lurking near the pay phones. I did not want to talk to Jenn any more.

The car drove closer to the stragglers and kept honking. People in the procession turned and shouted at the driver. The driver just honked more. He stopped diagonally in the middle of the road. I heard the crank of the emergency brake.

He got out of the car. His seat belt was still retracting when he began yelling. "You know what's behind that rouge!" he said. "You know I'm right!" He was an older man. "She killed him!" he yelled. "Poison! Would you stop? Stop walking!"

He got in the car again. The car started up, and lurched forward, and pulled around them, and jerked to a stop in front of them. The procession halted. There was nowhere to go. The car was diagonally in the way. The driver got out again. He was still shouting something. Jenn was stopped now, and turned away. She looked sad.

"She killed him," the man said.

I should have stayed behind the phones. Everyone was curious, though. Everyone on the sidewalks was wandering closer. I went with them.

"Charlie and her," said the old man. "With something." He shook his finger. "Something!"

She looked up and saw me. I thought she wanted to ask me a favor.

I stood there for a second. She didn't say a word. There was a big crowd.

I backed away. She closed her eyes.

I went inside the market. I thought that would be better. I didn't want to see her anymore. It was a close escape, and I did not want any more questions.

I sat on a plastic crate near the magazines and read birthday cards. Over the music on the radio, I could hear shouting. Something was happening outside. I kept reading the cards. Most of them were either flowers or dentures and greased men in Speedos.

Some kid ran into the market. He said to the girl at the counter, "His father says she killed him. He's accusing her."

"Yeah?"

"They're going to raise the dead. To ask him."

"Now?" she said.

"They've got the necromancer."

The girl looked out the window between the light-up cigarette signs. She called over her shoulder to me, "You need help with anything, sir?"

I put back the dog card I was reading.

"There's a guy," the kid told me, "who's dead." He jerked his thumb outside.

I went with them to watch.

It was not a good idea.

The necromancer was dressed in jeans and a stupid sweater. He had these yellow-colored lenses in his glasses, and he was kneeling by the corpse on the side of the road. He was sticking little plastic wedges into the flesh. The wedges were all over the body.

There was a pretty big crowd. Jenn was crying, and her mother and father, probably, were standing on either side of her. I saw Charlie, too, standing and looking at the dotted line in the middle of the road. He had on a suit. He scratched under his beard.

Everyone could see the dead man in his nudity. I didn't think about it, until I heard one woman whisper to her friend, "God. I'm glad I decided not to date him."

"Could people stand back?" said the necromancer. "One, two, three steps?"

We all moved away. The necromancer started tying the soul back to the body with lengths of black rubber. He twisted knots.

A man next to me asked a woman, "Did you leave Jarv on the phones?"

"No," she said.

"Who's on the phones?"

"I turned on the machine."

"You can't use the machine," he said. "It's eleven-thirty."

The body had started to move. It was clumsy, because the soul was slipping.

Everyone fell silent. The necromancer rose. The corpse was writhing on the sheet, which lay on the grass. The eyes were open.

The dead man looked down at his own body. He held out his fingers. He said, softly, "I'm dead. . . . That's it. . . ." He sounded surprised.

His father went and embraced him. He knocked something, and the head rocked back. The head was dead again. The tongue came out. The necromancer squatted and adjusted the rubber cinches, sending the father back with a wave.

The corpse sagged, but its eyes were open. "She killed me," said the dead man. "It was in the vinegar."

We looked at Jenn. She didn't move.

"You killed me," he said. "You and Charlie. It was the vinegar, wasn't it?"

"He's lying," she said. "It's not really him."

"It's me," he said.

"It's not him." She scolded the necromancer, "You were paid to get someone to say this. This is someone else."

The dead man said, "You watched while I fell down."

"This isn't him," she said. "I'd recognize him."

"It's him," said the father. "I can tell."

"You lying, cheating bastard," said Jenn to the necromancer. "How much is the old guy paying you?"

"This is him," said the necromancer. "It's a perfect fit."

"Show me," she said. "Show us that it's him. Because it's not."

"It's me," said the dead man. "And I'll prove it by telling you something that no one else living knows."

"Don't bother," she said.

"I'll tell you," said the dead man.

We waited.

And then he turned and looked around. He searched the crowd. And he turned to me. The dead man turned and raised his sloppy arm and waved his hand toward me. He said, "You left this kid to guard me last night. Sitting by my side. He fell asleep."

She looked at me. Everyone looked at me.

I shook my head.

I tried to back up, but there were people there.

The corpse said to Jenn, "You dressed like a weasel, in a weasel's skin. Then you came for me. He stopped you, so you sent him to sleep."

The necromancer rose and looked at me curiously, as if he saw something. He lightly held out his hands to part the crowd, and said, "Come forward."

They were waiting.

I wanted to run, but they were all waiting for me. I couldn't just turn away and run. Everyone was waiting. So I walked forward.

I stood beside the corpse. The necromancer inspected me.

The dead man said to his wife, "You and your sisters called my name. I heard you saying, 'Jim. Come to our feast, Jim.'"

"That's my name," I said. "My name is Jim."

"There are a lot of people named Jim," said the dead man. "I was once one of them. You were asleep, Jim, and I was dead, and they called my name. But you got up first. You went with them. Sleep is like death. They feasted on your face."

"This is—" I said. "I can't believe this."

"They hid what they had done," said the corpse.

"This—"

The necromancer reached up and touched me gently, like a lover. He pulled off my nose. It was wax.

"No," he said glumly, "it's true. Look."

I had no nose. It had been eaten.

I stumbled, but there were hands to hold me upright. The wax nose lay on the tarmac. He reached up and pressed my cheek. "I'm going home," I said. "Just leave it all on until I get home. Leave it on. . . ." But he was tearing off my ear and casting it on the ground. "It will be fine," I said. "I want a face. They can sew. . . . A doctor will help. I'll go to a doctor. When I get home. When I get home, they'll see me and—"

But the necromancer was gouging around my eyes, pulling pieces of my face off, casting them on the ground, and more and more was wax, and pieces fell, and I saw my lashes on the dirt, and felt the tugging of rind after rind peeled from my cheeks, my forehead, my chin, and did not know any longer who I was, or where I was going, or how I would ever get home.

CATHERYNNE M. VALENTE

The Oracle Alone

Catherynne M. Valente was born on Cinco de Mayo, 1979, in Seattle, Washington, but grew up in the wheatgrass paradise of Northern California. She graduated from high school at age fifteen, going on to UC San Diego and Edinburgh University, receiving her B.A. in Classics with an emphasis in Ancient Greek Linguistics. She currently resides in Virginia Beach with her husband.

Her work in poetry and short fiction can be found online and in print in such journals as The Pedestal Magazine, NYC Big City Lit, The Pomona Valley Review, *and the forthcoming PEN anthology,* The Book of Voices.

Her first chapbook, Music of a Proto-Suicide, *was released in early 2004, and her first novel,* The Labyrinth, *was published at the end of that year. She has several books forthcoming, including a second novel and a full-length collection of poetry. "The Oracle Alone" is from her chapbook.*

—E.D.

Perhaps you enter a room, cool and dark, tattooed with shadows cast by brocade curtains and sheer veils over the mirrors, the floor stone and cobbled, and perhaps she is there—installed in a demure corner with her feet bare.

Perhaps you think to yourself *nam Sibyllam quidem cumis ego ipse oculis meis vidi* . . . it is possible that the tumbling rainclouds and crushed rubies of those ancient words shoot through your mind like a hunting hawk, all sleek wings and talons. You look at her, brushing a long strand of dark hair from her face, and for a moment her profile is the classical phantasm you expected to find. But she is younger than you thought, there are no lines that assure the presence of wisdom, no origami folds in her crane-neck, no silver arrows piercing her hair. She is smooth and curved as the spine of a harp. And now that you have come all this way, the fact of her youth and those liquid eyes frighten you, and you do not want to know what she portends.

She spreads her hands on the velvet table-cover, the light slants in from a dusty window in this high tower, and she is illuminated like a manuscript, a tongue of gold dust and cobalt. You do not want her to open her mouth, you are certain that moths and infant crows flutter within, behind her terrible lips. It is the mouth you fear, that likeness of a door, a crevice sinking deep within blue glaciers. Oh, little one, she wakes all your secret night tremors, she is the serpent chasing you down hallways, she is the drowning sea, she is the mocking moon. Her hands have drawn seven thousand ash-wood bows, and all found their mark in the flesh of your liver. She ululates, undulates, abrades your corneas, from her little corner she bends all the roads you've ever known towards her. If she were old it would be better, you could accept a crone. She would have been less annihilating if you been able to guess the date of her death from the lines on her throat. But it is perfect, long and lithe, and out of it will issue bats singing arias and owls like treble clefs. She is all darkness, enveloped in a body of light so full and thick you could plunge your hands into it and be purified for a century.

She has not moved, but you have, you have orbited her and fallen and escaped and fallen again. She is the fulcrum, and you swing from her like a fat copper pendulum, the arc of you a glowering black line on the floor of the world. Roots have ripped out of your feet and anchored you before her, great thick ropes of her silence diving through the earth like playing seals, and you want to move towards her, but cannot. You have paid your admission and she is yours for the moment, her mouth, round and clear as a crystal ball, is bought, to exhale stars into your palm and tattered asphodels into your chest. It is full of dragonflies. The buzz makes you drunk, and you waver a little, wanting, for a moment, to run and hide in any cavern that will bear you. But that maddening strand, that lock of blackness, the slick of her hair wafting onto her cheek like a bruise, will hold you to her forever. She brushes it away again, uselessly, into the long mass gathered at her neck.

You commit the only act which was ever possible, you walk to her, three steps (it had seemed so much farther) and you sit beside her pale skin and dusty green eyes, the shade of a bottle of wine in the cellar. And you do not know why the words which fly up to your tongue like mezzo-soprano sparrows are Greek, except that once in a classroom with a view of the sea you read Eliot and wept. Those same tears fall now, hot and bright as Mars in the summer sky, the secret crimson of passion.

"Σιβυλλα, τι θελεις?"
"Sibyl, what do you want?"
And she inclines her head like a heron, looking at you with eyes full of pity and warning, of oracles and tombs, of oceanic tremors and lunar siroccos. She blurs like an impressionistic landscape through your tears as that seraphim-mouth opens and her voice, voice of blood-maps and continental drift, a voice like the opening of a door. She answers you in that same tongue, vowels like milky breasts and consonants pregnant with swords.

"Εμου τεκνον, τι κλαλεις?"
"My child, why do you weep?"
And it begins, and you listen, and she speaks.

JEFFREY FORD

A Night in The Tropics

Jeffrey Ford is the author of a trilogy of novels: The Physiognomy, Memoranda, The Beyond. *His most recent novels are* The Portrait of Mrs. Charbuque *and* The Girl in the Glass. *His short fiction has appeared in the magazines* Fantasy & Science Fiction, SCIFICTION, MSS, The Northwest Review, Puerto del Sol, *and in the anthologies* The Green Man, Leviathan 3, Trampoline, The Silver Gryphon, Polyphony 3, The Faery Reel, The Dark, *and* Flights. *His short fiction has been collected in* The Fantasy Writer's Assistant & Other Stories *and some of it has been reprinted in earlier volumes of this anthology and in* Fantasy: Best of 2002. *His second collection,* Empire of Ice Cream, *is forthcoming in 2006, as is a novella chapbook,* The Cosmology of the Wider World.

He is a three-time recipient of The World Fantasy Award *(for best novel, story, and collection), and has also won the* Nebula Award *for best novelette of 2003. Ford lives in southern New Jersey with his wife and two sons, and is a professor of Writing and Literature at Brookdale Community College.*

"A Night in The Tropics" was originally published in Argosy.

—E.D., K.L. & G.G.

The first bar I ever went to was The Tropics. It was and still is situated between the grocery store and the bank along Higbee Lane in West Islip. I was around five or six, and my old man would take me with him when he went there to watch the Giant games on Sunday afternoon. While the men were all at the bar, drinking, talking, giving Y.A. Tittle a piece of their minds, I'd roll the balls on the pool table or sit in one of the booths in the back and color. The jukebox always seemed to be playing "Somewhere, Beyond the Sea" by Bobby Darin while I searched for figures, the way people do with clouds, in the swirling cigar and cigarette smoke. I didn't go there for the hard-boiled eggs the bartender proffered after making them vanish and pulling them out of my ear, or for the time spent sitting on my father's lap at the bar, sipping a ginger ale with a cherry in it, although both were welcome. The glowing, bubbling beer signs were fascinating, the foul language was its own cool music, but the thing that drew me to The Tropics was a thirty-two-foot vision of paradise.

Along the south wall of the place, stretching from the front door back to the entrance of the bathrooms, was a continuous mural of a tropical beach. There were palm trees with coconuts and stretches of pale sand sloping down to a shoreline where the serene sea rolled in lazy wavelets. The sky was robin's egg blue, the ocean, six different shades of aquamarine. All down the beach, here and there, frozen forever in different poses, were island ladies wearing grass skirts but otherwise naked save the flowers in their hair. Their smooth brown skin, their breasts, their smiles, were ever-inviting. At the center of the painting, off at a distance on the horizon, was depicted an ocean liner with a central funnel issuing a smudgy trail of smoke. Between that ship and the shore, there bobbed a little rowboat with one man at the oars.

I was entranced by that painting and could sit and look at it for long stretches at a time. I'd inspected every inch of it, noticing in the bend of the palm leaves, the sweep of the women's hair, the curling edges of the grass skirts, which way the breeze was blowing and at what rate. I could almost feel it against my face. The cool clear water, the warmth of the island light, lulled me into a trance. I noticed the tiny crabs, shells, starfish, on the beach, the monkey peering out from within the fronds of a palm. The most curious item, though, back in the shadows of the bar, just before paradise came to an end by the bathroom door, was a hand, pushing aside the wide leaf of some plant as if it was *you* standing at the edge of the jungle, spying on that man in the rowboat.

Eventually, as time went on and life grew more chaotic, my father stopped going to The Tropics on Sundays. Supporting our family overtook the importance of the Giants, and until my mother passed away only a few years ago, he worked six days a week. When my own bar years began, I never went there as it was considered an old man's bar, but the memory of that mural stayed with me through the passing seasons. At different times in my life when things got hectic, its placid beauty would come back to me, and I'd contemplate living in paradise.

A couple of months ago, I was in West Islip, visiting my father, who still lives, alone now, in the same house I grew up in. After dinner we sat in the living room and talked about the old times and what had changed in town since I'd been there last. Eventually, he dozed off in his recliner, and I sat across from him contemplating his life. He seemed perfectly content, but all I could think about were those many years of hard work drawing to a close in an empty house, in a neighborhood where he knew no one. I found the prospect depressing, so as a means of trying to disperse it I decided to go out for a walk. It was a quarter after ten on a weeknight, and the town was very quiet. I traveled up onto Higbee Lane and turned down toward Montauk. As I passed The Tropics, I noticed the door was open and the old beer sign in the window was bubbling. No lie, the jukebox was softly playing Bobby Darin. Through the window I could see that the year-round Christmas lights bordering the mirror behind the bar were lit. On a whim, I decided to go in and have a few, hoping that in the decades since I'd last been in there no one had painted over the mural.

There was only one patron, a guy sitting at the bar, who was so wrinkled, he looked like just a bag of skin with a wig, wearing shoes, pants, and a cardigan. He had his eyes closed, but he nodded every now and then to the bartender, who towered over him, a huge, bloated hulk of a man in a T-shirt that only made it a little past the crest of his gut. The bartender was talking almost in whispers, smoking a cigarette. He looked up when I came in, waved, and asked me what I wanted. I ordered a VO and water. When he laid my drink down on a coaster in front of me, he said, "Play much hoop lately?" and smirked. I'm no paragon of physical fitness, myself, these days, so I laughed. I took it as a joke on all three of us beat-up castaways in The Tropics. After paying, I chose a table where I could get a good look at the south wall but sat facing the distant bathroom doors instead of rudely turning my back on my bar mates.

To my relief, the mural was still there, almost completely intact. Its colors had faded and grown dimmer with the buildup of tobacco smoke through the years, but I beheld paradise once again. Someone had drawn a mustache on one of the hula ladies, and the sight of the indiscretion momentarily made my heart sink. Otherwise, I just sat there, reminiscing and digging the breeze in the palms, the beautiful ocean, the distant ship, that poor bastard still trying to reach the shore. It came to me that the town should declare the mural a historic treasure or something. My reverie was interrupted when the old guy pushed back his bar stool and slouched toward the door. I watched him as he passed, his eyes glassy, his hand in the air, trembling. "Okay, Bobby," he barked, and then he was out the door.

"Bobby," I said to myself and looked over at the bartender as he started wiping down the bar. When he looked back at me, he smiled, but I turned quickly away and concentrated on the mural again. A couple of seconds later, I snuck another look at him because it was beginning to dawn on me that I knew the guy. He was definitely somebody from the old days, but time had disguised him. I went back to paradise for a few seconds, and there, in the sun and the ocean breeze, I remembered.

Bobby Lennin had been what my mother called a *hood*. He was a couple years ahead of me in school and light years ahead of me in life experience. I'm sure by the time he was in the sixth grade he'd gotten laid, gotten drunk, and gotten arrested. By high school, he was big, and though always in kind of sloppy shape, with a gut, his biceps were massive and the insatiable look in his eyes left no doubt that he could easily kill you with little remorse. His hair was long and stringy, never washed, and he wore, even in summer, a black leather jacket, jeans, a beer-stained white T-shirt, and thick, steel-toed black boots that could kick a hole in a car door.

I'd seen him fight guys after school by the bridge, guys who were bigger than him, cut with muscles, athletes from the football team. He wasn't even a good boxer, all his swings were these wild, roundhouse haymakers. He could be bleeding out of his eye and have been kicked in the stomach, but he was relentlessly fierce, and wouldn't stop till his opponent was on the ground unconscious. He had a patented throat punch that put the school's quarterback in the hospital. Lennin fought someone almost every day; sometimes he'd even take a swing at a teacher or the principal.

He had a gang, three other misfits in leather jackets, nearly as mean but minus their leader's brains. Whereas Lennin had a wicked sense of humor and a kind of sly intelligence, his followers were confused lunkheads who needed his power and guidance in order to be anyone at all. His constant companion was Cho-cho, who, when a kid in Brooklyn, had been hung by a rival gang to his older brother's. His sister had found him before he died and cut him down. Ever since, he wore the scar, a melted flesh necklace he tried to hide with the chain of a crucifix. The lack of oxygen to his brain had made him crazy, and when he spoke, in a harsh whisper, usually no one understood him except Lennin.

The second accomplice was Mike Wolfe, whose favorite pastime was huffing paint remover in his grandfather's shed. He actually had a lupine look to his face, and with his pencil mustache and sort of pointed ears, reminded me of Oil Can Harry. Then there was Johnny Mars, a thin, wiry guy with a high-pitched, annoying laugh you could light a match on and a strong streak of paranoia. One night, because of some perceived slight by a teacher, he shot out all of the windows on one side of the high school with his old man's twenty-two rifle.

Lennin and his gang scared the shit out of me, but I was lucky, because he liked me. My connection to him went back to when he was younger and played little league football, before he fell totally down the chute into delinquency. He was trouble even back then, but he was a good tackle and played hard. His problem was he didn't take direction all too well and would tell the coaches to fuck off. This was back in the days when saying *fuck* meant something, and it didn't endear him to the folks in charge.

One day when he was in seventh grade, he threw a rock at a passing car up on Higbee and broke the side window. The cops caught him and had him on the side of the road. My father happened to be passing by at the time, and he saw what was going on and pulled over. He knew Bobby because he had been a ref for a lot of the games in the football league. The cops told him they were going to book Lennin, and somehow my father worked it out with them to let him go. He paid the driver of the car to get his window fixed, and then drove Bobby home.

For whatever reason, maybe because he never knew his own father, that incident stuck with Lennin, and although he couldn't follow the advice my old man gave him that day and would continue to screw up, he took it upon himself to watch out for me as repayment for the kindness shown. The first time I had an inkling that this was the case: I was riding my bike through the grade school grounds on my way to the basketball courts. To get there, I had to pass by a spot where the hoods played handball against the tall brick wall of the gym. I was always relieved when they weren't there, but that day they were.

Mike Wolfe, eyes red, snarling like his namesake, ran out and grabbed my bike by the handlebars. I didn't say anything; I was too scared. Joey Missoula and Stinky Steinmuller, hood hangers-on, were ambling over to join him in torturing me. Just then Lennin appeared from somewhere with a quart bottle of beer in his hand, and he bellowed, "Leave him alone." They backed off. Then he said, "Come over here, Ford." He asked me if I wanted any beer, which I turned down, and then told me to hang out if I wanted to.

I didn't want to seem scared or ungrateful, so I stayed for a while sitting on the curb, watching them play handball while Johnny Mars explained how if you jerked off into a syringe and then gave yourself a shot with it and then fucked your wife, your kid would come out a genius. When I finally rode away, Lennin told me to say hello to my father, and when I was well across the field, he yelled after me, "Have a fucking nice summer."

Lennin's interest in protecting me made it possible for me and my brother to pass through the school field after dark, whereas anyone else would have had their asses beaten. One night we ran into Lennin and his gang there down by the woods, where Minerva Street led to the school grounds, and he had a silver handgun in his belt. He told us he was waiting for a guy from Brightwaters to show up and they were going to have a duel. "For my honor," he said and then drained his beer, smashed the bottle against the concrete opening of the sewer pipe, and belched. When a car pulled up on Minerva and blinked its lights on and off twice, he told us we better get going home. We were almost around the block to our house when, in the distance, we heard a gunshot.

Occasionally, Lennin would surface and either save me from some dire situation, like the time I almost got mixed up in a bad dope deal at this party, and he came out of the dark, smacked me in the side of the head, and told me to go home; or I'd hear about him through gossip. He and his gang were forever in trouble with the cops—knife fights, joy rides in hot-wired cars, breaking and entering. I know each of them did some time in the juvenile lockup out in Central Islip before I graduated. Finally, I finished high school, moved away from home to go to college, and lost track of him.

Now I was in The Tropics, just coming out of a daydream of paradise and the past, and there he was, standing at my table, holding a bottle of VO, a bucket of ice and a tumbler, looking like someone had taken him down to the gas station and put the air hose in his mouth.

"You don't remember me, do you?" he asked.

"I thought it was you," I said and smiled. "Bobby Lennin." I stuck my hand out to shake.

He laid the bottle and bucket on the table and then reached out and shook my hand. His grip didn't have any trace of the old power. He sat down across from me and filled my glass before pouring himself one.

"What are you doin' here?" he asked.

"I came in to see the mural," I said.

He smiled and nodded wistfully, as if he completely understood. "You visiting your old man?" he asked.

"Yeah, just for an overnight."

"I saw him in the grocery store a couple of weeks ago," said Bobby. "I said hi but he just nodded and smiled. I don't think he remembers me."

"You never know," I said. "He does the same thing with me half the time now."

He laughed and then asked about my brother and sisters. I told him my mother had passed away, and he said his mother had also died quite a while back. He lit a cigarette and then reached over to another table to get an ashtray. "What are you up to?" he asked.

I told him I was teaching college and was a writer. Then I asked if he still saw Cho-cho and the other guys. He blew out a stream of smoke and shook his head. "Nah," he said, looking kind of sad, and we sat there quietly for a time. I didn't know what to say.

"You're a writer?" he asked. "What do you write?"

"Stories and novels—you know, fiction," I said.

His eyes lit up a little and he poured another drink for each of us. "I got a story for you," he told me. "You asked about Cho-cho and the gang? I got a wild fuckin' story for you."

"Let's hear it," I said.

"This all happened a long time ago, after you left town but before Howie sold the pizza place, around the time Phil the barber's kid got knocked off at the track," he said.

"Yeah, I remember my mother telling me about that," I said.

"Well, anyway, none of us, me, Cho-cho, Wolfey, the Martian, ever graduated high school, and we were all hanging out doing the same old shit, only it was getting deeper all the time. We were all drinking and drugging and beginning to pull some serious capers, like once we broke into the grocery store and stole a couple of hundred dollars worth of cigarettes or we'd heist a car now and then and sell it to a chop shop one of Mars's relatives owned. Occasionally we'd get caught and do a little time, a couple of months here or there.

"We weren't pros by any means, and so we would have to get real jobs from time to time, and, of course, the jobs sucked. One night I was in here, having a few beers and this guy came in who I remembered from high school. Your brother would probably remember him. Anyway, he starts talking to the bartender. Remember old man Ryan?"

"Yeah," I said. "He served me my first drink—a Shirley Temple."

Lennin laughed and went on. "Well this guy was back in town, and he'd graduated from college with a degree in engineering, had a cushy job at Grumman, was getting married and had just bought a big house down by the bay. I overheard this, and I thought to myself, shit, I could go for some of that. But there was no way it was going to happen. And matter of fact, I was looking at the mural and thinking I was like that guy in the boat in the painting there, stuck forever outside the good life. In other words I was starting to see that the outlaw scene was going to get very old very soon.

"Now, I'm not crying in my beer, but let's face it, me and the group didn't have much help in life—busted homes, alcoholic parents, head problems . . . We were pretty fucked from word Go. It was easier for us to scare people into respecting us than it was ever going to be for them to just do it on their own. It seemed like everyone else was heading for the light and we were still down in the shadows munching crumbs. I wanted to be on the beach, so to speak. I wanted a home and a wife and kid and long quiet nights watching the tube and holidays. As for the other guys, I don't think they got it. Shit, if God would have let them, they'd still be muscling high-school kids for pocket change.

"Since it was clear I wasn't going to get there by regular means, I decided what we needed was one big heist, one real job in order to get the cash necessary to live in the real world. After that, I'd part company with them and move on. So I spent a long time thinking about what kind of scam we could pull, but I was blank. We'd spent so many years nickel-and-diming, I couldn't get out of that head. Until, one night, we were sitting at that table right over there, drinking, and a ragged, hopped-up Wolfey, eyes showing almost nothing but white, mentioned something, and I thought I felt the rowboat move a few feet closer to shore.

"This old guy had just moved in on Wolfey's block. What is it, over there by Minerva, Alice Road? Anyway, this old guy, blind, in a wheelchair, moved in. Remember Willie Hart, the guy in high school with the plastic arm? Well, his younger sister, Maria, who, by the way, the Wolfeman was banging every once in a while back in his grandfather's shed in between hits of Zippoway, went to work for the old guy. She cleaned his house and would take him out for walks in his wheelchair and so forth.

"Maria told Wolfey that the old fart was super strange and although he knew English and could talk it, he spoke to himself in another language she thought was Spanish. Maria, if you remember her, was no genius, and for all she knew the guy could have been talking fucking Chinese. Anyway, she said he was kind of feeble in the head, because he had this chess set he would take out and play against himself.

She asked him once if he was winning or losing, and he responded, 'Always losing. Always losing.'"

"What really caught her interest, though, were the pieces. She said they were beautiful, golden monsters. The guy didn't like to be disturbed in the middle of a game, but she had to ask him if they were real gold. He told her, 'Yes, solid gold. This set is very rare, worth hundreds of thousands of dollars. Very old—goes back to the sixteenth century.' The best part of Maria's story was that he kept the set in a drawer in his hutch—no lock.

"So we had a blind guy in a wheelchair with hundreds of thousands of dollars of gold without a lock. Of course, I made a plan to swipe it. I had Wolfe get Maria to tell him what time she walked the guy—Mr. Desnia was his name—in the afternoon, so we could get a look at him. I thought about doing the job when they were out of the house, but in that neighborhood during daylight hours, I knew someone would see us. We drove by them slowly a couple of days later as she pushed him down the street.

"He was bent over in the chair, his bald head like a shelled peanut, looking thin and haggard. His hands shook slightly. He wore dark glasses, no doubt to cover his fucked-up eyes, and a black, tight-fitting get-up like what a priest would wear but with no white collar. 'That's the guy with our gold,' I said after we were past them. 'A blind guy in a wheelchair?' said Mars. 'Jesus, he might as well just hand it over now.' We decided not to wait but to do the job the next night.

"The cops had our prints, so we went and stole some plastic gloves from the grocery store, you know, the kind you could pick a dime up with. We told Maria we'd cut her in if she kept her mouth shut and left the back door unlocked on her way out on the night of the job. She agreed, I think because she was in love with Wolfe, which will show you where her head was at. I warned the other guys, whatever they did, not to speak each other's names during the job. The plan was to get in there, cut the phone wire, put a gag over the old guy's mouth, and swipe the gold. Plain and simple, no one had to get hurt.

"The big night came and we spent the early part of it here, in The Tropics, building up our courage with shots of Jack. When it got to be about midnight, we set out in Mars's Pontiac. We parked on the next street over, snuck through the yard there, and scaled this ten-foot stockade fence into Desnia's backyard. We were all a little high, and climbing over was rough. I didn't bother bringing a flashlight, cause I figured if the guy was blind, we could just put the lights on, but I did bring a pillowcase to carry the gold in and a crowbar in case Maria was wrong about the lock.

"Maria had left the back door open as planned. We sent Cho-cho in first, as usual. Then, one at a time, we entered into the kitchen. The lights were out there and it was perfectly quiet in the house. All I remember was hearing the wall clock ticking off the seconds. A light was shining in the next room over, the living room. I peeked around the corner and saw Desnia sitting in his wheelchair, a big blanket covering his legs and midsection, dark glasses on. If he could see, he would have been looking straight at me, which was a little nerve wracking. To his left was the hutch.

"'Let's go,' I whispered.

"The second I spoke, he called out, 'Who's there? Maria?'

"Cho-cho moved around behind him with a piece of duct tape for his mouth.

Mars said to him, 'Take it easy and you won't get hurt.' Wolfe stood there looking confused, as if he had just come off his high. I got down on my haunches and had to open two drawers before I found the board and pieces. It struck me as odd that he didn't keep them in a box or a bag or something, but the entire board was set up inside the drawer. It took only a second to swipe every one of them up and toss them in the pillowcase. I didn't bother with the board.

"I was just going to tell the others, 'Let's get out of here,' when Desnia reached up and pulled the tape off his mouth. Cho-cho tried to lean over and stop him, but the old man drove his fist straight up, connected with Cho-cho under the chin, and sent him sprawling backward into the corner of the room where he knocked over a lamp and fell on his back.

"With his other hand, the old man flung something at Wolfe that moved through the air so fast I could hardly see it. A split second later, Mike had his hand to the side of his head and there was a sharp piece of metal sticking out of it, blood running down across his face. He went over like a ton of shit. Me and Mars were in shock, neither of us moving, when Desnia flung off the blanket and pulled out this big fucking sword. I'm not shitting you, this sword was like something out of a movie. Then he leaped out of the chair. That's when Johnny decided it was time to book. Too late, though—the old guy jumped forward into a crouch, swung that sword around and took a slice out of Mars's leg like you wouldn't believe. I mean the blood just sort of fell out all over the place and from the lower thigh down was hanging on by a piece of gristle. He hit the deck and started howling like a banshee.

"Desnia wasn't done yet, though. Following the slash on Johnny, like a goddamn dancer, he twirled around toward me and swung the sword again. Luckily, I had the crow bar and held it up in front of me at the last second. It deflected the blow but the blade still cut me on the left side of my chest. I don't know where it came from, just an automatic reaction, I swung the crow bar and took him out at the ankles. As he went down, I looked up and saw Cho-cho crawling out through an open window. I dropped the crowbar, grabbed the bag tight, ran across the room, and dove, head-first, right behind him.

"Man, I wasn't even on my feet before Desnia was sticking his bald head out the window, getting ready to leap through after us. We ran into the backyard, to a corner where there was a shed with a light over it, but there was that damn ten-foot fence. My first thought was to try to jump it, but forget it, he was already there behind us. He would have just slashed our asses. We backed against the fence and got ready to brawl.

"He walked slowly up to us, with the blade at his side. In the light from over the shed, I could see he had lost his glasses, and I don't know how he could have swung that sword the way he did, because his eyes weren't just fucked up, he had none. No eyes, just two puckered little assholes in his head.

"When Desnia was no more than three feet away, Cho-cho held up the crucifix that hung around his neck, like in a vampire movie, to protect himself. The old guy laughed without hardly a sound. Then he lifted the sword slowly, brought it to Cho-cho's neck, and with a flick of the wrist just nicked him so he started to bleed. With that, Desnia dropped the sword and turned around. He took two steps away and his legs buckled. He went down like a sack of turnips. In the distance I could hear Johnny still screaming like mad, and above his racket the sound of the police siren.

Cho-cho and I used the side of the shed to scrabble up over the fence, and we got away with the gold.

"Sounds crazy, right? The old man turning into fucking Zorro at the drop of a hat? But, I'm telling you it was serious. The Martian died that night on the old man's living-room rug. The blade had sliced an artery and he bled out before the ambulance could get there. On top of that, the old man was found dead from a heart attack. But get this, Wolfey got away. While we were out in the backyard up against the fence, he came to, pulled the metal thing out of his head, and split before the cops got there.

"We left Mars's car where it was and he took the rap for the whole caper. Maria kept her mouth shut. We all went into hiding, laying low for a while. I had the chess pieces stashed under a loose floorboard in my mother's bedroom. What was good was that I was pretty sure no one else even knew Desnia had had them to be stolen. I thought if we just chilled for a while, I could fence them and we'd be set. Still, I was spooked by what had happened, Johnny's death and the way it went down. I could feel something wasn't right.

"About two months after the heist, I got a call at like three in the morning from Cho-cho. He said he knew he wasn't supposed to call but he couldn't take it anymore. He was having these dreams that scared him so much he couldn't sleep. I asked him what he was dreaming about and he just said, 'Really evil shit.' A month after that, I heard from someone that he'd finished the job they started in Brooklyn when he was a kid. Yeah, he'd hung himself in his mother's attic.

"The year wasn't out before both Maria and Wolfe went down too. I'd heard that he'd taken to staying in his grandfather's shed all the time. She was joining him now on a regular basis, and they had begun taking pills, ludes and darvon, and drinking while huffing the Zippoway, and that just ate what little there was of their brains, melted that swiss cheese like acid one night. I should have been sadder at losing all my friends, but instead I was just scared to death and started living the clean life, laying off the booze and dope and getting to my crappy job at the metal shop every day on time. I never even went to Cho-cho's funeral.

"After that year ended, I let another six months go by before I started looking around for a fence. I knew it would have to be somebody high class, who dealt in antiques but was willing to look the other way when it came to how you acquired what you were selling. I did some studying up on the way it worked and spoke to a few connections. Eventually, I got the phone number of a guy in New York and the green light to give him a call. Nothing in person until he checked out you and the goods you claimed to have.

"I got the pieces out from under the floorboards and really looked at them for the first time. The bigger pieces were about four inches tall, and the smaller ones, which I guess were pawns—I don't know gots about chess—were three inches. They definitely seemed to be made of solid gold. Half of them were figures of monsters, each one different, the work on them really detailed. The other half, I don't know what they were, but I recognized one as being Christ. The smaller ones looked like angels. I couldn't make heads or tails of it.

"The day finally came when I was supposed to call the guy. I did, from the pay phone in the back of Phil's barbershop. I was nervous, you know, sweating how much I was gonna get and still scared at all the ill stuff that had gone down. Well, the phone rings, a guy answers, he tells me, 'No names. Describe what you have.' So I told him, 'Gold chess set from the sixteenth century.' But the minute I started describing the individual pieces, the line went dead. That was it. At first I thought it was just a bad connection, or I needed more change. I called back, but no one would pick up.

"Then shit started to really slide. Dreams like Cho-cho described, and I took to drinking again, but drinking in a way I never did before. I lost my job, and on top of it all my mother got the cancer. I was reeling and it took me a while, like two years, to get it together to deal with the damn gold again. Just by luck, I guess, I ran into a guy who knew this guy, a Dominican, who fenced stuff from break-ins out in the Hamptons. I met him one winter afternoon over in the parking lot at Jones Beach. Thinking it might be a setup, I only took three pieces with me.

"The wind was blowing like a motherfucker that day. It was like a sand storm even in the parking lot. The guy was there when I pulled up, sitting in a shiny black Cadillac. We got out of the cars. He was short, dark skinned, wore sunglasses and a rain coat. We shook hands, and he asked to see what I had. I took two of the pieces out and held them up for him to see. He took one look at them and said, 'Isiaso,' and then made a face like I was holding a couple of turds. The guy didn't say anything else, he just turned around, got in his car and drove away.

"And that's the way it went in trying to fence them. I'd give it a shot, be turned down and then get swamped in a lot of bad circumstance. Then I just wanted to unload them and take whatever I could get. Even this guy, Bowes, who bought gold teeth down on Canal Street in the city wouldn't touch them. He called them *La Ventaja del Demonio*, and threatened to call the cops if I didn't leave his shop. It wasn't until after my mother passed away that I decided to try to find out about them.

"Imagine me, Bobby Lennin, failer of classes and king of detention, in the library. I don't think I'd ever been in the fucking place in my life. But I started there, and you know what? I discovered I wasn't as stupid as I looked. There was some real pleasure in researching them. It was the only thing that offset the depression of drinking. In the meantime, old man Ryan took pity on me and gave me a job bartending here at The Tropics. I barely managed to keep myself from getting too screwed up until he went home in the evening, so as to keep the job.

"Yeah, I scoured the library, got interlibrary loans, all that good stuff, and I started to crack the story on the chess set. Then, when the Internet came in, I got with that too, and over a period of long years, I put it together. The set was known as *The Demon's Advantage*. Scholars talked about it like it was more a legend than anything that actually existed. It was supposedly crafted by this goldsmith in Italy, Dario Foresso, in 1533, commissioned by a strange cat who went by the name of Isiaso. The dude had no last name as far as anyone could tell.

"Anyway, this Isiaso was from Hispaniola, now the Dominican Republic. In 1503, I think it was Pope Julius III, declared Santo Domingo an official city of Christendom. It was the jumping-off place for European explorers who were headed to South and North America. Isiaso was born the year the Pope gave the two-fingered salute to the city. Our boy's father was Spanish, an attaché to the crown, there to oversee the money to be spent on expeditions. You know, basically an accountant. But his mother was a native, and, here's where it gets creepy, said to be from a long line of sorcerers. She was an adept of the island magic. Isiaso, who was supposed to be like a genius kid, learned the ways of both parents.

"When he's in his twenties, his old man ships him out to Rome to finish his education. He goes to the university and studies with the great philosophers and theologists of the time. It was during these years that he comes to see the battle between good and evil in terms of chess—the dark versus the light, et cetera, with the advantage going back and forth. Strategy was part of it and mathematics along with faith, but, to tell you the truth, I never really completely understood what he was supposed to be getting at.

"Somehow Isiaso gains wealth and power very quickly. Rises to the top of the heap. No one can figure out how he came by his wealth and those who cross him meet with weird and ugly deaths. Anyway, he has the funds to get Foresso to undertake the set. And Foresso is no slouch—an apprentice to Benvenuto Celini, greatest goldsmith who ever lived. 'Many thought Foresso was his master's equal,' was how one book put it.

"Okay, you with me? Enter Pope Paul III, Julian's successor. He's this big patron of the arts. Michelangelo worked for him at one time. He hears tell of this incredible chess set being created by Foresso and goes to the guy's studio and checks it out. Later, he lets it be known to his underlings that he wants the chess set for himself. He sends someone to see Isiaso, and the guy tells him the Pope wants to buy it off him. Isiaso has other plans. He knows the Vatican's going to be funding a university in Santo Domingo, and he tells him what he wants in exchange is passage home and a professor job at the university. I got the idea from my reading that it might have been difficult for him to get the job because he was half-native.

"He's surprised when the Pope's go-between says, 'Cool, we'll cut the deal.' What he doesn't know is that the Vatican has had their eye on him as a troublemaker, and they want him out of Rome anyway. On the voyage home, the ship drops anchor for a day off a small, uninhabited island. Isiaso is asked if he would like to go ashore and witness a true paradise on earth. Being a curious guy, he says yes. He and a sailor go to the island in a rowboat. They explore the place, but in the middle of them looking around, Isiaso notices all of a sudden that he's alone. When he makes it back to the beach, he sees the other guy in the rowboat heading back to the ship.

"The ship pulls up anchor and splits, stranding him there. It was the plan all along. They wanted him out of Rome, but they were too afraid of his supposed magic to come right out and boot his ass. So they got the chess set and got rid of him, and the legend has it that he put a curse on the chess set. Legend also has it that if you play the demon side of the board, you can never lose. You could play fucking Gary Kasparov and not lose. But at the same time, the person who owns it is doomed, cursed, screwed, blued and tattooed, and you can't give it away, you can't throw it away. Believe me, I've tried and it's a shit storm of misery and the dreams just get too intense. The only way to unload it is to have it stolen from you, and in the process blood must be drawn. Die with it in your possession, and you ain't going to be seeing paradise."

"Now," said Lennin, "what do you think of that? I swear on my mother's grave that it's all completely true." He lifted the bottle and filled each of our glasses. "And the biggest kicker of all is that I dug all this up on my own. Man, I could have gotten through high school and college, for Christ's sake."

"So, you believe in the curse?" I asked.

"I'm not gonna bore you with how many times I tried to dump the pieces," he said.

"You don't seem cursed, though," I said.

"Well, there's cursed and then there's cursed. Look at me. I'm a wreck. My liver is shot. I've been in and out of the hospital five times in the last year. They told me if I don't quit drinking, I'm gonna die very soon."

"What about some kind of addiction center where they can treat you?" I asked.

"I've tried it," he said. "I just can't stop. It's my part of the curse. I'm in here every day, throwing back the booze, it doesn't matter what kind it is, and staring at that mural, a castaway like Isiaso. It doesn't make any sense, but I swear that's his hand in the picture, down in the corner by the bathroom. All my attempts at relationships went south, all my plans to better myself dried up and blew away. I'm slowly killing myself. You see," he said, lifting his shirt to show me his sagging chest, "the scar is right here, over my heart, and my heart is poisoned."

"I don't know what to say," I told him. "You were always kind to me when I was a kid."

"Thanks," he said. "Maybe if I can unload the set eventually that'll be at least one thing on the scale in my favor." He got up then and went behind the bar. When he came back, he was carrying a chessboard and on it were the golden pieces. He laid it down on the table between us.

"Man, they're beautiful," I told him.

"Listen, you gotta get going home now," he said, the same as he had so many years ago. "I had a couple of rough-looking characters in here the other day, and I showed them the set, told them how much it was worth and that I kept it behind the bar all the time. It's getting past midnight, and there's a chance they'll show up. I know the old man let Maria see it and told her about it for the same reason I've been flaunting it lately. Maybe when they come for it, I'll get some of the old juice back like Desnia did, and we'll have a good brawl."

I stood up, a little wobbly from the bottle of VO we'd finished. "There's no other way?" I asked.

He shook his head.

I turned and took in the mural one last time, because I knew I would never come back again. Bobby looked it over too.

"You know," he said, "I bet you always thought that guy in the boat was trying to get to the island, right?"

"Yeah," I said.

"The truth is, he's been trying to escape all these years. Those women look like women to you, but count 'em, there are as many as pieces in a chess set."

"I hope he makes it," I said, and then reached out and shook his hand.

Leaving The Tropics behind, I stepped onto the sidewalk and stood there for a minute to get my bearings. The night was cold, and I realized autumn was only a week away. I turned my collar up and walked along, searching my mind, without success, for the warmth from that painted vision of paradise. Instead, all I could think of was my old man, sitting in his recliner, smiling like the Buddha, while the world he once knew slowly disintegrated. I turned off Higbee onto my block and was nearly home, when from somewhere away in the distance, I heard a gunshot.

TERRY DOWLING

Clownette

Terry Dowling continues to be one of Australia's most lauded and internationally acclaimed writers of science fiction, fantasy, and horror. He is author of Rynosseros, Blue Tyson, Twilight Beach, Wormwood, The Man Who Lost Red, An Intimate Knowledge of the Night, Antique Futures: The Best of Terry Dowling, *and* Blackwater Days, *and of the computer adventures* Schizm: Mysterious Journey, Mysterious Journey II: Chameleon, *and* Sentinel: Descendants in Time. *He is also co-editor of* Mortal Fire: Best Australian SF *and* The Essential Ellison.

Dowling's stories have appeared in numerous best-of compilations, including The Year's Best Science Fiction, The Year's Best SF, The Year's Best Fantasy, The Best New Horror, *and* The Year's Best Fantasy and Horror, *as well as anthologies as diverse as* Dreaming Down Under, Centaurus, Gathering the Bones, *and* The Dark. *He is a communications instructor, a musician and songwriter, and has been genre reviewer for* The Weekend Australian *for the past fifteen years.*

"Clownette" was originally published on SCI FICTION.

—E.D.

I've always had a love-hate relationship with Macklin's. When the place is full, when there are conventions or tour groups booked in, then relatives, friends, and discount regulars like me get offered the Clownette. There's no other choice.

Not that it's a bad room. There are darker, far worse rooms at Macklin's, many with brick-wall views. The Clownette opens onto a back lane, true, but it's on the top floor and there's sky and light. That's the upside. That's by day. At night—well, it changes.

And this time, for maybe the eighteenth, nineteenth time in six years, it was a full house and the Clownette or nothing.

No big deal, never a big deal. But there's always ten, twenty seconds or so when it almost matters a lot. I could trek over to Wright's or the Walden; they have budget plans as well, not that that's any kind of issue with my Hopeton's expense account. But, taking the good with the bad, there's something about the Clownette. Once those ten, twenty seconds are done, you see it as clear as day. You get the sky and the light—at least until nightfall. You get to check out the latest additions to the décor. You get to see the face, the "Motley," the Macklin Hotel's very own Shroud of Turin right there in the wall.

Dry-staining as art. A platter-sized discoloration that spoils the room, does so crucially for some. And it does look like a clown in a sketchy, man-in-the-moon fashion, with blotchy there-but-never-quite-there features. Paint it over as often as you like, the Motley creeps back, pushing through bit by bit, first as the barest hint of shadow, then as a chain of dusky fractals linking up. And once they connect: hey presto! Peekaboo! Bozo in the wall!

I took the news about the hotel being full with passable grace, expecting one of Gordon's usual quips. "Off to see the Wizard again, I'm afraid, Mr. J." Or "Tell me again, Mr. J., how you always wanted to join a circus as a kid!" Or, perfectly po-faced, as if taking the straight part in our long-standing, front-desk double act: "So he misses you, Mr. J. You see the kid, he says, you send him right up."

Six years of staying at Macklin's, and to Gordon—and the Motley, to hear Gordon tell it—I'm still the kid!

None of that today. Maybe there were things on his mind. Maybe he'd had bad news. He just gave me a warm-up smile straight out of Hospitality 101 and handed me a new-style magnetic key.

"Made some changes since your last visit, Mr. Jackson," he said.

There it was again, the Mr. Jackson! I'd thought it had been a natural enough slip when he'd said it the first time, some automatic holdover from dealing with too many new guests at once.

Thrown by how correct he was being, I was an extra second or two answering. "Don't tell me it's gone!"

"No, sir. I meant the key. The wall's been painted again since your last visit, but you know how it is."

Sir? Mr. Jackson; now *sir!*

"Wouldn't be the same without it, Gordon," I said to keep the patter going, trying for a handle on what was amiss here. These Gordon glitches overshadowed getting the Clownette, stopped me switching modes and welcoming the news that my special contingency plan for this particular "Meet the Motley" visit could be put into effect after all. Maybe the staff were being assessed. Maybe there were new owners, time-and-motion people on the premises, efficiency appraisals and staff cutbacks looming, even video surveillance right now. I'd seen it in so many other places: three-star establishments trying for four-star status. I forced myself not to look for cameras.

"Guess I'm off to see the Wizard then!" I said, making one last attempt to rebuild the old Gordon Maher and Bob Jackson bridges, and the smile did widen a bit, though a wink would have helped enormously.

I'd ask about it later. Now I reached for my bag.

"Let me get someone to help with—"

"Gordon, how many years have I been coming here?"

"A lot, Mr. Jackson."

"Then you know the drill. This front desk is yours. This bag is mine. Want to swap?"

The silly Gordon grin switched up a notch, seemed almost normal now. Much better. *Call me Mr. J.! Just once! Call me the kid!*

"No, Mr. Jackson."

Damn! One more try. "You still sleep over on-shift?"

"Sometimes."

"Then how about we swap digs? *You* can have the Clownette?"

"Never again, Mr. Jackson!" Gordon was really grinning now, as if finally braving the old Jackson-Maher routines in spite of himself.

"Then off I go."

Let the unseen time-and-motion gremlins add compassion and humor to their ticket and we might save Macklin's yet, keep it a strictly three-star haven in a cold and busy world.

I took my bag across to the elevators, rode one to the fifth floor, then followed the long, softly lit corridor toward the rear of the hotel and Room 516.

Other hotels had trained me well. I swiped the card in the new magnetic lock and pushed back the familiar old door.

And there it was.

Both parts of the 516 experience for me. First the "Rush of Weird," as I called it, the deep-anxiety, almost-dread stab of whatever it was I felt whenever I first opened the door on any visit. More than the Motley itself, it was *that* feeling that struck the brain, poleaxed the spirit, made me want to turn and run. It only happened on that first opening of the door during any stay.

Then there was the face.

Beyond the old queen-sized bed I knew so well, left of the same curtained triple windows, it blossomed against the load-bearing wall that somehow kept bringing damp up from the core of the old building, one and a half meters above the floor on the only wall not papered over, *never* papered over.

The Motley. Seven main blotches, enough of a man-in-the-moon soot-smudge face, but nothing that definite, just a grey-scale glitch in the latest color field.

They'd tried covering it with paintings, mirrors, other decorative features, but that's where things became truly wacky. It wasn't that screws and bolts gave, nothing as simple and conclusive as that, or that the damp leached out to create penicillin fields. It wasn't that furnishings placed in front soon had sprung backs and internal mold. This was *dry* staining—*dry* to the touch, no damp smell at all.

The Motley moved.

Put something in front, a painting, a cupboard, and within the week, sometimes overnight, Bozo would be starting to peer over the top or around the sides. A few more days and it was out of hiding altogether. Remove the obstacle and gradually, over days, nights, a week or two, back it went to its original position—but without any sign of a relocation trail. That was the real wonder of the thing for me.

Experts spoke of microclimates, of internal convection variables in the space between the stain and whatever fronted it, rerouting the damp-track, some central-core problem, whatever. No rising damp anywhere else in the building. No explaining the lack of residual staining left behind when it did relocate. It just—moved.

Make it a discount room, they said, or a freebie. *Not* a storeroom. Keep it open and airy. Count your losses. One room out of nearly sixty wasn't bad, considering.

Which is what Macklin's was given in lieu of any kind of adequate scientific explanation.

There'd been a fleeting Indian summer of notoriety: a month or two of minor tabloid features, even a guest spot on Ross Haslan's *Mysterious Houses*. But that kind of publicity drew the weirdos, management quickly discovered. They issued a press statement saying that modern damp-proofing techniques had fixed the problem. When journos phoned and the weirdos enquired, they were told the face was gone.

But here it was in all its dusky, smudgy, chimney-soot glory. And, oddly enough, management had found a winner with the latest color scheme. They'd painted the wall a soft tan, quite a nice contrast to the three papered walls with their familiar, muted yellow-and-white pattern. The blotches were less intense, less ominous somehow. I'd been here for olive, russet, even for an overkill chocolate brown. But darker colors had made the blemish seem more intense—another trick of the staining, the lighting, Room 516's Turin Effect, as if the Motley was determined to secure its place in the world.

My thoughts were definitely elsewhere, so the knock at the door startled me.

I hurried to answer it, first peering through the spy-hole to see who it was. When no one was visible, I just assumed there would be fresh towels left on the floor, or a fruit bowl, something that hadn't needed personal attention.

But when I opened the door, there was nothing. *Seemed* to be nothing, for when I glanced down the hall toward the lifts, there was Gordon standing right there, a few steps back from the doorway.

"Shit!" I cried, badly startled. Then I saw the bottle of wine he was holding out for me to take and immediately flashed the best smile I could manage.

"Look—er—Mr. J.," Gordon said. "About before. I'm sorry. I just wanted to give you this. With my compliments."

"Gordon, what's going on? Are they doing staff evaluations? You were so formal down there."

"That's it." He cast a quick glance back along the corridor. He was still edgy.

"Is your job at risk?"

"Maybe. Not sure. Something's happening, Mr. J. They won't tell us. We just need to be careful. I—wanted you to know."

"Well, hey, thanks, Gordon. I was worried. Hope it goes okay for you."

"Thanks. Thanks, Mr. J. You want anything, you just call down to the desk."

"Will do. Thanks for this."

He smiled, nodded, then turned and headed for the lifts.

I locked the door and went back to laying out my things. I felt a lot better about the business at the front desk now, though something still felt wrong. But what? What?

Then I knew.

Gordon hadn't wanted to be in line of sight of the open door. He was scared of the Motley!

I could hardly blame him. Some people flatly refused to stay in 516. With its Rush of Weird and its "what-do-you-see-in-this-picture" Rorschach feature to grab your attention, the room had a survival potential of five guests in ten. Gordon had given me the statistic on my third visit. Once the stain was seen as a face, he'd said, five out of ten first-time occupants refused to stay. I just hadn't for a moment considered that Gordon might be one of those who found it too much.

Who could blame him, any of them for that matter? In daylight the Motley was fine. Once your eye had resolved it as a face, it was a bit like having one of those cardboard cut-outs of cops used as thief deterrents in stores constantly staring at you. But at night—a few of the more forthcoming refugees from 516 had admitted—

especially once the lights were out, it just became too much. *Knowing* it was there, leering in the dark, big blotchy grin twitching up, smudge eyes staring.

The remaining five guests in ten did better apparently, and I was a borderline member of that line-up. We endured it, were either too drunk, too stolid, or too budget conscious. The last two probably did apply to me, but only if you added curious to the mix. With my plan for this latest stay, I was probably closer to the journo/weirdo margin than I cared to admit.

The Motley fascinated me. I'd balked at the front desk, sure, hesitated that ten to twenty seconds, but that was because of the anticipation, the weird feeling I knew I'd have when I first opened the door. That was because of—something. It didn't last more than a few seconds, otherwise no cut-rate plan on earth would have made me keep taking the Clownette. It was the love-hate, yes-no of it for me, the whole complex mix of "What's going on here?"/"You won't get me this time!" bravado and determination.

I smiled at how intense I was being. These were pretty much my usual daytime observations for 516 anyway, the ones I always had after I'd first felt the Rush of Weird again, but the business with Gordon—parts one *and* two!—had thrown me.

I checked my watch by the digital clock alongside the bed. Three forty-five on a bright, sunny afternoon. The Motley was in its day phase, its blotches so ordinary, so formless, like any of the other countless stainings in countless second-rate hotel rooms across the country, across the world.

I smiled at a wordplay that was suddenly there, paraphrasing the famous movie line.

Of all the grin joints in all the world, why did you have to walk into this one?

There was nothing like a face now, certainly no more than in any other set of stains in any other place. The day was too sunny, too bright.

And, to be fair, the features probably didn't get any more definite after dark. Not really. It was more to do with the ambient lighting, how the shift to evening let the room's lighting focus the observer's eye differently.

With the Rush of Weird behind me, I could deal with all that. I shifted my bag to the stand beside the bed and went to say hello.

"Tonight, Mr. Motley," I said, running my hand over the sooty spread of blotches as I always did, "we're going to try happy trails together. See if we can make you move a bit!"

There. Intentions declared. Our latest meeting formalized, everything stated up front. I sat on the edge of the bed then, studying how the smudges sat in the tan. Just an overnight stay, but somehow I felt this visit would be the one!

I *wanted* the Motley to move, wanted to be the one to make it move—see what Gordon and other hotel staff said happened.

"Guess we're just at that stage in our relationship, Mr. M.," I said, then went down to the bar to get a drink.

The sunlight was well and truly gone from the back lane when I returned at five thirty, and the Motley had fallen into shadow with the rest of the room's features. No face. Nothing like a face yet.

But I knew only too well how to hasten Bozo on his way, knew from experience to draw the curtains and switch on both bedside lamps to compensate.

The result was instantaneous and surprising, even reassuring in a way. The fall of artificial light in the room was such that the main features were evident almost immediately, first as the eyes and brow line, then, bit by smudgy bit, the grin, which always surprised me by how wide it actually was, how completely it had been there all along, waiting to be stitched up by just one more blotch resolving. Slowly, finally, the nose and cheeks emerged, cohered—there were no other words for it. It probably had more to do with an observer's brain providing whatever "nosing" and "cheeking" was needed, a few key bits of recognition cuing the rest.

Again I had to smile at what a good job we did when it came to haunting ourselves.

On other visits, I'd switched off the bedside lights, gone out to a movie or a restaurant, taken my time, then returned close on bedtime and slept through. I was still deciding how to fill this particular evening, but first there was work to do.

I set about moving the television cabinet out from the wall, disconnected the antenna cable and power lead, and dragged the unit across the carpet until it was in front of the stain. During my last stay in 516, I'd worked out that the cabinet with the black Akai television itself wasn't large enough to hide the Motley. But replacing the television with the large square painting above the bed would do the job nicely.

Unlike many of the more modern hotels and motels, Macklin's didn't bolt their prints to the walls. The copy of Van Gogh's *Sunflowers* hung by wire on a wall stud in the traditional manner, so it took surprisingly little time. I set the television on the floor, then placed the framed print on top of the cabinet so it was facing the wall. It covered the Motley completely.

Operation Happy Trails had begun. On the one hand I knew that nothing could come of it in the time available. I could hardly expect it. But on the other, there was a strange feeling that anything could happen. At least I was giving it a try, taking my relationship with Bozo to a new level.

I took the reports for the next day's sales meeting from my briefcase, called "Lazarus, come forth!" to my hidden roommate, then set off for Saffron's. No movie tonight. I'd read the Deane and the Warnock proposals again over dinner, have a few drinks, and turn in early.

I bid Gordon goodnight as I crossed the lobby. He flashed his smile, waved, and called, "Have a pleasant evening, Mr. Jackson!"

I smiled back. We were doing well. We were fellow conspirators now. Maybe we'd get a chance to laugh about it over a drink someday.

I was relieved to find Carmen at the front desk when I returned around ten. It had always been "Mr. Jackson" with her, so when she wished me a pleasant evening the world felt back on track again. I was surprised at how much I needed it right then.

My room was as I'd left it, of course, which suddenly made me wonder what other guests got up to in their rooms. I had plenty of horror stories from other establishments, and Gordon had shared some of Macklin's with me: about guests painting the walls with their feces, jumping into completely filled bathtubs, playing autoerotic hanging games from the pelmets and light fittings. Bob Jackson rearranging a few pieces of furniture was rather small-time in that larger scheme of things.

With the television cabinet borrowed for other duties, I had no choice but to turn in, though falling asleep took some doing. It only served me right, of course. Try as I might, I kept thinking of the Motley there in the darkness, grinning away. It'd been—what?—at least seven hours now, probably more. In a single night I could hardly expect anything. But what if there *was* a trace, some sign?

I switched on the bedside lamp. There was nothing visible around the edges of the painting that I could tell, but there simply wasn't enough light to be sure.

I reached along the headboard and switched on the main room lights. Nothing. The Motley was still in hiding.

I was tempted to leave a light on, but there was my nine-thirty sales meeting to consider. This would have to be just a rehearsal for the Happy Trails outing I'd originally planned. I'd try the whole thing again when I was in town for more than an overnighter.

I felt much better once that was decided. I switched off the lights and actually managed to doze for a few hours.

But just a few hours.

Something woke me at 1:47—a sound, a movement; I couldn't be sure.

The sense of the Motley's presence was stronger than ever. All imagined, no doubt, but such a thing had never happened before.

I didn't turn on the light this time, just lay in the dark thinking. The whole thing with Gordon had me again. There'd been something about him, the intensity. I couldn't shake it. It wasn't the "Mr. Jackson" or the "sir" business. That was easy enough to understand once staff appraisals were factored in, or the possibility of some influential guest complaining about too much familiarity among the staff.

It was *how* he was when he'd given me the wine. It should have made things better—that was clearly the intention—but it hadn't. It was like being with someone who thanked you too much or apologized too many times or asked if there was anything he could do once too often. It was overreaction.

That was part of it, most of it! Just a few words out in the hall and he'd said Mr. J.—what?—three, four times? As if overcompensating. As if he'd remembered to do it all of a sudden.

And there was something else, a body-language thing. Aside from the edginess, the anxiety, there'd been something about his eye line. His gaze had been wrong. What had those sales-training videos said? True friendly gaze went from the eyes in a triangle *down* to the smile. Formal business gaze went *up* from the eyes to a point on the forehead.

Hard to be sure now, but maybe that was it. Gordon may have been genuinely worried, but something had made him seem detached as well. Not sorry at all. It had happened all too quickly.

Another thought struck me then. Gordon had been standing to the side of the door, hadn't wanted to look in and see the Motley. What had he told me down at the front desk when I suggested he take 516? "Never again, Mr. Jackson!" That word! *Again!* Had he recently spent a night in the room? Had 516 done something to his memory, his way of looking at things? His personality?

Ludicrous, ridiculous, but the craziest things made sense in the small hours. And such late-night thoughts always seemed to drag their own wacky logic along with them. It worried me. Too much fear could trigger—what were the terms?—a behavioral shutdown or a post-traumatic adjustment of affect, a way of dealing with severe personal crisis. I'd read about that somewhere. Maybe this was something like that.

I smiled at myself in the darkness. I was haunting myself, using 516 and the Motley to do it.

Still, at 1:53 in the small hours, with newly limbered night at the windows, it did make sense. Provoking the Motley no longer seemed such a good idea.

I was half-asleep, being irrational, but enough was enough. I switched on the bedside light, got out of bed, crossed to the painting, hefted it, and prepared to set it on the floor. Before I could do that I dropped it in astonishment.

The Motley wasn't there!

I stood staring at where it had been, *should* have been, *had* to be! Then I broke free, stumbled across the room, switched on the main lights, and rushed back to the wall.

Not a trace. Not a sign.

It was gone!

Which wasn't possible. Not like that. Not after so little time.

It was 2:09, but I did the only sensible thing. I took a shower, turned it to cold at the end so I was completely awake. Then I made coffee, strong and black, and sat on the edge of the bed sipping it, relearning the room and trying to eliminate the things that almost make sense at that hour, can make too much sense if you're not careful.

"Serves you right, Jackson," I said, as much to hear a voice as anything. "Now you either call it quits and find another hotel or you work through this like an adult!"

I set my cup on the bedside table, went over to the television stand, and pulled it out from the wall.

Nothing. Not a smudge, not a hint that I could see. The tan was unblemished.

Which was impossible.

Maybe it was me. A vision thing. But after ten minutes of sightings from various points in the room, I was back sitting on the bed staring at the blank wall.

What to do? I could phone Rhonda or Bruce or Katie half a continent away, have friends talk me through this. Better yet, phone down to Carmen at the front desk, get her up here, let her be a witness to the whole thing.

I didn't, couldn't. Not yet.

What if the Motley reappeared just before she arrived? That's how these things happened, didn't they?

It was that certainty—absurd, laughable, vivid at this hour—that stopped me. Not because I truly believed it would or *could* happen, but because the certainty itself felt so real, had me so completely.

I couldn't help it. What if Carmen came up and the smudges *did* re-form just as she knocked at the door?

It took me back to my thoughts about Gordon staying the night in 516, being changed by the Motley. Maybe it adjusted your mind, how you saw things. That was it! The Motley was still there, had worked its special Bozo magic and done something to my ability to see it!

I grinned, laughed, was still able to, thank God, tracking my growing fear with an equally impressive detachment. I needed to act, do something.

"Clever, Mr. M.," I told the blank wall. "Seems this round might go to you unless a little Jackson finessing can save the day."

Save the day? I immediately corrected myself. *Save the night!* That was more like it, but definitely the wrong thought right then.

I grabbed the phone handset from the cradle by the bed and pressed the key for the front desk.

After a ten-second delay, Carmen answered. "Reception?"

"Carmen, it's Bob Jackson in 516."

"We don't talk to you."

I froze where I stood.

"What? What did you say?"

"I said: 'Yes, Mr. Jackson? How can I help?'"

"No, what did you just say before that?"

"I said, 'Yes, Mr. Jackson?' Is there something wrong?"

Sure is, kiddo. I've spooked myself good!

But no point pushing it. *It adjusts your mind.* "Ah—look, I know it's late, Carmen, but I'm really not sleeping too well. Would you have any sleeping pills down there?"

"Of course, Mr. Jackson. I can't leave the desk—"

"That's okay. That's fine. I'll be right down. Thanks, Carmen."

I fumbled getting the handset back into its cradle, fumbled pulling on my clothes.

What had she said? That other comment? So odd, so truly strange.

And now there was the prospect of actually leaving the room. Everything could change. Most certainly would, I was certain. That's how these things worked. I'd go down, get the pills, and the Motley would be back on the wall when I returned, grinning at me, its own Happy Trails maneuver wonderfully complete. *Not a bad trick, hey, Mr. J.? Motley one, Bob Jackson nil.*

I had to take charge, go down, anchor myself in the ordered, everyday world.

I grabbed the magnetic key from the nightstand and stepped out into the hall, waited till the door clicked shut behind me, then headed for the lifts.

And discovered Motley's next piece of trickery!

The corridor seemed longer, impossibly extended.

Adjusts your mind! How you see things.

My night logic snatched at it. Not surprising, not so strange, I told myself, dragged from sleep like this, primed with weird thoughts. Just another optical trick.

The setting encouraged it. By their very nature, hotel corridors exist in a state of timelessness. Day or night, the lights are always on. The carpeting steals sound. Every footstep is snatched away the moment you make it. You pass other rooms as if you never exist. And the doors! Blind, replicated, one after the other, just their vacant spy holes tracking you sightlessly like the eyes of figures in portraits.

Another key factor right there.

No portraits in hotel rooms or hotel corridors. Always landscapes, abstracts, vistas, safe, Impressionistic pieces. No one wanted eyes watching them in hotel rooms or down those long hallway approaches. Which explained 516's five refugees in ten, why the Motley had the impact it did. Of course! The portrait effect!

Almost at the lifts, I noticed Room 502 with its double spy hole: one at the usual eye level, one lower down for guests in wheelchairs, children, shorter people.

My rational mind understood, but the night terrors had me.

Being watched by something doubled over, folded on itself.

I laughed—my struggling, rational self did—and laughed again. I was imagining a third spy hole way down at floor level. For the snake, I thought. Or Randion the Living Torso from that old Tod Browning movie!

Crazy. All crazy. But what you did to cope. To turn it and make it right again.

Then I was safely past. I pressed the elevator call button, heard one, possibly both of the carriages responding, climbing the long dark throats of the old building.

One car signalled its arrival with a soft chime, a sound quickly snatched away by the carpeting. The doors slid back. I stepped into the plush interior and descended to the lobby, which seemed stark and overlit after the dim infinite corridor up there.

"Mr. Jackson," Carmen said from behind the reception desk. "Sorry you're having trouble sleeping. This should help."

She handed me a sleeping pill in its foil wrapping.

"Thanks, Carmen. I'm probably just overstressed. Got a big meeting tomorrow." *What was it you said before? What?*

"What time did you want to be woken? Just in case?"

"Good point. Make it seven A.M., okay?"

"Seven it is. Good night, Mr. Jackson."

"Good night, Carmen. Thanks."

It was easier going back, riding the lift up into the night, reaching the quiet fifth-floor elevator lobby, finding the hallway its normal self again. It was as if everything had been reset.

Not completely reset, thank goodness. When I swiped my card in the lock and pushed back the door, there was no Rush of Weird.

But the Motley was back on the wall!

Of course it was, back where it should have been, no doubt had been all along.

No more games. No more tricks. I rehung the Van Gogh print above the bed, moved the television cabinet back to its original place, reconnected the leads.

"You win this round, Mr. M.," I said, feeling exhausted, beaten, and yet strangely elated by the whole thing. Collateral damage, I told myself. Waking like this. Being primed. Seeing things.

I probably didn't need the sleeping pill, but when I was back in bed, ready to settle again, I popped it from its foil and swallowed it just the same. I was asleep in minutes.

And awake again at 3:17. The Motley woke me.

It was leering, shimmering on the wall, having itself a merry time! But glowing! Shining somehow!

Never knew I could be a night light, did you, Mr. J.?

I lurched from bed, leaden, dizzy but driven, and lunged at the wall.

Wrong way! Wrong thing to do, I knew, even as I did it. Should have turned on the light first! Should have kept away!

But it was panic. What passed for it in my drugged, terrified state. I went reeling, fell at the wall, with arms raised to stop myself.

But it wasn't there.

Now everything is different, of course. Not just because it's the view I've never had—looking *out* from the wall. It's because there are so many of us trapped in here, crowding behind, all in our turn, so needy, so frantic to look out again. It's knowing that the next too-curious guest will force me back into that darkness, that *all* the Clownette's guests checked out—just as I had, some tricked-up version of me—and that out there in the world a brand-new Bob Jackson was probably farewelling a brand-new Gordon and whatever other bits of itself this dark place has managed to squeeze through.

I'm beyond the revulsion and panic, the rage and disbelief. It adjusts your mind. Now there's just the numbness and despair, the agony of waiting. Feeling them crowding in behind, touching, snatching, muttering.

At least now I know what the sensation was whenever I first opened the door to 516—all that's left of a scream from a place where screams can no longer be heard.

Housemaid or guest, housemaid or guest—that's all that matters now, knowing that the day will come when Macklin's has a full house again and the scream is mine.

Stripping

In addition to being a respected novelist, story writer, playwright, and essay-ist, Joyce Carol Oates is the Roger S. Berlind Distinguished Professor in the Humanities at Princeton University. She has won the National Book Award and the Bram Stoker Award and is the 1994 recipient of the Bram Stoker Award for Life Achievement in Horror Fiction. Her most recent novels are We Were the Mulvaneys, Blonde, The Tattooed Girl, The Falls, Sexy, *and* The Stolen Heart *by Lauren Kelly. She has published several collections of short fiction, including three concentrating on her darker fiction:* Night-Side, Haunted: Tales of the Grotesque, *and* Demon and Other Tales.

"Stripping" was originally published in Postscripts.

—E.D.

S tripping the filthy things off. The stained things. The smells. Onto the floor with the filthy stripped-off things. Onto the floor with the stained things, the smells. Beneath the shower's nozzle. Hot hot as you can bear. Hot water streaming over shut eyes. *Why h'lo there! H'lo you. Do I know you?* Teasing smile. Taunting smile. *Think I do know you don't I?* Stripping off the smell of her. Onto the floor with the filth and the smell of her. And in the shower in the rising steam roughly soaping your hair that is strange to you so greasy, spiky like the coarse fur of a beast. Soaping your torso, armpits. Your torso an armor of flesh covered in coils of wire. Your armpits bristling with wire. Washing away the body-smells. And your filthy hands. Scratched knuckles, wrists. Broken fingernails and dried blood beneath. Draw your nails hard across the bar of soap, clean out the blood. Soap slipping from your clumsy hand you stoop to retrieve, grunting, the weight of your head suddenly heavy and pulses beating in your eyes, hearing her cry out in the terror of recognition *no no why? no let me go! why me, why? why hurt another person?* a riddle to echo in the shower's steam in the sharp needles of water erupting from the nozzle turned downward into your face. The soap is luminous-white like an object floating in a dream, you must not lapse into a dream but must carefully wash scrub cleanse yourself, lather away the blood and skin-particles beneath your fingernails broken against her skin repulsive to touch and the smell the sharp piercing cries quivering eyelids and bleeding mouth gaping like the mouth of a fish drowning in air *No no oh let me go let me—why are you doing this* flecks of dead skin washing away, soapy water tinged with red swirling down the drain faint and fading and your powerful lower body eel-like lathered in soap a luminous-white gossamer of soap through which the wire-hairs protrude. If the body could speak *Yes I am lonely, it is my loneliness that must be revenged* this is why you were born, the simplicity of life-in-the-body in-the-moment the instincts of the predator cruising rain-washed streets as a shark might cruise the ocean open-mouthed seeking prey cruising the night-time city, in the distance the sound of a train whistle melancholy and fading as the cry of a distant bird. Pleading for her life though such debased life! Pleading for her life but this is life. No need to force her, on her knees she sank willingly. *I know you think I know you hmmm?* Her soul was a frail fluttering butterfly. Her soul was soiled white wings beating. Her soul was torn wings beating wings, broken wings bravely beating. Her soul was a sudden sharp smell of animal terror. Saliva at the corners of the contorted mouth. In the ruins of the abandoned house. Crumbling bricks, rotted floorboards. Underfoot lay a child's mitten stiff with filth. Underfoot a torn calendar, stained newspapers. Stumbling in the dark laughing dared to take your hand *Come this way You know the way I think you do you* teasing taunting eyes glassy-festive high on methamphetamine picking her way through the filth to the mattress that was known to her stained beforehand with her blood or the blood of someone very like her *Where've I seen you before have you seen me* smiling as if laughing inside where her soul was filth and it came to you in a wave of disgust like filthy water in your mouth that maybe she was known to you, in your memory known to you, in an earlier life you had been a schoolteacher until the school was barred to you, the children's eyes sharp as beaks pecking, maybe the woman had been a child once in your classroom in St. Ignatius Middle School in an earlier life before the school was taken from you and all seemed clear to you suddenly *Yes I am lonely, it is my loneliness that feeds me* beneath the shower in the sharp-stinging needles of water, such pleasure, such happiness, now the filthy things have been stripped off, the stained things and the smells and blood swirling down the drain and gone and the fragrance of soap in your nostrils the simplicity of the naked body armored in flesh covered in wire-hairs thrumming with life, with heat *My loneliness I have come to love* this is why you were born, strip all else away and this is it.

CHRISTOPHER FOWLER

Seven Feet

Christopher Fowler is best known for his dark urban fiction; his thirteen novels all contain elements of black comedy, anxiety, and satire. He has written nine volumes of short stories; the latest, Demonized, *includes his 100th published short story.* Full Dark House, *the first of a six-volume series of dark crime novels was followed by* The Water Room *and* Seventy Seven Clocks. *He wrote the critically acclaimed graphic novel* Menz Insana. *His short story "The Master Builder" was made into a CBS TV movie. Another adaptation, "Left Hand Drive," was named Best British Short Film of 1993. He was the 1998 recipient of the British Fantasy Society award for Best Short Story, won their August Derleth Novel Award for* Full Dark House, *and their award for his story "American Waitress." He lives in London, England.*

The author says his story "came from a dire warning printed in the national press here about feral animals moving into inner cities vacated by humans. I've always felt that the breakdown of urban order is accompanied by the birth of new beliefs, and liked the idea of nature sparking the change. I also wrote a piece about squirrels mugging people for theater tickets which was a far sillier version of this scenario . . ."

"Seven Feet" was originally published in Demonized.

—E.D.

Cleethorpes was a crap mouser. She would hide underneath the sink if a rodent, a squirrel or a neighbor's cat even came near the open back door. Clearly, sleeping sixteen hours a day drained her reserves of nervous energy, and she was forced to play dead if her territory was threatened. She was good at a couple of things: batting moths about until they expired with their wings in dusty tatters, and staring at a spot on the wall three feet above the top of Edward's head. What could cats see, he wondered, that humans couldn't?

Cleethorpes was his only companion now that Sam was dead and Gill had gone. He'd bought her because everyone else had bought one. That was the month the price of cats skyrocketed. Hell, every cat's home in the country sold out in days, and pretty soon the mangiest strays were changing hands for incredible prices. It was the weirdest form of panic-buying Edward ever saw.

He'd lived in Camden Town for years, and had been thinking of getting out even before he met Gill; the area was being compared to Moscow and Johannesburg after eight murders on its streets in as many weeks earned the area a new nickname: "Murder Mile." There were 700 police operating in the borough, which badly needed over a thousand. It was strange, then, to think that the real threat to their lives eventually came not from muggers, but from fast-food outlets.

Edward lived in a flat in Eversholt Street, one of the most peculiar roads in the neighborhood. In one stretch of a few hundred yards there was a Roman Catholic church, a sports center, a legendary rock pub, council flats, a bingo hall, a juvenile detention center, an Italian café, a Victorian men's hostel for transients and an audacious green glass development of million-pound loft apartments. Edward was on the ground floor of the council block, a bad place to be as it turned out. The Regent's Canal ran nearby, and most of the road's drains emptied into it. The council eventually riveted steel grilles over the pipe covers, but by then it was too late.

Edward glanced over at Gill's photograph, pinned on the cork noticeboard beside the cooker. Once her eyes had been the color of cyanothus blossom, her hair saturated in sunlight, but now the picture appeared to be fading, as if it was determined to remove her from the world. He missed Gill more than he missed Sam, because nothing he could do would ever bring Sam back, but Gill was still around, living in Hackney with her two brothers. He knew he was unlikely to ever see her again. He missed her to the point where he would say her name aloud at odd moments for no reason at all. In those last days after Sam's death, she had grown so thin and pale that it seemed she was being erased from her surroundings. He watched helplessly as her bones appeared beneath her flesh, her clothes began hanging loosely on her thin arms. Gill's jaw-length blonde hair draped forward over her face as she endlessly scoured and bleached the kitchen counters. She stopped voicing her thoughts, becoming barely more visible than the water stains on the walls behind her. She would hush him with a raised finger, straining to listen for the scurrying scratch of claws in the walls, under the cupboards, across the rafters.

Rats. Some people's worst nightmare, but the thought of them no longer troubled him. What had happened to their family had happened to people all over the city. "Rats!" thought Edward as he welded the back door shut, "they fought the dogs and killed the cats, and bit the babies in the cradles . . ." He couldn't remember the rest of Robert Browning's poem. It hadn't been quite like that, because Camden Town was hardly Hamelin, but London could have done with a pied piper. Instead, all they'd got was a distracted mayor and his dithering officials, hopelessly failing to cope with a crisis.

He pulled the goggles to the top of his head and examined his handiwork. The steel plates only ran across to the middle of the door, but were better than nothing. Now he could sort out the chewed gap underneath. It wasn't more than two inches deep, but a cat-sized rat was capable of folding its ribs flat enough to slide through with ease. He remembered watching thousands of them one evening as they rippled in a brown tapestry through the back gardens. There had been nights when he'd sat in the darkened lounge with his feet lifted off the floor and a cricket bat across his knees, listening to the scampering conspiracy passing over the roofs, feet pattering in the kitchen, under the beds, under his chair. He'd watched as one plump brown rat with eyes like drops of black resin had fidgeted its way between books on a shelf, daring him into a display of pitifully slow reactions.

The best solution would be to rivet a steel bar across the space under the door, but the only one he had left was too short. He thought about risking a trip to the shops, but most of the ones in the high street had closed for good, and all the hardware stores had sold out of stock weeks ago. It was hard to imagine how much a city of eight million people could change in just four months. So many had left. The tubes were a no-go zone, of course, and it was dangerous to move around in the open at night. The rats were no longer frightened by people.

He was still deciding what to do when his mobile buzzed its way across the work counter.

"Is that Edward?" asked a cultured, unfamiliar voice.

"Yeah, who's that?"

"I don't suppose you'll remember me. We only met once, at a party. I'm Damon, Gillian's brother." The line fell warily silent. Damon, sanctimonious religious nut, Gill's older brother, what was the name of the other one? Matthew. Fuck. *Fuck.*

"Are you still there?"

"Yeah, sorry, you caught me a bit by surprise."

"I guess it's a bit of a bolt from the blue. Are you still living in Camden?"

"One of the last to leave the epicenter. The streets are pretty quiet around here now."

"I saw it on the news, didn't recognize the place. Not that I ever really knew it to begin with. Our family's from Hampshire, but I expect you remember that."

Stop being so damned chatty and tell me what the hell you want, thought Edward. His next thought hit hard: *Gill's condition has deteriorated, she's made him call me.*

"It's about Gillian, isn't it?"

"I'm afraid—she's been a lot worse lately. We've had a tough time looking after her. She had the problem, you know, with dirt and germs—"

Spermophobia, thought Edward, *mysophobia.* A lot of people had developed such phobias since the rats came.

"Now there are these other things, she's become terrified of disease."

Nephophobia, pathophobia. Once arcane medical terms, now almost everyday parlance. They were closely connected, not so surprising when you remembered what she'd been through.

"It's been making life very difficult for us!"

"I can imagine." Everything had to be cleaned over and over again. Floors scrubbed, handles and counters sprayed with disinfectant, the air kept refrigerated. All her foodstuffs had to be washed and vacuum-sealed in plastic before she would consider eating them. Edward had watched the roots of fear digging deeper within her day by day, until she could barely function and he could no longer cope.

"She's lost so much weight. She's become frightened of the bacteria in her own body. She was living on the top floor of the house, refused to take any visitors except us, and now she's gone missing."

"What do you mean?"

"It doesn't seem possible, but it's true. We thought you should know."

"Do you have any idea where she might have gone?"

"She couldn't have gone anywhere, that's the incredible part of it. We very badly need your help. Can you come over tonight?" *This is a turnaround,* Edward thought. *Her family spent a year trying to get me to clear off, and now they need me.*

"I suppose I can come. Both of you are still okay?"

"We're fine. We take a lot of precautions."

"Has the family been vaccinated?"

"No, Matthew and our father feel that the Lord protects us. Do you remember the address?"

"Of course. I can be there in around an hour."

He was surprised they had found the nerve to call at all. The brothers had him pegged as a man of science, a member of the tribe that had helped to bring about the present crisis. People like him had warmed the planet and genetically modified its harvests, bringing abundance and pestilence. Their religion sought to exclude, and their faith was vindictive. Men who sought to accuse were men to be avoided. But he owed it to Gill to go to them.

He used the short steel bar to block the gap in the door, and covered the shortfall by welding a biscuit-tin lid over it. Not an ideal solution, but one that would have to do for now. The sun would soon be setting. The red neon sign above the Kentucky Fried Chicken outlet opposite had flickered on. It was the only part of the store that was still intact. Rioters had smashed up most of the junk-food joints in the area, looking for someone to blame.

Pest controllers had put the massive rise in the number of rats down to three causes: the wetter, warmer winters caused flooding that lengthened the rats' breeding periods and drove them aboveground. Councils had reduced their spending on street cleaning. Most disastrously of all, takeaway litter left the street-bins overflowing with chicken bones and burger buns. The rat population rose by thirty percent in a single year. They thrived in London's Victorian drainage system, in the sewers and canal outlets, in the tube lines and railway cuttings. Beneath the city was a maze of interconnected pipework with openings into almost every street. They moved into the gardens and then the houses, colonizing and spreading as each property became vacant.

One much-cited statistic suggested that a single pair of rats could spawn a maximum number of nearly a hundred billion rats in just five years. It was a sign of the burgeoning rodent population that they began to be spotted during the day; starvation drove them out into the light, and into densely populated areas. They no longer knew fear. Worse, they sensed that others were afraid of them.

Edward had always known about the dangers of disease. As a young biology student he had been required to study pathogenic microbes. London had not seen a case of plague in almost a century. The Black Death of the Middle Ages had wiped out a third of the European population. The bacterium *Yersinia pestis* had finally been eradicated by fire in London in 1666. Plague had returned to consume ten million Indians early in the twentieth century, and had killed 200 as recently as 1994. Now it was back in a virulent new strain, and rampant. It had arrived via infected rat fleas, in a ship's container from the East, or perhaps from a poorly fumigated cargo plane, no one was sure, and everyone was anxious to assign blame. Rats brought leptospirosis, hantavirus, and rat bite fever, and they were only the fatal diseases.

Edward drove through the empty streets of King's Cross with the windows of the Peugeot tightly closed and the air-conditioning set to an icy temperature. Lying in the road outside McDonald's, a bloated, blackened corpse had been partially covered by a cardboard standee for Caramel McFlurrys. The gesture, presumably intended to provide some privacy in death, had only created further indignity. It was the first time he'd seen a body on the street, and the sight shocked him. It was a sign that the services could no longer cope, or that people were starting not to care. Most of the infected crept away into private corners to die, even though there were no red crosses to keep them in their houses this time.

The plague bacillus had evolved in terms of lethality. It no longer swelled the lymph glands of the neck, armpits and groin. It went straight to the lungs and caused catastrophic internal hemorrhaging. Death came fast as the lungs filled with septicemic pus and fluid. There was a preventative vaccine, but it proved useless once the outbreak began. Tetracycline and streptomycin, once seen as effective antibiotics against plague, also failed against the emerging drug-resistant strains. All you could do was burn and disinfect; the city air stank of both, but it was preferable to the smell of death. It had been a hot summer, and the still afternoons were filled with the stench of rotting flesh.

Edward had been vaccinated at the college. Gill had blamed him for failing to vaccinate their son in time. Sam had been four months old when he died. His cradle had been left near an open window. They could only assume that a rat had entered the room foraging for food, and came close enough for his fleas to jump to fresh breeding grounds. The child's pale skin blackened with necrosis before the overworked doctors of University College Hospital could get around to seeing him. Gill quickly developed a phobic reaction to germs, and was collected by her brothers a few weeks after.

Edward dropped out of college. In theory it would have been a good time to stay, because biology students were being drafted in the race to find more powerful weapons against the disease, but he couldn't bear to immerse himself in the subject, having so recently watched his child die in the very same building.

He wondered why he hadn't fled to the countryside like so many others. It was safer there, but no one was entirely immune. He found it hard to consider leaving the city where he had been born, and was fascinated by this slow decanting of the population. An eerie calm had descended on even the most populous districts. There were no tourists; nobody wanted to fly into Britain. People had become terrified of human contact, and kept their outside journeys to a minimum. *Mad cow disease was a comparative picnic,* he thought with a grim chuckle.

The little car bounced across the end of Upper Street, heading toward Shoreditch. The shadows were long on the gold-sheened tarmac. A blizzard of newspapers rolled across the City Road, adding to the sense of desolation. Edward spun the wheel, watching for pedestrians. He had started to think of them as survivors. There were hardly any cars on the road, although he was surprised to pass a bus in service. At Old Street and Pitfield Street, a shifting amoeba-shape fluctuated around the doorway of a closed supermarket. The glossy black rats scattered in every direction as he drove past. You could never drive over them, however fast you went.

There were now more rats than humans, approximately three for every man, woman and child, and the odds kept growing in their favor. They grew bolder each day, and had become quite brazen about their battle for occupancy. It had been said that in a city as crowded as London you were never more than fifteen feet away from a rat. Scientists warned that when the distance between rodent and human lowered to just seven feet, conditions would be perfect for the return of the plague. The flea, *Xenopsylla cheopis,* sucked up diseased rat blood and transported it to humans with shocking efficiency.

A great black patch shimmered across the road like a boiling oil slick, splitting and vanishing between the buildings. Without realizing it, he found himself gripping the sweat-slick wheel so tightly that his nails were digging into his palms.

Rattus rattus. No one knew where the black rat had originated, so their Latin name was suitably unrevealing. The brown ones—the English ones, *Rattus norvegicus*—lived in burrows and came from China. They grew to nearly a foot and a half, and ate anything at all. They could chew their way through brick and concrete; they had to keep chewing to stop their incisors from growing back into their skulls. The black ones were smaller, with larger ears, and lived off the ground in round nests. Edward had woken in the middle of the night two weeks ago and found a dozen of them in his kitchen, feeding from a wastebin. He had run at them with a broom, but they had simply skittered up the curtains and through a hole they had made in the ceiling to the drainpipes outside. The black ones were acrobats; they loved heights. Although they were less aggressive, they seemed to be outnumbering their brown cousins. At least, he saw more of them each day.

He fumigated the furniture and carpets for ticks and fleas, but still developed clusters of painful red welts on his ankles, his arms, his back. He was glad Gill was no longer here, but missed her terribly. She had slipped away from him, her mind distracted by a future she could not imagine or tolerate.

Damon and Matthew lived with their father above offices in Hoxton, having bought the building at the height of the area's property boom. These had once been the homes of well-to-do Edwardian families, but more than half a century of neglect had followed, until the district had been rediscovered by newly wealthy artists. That bubble had burst too, and now the houses were in fast decline as thousands of rats scampered into the basements.

As he climbed the steps, spotlights clicked on. He could hear movement all around him. He looked up and saw the old man through a haze of white light. Gill's father was silently watching him from an open upstairs window.

There was no bell. Edward slapped his hand against the front door glass and waited. Matthew answered the door. What was it about the over-religious that made them keep their hair so neat? Matthew's blonde fringe formed a perfect wave above his smooth scrubbed face. He smiled and shook Edward's hand.

"I'm glad you could make it," he said, as though he'd invited Edward to dinner. "We don't get many visitors." He led the way upstairs, then along a bare white hall into an undecorated space that served as their living quarters. There were no personal effects of any kind on display. A stripped oak table and four chairs stood in the center of the bright room. Damon rose to shake his hand. Edward had forgotten how alike the brothers were. They had the eyes of zealots, bright and black and dead. They spoke with great intensity, weighing their words, watching him as they spoke.

"Tell me what happened," Edward instructed, seating himself. He didn't want to be here any longer than was strictly necessary.

"Father can't get around anymore, so we moved him from his quarters at the top of the house and cleaned it out for Gillian. We thought if we couldn't cure her we should at least make her feel secure, so we put her up there. But the black rats . . ."

"They're good climbers."

"That's right. They came up the drainpipes and burrowed in through the attic, so we had to move her. The only place we could think where she'd be safe was within our congregation." *Ah yes,* thought Edward, *the Church Of Latter Day Nutters. I remember all too well.* Gill had fallen out with her father over religion. He had raised his sons in a far-right Christian offshoot that came with more rules than the Highway Code. Quite how he had fetched up in this biblical backwater was a mystery, but Gill was having none of it. Her brothers had proven more susceptible, and when the plague rats moved in adopted an insufferably smug attitude that drove the children further apart. Matthew was the father of three immaculately coiffed children whom Edward had christened "the Midwich Cuckoos". Damon's wife was the whitest woman he had ever met, someone who encouraged knitting as stress-therapy at Christian coffee mornings. He didn't like them, their politics or their religion, but was forced to admit that they had at least been helpful to his wife. He doubted their motives, however, suspecting that they were more concerned with restoring the family to a complete unit and turning Gill back into a surrogate mother.

"We took her to our church," Matthew explained. "It was built in 1860. The walls are three feet thick. There are no electrical cables, no drainpipes, nothing the smallest rat could wriggle its way into. The vestry doors are wooden, and some of the stained-glass windows are shaky, but it's always been a place of safety."

Edward had to admit it was a smart idea. Gill's condition was untreatable without access to a psychiatrist and medication, and right now the hospitals were nightmarish no-go areas where rats went to feast on the helpless sick.

Matthew seated himself opposite. "Gillian settled into the church, and we hoped she was starting to find some comfort in the protection of the Lord. Then some members of our congregation started spending their nights there, and she began to worry that they were bringing in plague fleas, even though we fumigated them before entering. We couldn't bear to see her suffer so we built her a special room, right there in the middle of the apse—"

"—we made her as comfortable as we could," Damon interrupted. "Ten feet by twelve. Four walls, a ceiling, a floor, a lockable door and a ventilation grille constructed from strong fine mesh." He looked as sheepish as a schoolboy describing a woodwork project. "Father directed the operation because he'd had some experience in carpentry. We moved her bed in there, and her books, and she was finally able to get some sleep. She even stopped taking the sleeping pills you used to give her." *The pills to which she had become addicted when we lived together,* thought Edward bitterly. *The habit I was blamed for creating.*

"I don't understand," he said aloud. "What happened?"

"I think we'd better go over to the church," said Matthew gently.

It was less than a thousand yards from the house, smaller than he'd imagined, slim and plain, without buttresses or arches, very little tracery. The former Welsh presbytery was sandwiched between two taller glass buildings, commerce dominating religion, darkening the streets with the inevitability of London rain.

Outside its single door sat a barrel-chested black man who would have passed for a night-club bouncer if it wasn't for the cricket pads strapped on his legs. He lumbered aside as Damon and Matthew approached. The small church was afire with the light of a thousand colored candles looted from luxury stores. Many were shaped like popular cartoon characters: Batman, Pokemon and Daffy Duck burned irreverently along the altar and apse. The pews had been removed and stacked against a wall. In the center of the aisle stood an oblong wooden box bolted into the stone floor and propped with planks, like the back of a film set. A small door was inset in a wall of the cube, and that was guarded by an elderly woman who sat reading in a high-backed armchair. In the nave, a dozen family friends were talking quietly on orange plastic chairs that surrounded a low oak table. They fell silent with suspicion as Edward passed them. Matthew withdrew a key from his jacket and unlocked the door of the box, pushing it open and clicking on a light.

"We rigged a bulb to a car battery because she wouldn't sleep in the dark," Damon explained, passing a manicured hand around the room, which was bare but for an unfurled white futon, an Indian rug and a stack of dog-eared religious books. The box smelled of fresh paint and incense.

"You built it of wood," said Edward, thumping the thin wall with his fist. "That makes no sense, Damon. A rat would be through this in a minute."

"What else could we do? It made her feel safer, and that was all that counted. We wanted to take away her pain. Can you imagine what it was like to see someone in your own family suffer so much? Our father worshipped her."

Edward detected an undercurrent of resentment in Damon's voice. He and Gill had chosen not to marry. In the eyes of her brothers, it was a sin that prevented Edward from ever being treated as a member of the family. "You're not telling me she disappeared from inside?" he asked. "How could she have got out?"

"That's what we thought you might be able to explain to us," snapped Matthew. "Why do you think we asked you here?"

"I don't understand. You locked her in each night?"

"We did it for her own good."

"How could it be good to lock a frightened woman inside a room?"

"She'd been getting panic attacks, growing confused, running into the street. Her aunt Alice has been sitting outside every night since this thing began. Anything Gillian's needed she's always been given."

"When did she go missing?"

"The night before last. We thought she'd come back."

"You didn't see her leave?" he asked the old lady.

"No," replied Alice, daring him to defy her. "I was here all night."

"And she didn't pass you. Are you sure you never left your chair?"

"Not once. And I didn't fall asleep, either. I don't sleep at night with those things crawling all over the roof."

"Did you let anyone else into the room?"

"Of course not," she said indignantly. "Only family and regular worshippers are allowed into the church. We don't want other people in here." *Of course not*, thought Edward, *what's the point of organized religion if you can't exclude disbelievers?*

"And no one except Gillian used the room," Damon added. "That was the point. That was why we asked you to come."

Edward studied the two brothers. He could just about understand Damon, squeaky clean and neatly groomed in a blazer and a pressed white shirt that provided him with an aura of faith made visible, but Matthew seemed in a state of perpetual anger, a church warrior who had no patience with the unconverted. He remained a mystery.

"Why me?" Edward asked. "What made you call me?"

Momentarily stumped, the brothers looked at each other awkwardly. "Well—you slept with her." Presumably they thought he must know her better for having done so.

"I knew her until our son died, but then—well, when someone changes that much, it becomes impossible to understand how they think anymore." Edward hoped they would appreciate his point of view. He wanted to make contact with them just once. "Let me take a look around, I'll see what I can do."

The brothers stepped back, cognizant of their ineffectuality, their hands awkwardly at their sides. Behind them, the church door opened and the congregation slowly streamed in. The men and women who arranged themselves at the rear of the church looked grey and beaten. Faith was all they had left.

"I'm sorry, it's time for our evening service to begin," Damon explained.

"Do what you have to do." Edward accepted the red plastic torch Matthew was offering him. "I'll call you if I find anything."

A series of narrow alleys ran beside the church. If Gill had managed to slip past the old lady, she would have had to enter them. Edward looked up at the dimming blue strip of evening sky. Along the gutters sat fat nests constructed of branches and binbags, the black plastic shredded into malleable strips. As he watched, one bulged and disgorged a family of coal-eyed rats. They clung to the drainpipes, staring into his torchbeam before suddenly spiralling down at him. He moved hastily aside as they scurried over his shoes and down the corridor of dirt-encrusted brick.

The end of the alley opened out into a small litter-strewn square. He hardly knew where to begin his search. If the family had failed to find her, how would he succeed? On the steps of a boarded-up block of flats sat an elderly man in a dirty green sleeping bag. The man stared wildly at him, as if he had just awoken from a nightmare.

"All right?" asked Edward, nodding curtly. The old man beckoned him. Edward tried to stay beyond range of his pungent stale aroma, but was summoned nearer. "What is it?" he asked, wondering how anyone dared to sleep rough in the city now. The old man pulled back the top of his sleeping bag as if shyly revealing a treasure, and allowed him to look in on the hundred or so hairless baby rats that wriggled over his bare stomach like maggots, pink and blind.

Perhaps that was the only way you could survive the streets now, thought Edward, riven with disgust, you had to take their side. He wondered if, as a host for their offspring, the old man had been made an honorary member of their species, and was therefore allowed to continue unharmed, although perhaps the truth was less fanciful; rats sensed the safety of their surroundings through the movement of their own bodies. Their spatial perception was highly attuned to the width of drains, the cracks in walls, the fearful humans who moved away in great haste. Gill might have been panicked into flight, but she was weak and would not have been able to run for long. She must have stopped somewhere to regain her breath, but where?

He searched the dark square. The wind had risen to disturb the tops of the plane trees, replacing the city's ever-present bass-line of traffic with natural sussurance. It was the only sound he could now hear. Lights shone above a corner shop. Slumped on the windowsill, two Indian children stared down into the square, their eyes half-closed by rat-bites.

He returned to the church, slipping in behind the ragged congregation, and watched Matthew in the dimly illuminated pulpit.

"For this is not the end but the beginning," said Matthew, clearly preaching a worn-in sermon of fire and redemption. "Those whom the Lord has chosen to keep in good health will be free to remake the land in His way." It was the kind of lecture to which Edward had been subjected as a child, unfocused in its promises, peppered with pompous rhetoric, vaguely threatening. "Each and every one of us must make a sacrifice, without which there can be no admittance to the kingdom of

Heaven, and he who has not surrendered his heart to Our Lady will be left outside, denied the power of reformation."

It seemed to Edward that congregations always required the imposition of rules for their salvation, and desperate times had forced them to assume that these zealous brothers would be capable of setting them. He moved quietly to the unguarded door of the wooden box and stepped inside, shutting himself in.

The sense of claustrophobia was immediate. A locked room, guarded from outside. Where the hell had she gone? He sat on the futon, idly kicking at the rug, and listened to the muffled litany of the congregation. A draught was coming into the room, but not through the door. He lowered his hand down into darkness, and felt chill air prickle his fingers. At first he failed to see the corner of the hatch, but as he focussed the torch more tightly, he realized what he was looking at; a section of flooring, about three feet by two, that had been sawn into the wooden deck beside the bed. The floor was plywood, easy to lift. The hatch covered the spiral stairwell to the crypt. A black-painted Victorian iron banister curved away beneath his feet. Outside, Matthew was leading a catechism that sounded more like a rallying call.

Edward dipped the light and stepped onto the fretwork wedges. Clearly Gill had been kept in the wooden room against her will, but how had she discovered the staircase to the chamber beneath her prison? Perhaps its existence was common knowledge, but it had not occurred to anyone that she might be able to gain access to it. The temperature of the air was dropping fast now; could this have been its appeal, the thought that germs would not be able to survive in such a chill environment?

He reached the bottom of the steps. His torchbeam reflected a fracturing moon of light; the flagstones were hand-deep in icy water. A series of low stone arches led through the tunneled crypt ahead of him. He waded forward and found himself beneath the ribbed vault of the main chamber. The splash of water boomed in the silent crypt.

With freezing legs and visible breath, he stood motionless, waiting for the ripples to subside. Something was wrong. Gillian might have lost her reason, but she would surely not have ventured down here alone. She knew that rats were good swimmers. It didn't make sense. Something was wrong.

In the church above, the steeple bell began to ring, cracked and flat. The change in the congregation was extraordinary. They dropped to their knees unmindful of injury, staring toward the tattered crimson reredos that shielded the choir stall. Damon and Matthew had reappeared in sharp white surplices, pushing back the choir screen as their flock began to murmur in anticipation. The dais they revealed had been swathed in shining gold brocade, discovered in bolts at a Brick Lane saree shop. Atop stood the enshrined figure, a mockery of Catholicism, its naked flesh dulled down with talcum powder until it resembled worn alabaster, its legs overgrown with plastic vines.

The wheels of the wooden dais creaked as Damon and Matthew pushed the wobbling tableau toward the altar. The voices of the crowd rose in adulation. The figure on the dais was transfixed in hysterical ecstasy, posed against a painted tree with her knees together and her palms turned out, a single rose stem lying across the right hand, a crown of dead roses placed far back on her shaved head, her eyes rolled to a glorious invisible heaven. Gillian no longer heard the desperate exultation of her worshippers; she existed in a higher place, a vessel for her brothers' piety, floating far above the filthy, blighted earth, in a holy place of such grace and purity that nothing dirty or harmful would ever touch her again.

Edward looked up. Somewhere above him the bell was still ringing, the single dull note repeated over and over. He cocked his head at the ribs of the vault and listened. First the trees, then the church bell, and now this, as though the forgotten order of nature was reasserting itself. He heard it again, the sound he had come to know and dread, growing steadily all around him. Raising the torch, he saw them scurrying over the fine green nylon webbing that had been stretched across the vault ceiling, thousands of them, far more than he had ever seen in one place before, black rats, quite small, their bodies shifting transversely, almost comically, as they weighed and judged distances.

They had been summoned to dinner.

They gathered in the roof of the main chamber, directly beneath the ringing bell, until they were piling on top of each other, some slipping and swinging by a single pink paw, and then they fell, twisting expertly so that they landed on him and not in the water, their needle claws digging into the flesh of his shoulders to gain purchase, to hang on at all costs. Edward hunched himself instinctively, but this exposed a broader area for the rats to drop onto, and now they were releasing themselves from the mesh and falling in ever-greater numbers, more and more, until the sheer weight of their solid, sleek bodies pushed him down into the filthy water. This was their cue to attack, their indication that the prey was defeatable, and they bit down hard, pushing their heads between each other to bury thin yellow teeth into his soft skin. He felt himself bleeding from a hundred different places at once, the wriggling mass of rat bodies first warm, then hot, now searing on his back until they made their way through his hair, heading for the tender prize of his eyes.

He was determined not to scream, not to open his mouth and admit their poisonous furred bodies. He did the only thing he could, and pushed his head deep under the water, drawing great draughts into his throat and down into his lungs, defeating them in the only way left to him, cheating them of live prey.

Gill, I love you, was his final prayer, *I only ever loved you, and wherever you are I hope you are happy.* Death etched the thought into his bones and preserved it forever.

In the little East End church, a mood of satiated harmony fell upon the congregation, and Matthew smiled at Damon as they covered the tableau once more, content that his revered sister was at peace. For now the enemy was assuaged, the commitment had been made, the congregation appeased.

Science had held sway for long enough. Now it was time for the harsh old gods to smile down once more.

Singing My Sister Down

Margo Lanagan, represented elsewhere in this anthology by her story "Rite of Spring," lives in Sydney, Australia.
    "Singing My Sister Down" was originally published in her story collection Black Juice.

                              —E.D., K.L. & G.G.

We all went down to the tar-pit, with mats to spread our weight.
    Ikky was standing on the bank, her hands in a metal twin-loop behind her. She'd stopped sulking; now she looked more stare-y and puzzled.
    Chief Barnarndra pointed to the pit. "Out you go then, girl. You must walk on out there to the middle and stand. When you picked a spot, your people can join you."

So Ik stepped out, very ordinary. She walked out. I thought—hoped, even—she might walk right across and into the thorns the other side; at the same time, I knew she wouldn't do that.

She walked the way you walk on the tar, except without the arms balancing. She nearly fell from a stumble once, but Mumma hulloo'd to her, and she straightened and walked upright out to the very middle, where she slowed and stopped.

Mumma didn't look to the chief, but all us kids and the rest did. "Right, then," he said.

Mumma stepped out as if she'd just herself that moment happened to decide to. We went after her—only us, Ik's family, which was like us being punished, too, everyone watching us walk out to that girl who was our shame.

In the winter you come to the pit to warm your feet in the tar. You stand long enough to sink as far as your ankles—the littler you are, the longer you can stand. You soak the heat in for as long as the tar doesn't close over your feet and grip, and it's as good as warmed boots wrapping your feet. But in summer, like this day, you keep away from the tar, because it makes the air hotter and you mind about the stink.

But today we had to go out, and everyone had to see us go.

Ikky was tall, but she was thin and light from all the worry and prison; she was going to take a long time about sinking. We got our mats down, all the food parcels and ice-baskets and instruments and such spread out evenly on the broad planks Dash and Felly had carried out.

"You start, Dash," said Mumma, and Dash got up and put his drum-ette to his hip and began with "Fork-Tail Trio," and it did feel a bit like a party. It stirred Ikky awake from her hung-headed shame; she lifted up and even laughed, and I saw her hips move in the last chorus, side to side.

Then Mumma got out one of the ice-baskets, which was already black on the bottom from meltwater.

Ikky gasped. "Ha! What! Crab! Where'd that come from?"

"Never you mind, sweet-thing." Mumma lifted some meat to Ikky's mouth, and rubbed some of the crush-ice into her hair.

"Oh, Mumma!" Ik said with her mouth full.

"May as well have the best of this world while you're here," said Mumma. She stood there and fed Ikky like a baby, like a pet guinea-bird.

"I thought Auntie Mai would come," said Ik.

"Auntie Mai, she's useless," said Dash. "She's sitting at home with her handker-chief."

"I wouldn't've cared, her crying," said Ik. "I would've thought she'd say good-bye to me."

"Her heart's too hurt," said Mumma. "You frightened her. And she's such a straight lady—she sees shame where some of us just see people. Here, inside the big claw, that's the sweetest meat."

"Ooh, yes! Is anyone else feasting with me?"

"No, darlin', this is your day only. Well, okay, I'll give some to this little sad-eyes here, huh? Felly never had crab but the once. Is it yum? Ooh, it's yum! Look at him!"

Next she called me to do my flute—the flashiest, hardest music I knew. And Ik listened; Ik who usually screamed at me to stop pushing spikes into her brain, she watched my fingers on the flute-holes and my sweating face and my straining, bow-ing body and, for the first time, I didn't feel like just the nuisance-brother. I played well, out of the surprise of her not minding. I couldn't've played better. I heard everyone else being surprised, too, at the end of those tunes that they must've known, too well from all my practicing.

I sat down, very hungry. Mumma passed me the water cup and a damp-roll.

"I'm stuck now," said Ik, and it was true—the tar had her by the feet, closed in a gleaming line like that pair of zipper-slippers I saw once in the shoemaster's vitrine.

"Oh yeah, well and truly stuck," said Mumma. "But then, you knew when you picked up that axe-handle you were sticking yourself."

"I did know."

"No coming unstuck from this one. You could've let that handle lie."

That was some serious teasing.

"No, I couldn't, Mumma, and you know."

"I do, baby chicken. I always knew you'd be too angry, once the wedding-glitter rubbed off your skin. It was a good party, though, wasn't it?" And they laughed at each other, Mumma having to steady Ikky or her ankles would've snapped over. And when their laughter started going strange Mumma said, "Well, this party's going to be almost as good, 'cause it's got children. And look what else!" And she reached for the next ice-basket.

And so the whole long day went, in treats and songs, in ice and stink and joke-stories and gossip and party-pieces. On the banks, people came and went, and the chief sat in his chair and was fanned and fed, and the family of Ikky's husband sat around the chief, being served, too, all in purple-cloth with flashing edging, very prideful.

She went down so slowly.

"Isn't it hot?" Felly asked her.

"It's like a big warm hug up my legs," said Ik. "Come here and give me a hug, little stick-arms, and let me check. Oof, yes, it's just like that, only lower down."

"You're coming down to me," said Fel, pleased.

"Yeah, soon I'll be able to bite your ankles like you bite mine."

Around midafternoon, Ikky couldn't move her arms any more and had a panic, just quiet, not so the bank-people would've noticed.

"What'm I going to do, Mumma?" she said. "When it comes up over my face? When it closes my nose?"

"Don't you worry. You won't be awake for that." And Mumma cooled her hands in the ice, dried them on her dress, and rubbed them over Ik's shoulders, down Ik's arms to where the tar had locked her wrists.

"You better not give me any teas, or herbs, or anything," said Ik. "They'll get you, too, if you help me. They'll come out to make sure."

Mumma put her hands over Felly's ears. "Tristem gave me a gun," she whispered.

Ikky's eyes went wide. "But you can't! Everyone'll hear!"

"It's got a thing on it, quietens it. I can slip it in a tar-wrinkle, get you in the head when your head is part sunk, fold back the wrinkle, tell 'em your heart stopped, the tar pressed it stopped."

Felly shook his head free. Ikky was looking at Mumma, quietening. There was only the sound of Dash tearing bread with his teeth, and the breeze whistling in the thorn-galls away over on the shore. I was watching Mumma and Ikky closely—I'd wondered about that last part, too. But now this girl up to her waist in the pit didn't even look like our Ikky. Her face was changing like a cloud, or like a masque-lizard's colors; you don't see them move but they *become* something else, then something else again.

"No," she said, still looking at Mumma. "You won't do that. You won't have to." Her face had a smile on it that touched off one on Mumma's, too, so that they were both quiet, smiling at something in each other that I couldn't see.

And then their eyes ran over and they were crying *and* smiling, and then Mumma was kneeling on the wood, her arms around Ikky, and Ikky was ugly against her shoulder, crying in a way that we couldn't interrupt them.

That was when I realized how many people were watching, when they set up a big, spooky oolooling and stamping on the banks, to see Mumma grieve.

"Fo!" I said to Dash, to stop the hair creeping around on my head from that noise. "There never was such a crowd when Chep's daddy went down."

"Ah, but he was old and crazy," said Dash through a mouthful of bread, "and only killed other olds and crazies."

"Are those fish-people? And look at the yellow-cloths—they're from up among the caves, all that way!"

"Well, it's nearly Langasday, too," said Dash. "Lots of people on the move, just happening by."

"Maybe. Is that an honor, or a greater shame?"

Dash shrugged. "This whole thing is upended. Who would have a party in the tar, and with family going down?"

"It's what Mumma wanted."

"Better than having her and Ik be like this *all day*." Dash's hand slipped into the nearest ice-basket and brought out a crumb of gilded macaroon. He ate it as if he had a perfect right.

Everything went slippery in my mind, after that. We were being watched so hard! Even though it was quiet out here, the pothering wind brought crowd-mumble and scraps of music and smoke our way, so often that we couldn't be private and ourselves. Besides, there was Ikky with the sun on her face, but the rest of her from the rib-peaks down gloved in tar, never to see sun again. Time seemed to just have *gone*, in big clumps, or all the day was happening at once or something, I was wondering so hard about what was to come, I was watching so hard the differences from our normal days. I wished I had more time to think, before she went right down; my mind was going breathless, trying to get all its thinking done.

But evening came and Ik was a head and shoulders, singing along with us in the lamplight, all the old songs—"A Flower for You," "Hen and Chicken Bay," "Walking the Tracks with Beejum Singh," "Dollarberries." She sang all Felly's little-kid songs that normally she'd sneer at; she got Dash to teach her his new one, "The Careless Wanderer," with the tricky chorus. She made us work on that one like she was trying to stop us noticing the monster bonfires around the shore, the other singing, of fishing songs and forest songs, the stomp and clatter of dancing in the gathering darkness. But they were there, however well we sang, and no other singing in our lives had had all this going on behind it.

When the tar began to tip Ik's chin up, Mumma sent me for the wreath. "Mai will have brought it, over by the chief's chair."

I got up and started across the tar, and it was as if I cast magic ahead of me, silence-making magic, for as I walked—and it was good to be walking, not sitting—musics petered out, and laughter stopped, and dancers stood still, and there were eyes at me, all along the dark banks, strange eyes and familiar both.

The wreath showed up in the crowd ahead, a big, pale ring trailing spirals of whisper-vine, the beautifullest thing. I climbed up the low bank there, and the ground felt hard and cold after a day on the squishy tar. My ankles shivered as I took the wreath from Mai. It was heavy; it was fat with heavenly scents.

"You'll have to carry those," I said to Mai, as someone handed her the other garlands. "You should come out, anyway. Ik wants you there."

She shook her head. "She's cloven my heart in two with that axe of hers."

"What, so you'll chop hers as well, this last hour?"

We glared at each other in the bonfire light, all loaded down with the fine, pale flowers.

"I never heard this boy speak with a voice before, Mai," said someone behind her.

"He's very sure," said someone else. "This is Ikky's Last Things we're talking about, Mai. If she wants you to be one of them . . ."

"She shouldn't have shamed us, then," Mai said, but weakly.

"You going to look back on this and think yourself a po-face," said the first someone.

"But it's like—" Mai sagged and clicked her tongue. "She should have *cared* what she did to this family," she said with her last fight. "It's more than just herself."

"Take the flowers, Mai. Don't make the boy do this twice over. Time is short."

"Yeah, *everybody's* time is short," said the first someone.

Mai stood, pulling her mouth to one side.

I turned and propped the top of the wreath on my forehead, so that I was like a little boy-bride, trailing a head of flowers down my back to the ground. I set off over the tar, leaving the magic silence in the crowd. There was only the rub and squeak of flower stalks in my ears; in my eyes, instead of the flourishes of bonfires, there were only the lamps in a ring around Mumma, Felly, Dash, and Ikky's head. Mumma was kneeling bonty-up on the wood, talking to Ikky; in the time it had taken me to get the wreath, Ikky's head had been locked still.

"Oh, the baby," Mai whimpered behind me. "The little darling."

Bit late for darling-ing now, I almost said. I felt cross and frightened and too grown-up for Mai's silliness.

"Here, Ik, we'll make you beautiful now," said Mumma, laying the wreath around Ik's head. "We'll come out here to these flowers when you're gone, and know you're here."

"They'll die pretty quick—I've seen it." Ik's voice was getting squashed, coming out through closed jaws. "The heat wilts 'em."

"They'll always look beautiful to you," said Mumma. "You'll carry down this beautiful wreath, and your family singing."

I trailed the vines out from the wreath like flares from the edge of the sun.

"Is that Mai?" said Ik. Mai looked up, startled, from laying the garlands between the vines. "Show me the extras, Mai."

Mai held up a garland. "Aren't they good? Trumpets from Low Swamp, Auntie Patti's whisper-vine, and star-weed to bind. You never thought ordinary old stars could look so good, I'll bet."

"I never did."

It was all set out right, now. It went in the order: head, half-ring of lamps behind (so as not to glare in her eyes), wreath, half-ring of garlands behind, leaving space in front of her for us.

"Okay, we're going to sing you down now," said Mumma. "Everybody get in and say a proper good-bye." And she knelt inside the wreath a moment herself, murmured something in Ikky's ear and kissed her on the forehead.

We kids all went one by one. Felly got clingy and made Ikky cry; Dash dashed in and planted a quick kiss while she was still upset and would hardly have noticed him; Mumma gave me a cloth and I crouched down and wiped Ik's eyes and nose—and then could not speak to her bare, blinking face.

"You're getting good at that flute," she said.

But this isn't about me, Ik. This is not at all about me.

"Will you come out here some time, and play over me, when no one else's around?"

I nodded. Then I had to say some words, of some kind, I knew. I wouldn't get away without speaking. "If you want."

"I want, okay? Now give me a kiss."

I gave her a kid's kiss, on the mouth. Last time I kissed her, it was carefully on the cheek as she was leaving for her wedding. Some of her glitter had come off on my lips. Now I patted her hair and backed away over the wreath.

Mai came in last. "Fairy doll," I heard her say sobbingly. "Only-one."

And Ik, "It's all right, Auntie. It'll be over so soon, you'll see. And I want to hear your voice nice and strong in the singing."

We readied ourselves, Felly in Mumma's lap, then Dash, then me next to Mai. I tried to stay attentive to Mumma, so Mai wouldn't mess me up with her weeping. It was quiet except for the distant flubber and snap of the bonfires.

We started up, all the ordinary evening songs for putting babies to sleep, for farewelling, for soothing broke-hearted people—all the ones everyone knew so well that they'd long ago made rude versions and joke-songs of them. We sang them plain, following Mumma's lead; we sang them straight, into Ikky's glistening eyes, as the tar climbed her chin. We stood tall, so as to see her, and she us, as her face became the sunken center of that giant flower, the wreath. Dash's little drum held us together and kept us singing, as Ik's eyes rolled and she struggled for breath against the pressing tar, as the chief and the husband's family came and stood across from us, shifting from foot to foot, with torches raised to watch her sink away.

Mai began to crumble and falter beside me as the tar closed in on Ik's face, a slow, sticky, rolling oval. I sang good and strong—I didn't want to hear any last whimper, any stopped breath. I took Mai's arm and tried to hold her together that way, but she only swayed worse, and wept louder. I listened for Mumma under the noise, pressed my eyes shut and made my voice follow hers. By the time I'd steadied myself that way, Ik's eyes were closing.

Through our singing, I thought I heard her cry for Mumma; I tried not to, yet my ears went on hearing. *This will happen only the once—you can't do it over again if ever you feel like remembering.* And Mumma went to her, and I could not tell whether Ik was crying and babbling, or whether it was a trick of our voices, or whether the people on the banks of the tar had started up again. I watched Mumma, because Mumma knew what to do; she knew to lie there on the matting, and dip her cloth in the last water with the little fading fish-scales of ice in it, and squeeze the cloth out and cool the shrinking face in the hole.

And the voice of Ik must have been ours or others' voices, because the hole Mumma was dampening with her cloth was, by her hand movements, only the size of a brassboy now. And by a certain shake of her shoulders I could tell: Mumma knew it was all right to be weeping now, now that Ik was surely gone, was just a nose or just a mouth with the breath crushed out of it, just an eye seeing nothing. And very suddenly it was too much—the flowers nodding in the lamplight, our own sister hanging in tar, going slowly, slowly down like Vanderberg's truck that time, like Jappity's cabin with the old man still inside it, or any old villain or scofflaw of around these parts, and I had a big sicking-up of tears, and they tell me I made an awful noise that frightened everybody right up to the chief, and that the husband's parents thought I was a very ill-brought-up boy for upsetting them instead of allowing them to serenely and superiorly watch justice be done for their lost son.

I don't remember a lot about that part. I came back to myself walking dully across the tar between Mai and Mumma, hand-in-hand, carrying nothing, when I had come out here laden, when we had all had to help. *We must have eaten everything,* I thought. *But what about the mats and pans and planks?* Then I heard a screeking clanking behind me, which was Dash hoisting up too heavy a load of pots.

And Mumma was talking, wearily, as if she'd been going on a long time, and soothingly, which was like a beautiful guide-rope out of my sickness, which my brain was following hand over hand. *It's what they do to people, what they have to do, and all you can do about it is watch out who you go loving, right? Make sure it's not someone who'll rouse that killing-anger in you, if you've got that rage, if you're like our Ik—*

Then the bank came up high in front of us, topped with grass that was white in Mumma's lamp's light. Beyond it were all the eyes, and attached to the eyes the bodies, flat and black against bonfire or starry sky. They shuffled aside for us.

I knew we had to leave Ik behind, and I didn't make a fuss, not now. I had done my fussing, all at once; I had blown myself to bits out on the tar, and now several monstrous things, several gaping mouths of truth, were rattling pieces of me around their teeth. I would be all right, if Mai stayed quiet, if Mumma kept murmuring, if both their hands held me as we passed through this forest of people, these flitting firefly eyes.

They got me up the bank, Mumma and Auntie; I paused and they stumped up and then lifted me, and I walked up the impossible slope like a demon, horizontal for a moment and then stiffly over the top—

—and into my Mumma, whose arms were ready. She couldn't've carried me out on the tar. We'd both have sunk, with me grown so big now. But here on the hard ground she took me up, too big as I was for it. And, too big as I was, I held myself onto her, crossing my feet around her back, my arms behind her neck. And she carried me like Jappity's wife used to carry Jappity's idiot son, and I felt just like that boy, as if the thoughts that were all right for everyone else weren't coming now, and never would come, to me. As if all I could do was watch, but not ever know anything, not ever understand. I pushed my face into Mumma's warm neck; I sealed my eyes shut against her skin; I let her strong warm arms carry me away in the dark.

LAIRD BARRON

Bulldozer

Laird Barron was born in Alaska, where he raised and trained sled dogs for many years. Later, he moved to Seattle and began writing poetry and fiction. His work has appeared in numerous publications, including the Melic Review *and* The Magazine of Fantasy & Science Fiction. *In 2004, his novelette "Old Virginia" was nominated for the International Horror Guild Award and appeared in* The Year's Best Fantasy and Horror: Seventeenth Annual Collection. *Mr. Barron currently resides in Olympia, Washington, and is working on a novel.*

"Bulldozer" originally appeared on SCI FICTION.

—E.D.

1.

Then He bites off my shooting hand.

Christ on a pony, here's a new dimension of pain.

The universe flares white. A storm of dandelion seeds, a cyclone of fire. That's the Coliseum on its feet, a full-blown German orchestra, a cannon blast inside my skull, the top of my skull coming off.

I better suck it up or I'm done for.

I'm a Pinkerton man. That means something. I've got the gun, a cold blue Colt and a card with my name engraved beneath the unblinking eye. I'm the genuine article. I'm a dead shot, a deadeye Dick. I was on the mark in Baltimore when assassins went for Honest Abe. I skinned my iron and plugged them varmints. Abe should've treated me to the theater. Might still be here. Might be in a rocker scribbling how the South was won.

Can't squeeze no trigger now can I? I can squirt my initials on the ceiling.

I'm a Pinkerton I'm a Pinkerton a goddamned Pinkerton.

That's right you sorry sonofabitch you chew on that you swallow like a python and I'll keep on chanting it while I paint these walls.

Belphegor ain't my FatherMother Father thou art in Heaven Jesus loves me.

Jesus Christ.

My balls clank when I walk.

I'm walking to the window.

Well I'm crawling.

If I make it to the window I'll smash the glass and do a stiff drop.

I've got to hustle the shades are dropping from left to right.

Earth on its axis tilting to the black black black iris rolling back inside a socket.

I'm glad the girl hopped the last train. Hope she's in Frisco selling it for more money than she's ever seen here in the sticks.

I taste hard Irish whiskey sweet inside her navel. She's whip smart she's got gams to run she's got blue eyes like the barrel of the gun on the floor under the dresser I can't believe how much blood can spurt from a stump I can't believe it's come to this I hear Him coming heavy on the floorboards buckling He's had a bite He wants more meat.

Pick up the iron southpaw Pinkerton pick it up and point like a man with grit in his liver not a drunk seeing double.

Hallelujah.

Who's laughing now you slack-jawed motherfucker I told you I'm a dead shot now you know now that it's too late.

Let me just say kapow-kapow.

I rest my case, ladies and gennulmen of the jury. I'm

2.

"A Pinkerton man. Well, shit my drawers." The engineer, a greasy brute in striped coveralls, gave me the once-over. Then he spat a stream of chaw and bent his back to feeding the furnace. Never heard of my man Rueben Hicks, so he said. He didn't utter another word until the narrow-gauge spur rolled up to the wretched outskirts of Purdon.

Ugly as rot in a molar, here we were after miles of pasture and hill stitched with barbwire.

Rude frame boxes squatted in the stinking alkaline mud beside the river. Rain pounded like God's own darning needles, stood in orange puddles along the banks, pooled in ruts beneath the awnings. Dull lamplight warmed coke-rimed windows. Shadows fluttered, moths against glass. Already, above the hiss and drum of the rain came faint screams, shouts, piano music.

Just another wild and wooly California mining town that sprang from the ground fast and would fall to ruin faster when the gold played out. Three decades was as the day of a mayfly in the scope of the great dim geography of an ancient continent freshly opened to white men.

Industry crowded in on the main street: Bank. Hotel. Whorehouse. Feed & Tack. Dry Goods. Sawbones. Sheriff's Office. A whole bunch of barrelhouses. Light of the Lord Baptist Temple up the lane and yonder. Purdon Cemetery. A-frame houses, cottages, shanties galore. Lanky men in flannels. Scrawny sows with litters of squalling brats. A rat warren.

The bruised mist held back a wilderness of pines and crooked hills. End of the world for all intents and purposes.

I stood on the leaking platform and decided this was a raw deal. I didn't care if the circus strongman was behind one of the piss-burned saloon facades, swilling whiskey, feeling up the thigh of a horse-toothed showgirl. I'd temporarily lost my hard-on for his scalp with the first rancid-sweet whiff of gunsmoke and open sewage. Suddenly, I'd had a bellyful.

Nothing for it but to do it. I slung my rifle, picked up my bags and began the slog.

3.

I signed *Jonah Koenig* on the ledger at the Riverfront Hotel, a rambling colonial monolith with oil paintings of Andrew Jackson, Ulysses S. Grant and the newly anointed Grover Cleveland hanging large as doom in the lobby. This wasn't the first time I'd used my real name on a job since the affair in Schuylkill, just the first time it felt natural. A sense of finality had settled into my bones.

Hicks surely knew I was closing in. Frankly, I didn't much care after eleven months of eating coal dust from Boston to San Francisco. I cared about securing a whiskey, a bath and a lay. Not in any particular order.

The clerk, a veteran of the trade, understood perfectly. He set me up on the third floor in a room with a liquor cabinet, a poster bed and a view of the mountains. The presidential suite. Some kid drew a washtub of lukewarm water and took my travel clothes to get cleaned. Shortly, a winsome, blue-eyed girl in a low-cut dress arrived without knocking. She unlocked a bottle of bourbon, two glasses and offered to scrub my back.

She told me to call her Violet and didn't seem fazed that I was buck naked or that I'd almost blown her head off. I grinned and hung gun and belt on the back of a chair. Tomorrow was more than soon enough to brace the sheriff.

Violet sidled over, got a handle on the situation without preamble. She had enough sense not to mention the brand on my left shoulder, the old needle tracks or the field of puckered scars uncoiling on my back.

We got so busy I completely forgot to ask if she'd ever happened to screw a dear chum of mine as went by Rueben Hicks. Or Tom Mullen, or Ezra Slade. Later I was half seas over and when I awoke, she was gone.

I noticed a crack in the plaster. A bleeding fault line.

4.

"Business or pleasure, Mr. Koenig?" Sheriff Murtaugh was a stout Irishman of my generation who'd lost most of his brogue and all of his hair. His right leg was propped on the filthy desk, foot encased in bandages gone the shade of rotten fruit. It reeked of gangrene. "Chink stabbed it with a pickaxe, can y'beat that? Be gone to hell before I let Doc Campion have a peek—he'll want to chop the fucker at the ankle." He'd laughed, polishing his tarnished lawman's star with his sleeve. Supposedly there was a camp full of Chinese nearby; the ones who'd stayed on and fallen into mining after the railroad pushed west. Bad sorts, according to the sheriff and his perforated foot.

We sat in his cramped office, sharing evil coffee from a pot that had probably been bubbling on the stove for several days. At the end of the room was the lockup, dingy as a Roman catacomb and vacant but for a deputy named Levi sleeping off a bender in an open cell.

I showed Murtaugh a creased photograph of Hicks taken during a P.T. Barnum extravaganza in Philadelphia. Hicks was lifting a grand piano on his back while ladies in tights applauded before a pyramid of elephants. "Recognize this fellow? I got a lead off a wanted poster in Frisco. Miner thought he'd seen him in town. Wasn't positive." The miner was a nice break—the trail was nearly three months cold and I'd combed every two-bit backwater within six hundred miles before the man and I bumped into each other at the Gold Digger Saloon and started swapping tales.

"Who wants to know?"

"The Man himself."

"Barnum? Really?"

"Oh, yes indeed." I began rolling a cigarette.

Murtaugh whistled through mismatched teeth. "Holy shit, that's Iron Man Hicks. Yuh, I seen him around. Came in 'bout June. Calls hisself Mullen, says he's from Philly. Gotta admit he looks different from his pictures. Don't stack up to much in person. So what's he done to bring a Pinkerton to the ass-end o' the mule?"

I struck a match on the desk, took a few moments to get the cigarette smoldering nicely. There was a trace of hash mixed with the tobacco. Ah, that was better. "Year and half back, some murders along the East Coast were connected to the presence of the circus. Ritual slayings—pentagrams, black candles, possible cannibalism. Nasty stuff. The investigation pointed to the strongman. Cops hauled him in, nothing stuck. Barnum doesn't take chances; fires the old boy and has him committed. Cedar Grove may not be pleasant, but it beats getting lynched, right? Iron Man didn't think so. He repaid his boss by ripping off some trinkets Barnum collected and skipping town."

"Real important cultural artifacts, I bet," Murtaugh said.

"Each to his own. Most of the junk turned up with local pawn dealers, antiquarians' shelves, spooky shops and you get the idea. We recovered everything except the original translation of the *Dictionnaire Infernal* by a dead Frenchman, Collin de Plancy."

"What's that?"

"A book about demons and devils. Something to talk about at church."

"The hell y'say. Lord have mercy. Well, I ain't seen Mullen, uh, Hicks, in weeks, though y'might want to check with the Honeybee Ranch. And Trosper over to the Longrifle. Be advised—Trosper hates lawmen. Did a stretch in the pokey, I reckon. We got us an understandin', o' course."

"Good thing I'm not really a lawman, isn't it?"

"What's the guy's story?" Murtaugh stared at the photo, shifting it in his blunt hands.

I said, "Hicks was born in Plymouth. His father was a minister, did missionary work here in California—tried to save the Gold Rush crowd. Guess the minister beat him something fierce. Kid runs off and joins the circus. Turns out he's a freak of nature and a natural showman. P.T. squires him to every city in the Union. One day, Iron Man Hicks decides to start cutting the throats of rag pickers and whores. At least, that's my theory. According to the docs at Cedar Grove, there's medical problems—might be consumption or syph or something completely foreign. Because of this disease maybe he hears voices, wants to be America's Jack the Ripper. Thinks God has a plan for him. Who knows for sure? He's got a stash of dubious bedside material on the order of the crap he stole from Barnum, which was confiscated; he'd filled the margins with notes the agency eggs still haven't deciphered. Somebody introduced him to the lovely hobby of demonology—probably his own dear dad. I can't check that because Hicks senior died in '67 and all his possessions were auctioned. Anyway, Junior gets slapped into a cozy asylum with the help of Barnum's legal team. Hicks escapes and, well, I've told you the rest."

"Jesus H., what a charmin' tale."

We drank our coffee, listened to rain thud on tin. Eventually Murtaugh got around to what had probably been ticking in his brain the minute he recognized my name. "You're the fellow who did for the Molly Maguires."

"Afraid so."

He smirked. "Yeah, I thought it was you. Dirty business that, eh?"

"Nothing pretty about it, Sheriff." Sixteen years and the legend kept growing, a cattle carcass bloating in the sun.

"I expect not. We don't get the paper up here, 'cept when the mail train comes in. I do recall mention that some folks are thinkin' yer Mollys weren't really the bad guys. Maybe the railroad lads had a hand in them killin's."

"That's true. It's also true that sometimes a horse thief gets hanged for another scoundrel's misdeed. The books get balanced either way, don't they? Everybody in Schuylkill got what they wanted."

Murtaugh said, "Might put that theory to the twenty sods as got hung up to dry."

I sucked on my cigarette, studied the ash drifting towards my knees. "Sheriff, did you ever talk to Hicks?"

"Bumped into him at one of the saloons durin' a faro game. Said howdy. No occasion for a philosophical debate."

"Anything he do or say seem odd?" I proffered my smoke.

"Sure. He smelled right foul and he wasn't winnin' any blue ribbons on account o' his handsome looks. He had fits—somethin' to do with his nerves, accordin' to Doc Campion." Murtaugh extended his hand and accepted the cigarette. He dragged, made an appreciative expression and closed his eyes. "I dunno, I myself ain't ever seen Hicks foamin' at the mouth. Others did, I allow."

"And that's it?"

"Y'mean, did the lad strike me as a thief and a murderer? I'm bound to say no more'n the rest o' the cowpunchers and prospectors that drift here. I allow most of 'em would plug you for a sawbuck . . . or a smoke." He grinned, rubbed ashes from his fingers. "Y'mentioned nothing stuck to our lad. Has that changed?"

"The evidence is pending."

"Think he did it?"

"I think he's doing it now."

"But you can't prove it."

"Nope."

"So, officially you're here to collect P.T.'s long lost valuables. I imagine Hicks is mighty attached to that book by now. Probbly won't part with it without a fight."

"Probably not."

"Billy Cullins might be fittin' him for a pine box, I suppose."

I pulled out a roll of wrinkled bills, subtracted a significant number and tossed them on the desk. Plenty more where that came from, hidden under a floorboard at the hotel. I always travel flush. "The agency's contribution to the Purdon widows and orphans fund."

"Much obliged, Mr. K. Whole lotta widows and orphans in these parts."

"More every day," I said.

5.

BELPHEGOR IS YOUR FATHERMOTHER. This carmine missive scrawled in a New Orleans hotel room. In the unmade bed, a phallus sculpted from human excrement. Flies crawled upon the sheets, buzzing and sluggish.

In Lubbock, a partially burned letter—"O FatherMother, may the blood of the-(indecipherable)-erate urchin be pleasing in thy throat. I am of the tradition."

Come Albuquerque, the deterioration had accelerated. Hicks did not bother to destroy this particular letter, rather scattered its befouled pages on the floor among vermiculate designs scriven in blood—"worms, godawful! i am changed! Blessed the sacrament of decay! Glut Obloodyhole O bloodymaggots Obloodybowels OLordof shite! Fearthegash! iamcomeiamcome"

Finally, Bakersfield in script writ large upon a flophouse wall—

EATEATEATEATEAT! Found wedged under a mattress, the severed hand and arm of an unidentified person. Doubtless a young female. The authorities figured these remains belonged to a prostitute. Unfortunately, a few of them were always missing.

The locket in the delicate fist was inscribed, For my little girl. *I recalled the bulls that stripped the room laughing when they read that. I also recalled busting one guy's jaw later that evening after we all got a snoot-full at the watering hole. I think it was a dispute over poker.*

6.

Trosper didn't enjoy seeing me at the bar. He knew what I was and what it meant from a mile off. First words out of his egg-sucker's mouth: "Lookit here, mister, I don't want no bullshit from you. You're buyin' or you're walkin'. Or Jake might have somethin' else for you."

I couldn't restrain my smile. The bandy roosters always got me. "Easy, friend. Gimme two fingers of coffin varnish. Hell, make it a round for the house."

The Longrifle was a murky barn devoid of all pretense to grandeur. This was the trough of the hard-working, harder-drinking peasantry. It was presently dead as three o'clock. Only me, Trosper and a wiry cowboy with a crimped, sullen face who nursed a beer down the line. Jake, I presumed.

Trosper made quick work of getting the whiskey into our glasses. He corked the bottle and left it in front of me.

I swallowed fast, smacked the glass onto the counter. "Ugh. I think my left eye just went blind."

"Give the Chinaman a music lesson or shove off, pig. You ain't got no jurydiction here."

"Happy to oblige." I did the honors. Flames crackled in my belly, spread to my chest and face. Big grandad clock behind the bar ticked too loudly.

Good old Jake had tipped back his hat and shifted in his chair to affright me with what I'm sure was his darkest glare. Bastard had a profile sharp as a hatchet. A regulator, a bullyboy. He was heeled with a fair-sized peashooter in a shoulder rig.

I belted another swig to fix my nerves, banged the glass hard enough to raise dust.

Motes drifted lazily, planetoids orbiting streams of light from the rain-blurred panes. I said to Trosper, "I hear tell you're chummy with a bad man goes by Tom Mullen."

Jake said, soft and deadly, "He told you to drink or get on shank's mare." Goddamned if the cowboy didn't possess the meanest drawl I'd heard since ever. First mistake was resting a rawboned hand on the butt of his pistola. Second mistake was not skinning said iron.

So I shot him twice. Once in the belly, through the buckle; once near the collar of his vest. Jake fell off his stool and squirmed in the sawdust. His hat tumbled away. He had a thick mane of blond hair with a perfect pink circle at the crown. That's what you got for wearing cowboy hats all the fucking time.

Making conversation with Trosper, who was currently frozen into a homely statue, I said, "Don't twitch or I'll nail your pecker to the floor." I walked over to Jake. The cowpoke was game; by then he almost had his gun free with the off hand. I stamped on his wrist until it cracked. He hissed. I smashed in his front teeth with a couple swipes from the heel of my boot. That settled him down.

I resumed my seat, poured another drink. "Hey, what's the matter? You haven't seen a man get plugged before? What kind of gin mill you running?" My glance swung to the dim ceiling and its mosaic of bullet holes and grease stains. "Oh, they usually shoot the hell out of your property, not each other. Tough luck the assholes got it all backwards. Come on, Trosper. Take a snort. This hooch you sling the shit-kickers kinda grows on a fellow."

Trosper was grey as his apron and sweating. His hands jerked. "H-he, uh, he's got a lotta friends, mister."

"I have lots of bullets. Drink, amigo." After he'd gulped his medicine I said, "All right. Where were we? Oh, yes. Mr. Mullen. I'm interested in meeting him. Any notions?"

"Used to come in here every couple weeks; whenever he had dust in his poke. Drank. Played cards with some of the boys from the Bar-H. Humped the girls pretty regular over to the Honeybee."

"Uh, huh. A particular girl?"

"No. He din't have no sweetheart."

"When's the last time you saw him?"

Trosper thought about that. "Dunno. Been a spell. Christ, is Jake dead? He ain't movin'."

"I'll be damned. He isn't. Pay attention. Mullen's gone a-prospecting you say?"

"Wha—yeah. Mister, I dunno. He came in with dust is all I'm sayin'." Trosper's eyes were glassy. "I dunno shit, mister. Could be he moved on. I ain't his keeper."

"The sheriff mentioned Hicks had a condition."

"He's got the Saint Vitus Dance. You know, he trembles like a drunk ain't had his eye-opener. Saw him fall down once; twitched and scratched at his face some-thin' awful. When it was over, he just grinned real pasty like, and made a joke about it."

I got the names and descriptions of the Bar-H riders, not that I'd likely interview them. As I turned to leave, I said, "Okay, Trosper. I'll be around, maybe stop in for a visit, see if your memory clears up. Here's a twenty. That should cover a box."

7.

I was riding a terrific buzz, equal parts whiskey and adrenaline, when I flopped on a plush divan in the parlor of the Honeybee Ranch. A not-too-uncomely lady-of-the-house pried off my muddy boots and rubbed oil on my feet. The Madame, a frigate in purple who styled herself as Octavia Plantagenet, provided me a Cuban cigar from a velvet humidor. She expertly lopped the tip with a fancy silver-chased cutter and got it burning, quirking suggestively as she worked the barrel between her fat red lips. The roses painted on her cheeks swelled like bellows.

The Honeybee swam in the exhaust of chortling hookahs and joints of Kentucky bluegrass. A swarthy fellow plucked his sitar in accompany to the pianist, cementing the union of Old World decadence and frontier excess. Here was a refined wilderness of thick Persian carpet and cool brass; no plywood, but polished mahogany; no cheap glass, but exquisite crystal. The girls wore elaborate gowns and mink-slick hair piled high, batted glitzy lashes over eyes twinkly as gemstones. Rouge, perfume, sequins and charms, the whole swarming mess an intoxicating collaboration of artifice and lust.

Madame Octavia recalled Hicks. "Tommy Mullen? Sorry-lookin' fella, what with the nerve disorder. Paid his tab. Not too rough on the merchandise, if he did have breath to gag a maggot. Only Lydia and Connie could stomach that, but he didn't complain. Lord, he hasn't been by in a coon's age. I think he headed back east."

I inquired after Violet and was told she'd be available later. Perhaps another girl? I said I'd wait and accepted four fingers of cognac in King George's own snifter. The brandy was smooth and I didn't notice the wallop it packed until maroon lamp-shades magnified the crowd of genteel gamblers, businessmen and blue-collar stiffs on their best behavior, distorted them in kaleidoscopic fashion. Tinkling notes from Brahms reverberated in my brain long after the short, thick Austrian player in the silk vest retired for a nip at the bar.

Fame preceded me. Seemed everybody who could decipher newsprint had read about my exploits in Pennsylvania. They knew all there was to know about how I infiltrated the Workers Benevolent Association and sent a score of murderous union extremists to the gallows with my testimony. Depending upon one's social inclinations, I was a champion of commerce and justice, or a no-good, yellow-bellied skunk. It was easy to tell who was who from the assorted smiles and sneers. The fact I'd recently ventilated a drover at the Longrifle was also a neat conversation starter.

Octavia encouraged a muddled procession of counterfeit gentry to ogle the infamous Pinkerton, a bulldozer of the first water from the Old States. Deduction was for the highbrows in top hats and greatcoats; I performed my detecting with a boot and a six-gun. I'd bust your brother's head or bribe your mother if that's what it took to hunt you to ground and collect my iron men. Rumor had it I'd strongarm the pope himself. Not much of a stretch as I never was impressed with that brand of idolatry.

Introductions came in waves—Taylor Hackett, bespectacled owner of the Bar-H cattle ranch; Norton Smythe, his stuffed-suit counterpart in the realm of gold mining; Ned Cates, Bob Tunny and Harry Edwards, esteemed investors of the Smythe & Ruth Mining Company; each beaming and guffawing, too many teeth bared. An

Eastern Triad. I asked them if they ate of The Master's sacrifice, but nobody appeared to understand and I relented while their waxy grins were yet in place. Blowsy as a poleaxed mule, I hadn't truly allowed for the possibility of my quarry snuggled in the fold of a nasty little cult. Hicks was a loner. I hoped.

After the contents of the snifter evaporated and got replenished like an iniquitous cousin to the Horn of Plenty, the lower caste made its rounds in the persons of Philmore Kavanaugh, journalist for some small-town rag that recently folded and sent him penniless to the ends of creation; Dalton Beaumont, chief deputy and unloved cousin of Sheriff Murtaugh; John Brown, a wrinkled alderman who enjoyed having his toes sucked and daubed mother-of-pearl right there before God and everyone; Michael Piers the formerly acclaimed French poet, now sunk into obscurity and bound for an early grave judging from the violence of his cough and the bloody spackle on his embroidered handkerchief. And others and others and others. I gave up on even trying to focus and concentrated on swilling without spilling.

There wasn't any sort of conversation, precisely. More the noise of an aroused hive. I waded through streams and tributaries from the great lake of communal thrum—

"—let some daylight into poor Jake. There'll be the devil to pay, mark me!"

"Langston gone to seed in Chinatown. A bloody shame—"

"First Holmes, now Stevenson. Wretched, wretched—"

"—the Ancient Order of Hibernia gets you your goddamned Molly Maguires and that's a fact. Shoulda hung a few more o' them Yankee bastards if you ask me—"

"—Welsh thick as ticks, doped out of their faculties on coolie mud. They've still got the savage in them. Worse than the red plague—"

"Two years, Ned. Oh, all right. Three years. The railroad gobbles up its share and I get the pieces with promising glint. California is weighed and measured, my friend. We'll run the independent operations into the dirt. Moonlighters don't have a prayer—"

"—Barnum, for gawd's sake! Anybody tell him—"

"I hate the circus. Stinks to high heaven. I hate those damned clowns too—"

"No. Langston's dead—"

"—poked her for fun. Dry hump and the bitch took my folding—"

"—Mullen? Hicks? Dunno an don' care. Long gone, long gone—"

"The hell, you say! He's bangin' the gong at the Forty-Mile Camp, last I heard—"

"—the Professor's on the hip? I thought he sailed across the pond—"

"My dear, sweet woman-child. As quoth Lord Baudelaire:

"Madonna, mistress I shall build for you
An altar of misery and hew—"

"It wasn't enough the cunt sacked me. 'E bloody spit in my face, the bloody wanker—"

"—stones to *kill* a man—"

"Ah, I could do the job real nice—"

" '*Et creuser dans le coin*—' "

"—I mean, look at 'im. He's a facking mechanical—"

"So, I says, lookee here, bitch, I'll cut your—"

"'Une niche, d'azur et d'or tout—'"

"—suck my cock or die! Whoopie! I'm on a hellbender, fellas!"

"—don't care. Murtaugh should string his ass from the welcome sign—"

"I met your Hicks. He was nothing really special." Piers blew a cloud of pungent clove exhaust, watched it eddy in the currents. "Thees circus freak of yours. He had a beeg mouth."

My head wobbled. "Always pegged him for the strong silent type. Ha, ha."

"No." Piers waved impatiently. "He had a beeg mouth. Drooled, how do you say?—Like an eediot. A fuck-ing eediot."

"Where?" I wheezed.

"Where? How do I know where? Ask the fuck-ing Professor. Maybe he knows where. The Professor knows everyone."

"There you are, darling," crooned Madame Octavia as if I had suddenly re-materialized. Her ponderous breasts pressed against my ribs. Her choice of scent brought tears to my eyes. "This gig is drying up, baby. It's a tourist trap. Ooh, Chi-Town is where the action is. Isn't Little Egypt a pistol? Hoochie-Koochie baby!"

Red lights. White faces. Shadows spreading cracks.

I dropped the snifter from disconnected fingers. Thank goodness Octavia was there with a perfumed cloth to blot the splash. I was thinking, yes, indeed, a tragedy about Robert Louis; a step above the penny-dreadfuls, but my hero nonetheless.

Where was Violet? Coupled to a banker? A sodbuster? Hoochie-Koochie all night long.

"Excuse, me, Mr. Koenig." An unfamiliar voice, a visage in silhouette.

"Ah, Frankie, he's just laying about waiting for one of my girls—"

"Sheriff's business, Miss Octavia. Please, sir. We've been sent to escort you to the office. Levi, he's dead weight, get his other arm. You too, Dalton. There's a lad." The sheriff's boys each grabbed a limb and hoisted me up as if on angels' wings.

"The cavalry," I said.

Scattered applause. A bawdy ragtime tune. Hungry mouths hanging slack.

And the muzzy lamps. Red. Black.

8.

"What do you call him?"

"Chemosh. Baal-Peeor. Belphegor. No big deal, the Moabites are dust. They won't mind if the title gits slaughtered by civilized folks."

"We're a fair piece from Moab."

"Belphegor speaks many tongues in many lands."

"A world traveler, eh?"

"That's right, Pinky."

"This friend of yours, he speaks to you through the shitter?"

"Yeah."

"Interesting. Seems a tad inelegant."

"Corruption begets corruption, Pinky," says Hicks. His eyes are brown, hard as baked earth. Gila monster's eyes. He once raised a four-hundred-pound stone above his head, balanced it in his palm to the cheers of mobs. Could reach across the table and crush my throat, even with the chains. Calcium deposits mar his fingers, distend *from his elbows not unlike spurs. There is a suspicious lump under his limp hair, near the brow. He's sinewy and passive in the Chair of Questions. "What's more lunatic than fallin' down before the image of a man tacked to a cross? Nothin'. You don't even git nothin' fun. I aim to have fun."*

I'm fascinated by the wet mouth in the bronzed face. It works, yes indeed it articulates most functionally. Yet it yawns, slightly yawns, as if my captive strongman was victim of a palsy, or the reverse of lockjaw. Saliva beads and dangles on viscous threads. I gag on the carnivore's stench gusting from the wound. His teeth are chipped and dark as flint. Long. I ask, "What are you?"

"Holes close. Holes open. I'm an Opener. They Who Wait live through me. What about you?"

"I'm an atheist." That was a half-truth, but close enough for government work.

"Good on you, Pinky. You're on your way. And here's Tuttle." He indicated a prim lawyer in a crisp suit. "P.T. only hires the best. Adios, pal."

Three weeks later, when Hicks strolls out of Cedar Grove Sanitarium, I'm not surprised at the message he leaves— CLOSE A HOLE AND ANOTHER OPENS.

Funny, funny world. It's Tuttle who pays the freight for my hunting expedition into the American West.

9.

Deputy Levi called it protective custody. They dumped me on a cot in a cell. Murtaugh's orders to keep me from getting lynched by some of Jake's confederates. These confederates had been tying one on down at the Longrifle, scene of the late, lamented Jake's demise. Murtaugh wasn't sorry to see a "cockeyed snake like that little sonofabitch" get planted. The sheriff promised to chat with Trosper regarding the details of our interview. It'd be straightened out by breakfast.

I fell into the amber and drowned.

Things clumped together in a sticky collage—

Hicks leering through the bars, his grin as prodigious as a train tunnel.

Violet's wheat-blonde head bowed at my groin and me so whiskey-flaccid I can only sweat and watch a cockroach cast a juggernaut shadow beneath a kerosene lamp while the sheriff farts and snores at his desk.

Jake shits himself, screams soundlessly as my boot descends, hammer of the gods.

Lincoln waves to the people in the balconies. His eyes pass directly over me. I'm twenty-two, I'm hell on wheels. In three minutes I'll make my first kill. Late bloomer.

"I once was lost. Now I'm found. The Soldier's Friend, Sister M, had a hold on me, yes sir, yesiree."

"I give up the needle and took to the bottle like a babe at his mama's nipple."

"Never had a wife, never needed one. I took up the traveling life, got married to my gun."

A man in a suit doffs his top hat and places his head into the jaws of a bored lion. The jaws close.

A glossy pink labium quakes and begins to yield, an orchid brimming with ancient stars.

"How many men you killed, Jonah?" Violet strokes my superheated brow.

"Today?"

"No, silly! I mean, in all. The grand total."

"More than twenty. More every day."

Sun eats stars. Moon eats sun. Black hole eats Earth.

Hicks winks a gory eye, an idiot lizard, gives the sheriff a languid, slobbery kiss that glistens snail slime. When the sackcloth of ashes floats to oblivion and I can see again, the beast is gone, if he ever was.

The door creaks with the storm. Open. Shut.

Violet sighs against my sweaty chest, sleeps in reinvented innocence.

There's a crack in the ceiling and it's dripping.

10.

I did the expedient thing—holed up in my hotel room for a week, drinking the hair of the dog that bit me and screwing Violet senseless.

I learned her daddy was a miner who was blown to smithereens. No mother; no kin as would take in a coattail relation from the boondocks. But she had great teeth and a nice ass. Fresh meat for Madame Octavia's stable. She was eighteen and real popular with the gentlemen, Miss Violet was. Kept her earnings tucked in a sock, was gonna hop the mail train to San Francisco one of these fine days, work as a showgirl in an upscale dance hall. Heck, she might even ride the rail to Chicago, meet this Little Egypt who was the apple of the city's eye. Yeah.

She finally asked me if I'd ever been married—it was damned obvious I wasn't at present—and I said no. Why not? Lucky, I guessed.

"Mercy, Jonah, you got some mighty peculiar readin' here." Violet was lying on her belly, thumbing through my Latin version of the *Pseudomonarchia Daemonum*. Her hair was tangled; perspiration glowed on her ivory flanks.

I sprawled naked, propped against the headboard, smoking while I cleaned and oiled my Winchester Model 1886. Best rifle I'd ever owned; heavy enough to drop a buffalo, but perfect for men. It made me a tad wistful to consider that I wasn't likely to use it on Hicks. I figured him for close quarters.

Grey and yellow out the window. Streets were a quagmire. I watched figures mucking about, dropping planks to make corduroy for the wagons. Occasionally a gun popped.

For ten dollars and an autograph, Deputy Levi had compiled a list of deaths and disappearances in Purdon and environs over the past four months, hand delivered it to my doorstep. Two pages long. Mostly unhelpful—routine shootings and stabbings, claim-jumping and bar brawls, a whole slew of accidents. I did mark the names of three prospectors who'd vanished. They worked claims separated by many miles of inhospitable terrain. Each had left a legacy of food, equipment and personal items—no money, though. No hard cash. No gold dust.

Violet gasped when she came to some unpleasant and rather florid illustrations. "Lordy! That's . . . awful. You believe in demons and such, Jonah?" Curiosity and suspicion struggled to reconcile her tone.

"Nope. But other folks do."

"Tommy Mullen—he does?" Her eyes widened. I glimpsed Hicks, a gaunt satyr loitering in the Honeybee parlor while the girls drew lots to seal a fate.

"I expect he does." I slapped her pale haunch. "Come on over here, sweetness. It isn't for you to fret about." And to mitigate the dread transmitted through her trembling flesh, I said, "He's hightailed to the next territory. I'm wasting daylight in this burg." Her grateful mouth closed on me and her tongue moved, rough and supple. I grabbed the bed post. "Pardon me, not completely wasting it."

Three miners. Picture-clear, the cabins, lonely, isolated. A black shape sauntering from an open door left swinging in its wake. Crows chattering in poplar branches, throaty chuckle of a stream.

I drowsed. The hotel boy knocked and reported a Chinaman was waiting in the lobby. The man bore me an invitation from Langston Butler. Professor Butler, to his friends. The note, in handsome script, read:

Sashay on out to Forty-Mile Camp and I'll tell you how to snare the Iron Man. Cordially, L. Butler.

I dressed in a hurry. Violet groaned, started to rise, but I kissed her on the mouth and said to take the afternoon off. Indulging a bout of prescience, I left some money on the dresser. A lot of money. The money basically said, "If you're smart you'll be on the next train to San Francisco; next stop the Windy City."

I hoped Murtaugh had successfully smoothed all the feathers I'd ruffled.

This was my best suit and I sure didn't want to get any holes in it.

11.

Forty-Mile Camp was not, as its appellation suggested, forty miles from Purdon. The jolting ride in Hung Chan's supply wagon lasted under three hours by my pocket watch. Hung didn't speak to me at all. I rode shotgun, riveted by the payload of flour, sugar and sundries, not the least of which happened to include a case of weathered, leaky dynamite.

We wound along Anderson Creek Canyon, emerged in a hollow near some dredges and a mongrel collection of shacks. Cookfires sputtered, monarch butterflies under cast iron pots tended by women the color of ash. There were few children and no dogs. Any male old enough to handle pick, shovel or pan was among the clusters of men stolidly attacking the earth, wading in the frigid water, toiling among the rocky shelves above the encampment.

Nobody returned my friendly nod. Nobody even really looked at me except for two men who observed the proceedings from a copse of scraggly cottonwoods, single-shot rifles slung at half mast. My hackles wouldn't lie down until Hung led me through the camp to a building that appeared to be three or four shanties in combination. He ushered me through a thick curtain and into a dim, moist realm pungent with body musk and opium tang.

"Koenig, at last. Pull up a rock." Butler lay on a pile of bear pelts near a guttering fire pit. He was wrapped in a Navajo blanket, but clearly emaciated. His misshapen skull resembled a chunk of anthracite sufficiently dense to crook his neck. His dark flesh had withered tight as rawhide and he appeared to be an eon older than his stentorian voice sounded. In short, he could've been a fossilized anthropoid at repose in Barnum's House of Curiosities.

Butler's attendant, a toothless crone with an evil squint, said, *"Mama die?"* She gently placed a long, slender pipe against his lips, waited for him to draw the load. She hooked another horrible glance my way and didn't offer to cook me a pill.

After a while Butler said, "You would've made a wonderful Templar."

"Except for the minor detail of suspecting Christianity is a pile of crap. Chopping down Saracens for fun and profit, that I could've done."

"You're a few centuries late. A modern-day crusader, then. An educated man, I presume?"

"Harvard, don't you know." I pronounced it *Hah-vahd* to maximize the irony.

"An *expensive* education; although, aren't they all. Still, a Pinkerton, tsk, tsk. Daddy was doubtless shamed beyond consolation."

"Papa Koenig was annoyed. One of the slickest New York lawyers you'll ever do battle with—came from a whole crabbed scroll of them. Said I was an ungrateful iconoclast before he disowned me. Hey, it's easier to shoot people than try to frame them, I've discovered."

"And now you've come to shoot poor Rueben Hicks."

"Rueben Hicks is a thief, a murderer and a cannibal. Seems prudent to put him down if I get the chance."

"Technically a cannibal is one that feeds on its own species."

I said, "Rueben doesn't qualify as a member?"

"That depends on your definition of human, Mr. Koenig," Butler said and smiled. The contortion had a ghoulish effect on his face. "Because it goes on two legs and wears a coat and tie? Because it knows how to say please and thank you?"

"Why do I get the feeling this conversation is headed south? People were talking about you in town. You're a folk legend at the whorehouse."

"A peasant hero, as it were?"

"More like disgraced nobility. I can't figure what you're doing here. Could've picked a more pleasant climate to go to seed."

"I came to Purdon ages ago. Sailed from London where I had pursued a successful career in anthropology—flunked medical school, you see. Too squeamish. I dabbled in physics and astronomy, but primitive culture has always been my obsession. Its rituals, its primal energy."

"Plenty of primitive culture here."

"Quite."

"*Mama die?*" said the hag as she brandished the pipe.

Butler accepted the crone's ministrations. His milky eyes flared, and when he spoke, he spoke more deliberately. "I've been following your progress. You are capable, resourceful, tenacious. I fear Rueben will swallow you alive, but if anyone has a chance to put a stop to his wickedness it is you."

"Lead has a sobering effect on most folks," I said. "Strange to hear a debauched occultist like yourself fussing about wickedness. I take it you've got a personal stake in this manhunt. He must've hurt your feelings or something."

"Insomuch as I know he intends to use me as a blood sacrifice, I'm extremely interested."

"You ever thought of clearing out?"

"Impossible."

"Why impossible?"

"Gravity, Mr. Koenig." Butler took another hit. Eventually, he said in a dreamy tone, "I'm a neglectful host. Care to bang the gong?"

"Thanks, no."

"A reformed addict. How rare."

"I'll settle for being a drunk. What's your history with Hicks?"

"We were introduced in '78. I was in Philadelphia and had taken in the circus with some colleagues from the university. I fell in with a small group of the players after the show, Rueben being among this number. We landed in a tiny café, a decadent slice of gay Paris, and everybody was fabulously schnockered, to employ the argot. Rueben and I got to talking and we hit it off. I was amazed at the breadth, and I blush to admit, scandalous nature of his many adventures. He was remarkably cultured behind the provincial façade. I was intrigued. Smitten, too."

I said, "And here I thought Hicks was a ladies man."

"Rueben is an opportunist. We retired to my flat; all very much a night's work for me. Then . . . then after we'd consummated our mutual fascination, he said he wanted to show me something that would change my life. Something astounding."

"Do tell."

"We were eating mushrooms. A mysterious variety—Rueben stole them from P.T. and P.T. obtained them from this queer fellow who dealt in African imports. I hallucinated that Rueben caused a window to open in the bedroom wall, a portal into space. Boggling! Millions of stars blazed inches from my nose, a whole colossal bell-shaped galaxy of exploded gases and cosmic dust. The sight would've driven Copernicus insane. It was a trick, stage magic. Something he'd borrowed from his fellow performers. He asked me what I saw and I told him. His face . . . there was something wrong. Too rigid, too cold. For a moment, I thought he'd put on an extremely clever mask and I was terrified. And his mouth . . . His expression melted almost instantly, and he was just Rueben again. I knew better, though. And, unfortunately, my fascination intensified. Later, when he showed me the portal trick, this time sans hallucinogens, I realized he wasn't simply a circus performer. He claimed to be more than human, to have evolved into a superior iteration of the genus. A flawed analysis, but at least partially correct."

Hick's rubbery grin bobbed to the surface of my mind. "He's crazed, I'll give you that."

"Rueben suffers from a unique breed of mycosis—you've perhaps seen the tumors on his arms and legs, and especially along his spinal column? It's consuming him as a fungus consumes a tree. Perversely, it's this very parasitic influence that imbues him with numerous dreadful abilities. Evolution via slow digestion."

"Dreadful abilities? If he'd showed me a hole in the wall that looked on the moon's surface I might've figured he was a fakir, or Jesus's little brother, or what have you. He didn't. He didn't fly out of Cedar Grove, either."

"Scoff as you will. Ignorance is all the blessing we apes can hope for."

"What became of your torrid love affair?"

"He and I grew close. He confided many terrible things to me, unspeakable deeds. Ultimately I determined to venture here and visit his childhood haunts, to discover the wellspring of his vitality, the source of his preternatural affinities. He warned me, albeit such caveats were mere inducements to an inquisitive soul. I was so easily corrupted." Butler's voice trailed off as he was lost in reflection.

Corruption begets corruption, copper. "Sounds very romantic," I said. "What were you after? The gold? Nah, the gold is panned out or property of the companies. Mating practices of the natives?"

"I coveted knowledge, Mr. Koenig. Rueben whispered of a way to unlock the secrets of brain and blood, to lay bare the truth behind several of mankind's squalid superstitions. To walk the earth as a god. His mind is far from scientific, and but remotely curious. One could nearly categorize him as a victim of circumstance in this drama. I, however, presumably equipped with superior intellect, would profit all the more than my barbarous concubine. My potential seemed enormous."

"Yes, and look at you now, Professor," I said. "Do these people understand what you are?"

"What do you think I am, detective?"

"A Satan-worshipping dope fiend."

"Wrong. I'm a naturalist. Would that I could reinvent my innocent dread of God and Satan, of supernatural phenomena. As for these yellow folk, they don't care what I am. I pay well for my upkeep and modest pleasures."

"For a man who's uncovered great secrets of existence, your accommodations lack couth."

"Behold the reward of hubris. I could've done as Rueben has—descended completely into the womb of an abominable mystery and evolved as a new and perfect savage. Too cowardly—I tasted the ichor of divinity and quailed, fled to this hovel and my drugs. My memories. Wisdom devours the weak." He shuddered and spat a singsong phrase that brought the old woman scuttling to feed him another load of dope. After he'd recovered, he produced a leather-bound book from beneath his pillow. The *Dictionnaire Infernal*. "A gift from our mutual acquaintance. Please, take it. These 'forbidden' tomes are surpassingly ludicrous."

I inspected the book; de Plancy's signature swooped across the title page. "Did Rueben travel all this way to fetch you a present and off a few hapless miners as a bonus?"

"Rueben has come home because he must, it is an integral component of his metamorphosis. Surely you've detected his quickening purpose, the apparent degeneration of his faculties, which is scarcely a symptom of decay, but rather a sign of fundamental alteration. Pupation. He has returned to this place to commune with his benefactor, to disgorge the red delights of his gruesome and sensuous escapades. Such is the pact between them. It is the pact all supplicants make. It was mine, before my defection."

My skin prickled at the matter-of-fact tone Butler affected. I said, "I don't get this, Professor. If you don't hold with demons and all that bunkum, what the hell are you worshipping?"

"Supplicating, dear boy. I didn't suggest we are alone in the cosmos. Certain monstrous examples of cryptogenetics serve the function of godhead well enough. That *scholars* invent fanciful titles and paint even more fanciful pictures does not diminish the essential reality of these organisms, only obscures it."

My suspicions about Butler's character were sharpening with the ebb and pulse of firelight. He lay coiled in his nest, a diamondback ready to strike. Not wanting an answer, I said, "Exactly what did you do to acquire this . . . knowledge?"

"I established communion with a primordial intelligence, a cyclopean plexus rooted below these hills and valleys. An unclassified mycoflora that might or might not be of terrestrial origin. There are rites to effect this dialogue. A variety of osmosis ancient as the sediment men first crawled from. Older! Most awful, I assure you."

"Christ, you've got holes in your brain from smoking way too much of the black O." I stood, covering my emotions with a grimace. "Next thing you'll tell me is Oberon came prancing from under his hill to sprinkle that magic fairy shit on you."

"You are the detective. Don't blame me if this little investigation uncovers things that discomfit your world view."

"Enough. Tell it to Charlie Darwin when you meet in hell. You want me to nail Hicks, stow the campfire tales and come across with his location."

"Rueben's visited infrequently since late spring. Most recently, three days ago. He promised to take me with him soon, to gaze once more upon the FatherMother. Obviously I don't wish to make that pilgrimage. I'd rather die a nice peaceful death—being lit on fire, boiled in oil, staked to an ant hill. That sort of thing."

"Is he aware of my presence in Purdon?"

"Of course. He expected you weeks ago. I do believe he mentioned some casual harm to your person, opportunity permitting. Rest assured it never occurred to him that I might betray his interests, that I would dare. Frankly, I doubt he considers you a real threat—not here in his demesne. Delusion is part and parcel with his condition."

"Where is he right now?"

"Out and about. Satiating his appetites. Perhaps wallowing in the Presence. His ambit is wide and unpredictable. He may pop in tomorrow. He may appear in six months. Time means less and less to him. Time is a ring, and in the House of Belphegor that ring contracts like a muscle."

"The house?"

Butler's lips twitched at the corners. He said, "A cell in a black honeycomb. Rueben's father stumbled upon it during his missionary days. He had no idea what it was. The chamber existed before the continents split and the ice came over the world. The people that built it, long dust. I can give directions, but I humbly suggest you wait here for your nemesis. Safer."

"No harm in looking," I said.

"Oh, no, Mr. Koenig. There's more harm than you could ever dream."

"Enlighten me anyhow."

Butler seemed to have expected nothing less. Joyful as a sadist, he drew me a map.

12.

The cave wasn't far from camp.

Long-suffering Hung Chan and his younger brother Ha agreed to accompany me to the general area after a harangue from Butler and the exchange of American currency.

We essayed a thirty-minute hike through scrub and streams, then up a steep knoll littered with brush and treacherous rocks. Invisible from a distance, a limestone cliff face split vertically, formed a narrow gash about the height of the average man. The Chan brothers informed me through violent gestures and pidgin English they'd await my return at the nearby riverbank. They retreated, snarling to themselves in their foreign dialect.

I crouched behind some rocks and cooled my heels for a lengthy spell. Nothing and more nothing. When I couldn't justify delaying any longer, I approached cautiously, in case Hicks was lying in ambush, rifle sights trained on the rugged slope. Immediately I noticed bizarre symbols scratched into the occasional boulder. Seasonal erosion had obliterated all save the deepest marks and these meant little to me, though it wasn't difficult to imagine they held some pagan significance. Also, whole skeletons of small animals—birds and squirrels—hung from low branches. Dozens of them, scattered like broken teeth across the hillside.

According to my watch and the dull slant of sun through the clouds, I had nearly two hours of light. I'd creep close, have a peek and scurry back to the mining camp in time for supper. No way did I intend to navigate these backwoods after dark and risk breaking a leg, or worse. I was a city boy at heart.

I scrambled from boulder to boulder, pausing to see if anyone would emerge to take a pot shot. When I reached the summit I was sweating and my nerves twanged like violin strings.

The stench of spoiled meat, of curdled offal, emanated from the fissure; a slaughterhouse gone to the maggots. The vile odor stung my eyes, scourged deep into my throat. I knotted a balaclava from a handkerchief I'd appropriated from the Honeybee Ranch, covered my mouth and nose.

A baby? I cocked my ears and didn't breathe until the throb of my pulse filled the universe. No baby. The soft moan of wind sucked through a chimney of granite.

I waited for my vision to clear and passed through the opening, pistol drawn

13.

so beautiful.
I

14.

stare at a wedge of darkening sky between the pines.

My cheeks burn, scorched with salt. I've been lying here in the shallows of a pebbly stream. I clutch the solid weight of my pistol in a death grip. The Chan brothers loom, hardly inscrutable. They are pale as flour. Their lips move silently. Their hands are on me. They drag me.

I keep staring at the sky, enjoy the vibration of my tongue as I hum. Tralalala.

The brothers release my arms, slowly edge away like automata over the crushed twigs. Their eyes are holes. Their mouths. I'm crouched, unsteady. My gun. Click. Click. Empty. But my knife my Jim Bowie special is here somewhere is in my hand. Ssaa! The brothers Chan are phantoms, loping. Deer. Mirages. My knife. Quivers in a tree trunk.

Why am I so happy. Why must I cover myself in the leaves and dirt.

Rain patters upon my roof.

15.

Time is a ring. Time is a muscle. It contracts.

16.

colloidal iris

17.

the pillar of faces

18.

migrant spores

19.

maggots

20.

glows my ecstasy in a sea of suns

21.

galactic parallax

22.

I had been eating leaves. Or at least there were leaves crammed in my mouth. Sunlight dribbled through the gleaming branches. I vomited leaves. I found a trickle of water, snuffled no prouder than a hog.

Everything was small and bright. Steam seeped from my muddy clothes. My shirt was starched with ejaculate, matted to my belly as second skin. I knelt in the damp needles and studied my filthy hands. My hands were shiny as metal on a casket.

Butler chortled from a spider-cocoon in the green limbs, *"Now you're seasoned for his palette. Best run, Pinkerton. You've been in the sauce. Chewed up and shat out. And if you live, in twenty years you'll be another walking Mouth."* He faded into the woodwork.

I made a meticulous job of scrubbing the grime and blood from my hands. I washed my face in the ice water, hesitated at the sticky bur of my mustache and hair, finally dunked my head under. The shock brought comprehension crashing down around my ears.

I remembered crossing over a threshold.

Inside, the cave is larger than I'd supposed, and humid.

Water gurgling in rock. Musty roots the girth of sequoias.

Gargantuan statues embedded in wattles of amber.

The cave mouth a seam of brightness that rotates until it is a blurry hatch in the ceiling.

My boots losing contact with the ground, as if I were weightless.

Floating away from the light, towards a moist chasm, purple warmth.

Darkness blooms, vast and sweet.

Gibberish, after.

I walked back to Forty-Mile Camp, my thoughts pleasantly disjointed.

23.

Labor ground to a halt when I stumbled into their midst. None spoke. No one tried to stop me from hunching over a kettle and slopping fistfuls of boiled rice, gorging like a beast. Nor when I hefted a rusty spade and padded into Butler's hut to pay my respects. Not even when I emerged, winded, and tore through the crates of supplies and helped myself to several sticks of dynamite with all the trimmings.

I smiled hugely at them, couldn't think of anything to say.

They stood in a half-moon, stoic as carvings. I wandered off into the hills.

24.

The explosion was gratifying.

Dust billowed, a hammerhead cloud that soon collapsed under its own ambition. I thought of big sticks and bigger nests full of angry hornets. I wasn't even afraid, really.

Some open, others close.

25.

After I pounded on the door for ten minutes, a girl named Evelyn came out and found me on the front porch of the whorehouse, slumped across the swing and muttering nonsense. Dawn was breaking and the stars were so pretty.

I asked for Violet. Evelyn said she'd lit a shuck from the Honeybee Ranch for parts unknown.

Octavia took in my frightful appearance and started snapping orders. She and a couple of the girls lugged me to a room and shoved me in a scalding bath. I didn't protest; somebody slapped a bottle of whiskey in my hand and lost the cork. Somebody else must've taken one look at the needle work on my arm and decided to snag some morphine from Doc Campion's bag of black magic. They shot me to the moon and reality melted into a slag of velvet and honey. I tumbled off the wagon and got crushed under its wheels.

"You going home one of these days?" Octavia squeezed water from a sponge over my shoulders. "Back to the Old States?" She smelled nice. Everything smelled of roses and lavender; nice.

I didn't know what day this was. Shadows clouded the teak panels. This place was firecracker hot back in the '50s. What a hoot it must've been while the west was yet wild. My lips were swollen. I was coming down hard, a piece of rock plunging from the sky. I said, "Uh, huh. You?" It occurred to me that I was fixating again, probably worse than when I originally acquired my dope habits. Every time my eyes dilated I was thrust into a Darwinian phantasm. A fugue state wherein the chain of humanity shuttered rapidly from the first incomprehensible amphibian creature to slop ashore, through myriad semi-erect sapiens slouching across chaotically shifting landscapes, unto the frantic masses in coats and dresses teeming about the stone and glass of Earth's megalopolises. I had vertigo.

"Any day now."

My ears still rang, might always.

Fading to a speck—the hilltop, decapitated in a thunderclap and a belch of dust. Boulders reduced to shattered bits, whizzing around me, a miracle I wasn't pulverized. Was that me, pitching like Samson before the Philistine army? More unreal with each drip of scented wax. My eyes were wet. I turned my head so Octavia wouldn't notice.

"Tommy Mullen came around today. You're still lookin' for Tommy. Right?"

"You see him?"

"Naw. Kavanaugh was talkin' to Dalton Beaumont, mentioned he saw Tommy on the street. Fella waved to him and went into an alley. Didn't come out again. Could be he's scared you'll get a bead on him."

"Could be."

Octavia said, "Glynna heard tell Langston Butler passed on. Died in his sleep. Guess the yellow boys held a ceremony. Reverend Fuller's talkin' 'bout ridin' to Forty-Mile, see that the Professor gets himself a Christian burial." She became quiet, kneading my neck with steely fingers. Then, "I'm powerful sad. The Professor was a decent man. You know he was the sawbones for three, four years? He did for the young 'uns as got themselves with child. Gentle as a father. Campion came along and the Professor fell to the coolie mud. Shame."

My smile was lye-hot and humorless. "He didn't limit his moonlighting to abortions. Butler did for the babies too, didn't he? The ones that were born here at the Ranch."

Octavia didn't answer.

All those whores' babies tossed into a pitchy shaft, tiny wails smothered in the great chthonian depths. I laughed, hollow. "The accidents. Don't see many orphanages this far north."

Octavia said, "How do you mean to settle your tab, by the by?" She was getting colder by the second. She must've gone through my empty wallet.

"For services rendered? Good question, lady."

"You gave your *whole* poke to Violet?" Her disbelief was tinged with scorn. "That's plain loco, mister. Why?"

The room was fuzzy. "I don't suppose I'll be needing it, where I'm going. I did an impetuous deed, Octavia. Can't take back the bet once it's on the table." Where was I going? Into a box into the ground, if I was lucky. The alternative was just too unhappy. I listened for the tick-tock of transmogrifying cells that would indicate my descent into the realm of superhuman. Damnation; the bottle was dry. I dropped it into the sudsy water, watched it sink. Glowed there between my black and blue thighs.

"Musta been a heap of coin. You love her, or somethin'?"

I frowned. "Another excellent question. No, I reckon I don't love her. She's just too good for the likes of you, is all. Hate to see her spoil."

Octavia left without even a kiss good-bye.

26.

At least my clothes were washed and pressed and laid out properly.

I dressed with the ponderous calculation of a man on his way to a funeral. I cleaned my pistol, inspected the cylinder reflexively—it's easy to tell how many bullets are loaded by the weight of the weapon in your hand.

The whores had shaved me and I cut a respectable figure except for the bruises and the sagging flesh under my eyes. My legs were unsteady. I went by the back stairs, unwilling to list through the parlor where the piano crashed and the shouts of evening debauchery swelled to a frenzied peak.

It was raining again; be snowing in another week or so. The mud-caked board-walks stretched emptily before unlit shop windows. I shuffled, easily confused by the darkness and the rushing wind.

The hotel waited, tomb-dark and utterly desolate.

Like a man mounting the scaffold, I climbed the three flights of squeaking stairs to my room, turned the key in the lock after the fourth or fifth try, and knew what was what as I stepped through and long before anything began to happen.

The room stank like an abattoir. I lighted a lamp on the dresser and its frail luminance caught the edge of spikes and loops on the bathroom door. This scrawl read, BELPHEGORBELPHEGORBELPHEGOR.

The mirror shuddered. A mass of shadows unfolded in the corner, became a tower. Hicks whispered from a place behind and above my left shoulder, "Hello again, Pinky."

"Hello yourself." I turned and fired and somewhere between the yellow flash and the new hole in the ceiling He snatched my wrist and the pistol went caroming across the floor. I dangled; my trigger finger was broken and my elbow dislocated, but I didn't feel a thing yet.

Hicks smiled almost kindly. He said, "I told you, Pinky. Close one hole, another opens." His face split at the seams, a terrible flower bending toward my light, my heat.

The poem quoted on pages 352–357 is cited as follows:
Baudelaire, Charles. "To A Madonna" (pp. 73). *The Flowers of Evil* (sixth ed.). New York: New Directions Publishing Corporation, 1989.

ANNA ROSS

These Various Methods of Brightness

Anna Ross holds an MFA in poetry from Columbia University, where she was a poetry editor for Columbia: A Journal of Literature and Art. She is the winner of the 2004 poetry prize from GSU Review. Her poetry has appeared or is forthcoming in The New Republic, The Paris Review, Southwest Review, and Rattapallax, among other journals, and her translations have appeared in Poetry Wales. She teaches in the English Department at Suffolk University and lives in Dorchester, Massachusetts.

Anna Ross's poem "These Various Methods of Brightness" was first published in Southwest Review.

—K.L. & G.G.

When the One Who Fills the Room with Hurricanes
has gone, there is nothing you can do
but get down on your knees and scrub.

Like all winds, this one too will leave
her mark: coarse oblongs on the joined
and leveled boards, every smoking mechanism

overturned. Check your vessels
for containing water, one will be missing.
Every animal will have achieved height.

When the One Who Arranges Floods
moves in upstairs, turn your listening devices
to the wall, remove all coverings and wait for sun.

Do not attempt negotiation. There is no code
of letters for her sorrow. Take care not to disturb
the One Who Creates Earthquakes,

she is sleeping. When the One Who Steals Rivers
pays a visit, you must get out the instruments
for boiling, sweetening, stirring

and offer her a seat. Fairly soon she will evaporate,
taking with her your smallest potted twigs
and two burnt loaves. You will not know

when the One Who Carries Fog arrives
until she wears your most secret, pleated gown.
She is the one who stays.

MÉLANIE FAZI

The Cajun Knot

Mélanie Fazi was born in Dunkirk, France in 1976 and currently lives in Paris where she works as a translator (mostly in the field of fantasy and science fiction). She has published two novels in France as well as a collection of stories, "Serpentine," which received the Grand Prix de l'Imaginaire in 2004.

"The Cajun Knot" was the first story she sold. It was published in French in 2000, and is her second story to be translated into English. Its first English-language publication was in The 3rd Alternative, translated from the French by Brian Stableford.

—E.D.

The summer stretched itself out like a serpent, all moistness and languor. The air above the housetops seemed clotted; the tension was manifest: the anticipation of a storm that never arrived. It was said in jest that the wind had been stopped at the border, refused permission to take up residence in Alabama. I knew more than one man who would have sold his wife and children for a few drops of rain, in order to sweep away that glutinous torpor. But the sky remained empty, day after day, and hopelessly blue: a uniform, nauseating blue.

It was a difficult time for a pregnant woman. At the height of the spell, during the month of August, I had watched Cora Ellis drag her weary carcass through the streets of the town. A long time—six years at least—had passed since she expended the energy of her previous pregnancy in cleaning the church and helping the neighbors. Juniper had been born in the tobacco field where Cora brought a snack to the older of the Quigley brothers while he worked.

"That one loves the earth so much that she'll never leave it," she had said, laughing, with her newborn in her arms.

She was a solid woman, Cora Ellis. A child of the country brought up in the open air, built to beget an entire dynasty and repopulate the whole state. But at twenty-nine, this infant was to be her last. It was her third pregnancy, perhaps one too many. Soon, it was not only her body that advertised her impending maternity—a belly inflated like a bloated watermelon, the skin stretched like that of a tambourine—but her face too, even her adorable eyes: veritable pecan nuts, which had acquired the dull color of scorched earth. Her laughter lost its spontaneity, as if the effort of provision were reducing the old Cora to a ruin, cut a little more out of her every day.

Now, she resembled a desiccated plant, nourishing her baby with her own sap, making a bulwark of her entire body in order to protect it from the summer.

At the beginning of September, when the laws of gravity had had their way with her health, Cora stopped coming to the village. One morning, I waited in vain for her to arrive in the grocery store, escorted by her two children, with all the grace of a tortoise pregnant with an anvil. Even Jackson and Juniper no longer came to plunder my sweet-jars. The neighborhood deduced that Cora would only reappear with a baby in her arms and a smile on her lips; tongues wagged happily in anticipation of the news. That's the most widespread pastime hereabouts—the only one that fills your head without emptying your pockets. There were even a few who bet money on the sex of the baby, in order to kill time when the evenings were slow.

And the days went by.

Three weeks had passed when the rumors took a more serious turn, perhaps because Cora's prolonged absence had become a puzzle requiring a solution. As ever, there was no lack of speculation. Some claimed to have seen Eugene Ellis, rifle in hand, spending entire afternoons sitting on the porch of his house. Luther Owens, the cabinet-maker, spoke in hushed tones of an explosion heard in mid-afternoon, as he passed in front of the Ellis house. I'm leaving out the more extravagant rumors— stories of phantoms sighted in the fields behind the house. I remained frankly skeptical when told the story of old Gavin Oakley—already more than a little senile, even when he was sober—who swore that he had encountered Jester, Eugene's dog, when he got back home returning from his usual session with the local boozers (which was his substitute for a social life). According to him, the hound had asked him the time before slinking off without a word of thanks.

I'm not a man to interest myself in the tittle-tattle of idle peasants, but the facts spoke for themselves. It was the absence of the kids from mass that had attracted attention in the first place. Even when he couldn't go himself, Eugene never failed to send his children to the service; it was a point of honor with him. Always in the first row, standing up so straight they might have had broomsticks for spinal columns; always spick and span—Jackson in a white shirt buttoned up to the collar, Juniper in her Sunday best dress, cut from the cloth of one of her mother's old gowns. It's rather bad form to refuse to join the community on a Sunday morning—an hour a week is hardly asking for the moon. Cora had good reason for remaining indoors, and Eugene might well be fully occupied at such a time—but what of the two little Ellises?

And then Jackson had failed to attend his classes for several days after school resumed, without offering any excuses and without a word from his parents. Sometimes, he was still seen accompanying Juniper as far as the gate and going home unhurriedly, to the little house some distance from the town—which immediately demolished the hypothesis that he was playing truant. To be sure, there's nothing very tempting in passing four hours in a stifling classroom, regurgitating multiplication tables by the dozen, but if the desire had overtaken him to go running through the fields with other street-corner kids, Jackson would have acted with discretion, without taking the risk that Eugene would catch wind of it. Eugene, keen to bring up his kids properly, had his own educational principles. An Ellis *never* ducked out. Even if an earthquake were to sweep away the school like a house of cards, an Ellis would still be at his desk. The day when Jackson had reappeared in my shop to buy a Coca-Cola and a comic book, he had avoided my questions by playing particularly dumb—although the fact was that the kid had never been very loquacious. "Must go back and help my father," was all that I could extract from him. Instead of sitting down by the door to read his comic, as was his habit, Jackson had gone straight home, his booty in his pocket.

The baby had doubtless arrived; that was what I had deduced at first. When another week passed without any news of Cora, though, I was no longer so sure. Eugene would surely have come into the shop eventually, if not for provisions at least to let us know. He adored his children, that one. He would have never let the arrival of the latest addition to his family pass in silence; he was more the sort to shout it from the rooftops before cockcrow, at an hour when honest men were asleep in bed. (Eugene's voice was scarcely more harmonious than a cock's, in my experience—during one memorable drinking session in the fields, to wet the head of the new year, he had sung a serenade to a nearby scarecrow before demanding that it marry him.)

I'd be lying if I said that it wasn't curiosity that pushed me to pay them a visit. Oh, to be sure, I'd have found a good excuse, if the need arose, to justify myself—to verify that all was well, to obtain news of Cora, to let slip a few anodyne remarks about Jackson's absence, that sort of thing. And I was sincere, or nearly. But more than anything else, I wanted to know—that's only human. No one can keep a secret to himself in such a little town. If Eugene was hiding something from us, if he needed our help—who could tell?—it was as well to make the first move while I could still make myself useful.

Some considerable time had passed since I'd last gone out to the Ellis house. Most of the time, it was Cora who came to us, to dispense a little of her good humor like a whiff of fragrance, exchange a few words with my wife and empty the shelves of the shop to fill her larder. By that time, I no longer went to the Ellises unless I received an invitation—a favor that had become increasingly rare. How long had it been since I shared a beer with Eugene, staring at the stars like two cows watching the trains pass by?

The house had been repainted since my last visit—or, to be accurate, the repainting had been started. The rusty mailbox, whose inscription of EUGENE D. ELLIS would soon be no more than a memory, was perched like a vulture above the recently renewed whiteness of the gate—to which the dust, after two blinks of an eye, was already restaking its claim. But the work remained incomplete, whether from lack of time or shortage of paint it was impossible to tell. The other half of the gate still looked as if it hadn't seen the paintbrush since the time when Eugene's grandfather was in his cradle. Shoots of kudzu had crept to the foot of the fence, ready to take up residence there.

The house's own metamorphosis had been arrested in a similar hybrid state. It was as if a far-reaching project, intended to renew everything—for the birth of the little Ellis, no doubt—had had to be abandoned because of some sudden catastrophe. It was perhaps as well that the wind had deserted Alabama that summer—if not, I wouldn't have given much for that poor excuse for a roof. On a dark night, the light of the hayloft must have been visible, escaping between the dislodged tiles.

Eugene was waiting, sitting on the steps of the porch, his rifle laid across his knees. He got up when he saw me approaching, without taking his eyes off me for a second.

My gaze slid towards the bottle posed unceremoniously beside him, directly in front of Jester's empty kennel. It was three-quarters full of some home made cocktail whose recipe I preferred not to know. The turbid liquid was the same indeterminate color as the stain on his trousers, shaped like a map of the States. His crumpled clothes didn't seem to be very clean either—as if he slipped on the same ones every morning, without question. His cheeks resembled a badly kept garden, cut by hurried sweeps of a razor—with the result that, for once in his life, he was showing his age.

Eugene had always seemed too young to be Jackson's father. Cora and he had not yet reached their twentieth years when their son was born, and the boy was now ten. Perhaps it was because of his pale complexion and his blond hair, like a Viking—not really the image of a man who toiled beneath the southern sun from dawn to dusk.

When I reached him, Eugene fixed me with the oblique gaze that he had bequeathed to Jackson—as if he were looking at me over the rims of imaginary spectacles. He tightened his grip on the rifle that he was clasping firmly between his grubby fingers. He'd doubtless spent long hours making it shine like some precious silver trinket—the weapon glistened like a bolt of cold lightning. I licked my lips before sketching out—not at all convincingly—the ghost of a smile.

"Hi there, Gene."

It was not until that moment that he seemed to recognize me. He took on the expression of a man who had woken up in the middle of the night in an unfamiliar bedroom. For a moment, I wondered whether he might have been abusing unorthodox substances. Who knows what temptations a man might yield to, left to his own devices?

"Elmo?"

"I thought I might bring you a few provisions. Lucy's made fried bread and rice with beans. There's also the remains of a pumpkin pie, for the children. I suppose Cora isn't in any state to cook for you just now, unless I'm mistaken."

I was waiting for Eugene to grab the helping hand that I was waving under his nose, but he hadn't budged an inch. I wondered if he'd understood a single word I'd said.

"Perhaps I should put them in the kitchen?"

"Wait!" The answer was a little too quick, like a cry from the heart. "I'll put them away myself." Then, by way of apology: "I don't want to wake Cora. Thanks, Elmo . . ."

I gave him the package, which he placed on the steps of the porch one-handed, always keeping the rifle in the other—as if he had a superstitious dread of letting go of it. It was only then that I noticed the odor—or, rather, the absence of odor. Each of the other houses in the neighborhood had its own distinctive reek, most often the effluvia of frying bacon and eggs, or meat grilled on those barbecues that continued far into the night: the perfume of summer, tenacious and haunting.

The Ellis house emitted none but faded and diffuse odors: dead odors, of hay or tobacco. Any others remained imprisoned by the closed shutters that barred the passage of the sun's rays. Even the half-open door revealed the hostile grille of a fly-screen.

There was the silence as well.

All I could hear was the clicking chains of the swing suspended from the branches of a tree behind the house—Jackson, presumably. The noise of every one of Eugene's gestures was amplified in consequence; the rustling resonated in the emptiness like the crackling of dry twigs under a boot-heel. I had expected to be greeted by the staccato murmur of Eugene's radio. That was what one usually heard first, before even passing through the door. Distant voices stifled by parasitic noises, like clandestine messages thrown out at hazard and picked up in error. Nameless pieces of music, emerging from nowhere, which served as a sonic backcloth to our card games. Joyful tunes that made Juniper warble when she was a baby. They had even accompanied her first steps; one day, she had wanted to dance to the sound of a violin's melody and had simply got to her feet.

"I just wondered what had become of the baby. I suppose . . ."

"Not yet," Eugene cut me off. "It's late coming."

"Cora must be finding the long wait wearisome."

"Not as much as me." The remark was made in a single breath, almost a whisper.

Eugene didn't exactly seem overjoyed by the prospect of his impending paternity. Do you know many fathers who talk about the birth of their latest child while tightening their grip on the butts of their rifles? Perhaps the summer had begun to weigh heavily on him, I thought—and on her too. When the heat makes the blood boil in our veins, is it any wonder that minds become unhinged?

"If you've come for news, Elmo, I'm afraid that I've none of importance to give you."

"Actually, I'm just a little anxious for Cora. As we haven't seen you in town lately . . ."

". . . you're wondering, of course, why I no longer send my boy to school. Is that it, Elmo? Have the others sent you to spy on me?"

I saw Eugene hesitate momentarily, considering different alibis—"I send my kids to school when I want to" (rather suspect); "the farm's afflicted by a virus" (hardly a reason to cut oneself off from the world, especially with a pregnant wife)—before choosing the most neutral option. "I need Jack here to give me a hand, if you must know. He's a great help."

"Repainting the house?"

"Among other things."

He had a damned cheek to reply to me as if the job had been started up again; it obviously hadn't been touched for some time.

Behind him, at the corner of he house, a face appeared that was a little too pale, topped with red hair as fine as his father's. Jackson must have come running after hearing his name pronounced.

He was rather small for his age, and his puppy fat hadn't yet disappeared completely. The dungarees he was wearing were threadbare at the knees and two sizes too big for him—the gift of a neighbor whose son had grown out of them too quickly. Even with the legs turned up and the shoulder straps shortened as far as possible, it was reminiscent of the ancient outfits with which one rigs out scarecrows.

Jackson stepped back a pace on seeing that I had noticed him. He put his hand on Jester's collar to restrain the dog, who only wanted to lick me clean with his long tongue. I winked at the boy, without any response.

"Jackson Ellis," Eugene said, without turning round, "will you please go and play, and let us men talk." His voice was almost calm, without a trace of severity. To talk to his son, Eugene abandoned the brittle tone that he reserved for intruders—a role in which he seemed to have cast me.

Jackson grudgingly obeyed and took himself off, still holding Jester's collar—but not without throwing me one last inquisitive glance. Beside him, the dog seemed so massive that I couldn't tell which of the two was directing the other.

"I suppose Jackson's also helping you with the birds?"

"The birds?"

"I notice that you've fetched out your hunting rifle—that's to scare off the birds and small animals prowling around the fields, isn't it?"

One of the corners of his mouth was raised in a rictus of amusement, so conspicuously that he almost seemed to be winking his eye. Eugene had never been able to produce a symmetrical smile.

"Do you really think I have ammunition to waste on feathered creatures, Elmo? Honestly? I'm expecting a visit, to tell you the truth." There was a moment's silence, then a sentence that had been held up for too long sprang forth like a bullet: precise, murderous, definitive. "I'm waiting for the son of a bitch who's made a kid with Cora."

I couldn't tell whether Eugene was embarrassed or relieved to have spat out that particular morsel. He was never in a mood to share confidences, though—unless he was drunk, with the night air for a witness.

So that was the reason for the rifle, and the hours spent mounting guard on the porch. Eugene was simply furious—as furious as only a jealous husband knows how to be. Above all else, he had always had absolute trust in his wife.

"What's that supposed to mean, Gene?"

"You understood me well enough. A father can recognize his children, can't he? I tell you this one isn't mine."

"I thought it wasn't born yet?"

"Don't push me, Elmo, okay? Don't make me say any more than I already have. Sure, it isn't born—but I've good reason to believe that it isn't mine. Well, I'm waiting for the other dirty bastard to come back to see his son. He'll come back in the end. I want to see the sort of man that could father that kind of . . ."

"Has Cora . . . ?"

"No, she's never said a word. No need. I know what I'm talking about."

Jackson came back, insinuating himself at his father's side with all the discretion of a field-mouse. I hadn't noticed his presence until he pulled at his father's sleeve to attract his attention.

"Papa," he ventured, timidly.

"What, Jack?"

"I think it will soon be time."

From his pocket, Jackson took an imposing watch that Eugene had entrusted to him, and deposited it in his father's open palm. He swayed from one leg to the other, with a slightly embarrassed air, gazing at me earnestly. He was careful to keep a respectful distance between us.

"You're right, Jack. I'd begun to lose track of time. Listen Elmo, thanks for the provisions and the visit—truly, from the bottom of my heart—but I've a lot to do today, as you'll understand . . ."

"Gene!"

Cora's voice reached us through the half-open door, from the shuttered room. I saw Eugene stiffen in front of me and exchange an indecipherable glance with Jackson.

"You have to go now, Elmo."

"You're sure that you don't need my help?"

"It's a family matter. We can straighten it out perfectly well between ourselves, thanks."

"It's here, Gene! It's coming!"

The voice became more urgent, impatient and slightly anxious at the same time: that of a woman who has reached the stage of having contractions and is beginning to anticipate the pain that will precede the delivery. Eugene leapt towards the door, every sense alert, before turning towards me one last time.

"Listen to me good, Elmo—I want you to know that whatever happens, it's not my fault. Go away, now."

A moment later, he disappeared into the suffocating darkness of the house. I found myself alone again with his son, who seemed anything but delighted by my presence.

With his fists deeply thrust into the pockets of his dungarees, Jackson distractedly shifted pebbles with the tips of his bare toes, while installing himself on the step in order to force me to be on my way. But Eugene had only had to order me to go to make it impossible for me to turn around.

I simply wanted to know what was going on—and to be there when Cora needed me. I couldn't leave a woman on the point of childbirth in the hands of a man alone, even though it would be her husband.

My gaze flickered over the layer of dust that covered the swinging armchair set in the corner of the porch, where Cora spent the summer nights. I had seen her nursing Juniper there, six years ago. I had seen her burst out laughing on Eugene's knees while they rocked back and forth together in unstable equilibrium. I had expected that she would pass the last hours of her pregnancy there, in the shelter of the shady porch, outside the stifling walls of the house.

I don't know which came first—the explosion or the gasp of surprise that hadn't time to develop into a cry. I only remember clearing the steps with a single bound, pushing Jackson back as he tugged at my sleeve and begged me not to go in.

And suddenly, I was planted in front of the door of the master bedroom, incapable of crossing the threshold.

I hadn't had the time to see very much before Eugene slammed the door in my face.

Cora's emaciated face, emptied of all substance, clotted by stupor. Her lips scarcely thicker than a leaf of parchment.

The third red eye in the dead center of her forehead.

The brown hair strewn across the patchwork quilt, soiled with the same sticky substance that flooded her face.

The arms of a desiccated mummy, folded in a reflexive gesture of a self-protection. The inflated belly, fit to burst.

Lower down—much lower down—between the legs opened to let the infant emerge, a dark form, moving slowly and sinuously.

I can't be certain now of what I thought I'd seen. It had all happened so quickly. At the time, however, I was convinced. The door had closed on the image of one serpent preceding a second, with other heads emerging in their train. About ten, at a conservative estimate.

But I could have been mistaken.

The noises went on and on within the secrecy of the bedroom. Even passing through the wooden door, some were still clear enough to stimulate the imagination. Including the most anodyne: the demented cadence of Eugene's footsteps on the floorboards; the dull impact of a body falling back on a mattress.

Images rose up spontaneously before my eyes, like a collage with neither head not tail, but already too precise. I didn't want to hear those sucking noises, like boots plunging in and out of mud. I didn't want those visions of broken bones, of flesh ravaged by a blade.

All the noises had the dirty red color of Cora's blood.

The house spat me out again upon the porch, into the open air. My eyelids clamped themselves shut, like shutters in a storm, to banish the white glare of the sun—our eyes lose the memory of light as soon as they're deprived of it. I would have sold my grocery store to the devil for a breath of wind, let alone a few drops of rain.

Without quite understanding how, I found myself stuck fast to the porch steps, convinced that I was about to cough up my guts and perish where I lay—but my stomach was more solidly entrenched than I thought.

When Eugene had come out in his turn, I heard Jackson turn the key to lock the bedroom door. Eugene was holding a linen sack in his clenched fist, sealed by several knots. It was soiled with dark marks, as if he had wiped his hands on it.

On reflection, the traces on his trousers might not all have been wine-stains.

Eugene held his burden at arm's length in order to avoid any contact with the contents, whose nature I preferred not to know. When he had thrown it into the grass, I thought I saw movement under the linen.

The other hand held the rifle by the barrel, with the butt extended towards the ground. I saw Eugene lift it up towards the sky in order to bring it down with all his strength on the linen sack, and then again and again—ten times in all. The mighty blows were delivered in a blind fury. He finished the job with the heel of his boot.

I watched him as one watches a madman discharge his nervous energy on the first thing that comes to hand, unsure as to whether I ought to intervene. Having run out of breath, Eugene finished up by sending his punch-bag flying with a savage kick, before signalling to his son to pick it up.

"In the well, Jack. You know the way."

Jackson obeyed, with all the enthusiasm of a condemned man marching to the scaffold. He advanced slowly, placing one foot exactly in front of the other with the extreme concentration of which only children are capable. Jester went after him, tongue scraping along the ground like an anteater's.

Jackson chased the dog away with a brusque gesture, only to see him return a moment later with the alacrity of a boomerang, sticking fast to his coattails.

Beside me, Eugene had slumped down on the steps again, at the exact spot where he had mounted guard for six weeks. All trace of anger had vanished from his face; nothing remained but lassitude. *I warned you, didn't I?* his eyes seemed to be saying.

"Don't look at me like a criminal. Do you think I like spending every day like this? Telling stories to my little girl, at night. *Your mummy's tired, June—you'll see her tomorrow . . .*"

He lowered his eyes towards his blood-encrusted fingers. He wiped them clean on the wood of the porch, mechanically.

"I truly had no choice, you know. It was to spare her all the rest. One way or another, she would have been dead before June came back from school. That was settled on the first day."

Then Eugene stared at me again over his invisible spectacle-rims, his lips twisted into a sick smile. Beneath his bushy eyebrows, his eyes shone like those of a man who was preparing to tell a good joke.

"Go ahead, say it—I'm crazy. You find that funny, eh? A miserable degenerate who shoots his wife like a dog. Say it, if it's what you think. But I'll tell you a funny thing, Elmo. Come back tomorrow morning, if you dare, and you'll find Cora still living. In a terrible state, but always alive. That amazes you, eh? Do you have the guts to show up here tomorrow morning? Are you man enough?"

"Stop it, Gene. What do you want?"

The sound of my voice sobered him up like a smack in the face or a bucketful of water poured over his head.

"You're dying to tell me your version of the facts, aren't you? Well, go ahead."

Eugene passed the palm of his left hand over the stubble on his cheeks, mechanically. He gave every indication of never having thought that he might have to justify Cora's murder before a truly attentive audience.

"It's . . . I don't really know where to begin . . ."

"You said *that was settled on the first day.* Do you want to start from there?"

With a piteous little giggle, he pointed his thumb at the door behind him. "It's been right in front of your eyes since you arrived, and you still don't understand . . ."

I have to admit, frankly, that it was not the kind of decoration that my neighbors stuck on their doors to welcome visitors. It was curious that I hadn't seen it sooner, even fully occupied as I was by Eugene: the tree that had hidden the forest close at hand.

I knew what it was—in theory, at least, since it was the first I had seen with my own eyes. A *vèvè*: a voodoo spell, all curlicues and crosses, inscribed in chalk on the wooden door by a beginner's hand. The contours of some of the symbols were blurred, as if they had been redesigned several times before the chalk was reduced to a stump.

The design was set in the center of a circular device reminiscent of the image of a serpent devouring its tail. A bulging sachet, sealed by a cord—doubtless a mojo amulet—was nailed in the middle of the largest cross.

Suddenly, I had an absurd vision of Eugene in the process of cutting the throat of a black cockerel over a tin-plated bucket held out at arm's length by Jackson. Only moonlight was lacking to complete the tableau.

"It's a loop," Eugene explained. "A little souvenir of three years spent in Louisiana, with Cora and Jack. The guy who showed it to me was a Cajun—a lowlife who knew New Orleans like the back of his hand. The kind of creep who tried to lay his hands on my wife as soon as my back was turned. Who knew what dirty business he was mixed up in, until the day he disappeared into the wilderness? For no apparent reason, he showed me some pretty tricks after nightfall—really weird things, like you'd never believe. But if anyone had told me that I'd be doing them one day under my own roof . . ."

"What do you mean, a *loop*?"

"I mean that within these four walls, the same day has repeated itself for six weeks. And it will go on and on for as long as I don't untie the knot—until that other son of a bitch comes back for his kid."

Have you ever seen the desire for revenge lurking in a man's gaze? It's a sad sight: something fugitive, elusive, like the reflection of the moon at the bottom of a well. It's there, before our very eyes, but always out of reach. It was at such moments that Eugene seemed most distant of all—and the most alone, busy digging himself a hole into which he might sink.

"I must say that Jack's been a great help. A brave lad, that—a chip off the old block. I didn't want him to know at first, you know, but he figured it out for himself. He's a little devil, my Jack. It's only Juniper that hasn't caught on. And I swear to you that she'll never know what happens here while she's at school—not as long as I'm alive. She stays in the loop after nightfall, of course—within the walls. Jackson and me, we see that she leaves the house when the moment comes. For June, it's always the same day, one morning after another."

That was when the sun began to set. It cast a threadlike shadow at Eugene's feet, armed with an unnaturally extended rifle. When I saw that it had already swallowed up the toes of my boots, I couldn't help stepping back. On a dog-day like that, I must have been the only man in the state to flee the shade.

"It's like the story of the hydra, you see—the creature with all the serpent's heads. I cut one of them off, and the following day it's already regrown, and I have to begin all over again. I can show you, if you don't believe me. You know the well, close to the railway track? That's where I chuck them away, mostly . . ."

(The following day, I went to the place to check out his story. I stayed there for a long time, gazing at the wellhead, besieged by honeysuckle—but I dared not go too close.)

". . . the rest, I buried. There was one I left on the rails to wait for the train. I even tried to feed them to the dog, but that brute Jester didn't want to know."

He had instinctively resumed his sentinel pose, with his bottle of liquor standing in for a guard-dog. Legs apart and firmly anchored to the ground, back very straight, rifle laid across his knees. The sun and the shadows wrangled over the burnished skin of his shoulders, which brought out the dirty whiteness of his smock.

The world was effacing itself anew; there was no more shuttered house, no more leaden sun descending at a snail's pace, no more insects that stick to your skin to while away their tedium. All of that had perhaps existed one day, in another era, in a parallel world—but for the moment, there was nothing but Eugene D. Ellis, and a mission that looked as if it might never end.

"But that's no big deal. I'll take my time. He'll come back in the end. They always do. And I swear to you that the loop will stay knotted until he does. There'll be a birthday party then, you can take it from me. I'll force him to tell me how to deliver Cora. After that, I'll shoot him like a dog. A bullet between the eyes, no hesitation at all."

I too had been erased from his mind. He was only talking to himself, like some senile dotard replaying scenes from the good old days. The Ellis house had no more need of me, now that his story had found an audience. I had no other role to play but to listen, to understand and to disappear. To keep up appearances. Then again, Juniper would soon be home from school, and I preferred to avoid having to cross her path. And Eugene and Jackson needed time to cover up the traces, to go through the routine.

I knew well enough what I had to do: to go back to Lucy at the grocery store, take my place behind the counter, surrounded by jars and laden shelves; to say "yes, Eugene thanks you for the provisions, everything's all right, no, the baby hasn't come yet"—although I'm such a wretched actor that Lucy knows how to read my face well enough to count the glasses I've downed; to wait for the time to pass and the affair to be settled, in whatever manner it will be; to resume a normal life, regulated by the rhythm of the cash register and the tinkle of the bell that announces the advent of customers.

Every afternoon, at about four o'clock, I would try to not to think about it.

There remained, even so, one detail that bothered me. I had tried to picture in my mind the man to be shot: the one who had taken Eugene's place in Cora's bed. The kind of person who might be capable of planting those degenerate seeds and vanishing, leaving someone else to pick up the pieces. But no matter how I imagined him, he always had Eugene's features. I had changed the color of his hair, remodeled his build, added forty pounds, with no effect. All those small brown fat people, those mountains of muscle, those giant moustaches, had but a single face. Perhaps I'm naively old-fashioned, but I had never believed that Cora was the sort who would seek satisfaction away from home.

"Just one last thing, Gene. What if you *were* the father, after all?"

His stance changed as if to recall my presence, but the face that he turned towards me was closed upon itself. His fingers were clenched upon the butt of the rifle, mechanically.

"I'll wait until the son of a bitch has the guts to show up. Then—a bullet between the eyes. No hesitation."

GREG VAN EEKHOUT

Tales from the City of Seams

Greg van Eekhout sold his first story in 1996. Since then he has published a number of stories which might vary widely in both subject and tone, yet always have a deeply humanist focus. His stories have appeared in the periodicals The Magazine of Fantasy & Science Fiction, Asimov's Science Fiction, Strange Horizons, Flytrap, Lady Churchill's Rosebud Wristlet, and in the anthologies Starlight 3, So Long Been Dreaming, and New Skies. He lives in Tempe, Arizona, chronicles the minutiae of his life on his live journal (www.journalscape.com/greg), and is working on two young adult novels. This story suite, "Tales from the City of Seams," was published in the fourth volume of Polyphony, Wheatland Press's annual anthology of slipstream and speculative fiction.

K.L. & G.G.

Lovers Lookout

In the hills above the city, among the ruins of the old zoo, the kids come to screw. They cage themselves inside the animal enclosures and kick away the cigarette butts and the crushed beer cans and the brittle snakeskin condoms, and then, with the city glittering below, they fill the hot-smog nights with their whispers. They are not alone.

There is a sort of cave in the hillside behind the picnic grounds. It used to be the bear grotto, but over the decades, the cave has grown deeper. It goes far back, now, and down. Over the grotto's entrance hangs a sign that says something to the effect of Abandon hope, all ye who enter.

Understandably, this gives the dead pause. They tend to linger here.

Hearing the sighs and groans of the living young, the dead get ideas. They shed their frail uniforms and gossamer business suits and wispy club wear. They strip down to silver-moon flesh and lie in the grass one final time.

Like all lovers lanes and modern ruins, the old zoo accumulates stories. One of these tales is that, when the zoo was shut down some three generations ago, most of the animals were sold to circuses and other zoos and private collections. A few escaped, however. There are jaguars in the hills, it is said, and vultures, and kudu.

Sometimes at night, when the zoo reaches its height of passion, hyenas howl in ghostly sympathy.

Or so the tales go.

But the dead are wise, and they know these stories for the urban legends they are. They know that the cries aren't from the descendents of escaped animals.

No, the cries are from the living, unknowingly exhorting the dead to abandon, but not to abandon hope.

Chinatown

When I worked for a plumbing supply wholesaler in Chinatown, the best part of my day was lunch. I'd walk by the window displays of tobacco-colored ducks strung up by their necks, the scents of grease and ginger trying to draw me in. But I was like a man passing a row of prostitutes without interest, secure in the knowledge that a more desirable lover awaits him at home. Lady Sze's Golden Crown Café was my destination, the only place in town where you could get a bowl of soup that had been simmering for a thousand years.

A thousand years was actually a bit of an exaggeration. A forgivable fib of marketing. Truthfully, the thousand-year soup had been cooking in its pot for only eight centuries, born in the latter days of Genghis Khan. The great Mongol warlord had been displeased by a subordinate, one Lu Ch'eng-Huan, in some small way forgotten to history (although the most recent Lady Sze once suggested to me that it had something to do with a concubine, a canary, and a paintbrush). Wishing to discipline Lu Ch'eng-Huan, the Khan had his head removed and boiled in a golden pot. The Khan kept the skull as a trophy, but, not realizing Lu Ch'eng-Huan was a sorcerer, permitted Lu's wife to claim the pot, the water, and the gray film floating on top. After taking it back to her home village, she added salt, leeks, onions, and garlic, and made a soup of her beloved husband's dissolved head. Every day she would add some more water, more vegetables and seasoning, and thus the soup was kept going.

Hundreds of years later, when Lu's descendents came to American shores, they brought the soup with them, keeping vigil over the cook fires on the deck of the brig *Prometheus*.

I had no idea how much of that was true, but the soup tasted wonderful and kept me cold-free, and Lady Sze (her actual name was Michelle) charged only three bucks a bowl.

One day as I sat in the restaurant savoring my lunch, a man in an ivory suit came into the place. His head was as white and hairless as an eggshell, and when he spoke, every syllable came out twisted into an odd shape. I think he was Belgian. "Daughter of Lu Ch'eng-Huan, far removed," he said, "I have grown impatient with your truculence. I have dealt with you in good faith. I have offered you riches—gems and antiques, property and estates, significant shares in profitable concerns—but you have mistaken my generosity for desperation. If you will not part with the soup in a fair exchange, I shall have to take it by force."

Michelle Sze was over at a corner table, taking care of some accounting matters. "Get lost," she said.

The white man smiled tightly. His blue eyes darkened as through glazed over by a layer of ice. "Boys?" he said, and, on cue, two men entered the restaurant and stood behind him. Their faces were broad, with mouths so wide their lips seemed to curve back behind their huge ears. Long-fingered hands twitched down low near their bowed knees. I somehow knew that these were not true men, but monkeys grown and reshaped to pass as men. They leered at Michelle Sze, rocking on their strange, short legs.

Michelle Sze barely glanced up at them. "Brothers," she said. And five men came out of the kitchen. They stood shoulder to shoulder, forming a wall. "To get to my soup," Michelle said, "you will first have to overcome my brothers. This will be more difficult than you might suppose. First brother is like stone. His flesh cannot be penetrated. Second brother has the strength of ten men concentrated in his right hand. Third brother is tireless and needs neither food nor water, neither sleep nor breath. Fourth brother can outrun a horse, a hawk, an arrow shot from a bow. Fifth brother, though he still walks among us, is already dead and cannot be harmed. Sixth brother can see a moth twitch its antennae from a hundred miles away. Seventh brother can hear the creak and groan of grass growing." Michelle wrote something on her spreadsheet. "Let's see your monkeys get past them."

The white man smiled as though Michelle Sze had said something cute but stupid. And then his smile faltered. "Wait a minute. Seven brothers? I count only five."

"Yes. Sixth and Seventh brothers took the soup out the back door as I was introducing you to First through Fifth." She scratched out something on the spreadsheet.

"Then you are defeated," the white man said, "for I had more monkeys posted in the alley."

"Yes," Michelle said, "and Eighth brother of the poison touch took care of them."

"Ah," said the white man, shutting his eyes. He rubbed the bridge of his nose. "Ah." A silence followed. One of the monkeys scratched its ass and sniffed its fingers.

"Well, then," the white man said, finally, "another day."

"Another day," Michelle agreed.

And the white man took his leave with all the straight-backed dignity he could muster in the face of this setback, his monkeys ook-ooking behind him with disappointment and confusion.

The brothers stood around grinning at one another for a few moments until Michelle snapped at them to go back to work. Chagrined, they filed back into the kitchen.

I tipped my bowl to drink the last of my soup. "That turned out pretty well," I said.

She released a long, sad sigh. "Not really. We've been here for three generations, but now we're done with this city. We'll have to move the restaurant."

I choked on the broth. "Move? But . . . Why? Your brothers . . ."

"The Belgian will be back. And he can make monkeys faster than I can make brothers. So, we move." She got up and flipped the OPEN sign to CLOSED.

"But . . . where will you go?" I asked, knowing I wouldn't like the answer.

"Far away. Across one ocean, perhaps two. Now, if you'll excuse me, sir, you've been a good customer, but I do have some arrangements to make . . ."

And that was it. By the very next day, Lady Sze's Golden Crown Café had been abandoned. A week later, a donut shop had replaced it.

It took me months to find another regular lunch place, but I eventually settled on a Texas barbecue joint on the south 400 block of Milton. Their secret lay in the heated rocks that lined the bottom of the barbecue pit, brought here by way of Texas and Mexico. They were fragments of an Aztec pyramid and had been splashed with the blood of more than a thousand human sacrifices.

The ribs are pretty good, but I'm more a fan of the pulled pork sandwich.

Harbor District

I walked along the row of aquariums and pressed my nose against miniature worlds. Treasure chests spewed bubbles. Skeletal pirates gripped ship wheels. Fish nipped pink rocks.

PLEASE DON'T TAP THE GLASS, the signs said, so I refrained.

My kid's birthday was coming up. I'd been thinking about giving him an ant farm but changed my mind and decided he could do with some fish. When ants get out you've got them all over the house. When fish get out, they die. Lots of arguments in favor of fish. The only question was, what kind? I had it in my head that goldfish die as soon as you get them home. They're programmed that way, with this little chip inside their bellies that somehow knows the second you've got them through the door, and then, *zap*, time to meet the Ty-D-Bol Man.

The shop was dark, hot and moist. Humming and gurgling filled the air. It was hard to breathe, and I loosened my tie. So many weird fish: ear-spot angels, convict tangs, chevroned butterflies, clown knives, blue-sided fairy wrasses. Near the back of the store, I paused before a ten-gallon tank with a porcelain castle. There was something different about the fish inside. About as long as my thumb, they weren't covered in scales, but rather emerald-bright skin from their midsections to their tails, which ended in horizontal flukes, like a dolphin's. From the midsection forward, they were human-shaped: brown-skinned, with long, graceful arms; round breasts with little pencil-dot nipples; long, flowing black hair. Their eyes were like tiny diamond chips.

"Hey, what are these?" I called to the front of the store.

The shopkeeper—a tall hippie with a blurred U.S. Navy tattoo on his arm— sauntered over to me. "Mermaids," he said. "Pretty rare."

I spent a moment watching them swim. One broke the surface, arching her back and stretching. Another swam up to her and started braiding her hair. I felt a slight twitch in my crotch.

"How much?"

"Forty each," he said with the tone of someone trying to conceal the sound of hope in his voice. "And they go as a group."

There were six mermaids in the tank.

"Okay," I said. "I'll just take a couple of those Siamese fighting fish in the front of the store."

"More than one and they'll kill each other. That's why they call them *fighting* fish."

I got out my wallet. "How about three goldfish?"

As it turned out, my kid was pretty happy with his gift. I got him a nice little tank, some plastic plants for decoration, and only one of the goldfish died before we could get it all set up. It was nice to see him learning to take care of something, making sure the water didn't get too grimy, feeding the fish just the right pinch. I enjoyed going into his room when he was over at a friend's or at his mom's. I'd sit on the bed and watch the fish go back and forth. I could stare at them for hours. It was fun. Better than TV.

I figured the kid might enjoy some more fish, so I went back to the shop. The mermaids didn't look so good now. Their green tails were the color of wilted lettuce, and their hair was patchy, showing too much scalp. Their eyes had grown red. And one of the mermaids was gone. There were only five now.

Taped to the glass was a handwritten sign: 50% OFF. ASK AT COUNTER. PLEASE DON'T TAP ON THE GLASS.

I saw the shopkeeper's reflection in the tank, and I turned around. "What's wrong with them?" I asked.

"You're really not supposed to break up the group," he said, sheepishly. "But, you know, rent's climbing, economy's screwed . . . I sold one of them. I thought they'd get over it."

I bent back down to the tank. Their eyes actually weren't red. They were gone. Just bloody sockets left, trailing threads of blood through the water.

"They grieve pretty dramatically," the shopkeeper explained.

I straightened and got out my wallet. "Think I'd like four neon tetras and three tiger barbs, please."

As he went off to net me my fish, I lingered a while longer by the mermaids. When I could stand it no more, I tapped lightly on the glass. They darted off in all directions, their mouths stretched in silent screams.

College Square

First of all, it's not a fetish; it's a preference.

Most guys have one. Maybe it's redheads, or poet chicks with tight sweaters and little round glasses, or girls who remind them of a their third-grade teacher who was careless with her bra straps. Me, I like dangerous girls. Femme fatales. Exotic spies from foreign lands. Girls with knives who put you through your paces on the backs of their Harleys. I like being pursued by perilous women, and I don't mind if I get pounced on, or even roughed up a little. As long as I get away in the end.

I'm neither proud nor ashamed of this. I just know what makes me tick.

I watch them from across the street.

The tawny-haired one sweeps the walk in front of her café, her eyes green as a traffic light saying go. When she pauses, puts a hand against the small of her back and stretches, her dress draws taut against her curves. Then she catches me watching her. Her lips curl into a small smile and she goes back to her sweeping.

One door down, another café, and here a woman with black curls that fall over her shoulders waters hydrangeas in terra cotta pots. She bends forward, and water trickles from her watering can.

They don't look much alike, these two witches, but I'm sure they're sisters. And not the kind who stir the same pot and feed the same cats. These are sisters who, perhaps, shared the womb, and were it not for the intervention of calming teas drunk by their mother, they would have strangled each other with their own umbilical cords.

The broom stops moving. The watering can stops trickling. The sister-witches tilt their heads, both giving me questioning looks, and go inside their respective cafés.

I choose the establishment of the tawny-haired one, because from where I'm standing, her place is on my left, and I read left to right. Through the doors I go, only to find that her café is disappointingly uninviting. Mismatched folding chairs are arranged haphazardly around wobbly tables. The prints on the wall are whatever was cheap at the mall poster shop.

With a scrape of metal legs against yellowing vinyl floor, I pull out a chair and take a seat.

The tawny witch is less attractive up close. Her arms are skinny, with thick blue veins pushing up the skin. And those once-amazing green eyes—contacts, surely—sit inside deep hollows.

It doesn't matter. The aromas will keep me here. Warm, buttery scents, with vanilla and light dancing over rich, dark coffee. My stomach rumbles, my mouth waters, my hamstrings tingle.

Eat not the food of witches, warn my thoughts, in an urgent voice of authority, like Ahab, or a Scottish preacher. *Eat not the food of witches.*

"A croissant and a large drip," I say, swallowing.

She sets a golden, pillowy croissant on a polystyrene plate, fills a paper cup with night, and sets both on my table. She tries to shake her hips as she returns to her place behind the counter.

I bite into the croissant.

Flaky crust gives way to soft wisps of pastry, soaking my tongue in a warmth that spreads to my chest and belly. Despite myself, I moan softly, and the tawny witch smiles now, a smile that softens the angles of her face and brings a glow to her cheeks. Her green eyes come to life.

She's got me, I realize with a panicky intake of breath. Caught. Trapped. No escape this time. Why, oh, why didn't I listen to Ahab?

I will come here every day for the rest of my life. I will have no meals other than what she makes for me.

Eventually, though, my plate is empty, even the crumbs gone, and I can see the bottom of my cup. And once more the tawny witch is too pale, too stretched out. Her smile reveals a bit too much gum. So, I put six dollars on the table and run out, her curses thrown at my back.

Outside, I catch my breath, craving a cigarette. My heart jackhammers in my chest, and this is the part I like best: The light-legged, dizzy buzz that follows an escape.

Is this how Harry Houdini felt after throwing off straitjacket and shackles and bursting naked through the surface of a half-frozen river?

What a great feeling. Nice going, Harry.

But I need more.

Only a few moments later I find myself moving toward the café next door.

Overstuffed chairs and throw pillows suggest long, rainy afternoons with steaming mugs and good books. The windows cast honey-colored light on warm wood floors.

The black-haired one has been waiting.

"Sit," she says. "Tell me what you want."

I take the chair nearest the counter, nearest her. "A croissant, please, and a large coffee."

"Cream and sugar?"

I like the way her lips form the word *cream*.

Not trusting my voice, I leave it at a mute nod.

She brings me a plate ringed with small green leaves and a cup painted with night sky and stars. Then she takes a seat in the chair opposite me. When I bite into the croissant, she moves her legs and exhales.

I chew. Hard, burnt crust gives way to something the texture of wood. I sip the coffee and get a mouthful of sour water and bitter grounds.

As I eat and drink, the witch's lips part and her chest rises and falls. I squirm in my seat, tension gathering in my thighs.

The awful taste of her food is no matter when she tilts her head back and shows me the exquisite long curve of her neck. For a moment, I even entertain the notion that I am seducing her.

But one does not seduce a witch. Not in her own café. Not when eating her food. And soon, I am in love with her, with her midnight forest of black curls, and her eyes, blue as glacial ice. And though I would be her captive lover, a pet of sorts, or a slave, I would not mind so much, because she has worked magic on my glands, and what is love but a product of pheromones and the promise of long, pleasant afternoons?

But is that what I want? Long, pleasant afternoons? Better loving through chemistry?

And, in the end, it is not. And I put down plate and cup, and leave six dollars on the table, and run out the door, plugging my ears against her strange, angry, hissed words.

I'm so good at this, this escaping thing. Two in one day. I am a young, virile, fleet-footed gazelle, and I'm still congratulating myself when I realize my legs are carrying me to a third door, one I hadn't noticed before, placed right between the two café's. And that's where I go.

Inside, the tawny-haired witch smiles and grinds coffee beans by hand. The black-haired one makes slow circles on a table with a polishing cloth.

I have been in the houses of two witches, and I have eaten the food of two witches, and I have risked the ire of two witches. And today I heave learned that I can resist witchcraft in matters of lust, and I can resist witchcraft in matters of breakfast.

But lust *and* breakfast?

That's a pretty damn good trap.

I close the door behind me.

The black-haired one polishes. The tawny-haired one grinds. Then, their hands fall motionless, and the witches come towards me, reaching.

Old Heights

Maybe he's a retired heavyweight who owns a cigar-stained Italian restaurant downtown and still spars with the kids when he runs his youth boxing camp. Or maybe he's a cowboy actor who exaggerates his Texas drawl when he does commercials for his Ford dealership. Possibly, he's an old news anchor who emcees the annual leukemia telethon and does a radio show early on Sunday mornings. Every town has one, the old local celebrity who represents the people in a way an elected politician never could. Whoever he is, you can be sure he's a raconteur, that he's been entertaining people for as long as anyone can remember. People agree that he's simply the nicest guy in town, though there are some faded rumors about womanizing, and some drunk driving allegations. But those happened so long ago, and anyway, they somehow make him human and better loved.

Around here, for my generation, at least, that guy was the Green Thunder.

The Green Thunder was the grand marshal in the Settler's Day parade.

The Green Thunder visited kids in the hospital.

The Green Thunder judged the Daffodil Queen pageant.

You remember that commercial campaign the city did? A guy throws his fast-food garbage out his car window, and a kid walks up, and he stares at the garbage, and he stares at the trash can across the street, and the voice-over says, "What would the Green Thunder do?" I still think of that commercial every time I see litter in the street.

The Green Thunder once had his cape pressed at my dry cleaner shop. Dropped it off himself, paid cash, and when I asked him for an autograph, he gave me that billion-dollar grin and got out an 8×10 glossy. He signed it, *To Sidney, My Dry Cleaning Hero. Thanks! Green Thunder.* Drew a little thunder bolt and everything.

His dry-cleaning hero? It was the first time he'd ever been to my shop, and I hadn't even pressed his cape yet. He didn't have to do that for me, but that's the kind of guy he was.

And, look, I'm not defending what he said to that reporter. It was dead wrong. I think he was just trying to be funny, and that's how people talked in the neighborhood when guys like Green Thunder and me were growing up. When it comes right down to it, didn't he help a lot of people, no matter who they were? He didn't care if you were black or white or yellow or green. If you needed help of any kind, the Green Thunder was there.

On the other hand, I understand why people got upset. My wife, she's Korean, and when we were driving cross-country on our honeymoon, some of the looks we used to get . . .

I keep telling people the Green Thunder was more than a remark made in a moment of bad judgment. He was a real part of this city for a long time.

They say he and that reporter had some history between them. They'd been friends back in the old days but had a falling-out of sorts. Something about a signal watch, something trivial.

Anyway.

It's just sad.

I was sweeping in front of my shop the day he left. I heard the boom, the bang, the sound of the sky ripping apart that people who grew up when and where I did had come to associate with hope, and I looked to the sky, and there he was. Not the fast streak of green across the morning blue. Just an old man, slowly passing out of view.

He wasn't even wearing his cape.

Some people get a little upset when they see his photo hanging on my wall. I've had once-loyal customers stop coming in because I won't take it down.

Heck, sometimes I want to take it down myself.

What's the right thing to do?

I don't know.

I don't know what the Green Thunder would do.

Carnival Park

We knew there'd be trouble when the new balloon man showed up. Orange John had been working Carnival Park for as long as there'd been a Carnival Park, tying his balloon animals with rope-strong hands. He always had that faraway look in his eyes, as if expecting something to appear on the horizon. And one day, something did. A new balloon man.

You have guys like Orange John where you come from? You know what I mean. Guys who do one thing in one place, like the Knife Guy, or Mr. Rags and Mr. Rags, Jr.? They do their one thing, and you can't imagine them having a life outside that thing, like a home, or a family, or a bank account. These guys make a place what it is, as surely as pigeon-crapped statues and old buildings with columns and stone lions out front.

So there was Orange John near the war fountain in his oversized orange suit and Bozo hair, knotting himself up a real nice stegosaurus, when up came the young balloon man. He was a skinny boy in a black T-shirt, rainbow vest, and jeans painted like all the sample chips in a paint store. His uninflated balloons hung from his waistband like little tongues, and he stopped a dozen or so yards away from Orange John.

"Jack Many-Colors," he said, tipping an imaginary hat.

"Orange John," said Orange John, with a squint and a nod.

And so it began.

Many-Colors was the challenger, so he went first. He took out a brown balloon, put it to his lips, and blew. It extended like a time-lapse video of a growing vine, curving in on itself before he pinched the spout, grabbed the far end, and made a series of deft twists and knots. The end result: an odd sort of elephant with a weird, humped head, and squat, fat legs. Not terrible, but not a very good likeness. But then he took a white balloon from his waistband, and before we knew it, the elephant had huge, curving tusks. A mammoth, then. A good one.

A crowd had started gathering, and they *oohed* appreciatively around mouthfuls of hot dogs and soft pretzels. He handed the mammoth to a young boy who ran off, trumpeting mammoth sounds.

It was Orange John's turn. He gazed up at the sky, as if searching the clouds for inspiration. Then, after a few moments, he reached into his breast pocket and took out a red balloon and a yellow balloon. He put both to his mouth and blew into them, his eyes distant, like a smoker deep in thought. When the balloons were inflated to his satisfaction, he grabbed them roughly and wrestled them into a red hawk with yellow eyes and talons. He held it aloft and gave it a toss. The wind caught it, and it sailed over the fountain, over the trees, out of sight.

Many-Colors clapped his hands in silent applause, then went to work. One by one he inflated about a dozen orange and black balloons, storing them under his armpit until he'd accumulated an unwieldy bundle. There was a flurry of rubber squeaking against rubber, and then before him in the grass crouched a life-sized tiger.

He grabbed it by the scruff of the neck and tugged. It walked on articulated legs. The jaw fell open to reveal long fangs and a lolling tongue.

It was a fine balloon animal.

Orange John placed his palms flat against each other as if in prayer and bowed deeply toward Many-Colors. From his pocket he drew a number of black balloons, and when he was finished blowing them up, he panted, out of breath, his face red. With shaky hands, he made a spider and set it against Many-Colors' tiger. The spider grasped the tiger in its legs and squeezed, destroying the tiger with small pops. Then it slowly scuttled back to its maker, exhausted, and deflated itself empty.

Many-Colors's eyes went wide, and his mouth formed an O. But his expression of surprise wasn't genuine. He was mocking Orange John.

Reaching to his waist, Many-Colors pulled out every green balloon he had, and when he seemed to be looking for more, Orange John took out a handful of his own and held them out in offering. But Many-Colors just sneered at him and pulled more green balloons from the air until his sleight-of-hand had given him an adequate supply for his next sculpture. This one took a while. Sweat glistened on his brow, and his lips moved as though he were reading aloud as his hands did their work.

His dragon reared up on its bulbous haunches, black claws gleaming. Its red eyes seemed lit from within, and from its great maw came long, sinuous twists of red and yellow balloon flame.

Orange John didn't waste time acknowledging his opponent, for the dragon was lurching towards him. With desperate speed, he tied and twisted and knotted. The dragon was almost on him, and Orange John's lattice of balloon-work had yet to take form. We could hear him release small grunts of pain or frustration as he worked. For the first time ever, we noticed the way his fingers curled, the knots in his knuckles. Orange John had arthritis.

The dragon stretched its jaws wide, revealing more rubber flame, and Orange John jumped back from his own animal—a large feline body with the head of a bird of prey and graceful back-swept wings. A griffin.

Well-chosen, we agreed among ourselves.

The two animals leapt at one another, and for the next several minutes, an epic battle raged above Carnival Park. Flashes of color. Rubber squeaks drawn out into screams. Tiny pops of injury.

When the dragon of Many-Colors floated back down to earth, half its jaw was missing. One of its bat wings hung limp, barely attached.

But at least it was still recognizable.

Not so for Orange John's griffin. Shredded bits of rubber rained on us.

The contest was over. Orange John kept his back rigid with dignity, but he already looked half dead. Perhaps, long ago, he had humiliated an older, more fatigued balloon man in this very spot. Perhaps it was simply the way of things.

Many-Colors offered his dragon to a little girl, but the little girl refused to take it. Tears streaming down her eyes, she crossed her arms and looked away from the younger balloon man. Then the rest of us exchanged glances, and we knew what was right.

"A giraffe, Orange John?" someone said.

"And after that, a big dinosaur with spikes," said someone else.

Many-Colors looked at us, not understanding. "But . . . I defeated Orange John. I'm your balloon man now."

We told him he'd never be our balloon man. Carnival Park belonged to Orange John. Orange John was this place. This place was Orange John.

Many-Colors made a lot of noise—he never really wanted to be our balloon man anyway, he said; and Orange John's balloons smelled like cigarettes (which was true); and we wouldn't know a good balloon man if he blew a poodle up our asses. But it was no use. With more grumbling and curses, he left, going wherever balloon men with no parks go.

Orange John didn't thank us. He didn't need to. He just began working on a beautiful long-necked giraffe with spindly long legs, which was exactly what we needed of him.

To tie balloons. To be here. To always be here.

Those of us who live and work around Carnival Park had never asked for a champion.

All we'd ever wanted was a good balloon man.

The Strip

My hand reaches for the toilet stall door, and he says, "You ever hear of a zero room?"

Restroom attendants make me nervous. I've been going to the bathroom on my own since I was three, and I don't need help.

"Every city's got a zero room," he says, "but it's never in the same place. Not from city to city, not from moment to moment."

He sits over there on his little stool, his bottles of cologne gleaming in the spotlights over the mirror. The bright reflections hurt my eyes.

"They say zero rooms were built by the man who made all the cities. They connect places. Or, to put it another way, every door, every single one, connects to the same zero room. When you open a door, maybe it goes somewhere you didn't expect it to. Or maybe it goes to everywhere at once. Or maybe everywhere comes spilling through the door, like a great tidal wave, and all the places behind all the doors smash into each other and get mixed up and cancel each other out, and it's the end of everything." He moves some of his cologne bottles around as if they're chess pieces. "Or maybe nothing at all happens. You never know."

I stare at him a while longer, but he seems to be done with me. He arranges breath mints on a silver tray.

I turn back to the toilet stall. With my hand hovering near the door, I flirt nervously with godhood.

ALISON SMITH

The Specialist

Alison Smith's memoir, Name All the Animals, *was a winner of the 2004* Barnes & Noble Discover Award. *Her writing has appeared in* McSweeney's, The London Telegraph, Best American Erotica, *and other publications. She lives in Brooklyn, New York.*

"The Specialist" first appeared in McSweeney's *No. 11. It won the first Fountain Award, an award given by the Speculative Literature Foundation to a speculative short story of exceptional literary quality.*

—K.L. & G.G.

The first one said it was incurable. The next agreed. "Incurable," he sighed. The third one looked and looked and found nothing. He tapped her temple. "It's all in your head," he said. The fourth one put his hand in and cried, "Mother! Mother!" The fifth never saw anything like it. "I never saw anything like it," he gasped as he draped his fingers over his stethoscope. The sixth agreed with the first and the seventh agreed with the third. He parted her legs and said, "There's nothing wrong with you."

Alice sat up. The paper gown crinkled. Her feet gripped the metal stirrups. "But it hurts," she said and she pointed.

"Maybe it's a rash," Number Seven said and he gave her some small white pills. They did not help. "Maybe it's spores," he said and he gave her a tube of gel. This made it worse. "Maybe it's a virus." He gave her a bottle of yellow pills. When Alice returned for the fourth time and told Number Seven it was not better, he slumped against the examining table, his white coat trailing. "There's nothing left," he said.

"Nothing?" Alice asked. "What am I going to do?"

He put his finger to her lips and shook his head. "Not here," he said.

That evening, Number Seven took Alice out to dinner. He leaned in over the herb-encrusted salmon croquettes. "Do you mind if I call you Alice?" he asked.

Alice frowned. "What's wrong with me?"

Number Seven pushed the fish around his plate. "I don't know," he said and then he started to cry.

"It's okay," Alice murmured. "At least you tried."

He touched her hand. She held her napkin. She could not eat. Everything tasted

incurable. The rice, the saffron asparagus soufflé, the flaming liquor in the dessert—
all of it, incurable.

The eighth told her it was the feminine bleeding wound. "All women have it," he
said. The ninth told her she didn't use it enough. "It's atrophied," he said as he
peeled off his latex gloves with a little shiver.

"But," said Alice as she sat up on her elbows, "it hurts."

The tenth said, "Call me Bob, why don't you?" He looked inside and shook his
head. He sat next to her. Alice held on to the edge of the metal table. "I've been
thinking," he whispered. She could smell the Scope on his breath. "I've got something that could fix this."

"Oh?" said Alice and she brightened. She felt the hair on his arm brush against
her thigh.

"Yes," said Bob. He nodded his head up and down. It was then that she caught
sight of the bulge inside Number Ten's slacks.

Alice decided to try a new town, a larger one. Back east, she thought, where the
civilized people live. This town had underground tunnels with trains inside. On her
first day, Alice descended the cement stairs, walked onto a waiting car and sat down.
The orange plastic seat cupped her thighs. The doors sighed shut. The rails rushed
along beneath her. She liked the dark, jerking movement of it, the idea of the
ground flying by, right beside her. When the car stopped and the doors flew open,
Alice emerged. She walked up another cement staircase and found herself in an entirely different part of the city.

"Brilliant," Alice thought.

She rode the underground trains for days.

Then Alice discovered take-out. As she did not have a phone in her one-room
walk-up, she had to call from the pay phone on the corner when she wanted to place
an order. But she did not mind. Alice liked everything about take-out. She liked the
warm white boxes with their fold-away lids, the plastic utensils, the stiff paper bags
that held in the gooey warmth. She believed that a city which could deliver such del-
icacies right to your door was a city of great promise. Alice stayed up late, ate Indian
lentil soup from a box and said, out loud, "This is it. This is where I'll find it."

She found a job stocking shelves in a bookstore.

The eleventh told her try something different.

"I've seen this before. There's nothing for it," he said and he gave her a card with
a number on it. "Try this anyway." Under the number were printed the words, "Psychic Healer."

This card led Alice to Number Twelve. She was alternative. "Find a piece of
gold," Number Twelve said, "real gold. Boil it for three days and keep the water.
Store it in a cool place. Drink this water every day for a month."

Number Twelve nodded. Alice nodded. "It aches," she said.

A pinched smile lighted across Number Twelve's face. She clasped her hands together. Gold bangles tripped down her arms and she nodded some more.

Alice did not have any gold. No ring, no brooch, not even a pendant. So she
bought a set of gold-rimmed plates at the Salvation Army and boiled them for three
days. The painted flowers dissolved into the water, turning it pink, then green and
then, finally, the color of mud. Alice slurped at her box of green lentil soup and
stared into the murky liquid.

The thirteenth was also alternative. He said, "Imagine a white light entering your body. Its energy fills you. Imagine this white light healing your internal wound."

"A wound?" Alice thought. "Is that what I have?"

Alice ordered more take-out.

The fourteenth was recommended by the thirteenth. This one did not even have a card. Instead, he had fountains, dozens of them. In the waiting room tiny gurgling pumps sprouted out of copper bowls. Held in place with river stones, they bubbled and chattered all around her.

Number Fourteen was a mumbler. He swallowed his words, half-spoken. He talked into the collar of his shirt. Alice leaned in. She could not hear him over the sound of running water. "I beg your pardon?" she asked.

"Become one with the water," Number Fourteen mumbled, "and you will find your cure."

"How?" asked Alice.

Number Fourteen spread his arms. He smiled. He closed his eyes. Alice leaned in and waited. He said nothing. She thought perhaps he had fallen asleep. "Sir," she whispered. "Sir?"

But Number Fourteen did not answer.

Alice found an indoor lap pool. After her morning shift at the bookstore, she swam up and down between the ropes. The water soothed her—the buoyancy of it, the soft fingers of cold. That winter, Alice swam and swam. She swam so many laps that her fingers pruned and her shoulders grew broad and taut. Every day, when she had completed her laps, Alice would linger in the pool. She held on to the side, gasping for breath, and floated. She spread her arms, tilted her head back and let the water surround her like a shapeless, soft eraser. But every time she stepped out of the pool, the ache returned.

Alice waited. She thought perhaps what she needed was rest. Perhaps what the ache wanted was to be left alone. So for an entire year she tried to ignore it. She did not see a single doctor. She swam up and down between the ropes. She shelved books. She rode the subway. Closing her eyes, she leaned her head against the plastic seat and waited for her life to change. Every night, she called for take-out from the pay phone on the corner. Every day, she gazed down at the neat lines of bills in the bookstore cash register.

Through it all, the ache zinged and popped. It burned and festered. And the pain of it began to eat away at her. At times, Alice felt certain there must be little left inside her. And that year, the-year-of-not-trying, something cold and hard slipped inside Alice and her heart became like a knife drawer. Sharp and shining, she kept it closed.

Then Alice met the Specialist.

"The best in the city," her coworker whispered handing her a card as she adjusted the sale sign by the overstock books. "He's a specialist."

Alice shook her head. "I'm done with doctors," she whispered back.

"Just try," her coworker said. "Try this one."

Alice had to wait a month for an appointment and when she did finally see him, when at last she climbed up onto his metal table and leaned back, the Specialist said she was empty.

"Empty!" he shrieked, his head popping up from behind the paper sheet. "There's nothing there!" He probed deeper. "It's cold," he cried. "It's so cold!" And then something strange happened, something entirely new. Alice heard a muffled shrieking and a great sucking sound. The room filled with a gust of cold air and then—silence. The Specialist was gone.

Alice sat up on her elbows and looked around her. "Where is he?" she asked the nurse.

"In there!" the nurse cried as she pointed between Alice's legs. "And he's caught!"

Alice plucked at the sheet, looking beneath it. Nothing. She leaned over and peered under the table. Still nothing. The Specialist was nowhere. Alice sat back on the metal table, her feet suspended in the stirrups. She lay very still and listened. She could hear a distant sound. The Specialist's voice, frantic and screaming, echoed somewhere below her. Alice looked over at the nurse. The nurse shook her head. Alice crossed her arms and waited.

After twenty minutes Alice shifted her weight and moved to rise. As she did, the distant echo grew louder. Then, with a terrible rush of cold air, the Specialist reemerged. His head rising above the paper sheet, his teeth chattering, a single icicle hung from the end of his nose.

"This is unbelievable," cried the Specialist. He pressed a red button. "Code Blue," he screamed into a mesh speaker in the wall. "I need a second opinion!" He paced. The icicle at the end of his nose began to melt. "I've got to get documentation," he said. "I need pictures. I need verification." He pressed the red button again and called into the mesh speaker. "Please, can I get some help in here!" His icicle dripped on the paper sheet.

"I'll help," the nurse said. She set down her clipboard.

"No," said the Specialist. "I need a doctor. This is, is . . ." he looked down at Alice and shook his head, "unprecedented."

"I don't know about that," said the nurse and she ducked her head below the paper sheet. "How deep did you get?" she asked.

"Deep enough," the Specialist said.

"Hmm," said the nurse.

"Oh!" said the Specialist. "If you don't believe me, I'll prove it."

The Specialist rushed out of the room. He returned moments later with a snowsuit, a pith helmet and a flashlight. He suited up. "I'm going in," he said. "Do you need anything?" he asked Alice.

Alice shrugged.

"Why don't you order Chinese," he said. "I may be a while."

"Take-out," thought Alice, and she warmed to the Specialist. "Even if he did say I was empty and cold inside."

The Specialist put his hand inside Alice, then his arm. Before he could say another word, there was a great sucking sound, the room filled with a gust of cold air and, for the second time that day, the Specialist fell inside Alice.

The hours passed. The take-out arrived. Alice slurped her noodles. She asked for a pillow, but the nurse was busy peering into the pages of an enormous black book. She wondered where the Specialist had gone. She stretched her arms up over her head, sat back and picked up her box of noodles.

An hour later, the Specialist emerged. When she saw him rise up from between her legs, covered in icicles and shivering, Alice set down her chopsticks.

"My God, there's nothing in there!" the Specialist cried, his face shining with cold. "Nothing! Miles of it! I could not even find the edges of her."

Alice gazed at the Specialist's chapped hands. She had to admit that they did look quite frostbitten. Alice reached for her sweater. The Specialist set down his flashlight and rushed away to record his findings. The nurse followed, waving a clipboard. Alice was alone.

One at a time, she removed her feet from the stirrups. She stretched out. She pulled the paper gown tight against herself. She looked around the room. On one wall hung a print of a field of poppies, red and bursting. On the other, a picture of a snowy tundra. After waiting on the table for quite a while, Alice sighed. "They must have forgotten about me," she thought. She looked at her watch. If she didn't leave now, she would be late for her shift at the bookstore. She stood up, found her slacks and blouse, and began to dress.

Just as she was stepping into the second pant leg, the Specialist burst into the room holding a camera. "I must have you for my new research project," he cried. "You must stay with me and work." He grasped her shoulders. Alice held on to the waist of her slacks. "A woman with nothing inside but a cold, hard breeze!" He gazed out beyond her, at the field of poppies. Then he looked down at Alice, as if He were seeing her for the first time. "I've never found anything like you." He smiled. "Come with me! We'll travel the world. We'll meet all the great doctors. We'll stay in the best hotels. Separate rooms, of course."

Alice thought for a moment. She knew it could not be true. She knew that there was something inside her, something more than a cold, hard breeze. But no one had made this much of a fuss over her before. No one had ever seemed to care like he did. This Specialist may not have understood her, but something about her thrilled him.

"Maybe that's more important than understanding," Alice thought. She looked into the Specialist's eyes. They were green, the color of shallow ocean water. She felt a little pull in her chest, a soft tug, as if the drawer of her heart were opening. She saw the roped lane at the swimming pool and the beige mouth of the bookstore cash register gaping and she realized that she was lonely.

"Will you help me, then?" she asked. "If I go with you, will we find a cure for the constant ache? The pain of it, it tires me so."

"Pain?" The Specialist tilted his head to one side. No one had told him this. "You have pain?" He paused a moment, then he shrugged and embraced Alice. He picked her up and swung her around twice.

The rush of air past her face, the whirl of the white, sanitary room as it flew by, it startled Alice. A new feeling, a feeling she could not quite describe, flooded her veins. It was not happiness, but it was close. The closest she had been in a long time.

In Atlantic City they praised her, treated her like royalty. "The Queen of Emptiness!" they said. In Hershey they offered her a complimentary sunsuit with a picture of the arctic printed on it, and a sash that read: "Miss Iceberg," its pink letters marching across the white satin.

The Specialist developed a slide show to accompany his demonstration. "Dim the lights," he said. Alice liked this part best. She hated it when he called her up on stage, when he poked and prodded with his cold, clammy hands. Alice sunk back in her seat and watched the photographs glow and shimmer against the white screen. She never tired of looking at them. "A distant landscape," the Specialist barked, his hand on the remote. "Cold, empty, devoid of life as we know it." Alice watched as the mysterious vistas appeared before her: a blue wash of glaciers, a white seamless line of snow. "The interior of Alice N. is like a frozen tundra. Nothing can live there!" the Specialist bellowed across the darkened room.

This is where Alice always lost track. It never failed. Every time the Specialist started in on the part about the cold and the snow stuck up inside her, Alice felt the room begin to spin. Her vision tunneled. She watched the Specialist's mouth move and she knew that he was talking, that he was explaining to the crowd of doctors behind her what it was like to be her, what it was like to be inside of her. But she could not make out what he said.

In Gainesville she could smell the ocean, but it was too far to reach. She wanted to swim. The Specialist said, "We have no time for recreation." And so she lay on the bed while he rifled through his papers. She imagined herself in the water, the salt shine rising up, coating her white arms.

In Louisville they laughed her off stage and the Specialist after her. "There's no such thing," the doctors said. "No such thing as a woman with nothing inside but a cold, hard breeze!"

"You don't believe me?" the Specialist said. He pointed at Alice. "Then why don't you look for yourself?"

The room fell silent. The doctors blanched. They stepped away from the stage. Someone dropped a clipboard. It skittered across the concrete floor.

The Specialist nodded. He stepped up to the podium once again. "I thought so," he said. "I thought that would stop you." He put his arm around Alice. "When you're ready to do some real research, you'll know where to find us." He guided her off.

They headed west. Later, years later, long after the National Guard had captured him, the Specialist would say that it was Los Angeles where it all started to go wrong. For it was there, swept along by the bright lights and the promise of fame, that he decided to put Alice in the talk show circuit. "To broaden your audience," the Specialist said and he spread his arms wide to make his point.

The Specialist bought her a new suit. He said it was a present for their success. "Now we've hit the big time!" he beamed at her.

Alice met the talk show host in the dressing room moments before she was to go on air.

"It is a pleasure to meet you, Miss Empty," he said and he kissed her cheek.

His mustache made her sneeze. Alice wiped her nose and asked for a glass of water. The host smiled at Alice. His white teeth shimmered under the green room lights. He leaned in close to Alice and looked at her, into her face, closely. It had been so long since someone had looked at her like that. Alice tipped her head down. She blushed. She placed the rim of the glass against her lips and sipped.

"She's going to need makeup!" the Host bellowed.

After her makeup session, the Host guided her on stage. Under the bright lights, the makeup felt like a thick, gooey mask.

"Here's the little lady with the big empty!" the Host said.

An applause sign popped up. The Host turned toward the Specialist. He wanted to see all the comparative charts. He wanted the entire history of his research. "Start from the beginning," the Host said, leaning forward in his overstuffed chair, "and don't leave out a thing."

The Specialist was happy to oblige. He pulled out statistics on the discrepancy between the size of Alice's outside and her inside. "The circumference of her torso," he said and he pointed at one chart, "as opposed to the circumference of her interior." He pointed to a second chart. "Alice defies logic!" This is where he always got excited. "She's an impossibility!" he cried. "And here she sits before you."

The Host smiled. "A woman who laughs in the face of science!"

The camera cut to a psychiatrist who spoke about the physical-manifestation-of-a-mental-state-brought-on-by-extreme-stress. He ended with, "It's remarkable. Quite remarkable."

The Host opened the discussion up to the audience. Alice was asked questions about her personal life that puzzled her. "How much do you eat?" "Do you like cold weather?" "Do you have a boyfriend?" Alice squirmed in her seat. The Host broke in. "Don't worry." He patted Alice's hand. "We'll find you a boyfriend," he said. "No doubt about that!" The audience cheered. Then a woman from the back row stood up, tapped the mike, and asked, "Does it ever hurt? I mean, does it ache?"

Alice felt her face flush and tingle. Finally, a question that she wanted to answer. She cleared her throat. "As a matter of fact," Alice began and then she lost the thread of her thought. She faltered.

The Host tapped his fingers together and waited. The Specialist shifted in his seat. "Go on," he nodded.

"As a matter of fact," she tried again, but the words would not come.

The Host put his hand on Alice's shoulder. "Hold that thought," he smiled. He turned and spoke to the camera lens. "We'll be right back."

"We're going back to Gainesville," the Specialist said the following morning while they were in a cab on the way to the airport. "You're not ready for the big time. We need to rehearse."

As they handed in their boarding passes and headed for the gate, they were intercepted by a man in a black suit with an ear prompt. "Excuse me," he said. "I've been sent by the talk show. They want you back."

The Specialist blinked. "Really? They want us?"

The man held his ear prompt and nodded. It turned out that Alice was a hit. Alice and her frozen tundra were the topic-of-the-day on every major morning newscast.

So Alice and the Specialist returned to the studio. Alice submitted to the creams and cover-up, the blush and shadow of the makeup artist. Once again, Alice and the Specialist found themselves under the hot studio lights, awaiting further instruction. The Host beamed at them. The second interview went better than the first. The Specialist showed more slides.

Alice was relieved when they dimmed the lights. The monitor flooded with the bright grays and whites of the frozen tundra. A distant sun bounced off all that glacial terrain. Before she knew it, the show was over and Alice found herself in her new suit in the green room once again, scraping makeup off her face.

By the end of the week Alice and the Specialist were regulars on the talk show. "It seems like everybody wants a piece of the little girl with the big empty," the Host smiled. He winked at Alice.

Reporters hounded them. Hotel staff hovered. Crowds formed around them wherever they went. And then, one day, the tide turned. The skeptics arrived—researchers and doctors, lab technicians and the geologists—all of whom did not believe in the cold-and-empty theory. They sat in the studio audience, crossed their arms and waited. "For some solid evidence," they whispered. "For one verifiable fact," they sneered.

The skeptics stared dubiously at the Specialist's charts. They recalculated his measurements. They scratched their heads. They lifted their chins. "Impossible," they said. "There's no such thing."

The Specialist was right there, his hand on Alice's shoulder, starting in with his challenge. "If you don't believe me," he began, "then why don't you see for yourself?"

Again, the room fell silent. Someone dropped a pen. They all stepped back.

"I thought so," the Specialist said.

But he spoke too soon. From the back, a white-coated lab technician with a shock of bright red hair stepped out of the crowds and raised his hand. "I'll go," he said. "I'd like to see."

And then another stepped forward. And another. And another. They all wanted to see this empty landscape, firsthand. Soon there was a line forming at the edge of the stage.

"We'll go," they cried. "We want to see this cold, hard breeze for ourselves."

"But," the Specialist stammered, waving his arms above his head, "it's too dangerous! It's not for the faint of heart!"

They would not listen to reason.

In the end, four men suited up and approached Alice. Each one ducked below the paper sheet. Each one slipped in, slowly at first, and then, with a rush of cold air, they disappeared.

Only three came back. Snow-crusted and shivering, one by one they climbed out of her, a gust of wind sweeping through the studio as they stepped onto solid ground. They brushed the snow off their shoulders. They straightened their wool caps. They rubbed their chapped hands together. They clapped each other on the back and nodded.

"It's true," they said. "It's huge and empty."

They nodded. They smiled. They looked around and counted. One. Two. Three. Their smiles faded. The fourth man was not among them. The three men turned around and stared at Alice. They gazed at the modesty sheet draped over her knees. They peeked under it. Nothing. So they sat down and waited.

"I'm sure he's just late," said the first man. "He stopped to take some photos," said the second. The third shifted in his seat, brushed the snow off his mittens and said nothing.

And so they waited, all of them, the three men, the Specialist and the studio audience. The Host paced. "This is highly irregular," he muttered. Then the network offered him round-the-clock coverage till the fourth man returned and the Host brightened.

The hours turned into days and still they waited. A vigil formed around the examination table. Doctors trickled in throughout the day, journalists clamored at the studio doors. The three men sat up front, right next to Alice. They called for him, the lost man, alone and wandering up inside Alice.

"I told you," the Specialist cried. "I warned you all!"

But no one was listening to him. The three men talked of extreme temperatures, the endless landscape, and lost provisions.

"Did he bring any food?" an audience member asked. "Did he pack his canteen?" asked another. "Did he wear his long johns?" his mother cried over the television satellite. Then someone suggested forming a search party. The three men who had survived to tell the story of Alice's insides shook their heads. "Why?" the people asked.

"Because it's cold in there," the three who came back said. "It's damn cold." They held their arms and shivered.

The Specialist nodded. "That's true," he mumbled as he sidled toward the door.

Someone grabbed his arm. "Where are you going?"

"I forgot my lunch," he said. "I'll be right back."

The doctors all shook their heads. "You'll stay right here," they said, "until you return the fourth man."

The Specialist threw up his hands. "Don't look at me! I didn't take him." He pointed at Alice. "She did."

Alice lay on the studio's examination table. By the third day, her back was in knots. Bedsores formed on Alice's skin. They grew weepy with infection. She asked if she could get up and try shaking him out. The doctors huddled in the corner and discussed the possibility. They nodded at each other. One of them stepped forward. "It might work."

Slowly, very slowly, Alice removed her feet from the stirrups, first the right and then the left. She slid her body to the edge of the examination table and placed one foot on the ground.

Alice shook and shook. She stomped her feet. She jumped up and down. She walked up the center aisle of the auditorium. She walked down the side aisle. She held on to the edge of the stage and stomped until her feet burned and her breath came hard. But it did not work. The fourth man did not emerge.

The three men who made it back alive helped her up onto the examination table. They tried calling his name. They tried playing his favorite music, pressing the speaker against Alice's exposed abdomen. They tried baking his favorite foods. They called in a diviner with his forked stick. They called in a meteorologist. He lined his instruments up and down her body, and shook his head. "Storm's coming," he said.

The doctors leaned in. "Storm's coming?" they asked. "Where?"

The meteorologist pointed at Alice. "In there."

They called in an Eskimo. "There are 437 words for snow," he whispered.

"But how do we get him out?" the doctors asked.

The Eskimo nodded, his fur cap shining under the examination lamp. "437 words," he said.

By then, it was day six. The doctors shook their heads. "There's no way," they whispered, "what with the exposure and the lack of food, there's no way he's still alive."

On the seventh day of the vigil, they sent for the lost man's wife. She spread Alice's legs, bent down and shivered. "What do I do?" she trembled. "What do I do down here?"

"Call to him," the doctors urged. "Call his name."

She called. "Honey?" she crooned. "Come out, come home!"

There was no answer. The wife began to sob. She clung to Alice. Her arms wrapped around Alice's bent legs, "Give him back," she pleaded. "Give him back!"

For a while, the story of the girl with nothing but a cold, hard breeze inside her swept through all the news stations. When the drama heightened with the missing fourth man, the network's ratings went through the roof. It was all anybody could talk about: "What does it mean that she is cold and empty inside?" they asked. "Where did the fourth man go?" When Alice and the Specialist disappeared, the story made international news.

They had slipped out one night, three weeks into the vigil for the fourth man. It was not a well-planned escape, but somehow it worked. They tiptoed right past the studio security guards, cut the wire that led to the exit alarm and crawled out onto the highway. They flagged down a passing car. The driver took them all the way to the Nevada border. Desert rain washed across the stranger's windshield as Alice huddled close to the Specialist. They were on the lam together. For once, they were running in the same direction, with the same goal in mind—to get away from the doctors. A week later, he left her.

It was an eerily still day. They were holed up in an Econo Lodge outside Las Vegas. "We're going to split up," he had whispered, his hands grasping her shoulders as they had on their first meeting. "I'll go north. You go west."

"Why?" she asked.

He let go of her, walked over to the motel window. Parting the curtain an inch with his index finger, he stared out at the parking lot. "If you don't know that by now, I'm not going to be the one to tell you."

Alice gazed at him. There he stood in his rumpled seersucker suit, pigeon-toed and balding, a slice of desert sunlight cutting across his stricken face. Despite his odd theories, Alice had grown fond of the Specialist. She stood up, smoothed her skirt and crossed to him. He held a photo in his hand. In it, the Specialist stands in full gear, his bright blue parka shining in the winter sunlight, surrounded by vast fields of snow, miles of it mounding up, soft and seamless and white. He smiles into the camera. Alice took his shaking hand in hers. "That's not really me," she said. She looked into his eyes—warm and moist, green as the sea.

"But I have evidence," he whispered back. "I have irrefutable evidence." He looked away again, out at the cactus shivering in the hot wind, just beyond the motel parking lot.

He left the next morning, before dawn, with one blue Samsonite carry-on and a hotel facecloth shielding his balding head from the hot Nevada sun. Alice feigned sleep throughout this long departure. As he folded his three dress shirts and zipped up his utility bag, as he combed the last few strands of hair over the crown of his head and trimmed his beard, Alice watched. Through half-closed eyes she saw him place a single envelope on the bedside table, cross to the motel door, unbolt the lock and slip away into the rising heat. After he left, she opened the envelope. There was no note, no instructions, no forwarding address, nothing, but a single photograph of a man standing in a field of snow.

That afternoon, Alice dyed her hair. She slipped into the motel laundry facility and quietly removed a pair of jeans and a new T-shirt from one of the dryers. Alice had never stolen anything before and the thrill of it, the getting-away-with-it feeling flooded her veins. Flushing with pleasure, she shimmied into the jeans. She sold her one good suit and bought a bus ticket back to California where she found work at a bakery on a strip right near the boardwalk. From her station behind the kneading tables, she could smell the ocean.

Back at the studio the Host was shocked by their disappearance. "How could you let this happen?" he asked his staff. "Right out from under my nose." But the two were gone. Not a single trace of them remained. A search party was formed, the Host leading the effort. "In the name of science," he blustered. "In the name of justice!" The camera recorded it all.

Following an anonymous tip, they headed north. They hired dogsleds and glided through the Yukon. They assumed that Alice and the Specialist, partners in this absurd crime, would always be together. The fourth man's wife came along. She rode just behind the dogs, a fur-lined parka framing her face. She called his name. Her voice echoed across the frozen landscape.

And for a while, that was all Alice saw. Every night before she fell asleep in her little apartment above the bakery, Alice turned on the evening news and there she was, the fourth man's wife. Chilblains had swollen her fingers. Her nose and cheeks were rubbed raw from exposure. She blinked into the camera. "Wherever you are, if you can hear me, call this number," the wife pleaded. "We don't want to hurt you. I just want my husband back."

The heat from the large ovens burned the hair off Alice's arms. It opened her pores and sweat ran down her back, formed half-moons under her shirtsleeves. She reveled in the sloppy warmth of the bakery, in the easy camaraderie with her coworkers. Evenings, after the baking was done, her coworkers unfolded lawn chairs on the boardwalk and watched the red ball of the sun slide lower in the sky till it sat on the edge of the ocean. When it broke open and began to sink, the colors bled across the water. Alice often joined them. She liked the feel of the ocean breeze on her arms and neck. The wind lifted her hair and fluttered across her cheeks. She closed her eyes, leaned back and listened to the bakery girls talk about their boyfriends.

In the mornings, when the other bakers wandered outside for a smoke break, Alice would slip into the back room. Nestled into the tiered rising racks, lay warm mounds of dough, resting like sleeping bodies, between the sheets of metal shelving. She gazed at the pastries. The raw, white buns, dusted in a soft layer of flour, slowly expanded as the yeast pulled in the surrounding air and the soft buns of dough rose. One morning, when the owner was late and the other girls lingered over their cigarettes, taking one last pull, wandering further away from the back door out toward the beach, Alice slipped her hand in between the rising racks and caressed the new, white flesh.

All the while, miles away, deep in the north country, a search party combed Alaska and the Northern Territory. They found nothing. No sign of Alice. No trace of the fourth man. For eleven months they rode up and down over the snow-packed ground, the dogs barking in the cold, the fourth man's wife crying into the wilderness.

Then, a year later, the Host got a new tip and this one was solid. It led them right to the Specialist. He had taken refuge in a tiny Inuit community, trading his gold watch for the price of a safe haven for twelve months. But, at the end of the year, when he started conducting research, running experiments on the local girls, looking for another Alice, the villagers turned him in.

The morning the authorities went out and found him, Alice was in the middle of cutting dough for hot-crossed buns. The girl who ran the cash register rushed in, calling, "They caught him!"

"Who?" asked Alice, sliding a baker's knife through the dough.

"The Specialist! They caught the Specialist."

Alice let her hands fall to her sides. The girl turned on the TV. Once again Alice found herself gazing into the frozen tundra. The dogs barked outside the igloo. The snow was so cold it had turned icy and blue. They had the igloo surrounded and still, the Specialist would not give himself up. In the end, they smoked him out. Alice watched as the Specialist ran, half-naked, across the fields of snow. They shot him with a stun gun and he fell like a wild deer, his body sliding across the ice.

Alice stepped out onto the beach. The sign above the bakery switched on. Neon flooded the glass tubes, hovering and jumping to life in the crystalline air, calling to her, calling out OPEN. She remembered the poppies, bright and red on the wall in the examination room, and the Specialist's shallow-water eyes. She remembered the hotel in the desert, the stillness of the morning air, the cactus shuddering outside her window and the moment—before he left her, before he was gone—when she held his hands, still and cold, in her own. It had been years of waiting and holding herself, of trying to find the answer, the end, the other side of the mysterious pain, and how it had changed her, carved out her insides.

Alice walked toward the shore, stepping closer to the ocean than she had allowed herself to go in a long time. At the edge, she bent down and placed her fingers in the water. Her hands and arms were coated with pastry flour, rendering her whiter than usual, white as a ghost. The flour dissolved off her skin. It shimmered and flickered, falling away from her, toward the sand below. She let her wrists slip into the water, then her forearms, and her elbows. Waves crawled up her skin, licking the clouds of flour until the whiteness shifted. It moved off of Alice and into the water. The air around her grew solid and soft, as if it were made of pillows. And the ocean, which for hundreds of thousands of years had been whining outside the door, falling over and over itself, reaching for the shore, the ocean stopped. The white foaming crests of the waves stilled. The green water, shallow and undulating below her, grew viscous; it grew hard as fine crystal. Slowly, what lived inside Alice—the bright, soft, swelling snow, the cold, hard breeze, all of it—slipped out, and the ocean became a field, and the field became a tundra and it rolled out, like a door opening up, swinging loose on its hinges.

As Alice gazed out on the tundra she noticed beyond the last snowy hill, something bright and shining, something calling to her, crying, "Alice, Alice, I'm here." She stepped forward, away from the huddle of shops by the boardwalk and the flickering light of the neon sign and onto the white glaciers. She walked toward the tiny speck and as she walked the speck divided into a shock of red hair and a white lab coat and there before her in the distance stood the fourth man. His hand floated above his head as he waved and he called to her, his voice bugling out, a reveille, calling her name, calling out across the frozen fields of snow.

SHELLEY JACKSON

Here Is the Church

Shelley Jackson is the author of the collection The Melancholy of Anatomy, *the acclaimed hypertexts* Patchwork Girl, The Doll Games, *and* My Body, *and several children's books. Her stories and essays have appeared in* Grand Street, Conjunctions, *and* The Paris Review. *One current project is the story "Skin," published one tattoo at a time, on the skin of volunteer "words." Jackson and artist Christine Hill have founded The Interstitial Library, to "champion the incomplete, temporary, provisional, circulating and, of course, interstitial. Above all, we aim to acquire and catalogue those books that are themselves interstitial: that fall between obvious subject categories; that are notable for qualities seldom recognized by traditional institutions; that no longer exist, do not yet exist, or are entirely imaginary. [Its] holdings are dispersed throughout private collections, used bookstores, other libraries, thrift stores, garbage dumps, attics, garages, hollow trees, sunken ships, the bottom desk-drawers of writers, the imaginations of non-writers, the pages of other books, the possible future, and the inaccessible past."*

"Here Is the Church" appeared in the second issue of Black Clock, *a CalArts literary magazine edited by Steve Erickson.*

— K.L. & G.G.

"This is a show tune, but the show hasn't been
written for it yet"

— Nina Simone

I n 1974, on the advice of a witchdoctor, Eunice Waymon lay in bed for three days with a can of Carnation milk under her pillow.

On the first day she put the can of milk under her pillow like a gun, something she could use to defend herself, if the need arose.

The guest room was small and shadowed and almost cool, softly breathing under the shush of an overhead fan. It contained very little. There was a long mirror on a stand, slightly inclined toward the floor. There was a tremendous white nightgown laid out on the bed. Of course she had brought along a negligée, a Parisian concoction of silk panels held together with ribbons, like a fantastic kite. But she had been told to put aside the trappings of her adult life, of the *chanteuse*, the star. She unfastened her hoop earrings and clunked them onto the bedstand. Her batiked headcloth had come loose at the back and she unwound it, coiled it, looked around, finally dropped it into the open mouth of her purse. Her hair she fidgeted into loose braids. The halter neck undone, her dress slid to the floor and she stepped out of the soft ring of fabric, hooked it up with one foot, shook the folds out of it and draped it over the headboard. Then took it back and hung it in the closet above her shoes.

The nightgown was heavy and stiff and the collar scraped her ears when she pulled it over her head. She touched the mirror experimentally. It pivoted smoothly around its central axis. Up rose an apparition: Little Eunice in big sister Lucille's hand-me-downs. She considered her without especial friendliness, then banished her with a touch.

The bedposts and headboard, of soft wood, had been minutely perforated by some methodical insect. They looked carved out of bread. The bed did not appear sleepworthy. She boarded gingerly, slid her legs under the covers. The nightgown did not slide with them. She had to clench its hem between her toes to pull it down. Once it was in place, she could barely move. She stared up at the ceiling fan, at the dozy countercircles its hub described within the orbit of the vanes. She felt foolish lying in bed in the middle of the afternoon, wide awake.

When she had arrived in Liberia, the friend who met her at the airport had narrowed her eyes at her and said, "I have to take you somewhere right away." Eunice had let herself be taken to a small, ordinary house where they were met by a small, ordinary witchdoctor. He waved her to a chair at a dining room table, and took a seat opposite. She noticed he had a limp. She did not like cripples, they reminded her of failure. The witchdoctor opened his briefcase and took out a scuffed white dinner plate with flowers daubed on it, maybe roses, maybe poppies. Out of one pocket of his cheap suit jacket he took a knotted plastic baggie. He picked open the knot over the plate and shook out some tiny bones.

He studied the bones. Eunice studied his powdery lashes, the fine lines in his forehead, the welts in the shoulders of his jacket inflicted by the points of a wire hanger. He gathered the bones up, tossed them, studied them some more. He sucked his teeth. To keep from laughing, Eunice played scales on her thigh under the table. For a moment, she had actually thought he might be able to help her.

Then, "Who is this person on the other side who is so fond of Carnation milk?" he had said.

She was tired after all. She closed her eyes and saw a hog, axe-whacked, slump to his knees in astonishment and sorrow. His blood uglied the straw in long squirts. She saw this happen over and over, different hogs each time. As a girl she had watched many hogs die. It had been an occasion for joy, because afterwards the kitchen would be hung with sausages, roasts, sweetbreads, bacon. It was magic: The hog had ceased to be a hog and had become a place, a fairy-tale room made entirely out of food. This was what was meant by hog heaven, she supposed. Of course it was not heaven for the hog.

The curtain bellied in and out. Behind it Africa waited. She had left the mirror at such an angle that, from the bed, she could see the floor tilting up like a ramp. She imagined herself walking up it.

She woke up holding a gun. It was still day. She saw a shadow by the window. She waved the gun, which sloshed strangely, and a fold in the curtain unkinked itself, enlightening an unmarked stretch of wall.

Once, something in the news had angered her beyond reason. She had fetched junk from the garage: wire, a padlock with no key, a stiletto heel, a pipe, a little gold woman from a bowling trophy with a globe stuck to her hand. Weeping, she had attempted to put these together into a gun. She intended to kill someone. A white person, any white person. Except Miz Mazzy. And her first husband, even if he was a creep.

Her second husband had come into the room like a familiar smell, unnoticed at first. "You don't know anything about killing people," he said after a while. "All you have is music."

With this formula, which she hated but believed, he had turned the gun back into junk and her music into a gun—maybe the gun she was holding now, with its tight, handsome paper wrapper.

She held it steady. There was something coming down from inside the mirror.

Her dead father stepped into the room.

He was not exactly standing. His feet occasionally bumped the floor, but in the soft way swimmer's feet do. It was as though they remembered that the floor had been important to them, but not exactly how. He stood at an angle that seemed to misunderstand gravity in some slight but fundamental way. His weight was withheld. This hurt her feelings somehow, like an intentional display of reserve.

He was naked, and he was young. Younger than she was, now, and a fine-looking man. Except he had the old wound back, and its leakage drizzled into his pubic hair and down one inner thigh to his ankle bone and along the fine arch of his foot and between the long toes and then across the half inch or so between his curved nail and the floor in a shining line that stretched and angled with him as he swayed, like the tether of a balloon.

He raised his arms in an ambiguous gesture. He might have been acknowledging the gun. Might have been asking for a hug. "Together again," he said. He had a look of secret mirth, the exaggerated calm of someone waiting for the joke to take. "Me and my daughter, close as flies."

"That's my line," she said, keeping the gun on him. "Don't take credit for things you didn't do. That's how we came to grief in the first place."

"Your line?"

"It's from a song I wrote the day you died. I performed it that same night in Washington. At the Kennedy Center. If you don't believe me look it up."

"Died?"

"I thought I had learned not to rely on anyone but myself. But you, I thought I could—"

"I died?" He lowered his head and threw himself, keening, through the hole in his side. He did this so quickly she could not make out whether it was more like a sock turning inside out or more like a chord dying down of itself in a quiet room. For a second, impossibly, she saw him vignetted in himself, walking away.

On the second day she put the can of milk under her pillow like a tooth, a part of herself she put aside in hopes of getting something better in return.

The room had begun to smell of milk, although the can was sealed. Not fresh milk, but the thick sweet smell of evaporated milk, warming up in a pan.

When she was four, her father had had an operation. While he was sleeping, they drew his stomach out through his side and washed it. She pictured it clean and pink, purse-like. Then they put it back. When she heard he was coming home with a hole in his side, she imagined spotting his heart in the hole, and saying to herself, *This is the heart that loves me!* But when she unstuck the bandage, rather than a neat porthole, there was a mess of proud flesh standing up around a smeary tube. Out of the tube dripped something that looked like cane syrup, streaked with blood.

Eunice was nurse. Everyone else had work. She sat by him all day, every day of his slow convalescence. She washed his wound with cotton napkins that she boiled clean in a big pot. She was aware of being indispensable. Sometimes she caught herself thinking something terrible, that she never wanted him to get better. When he felt strong, they played games: He'd lace his fingers together, all except for the index fingers pointing up. "Here's the church and here's the steeple," he'd whisper. "Open the door"—he'd let her pull his thumbs apart—"Where's all the people?"

Eunice stuck her face into the vault to look for them, pulled it out again. "I don't know!" she wailed.

"Here's the church and here's the steeple," he said, reassembling them. "Open the doors . . . There's all the people!" And there they were, filling the vault, pink and wiggling. The church flew apart, and they both sat back, exhausted.

She washed his wound. Then she fixed him the only food he could eat: Carnation milk, with egg, vanilla and a little sugar beaten into it.

Someone knocked. The door opened a chink. "I'm sorry," her friend said. "I thought you might like some music to pass the time." She brought in a small record player, then a stack of records. "Want me to put anything on for you?"

"Not right now," Eunice said.

"I'm sorry," her friend said again. Eunice tended to have that effect on people. Imperious, reporters called her. Not one to suffer fools. She waited until her friend left before going through the records, which included some of Eunice's own, with unfamiliar covers—bootlegs, probably, she thought with a twinge of annoyance. She lay back on top of the covers and fell asleep.

When she woke up, her father was squatting by the turntable, flipping through the records. He seemed to have settled more firmly on the ground. She noticed that she could see right through the hole in his stomach. "Nina Simone," said her father without turning around. "Is that what they call you now?"

As a girl she had been baptized and rebaptized. Every time, her name soaked in deeper. This name belonged to the town, which had paid for her piano lessons. Her future as a concert pianist was a municipal project. But her future, in the form of the Curtis Institute of Music, had turned her down. Nobody mentioned until considerably later that this might be because she was poor and black and female. She took a job playing in a bar in Atlantic City. So as not to shame her town, she performed under a different name, a name she made up. She would close her eyes while she played, pretending to be someone else. Between sets, she would sit at the bar in a long gown and drink a glass of milk.

Eventually, the person she pretended to be became the person she was.

Without moving his feet, her dead father turned. His fingers were laced together, pointers steepling. He raised his eyebrows at Eunice.

"Here's the church and here's the steeple," Eunice recited. "Open the doors—"

But this time he folded his hands out flat to show her the floor of her mother's church. The fingers wiggling in a line down the center aisle were the Saints rising up out of their pews, eyeballing God above, throwing up their hands to show their blue dresses blackening under the arms. When Eunice played the organ, grown women had dropped to their knees in the aisle, neck flesh wobbling and shining with sweat, and started gibbering, ululating, speaking in tongues.

He replaited his fingers in a different way and showed her again: the church, the steeple. She nodded. He waited. "Okay, Dad," she sighed. "'Here's the church and here's the steeple, open the doors, where's all the people.'"

He spread his hands flat again. Somehow, he drew her attention to four fingers that were laid out in the middle of the floor, you might say head to toe. They were very still.

Yes, that was what had made her so angry, that time. Those four girls killed in church, in Birmingham, Alabama. They had been changing into their choir robes when the bomb went off. The youngest was eleven. What were their names?

"Aunt Sarah," said her father, folding down one finger, "Siffronia, Sweet Thing," folding down three more, "and Peaches," folding down all the rest of them.

She looked at him weirdly. "No," she said. "That's from a song I wrote. It's called Four Women."

"Why is your father like a record?" he said.

"I don't know."

"He's black, groovy, and has a hole right through the middle." Laughing, he did his disappearing trick again.

On the floor where he had stood there was a puddle. She touched it. It was not liquid. She pried it off the floor with her fingernails. It was light, flat, superficially knobbly, cloudy, translucent, with a blush to it, and it had a perfect round hole through the center of it.

She laid it on the record player and lowered the needle cautiously. The diamond nicked the top of a blister and the speaker cried out. The needle skidded and fishtailed, then steadied. There was a stuttering, seething sound, like rain or applause. Then something came through. She recognized the tune: "The Darktown Strutters' Ball." Her father had taught her to play it with him—the way he had learned it, using only the black keys. When they heard her mother coming up the stairs, they would switch to "God Be With You 'Til We Meet Again." Her mother did not approve of worldly music. For her mother, and the congregation, she played hymns. But for herself, and her teacher Miz Mazzy? *The Well-Tempered Clavier.*

She had wanted to be a concert pianist and perform at Carnegie Hall. Instead she had sung protest songs on a stage held up by coffins. That part sounds like a dream or the setup of a joke, but it is a fact. The local black funeral parlor had provided them. That was when the movement was still moving.

Later the coffins had proved useful in more conventional ways.

It was not "The Darktown Strutters' Ball" after all, though it was hard to understand how she could have been so mistaken. It was Bach's Prelude and Fugue in F# Minor.

"Once more, Eunice. From the beginning," said the voice of Miz Mazzy.

"Another goddam bootleg," said Eunice.

––––––––––

On the third day she put the can of milk under her pillow like a charm to bring true dreams of love, but then she lay awake and watched the light drag itself across the ceiling. A fly spoiled the silence. She could see her sour face in the mirror. Well, why shouldn't she be sour? Unlike her mother, she did not feel obliged to approve of God's creation. Eunice Waymon had found the world wanting. It wanted, among other things, a mother who loved her daughter as much as she loved God. Also, an honest record company. A good manager, a kind, loving husband. She had allowed various men to apply themselves to her. They had used a little elbow grease, then slipped away. Many things had slipped away: Lorraine, Malcolm, Dr. King, the hopes of the movement.

One day her father, too, failed her: He told a lie. What the lie was is not important. Not too long after that, he started to die. He grew thinner and thinner, and he asked for Eunice, but she did not come.

She closed her eyes and tried to call up a worn but still comforting image: Eunice Waymon at Carnegie Hall, smoothing her gown under her as she sat down, raising her wrists. But the hall kept changing, the walls turning pink, greasy, and when she brought her fingers down on the keys in a thunderous chord, the walls opened like hands, and she had the feeling that something terrible was going to happen.

That fly was buzzing around her head again. She flapped her hand, hit something and opened her eyes. Her father was sitting on the bed beside her. The buzzing was coming from the hole in his side. She craned her neck and peered into the hole. Then her father clamped his hand on the back of her neck and pulled her toward him.

He had the smell he had had when he was sick, a sweetish funk which had become so confused in her mind with the thick rich smell of Carnation that she could not now taste evaporated milk without the feeling that she was taking her own father into her mouth. As her face neared the crimped, inflamed rim of the hole, she reared back, but he was too strong. The hole, which had seemed no bigger than a mouth, sealed lightly around her face, and now she realized what she was seeing and she forgot to fight.

Inside her father was a dark barroom with a rudimentary stage at one end. A small audience lounged in the shadows, their faces unclear, though some of them looked familiar. There were four black girls onstage. They were so young they still had chubby cheeks and they were wearing choir robes open over matching flowered panties and undershirts like they had nobody to tell them how to make themselves decent. The one on drums was staring intently past the audience as if she saw something far away coming slowly toward her and was trying to make out what it was. She was drumming steady and fast, bouncing tensely on her skinny flanks, undershirt sweat-glued to her chest, though it revealed nothing you couldn't see on a twelve-year-old boy. The little girl on keyboards had her eyes cast up to the rafters. The biggest girl was playing the bass and she was looking right at Eunice with a scowl that reminded her of Lucille when she decided to play mother to the younger kids. The girl on guitar was switching her scrawny behind. Her guitar, carnation-red with long white scars in the varnish, had a peeling sticker on it that seemed to say *The Simones*. It was much too big for her, but now she was jumping up and down as if it were no burden at all.

Was it a guitar? All the instruments reminded her of other things entirely: shovels, pickaxes, crowbars, wheelbarrows. Made noises like them too: clank, crash, screech. And the girls were not singing but bawling, squalling, ballyhooing. Their voices echoed strangely. Though it looked tiny, the room had the dynamics of a concert hall. "Mississippi *Goddam*," the guitarist snarled, and Eunice sucked in her breath and sat back. They were playing her song. But their version was ugly. It didn't have a trace of jaunty. If it had hope, it was the last-ditch hope of a hog getting its throat cut and keeping right on screaming through the slit. It was too fast and off-key and you could hardly make out a word, but it was the gun she had been trying to make.

"Ever seen a little girl look so determined?" her father said. "I have." He groped around in the hole in his side and brought out a can opener. He nipped two triangular holes in the can of milk and drank. Then he passed it to her. "I think they're going places. But they need some new songs and a real lead singer." For a moment she had the feeling that he was something else altogether, something that only cropped up to her as a father, but went way back, making some surprising turns as it did so.

She took a sip of milk. Then she went through the hole in her father's side. She was going on.

ALICE HOFFMAN

The Witch of Truro

Alice Hoffman has published over fifteen novels, two books of short fiction, and six books for children. Her writing is notable for its use of fairy tales and magic, and its generous, dreamlike sensibility. Her most recent books include Green Angel, *a novel for teens, the* New York Times *bestselling novels* The River King *and* Blue Diary, *and the suite of stories,* Blackbird House, *from which this story is taken. Hoffman is married, lives outside Boston, and is the mother of two sons.*

Hoffman's delicately fantastical story "The Witch of Truro" was first published in The Kenyon Review.

—K.L. & G.G.

1801

Witches take their names from places, for places are what give them their strength. The place need not be beautiful, or habitable, or even green. Sand and salt, so much the better. Scrub pine, plumberry and brambles, better still. From every bitter thing, after all, something hardy will surely grow. From every difficulty, the seed that's sown is that much stronger. Ruin is the milk all witches must drink; it's the lesson they learn and the diet they're fed upon. Ruth Declan lived on a bluff that was called Blackbird's Hill, and so she was called Ruth Blackbird Hill, a fitting name, as her hair was black and she was so light-footed she could disappear right past a man and he wouldn't see anything, he'd just feel a rush of wind and pick up the scent of something reminiscent of orchards and the faint green odor of milk.

Ruth kept cows, half a dozen, but they gave so much into their buckets she might have had twenty. She took her cows for walks, as though they were pets, along the sand-rutted King's Highway, down to the bay where they grazed on marsh grass. Ruth Blackbird Hill called her cows her babies and hugged them to her breast; she patted their heads and fed them sugar from the palm of her hand, and that may have been why their milk was so sweet. People said Ruth Blackbird Hill sang to her cows at night, and that whoever bought milk from her would surely be bewitched. Not that anyone believed in such things anymore. All the same, when Ruth came into town, the old women tied bits of hemp into witchknots on their sleeves for protection. The old men looked to see if she was wearing red shoes, always the mark of a witch. Ruth avoided these people; she didn't care what they thought. She would have happily stayed on Blackbird Hill and never come down, but two things happened: first came smallpox, which took her father and her mother, no matter how much sassafras tea they were given, and how tenderly Ruth cared for them. Then came the fire, which took the house and the land.

On the night of the fire, Ruth Blackbird Hill stood in the grass and screamed. People could hear her in Wellfleet and in Eastham and far out to sea. She watched the pear and the apple and the peach trees burning. She watched the grass turn red as blood. She had risked her life to save her cows, running into the smoky barn, and now they gathered round her, lowing, leaking milk, panicked. It was not enough that she should lose her mother and her father, one after another, now she had lost Blackbird Hill, and with it she had lost herself. The fire raged for two days until a heavy rain began to fall. People in town said that Ruth killed a toad and nailed it to a hickory tree, knowing that rain would follow, but it was too late. The hill was burned to cinders; it was indeed a blackbird's hill, black as night, black as the look in Ruth's eyes, black as the future that was assuredly hers.

Ruth sat on the hillside until her hair was completely knotted and her skin was the color of the gray sky up above. She might have stayed there forever, but after some time went by, her cows began to cry. They were weak with hunger, they were her babies still, and so Ruth took them into town. One day, people looked out their windows and a blackbird seemed to swoop by, followed by a herd of skinny milkcows that had all turned to pitch in the fire. Ruth Blackbird Hill made herself a camp right on the beach; she slept there with no shelter, no matter the weather. The only food she ate was what she dug up in the shallows: clams and whelks. She may have drunk the green, thin milk her cows gave, though it was still tinged with cinders. She may have bewitched herself to protect herself from any more pain. Perhaps that was the reason she could sleep in the heat or the rain; why it was said she could drink saltwater.

Anyone would have guessed the six cows would have bolted for someone else's farmland and a field of green grass, but they stayed where they were, on the beach, beside Ruth. People in town said you could hear them crying at night; it got so bad the fish were frightened out of the bay, and the whelks disappeared, and the oysters buried themselves so deeply they couldn't be found.

It was May, the time of year when the men were at sea. Perhaps there might have been a different decision made if the men had been home from the Great Banks and the Middle Banks, where their sights were set on mackerel and cod. Perhaps Ruth would have been run out of town. As it was, Susan Crosby and Easter West devised a plan of their own. They won Ruth Blackbird Hill over slowly, with plates of oatcakes and kettles of tea. They took their time, the way they might have with a fox or a dove, any creature that might be easily startled. They sat on a log of driftwood and told Ruth that sorrow was what this world was made of, but that it was her world still. At first she would not look at them, yet they could tell she was listening. She was a young woman, a girl really, nineteen at most, although her hands looked as hard as an old woman's, with ropes of veins that announced her hardships.

Susan and Easter brought Ruth over to Lysander Wynn's farm, where he'd built a blacksmithing shed. It took half the morning to walk there, with the cows stopping to graze by the road, dawdling until Ruth coaxed them on. It was a bright blue day and the women from town felt giddy now that they'd made a firm decision to guide someone else's fate, what their husbands might call interference had they but known. As for Ruth, she still had a line of black cinders under her fingernails. There was eelgrass threaded through her hair. She had the notion that these two women, Susan and Easter, known for their good works and their kindly attitudes, were about to sell her. She simply couldn't see any other reason for them to be walking along with her, swatting the cows on the rear to speed them on, waving away the flies. The awful thing was that Ruth wasn't completely opposed to being sold. She didn't want to think. She didn't want to ask questions. She didn't even want to speak.

They reached the farm that Lysander had bought from the Hadley family. He'd purchased the property mainly because it was the one place in the area from which there was no view of the sea, for that was exactly what he wanted. The farm was only a mile from the closest shore, but it sat in a hollow, with tall oaks and scrub pine and a field of sweet peas and brambles nearby. As a younger man, Lysander had been a sailor, he'd gone out with the neighbors to the Great Banks, and it was there he'd had his accident. A storm had come up suddenly, and the sloop had tilted madly, throwing Lysander into the sea. It was so cold he had no time to think, save for a fleeting thought of Jonah, of how a man could be saved when he least expected it, in ways he could have never imagined.

He wondered if perhaps the other men on board, Joseph Hansen and Edward West, had had the foresight to throw him a side of salt pork for him to lean on, for just when he expected to drown, something solid was suddenly beneath him. Something hard and cold as ice. Something made of scales rather than flesh or water or wood; a creature who certainly was not intent on Lysander's salvation. The fish to whose back he clung was a halibut, a huge one, two hundred, maybe three hundred pounds, Edward West later said. Lysander rode the halibut like he rode his horse, Domino, until he was bucked off. All at once his strength was renewed by his panic; he started swimming, harder than he ever had before. Lysander was almost to the boat when he felt it, the slash of the thing against him, and the water turned red right away. He was only twenty at the time, too young to have this happen. Dead or alive, either would have been better than what had befallen him. He wished he had drowned that day, because when he was hauled into the boat, they had to finish the job and cut off the leg at the thigh, then cauterize the wound with gunpowder and whiskey.

Lysander had some money saved, and the other men in town contributed the rest, and the farm was bought soon after. The shed was built in a single afternoon, and the anvil brought down from Boston. Luckily, Lysander had the blacksmith's trade in his family, on his father's side, so it came naturally to him. The hotter the work was, the better he liked it. He could stick his hand into the flame fueled by the bellow and not feel a thing. But let it rain, even a fleeting drizzle, and he would start to shiver. He ignored the pond behind the house entirely, though there were catfish there that were said to be delectable. Fishing was for other men. Water was for fools. As for women, they were a dream he didn't bother with. In his estimation, the future was no farther away than the darkness of evening; it consisted of nothing more than a sprinkling of stars in the sky.

Lysander used a crutch made of applewood that bent when he leaned upon it, but was surprisingly strong when the need arose. He had hit a prowling skunk on the head with the crutch and knocked it unconscious. He had dug through a mat of moss for a wild orchid that smelled like fire when he held it up to his face. He slept with the crutch by his side in bed, afraid to be without it. He liked to walk in the woods, and sometimes he imagined he would be better off if he just lay down between the logs and the moss and stayed there, forevermore. Then someone would need their horse shod; they'd come up the road and ring the bell hung on the wall of the shed, and Lysander would have to scramble back from the woods. But he thought about remaining where he was, hidden, unmoving; he imagined it more often than anyone might have guessed. Blackbirds would light upon his shoulders, crickets would crawl into his pockets, fox would lie down beside him and never even notice he was there.

He was in the woods on the day they brought Ruth Blackbird Hill and her cows to the farm. Sometimes when he was very quiet Lysander thought he saw another man in the trees. He thought it might be the sailor who'd built the house, the widow Hadley's husband, who'd been lost at sea. Or perhaps it was himself, weaving in and out of the shadows, the man he might have been.

Susan Crosby and Easter West explained the situation, the parents lost, the house and meadows burned down, the way Ruth was living on the beach, unprotected, unable to support herself, even to eat. In exchange for living in Lysander's house, she would cook and clean for him. Ruth kept her back to them as they discussed her fate; she patted one of her cows, a favorite of hers she called Missy. Lysander Wynn was just as bitter as Ruth Blackbird Hill was. He was certain the women from town wouldn't have brought Ruth to the farm if he'd been a whole man, if he'd been able to get up the stairs to the attic where they suggested Ruth sleep. He was about to say no, he was more than willing to get back to work in the fires of his shop, when he noticed that Ruth was wearing red boots. They were made of old leather, mud-caked, but all the same, Lysander had never seen shoes that color, and he felt touched in some way. He thought about the color of fire. He thought about flames. He thought he would never be hot enough to get the chill out of his body or the water out of his soul.

"Just as long as she never cooks fish," he heard himself say.

Ruth Blackbird Hill laughed at that. "What makes you think I cook at all?"

Ruth took the cows into the field of sweet peas. Lysander's horse, Domino, rolled his eyes and ran to the far end of the meadow, spooked. But the cows paid no attention to him whatsoever, they just huddled around Ruth Blackbird Hill and calmly began to eat wild weeds and grass. What Lysander had agreed to didn't sink in until Susan Crosby and Easter West left to go back to town. "Hasn't this woman any belongings?" Lysander had called after them. "Not a thing," they replied. "The cows that follow her and the shoes on her feet."

Well, a shoe was the one thing Lysander might have offered. He had several old boots thrown into a cabinet, useless when it came to his missing right foot. He put out some old clothes and some quilts at the foot of the stairs leading to the attic. He'd meant to finish the attic, turn the space into decent rooms, but he'd had to crawl up the twisting staircase to check on the rafters, and that was enough humiliation to last him for a very long time. Anyway, the space was good enough for someone used to sleeping on the beach. When Ruth didn't come in to start supper, Lysander made himself some johnnycake, half-cooked, but decent enough, along with a plate of turnips; he left half of what he'd fixed on the stair as well, though he had his suspicions that Ruth might not eat. She might just starve herself sitting out in that field. She might take flight and he'd find nothing when he woke, except for the lonely cows mooing sorrowfully.

As it turned out, Ruth was there in the morning. She'd eaten the food he'd left out for her and was already milking the cows when Lysander went out to work on a metal harness for Easter West's uncle, Karl. Those red shoes peeked out from beneath Ruth's black skirt. She was singing to the cows and they were waiting in line, patiently. The horse, Domino, had come closer and Ruth Blackbird Hill opened her palm and gave him a lick of sugar.

In the afternoon Lysander saw her looking in the window of the shed. The fire was hot and he was sweating. He wanted to sweat out every bit of cold ocean water. He always built the fire hotter than advisable. He needed it that way. Sometimes he got a stomachache, and when he vomited, he spit out the halibut's teeth. Those teeth had gone right through him, it seemed. He could feel them, cold, silvery things.

He must have looked frightening as he forged the metal harness, covered with soot, hot as the devil, because Ruth Blackbird Hill ran away, and she didn't come to fetch the dinner he placed on the stair—though the food was better than the night before, cornbread with wild onions this time, and greens poured over with gravy. All the same, the following morning, the plate was clean and resting on the table. Every morsel had been eaten.

Ruth Blackbird Hill didn't cook and she didn't clean, but she kept on watching him through the window that was made out of bumpy glass. Lysander didn't look up, didn't let on that he knew she was staring, and then one day she was standing in the doorway to the shed. She was wearing a pair of his old britches and a white shirt, but he could see through the smoke that she had on those red shoes.

"How did you lose your leg?" Ruth asked.

He had expected nearly anything but that question. It was rude; no one asked things like that.

"A fish bit it off," he said.

Ruth laughed and said, "No."

He could feel the heat from the iron he was working on in his hands, his arms, his head.

"You don't believe me?" He showed her the chain he wore around his neck, strung with halibut teeth. "I coughed these up one by one."

"No," Ruth said again, but her voice was quieter, like she was thinking it over. She walked right up to him and he felt something inside him quicken. He had absolutely no idea of what she might do.

Ruth Blackbird Hill put her left hand in the fire, and she would have kept it there if he hadn't grabbed her arm and pulled her back.

"See?" she said to him. Her skin felt cool and she smelled like grass. "There are things I'm afraid of, too."

People in town forgot about Ruth; they didn't think about how she was living out at the farm any more than they remembered how she'd been camped on the beach for weeks without anyone offering her help until Susan and Easter could no longer tolerate her situation. Those two women probably should have minded their own business as well, but they were too kindhearted for that, and too smart to ever tell their husbands what part they had played in Ruth Blackbird Hill living at Lysander's farm. In truth, they had nearly forgotten about her themselves. Then one day Easter

West found a pail of milk at her back door. As it turned out Susan Crosby discovered the very same thing on her porch—cool, green milk that tasted so sweet, so very filling, that after a single cup a person wouldn't want another drop to drink all day. Susan chose to go about her business, but Easter was a more curious individual. One night, Easter had dreamed of blackbirds, and of her husband, who was out in the Middle Banks fishing for mackerel. When she woke she had a terrible thirst for fresh milk. She went out to the farm that day, just to have a look around.

There was Ruth in the field, riding that old horse Domino, teaching him to jump over a barrel while the cows gazed on, disinterested. When she saw Easter, Ruth left the horse and came to meet her at the gate. That past night, Ruth herself had dreamed of tea, and of needles and thread set to work, and of a woman who was raising three sons alone while her husband was off to sea. She had been expecting Easter, and had a pail of milk waiting under the shade of an oak tree. The milk was greener than ever, and sweeter than ever too; Easter West drank two tin cupfuls before she realized that Ruth Blackbird Hill was crying.

It was near the end of summer. Everything was blooming and fresh, but it wouldn't last long.

"What is it?" Easter said. "Does he make you work too hard? Is he cruel?"

Ruth shook her head. "It's just that I'll never get what I want. It's not possible."

"What is it you want?"

There was the scent of cows, and of hay, and of smoke from the blacksmith's shop. Ruth had been swimming in the pond behind the house earlier in the day and her hair was shiny; she smelled like water and her skin was cool even in the heat of the day.

"It doesn't matter. Whenever I want something, I don't get it. No matter what it might be. That's the story of my life."

When Easter was leaving, Lysander Wynn came out of his shop. He was leaning on his crutch. He wanted something, too. He wasn't yet thirty, and his work made him strong in his arms and his back, but he felt weak deep inside, bitten by something painful and sharp.

"What did she tell you?" he asked Easter West.

"She's afraid she won't get what she wants," Easter said.

Lysander thought this over while he finished up working. He thought about it while he made supper, a corn and tomato stew. When he left Ruth's dinner on the stair he left a note as well. *I'll get you anything you want.*

That night, Lysander dreamed he wouldn't be able to give Ruth what she asked for, despite his promise. She would want gold, of which he had none. She would want to live in London, on the other side of the ocean. She would want another man, one with two legs who didn't spit out halibut teeth, who didn't fear rain and pondwater. But in the morning, he found a note by the anvil in his shed. What she seemed to want was entirely different from anything he had imagined. *Bring me a tree that has pears the color of blood. The same exact color as my shoes.*

The next day, Lysander Wynn hitched up his horse to a wagon and left on the King's Highway. He went early, while the cows were still sleeping in the field, while the blackbirds were quiet and the fox were still running across the sandy ruts in the road. Ruth knew he was gone when she woke because there was no smoke spiraling from the chimney in the shed; when Edward Hastings came to get his horse shod, no one answered his call. Ruth Blackbird Hill took care of the cows, then she went into the shed herself. She put her hand into the ashes—they were still hot, embers continuing to burn from the day before. She thought about red grass and burning trees and her parents calling out for her to save them. She kept her hand there, unmoving, until she couldn't stand the pain anymore.

He was gone for two weeks, and he never said exactly where he'd been. He admitted only that he'd been through Providence and on into Connecticut. What he didn't say was that he would have gone farther still if it had been necessary. He had no time frame in mind of when he might return. He would have kept on even if snow had begun to fall, if the orchards had turned so white it would have been impossible to tell an apple tree from a plum, a grapevine from a trellis of wisteria.

Lysander planted the pear tree right in front of the house. While he was working, Ruth brought him a cold glass of milk that made him feel like weeping. She showed him her burned hand, then she took off her shoes and stood barefoot in the grass. He hoped what he'd been told in Connecticut was true. The last farmer he'd gone to was experienced with fruit trees, and his orchard was legendary. When Lysander had wanted a guarantee, the old farmer had told him that often what you grew turned out to be what you had wanted all along. He said there was a fine line between crimson and scarlet, and that a person simply had to wait to see what appeared. Ruth wouldn't know until the following fall whether or not the pears would be red, nearly a full year, but she was hopeful that by that time, she wouldn't care.

PETER STRAUB

Lapland, or Film Noir

Peter Straub, represented elsewhere in this anthology with "Mr. Aickman's Air Rifle," here shows his versatility with a very different sort of tale.
"Lapland, or Film Noir" was originally published in Conjunctions 42: Cinema Lingua: Writers Respond to Film.

—E.D., K.L. & G.G.

A General Introduction

Our initial purpose is to discuss the effect, the *feeling tone* of headlights reflected on wet urban streets in Lapland, Florida. This is central to our discourse, the feeling tone of those reflections. By implication, then, rain; cars veering at great speed around sharp corners; upholstered pistols, brandished; desperate men; a sick, thrilled sense of impendingness. The immediate historical context plays a central role, as does a profound national sense of the shameful, the squalid, matters never acknowledged in the golden but streaky Florida light. You'd need a spotlight and a truncheon to beat it out of these people. Florida, it will be remembered, tends toward the hot, the dark, the needy, the rotting, the "sultry." The stunted and unnatural. Lapland, i.e., someone's (theoretically) warm yet not really comfortable, in fact impossibly dispossessing . . .

Steam rises through the grates.

We are in . . . .

. . . . gulf coast. . . . .

. . . . sempiternal darkness. . . . .

. . . . without surcease, without hope for Silky's. . . . .

In Lapland, all the women are always awake. Even your *mother* lies awake all the night through, drawing essential feminine nourishment from the bottomless communal well. Headlights shine in long streaks on the rain-soaked streets. Just outside the city limits, a gas station attendant named Bud Forrester rolls on his side in bed, thinking of a woman named Carole Chandler. Carole Chandler is his boss's wife, and she has no conscience whatsoever. Bud does possess a conscience, rudimentary though it is. He wishes he could amputate it, without pain, like a sixth finger no thicker around than a twig. In Bud Forrester's past lies a tremendous crime for which his simple duties at the gas station represent a conscious and ongoing penance.

During the commission of the crime, Frank Bigelow took two rounds in the gut, and he will never again void his bowels without whimpering, cursing, sweating. He walks with a limp, Frank. He isn't the kind of guy who can accept stuff like the whimpering, the sweating, the limping with every step of his beautifully shod feet. And when everything depended on where the money was, the money was lifting and blowing all across the tarmac, jittering through the air, like leaves, falling earthward in zigzags, like leaves. Bud Forrester always had a little tingle of a premonition that it was going to end this way. The other guys, they didn't want to hear about it. Bradford Galt and Tom Jardine, Bigelow had them hypnotized, *in thrall.* If Bud had tried to tell them about his little tingle, Galt and Jardine would have taped his mouth shut, bound his arms and legs, and locked him in a closet. That's the way these boys operate — on only a couple of very simple levels.

Frank Bigelow, though, is another matter. One night, over a lamplit table littered with charts and maps, he had observed a certain shine in the whites of Bud's eyes, and immediately he had known of his underling's traitorous misgivings.

One more detail, essential to the coils of the plot: Frank Bigelow also thinks endlessly and without. . . . . . . upon Carole Chandler. These thoughts, alas, have darkened since he wound up impotent. Deep in his heart what he'd like to do is sic Tom Jardine on Carole; brutal, stupid Jardine is hung like a stallion (off-camera, the guy is always inventing excuses for showing off his tool) and while Tom makes Carole Chandler beg for more like the bitch she is, Frank would like to be watching through a kind of peephole arrangement. Trouble is, after that he would have to murder Tom Jardine, and Tom is one of his main guys, he's like one of the family, so that's out.

Every film noir has one impossible plot convenience, in this instance: despite his frustrated passion for wicked Carole Chandler, Frank Bigelow has no idea that Bud Forrester is employed at her husband's Shell station, because he sees her only at the Black Swan, the gambling club of which he is part-owner with Nicky Drake, a smooth, smooth operator. In Lapland, one always finds gambling clubs; also, drunken or corrupt night watchmen; a negligée; a ditch; a running man; a number of raincoats and hats; a man named "Johnny"; a man named "Doc," sometimes varied to "Dad"; an alcoholic; a penthouse; a beach shack; a tavern full of dumbbells; an armored car; a racetrack; a. . . . . ; a shadowy staircase. These elements commonly participate in and enhance the effect of headlights reflected on wet urban streets.

The Women of Lapland

When young, remarkably beautiful. When aged, negligible. This disparity passes without notice because few of the women of Lapland outlive their youth. They often hiss when they speak, or exhibit some other charming speech defect. Their reflections can be seen in rearview mirrors, the windows of apartments at night, the surfaces of slick wooden bars, the surfaces of lakes and pools, in the eyes of dead men. Carole Chandler likes the look of Bud Forrester, she "fancies" the "cut of his jib," but he strikes her as strangely inert, withdrawn, passive. Of course Carole takes these qualities both at face value and as a personal challenge. Nicky Drake wouldn't fuck this dame for, oh, a hundred million bucks, and his partner's obsession with her makes him. . . . . When Carole slinks into the Black Swan, handsome Nicky looks away and frowns in disgust.

Having the life expectancy of mayflies, these women dress like dragonflies, for like cigarette smoking and cocktail drinking the wearing of dragonfly-attire is a means of slowing time. The most gifted women in Lapland live in virtual dog years, or on a seven to one ratio. Time is astonishingly relative for everyone in Lapland. That it is especially so for the women allows them a tremendous advantage. They can outthink any man who wanders into their crosshairs because they have a great deal more time to do their thinking in.

In Lapland, no woman ever speaks to another woman, there'd be no point in wasting valuable time like that. What would they talk about, their feelings? They already understand everything they have to know about their feelings. In Lapland, no woman ever speaks to a child, for they are all barren, although some may now and again pretend to be pregnant. It follows that there are no children in Lapland. However, in a location error that went largely unnoticed, Frank Bigelow once drove past an elementary school. In Lapland, women speak only to men, and these interchanges are deeply codified. The soundtrack (see below) becomes especially intrusive at such moments. It is understood that the woman is motivated by a private scheme, of which the man is entirely ignorant, though he may be suspicious, and it's always better, more dramatic, if he is.

Lapland women all have at least two names, the old one that got used up, and the new one, which gets a little more tarnished every day. Carole Chandler used to be Dorothy Lyons, back when she lived in Center City and engineered the moral ruin and financial collapse of Nicky Drake's best friend, Rip Murdock, the owner of the Orchid Club, a gambling establishment with a private membership.

Rip, a dandy at the time, used to. . . . . , and Carol/Dorothy, then a cocktail waitress at his club, ... his beach shack. . . . . a moue. . . . . a stranger with a gun. . . . . bloody rags. . . . . off the cliff. . . . . arched an eyebrow.

Once in her life, every woman in Lapland gazes through lowered eyelids at a man like Nicky, or Frank, or Rip, or even Doc/Dad (but never at a man like Bud), and says, "You and me, we're the same—a no-good piece of trash." In every case, this declaration is meant as, and is taken to be, a compliment.

Social Criticism

In Lapland, the spectator observes a world characterized by deliberate dislocations, complex and indirect narratives, flawed protagonists, ambiguous motives and resolutions, a fascination with death. . . . .

.... "the blood in her hair, the blood on the floor, the blood in her hair". .... and an atmosphere of nightmare.

When Rusty Fontaine blew into town, he took a room at the Mandarin hotel and started spreading his money around. He was so successful at exploiting middle-class greed and veniality that in six months every square in Lapland owed him a fortune. To get out of debt, a consortium of the squares lured a banker, Chalmers Vermilyea, into an abandoned warehouse and, assisted by Rusty's luscious and treacherous female sidekick, Marie Gardner, persuaded him to embezzle. ....
...............................sprinkled gasoline over the corpse. ...
...........................off the cliff.

To the extent that Lapland is a style and not a genre, the vertiginous camera angles, broken shadows, neon-lit interiors, hairpin staircases, extreme high-angle long shots, graphics specific to entrapment, represent a radically disenchanted vision of postwar American life and values.

Psychopaths

Because paranoia is always justified in Lapland, psychopathology becomes an adaptive measure. Johnny O'Clock runs a gambling casino, the Velvet Deuce. He knew Bud Forrester in the war, when they fought across France, killing hundreds of Krauts in one bombed-out village after another. Forrester was his sergeant, and he always respected the man. When one day O'Clock stops for gas at a Shell station on the edge of town, he recognizes his old friend in the station attendant and, acting on impulse, offers him a job in the casino. Forrester accepts, thinking that he might escape his obsession with Carole Chandler. Unknown to Forrester, Johnny O'-Clock was unable to stop killing after returning to civilian life and now, under the cover of his job at the Velvet Deuce, hires himself out as a contract killer. He intends to recruit his old sergeant into. ....
.................velvet gloves, his trademark. ....
....
.........................Frank Bigelow. ....
...steam rising through the grates. ....
.... to the beach shack. ....
with the alcoholic security guard in a stupor. ....
...........................aflame, the Dodge. ....
......two corpses in the back seat and six thousand dollars in cash.

World War II, it must be remembered, serves as the unspoken background for these films and defines their emotional context. Eight percent of adult males in Lapland served as snipers in the war, and a good twelve percent have metal plates in their heads. These men drink too much and mutter to themselves. Because it gives them red-rimmed headaches, they detest big-band jazz, which they refer to as "that monkey music." They are prone to blackouts and spells of amnesia. They often marry blind women and/or nymphomaniacs. Unlike them, the former snipers display no visible emotion of any kind. The men with plates in their heads are completely devoted to the ex-snipers, who reward their loyalty with. .... with onions.

Brace Bannister threw an old woman down the stairs. For pleasure, Johnny O'-Clock shot Nelle Marchetti, a prostitute, in the head, and got clean away with it. Norman Clyde existed entirely in flashbacks. Old Man Tierney poisoned a girl visiting from California and kept her severed hand in his pocket. Carole Chandler's husband, Smokey Chandler, molests small boys on "business trips" to Center City. Nicky Drake has assigned a number to everyone in the world. Carter Carpenter, the Vice Mayor of Lapland, sleeps on a mattress stuffed with human hair.

Private Eyes

Most noncriminal adult males in Lapland, apart from the doomed squares, are either policemen or private eyes. It is the job of the policemen to accept bribes and arrest the innocent. It is the job of the private investigators to discover bodies, to be interrogated, to drink from the bottle, to wear trench coats, to smoke all the time, to rebuff sexual invitations from females with charming lisps and hair that hangs, fetchingly, over one eye. The private eyes distrust authority, even their own. Nick Cochran is a rich private eye, and Eddie Willis, Mike Lane, and Tony Burke struggle to make the rent on their ugly little offices, where they sleep on. . . . . .Frank Bigelow hired Eddie Willis to find Bud Forrester, but Johnny O'Clock followed Eddie into an alley behind the Black Swan and shot him dead. In Nick Cochran's penthouse, Nicky Drake persuaded Rusty Fontaine to. . . . . , but Marie Gardner, who was hiding on the. . . . . , overheard and. . . . . with Chalmers Vermilyea. Esther Vermilyea (no relation), made an anonymous call to Nick Cochran and. . . . .

Two corpses in the back seat and a man with a plate in his head. . . . . screaming and sobbing in the dark and rainy street.

Six thousand dollars blew away in the wind, and Tom Jardine. . . . . for the first time since the landing at Anzio. Frank Bigelow could protect him no longer. The armored car left the racetrack. The wrinkled old criminal mastermind known as Dad, whose. . . . . had never left him, led Carole Chandler up the shadowy staircase and. . . . . with a new negligée from the Smart Shoppe.

The Role of Alan Ladd

Alan Ladd attracts the light.

The Other Role of Alan Ladd

He hovers at the edge of the screen, reminding you that you are, after all, in Lapland, and in some sense always will be. When he smiles, his hair gleams. The smile of Alan Ladd is both tough and wounded, an effect akin to that of headlights reflected on a dark, rain-wet street in downtown Lapland, his turf, his home territory. A sick, shameful nostalgia leaks from every frame, and it is abetted, magnified, amplified by the swooning strings on the sound track. The sound track clings to you like grease. You carry it with you out of the theater, and it swells between the parked cars baking in the sunlight, indistinguishable from the sounds in your head.

Alan Ladd Considered as Extension of the Sound Track

His name is. . . . ., says Alan Ladd, whose name is Ed Adams, or Johnny Morrison. *That man's name is*. . . . . *He is known as Slim Dundee and Johnny O'Clock, also*. . . . . *and*. . . . . *His names surround him like a cloud of flies. At the center of his names, he*. . . . . *and*. . . . . A speaking shadow rises from between the parked cars, and you wish for it to follow you home.

. . . ., Alan says in musical italics, coming along steadily behind. Sirens flare. A man with a gun flees into a dark, sunlit alley. The hot white stripes of headlights reflected on rainy asphalt shine and shine and shine on the street. Beneath a car farther down the block an oily shadow moves, and the name of that shadow is. . . . .

Forget him, Alan says. *Forget IT.* Underneath his warm deep grainy voice, that of a tender and exhausted god, a hundred stringed instruments swoop and twirl, following its music. *Do it for my sake. If not for*. . . . . . . *sake, for mine. I know*. . . . . . . *can hear me, kid. Kiddo. Little guy.*

I always liked. . . . . ., *did you know that?*

And at night, when. . . . . lie in the bottom bunk with your face to the onyx window, only. . . . . awake in all the house, a streak of blond hair shines in the corner of the window frame, the music stirs like the sound of death and heartbreak, and when his wounded face slips into view, he says, A *lot of this is gonna disappear forever. If you remember anything, remember that it's*. . . . .*fault*. . . . . *mber that. Little guy. If you can't remember that, remember me.*

THEODORA GOSS

What Her Mother Said

*Theodora Goss is represented elsewhere in this anthology with her poem
"The Changeling."*

  *"What Her Mother Said" was inspired by the story of Little Red Riding
Hood. It first appeared online at* The Journal of Mythic Arts.

—K.L. & G.G.

Go, my child, through the forest
To your grandmother's house, in a glade
Where poppies with red mouths grow.

In this basket is an egg laid
Three days ago,
The three days our Lord lay sleeping,
Unspotted, from a white hen.
In this basket is also a skein
Of wool, without stain,
Unspun. And a comb that the bees
Industriously filled
From the clover in the far pasture,
Unmown since the sun
Thawed it, last spring.

If you can take it without breaking
Anything, I will give you
This ring.

Stay, child, and I'll give you this cap
To wear, so the forest creatures whose eyes
Blink from the undergrowth will be aware
That my love protects you. The creatures
Lurking beneath the trees,
Weasels and stoats and foxes, and worse
Than these.

And child, you must be wise
In the forest.

When the wolf finds you, remember:
Be courteous, but evasive. No answer
Is better than a foolish one.

If you stray from the path, know
That I strayed also. It is no great matter,
So long as you mark the signs:
Where moss grows on bark, where a robin
Builds her nest. The sun
Sailing west.

But do not stop to gather
The hawthorn flowers, nor yet
The red berries which so resemble
Coral beads. They are poisonous.
And do not stop to listen
To the reeds.

He must not be there first,
At your grandmother's house.

And when your grandmother serves you,
With a silver spoon, on a dish
Like a porcelain moon, Wolf Soup,
Remember to say your grace
Before you eat.

And know that I am pleased
With you, my child.

But remember, when returning through the forest,
Kept warm against the night by a cloak
Of the wolf's pelt:
The hunter is also a wolf.

CONRAD WILLIAMS

The Owl

Conrad Williams is the award-winning author of the novels Head Injuries
and London Revenant. *He has also written two novellas, "Nearly People"
and "Game," and a collection of short stories,* Use Once, then Destroy. *He
is currently working on a new novel,* The Unblemished. *He divides his time
between the U.K. and France with his wife and their two sons.*
"The Owl" was originally published in Use Once, then Destroy.

—E.D.

Walk continuously around a tree with an owl in it: the owl will keep its
eye on you until it has wrenched off its own head.

He couldn't remember where the words had come from, but he
knew they were old and the last time he had heard them he could have
been little more than five years of age.

Luc, the estate agent, turned the stiff corpse of the barn owl over with his foot so
that they could all get a better view. "*Hibou,*" he said, and smiled, almost apologeti-
cally. "This place, they have lots of owl."

"One less, now," Ian said.

"Yes, well," Molly said, giving him a look. "No need to go stating the obvious, is
there? Poor thing. It's beautiful."

"It won't be for long," Ian said, and wished he'd kept his mouth shut. She was
right: the bird *was* beautiful. He had never been this close to an owl before, and was
struck by the size of its head, how round it was. Luc shuffled, clearly indicating that
they should move on. There was much more of the house to see and dusk was pouring oil over the garden; soon it would be too dark to see anything.

"I forget my torch," he said, and shrugged. "This house has good electric. But not
switched on at present. Come."

They proceeded up a makeshift wooden staircase that would not be safe for too
much longer; tiny holes were scattered across the grain, fresh frass on the floorboards. Ian felt his wallet wince. He plucked at Molly's sleeve. "This whole
house . . . you know, we're going to have to get it *all* treated for woodworm."

She moved away from him, clearly annoyed by his pettifogging. "I'll wait here.
I'm not going up there, not in my condition."

Ian followed Luc up into the attic. He couldn't speak much French, beyond *Bon-*

jour, ça va? Au revoir, so the atmosphere grew slightly strained, despite his liking the estate agent. Luc was pointing at the curious circular windows low on the wall, a peculiarity of the Charente region. *"Très jolie, non?"*

"Like portholes," Ian said.

Luc smiled, frowned, shook his head.

"Never mind."

There wasn't much else to see in the attic, except for the awkward, low beams and a few rotting *batons* that would need to be tackled quickly if they weren't to deteriorate further over the coming winter.

"Good space for children," Ian said to Molly as he carefully returned down the stairs. He pressed his hand against the firm swell of her belly, and kissed her cheek.

The storms in the Charente were spectacular affairs, Ian had been promised. He had always fancied himself as a stormchaser, and harbored a wish to one day visit Tornado Alley, go in search for some big game like the guys he saw on the Discovery Channel. There was something about lightning and the brightness in the sky turned right down that appealed to a raw and ancient part of him. The lowing of thunder, miles away, getting closer. The air pressure, grinding down on you.

In the Charente, the flat countryside offered nothing upon which the storms might spend themselves. They drifted away but then they might come back again. On very rare occasions, two storms might gather in the same area, and revolve around each other. One of these broke the first night they spent in the house, after the contracts had been signed in the presence of the solicitor in Matha, the nearest town to their little village.

"It's a double-yolker," Ian said, face pressed against the window of what they had chosen for their bedroom, a ridiculously large room that could have easily accommodated a walk-in wardrobe and an en suite bathroom and still left them with more space than they had known in their one-bedroom flat in London. "Listen to that thunder. It's practically on top of us."

Molly was lying on the inflatable bed, watching the steam rise from her mug of raspberry leaf tea. She was trying to read a book about herbal remedies especially aimed at pregnant women but the candlelight was too faint, or too agitated for her to concentrate properly, because she gave up after only a short while, tossing the book to the side of the bed. She ran a hand through her hair. The fingers of her other hand were absently toying with her belly button, which had recently become convex. Ian had altered the depth of his focus so that he could watch her reflection in the window, her transparent face blitzed by raindrops. He liked the way she always seemed to be able to find the most comfortable position with apparently minimum effort. In this way, she reminded him of a cat. She could fall asleep anywhere. There was a photograph of her as a young girl, half hanging out of a wicker chair, her head almost touching the floor, as content in sleep as she might have been in a deluxe bed.

They had met on Brighton beach, a little over two years previously. She had been kneeling on the shingle in such a bizarre way—her almost supernaturally long legs somehow splayed out and tucked beneath each other—that it seemed more like a torture than a position of rest. The first time they made love, she had hooked her legs over his shoulders and then, hushing his protests, detached herself from him, lifted herself up on her neck muscles alone, twisted around and lowered herself slowly into a new position, presenting her rear to him, laughing deeply in the dark.

She seemed double-jointed, treble-jointed. She folded herself around him like strange origami.

"I love you," he said, the words falling out of him, coming from somewhere beyond his control, fueled by the sentiment in his memories. Rain, like buckshot, scattered across the glass. The sky was so alive with pulses of lightning now, constant, random, that it could pass for day.

Molly laughed and reached out her hand to him. He could not remember the last time he had told her he loved her and didn't know whether that was a good thing. He joined her on the inflatable bed and she pressed his hand against her stomach, the skin as tight as that on a drum. "Say hello to the baby," she whispered. He did so, touching his lips to that warm curve, passing on a message of love, of hope.

"Hello baby . . . Daddy here . . ."

Molly moved against the tickle of his mouth, gently touching his face with her fingers, nudging him lower.

Some time later, the storm having finally tired itself out, they lay awake, listening to each other breathing in the dark, and the beat of water as it leaked from the roof onto the attic floor above them.

"I wonder if all the houses, even the ones in good order, have leaks?" Ian said.

"This house *is* in good order," Molly said. "Or it will be soon. There's a lot of work needs doing, but we knew that at the start, when we first talked about this, remember?"

He remembered, but their moving here seemed to have come around so quickly. Too quickly, for him. He had been happy in their one-bedroom flat, even though the space seemed to shrink around them by the day. "I'm a DIY dunce, Mol," he said. "I see a claw hammer, I don't know if I should hit something with it, or pick my teeth."

"So you keep saying. But nobody is born with that kind of knowledge. You'll learn. You'll have to. *We'll* have to."

Sleep drew them down. Ian was on the edge of it, his thoughts deepening, fracturing into nonsense, into dreams, when the shriek slapped them both awake.

"What in Christ. . . ."

Molly was already up, standing at the window. Her naked body didn't appear pregnant from behind. A *boy, that means*, she had said. A *bulge out in front, that's a boy*. Light from the floods trained on the church outlined her. From where he lay, perched on one elbow, he could see a great sweep of stars spraying out across the sky, like spilled sugar on a dark tablecloth.

"Bats?" Ian asked.

"Maybe. Maybe owls."

"Owls make that kind of noise? I thought they hooted. It sounds like someone being torn apart."

He saw her shrug. "Maybe it was. I'm no wildlife expert. Maybe it was a rabbit or a mouse being killed. Maybe it was the local cat being fucked. Maybe it was somebody's hinges need oiling."

He could never tell, when Molly was in this mood, whether she was merely teasing him or being more aggressively dismissive. He was aware that his questions tended to be on the pointless side, begging, for the most part, confirmation of something already said. It needled him that, two years on—married, with a kid on the way—he still did not know his wife as well as he felt he ought to.

The noise came again, a truly creepy rasp vented somewhere from the lime trees that shivered outside their window, and Ian saw how it could not possibly belong to an animal being hunted. It was a predator's cry. It was what bloodlust sounded like.

"Come back to bed," he said.

He dreamed of climbing the church tower from within. It was an old building—thirteenth century—and the interior stone, though initially pale and attractive, was, up close, failing rapidly. A wooden staircase took him only so far. He had to ascend the remaining darkness by a rickety ladder, some of the rungs of which had rotted away and been replaced by lengths of rusting iron, or sawn-off shafts of broom handles. The smell of bird shit was intense, it burned his nostrils. The netting, hung over the open arches to prevent the belltower from being invaded by wildlife, had decayed badly. It flapped ineffectually in the breeze. Night shifted beyond it like something that could be touched. As he reached the landing, a group of pigeons leapt nervously away from him, heads cocked, eyeing him with suspicion. He paused for a moment, the shape of the great bell within arm's reach. Its stillness was all wrong. Its size and silence seemed to go in direct contradiction of all that was meant for it. As if in acknowledgment of his thoughts, the bell began to move. Slowly at first, the sound of the cord as it was tugged fizzed lightly against the chamfered apertures of the landing. The bell tipped this way and that, gathering pace, and fear tipped with it, filling the gaps in his body with cold until his temperature had dropped so drastically it seemed he could be nothing but vacuum. He didn't want the bell to swing so violently. Not because of the immense sound that it would generate, but because it would mean he would be able to see through to the other side of the landing, and what waited there for him. He could not escape quickly enough. The pendulous slices showed him a scattering of picked corpses. The owl moved out of the shadows. It carried a dead rat in its beak. The owl's eyes held Ian like the headlights of a car will trap a rabbit. With a claw, the bird raked open the rat's stomach and half a dozen hairless, blind babies spilled from it.

Ian's laboring breath wakened him, more so than the dream. He lay listening to Molly sleep and tried to unpick the dream of its threat before his discomfort grew to the extent that he would have to get up, switch on some lights, make tea.

Owls don't leave bodies lying around like that. And not so big, either. The bones of their prey were evacuated in their spoors. Owl shit wasn't scary. Christ, *owls* weren't scary.

Before breakfast, still feeling jittery but much happier now that the night was over, Ian spent some time in the garden, acquainting himself with the flowers and shrubs as they solidified in the early morning mist. The field across the way was a featureless gray screen. The church tower was soft, like something captured out of focus on a camera. He paid it scant attention.

The hibiscus, the geranium, the hazel tree were known to him; pretty much everything else was not. Ivy scarred the walls and inserted damaging fingers under the pan tiles that protected them. The ground was covered with what seemed like thick grass, but it came away in great swatches when he pulled at it, like hair from the head of a person suffering from alopecia. The soil was stony, uncooperative. A tree had collapsed, possibly during one of the great storms, and a riot of ivy and convolvulus had knotted around it, anchoring it to the ground. The only tool he owned was a rusty scythe he had found lying in the grass. His own teeth were sharper. There was so much work, everywhere he looked, that it appeared insurmountable. He didn't know where to begin.

And then Molly was at the window, pushing back the shutters, smiling down at him above that splendidly proud stomach, and he realized that it didn't matter where he began. They had all the time in the world.

"What does a sodding starter motor look like, anyway?" he said, leaning over the Xantia's engine, trying to find some sense in its weird steel and plastic codes. "Have a look at the manual."

By the time they fired the engine up it was gone ten and the pleasant morning they had envisaged pottering around the market stalls of Saintes was steadily being eaten away. The N10, usually so quiet, a pleasure to drive along, was congested with great lorries. Added to that, the radio was asking him to input the security code and neither of them had noted down what it was when they picked the car up from the garage in Oxford.

"The guy who sold us this *Shitroën*, I'm taking a contract out on the bastard."

Molly ignored him. She was leafing through a baby catalogue, marking items they needed with a red highlighter pen. More money they didn't have. It didn't seem to make things any better to consider these things essentials: a car seat, a travel cot, changing mats; at least he hadn't yet bothered to work out how to convert Euros to Sterling. This way, the total would just be so many figures that he didn't understand; it might make the pain of unfolding his wallet that bit more bearable.

They arrived in Saintes as the stallholders were in the process of packing away their produce. Hastily, Molly hurried to buy vegetables and a few cuts of meat for that evening's meal, her easy way with the language never failing to impress Ian.

"Look at the cheeses," he said. "My God. Look at what we've missed."

"We can come again," Molly said. "There's always the market in Cognac we can go to. There's even one in Matha, although I'll have to find out when it's on."

The baby shop was on the other side of the market, on a one-way street. They passed the remaining few stalls, and their owners, who were hosing down their pitches and loading the last trays and cartons into their vans. A butcher wiped down his chopping blocks. Steel glinted. A pile of skinned rabbits gritted their teeth at Ian as they were tipped into a thick plastic bag. Their eyes seemed too big for the heads that contained them. Molly was hurrying on, aiming for a gap in the traffic. In the instant that Ian's attention swung back to his wife, he saw another pile of peeled bodies being swept into storage. When he checked himself and stepped back to have another look, to confirm they were what he thought they were, the butcher flipped the latch off the awning and drew it across the service hatch.

By the time he opened the baby shop door, and navigated a path through the prams and buggies, Molly had already gathered a number of items under her arm that hadn't been on the original list.

"What, do you want the baby to have nothing?" she asked, when he pointed out that their budget might not be sturdy enough to factor in these items.

"I didn't say that," he said. "But come on. Toys, night-lights. A bean bag. Hardly essentials, are they?"

She dropped the things at his feet. "You sort it out, then," she said.

He shrugged at the shop assistant as Molly slammed her way out of the shop. "*Je suis desolé*," he said, haltingly, and then paid for everything.

He found her sitting outside a café on the Cours Reverseaux. She was sipping a latté and flicking through a magazine at speed. Not reading anything, hardly looking at the pictures, just needing something to do with her fingers to deal with her anger. Her left foot bounced against her right. He watched it. He watched the sun glinting on the silver ring that encircled her little toe, a present he had given her on their honeymoon in Bali.

"I'm sorry," he said, but he had uttered the words too often for it to have any meaning.

She thawed a little, on the way back. It helped that he had bought something that wasn't on the list either: a small toy owl. It had seemed fitting, somehow. A tribute to the dead creature.

The traffic had dispersed for the legendary French lunch; they made good time going back, and could enjoy more of the scenery now that there were no tailgating Renault drivers, or swerving HGVs to keep an eye on. Crumbling farmhouses; fields freshly opened by the tractors, the soil dark and dense, brown as wet leather; long gray roads. They turned on to one now, flanked by elm trees, an object lesson in perspective.

"Now there's pretty for you," Molly said.

"There are moves to pull trees like that down," Ian said, and then mentally kicked himself for once again putting a downer on things. Why couldn't he just agree occasionally? It was what she wanted to hear.

"Why?"

"Too dangerous. They hide the junctions joining the main road. So if a car comes out and you swerve so as not to hit it, there's a tree waiting for you to wrap yourself around."

Silence.

"But you're right. Pretty. Reminds me of the opening titles to *Secret Army*."

Molly returned to her baby magazines and her yoga manuals. Ian switched on the radio. Normally he could not stomach the inane Euro-pop that tumbled from the speakers, but anything was better than this atmosphere. But then, a few minutes later, the signal faded, replaced by a wall of static so dense that Ian had to lash out at the volume control.

"Jesus," Molly said. "Do you mind?"

"It wasn't my fault," he said, but she had blanked him again. Ian swallowed against his rising anger—he didn't want to get into a fight with Molly in her state—and tried tuning the radio to a different station. Static followed him, wherever he sent the dial.

"This bastard car," he said. When he returned his full attention to the road, snapping off the radio with a curse, he flinched. A shaded figure was standing inches away from the Tarmac, a red fracture splitting his head. The fact that it was only a cardboard cut-out was no relief.

"Did you see that?" Ian asked. "Look, there's some more."

Single black figures, or pairs, were positioned by the road; they marched off into the distance, provocative, ineluctable, all of them with the same crude head injuries. Molly seemed unimpressed.

"They're *fantômes*," she said. "They're a warning to drivers. They signify that there have been deaths on these roads. Violent deaths. So slow down and watch what you're doing."

Ian said nothing more on the drive home. He stopped off in Matha and bought an English newspaper, then popped into the local *Bricomarché* and bought a garden fork, a spade, some pruning shears, a machete and a pair of gloves.

"Ian," Molly said, as he got back behind the wheel, "look, I know we're not going through the best of patches at the moment, but things will get better. What might help is if you lay off buying things that we don't need."

"The garden is in a mess, Molly. We need gardening equipment. What do you expect me to do? Kick the weeds into submission? Talk to them in a stern manner?"

"Darling, there's no need to be facetious. The garden can wait. We need to sort out a room for the baby."

"Which will be done."

"I know it will, but not if you're out in the garden all day."

He swallowed, counted to ten. There was no question of him returning the gardening tools. Just let her have her moment. *Let it slide over you.*

"And those newspapers. They're so expensive for what they are. Why don't you just check out the Beeb's website?"

Back home, he unloaded the car and made tea for them both. Molly watched him and then said she didn't want any tea when he handed her a cup. Ian stared at her, but kept his mouth shut. He emptied the cup, rinsed it, grabbed his paper and his own tea, and headed for the door.

"Where are you going?" she asked.

"I'm going for a shit. Is that okay with you?"

There were a couple of owl droppings on the cement floor of the *hangar*, he saw, as he was returning from the outhouse. He poked at them with his boot and they disintegrated: a tiny mandible, ribs like fishbones, half a skull, the size of a pistachio nut. Above him, a beam was spattered with white bird shit like pointless graffiti. He suddenly found himself thinking of his child, safe and warm inside Molly. It had been this size once, smaller, even, and just as fragile. Its own bones as thin as an eyelash. A heart beating, the size of a pinhead. He entered the house determined to make things better. Molly was in the room they had chosen for the baby, chosen for its lack of a window, painting the roughly plastered walls.

"You shouldn't be doing that," Ian said. "The fumes. Here, let me—"

"Get away from me!" Molly's eyes, in the gloom, glinted like scratched coal. The paintbrush had become a weapon she held out in front of her. "Just leave me alone. I'll have the baby without you, if that's what it takes to be happy. I'm sick of doing everything around here while you swan off buying garden tools. I'm the only one preparing for this child. You haven't even talked to me about what names you like."

He was too taken aback to retaliate, or to reason with her. He moved away from her as she returned to the wall, streaking the plaster with fiercely applied strokes.

Crazed thoughts descended on him as he stepped into the garden, like the leaves that spiraled down from the disrobing trees. *Leave now. Take the car and go. Fuck it. But the baby. The baby. Fuck it. She'll leave you in the end and take the baby with her. Stick around for the birth and it will only be worse. It will be impossible to leave once you've held the child in your arms. Leave. Leave now.*

An agonized cry caught in his throat. Tears of impotent rage made further nonsense of the wild garden. He stalked to the barn where he had stored his equipment and rammed his fingers into the gloves. He took the machete and walked around the house to the fallen bough. She couldn't let go anything he said; nothing he could do was good enough. Even this, trying to clear the garden of obstacles, she'd criticize.

I'm stuck here toiling and you're outside doing all the lovely creative stuff. Great. Thanks.

He attacked the naked limbs of the tree almost in a panic, shaking from the absurd interior arguments he was fashioning. Jesus, she wasn't even around and he could get into a row with her. What did that mean? Nothing good, nothing good. The virgin blade chewed into the damp wood, squealing as he recovered it. The shocks that flew up his arm were welcome distractions. After a couple of minutes of senseless hewing, he stopped, exhausted. Despite the cold, sweat coated his forehead and steam was rising from his muscles.

At the point where the tree had split from its roots, a great mass of stinging nettles had sprouted. Thick climbers and thorny vines moved through it, reminding him of Walt Disney scenes of enchanted castles guarded by menacing flora. He snorted and lifted the blade again. *And they lived happily ever after.* This time he worked more systematically, lopping off the branches close to the trunk and stacking them in a pile to be either burnt on the spot once it had dried, or to be stored as kindling. He thrashed at the nettles until enough of the climbers and vines had been exposed to be able to get at them. After half an hour he had cleared a goodly portion of the tangle and the underlying shape of the garden was coming through.

He felt calmer, and was beginning to enjoy himself, the sense of achievement as it grew, but the air was changing, deteriorating. The sky to the east was leaden, sucking all of the light into it. The hairs on Ian's arms shifted slowly, like the legs of a cautious spider making itself known to something it hasn't yet recognized on the web. A rumble shifted across the horizon.

The engine fired first time, thank God. He didn't relish the prospect of asking Molly to help him start the car, and the inevitable queries. He didn't bother closing the gates in case she was already on her way down to see where he was going. The country lane to the main road was less than a mile long; by the time he had covered it, rain was spitting against the windscreen. There was nothing else on the road. The countryside opened up around him. A village a couple of miles to his left was painted momentarily with gold through a rent in the black sheet. Rain hung like fishermen's nets, trawling the skies in great swathes. It must be ten miles across. Beyond it, or within it—Ian couldn't tell—a sudden trigger of lightning burnt everything onto his retina. It was followed almost immediately by the crash of thunder, so close it seemed it must split the sky above him. Ian heard it despite the protesting engine.

He pushed the car hard, hoping to intercept the storm as it passed over the N939. If he missed it, it would mean a pursuit along the smaller country thoroughfares, which would be impossible, especially if he had to slow down to fifty kph every time he hit a village. He wound down the window and was assaulted by the chill wind, the almost horizontal slanting of rain.

"Come on!" he screamed. "Come *on*!"

He took the car off the road at the top of a slight rise and parked without caring if he had spoiled the plowed patterns of the field, or whether he would be able to drive out of the mud when his adventure was over. He stumbled out of the car, unconsciously stooped because of the closeness of the sky. The darkness was alive. At its edges it trembled, where real light still existed, somehow compacted and intensified at the horizon, as if the pressure of the storm was affecting it. He could still make out the soft, black ribbons of rain as they approached, before they engulfed him and he became a part of their pattern. The howling of the wind went away as the storm's heart settled over him and for a moment he could hear nothing, except for the beating in his own chest. It felt as though something invisible was being drawn up from the ground. He felt his testicles contract; the hairs on his nape standing to attention. He felt as if the sky was breathing him in. And then the sky opened under a brilliant slash of a knife that drove the grim colors away for a beat. Thunder collapsed around him, shaking him. Again he screamed, as hard as he could, but the sound was lost; his was a tiny voice, an insignificance. He slumped back against the car as the storm left him, now one, now three, now five kilometers further west, still violent, but already sounding weak to Ian's ears. Rain continued to batter down, but he barely felt it. The sharp, almost sour taste of ozone flooded him. He felt alive for the first time in his thirty-odd years. He felt, somehow, defined. He watched the storm recede until it disappeared, and yet he stayed on, willing it to return, until the darkness around him no longer had anything to do with the weather.

When he arrived at the house, he found he could not remember his return journey. Maybe the electrical play had done something to his mind, short-circuited him, thrown a few switches. Maybe pure elation had wiped a little bit of him out. The clock on the dashboard read a quarter to midnight. He eased himself out of the car and trudged in the dark around to the front of the house. What he'd give for a hot, deep bath now, instead of the cold shower that was their only means of keeping clean. A cognac then, and a piece of last year's Christmas cake. He'd take some tea up to Molly and tell her about the storm. He would apologize, and promise to make things right between them. The storm had scored a line beneath him. Things could change. He wanted the best possible start for their baby.

His clothes were strewn about the garden like the remains of bodies that had decomposed into the grass. The photograph of him and Molly on their wedding day was hidden behind a white star in the grass. His love letters to her were torn and discarded, fluttering at his feet. The front door was locked. He rapped on it, but Molly was either asleep, or ignoring him. He moved back from the door and looked up at the bedroom window. The shutters had been closed.

"Molly? Molly, please?" he hated the wheedling tone that edged his voice. But she wasn't giving way this time.

Ian picked up his sopping clothes and the disintegrating cards and notes and dumped them in the outbuilding they were using for storage. He briefly considered spending the night in there, but it was cold, and there was an unpleasant smell of bleach from a sink where they washed their clothes. He went back to the car, shivering now. The storm had scoured the sky and it was eerily clean; there seemed to be more stars than the space they were studded into. Cold filled the gaps. Inside the car he started the engine and turned on the heating. It didn't take long to warm up. He dragged a blanket from the boot through the access hatch in the back seat and wrapped it around him. He tried the radio. No static this time. There was a faint classical music station and he felt himself drifting as a soft, soothing piece played. He wondered vaguely who might have composed it and what had driven him to do so.

As sleep came, he recalled the tableau from the road as the lightning's flash photography trapped it in his mind. The village, the black wet strip of Tarmac, the sheets of rain, the trees like shocked things staggering back from the ghastly breath of the weather. There was something else there, something, in his excitement, that he had missed the first time. A fat cuneiform shape, arresting itself against the thermals, talons outstretched in a classic pose of predation.

A shriek startled him out of a dream that he could not fully recall, other than it involved the machete, and dark parts of the garden that became more, not less, tangled as he scythed through to them. He moved in the seat and pain ricocheted through him like a hard steel ball in a game of bagatelle. His arms felt as if they had been wrenched into impossible positions, forced to do things beyond what human physicality ought to be able to achieve. They felt tenderized. His hands were raw and itchy, as they were when he washed lots of dishes in detergent without moisturizing them afterwards. Gingerly, he straightened and his gaze fell upon the rearview mirror. In it he saw three figures reduced by the night to faceless mannequins: two close to the rear of the car, one further behind, almost at the great arched gate. All of them approached stiffly, incrementally, their outlines filled in with a black that was deeper than their surroundings. They seemed, somehow, *damaged*. The click that jerked him from his paralysis was his throat reacting as he tried to swallow.

He got out of the car. He got out of the car and he did not look back because to do that was to confirm his own madness. He would not allow that. There was nobody else in the grounds of his house. Ian stood by the car long enough for them to be able to touch him, if that was what they wanted, and then, feeling vindicated, walked to the front of the house. Dawn light had set fire to the lowest edge of the gloom, but it was damp and it burned slowly, coming on with the same terrible slowness as the figures he had seen. Thought he had seen. He tried the door and felt a bitter victory to find that it was unlocked. Molly had capitulated. He was being offered an unspoken invitation to return to the fold.

He passed through the kitchen, which smelled faintly of the previous night's casserole and he broke off a piece of stale baguette to take the edge from his enormous hunger. Food could wait. At the top of the stairs he smelled the fresh paint in the nursery and felt cold fingers of rooms seldom used reaching out to him. In the bedroom he switched on the light and was greeted by an empty bed, the covers torn away from it, lying in a pile in the middle of the floor.

"Molly," he said, and his voice fell flat. Had she gone into labor while he was sleeping? Why didn't she come to him in the car? Surely her troubles with him could be forgotten if their baby were on the way. She wouldn't go to a neighbor for help instead, would she? Their first baby. How could she not want him with her?

He hurried downstairs, feverishly patting his pockets for the car keys. Presumably she would have been taken to Saintes to give birth. He ought to ring ahead, but he didn't have the number, and anyway, he was reluctant to talk to a voice that couldn't understand his urgency, and time was precious to him now.

All that was forgotten when he stepped into the cold mist of morning and saw the figures again, shifting slowly around the corner of the house—two walking abreast, the other still lagging behind—the jagged wounds in their heads clearly visible, shining wetly in the embryonic light.

He stepped away from them, into the shade thrown by the canopy of trees. He heard the ticking of long gone rain on a carpet of dead leaves as the branches gave up the water they had gathered the previous night. The owl landed on the wall and began to clean its bloodied beak.

The light's slow accretion, so subtle that it couldn't be measured.

Ian turned to look up at the crooks of the branches and waited for her wrenched shape to assume there, and that of the strange pendulum that swung bloodily from her guts. He retrieved his machete from the foot of the tree at the same moment that the third figure joined its companions. Ian rejoined his own moments later.

ELIZABETH A. LYNN

The Silver Dragon

Elizabeth A. Lynn received the World Fantasy Award for her novel Watch-tower, *and for her story "The Woman Who Loved the Moon." "The Silver Dragon," a stand-alone story set in the same world as Lynn's novels* Dragon's Winter *and* Dragon's Treasure, *was published in the fantasy anthology* Flights. *Lynn lives in the San Francisco Bay Area and teaches martial arts.*

—K.L. & G.G.

This is a story of Iyadur Atani, who was master of Dragon Keep and lord of Dragon's Country a long, long time ago.

At this time, Ryoka was both the same as and different than it is today. In Issho, in the west, there was peace, for the mages of Ryoka had built the great wall, the Wizards' Wall, and defended it with spells. Though the wizards were long gone, the power of their magic lingered in the towers and ramparts of the wall. The Isojai feared it, and would not storm it.

In the east, there was no peace. Chuyo was not part of Ryoka, but a separate country. The Chuyokai lords were masters of the sea. They sailed the eastern seas in black-sailed ships, landing to plunder and loot and carry off the young boys and girls to make them slaves. All along the coast of Kameni, men feared the Chuyokai pirates.

In the north, the lords of Ippa prospered. Yet, having no enemies from beyond their borders to fight, they grew bored, and impatient, and quarrelsome. They quarreled with the lords of Issho, with the Talvelai, and the Nyo, and they fought among themselves. Most quarrelsome among them was Martun Hal, lord of Serrenhold. Serrenhold, as all men know, is the smallest and most isolated of the domains of Ippa. For nothing is it praised: not for its tasty beer or its excellence of horseflesh, nor for the beauty of its women, nor the prowess of its men. Indeed, Serrenhold is notable for only one thing: its inhospitable climate. *Bitter as the winds of Serrenhold*, the folk of Ippa say.

No one knew what made Martun Hal so contentious. Perhaps it was the wind, or the will of the gods, or perhaps it was just his nature. In the ten years since he had inherited the lordship from his father Owen, he had killed one brother, exiled another, and picked fights with all his neighbors.

His greatest enmity was reserved for Roderico di Corsini of Derrenhold. There had not always been enmity between them. Indeed, he had once asked Olivia di Corsini, daughter of Roderico di Corsini, lord of Derrenhold, to marry him. But Olivia di Corsini turned him down.

"He is old. Besides, I do not love him," she told her father. "I will not wed a man I do not love."

"Love? What does love have to do with marriage?" Roderico glared at his child. She glared back. They were very alike: stubborn and proud of it. "Pah. I suppose you *love* someone else."

"I do," said Olivia.

"And who might that be, missy?"

"Jon Torneo of Galva."

"Jon Torneo?" Roderico scowled a formidable scowl. "Jon Torneo? He's a shepherd's son! He smells of sheep fat and hay!" This, as it happened, was not true. Jon Torneo's father, Federico Torneo of Galva, did own sheep. But he could hardly be called a shepherd: he was a wool merchant, and one of the wealthiest men in the domain, who had often come to Derrenhold as Roderico di Corsini guest.

"I don't care. I love him," Olivia said.

And the very next night she ran away from her father's house and rode east across the countryside to Galva. To tell you what happened then would be a whole other story. But since the wedding of Olivia di Corsini and Jon Torneo, while of great import to them, is a small part of this story, suffice it to say that Olivia married Jon Torneo and went to live with him in Galva. Do I need to tell you they were happy? They were. They had four children. The eldest—a boy, called Federico after his grandfather—was a friendly, sturdy, biddable lad. The next two were girls. They were also charming and biddable children, like their brother.

The fourth was Joanna. She was very lovely, having inherited her mother's olive skin and black, thick hair. But she was in no way biddable. She fought with her nurses and bullied her brother. She preferred trousers to skirts, archery to sewing, and hunting dogs to dolls.

"I want to ride. I want to fight," she said.

"Women do not fight," her sisters said.

"I do," said Joanna.

And her mother, recognizing in her youngest daughter the indomitable stubbornness of her own nature, said, "Let her do as she will."

So Joanna learned to ride, and shoot, and wield a sword. By thirteen she could ride as well as any horseman in her grandfather's army. By fourteen she could outshoot all but his best archers.

"She has not the weight to make a swordsman," her father's armsmaster said, "but she'll best anyone her own size in a fair fight."

"She's a hellion. No man will ever want to wed her," Roderico di Corsini said, so gloomily that it made his daughter smile. But Joanna Torneo laughed. She knew very well whom she would marry. She had seen him, shining brighter than the moon, soaring across the sky on his way to his castle in the mountains, and had vowed—this was a fourteen-year-old girl, remember—that Iyadur Atani, the Silver Dragon, would be her husband. That he was a changeling, older than she by twelve years, and that they had never met disturbed her not a whit.

Despite his age—he was nearly sixty—the rancor of the lord of Serrenhold toward his neighbors did not cool. The year Joanna turned five, his war band attacked and burned Ragnar Castle. The year she turned nine, he stormed Voiana, the eyrie of the Red Hawks, hoping for plunder. But he found there only empty chambers and the rushing of wind through stone.

The autumn Joanna turned fourteen, Roderico di Corsini died: shot through the heart by one of Martun Hal's archers as he led his soldiers along the crest of the western hills. His son, Ege, inherited the domain. Ege di Corsini, though not the warrior his father had been, was a capable man. His first act as lord was to send a large company of troops to patrol his western border. His next act was to invite his neighbors to a council. "For," he said, "it is past time to end this madness." Couriers were sent to Mirrinhold and Ragnar, to Voiana and to far Mako. A courier was even sent to Dragon Keep.

His councilors wondered at this. "Martun Hal has never attacked the Atani," they pointed out. "The Silver Dragon will not join us."

"I hope you are wrong," said Ege di Corsini. "We need him." He penned that invitation with his own hand. And, since Galva lay between Derrenhold and Dragon Keep, and because he loved his sister, he told the courier, whose name was Ullin March, to stop overnight at the home of Jon Torneo.

Ullin March did as he was told. He rode to Galva. He ate dinner that night with the family. After dinner, he spoke quietly with his hosts, apprising them of Ege di Corsini's plan.

"This could mean war," said Jon Torneo.

"It will mean war," Olivia di Corsini Torneo said.

The next day, Ullin March took his leave of the Torneo family and rode east. At dusk he reached the tall stone pillar that marked the border between the di Corsini's domain and Dragon's Country. He was about to pass the marker, when a slender form leaped from behind the pillar and seized his horse's bridle.

"Dismount," said a fierce young voice, "or I will kill your horse." Steel glinted against the great artery in the gray mare's neck.

Ullin March was no coward. But he valued his horse. He dismounted. The hood fell back from his assailant's face, and he saw that it was a young woman. She was lovely, with olive-colored skin and black hair, tied back behind her neck in a club.

"Who are you?" he said.

"Never mind. The letter you carry. Give it to me."

"No."

The sword tip moved from his horse's neck to his own throat. "I will kill you."

"Then kill me," Ullin March said. Then he dropped, and rolled into her legs. But she had moved. Something hard hit him on the crown of the head.

Dazed and astonished, he drew his sword and lunged at his attacker. She slipped the blow and thrust her blade without hesitation into his arm. He staggered, and slipped to one knee. Again he was hit on the head. The blow stunned him. Blood streamed from his scalp into his eyes. His sword was torn from his grasp. Small hands darted into his shirt, and removed his courier's badge and the letter.

"I am sorry," the girl said. "I had to do it. I will send someone to help you, I promise." He heard the noise of hoofbeats, two sets of them. Cursing, he staggered upright, knowing there was nothing he could do.

Joanna Torneo, granddaughter of Roderico di Corsini, carried her uncle's invitation to Dragon Keep. As it happened, the dragon-lord was at home when she arrived. He was in his hall when a page came running to tell him that a courier from Ege di Corsini was waiting at the gate.

"Put him in the downstairs chamber, and see to his comfort. I will come," said the lord.

"My lord, it's not a him. It's a girl."

"Indeed?" said Iyadur Atani. "See to her comfort, then." The oddity of the event roused his curiosity. In a very short time he was crossing the courtyard to the little chamber where he was wont to receive guests. Within the chamber he found a well-dressed, slightly grubby, very lovely young woman.

"My lord," she said calmly, "I am Joanna Torneo, Ege di Corsini's sister's daughter. I bear you his greetings and a letter." She took the letter from the pocket of her shirt and handed it to him.

Iyadur Atani read her uncle's letter.

"Do you know what this letter says?" he asked.

"It invites you to a council."

"And it assures me that the bearer, a man named Ullin March, can be trusted to answer truthfully any questions I might wish to put to him. You are not Ullin March."

"No. I took the letter from him at the border. Perhaps you would be so kind as to send someone to help him? I had to hit him."

"Why?"

"Had I not, he would not have let me take the letter."

"Why did you take the letter?"

"I wanted to meet you."

"Why?" asked Iyadur Atani.

Joanna took a deep breath. "I am going to marry you."

"Are you?" said Iyadur Atani. "Does your father know this?"

"My mother does," said Joanna. She gazed at him. He was a handsome man, fair, and very tall. His clothes, though rich, were simple; his only adornment, a golden ring on the third finger of his right hand. It was fashioned in the shape of a sleeping dragon. His gaze was very direct, and his eyes burned with a blue flame. Resolute men, men of uncompromising courage, feared that fiery gaze.

When they emerged, first the girl, radiant despite her mud-stained clothes, and then the lord of the Keep, it was evident to all his household that their habitually reserved lord was unusually, remarkably happy.

"This is the lady Joanna Torneo of Galva, soon to be my wife," he said. "Take care of her." He lifted the girl's hand to his lips.

That afternoon he wrote two letters. The first went to Olivia Torneo, assuring her that her beloved daughter was safe in Dragon Keep. The second was to Ege di Corsini. Both letters made their recipients very glad indeed. An exchange of letters followed: from Olivia Torneo to her headstrong daughter, and from Ege di Corsini to the lord of the Keep. Couriers wore ruts in the road from Dragon Keep to Galva, and from Dragon Keep to Derrenhold.

The council was held in the great hall of Derrenhold. Ferris Wulf, lord of Mirrin-hold, a doughty warrior, was there, with his captains; so was Aurelio Ragnarin of Ragnar Castle and Rudolf diMako, whose cavalry was the finest in Ippa. Even Jamis Delamico, matriarch of the Red Hawk clan, had come, accompanied by six dark-haired, dark-eyed women who looked exactly like her. She did not introduce them: no one knew if they were her sisters, or her daughters. Iyadur Atani was not present.

Ege di Corsini spoke first.

"My lords, honored friends," he said, "for nineteen years, since the old lord of Ser-renhold died, Martun Hal and his troops have prowled the borders of our territories, snapping and biting like a pack of hungry dogs. His people starve, and groan beneath their taxes. He has attacked Mirrinhold, and Ragnar, and Voiana. Two years ago, my lord of Mirrinhold, his archers killed your son. Last year they killed my father.

"My lords and captains, nineteen years is too long. It is time to muzzle the dogs." The lesser captains shouted. Ege di Corsini went on. "Alone, no one of us has been able to prevail against Martun Hal's aggression. I suggest we unite our forces and at-tack him."

"How?" said Aurelio Ragnarin. "He hides behind his walls, and attacks only when he is sure of victory."

"We must go to him, and attack him where he lives."

The leaders looked at one another, and then at di Corsini as if he had lost his mind. Ferris Wulf said, "Serrenhold is unassailable."

"How do you know?" Ege di Corsini said. "For nineteen years no one has at-tacked it."

"You have a plan," said Jamis Delamico.

"I do." And Ege di Corsini explained to the lords of Ippa exactly how he planned to defeat Martun Hal.

At the end of his speech, Ferris Wulf said, "You are sure of this?"

"I am."

"I am with you."

"And I," said Aurelio Ragnarin.

"My sisters and my daughters will follow you," Jamis Delamico said.

Rudolf diMako stuck his thumbs in his belt. "Martun Hal has stayed well clear of my domain. But I see that he needs to be taught a lesson. My army is yours to command."

Solitary in his fortress, Martun Hal heard through his spies of his enemies' machi-nations. He summoned his captains to his side. "Gather the troops," he ordered. "We must prepare to defend our borders. Go," he told his spies. "Watch the high-ways. Tell me when they come."

Sooner than he expected, the spies returned. "My lord, they come."

"What are their forces?"

"They are a hundred mounted men, and six hundred foot."

"Archers?"

"About a hundred."

"Have they brought a ram?"

"Yes, my lord."

"Ladders? Ropes? Catapults?"

"They have ladders and ropes. No catapults, my lord."

"Pah. They are fools, and overconfident. Their horses will do them no good here. Do they think to leap over Serrenhold's walls? We have three hundred archers, and a thousand foot soldiers," Martun Hal said. His spirits rose. "Let them come. They will lose."

The morning of the battle was clear and cold. Frost hardened the ground. A bitter wind blew across the mountain peaks. The forces of the lords of Ippa advanced steadily upon Serrenhold Castle. On the ramparts of the castle, archers strung their bows. They were unafraid, for their forces outnumbered the attackers, and besides, no one had ever besieged Serrenhold and won. Behind the castle gates, the Serrenhold army waited. The swordsmen drew their swords and taunted their foes: "Run, dogs! Run, rabbits! Run, little boys! Go home to your mothers!"

The attackers advanced. Ege di Corsini called to the defenders, "Surrender, and you will live. Fight, and you will die."

"We will not surrender," the guard captain said.

"As you wish," di Corsini said. He signaled to his trumpeter. The trumpeter lifted his horn to his lips and blew a sharp trill. Yelling, the attackers charged. Despite the rain of arrows coming from the castle walls, a valiant band of men from Ragnar Castle scaled the walls, and leaped into the courtyard. Back to back, they fought their way slowly toward the gates. Screaming out of the sky, a flock of hawks flew at the faces of the amazed archers. The rain of arrows faltered.

A second group of men smashed its way through a postern gate and battled in the courtyard with Martun Hal's men. Ferris Wulf said to Ege di Corsini, "They weaken. But still they outnumber us. We are losing too many men. Call him."

"Not yet," Ege di Corsini said. He signaled. Men brought the ram up. Again and again they hurled it at the gates. But the gates held. The men in the courtyard fought and died. The hawks attacked the archers, and the archers turned their bows against the birds and shot them out of the sky. A huge red hawk swooped to earth and became Jamis Delamico.

"They are killing my sisters," she said, and her eyes glittered with rage. "Why do you wait? Call him."

"Not yet," said Ege di Corsini. "Look. We are through." The ram broke through the gate. Shouting, the attackers flung themselves at the breach, clawing at the gate with their hands. Fighting with tremendous courage, the attackers moved them back from the gates, inch by inch.

But there were indeed many more defenders. They drove the di Corsini army back, and closed the gate, and braced it with barrels and wagons and lengths of wood.

"Now," said Ege di Corsini. He signaled the trumpeter. The trumpeter blew again.

Then the dragon came. Huge, silver, deadly, he swooped upon the men of Serrenhold. His silver claws cut the air like scythes. He stooped his head, and his eyes glowed like fire. Fire trickled from his nostrils. He breathed upon the castle walls, and the stone hissed and melted like snow in the sun. He roared. The sound filled the day, louder and more terrible than thunder. The archers' fingers opened, and their bows clattered to the ground. The swordsmen trembled, and their legs turned to jelly. Shouting, the men of Ippa stormed over the broken gates and into Serrenhold. They found the lord of the castle sitting in his hall, with his sword across his lap.

"Come on," he said, rising. "I am an old man. Come and kill me."

He charged them then, hoping to force them to kill him. But though he fought fiercely, killing two of them, and wounding three more, they finally disarmed him. Bruised and bloody, but whole, Martun Hal was bound and marched at swordpoint out of his hall to the courtyard where the lords of Ippa stood. He bowed mockingly into their unyielding faces.

"Well, my lords. I hope you are pleased with your victory. All of you together, and still it took dragonfire to defeat me."

Ferris Wulf scowled. But Ege di Corsini said, "Why should more men of Ippa die for you? Even your own people are glad the war is over."

"Is it over?"

"It is," di Corsini said firmly.

Martun Hal smiled bleakly. "Yet I live."

"Not for long," someone cried. And Ferris Wulf's chief captain, whose home Martun Hal's men had burned, stepped forward and set the tip of his sword against the old man's breast.

"No," said Ege di Corsini.

"Why not?" said Ferris Wulf. "He killed your father."

"Whom would you put in his place?" Ege di Corsini said. "He is Serrenhold's rightful lord. His father had three sons, but one is dead, and the other gone, who knows where. He has no children to succeed him. *I* would not reign in Serrenhold. It is a dismal place. Let him keep it. We will set a guard about his border, and restrict the number of soldiers he may have, and watch him."

"And when he dies?" said Aurelio Ragnarin.

"Then we will name his successor."

Glaring, Ferris Wulf fingered the hilt of his sword. "He should die *now*. Then we could appoint a regent. One of our own captains, someone honorable and deserving of trust."

Ege di Corsini said, "We could do that. But that man would never have a moment's peace. *I* say, let us set a watch upon this land, so that Martun Hal may never trouble our towns and people again, and let him rot in this lifeless place."

"The Red Hawk clan will watch him," Jamis Delamico said.

And so it came to pass. Martun Hal lived. His weapons were destroyed; his war band, all but thirty men, was disbanded and scattered. He was forbidden to travel more than two miles from his castle. The lords of Ippa, feeling reasonably secure in their victory, went home to their castles, to rest and rebuild and prepare for winter.

Ege di Corsini, riding east amid his rejoicing troops, made ready to attend a wedding. He was fond of his niece. His sister had assured him that the girl was absolutely determined to wed Iyadur Atani, and as for the flame-haired, flame-eyed dragon-lord, he seemed equally eager for the match. Remembering stories he had heard, Ege di Corsini admitted, though only to himself, that Joanna's husband was not the one he would have chosen for her. But no one had asked his opinion.

The wedding was held at Derrenhold and attended by all the lords of Ippa, except, of course, Martun Hal. Rudolf diMako attended, despite the distance, but no one was surprised; there was strong friendship between the diMako and the Atani. Jamis Delamico came. The bride was pronounced to be astonishingly beautiful, and the bride's mother almost as beautiful. The dragon-lord presented the parents of his bride with gifts: a tapestry, a mettlesome stallion and a breeding mare from the Atani stables, a sapphire pendant, a cup of beaten gold. The couple drank the wine. The priestess said the blessings.

The following morning, Olivia di Corsini Torneo said farewell to her daughter. "I will miss you. Your father will miss you. You must visit often. He is older than he was, you know."

"I will," Joanna promised. Olivia watched the last of her children ride away into the bright autumnal day. The two older girls were both wed, and Federico was not only wed but twice a father, as well.

I don't feel like a grandmother, Olivia Torneo thought. Then she laughed at herself and went inside to find her husband.

And so there was peace in Ippa. The folk of Derrenhold and Mirrinhold and Ragnar ceased to look over their shoulders. They left their daggers sheathed and hung their battle-axes on the walls. Men who had spent most of their lives fighting put aside their shields and went home, to towns and farms and wives they barely remembered. More babies were born the following summer than had been born in the previous three years put together. The midwives were run ragged trying to attend the births. Many of the boys, even in Ragnar and Mirrinhold, were named Ege or Roderico. A few of the girls were even named Joanna.

Martun Hal heard the tidings of his enemies' good fortune, and his hatred of them deepened. Penned in his dreary fortress, he took count of his gold. Discreetly, he let it be known that the lord of Serrenhold, although beaten, was not without resources. Slowly, cautiously, some of those who had served him before his defeat crept across the border to his castle. He paid them and sent them out again to Derrenhold and Mirrinhold, and even—cautiously—into Iyadur Atani's country.

"Watch," he said, "and when something happens, send me word."

As for Joanna Torneo Atani, she was as happy as she had known she would be. She adored her husband and was unafraid of his changeling nature. The people of his domain had welcomed her. Her only disappointment, as the year moved from spring to summer and to the crisp cold nights of autumn again, was that she was childless.

"Every other woman in the world is having a baby," she complained to her husband. "Why can't I?"

He smiled and drew her into the warmth of his arms. "You will."

Nearly three years after the surrender of Martun Hal, with the Hunter's Moon waning in the autumn sky, Joanna Atani received a message from her mother.

Come, it said. *Your father needs you.* She left the next morning for Galva, accompanied by her maid and escorted by six of Dragon Keep's most experienced and competent soldiers.

"Send word if you need me," her husband said.

"I will."

The journey took two days. Outside the Galva gates, a beggar warming his hands over a scrap of fire told Joanna what she most wanted to know.

"Your father still lives, my lady. I heard it from Viksa the fruit-seller an hour ago."

"Give him gold," Joanna said to her captain as she urged her horse through the gate. Word of her coming hurried before her. By the time Joanna reached her parents' home, the gate was open. Her brother stood before it.

She said, "Is he dead?"

"Not yet." He drew her inside.

Olivia di Corsini Torneo sat at her dying husband's bedside, in the chamber they had shared for twenty-nine years. She still looked young, nearly as young as the day she had left her father's house behind for good. Her dark eyes were clear, and her skin smooth. Only her lustrous thick hair was no longer dark; it was shot through with white, like lace.

She smiled at her youngest daughter and put up her face to be kissed. "I am glad you could come," she said. "Your sisters are here." She turned back to her husband.

Joanna bent over the bed. "Papa?" she whispered. But the man in the bed, so flat and still, did not respond. A plain white cloth wound around Jon Torneo's head was the only sign of injury: otherwise, he appeared to be asleep.

"What happened?"

"An accident, a week ago. He was bringing the herd down from the high pasture when something frightened the sheep: they ran. He fell among them and was trampled. His head was hurt. He has not woken since. The physician Phylla says there is nothing she can do."

Joanna said tremulously, "He always said sheep were stupid. Is he in pain?"

"Phylla says not."

That afternoon, Joanna wrote a letter to her husband, telling him what had happened. She gave it to a courier to take to Dragon Keep.

Do not come, she wrote. *There is nothing you can do. I will stay until he dies.*

One by one his children took their turns at Jon Torneo's bedside. Olivia ate her meals in the chamber and slept on a pallet laid by the bed. Once each day she walked outside the gates, to talk to the people who thronged day and night outside the house, for Jon Torneo was much beloved. Solemn strangers came up to her weeping. Olivia, despite her own grief, spoke kindly to them all.

Joanna marveled at her mother's strength. She could not match it: she found herself weeping at night and snapping by day at her sisters. She was even, to her shame, sick one morning.

A week after Joanna's arrival, Jon Torneo died. He was buried, as was proper, within three days. Ege di Corsini was there, as were the husbands of Joanna's sisters, and all of Jon Torneo's family, and half Galva, or so it seemed.

The next morning, in the privacy of the garden, Olivia Torneo said quietly to her youngest daughter, "You should go home."

"Why?" Joanna said. She was dumbstruck. "Have I offended you?" Tears rose to her eyes. "Oh, Mother, I'm so sorry. . . ."

"Idiot child," Olivia said, and put her arms around her daughter. "My treasure, you and your sisters have been a great comfort to me. But you should be with your husband at this time." Her gaze narrowed. "Joanna? Do you not know that you are pregnant?"

Joanna blinked. "What makes you—? I feel fine," she said.

"Of course you do," said Olivia. "di Corsini women never have trouble with babies."

Phylla confirmed that Joanna was indeed pregnant.

"You are sure?"

"Yes. Your baby will be born in the spring."

"Is it a boy or a girl?" Joanna asked.

But Phylla could not tell her that.

So Joanna Atani said farewell to her family, and, with her escort about her, departed Galva for the journey to Dragon Keep. As they rode toward the hills, she marked the drifts of leaves on the ground and the dull color on the hills, and rejoiced. The year was turning. Slipping a hand beneath her clothes, she laid her palm across her belly, hoping to feel the quickening of life in her womb. It seemed strange to be so happy, so soon after her father's untimely death.

Twenty-one days after the departure of his wife from Dragon Keep, Iyadur Atani called one of his men to his side.

"Go to Galva, to the house of Jon Torneo," he said. "Find out what is happening there."

The courier rode to Galva. A light snow fell as he rode through the gates. The steward of the house escorted him to Olivia Torneo's chamber.

"My lady," he said, "I am sent from Dragon Keep to inquire after the well-being of the lady Joanna. May I speak with her?"

Olivia Torneo's face slowly lost its color. She said, "My daughter Joanna left a week ago to return to Dragon Keep. Soldiers from Dragon Keep were with her."

The courier stared. Then he said, "Get me fresh horses."

He burst through the Galva gates as though the demons of hell were on his horse's heels. He rode through the night. He reached Dragon Keep at dawn.

"He's asleep," the page warned.

"Wake him," the courier said. But the page would not. So the courier himself pushed open the door. "My lord? I am back from Galva."

The torches lit in the bedchamber.

"Come," said Iyadur Atani from the curtained bed. He drew back the curtains. The courier knelt on the rug beside the bed. He was shaking with weariness, and hunger, and also with dread.

"My lord, I bear ill news. Your lady left Galva to return home eight days ago. Since then, no one has seen her."

Fire came into Iyadur Atani's eyes. The courier turned his head. Rising from the bed, the dragon-lord said, "Call my captains."

The captains came. Crisply their lord told them that their lady was missing somewhere between Galva and Dragon Keep, and that it was their task, their only task, to find her. "You *will* find her," he said, and his words seemed to burn the air like flames.

"Aye, my lord," they said.

They searched across the countryside, hunting through hamlet and hut and barn, through valley and cave and ravine. They did not find Joanna Atani.

But midway between Galva and the border between the di Corsini land and Dragon's Country, they found, piled in a ditch and rudely concealed with branches, the bodies of nine men and one woman.

"Six of them we know," Bran, second-in-command of Dragon Keep's archers, reported to his lord. He named them: they were the six men who Joanna Atani's escort had comprised. "The woman is my lady Joanna's maid. My lord, we have found the tracks of many men and horses, riding hard and fast. The trail leads west."

"We shall follow it," Iyadur Atani said. "Four of you shall ride with me. The rest shall return to Dragon Keep, to await my orders."

They followed that trail for nine long days across Ippa, through bleak and stony hills, through the high reaches of Derrenhold, into Serrenhold's wild, windswept country. As they crossed the borders, a red-winged hawk swept down upon them. It landed in the snow, and became a dark-eyed woman in a gray cloak.

She said, "I am Madelene of the Red Hawk sisters. I watch this land. Who are you, and what is your business here?"

The dragon-lord said, "I am Iyadur Atani. I am looking for my wife. I believe she came this way, accompanied by many men, perhaps a dozen of them, and their remounts. We have been tracking them for nine days."

"A band of ten men rode across the border from Derrenhold into Serrenhold twelve days ago," the watcher said. "They led ten spare horses. I saw no women among them."

Bran said, "Could she have been disguised? A woman with her hair cropped might look like a boy, and the lady Joanna rides as well as any man."

Madelene shrugged. "I did not see their faces."

"Then you see ill," Bran said angrily. "Is this how the Red Hawk sisters keep watch?" Hawk-changeling and archer glared at one another.

"Enough," Iyadur Atani said. He led them onto the path to the fortress. It wound upward through the rocks. Suddenly they heard the clop of horses' hooves against the stone. Four horsemen appeared on the path ahead of them.

Bran cupped his hands to his lips. "What do you want?" he shouted.

The lead rider shouted back, "It is for us to ask that! You are on our land!"

"Then speak," Bran said.

"Your badges proclaim that you come from Dragon Keep. I bear a message to Iyadur Atani from Martun Hal."

Bran waited for the dragon-lord to declare himself. When he did not, the captain said, "Tell me, and I will carry it to him."

"Tell Iyadur Atani," the lead rider said, "that his wife will be staying in Serrenhold for a time. If any attempt is made to find her, then she will die, slowly and in great pain. That is all." He and his fellows turned their horses and bolted up the path.

Iyadur Atani said not a word, but the dragon rage burned white hot upon his face. The men from Dragon Keep looked at him, once. Then they looked away, holding their breath.

Finally he said, "Let us go."

When they reached the border, they found Ege di Corsini, with a large company of well-armed men, waiting for them.

"Olivia sent word to me," he said to Iyadur Atani. "Have you found her?"

"Martun Hal has her," the dragon-lord said. "He says he will kill her if we try to get her back." His face was set. "He may kill her anyway."

"He won't kill her," Ege di Corsini said. "He'll use her to bargain with. He will want his weapons and his army back, and freedom to move about his land."

"Give it to him," Iyadur Atani said. "I want my wife."

So Ege di Corsini sent a delegation of his men to Martun Hal, offering to modify the terms of Serrenhold's surrender, if he would release Joanna Atani unharmed.

But Martun Hal did not release Joanna. As di Corsini had said, he used her welfare to bargain with, demanding first the freedom to move about his own country, and then the restoration of his war band, first to one hundred, then to three hundred men.

"We must know where she is. When we know where she is, we can rescue her," di Corsini said. And he sent spies into Serrenhold, with instructions to discover where in that bleak and barren country the lady of Ippa was. But Martun Hal, ever crafty, had anticipated this. He sent a message to Iyadur Atani, warning that payment for the trespass of strangers would be exacted upon Joanna's body. He detailed, with blunt and horrific cruelty, what that payment would be.

In truth, despite the threats, he did nothing to hurt his captive. For though years of war had scoured from him almost all human feeling save pride, ambition, and spite, he understood quite well that if Joanna died, and word of that death reached Dragon Keep, no power in or out of Ryoka could protect him.

As for Joanna, she had refused even to speak to him from the day his men had brought her, hair chopped like a boy's, wrapped in a soldier's cloak, into his castle. She did not weep. They put her in an inner chamber, and placed guards on the door, and assigned two women to care for her. They were both named Kate, and since one was large and one not, they were known as Big Kate and Small Kate. She did not rage, either. She ate the meals the women brought her and slept in the bed they gave her.

Winter came early, as it does in Serrenhold. The wind moaned about the castle walls, and snow covered the mountains. Weeks passed, and Joanna's belly swelled. When it became clear beyond any doubt that she was indeed pregnant, the women who served her went swiftly to tell their lord.

"Are you sure?" he demanded. "If this is a trick, I will have you both flayed!"

"We are sure," they told him. "Send a physician to her, if you question it."

So Martun Hal sent a physician to Joanna's room. But Joanna refused to let him touch her. "I am Iyadur Atani's wife," she said. "I will allow no other man to lay his hands on me."

"Pray that it is a changeling, a dragon-child," Martun Hal said to his captains. And he told the two Kates to give Joanna whatever she needed for her comfort, save freedom.

The women went to Joanna and asked what she wanted.

"I should like a window," Joanna said. The rooms in which they housed her had all been windowless. They moved her to a chamber in a tower. It was smaller than the room in which they had been keeping her, but it had a narrow window, through which she could see sky and clouds, and on clear nights, stars.

When her idleness began to weigh upon her, she said, "Bring me books." They brought her books. But reading soon bored her.

"Bring me a loom."

"A loom? Can you weave?" Big Kate asked.

"No," Joanna said. "Can you?"

"Of course."

"Then you can teach me." The women brought her the loom, and with it, a dozen skeins of bright wool. "Show me what to do." Big Kate showed her how to set up the threads, and how to cast the shuttle. The first thing she made was a yellow blanket, a small one.

Small Kate asked, "Who shall that be for?"

"For the babe," Joanna said.

Then she began another: a scarlet cloak, a large one, with a fine gold border.

"Who shall that be for?" Big Kate asked.

"For my lord, when he comes."

One gray afternoon, as Joanna sat at her loom, a red-winged hawk alighted on her windowsill.

"Good day," Joanna said to it. It cocked its head and stared at her sideways out of its left eye. "There is bread on the table." She pointed to the little table where she ate her food. She had left a slice of bread untouched from her midday meal, intending to eat it later. The hawk turned its beak and stared at her out of its right eye. Hopping to the table, it pecked at the bread.

Then it fluttered to the floor and became a dark-eyed, dark-haired woman wearing a gray cloak. Crossing swiftly to Joanna's seat, she whispered, "Leave the shutter ajar. I will come again tonight." Before Joanna could answer, she turned into a bird and was gone.

That evening Joanna could barely eat. Concerned, Big Kate fussed at her. "You have to eat. The babe grows swiftly now; it needs all the nourishment you can give it. Look, here is the cream you wanted, and here is soft ripe cheese, come all the way from Merigny in the south, where they say it snows once every hundred years."

"I don't want it." Big Kate reached to close the window shutter. "Leave it!"

"It's freezing."

"I am warm."

"You might be feverish." Small Kate reached to feel her forehead.

"I am not. I'm fine."

At last they left her. She heard the bar slide across the door. She lay down on her bed. As was their custom, they had left her but a single candle, but light came from the hearth log. The babe moved in her belly. "Little one, I feel you," she whispered. "Be patient. We shall not always be in this loathsome place."

Then she heard the rustle of wings. A human shadow sprang across the walls of the chamber. A woman's voice said softly, "My lady, do you know me? I am Madelene of the Red Hawk sisters. I was at your wedding."

"I remember." Tears—the first she had shed since the start of her captivity—welled into Joanna's eyes. She knuckled them away. "I am glad to see you."

"And I you," Madelene said. "Since first I knew you were here, I have looked for you. I feared you were in torment, or locked away in some dark dungeon, where I might never find you."

"Can you help me to escape this place?"

Madelene said sadly, "No, my lady. I have no power to do that."

"I thought not." She reached beneath her pillow and brought out a golden brooch shaped like a full-blown rose. It had been a gift from her husband on their wedding night. "Never mind. Here. Take this to my husband."

In Dragon Keep, Iyadur Atani's mood grew grimmer and more remote. Martun Hal's threats obsessed him: he imagined his wife alone, cold, hungry, confined to darkness, perhaps hurt. His appetite vanished; he ceased to eat, or nearly so.

At night he paced the castle corridors, silent as a ghost, cloakless despite the winter cold, his eyes like white flame. His soldiers and his servants began to fear him. One by one, they vanished from the castle.

But some, more resolute or more loyal, remained. Among them was Bran the archer, now captain of the archery wing, since Jarko, the former captain, had disappeared one moonless December night. When a strange woman appeared among them, claiming to bear a message to Iyadur Atani from his captive wife, it was to Bran the guards brought her.

He recognized her. Leading her to Iyadur Atani's chamber, he pounded on the closed door. The door opened. Iyadur Atani stood framed in the doorway. His face was gaunt.

Madelene held out the golden brooch.

Iyadur Atani knew it at once. The grief and rage and fear that had filled him for four months eased a little. Lifting the brooch from Madelene's palm, he touched it to his lips.

"Be welcome," he said. "Tell me how Joanna is. Is she well?"

"She bade me say that she is, my lord."

"And—the babe?"

"It thrives. It is your child, my lord. Your lady charged me to say that, and to tell you that no matter what rumors you might have heard, neither Martun Hal nor any of his men has touched her. Indeed, no torment has been offered her at all. Only she begs you to please, come quickly to succor her, for she is desperate to be home."

"Can you visit her easily?"

"I can."

"Then return to her, of your kindness. Tell her I love her. Tell her not to despair."

"She will not despair," Madelene said. "Despair is not in her nature. But I have a second message for you. This one is from my queen." She meant the matriarch of the Red Hawks, Jamis Delamico. "She said to tell you, where force will not prevail, seek magic. She says, go west, to Lake Urai. Find the sorcerer who lives beside the lake, and ask him how to get your wife back."

Iyadur Atani said, "I did not know there were still sorcerers in the west."

"There is one. The common folk know him as Viksa. But that is not his true name, my queen says."

"And does your queen know the true name of this reclusive wizard?" For everyone knows that unless you know a sorcerer's true name, he or she will not even speak with you.

"She does. And she told me to tell it to you," said Madelene. She leaned toward the dragon-lord and whispered in his ear. "And she also told me to tell you, be careful when you deal with him. For he is sly, and what he intends to do, he does not always reveal. But what he says he will do, he will do."

"Thank you," Iyadur Atani said, and he smiled, for the first time in a long time. "Cousin, I am in your debt." He told Bran to see to her comfort and to provide her with whatever she needed—food, a bath, a place to sleep. Summoning his servants, he asked them to bring him a meal and wine.

Then he called his officers together. "I am leaving," he said. "You must defend my people and hold the borders against outlaws and incursions. If you need help, ask for aid from Mako or Derrenhold."

"How long will you be gone, my lord?" they asked him.

"I do not know."

Then he flew to Galva.

"I should have come before," he said. "I am sorry." He assured Olivia that despite her captivity, Joanna was well, and unharmed. "I go now to get her," he said. "When I return, I shall bring her with me. I swear it."

Issho, the southeastern province of Ryoka, is a rugged place. Though not so grim as Ippa, it has none of the gentle domesticated peace of Nakase. Its plains are colder than those of Nakase, and its rivers are wilder. The greatest of those rivers is the Endor. It starts in the north, beneath that peak which men call the Lookout, Mirrin, and pours ceaselessly south, cutting like a knife through Issho's open spaces to the border where Chuyo and Issho and Nakase meet.

It ends in Lake Urai. Lake Urai is vast, and even on a fair day, the water is not blue, but pewter gray. In winter, it does not freeze. Contrary winds swirl about it; at dawn and at twilight gray mist obscures its contours, and at all times the chill bright water lies quiescent, untroubled by even the most violent wind. The land about it is sparsely inhabited. Its people are a hardy, silent folk, not particularly friendly to strangers. They respect the lake and do not willingly discuss its secrets. When the tall, fair-haired stranger appeared among them, having come, so he said, from Ippa, they were happy to prepare his food and take his money, but were inclined to answer his questions evasively, or not at all.

The lake is as you see it. The wizard of the lake? Never heard of him.

But the stranger was persistent. He took a room at The Red Deer in Jen, hired a horse—oddly, he seemed to have arrived without one—and roamed about the lake. The weather did not seem to trouble him. "We have winter in my country." His clothes were plain, but clearly of the highest quality, and beneath his quiet manner there was iron.

"His eyes are different," the innkeeper's wife said. "He's looking for a wizard. Maybe he's one himself, in disguise."

One gray March afternoon, when the lake lay shrouded in mist, Iyadur Atani came upon a figure sitting on a rock beside a small fire. It was dressed in rags and held what appeared to be a fishing pole.

The dragon-lord's heart quickened. He dismounted. Tying his horse to a tall reed, he walked toward the fisherman. As he approached, the hunched figure turned. Beneath the ragged hood he glimpsed white hair, and a visage so old and wrinkled that he could not tell if he was facing a man or a woman.

"Good day," he said. The ancient being nodded. "My name is Iyadur Atani. Men call me the Silver Dragon. I am looking for a wizard."

The ancient one shook its head and gestured, as if to say, Leave me alone. Iyadur Atani crouched.

"Old One, I don't believe you are as you appear," he said in a conversational tone. "I believe you are the one I seek. If you are indeed"—and then he said the name that Madelene of the Red Hawks had whispered in his ear—"I beg you to help me. For I have come a long way to look for you."

An aged hand swept the hood aside. Dark gray eyes stared out of a withered, wrinkled face.

A feeble voice said, "Who told you my name?"

"A friend."

"Huh. Whoever it was is no friend of *mine*. What does the Silver Dragon need a wizard for?"

"If you are truly wise," Iyadur Atani said, "you know."

The sorcerer laughed softly. The hunched figure straightened. The rags became a silken gown with glittering jewels at its hem and throat. Instead of an old man, the dragon-lord faced a man in his prime, of princely bearing, with luminous chestnut hair and eyes the color of a summer storm. The fishing pole became a tall staff. Its crook was carved like a serpent's head. The sorcerer pointed the staff at the ground and said three words.

A doorway seemed to open in the stony hillside. Joanna Torneo Atani stood within it. She wore furs and was visibly pregnant.

"Joanna!" The dragon-lord reached for her. But his hands gripped empty air.

"Illusion," said the sorcerer known as Viksa. "A simple spell, but effective, don't you think? You are correct, my lord. I know you lost your wife. I assume you want her back. Tell me, why do you not lead your war band to Serrenhold and rescue her?"

"Martun Hal will kill her if I do that."

"I see."

"Will you help me?"

"Perhaps," said the sorcerer. The serpent in his staff turned its head to stare at the dragon-lord. Its eyes were rubies. "What will you pay me if I help you?"

"I have gold."

Viksa yawned. "I have no interest in gold."

"Jewels," said the dragon-lord, "fine clothing, a horse to bear you wherever you might choose to go, a castle of your own to dwell in . . ."

"I have no use for those."

"Name your price, and I will pay it," Iyadur Atani said steadily. "I reserve only the life of my wife and my child."

"But not your own?" Viksa cocked his head. "You intrigue me. Indeed, you move me. I accept your offer, my lord. I will help you rescue your wife from Serrenhold. I shall teach you a spell, a very simple spell, I assure you. When you speak it, you will be able to hide within a shadow. In that way you may pass into Serrenhold unseen."

"And its price?"

Viksa smiled. "In payment, I will take—you. Not your life, but your service. It has been many years since I had someone to hunt for me, cook for me, build my fire, and launder my clothes. It will amuse me to have a dragon as my servant."

"For how long would I owe you service?"

"As long as I wish it."

"That seems unfair."

The wizard shrugged.

"When would this service start?"

The wizard shrugged again. "It may be next month, or next year. Or it may be twenty years from now. Do we have an agreement?"

Iyadur Atani considered. He did not like this wizard. But he could see no other way to get his wife back.

"We do," he said. "Teach me the spell."

So Viksa the sorcerer taught Iyadur Atani the spell which would enable him to hide in a shadow. It was not a difficult spell. Iyadur Atani rode his hired horse back to The Red Deer and paid the innkeeper what remained on his bill. Then he walked into the bare field beside the inn, and became the Silver Dragon. As the innkeeper and his wife watched openmouthed, he circled the inn once and then sped north.

"A dragon!" the innkeeper's wife said with intense satisfaction. "I wonder if he found the sorcerer. See, I told you his eyes were odd." The innkeeper agreed. Then he went up to the room Iyadur Atani had occupied and searched carefully in every cranny, in case the dragon-lord had chanced to leave some gold behind.

Now it was in Iyadur Atani's mind to fly immediately to Serrenhold Castle. But remembering Martun Hal's threats, he did not. He flew to a point just south of Serrenhold's southern border. And there, in a nondescript village, he bought a horse, a shaggy brown gelding. From there he proceeded to Serrenhold Castle. It was not so tedious a journey as he had thought it would be. The prickly stunted pine trees that grew along the slopes of the windswept hills showed new green along their branches. Birds sang. Foxes loped across the hills, hunting mice and quail and the occasional stray chicken. The journey took six days. At dawn on the seventh day, Iyadur Atani fed the brown gelding and left him in a farmer's yard. It was a fine spring morning. The sky was cloudless; the sun brilliant; the shadows sharp-edged as steel. Thorn-crowned hawthorn bushes lined the road to Serrenhold Castle. Their shadows webbed the ground. A wagon filled with lumber lumbered toward the castle. Its shadow rolled beneath it.

"Wizard," the dragon-lord said to the empty sky, "if you have played me false, I will find you wherever you try to hide, and eat your heart."

In her prison in the tower, Joanna Torneo Atani walked from one side of her chamber to the other. Her hair had grown long again: it fell around her shoulders. Her belly was round and high under the soft thick drape of her gown. The coming of spring had made her restless. She had asked to be allowed to walk on the ramparts, but this Martun Hal had refused.

Below her window, the castle seethed like a cauldron. The place was never still; the smells and sounds of war continued day and night. The air was thick with soot. Soldiers drilled in the courtyard. Martun Hal was planning an attack on Ege di Corsini. He had told her all about it, including his intention to destroy Galva. *I will burn it to the ground. I will kill your uncle and take your mother prisoner,* he had said. *Or perhaps not. Perhaps I will just have her killed.*

She glanced toward the patch of sky that was her window. If Madelene would only come, she could get word to Galva, or to her uncle in Derrenhold. . . . But Madelene would not come in daylight; it was too dangerous.

She heard a hinge creak. The door to the outer chamber opened. "My lady," Big Kate called. She bustled in, bearing a tray. It held soup, bread, and a dish of thin sour pickles. "I brought your lunch."

"I'm not hungry."

Kate said, troubled, "My lady, you have to eat. For the baby."

"Leave it," Joanna said. "I will eat." Kate set the tray on the table and left.

Joanna nibbled at a pickle. She rubbed her back, which ached. The baby's heel thudded against the inside of her womb. "My precious, my little one, be still," she said. For it was her greatest fear that her babe, Iyadur Atani's child, might in its haste to be born arrive early, before her husband arrived to rescue them. That he would come, despite Martun Hal's threats, she had no doubt. "Be still."

Silently, Iyadur Atani materialized from the shadows.

"Joanna," he said. He put his arms about her. She reached her hands up. Her fingertips brushed his face. She leaned against him, trembling.

She whispered into his shirt, "How did you—?"

"Magic." He touched the high mound of her belly. "Are you well? Have they mistreated you?"

"I am very well. The babe is well." She seized his hand and pressed his palm over the mound. The baby kicked strongly. "Do you feel?"

"Yes." Iyadur Atani stroked her hair. A scarlet cloak with an ornate gold border hung on a peg. He reached for it and wrapped it about her. "Now, my love, we go. Shut your eyes, and keep them shut until I tell you to open them." He bent and lifted her into his arms. Her heart thundered against his chest.

She breathed into his ear, "I am sorry. I am heavy."

"You weigh nothing," he said. His human shape dissolved. The walls of the tower shuddered and burst apart. Blocks of stone and splintered planks of wood toppled into the courtyard. Women screamed. Arching his great neck, the Silver Dragon spread his wings and rose into the sky. The soldiers on the ramparts threw their spears at him and fled. Joanna heard the screaming and felt the hot wind. The scent of burning filled her nostrils. She knew what must have happened. But the arms about her were her husband's, and human. She did not know how this could be, yet it was. Eyes tight shut, she buried her face against her husband's shoulder.

Martun Hal stood with a courier in the castle hall. The crash of stone and the screaming interrupted him. A violent gust of heat swept through the room. The windows of the hall shattered. Racing from the hall, he looked up and saw the dragon circling. His men crouched, sobbing in fear. Consumed with rage, he looked about for a bow, a spear, a rock . . . Finally he drew his sword.

"Damn you!" he shouted impotently at his adversary.

Then the walls of his castle melted beneath a white-hot rain.

In Derrenhold, Ege di Corsini was wearily, reluctantly preparing for war. He did not want to fight Martun Hal, but he would, of course, if troops from Serrenhold took one step across his border. That an attack would be mounted he had no doubt. His spies had told him to expect it. Jamis of the Hawks had sent her daughters to warn him.

Part of his weariness was a fatigue of the spirit. *This is all my fault. I should have killed him when I had the opportunity. Ferris was right.* The other part of his weariness was physical. He was tired much of the time, and none of the tonics or herbal concoctions that the physicians prescribed seemed to help. His heart raced oddly. He could not sleep. Sometimes in the night he wondered if the Old One sleeping underground had dreamed of him. When the Old One dreams of you, you die. But he did not want to die and leave his domain and its people in danger, and so he planned a war, knowing all the while that he might die in the middle of it.

"My lord," a servant said, "you have visitors."

"Send them in," Ege di Corsini said. "No, wait." The physicians had said he needed to move about. Rising wearily, he went into the hall.

He found there his niece Joanna, big with child, and with her, her flame-haired, flame-eyed husband. A strong smell of burning hung about their clothes.

Ege di Corsini drew a long breath. He kissed Joanna on both cheeks. "I will let your mother know that you are safe."

"She needs to rest," Iyadur Atani said.

"I do not need to rest. I have been doing absolutely nothing for the last six months. I need to go home," Joanna said astringently. "Only I do not wish to ride. Uncle, would you lend us a litter and some steady beasts to draw it?"

"You may have anything I have," Ege di Corsini said. And for a moment he was not tired at all.

Couriers galloped throughout Ippa, bearing the news: Martun Hal was dead; Serrenhold Castle was ash, or nearly so. The threat of war was—after twenty years—truly over. Martun Hal's captains—most of them—had died with him. Those still alive hid, hoping to save their skins.

Two weeks after the rescue and the burning of Serrenhold, Ege di Corsini died.

In May, with her mother and sisters at her side, Joanna gave birth to a son. The baby had flame-colored hair and eyes like his father's. He was named Avahir. A year and a half later, a second son was born to Joanna Torneo Atani. He had dark hair, and eyes like his mother's. He was named Jon. Like the man whose name he bore, Jon Atani had a sweet disposition and a loving heart. He adored his brother, and Avahir loved his younger brother fiercely. Their loyalty to each other made their parents very happy.

Thirteen years almost to the day from the burning of Serrenhold, on a bright spring morning, a man dressed richly as a prince, carrying a white birch staff, appeared at the front gate of Atani Castle and requested audience with the dragon-lord. He refused to enter or even to give his name, saying only, "Tell him the fisherman has come for his catch."

His servants found Iyadur Atani in the great hall of his castle.

"My lord," they said, "a stranger stands at the front gate, who will not give his name. He says, The fisherman has come for his catch.'"

"I know who it is," their lord replied. He walked to the gate of his castle. The sorcerer stood there, leaning on his serpent-headed staff, entirely at ease.

"Good day," he said cheerfully. "Are you ready to travel?"

And so Iyadur Atani left his children and his kingdom to serve Viksa the wizard. I do not know—no one ever asked her, not even their sons—what Iyadur Atani and his wife said to one another that day. Avahir Atani, who at twelve was already full-grown, as changeling children are wont to be, inherited the lordship of Atani Castle. Like his father, he gained the reputation of being fierce but just.

Jon Atani married a granddaughter of Rudolf diMako and went to live in that city.

Joanna Atani remained in Dragon Keep. As time passed and Iyadur Atani did not return, her sisters and her brother, even her sons, urged her to remarry. She told them all not to be fools; she was wife to the Silver Dragon. Her husband was alive and might return at any time, and how would he feel to find another man warming her bed? She became her son's chief minister, and in that capacity could often be found riding across Dragon's Country, and elsewhere in Ippa, to Derrenhold and Mirrinhold and Ragnar, and even to far Voiana, where the Red Hawk sisters, one in particular, always welcomed her. She would not go to Serrenhold.

But always she returned to Dragon Keep.

As for Iyadur Atani: he traveled with the wizard throughout Ryoka, carrying his bags, preparing his oatcakes and his bathwater, scraping mud from his boots. Viksa's boots were often muddy, for he was a great traveler, who walked, rather than rode, to his many destinations. In the morning, when Iyadur Atani brought the sorcerer his breakfast, Viksa would say, "Today we go to Rotsa"—or Ruggio, or Rowena. "They have need of magic." He never said how he knew this. And off they would go to Vipurri or Rotsa or Talvela, to Sorvino, Ruggio, or Rowena.

Sometimes the need to which he was responding had to do directly with magic, as when a curse needed to be lifted. Often it had to do with common disasters. A river had swollen in its banks and needed to be restrained. A landslide had fallen on a house or barn. Sometimes the one who needed them was noble, or rich. Sometimes not. It did not matter to Viksa. He could enchant a cornerstone, so that the wall it anchored would rise straight and true; he could spell a field, so that its crop would thrust from the soil no matter what the rainfall.

His greatest skill was with water. Some sorcerers draw a portion of their power from an element: wind, water, fire, or stone. Viksa could coax a spring out of earth that had known only drought for a hundred years. He could turn stagnant water sweet. He knew the names of every river, stream, brook, and waterfall in Issho.

In the first years of his servitude, Iyadur Atani thought often of his sons, and especially Avahir, and of Joanna, but after a while his anxiety for them faded. After a longer while, he found he did not think of them so often—rarely at all, in fact. He even forgot their names. He had already relinquished his own. *Iyadur is too grand a name for a servant*, the sorcerer had remarked. *You need a different name.*

And so the tall, fair-haired man became known as Shadow. He carried the sorcerer's pack and cooked his food. He rarely spoke.

"Why is he so silent?" women, bolder and more curious than their men, asked the sorcerer.

Sometimes the sorcerer answered, "No reason. It's his nature." And sometimes he told a tale, a long, elaborate fantasy of spells and dragons and sorcerers, a gallant tale in which Shadow had been the hero, but from which he had emerged changed— broken. Shadow, listening, wondered if perhaps this tale was true. It might have been. It explained why his memory was so erratic, and so vague.

His dreams, by contrast, were vivid and intense. He dreamed often of a dark-walled castle flanked by white-capped mountains. Sometimes he dreamed that he was a bird, flying over the castle. The most adventurous of the women, attracted by Shadow's looks and, sometimes, by his silence, tried to talk with him. But their smiles and allusive glances only made him shy. He thought that he had had a wife, once. Maybe she had left him. He thought perhaps she had. But maybe not. Maybe she had died.

He had no interest in the women they met, though as far as he could tell, his body still worked as it should. He was a powerful man, well formed. Shadow wondered sometimes what his life had been before he had come to serve the wizard. He had skills: he could hunt and shoot a bow, and use a sword. Perhaps he had served in some noble's war band. He bore a knife now, a good one, with a bone hilt, but no sword. He did not need a sword. Viksa's reputation, and his magic, shielded them both.

Every night, before they slept, wherever they were, half speaking, half chanting in a language Shadow did not know, the sorcerer wove spells of protection about them and their dwelling. The spells were very powerful. They made Shadow's ears hurt.

Once, early in their association, he asked the sorcerer what the spell was for.

"Protection," Viksa replied. Shadow had been surprised. He had not realized Viksa had enemies.

But now, having traveled with the sorcerer as long as he had, he knew that even the lightest magic can have consequences, and Viksa's magic was not always light. He could make rain, but he could also make drought. He could lift curses or lay them. He was a man of power, and he had his vanity. He enjoyed being obeyed. Sometimes he enjoyed being feared.

Through spring, summer, and autumn, the wizard traveled wherever he was called to go. But in winter they returned to Lake Urai. He had a house beside the lake, a simple place, furnished with simple things: a pallet, a table, a chair, a shelf for books. But Viksa rarely looked at the books; it seemed he had no real love for study. Indeed, he seemed to have no passion for anything, save sorcery itself—and fishing. All through the Issho winter, despite the bitter winds, he took his little coracle out upon the lake and sat there with a pole. Sometimes he caught a fish, or two, or half a dozen. Sometimes he caught none.

"Enchant them," Shadow said to him one gray afternoon, when his master had returned to the house empty-handed. "Call them to your hook with magic."

The wizard shook his head. "I can't."

"Why not?"

"I was one of them once." Shadow looked at him, uncertain. "Before I was a sorcerer, I was a fish."

It was impossible to tell if he was joking or serious. It might have been true. It explained, at least, his affinity for water.

While Viksa fished, Shadow hunted. The country around the lake was rich with game; despite the winter, they did not lack for meat. Shadow hunted deer and badger and beaver. He saw wolves, but did not kill them. Nor would he kill birds, though birds there were; even in winter, geese came often to the lake. Their presence woke in him a wild, formless longing.

One day he saw a white bird, with wings as wide as he was tall, circling over the lake. It had a beak like a raptor. It called to him, an eerie sound. Something about it made his heart beat faster. When Viksa returned from his sojourn at the lake, Shadow described the strange bird to him, and asked what it was.

"A condor," the wizard said.

"Where does it come from?"

"From the north," the wizard said, frowning.

"It called to me. It looked—noble."

"It is not. It is scavenger, not predator." He continued to frown. That night he spent a long time over his nightly spells.

In spring, the kingfishers and guillemots returned to the lake. And one April morning, when Shadow laid breakfast upon the table, Viksa said, "Today we go to Dale."

"Where is that?"

"In the White Mountains, in Kameni, far to the north." And so they went to Dale, where a petty lordling needed Viksa's help in deciphering the terms and conditions of an ancient prophecy, for within it lay the future of his kingdom.

From Dale they traveled to Secca, where a youthful hedge-witch, hoping to shatter a boulder, had used a spell too complex for her powers and had managed to summon a stone demon, which promptly ate her. It was an old, powerful demon. It took a day, a night, and another whole day until Viksa, using the strongest spells he knew, was able to send it back into the Void.

They rested that night at a roadside inn, south of Secca. Viksa, exhausted from his battle with the demon, went to bed right after his meal, so worn that he fell asleep without taking the time to make his customary incantations.

Shadow considered waking him to remind him of it, and decided not to. Instead, he, too, slept.

And there, in an inn south of Secca, Iyadur Atani woke.

He was not, he realized, in his bed, or even in his bedroom. He lay on the floor. The coverlet around his shoulders was rough, coarse wool, not the soft quilt he was used to. Also, he was wearing his boots.

He said, "Joanna?" No one answered. A candle sat on a plate at his elbow. He lit it without touching it.

Sitting up soundlessly, he gazed about the chamber, at the bed and its snoring occupant, at the packs he had packed himself, the birchwood staff athwart the doorway. . . . Memory flooded through him. The staff was Viksa's. The man sleeping in the bed was Viksa. And he—*he* was Iyadur Atani, lord of Dragon Keep.

His heart thundered. His skin coursed with heat. The ring on his hand glowed, but he could not feel the burning. Fire coursed beneath his skin. He rose.

How long had Viksa's magic kept him in thrall—five years? Ten years? More?

He took a step toward the bed. The serpent in the wizard's staff opened its eyes. Raising its carved head, it hissed at him.

The sound woke Viksa. Gazing up from his bed at the bright shimmering shape looming over him, he knew immediately what had happened. He had made a mistake. *Fool*, he thought, *Oh, you fool.*

It was too late now.

The guards on the walls of Secca saw a pillar of fire rise into the night. Out of it— so they swore, with such fervor that even the most skeptical did not doubt them— flew a silver dragon. It circled the flames, bellowing with such power and ferocity that all who heard it trembled.

Then it beat the air with its wings and leaped north.

In Dragon Keep, a light powdery snow covered the garden. It did not deter the rhubarb shoots breaking through the soil, or the fireweed, or the buds on the birches. A sparrow swung in the birch branches, singing. The clouds that had brought the snow had dissipated; the day was bright and fair, the shadows sharp as the angle of the sparrow's wing against the light.

Joanna Atani walked along the garden path. Her face was lined, and her hair, though still lustrous and thick, was streaked with silver. But her step was as vigorous, and her eyes as bright, as they had been when first she came to Atani Castle, over thirty years before.

Bending, she brushed a snowdrop free of snow. By midday, she judged, the snow would be gone. A clatter of pans arose in the kitchen. A clear voice, imperious and young, called from within. She smiled. It was Hikaru, Avahir's firstborn and heir. He was only two years old, but had the height and grace of a lad twice that age.

A woman answered him, her voice soft and firm. That was Geneva Tuolinnen, Hikaru's mother. She was an excellent mother, calm and unexcitable. She was a good seamstress, too, and a superb manager; far better at running the castle than Joanna had ever been. She could scarcely handle a bow, though, and thought swordplay was entirely men's work.

She and Joanna were as friendly as two strong-willed women can be.

A black, floppy-eared puppy bounded across Joanna's feet, nearly knocking her down. Rup the dog-boy scampered after it. They tore through the garden and raced past the kitchen door into the yard.

A man walked into the garden. Joanna shaded her eyes. He was quite tall. She did not recognize him. His hair was nearly white, but he did not move like an old man. Indeed, the height of him and the breadth of his shoulder reminded her of Avahir, but she knew it was not Avahir. He was hundreds of miles away, in Kameni.

She said, "Sir, who are you?"

The man came closer. "Joanna?"

She knew that voice. For a moment she ceased to breathe. Then she walked toward him.

It was her husband.

He looked exactly as he had the morning he had left with the wizard, sixteen years before. His eyes were the same, and his scent, and the heat of his body against hers. She slid her palms beneath his shirt. His skin was warm. Their lips met.

I do not know—no one ever asked them—what Iyadur Atani and his wife said to one another that day. Surely there were questions, and answers. Surely there were tears, of sorrow and of joy.

He told her of his travels, of his captivity, and of his freedom. She told him of their sons, particularly of his heir, Avahir, who ruled Dragon's Country.

"He is a good lord, respected throughout Ryoka. His people fear him and love him. He is called the Azure Dragon. He married a girl from Issho. She is cousin to the Talvela; we are at peace with them, and with the Nyo. She and Avahir have a son, Hikaru. Jon, too, is wed. He and his wife live in Mako. They have three children, two boys and a girl. You are a grandfather."

He smiled at that. Then he said, "Where is my son?"

"In Kameni, at a council called by Rowan Imorin, the king's war leader, who wished to lead an army against the Chuyo pirates." She stroked his face. It was not true, as she had first thought, that he was unchanged. The years had marked him. Still, he looked astonishingly young. She wondered if she seemed old to him.

"Never leave me again," she said.

A shadow crossed his face. He lifted her hands to his lips and kissed them, front and back. Then he said, "My love, I would not. But I must go. I cannot stay here."

"What are you saying?"

"Avahir is lord of this land now. You know the dragon-nature. We are jealous of power, we dragons. It would go ill were I to stay."

Joanna's blood chilled. She did know. The history of the dragon-folk is filled with tales of rage and rivalry: sons strive against fathers, brothers against brothers, mothers against their children. They are bloody tales. For this reason, among others, the dragon kindred do not live very long.

She said steadily, "You cannot hurt your son."

"I would not," said Iyadur Atani. "Therefore I must leave."

"Where will you go?"

"I don't know. Will you come with me?"

She locked her fingers through his huge ones and smiled through tears. "I will go wherever you wish. Only give me time to kiss my grandchild and write a letter to my son. For he must know that I have gone of my own accord."

And so, Iyadur Atani and Joanna Torneo Atani left Atani Castle. They went quietly, without fuss, accompanied by neither man nor maidservant. They went first to Mako, where Iyadur Atani greeted his younger son and met his son's wife, and their children.

From there they went to Derrenhold, and from Derrenhold, west, to Voiana, the home of the Red Hawk sisters. From Voiana, letters came to Avahir Atani and to Jon Atani from their mother, assuring them, and particularly Avahir, that she was with her husband, and that she was well.

Avahir Atani, who truly loved his mother, flew to Voiana. But he arrived to find them gone.

"Where are they?" he asked Jamis Delamico, who was still matriarch of the Red Hawk clan. For the Red Hawk sisters live long.

"They left."

"Where did they go?"

Jamis Delamico shrugged. "They did not tell me their destination, and I did not ask."

There were no more letters. Over time, word trickled back to Dragon Keep that they had been seen in Rowena, or Sorvino, or Secca, or the mountains north of Dale.

"Where were they going?" Avahir Atani asked, when his servants came to him to tell him these stories. But no one could tell him that.

Time passed; Ippa prospered. In Dragon Keep, a daughter was born to Avahir and Geneva Atani. They named her Lucia. She was small and dark-haired and feisty. In Derrenhold and Mako and Mirrinhold, memories of conflict faded. In the windswept west, the folk of Serrenhold rebuilt their lord's tower.

In the east, Rowan Imorin, the war leader of Kameni, summoned the lords of all the provinces to unite against the Chuyo pirates. The lords of Ippa, instead of quarreling with each other, joined the lords of Nakase and Kameni. They fought many battles. They gained many victories.

But in one battle, not the greatest, an arrow shot by a Chuyo archer sliced into the throat of Avahir Atani, and killed him. Grimly, his mourning soldiers made a pyre and burned his body. For the dragon-kindred do not lie in earth.

Hikaru, the Shining Dragon, became lord of Dragon Keep. Like his father and his grandfather before him, he was feared and respected throughout Ippa.

One foggy autumn, a stranger arrived at the gates of Dragon Keep, requesting to see the lord. He was an old man with silver hair. His back was stooped, but they could see that he had once been powerful. He bore no sword, but only a knife with a bone hilt.

"Who are you?" the servants asked him.

"My name doesn't matter," he answered. "Tell him I have a gift for him."

They brought him to Hikaru. Hikaru said, "Old man, I am told you have a gift for me."

"It is so," the old man said. He extended his palm. On it sat a golden brooch, fashioned in the shape of a rose. "It is an heirloom of your house. It was given by your grandfather, Iyadur, to his wife Joanna, on their wedding night. She is dead now, and so it comes to you. You should give it to your wife, when you wed."

Frowning, Hikaru said, "How do you come by this thing? Who are you? Are you a sorcerer?"

"I am no one," the old man replied, "a shadow."

"That is not an answer," Hikaru said, and he signaled to his soldiers to seize the stranger.

But the men who stepped forward to hold the old man found their hands passing through empty air. They hunted through the castle for him, but he was gone. They decided that he was a sorcerer, or perhaps the sending of a sorcerer. Eventually they forgot him. When the shadow of the dragon first appeared in Atani Castle, rising like smoke out of the castle walls, few thought of the old man who had vanished into shadow one autumnal morning. Those who did kept it to themselves. But Hikaru Atani remembered. He kept the brooch and gave it to his wife upon their wedding night. And he told his soldiers to honor the shadow-dragon when it came, and not to speak lightly of it.

"For clearly," he said, "it belongs here."

The shadow of the dragon still lives in the walls of Atani Castle. It comes as it chooses, unsummoned. And still, in Dragon's Country, and throughout Ippa and Issho, and even into the east, the singers tell the story of Iyadur Atani, of his wife, Joanna, and of the burning of Serrenhold.

Honorable Mentions: 2004

Abouzeid, Chris, "The Silence of the Iambs," *Agni* 59.

Abraham, Daniel, "Flat Diane," *The Magazine of Fantasy and Science Fiction*, Oct./Nov.

———, "Leviathan Wept," *SCI FICTION*, July 7.

Adams, Danny, "A Deconstruction of Beauty," *Not One of Us* 32.

Aegard, John, "The Golden Age of Fire Escapes," *Rabid Transit: Petting Zoo.*

Albrecht, Aaron, "Accursed," *All Hallows*, October.

Aletti, Steffan, "Yellow Shadows," *Strange Tales* 8.

Alexander, Maria, "Sighs from the Edda Over Iceland," (poem) *Dreams and Nightmares* 67.

Alexander, Maria, "When Gods Die," Gothic.net, April 19.

Allen, Angela C., "Vamp Noir," *Dark Thirst.*

Allen, Mike, "The Windows Breathe," (poem) *Dreams and Nightmares* 67.

Allyn, Doug, "Secondhand Heart," *Alfred Hitchcock's Mystery Magazine*, Jan./Feb.

Amis, Martin, "In the Palace of the End," *The New Yorker*, March 15.

Anders, Charlie, "The Sorcersoft Story," *Problem Child* 2.

Anderson, Barth, "Alone in the House of Mims," *Strange Horizons*, April 26.

Anderson, Kevin, "Ink Spot," *Lone Star Stories* 1.

Armstrong, Michael, "The Boy Who Chased Seagulls," *Powers of Detection.*

Arnzen, Michael A. "The Cow Café," *100 Jolts.*

———, "Nightmare Job #2," Ibid.

Aspey, Lynette, "Sleeping Dragons," *Asimov's Science Fiction Magazine*, Sept.

Attanasio, A. A., "Demons Hide Their Faces," *Flights.*

Ayres, Neil, "Sundrew," *Electric Velocipede* 6.

Bailey, Dale, "The End of the World as We Know It," *F&SF*, Oct./Nov.

———, "Passing to the Distant Shore," *Alchemy* 2.

Baker, James Ireland, "Worried Man Blues," *Cemetery Dance* 48.

Baker, Kage, "Leaving His Cares Behind Him," *Asimov's*, Apr./May.

Bamberg, Richard A., "Just 'Til I Need Glasses," *The Parasitorium.*

Barker, Trey, "The Regard of Oddities," *Carnival of Horrors.*

Barnes, Steven and Tananarive Due, "Danger Word," *Dark Dreams.*

Barnett, David G., "And the Lake Shall Cry No More," *Dead Souls.*

———, "Bully," Ibid.

———, "Libra," Ibid.

Barrett, Neil Jr., "Tourists," *Flights.*

Barry, Michael, "Sleeping with Monsters," *Encounters*.

Barzak, Christopher, "The Other Angelas," www.pindeldyboz.com.

Battersby, Lee, "Father Muerte and the Theft," *Tales of the Unanticipated* 25.

Bear, Elizabeth, "Seven Dragons Mountain," *All-Star Zeppelin Adventure Stories*.

Beatty, Greg, "Sometimes," *Neverary* 4.

Bender, Aimee, "Crew (Devilly & Skelly)," *Hobart* 4.

———, "Debbieland," *Black Clock March*.

Berg, T. J., "To Crown a Sand Castle Just Right," *Talebones* 28.

Berger, Paul, "Voice of the Hurricane," *All-Star Zeppelin*.

Berman, Judith, "The Poison Well," *Black Gate* 7.

Berman, Steve, "The Price of Glamour," *The Faery Reel*.

Bestwick, Simon, ". . . And Dream of Avalon," *A Hazy Shade of Winter*.

———, "A Hazy Shade of Winter," Ibid.

———, "Come with Me, Down This Long Road," Ibid.

———, "The Crows," Ibid.

———, "Until My Darkness Goes," (novella) Ibid.

Betancourt, John Gregory, "Dry Days in Yellow Gulch," *Weird Trails*, April.

Biancotti, Deborah, "Cinnamon Gate," *Orb* 6.

———, "Number 3 Raw Place," *Agog! Smashing Stories*.

Bick, Ilsa J., "Driving Blind," *Strange Bedfellows: The Hot Blood Series*.

Bidart, Frank, "The Third Hour of the Night" (poem), *Poetry*, Oct.

Bishop, Anne, "The Price," *Powers of Detection*.

Bishop, K. J., "Alsiso," *The Alsiso Project*.

———, "We the Enclosed," *Leviathan* 4.

Bishop, Michael, "'An Owl at the Crucifixion,' by Susannah Huckaby," (poem) *The Devil's Wine*.

Bisson, Terry, "Death's Door," *Flights*.

———, "Super 8," *SCI FICTION*, Nov. 24.

Black, Holly, "The Night Market," *The Faery Reel*.

Blair, David, "We Were Insanely Bored," (poem) *Harvard Review* 26.

———, "Diamond," (poem) *Lady Churchill's Rosebud Wristlet* 14.

Blaylock, James P., "Hula Ville," *SCI FICTION*, Nov. 3.

Bobet, Leah, "Sonnets Made of Wood," *Realms of Fantasy*, Dec.

Bonansinga, Jay, "Hair Cut," (poem) *The Devil's Wine*.

———, "My Boys," (poem) Ibid.

Bond, Lance, "Violation," *On Spec*, fall.

Boston, Bruce, "The Changing of the Flesh," (poem) *Star*Line*, July/Aug.

———, "Crow People," (poem) *Feralfiction* 1.

———, "Curse of the Siren's Suitors," (poem) *Weird Tales* 336.

———, "The Death of Statues," (poem) *Dreams and Nightmares* 65.

———, "In a Key of Shadow Horror," (poem) *Flesh and Blood* 15.

———, "Like a Bunch of Animals Pawing," (poem) *Dreams and Nightmares* 66.

———, "Noir Slash," *Dreams and . . .* 65.

———, "Rat People," (poem) *Feralfiction* 1.

Boston, Bruce and Marge Simon, "Counting the Cries," (poem) *EOTU*.

Boudinot, Ryan, "Civilization," *McSweeney's* 15.

Boyer, Judith, "The Ugly Stepsister," (poem) *Dreams and Nightmares* 68.

Bowen, Hannah Wolf, "My Kingdom," *Abyss and Apex* 7.

Bradbury, Ray, "A Careful Man Dies," *The Cat's Pajamas.*

——, "The Ghosts," Ibid.

——, "The House," Ibid.

——, "I Met Murder on the Way," (poem) *Cemetery Dance* 50.

——, "The Island," *The Cat's Pajamas.*

——, "Sixty-Six," Ibid.

Bradley, Lisa M., "Gehenesis," *The Brutarian Quarterly*, summer/fall.

Braunbeck, Gary A., "Just Out of Reach," *Cemetery Dance* 50.

——, "That, and the Rain," *Damned: An Anthology of the Lost.*

Brite, Poppy, "The Devil of Delery Street," *McSweeney's Enchanted Chamber of Astonishing Stories.*

Broadhurst, Lida, "Next Door," (poem) *Into the Beautiful Maze.*

Brown, Davit, "A Report on Making Out," *Denver Quarterly*, vol. 39, issue 1.

Brown, Simon, "Chlorine," *Borderlands* 3.

Brown, Toni, "Sometimes I See My Father," (poem) *Prairie Schooner*, vol. 78, issue 4.

Buckell, Tobias S., "Her," *Fortean Bureau* 18.

Budnitz, Judy, "Miracle," *The New Yorker*, July 12 and 19.

Bull, Scott Emerson, "Balance," *Outer Darkness* 30.

Bunn, Cullen, "Why Sing the Sirens?" *Horrorfind.*

Burgess, Donna Taylor, "Blue Monday," (poem) *A Song of Bones.*

Burke, Chesya, "Purse," *Tales from the Gorezone.*

Burke, John, "The Devil's Tritone," *The Mammoth Book of Vampires.*

Burke, Kealan Patrick, "The Number 121 to Pennsylvania," *C. Dance* 47.

Burrage, Nathan, "The R Quotient," *Orb* 6.

Burt, Steve, "The French Acre," *Oddest Yet.*

Butner, Richard, "House of the Future," *SCI FICTION*, Jan. 14.

——, "The Rules of Gambling," *Horses Blow Up Dog City.*

——, "The Wounded," *Crossroads.*

Butterworth, Christine, "Flounder," (poem) *Tales of the Unanticipated* 25.

Byatt, A. S., "The Pink Ribbon," *Little Black Book of Stories.*

Cacek, P. D., "The Following," *Flights.*

——, ". . . With Bright and Shining Eyes . . ." *Quietly Now.*

Cady, Jack, "Fog," *F&SF*, Dec.

Cafer, Judith Ortiz, "Rice," (poem) *Prairie Schooner*, vol. 78, issue 1.

Campbell, Ramsey, "Direct Line," *Postscripts*, spring.

Carey, Jacqueline, "The Isle of Women," *Emerald Magic.*

Carter, Scott William, "Front Row Seats," *Chizine* 20.

——, "The Woman Coughed Up by the Sea," *Chizine* 21.

Chabrai, Priya Sarukkai, "In Hospital" (poem), *Indian Literature* 221.

Channer, Laurie, "Pizza Night," *On Spec*, summer.

Chapman, Stepan, "The Stiff and the Stile," *Premonitions*, 2004.

Charnas, Suzy McKee, "Peregrines," *SCI FICTION*, Jan. 7.

Chen, E. L., "The Moment of Truth," *On Spec*, summer.

——, "Tickling the Siroko's Chin," *Challenging Destiny* 19.

Chernoff, Maxine, "[to bully the gods, we ask their blessings]," (poem) *Minnesota Review*, 61–62.

Choo, Mary E., "Christina," (poem) *Chizine* 22.

Chui, Janet, "Black Fish," *Say . . . Why Aren't We Crying?*

Cisco, Michael, "The City of God," *Leviathan* 4.

Clark, Lawrence Gordon, "Original Sin," *Postscripts*, spring.

——, "The Return," *Postscripts*, summer.

Clarke, Susanna, "Antickes and Frets," *The New York Times*, Oct. 31.

Claxton, Matthew, "The Anatomist's Apprentice," *SCI FICTION*, July 14.

Clegg, Douglas, "The Attraction," (novella) chapbook.

——, "The Dark Game," *Flesh and Blood* 14 and 15 / *The Machinery of Night*.

——, "Subway Turnstile," *The Machinery of Night*.

Cogman, Genevieve, "Snow and Salt," *Strange Horizons*, July 19.

Colburn, John, "Burning Up," (poem) *Jubilat* 8.

Collins, Morris, "Gwydion to Blodeuedd," (poem) *Magazine of Speculative Poetry*, autumn.

Collins, Tess, "Scarlet Ribbons," *Space and Time*, spring.

Congreve, Bill, "The Shooter at the Heartrock Waterhole," *The Faery Reel*.

Connolly, John, "The Cancer Cowboy Rides," (novella) *Nocturnes*.

——, "The Erlking," Ibid.

——, "The Furnace Room," Ibid.

——, "The Inn at Shillingford," johnconnolly.co.uk.

——, "Miss Froom, Vampire," *Nocturnes*.

——, "The New Daughter," Ibid.

——, "Nocturne," Ibid.

——, "Mr. Pettinger's Daemon," Ibid.

——, "The Reflecting Eye," (novella) Ibid.

——, "The Shifting of the Sands," Ibid.

——, "Some Children Wander by Mistake," Ibid.

——, "The Underbury Witches," Ibid.

Constantine, Brendan, "Cold Reading," (poem) *Ploughshares*, vol. 30, issue 4.

Cooney, Laura, "Number 808," *Lullaby Hearse* 5.

Cooper, Constance, "Necropolis," (poem) *Mythic Delirium* 10.

Copeland, Joy M., "Hair Dreams," *Dark Dreams*.

Costaris, Matthew, "The Office," *Tales from the Gorezone*.

Cowdrey, Albert E., "The Name of the Sphinx," *F&SF*, Dec.

——, "Rapper," *F&SF*, Feb.

——, "Silent Echoes," *F&SF*, April.

Cox, F. Brett, "Madeline's Version," *Crossroads*.

Crisp, Quentin S., "The Mermaid," (novella) *Morbid Tales*.

——"The Two-Timer," Ibid.

Crowther, Peter, "Conversation," (poem) *The Devil's Wine*.

——, "Outside," (poem) Ibid.

Cummins, Ann, "Pyromaniac," *Argosy*, Jan./Feb.

Curren, Tim, "The Grisly Race," *Cloaked in Shadow*.

Curtis, Rebecca, "The Wolf at the Door," *Story Quarterly* 40.

de Lint, Charles, "The Butter Spirit's Tithe," *Emerald Magic*.

——, "Riding Shotgun," *Flights*.

——, "The World in a Box," chapbook.

de Ory, Carlos Edmundo (translated by Steven J. Stewart), "Aerolites," (poem) *Jubilat* 9.

DeNiro, Alan, "The Keeper," *Electric Velocipede* 6.

——, "Tetrarchs," *Strange Horizons*, May 3.

De Noux, O'Neil, "Cruelty the Human Heart," *Argosy*, May/June.

De Winter, Corinne, "Before the Fall," (poem) *The Women at the Funeral.*

——, "Poe," (poem) Ibid.

——, "The Stranger," (poem) Ibid.

Decker, Sherry, "Chazzabryom," *Space and Time*, spring.

——, "Hook House," *Cemetery Dance* 49.

Dedman, Stephen, "Twilight of Idols," *Conqueror Fantastic.*

Dellamonica, A. M., "Origin of Species," *The Many Faces of Van Helsing.*

Detzner, Brendan, "Rolling Bones," Gothic.net, March 22.

Dietz, Michael, "On a Crooked Sixpence (Pantoum of Vulgar Errors)," (poem) *New England Review*, vol. 25, issue 1–2.

Di Filippo, Paul, "Observable Things," *Conqueror Fantastic.*

Dirda, Michael, "Dukedom Large Enough," *All Hallows*, Oct.

Dockins, Mike, "Zarathustra Paints Town," (poem) *Jubilat* 9.

Dodds, John, "A Crow Among the Starlings," *The Horror Express* 3.

Domina, Lynn, "Sabbath," (poem) *Prairie Schooner*, vol. 78, issue 2.

Donahoe, Erin, "Her Eyes," *Aoife's Kiss*, March.

——, "Woman with Webbed Fingers," (poem) *Dreams and Nightmares* 65.

Dornemann, Rudi, "The Labyrinth Tourist," *Flytrap* 2.

——, "Lantean Sands," *Fortean Bureau* 26.

Doyle, Roddy, "The Child," *McSweeney's Enchanted Chamber.*

Doyle, Tom, "The Floating Otherworld," *Strange Horizons*, Dec. 20.

Dubrow, Jehane, "Cinderella Summer," (poem) *Hudson Review*, vol. 57, issue 2.

Dunyach, Jean-Claude, "Scenes at the Exhibition," *The Night Orchid.*

——, "What the Dead Know," *On Spec*, winter.

Edelman, Scott, "I Wish I Knew Where I Was Going," *Quietly Now.*

Eller, Steve and Paul G. Tremblay, "Lies and Skin," *Razor Magazine*, March.

Emswiler, Tim, "Adagio," *Bare Bone* 6.

Emshwiller, Carol, "Gliders Though They Be," *SCI FICTION*, June 3.

——, "The Library," *F&SF*, August.

——, "On Display Among the Lesser," *SCI FICTION*, April 14.

Erickson, Steve, "Zeroville," *McSweeney's Enchanted Chamber.*

Etchemendy, Nancy, "Nimitseahpah," *F&SF*, Jan.

Evans, Kendall and David Kopaska-Merkel, "Of Time and the Teeth of the Black Dog," *Star*Line*, July/Aug.

Evans, S. E., "Louisa, Johnny, and the North Shore Huldre," *Strange Horizons*, March 8.

Evenson, Brian, "Helpful," *Bombay Gin.*

Everson, John, "The Beginning Was the End," *Black October*, vol. 1, issue 6.

Every, Gary, "Azurite Mine" (poem), *Mythic Delirium* 11.

Farris, John, "Waiting for Mr. Gillray," *Elvisland.*

Faust, Christa, "Tighter," *Strange Bedfellows.*

Feeley, Gregory, "Gilead," *The First Heroes.*

Files, Gemma, "Nigredo," *The Worm in Every Heart.*

Finch, Paul, "April," *All Hallows* 35.

——, "Bullbeggar Walk," *Inhuman* 1.

——, "Children Don't Play Here Anymore," *Quietly Now.*

——, "God's Fist," *A Walk on the Darkside.*

——, "The Other One," *Terror Tales* 2.

Findlay, David, "Recovery from a Fall," *Dark Matter: Reading the Bones*.

Finlay, Charles Coleman, "After the Gaud Chysalis," *F&SF*, June.

Fintushel, Eliot, "The Eye," *Polyphony* 4.

——, "Women Are Ugly," *Strange Horizons*, June 21.

Fishler, Karen D., "Country Life," *Realms of Fantasy*, June.

Fleming, Robert, "But Beautiful and Terrifying," *Dark Dreams*.

——, "Life after Bas," Ibid.

——, "The Tenderness of Monsieur Blanc," Ibid.

Ford, Jeffrey, "The Annals of Eelin-Ok," *The Faery Reel*.

——, "Jupiter's Skull," *Flights*.

Fowler, Christopher, "Dealing," *Demonized*.

——, "Personal Space," Ibid.

——, "Red Torch," *SFX Horror Special*.

——, "The Scorpion Jacket," *Demonized*.

Fox, D. S., "Dreads," *Dark Dreams*.

Freeman, Kyri, "The Elf Knight and Lady Isabelle," *Cloaked in Shadow*.

Frost, Gregory, "Dub," *Weird Trails*, April.

——, "Tengu Mountain," *The Faery Reel*.

Fry, Adrian, "Determining the Extent," *Nemonymous Four* (part 3).

Fry, Gary "Man's Best Friend," *Maelstrom*, Volume One.

Fuller, William, "Homburg," (poem) *Chicago Review*, 49:3/4 and 50:1.

Gabriel, Manfred, "The Correct Response," *Tales of the Unanticipated* 25.

Gaiman, Neil, "Forbidden Brides of the Faceless Slaves in the Nameless . . . ," *Gothic!*

——, "The Monarch of the Glen" (novella), *Legends II*.

——, "The Problem of Susan," *Flights*.

Galeano, Juan Carlos, "Amazon Show," (poem) *Stand*, vol. 5, issue 3.

Gallagher, Stephen, "Little Angels," *Out of His Head*.

Garcia, Victoria Elizabeth, "The Chitin Heart," (chapbook) *Unspeakable Vitrine*.

——, "Preserve Us," Ibid.

Gavin, Richard, "In the Shadow of the Nodding God," *Shadow Writers*.

——, "The Folly," *Charnel Wine*.

——, "The Physics of Unseen Puppeteers," Ibid.

Geiger, Barbara, "Songs," *Cloaked in Shadow*.

Gilman, Laura Anne, "Dragons," *Chizine* 21.

——, "Talent," *Realms of Fantasy*, Dec.

Godfrey, Darren O., "Night of the Puppet," *Tales from the Gorezone*.

Golaski, Adam, "From Colour Plates," *Supernatural Tales* 8.

goldberg, d.g.k., " 'Whatever Happened To?'," *A Walk on the Darkside*.

——, "Playthings of the Goddess," *Deathgrip* (2003).

Golden, Christopher, "Venus and Mars," *The Many Faces of Van Helsing*.

Goldstein, Lisa, "Finding Beauty," *F&SF*, Oct./Nov.

Golightly, Walton, "Russian Mail Order Brides," *NFG*, vol. 4, issue 2.

Gorman, Ed, "Riff," *Postscripts*, spring.

Goss, Theodora, "The Bear's Daughter," (poem) *The Journal of Mythic Arts*, winter.

——, "Her Mother's Ghosts," *The Rose in Twelve Petals and Other Stories*.

——, "Miss Emily Gray," *Alchemy* 2.

——, "The Wings of Meister Wilhelm," *Polyphony* 4.

Goto, Hiromi, "Camp Americana," *Hopeful Monsters*.

——, "Foxwife," *The Faery Reel*.

Gramlich, Charles A., "Thief of Eyes," *The Parasitorium*.

Grant, John, "Has Anyone Here Seen Kristie?," *The 3rd Alternative* 38.

——, "Q," *SCI FICTION*, Oct. 20.

Gregory, Daryl, "The Continuing Adventures of Rocket Boy," *F&SF*, July.

Gresham, Stephen, "Where No One Ever Dies Good," *Strange Bedfellows*.

Grey, Ian, "The Last Clean Spot," *The Urban Bizarre*.

Gunn, Eileen, "Coming to Terms," *Stable Strategies and Others*.

Haines, Paul, "The Gift of Hindsight," *Aurealis* 32.

——, "The Last Days of Kali Yuga," *NFG*, vol. 2, issue 4.

——, "They Say It's Other People," *Agog! Smashing Stories*.

——, "This is the End, Harry, Good Night," *NFG*, vol. 2, issue 5.

Haldeman, Joe, "Audience Participation," (poem) *The Devil's Wine*.

——, "Camouflage," (novella) *Analog*, March-May.

Harland, Richard, "The Border," *Agog! Smashing Stories*.

——, "Catabolic Magic," *Aurealis* 32.

——, "The Souvenir," *Encounters*.

Harmon, Christopher, "Old Pro," *Supernatural Tales* 7.

Harmon, Jim, "The Three Gray Wolves," *Weird Trails*, April.

Harris, Joanne, "Fish," *Jigs and Reels*.

——, "The Little Mermaid," Ibid.

——, "Waiting for Gandalf," Ibid.

Hawkey, Christian, "Hours," (poem) *Conjunctions* 43.

Hemmingson, Michael, "Long Island Iced Tea," *The Urban Bizarre*.

Henderson, C. J., "The Incident on Highway 19," *Book of Dark Wisdom*, fall.

Henderson, Samantha, "Grandma Came from Eldritch," (poem) *Neverary*, Oct.

Hendricks, Brent, "My Life as the Moon," (poem) *Black Warrior Review*, vol. 31, issue 1.

Hill, Joe, "The Black Phone," *The 3rd Alternative* 39.

Hirshberg, Glen, "Like a Lily in a Flood," *Cemetery Dance* 50.

Hitchcock, Karen, "In Formation," *Meanjin*, vol. 63, issue 4.

Hobb, Robin, "Homecoming," *Legends II*.

Hodge, Brian, "Brushed in Blackest Silence," *The Many Faces of Van Helsing*.

——, "An Ounce of Prevention Is Worth a Pound of Flesh," *Walk on the . . .*

——, "Sunrise, Dressed for Dusk," (poem) *The Devil's Wine*.

——, "When the Bough Doesn't Break," *Damned*.

Hoff, Bruce, "The Lost Pictures of Franklin Field," *Spooks!*

Hoffman, Alice, "The Conjurer's Handbook," *Southwest Review*, vol. 89, issues 2 & 3.

Hoffman, Nina Kiriki, "Hearts' Desires," *Realms of Fantasy*, Feb.

——, "The Laily Worm," *Realms of Fantasy*, Aug.

Hood, Robert, "Regolith," *Agog! Smashing Stories*.

Hopkins, Brian A., "The Secret Sympathy," *Haunted Holidays*.

Hopkinson, Nalo, "The Smile on the Face," *Girls Who Bite Back*.

——, "A Young Candy Daughter," www.sff.net/people/nalo.

Horsley, Ron, ". . . And the Red Light Was My Mind," *On Spec*, winter.

Houarner, Gerard, "Ash Man," *Flesh and Blood* 15.

——, "Celebrant," *Cloaked in Shadow*.

——, "Dead Cat's Lick," chapbook, *Bedlam Press*.

——, "No We Love No One," *Damned*.

——, "The Three Strangers," *The Last Pentacle of the Sun*.

Howkins, Elizabeth, "Children of the Wolves," (poem) *Penny Dreadful* 15.

Hughes, Rhys, "The Old House under the Snow Where Nobody Goes Except You and Me Tonight," *Postscripts* 2.

Hummell, Austin, "Nights Like Renfield," (poem) *Minnesota Review* 61–62.

Humphrey, Andrew, "Alsiso," *The Alsiso Project*.

——, "Other Voices," *Midnight Street* 1.

——, "Three Days," *Bare Bone* 6.

——, "War Stories," *Midnight Street* 1.

Hunter, Ian, "For One Night Only," *Carnival* (CD-ROM).

Huntington, Cynthia, "Bastard's Song," (poem) *Triquarterly* 119.

Hynes, Peter, "Gnaw," *Wicked Hollow*, May.

Ireland, Davin, "Resting Place," *Zahir* 5.

Irvine, Alex, "For Now It's Eight O'Clock," *Strange Horizons*, March 1.

Jablonsky, William, "Swimming with the Dead," *Harpur Palate*, summer.

Jackson-Adams, Tracina, "Death and Crow, Alone," *Flytrap* 2.

——, "Making a Sparrow," *Abyss and Apex* 8.

Jacob, Charlee, "Creases," (poem) *The Desert*.

——, "The Desert," (poem) Ibid.

——, "Rainmaker," (poem) *Cthulhu Sex*, vol. 2, issue 19.

——, "Second Thoughts," (poem) *The Desert*.

Jacobs, Sarah Ruth, "Stick Man," (poem) *Dreams and Nightmares* 65.

Jakeman, Jane, "Farmer's Market," *Supernatural Tales* 8.

Jarrar, Randa, "The Lunatic's Eclipse," *Ploughshares*, vol. 30, issue 2–3.

Jasper, Michael, "Coal Ash and Sparrows," *Asimov's*, Jan.

Jeffers, Honorée Fanonne, "A Plate of Mojo," *Crossroads*.

Jemison, N. K., "L'Alchimista," *Scattered, Covered, Smothered*.

Jens, Tina L., "Red Whiskey," *Spooks!*

Johnson, Alaya, "Good for Hanging," (poem) *Chizine* 22.

Johnson, Jeremy, "Walk on the Wild Side," *Cthulhu Sex*, vol. 2, issue 19.

Johnson, Kij, "The Empress Jingu Fishes," *Conqueror Fantastic*.

Jones, Howard Andrew, "Servant of Iblis," *Paradox* 5.

Jouet, Jacques, "Mountain R" (trans. by Brian Evenson), *Chicago Review*, 49:3/4 and 50:1.

Julavits, Heidi, "The Miniaturist," *McSweeney's Enchanted Chamber*.

Justice, Donald, "Angel Death Blues," (poem) *New England Review*, vol. 3, issue 25.

Kaysen, Daniel, "The Opposition," *The 3rd Alternative* 38.

Keene, Brian, "I Am an Exit," *Fear of Gravity*.

——, "The King, in: Yellow," Ibid.

Kees, S., "ghost hair," (poem) Magazine of Speculative Poetry, spring.

Kelderman, Sarah, "Ardelis," *The Many Faces of Van Helsing*.

Kelly, James Patrick, "Serpent," *F&SF*, May.

Kemble, Gary, "Ad Infinitum," *Shadowed Realms* 1.

Kemp, Lou, "The Wreck of the Virgo Idolin," *Black October*, vol. 1, issue 6.

Kenworthy, Christopher, "Alsiso," *The Alsiso Project*.

Keret, Etgar, "Pride and Joy" (trans. by Sondra Silverstone), *Swink* 1.

Kiernan, Caitlín R., "The Dead and the Moonstruck," *Gothic!*

——, "La Mer Des Rêves," *A Walk on the Darkside*.

——, "Mercury," (chapbook) Subterranean Press.

——, "Riding the White Bull," *Argosy*, Jan./Feb.

Kihn, Greg, "Abomination," *Strange Bedfellows*.

Kilby, Damien, "Pictures on a Café Wall," *The 3rd Alternative* 38.

King, Stephen, "Lisey and the Madman," *McSweeney's Enchanted Chamber*.

Koja, Kathe, "Anna Lee," *The Many Faces of Van Helsing*.

Konrath, J. A., "Forgiveness," *Cemetery Dance* 48.

——, "The Screaming," *The Many Faces of Van Helsing*.

Kopaska-Merkel, D. and Kendall Evans, "Variations on the Songs of Seriphim," *Star* Line*, Jan./Feb.

Lake, Jay, "Adagio for Flames and Jealousy," *Fortean Bureau*, June.

——, "Apologizing to the Concrete," *Nemonymous Four (Part 3)*.

——, "The Dying Dream of Water," *Flytrap* 3.

——, "Shattering Angels," *Dogs in the Moonlight*.

——, "Sloe-Eyed Jacks and the Homicide Kings," *Chizine* 19.

——, "The Soul Bottles," *Leviathan 4*.

——, "Tiny Flowers and Rotten Lace," *Realms of Fantasy*, Feb.

Lanagan, Margo, "House of the Many," *Black Juice*.

——, "Red Nose Day," Ibid.

——, "Wooden Bride," Ibid.

——, "Yowlinin," Ibid.

Lane, Joel, "Against My Ruins," *Midnight Street* 1.

——, "A Cup of Blood," *Supernatural Tales* 8.

——, "Facing the Wall," *The 3rd Alternative* 38.

——, "The Victim Card," *Midnight Street* 3.

Larbalestier, Justine, "Where Did You Sleep Last Night?" *Agog! Smashing Stories*.

LaValle, Victor, "I Left My Heart in Skaftafell," *Daedalus*, vol. 133, issue 4.

Leary, John, "Daddy," *Hobart* 3.

Lebbon, Tim, "Dead Man's Hand," (novella chapbook) Necessary Evil Press.

——, "In Perpetuity," (novella) *Night Visions* 11.

——, "Remnants," (novella) *Fears Unnamed*.

Lebbon, Tim and Brett Alexander Savory, "Shoes," *A Walk on the Darkside*.

Lecard, Marc, "Night Window," *Not One of Us* 31.

Lee, Edward, "The Angel," *Damned*.

——, "Edit from May Fifth at Three Thirty-seven A.M." (poem), *The Devil's Wine*.

Lee, Tanith, "Israbel," *Realms of Fantasy*, April.

——, "Remember Me," *The Many Faces of V. H.*

Leeming, Jay, "Ghazal in Which the Parthenon is Filled with Explosives," (poem) *Black Warrior Review*, vol. 1, issue 31.

Le Guin, Ursula K., "On the Hillside," *Denver Quarterly*, vol. 1, issue 39.

Lestewka, Patrick, "The Coliseum," (novella) *Damned*.

——, "The Count," *Chizine* 21.

Levine, Daniel Gould, "Joy," *Ellery Queen's Mystery Magazine*, May.

Levine, Richard, "Dancing to Restore an Eclipsed Moon," (poem) *Qagybul*.

Lewis, D. F., "Strollers," (novella) *Megazanthine*.

Lewis, Mike, "The Smell of Magic," *Realms of Fantasy*, Aug.

Libling, Michael, "Christmas in the Catskills," *F&SF*, Dec.

Lifshin, Lyn, "A Woman Goes into the Cemetery," (poem) *Harpur Palate*, summer.

Link, Kelly, "Stone Animals," *Conjunctions* 43.

Little, Bentley, "The Addition," *Cemetery Dance* 50.

Livings, Martin, "Maelstrom," *Agog! Smashing Stories.*

Locascio, Phil, "The Boy in the Corner," *Top International Horror.*

Lockley, Steve and Paul Lewis, "The Ice Maiden," (novella) chapbook.

Lofton, S. C., "Dark Drug," *Tales of the Unanticipated* 25.

Logan, Simon, "You Have to Know This," *The Last Pentacle of the Sun.*

Lomax, David, "How to Write an Epic Fantasy Novel," *Rabid Transit: Petting Zoo.*

Ludwigsen, Will, "Soured," Horrorfind.com.

Lynch, Mark Patrick, "Triangulation," *Zahir* 5.

Lyon, Annabel, "Saturday Night Function," *Harvard Review* 26.

Mackay, Erin, "Diminishing," *Cloaked in Shadow.*

Maclay, John, "Lynn," *Dreadful Delineations.*

MacLeod, Catherine, "Stick House," *On Spec*, spring.

Maguire, Gregory, "The Prank," *Gothic!*

——, "Rumplesnakeskin," *Leaping Beauty.*

Maloney, Geoffrey, "Birds of the Brushes and Scrubs," *TiconderogaOnline*, vol. 1, issue 2.

——, "Conversations with Eternity," *Orb* 6.

Mann, Antony, "Sweet Little Memory," *Midnight Street* 1.

Mannetti, Lisa, "The Haunted Lizzie Borden House," *Spooks!*

Martin, George R. R., "The Sworn Sword," *Legends II.*

Massie, Elizabeth, "Dooka Dee," *The Fear Report.*

——, "Frozen Orchard," (poem) *The Devil's Wine.*

——, "Pisspot Bay," *The Last Pentacle of the Sun.*

Masterton, Graham, "Camelot," *Strange Bedfellows.*

——, "Reflection of Evil," *The Mammoth Book of New Terror.*

——, "Sarcophagus," *Small Bites.*

——, "Sunday Prayer Meeting," (poem) *The Devil's Wine.*

Matheson, Richard, "Cassidy's Shoes," *Darker Places.*

——, "The Puppy," Ibid.

Maycock, Brian, "Where's the Matter," *Not One of Us* 32.

Maynard, L. H. and M.P.N. Sims, "Calling Down the Lightning," *Falling into Heaven.*

——, "Dancers," Ibid.

——, "Dead Man's Shoes," Ibid.

——, "Flour White and Spindle Thin," Ibid.

——, "Images," Ibid.

McDonald, Sandra, "Bluebeard by the Sea," *Talebones* 28.

McDowell, Ian, "They Are Girls, Green Girls," *Realms of Fantasy*, Oct.

——, "Under the Flag of the Night," *Asimov's*, March.

McGivney, Claudia, "Homicide," (poem) *Wicked Hollow* 8.

McIlvoy, Kevin, "Permission," *Harper's*, Nov.

McKenna, Claire, "Unreal City," *Borderlands* 3.

McKillip, Patricia, "The Gorgon in the Cupboard," *To Weave a Web of Magic.*

——, "Out of the Woods," *Flights.*

McMahon, Gary, "Her Sister's Dance," *Maelstrom*, Volume 1.

——, "My Burglar," *Nemonymous Four (Part 3).*

McNally, Sean, "Get to Know Your Presidential Pets (3)" (poem), *Lit* 9.

McVey, David, "The Fetcher," *All Hallows* 35.

Meaney, John, "Diva's Bones," *Interzone* 193.

Melko, Paul, "Ten Sigmas," *Talebones* 28.

Meloy, Paul, "Black Static," *The 3rd Alternative* 40.

Menge, Elaine, "A Period of Adjustment," *AHMM*, April.

Michel, Lincoln, "The Color of Mouse Trails on Snow," (poem) *The Pedestal Magazine* 24.

Mills, David, "Grey Zone," *All Hallows*, Feb.

Milosevic, Mario, "Bigfoot," (poem) *Journal of Mythic Arts*, summer.

——, "The Last Melody," (poem) *Fantasy Life*.

——, "We Are All Ghosts," (poem) *Magazine of Speculative Poetry*, spring.

Mingin, Bill, "The Haunting of Lew Salmonsen," *Black October*, vol. 1, issue 6.

Minton, Jeremy, "Nails," *The 3rd Alternative* 38.

Mohn, Steve, "We Must an Anguish Pay," *The 3rd Alternative* 40.

Moles, David, "Five Irrational Histories," *Rabid Transit: Petting Zoo*.

Monette, Sarah, "Bringing Helena Back," *All Hallows* 35.

——, "The Venebretti Necklace," *Alchemy* 2.

Monteleone, Thomas F., "Sideshow," *The Many Faces of Van Helsing*.

——, "The Three," *A Little Brown Book of Bizarre Stories*.

Moody, Rick, "Flap," *Post Road* 8.

——, "The Free Library," *Ploughshares*, vol. 30, issue 1.

Mor, Edo, "Tohil," *Chizine* 19.

Morrow, James, "Martyrs of the Upshot Knothole," *Conqueror Fantastic*.

Mosser, Susan, "For Norine, in Gratitude for Magic Beans," (poem) *Turbocharged Fortune Cookie* 2.

Murphy, Joe, "The Secret of Making Brains," *Realms of Fantasy*, Dec.

Murray, Will, "The Cow-Men of Coburn," *Weird Trails*, April.

Myers, Gary, "The End of Wisdom," *Strange Tales* 8.

Negus, Lisa, "Blueskin," *Terror Tales* 2.

Newman, Karen, "Absolute Zero," (poem) *EOTU*, Aug.

——, "Unspoken," (poem) *Aoife's Kiss*, Dec.

Newman, Kim, "The Chill Clutch of the Unseen," *Quietly Now*.

——, "Soho Golem," *SCI FICTION*, Oct. 13.

——, "Swellhead," (novella) *Night Visions* 11.

Newton, Kurt, "Cold as the Crow Flies," (poem) *Poe Little Thing* 2.

Niles, Angelo, "Maelstrom," *On Spec*, Dec.

Nix, Garth, "Endings," *Gothic!*

Noles, Pam, "Whipping Boy," *Dark Matter: Reading the Bones*.

O'Driscoll, Mike, "If I Should Wake before I Die," *The 3rd Alternative* 39.

O'Neal, C. Mitchell, "The Moon Shone on My Slumbers," *Paradox*, summer.

O'Neill, Gene, "Masquerade," *Bare Bone* 6.

O'Regan, Marie, "Alsiso," *The Alsiso Project*.

Oates, Joyce Carol, "The Banshee," *Ellery Queen's Mystery Magazine*, June.

——, "The Fabled Light-House at Viña Del Mar," *McSweeney's Enchanted Chamber*.

——, "The Fruit Cellar," *Ellery Queen's Mystery Magazine*, March/April.

——, "Six Hypotheses," *Flights*.

Oldknow, Anthony, "The Gollies," *All Hallows* 36.

Oliver, Reggie, "The Skins," *Weirdly Supernatural* 2.

Ozmert, Nicholas, "The Prairie Whales Are All Extinct," (poem) *Mythic Delirium* 11.

Palwick, Susan, "Beautiful Stuff," *SCI FICTION*, Aug. 18.

Payne, Ben, "Boys," *Encounters*.

Pearce, Richard William, "The Rat's Dream," (poem) *Space and Time*, spring.

Pearson, Lisa, "Alsiso," *The Alsiso Project*.

Peek, Ben, " 'R,' " *Agog! Smashing Stories*.

Pelan, John, "Homecoming," *The Last Pentacle of the Sun*.

——, "Memories Are Made of This," *A Walk on the Darkside*.

Penn, David, "The Condition," *Midnight Street* 2.

Phillips, Holly, "The Dead Boy," *On Spec*, Summer.

——, "In the Shadow of Your Head," *Flesh and Blood* 14.

Piccirilli, Tom, "Black," *A Little Black Book of Noir* (2003).

——, "In Bed with It," *Waiting My Turn to Go under the Knife*.

——, "Sins of the Sons," Ibid.

——, "These Strange Lays," *A Walk on the Darkside*.

——, "Thief of Golgotha," *Damned*.

——, "With an Ear for My Father's Weeping," *The Horror Express* 3.

Pietrzykowski, Marc, "The Tyranny of the Firmament," (poem) *Star*Line*, March/April.

Polack, Gillian, "Happy Faces for Happy Families," *Encounters*.

Pond, Whitt, "The Job," *Tales of the Unanticipated* 25.

Popkes, Steve, "The Old Woman in the Moon," *Realms of Fantasy*, Oct.

Porter, Karen R., "Unseen," (poem) *Not One of Us* 32.

Powers, Tim, "Pat Moore," *Flights*.

Pratt, Tim, "Life in Stone," *Lenox Avenue* 3.

——, "Hart and Boot," *Polyphony* 4.

——, "Terrible Ones," *The 3rd Alternative* 37.

Prineas, Sarah, "The Dog Prince," *Talebones* 29.

Prunty, Wyatt, "Times Train," (poem) *Poetry*, Nov.

Ptacek, Kathryn, "The Children's Hour," *Quietly Now*.

Purfield, Mike E., "Let Down," *Tales from the Gorezone*.

Raboteau, Emily, "Rum and the Flesh," *Argosy*, Jan./Feb.

Rath, Tina, "Mr. Polkington," *All Hallows*, Oct.

Read, Nigel, "The Dove," *Encounters*.

Rector, John, "The Long Road Back," *Maelstrom, volume One*.

Reed, Kit, "The Family Bed," *SCI FICTION*, May 12.

——, "The Zombie Prince," *F&SF*, June.

Reed, Robert, "Daily Reports," *Asimov's*, July.

——, "Designing with Souls," *F&SF*, Sept.

——, "The Dragons of Summer Gulch," *SCI FICTION*, Dec. 1.

Rees, Celia, "Writing on the Wall," *Gothic!*

Reibe, Neil, "Dagon's Mistress," *Eldritch Blue*.

Reifler, Nelly, "The River and Una," *Land Grant College Review* 2.

Richards, Tony, "Misdirection," *Cemetery Dance* 49.

Rickert, M., "Art Is Not a Violent Subject," *Rabid Transit: Petting Zoo*.

——, "Many Voices," *F&SF*, March.

Riedel, Kate, "The Pear Orchard," *Not One of Us* 31.

Roberson, Chris, "In Sheep's Clothing," *Black October*, vol. 1, issue 6.

Roberts, Adam, "Eleanor," *Swiftly*.

——, "Roads Were Burning," *Postscripts* 1.

——, "The Siege of Fadiman," *Swiftly*.

Roberts, Jason, "7C," *McSweeney's Enchanted Chamber*.

Roberts, Tansy Rayner, "Garments of the Dead," *Aurealis* 32.

Robins, Maureen Picard, "Deliver Her," (poem) *Prairie Schooner*, vol. 78, issue 1.

Robson, Barbara, "Lizzy Lou," *Borderlands* 3.

Roessner, Michaela, "Inside Outside," *SCI FICTION*, Jan. 21.

Rogers, Bruce Holland, "A Baker's Dozen," *NFG*, vol. 4, issue 2.

——, "Recovering the Body," *flashquake*, summer.

——, "Tiny Bells," *Realms of Fantasy*, June.

——, and Ray Vukcevich and Holly Arrow, "The Train There's No Getting Off," *Polyphony* 4.

Rogers, Lenore K., "The Open Arms of Bellamy," *Outer Darkness* 28.

Rogers, Stephen D., "Laune's Lesson," *Cloaked in Shadow*.

Rosen, Jamie, "Creek Man," *Nemonymous Four (Part 3)*.

Rosenbaum, Benjamin, "Biographical Notes to 'A Discourse on the Nature of Causality, with Air-Planes,'" *All-Star Zeppelin*.

——, "Embracing-the-New," *Asimov's*, Jan.

Rowan, Iain, "Lilies," *Postscripts* 1.

——, "The Marsh," *All Hallows*, Oct.

——, The Walker on the Wall," *Supernatural Tales* 7.

Rowlands, David G., "Long Service," *Weirdly Supernatural* 2.

Royle, Nicholas, "The Performance," *Matter* 4.

Rubins, Jodee, "Bob's Witch," *Electric Velocipede* 6.

Russo, Patricia, "Suckling," *Not One of Us* 31.

Ryan, Kay, "Rubbing Lamps," (poem) *Poetry*, Nov.

Safran Foer, Jonathan, "The Sixth Borough," *The New York Times*, Sept. 17.

Sala, Jerome, "The Four Visions of St. Nemo," (poem) *Lit*, 9.

Salaam, Kiini Ibura, "Desire," *Dark Matter: Reading the Bones*.

Sallis, James, "The Museum of Last Week," *Lady Churchill's Rosebud Wristlet* 14.

Sanders, Milly, "Recipe for Raise the Dead," *Suspect Thoughts*.

Santoro, Lawrence, "So Many Tiny Mouths," *FeralFiction*, Sept.

Saplak, Charles M., "The Submergence and Re-emergence of John Starkey," *Dreams and Nightmares* 87.

Sarrantonio, Al, "Sleepover," *Flights*.

Saunders, George, "Adams," *The New Yorker*, Aug. 9 & 16.

Savile, Steven, "All That Remains of You," *Angel Road*.

——, "Alsiso," *Alsiso*.

——, "Angel Road," (poem) *Angel Road*.

——, "Malice," Ibid.

——, "The Pain, Heartbreak and Redemption of Owen Frost," Ibid.

——, "Two Stones in My Heart," (poem) Ibid.

Schaeffer, Susan Fromberg, "Wolves," (poem) *Prairie Schooner*, vol. 78, issue 3.

Schneider, Peter, "Tots," *Flights*.

Schoffstall, John, "Clockwork Dragons Must Die!" *Fortean Bureau* 26.

Schow, David J., "Expanding Your Capabilities Using Frame/Shift™ Mode," *DTOT Light*.

Schwader, Ann K., "Mr. Marmalade," *Strange Suns and Alien Shadows*.

——, "Objects from the Gilman-Waite Collections," Ibid.

——, "Tattered Souls," Ibid.

Schwartz, David J., "Breaking Glass," *The 3rd Alternative* 40.

——, "The Colossus Vignettes," *Fortean Bureau* 25.

——, "Iron Ankles," *Strange Horizons*, Aug. 16.

Schweitzer, Darrell, "The Order of Things Must be Preserved," *Interzone* 193.

Schweitzer, Darrell and Jason Van Hollander, "The Scroll of the Worm," *The Horror Express* 2.

Searles, Vera, "The Man Who Hated Memories," *Mudrock*, spring/summer.

Sevin, R. J., "Blood and Sand," *Maelstrom, Volume One*.

Shannon, Harry, "Blacktop," *Tales from the Gorezone*.

Shaw, Paul J., "Beneath the Hood," *All Hallows* 35.

Shawl, Nisi, "Looking for Lilith," *Lenox Avenue* 1.

Shea, Michael, "Incident Report," *A Walk on the Darkside*.

——, "The Growlimb," *F&SF*, Jan.

Shepard, Lucius, "Hands Up! Who Wants to Die?" (novella) *Night Visions* 11.

——, "Viator," (novella) chapbook.

Sherman, Delia, "CATNYP," *The Faery Reel*.

Sherrard, Cherene, "The Quality of Sand," *Dark Matter*.

Shippy, Peter Jay, "Genre Fiction," (poem) *Harvard Review* 27.

Siddall, D., "Melody," *Supernatural Tales* 8.

Silva, David B., "Through Desmond's Eyes," *Cemetery Dance* 48.

——, "Wrinkles," *Quietly Now*.

Silverman, Sue William, "Queen Hatasu Descends to Throne," (poem) *Prairie Schooner*, vol. 78, issue 4.

Simmons, Meredith, "Milk in a Silver Cup," *Paradox*, winter '04–'05.

Simmons, William P., "Skin," *By Reason of Darkness*.

——, "Small Decisions," Ibid.

Simner, Janni Lee, "Stone Tower," *Gothic!*

Simon, Marge, "Blood on My Tongue," *The Pedestal Magazine* 24.

——, "Performance in a Cemetery," (poem) *Flesh and Blood* 15.

——, "The Seasons of Death," (poem) *The Pedestal Magazine* 21.

——, "The Significance of Being a Luminary," (poem) *Chizine* 21.

Singh, Vandana, "Three Tales from Sky River," *Strange Horizons*, Jan. 5.

——, "Thirst," *The 3rd Alternative* 40.

Sjolie, Dennis, "Edges," *Flesh and Blood* 15.

Skillingstead, Jack, "Reunion," *On Spec*, spring.

Slay, Jack Jr., "Chase's Fairy," *Cemetery Dance* 50.

Smiderle, Wes, "The Art of Dying Well," *On Spec*, winter.

Smith, Chad L., "The Neighbor," *Tales from the Gorezone*.

Smith, Daniel C., "Somewhere in Kansas," (poem) *Bare Bone* 6.

Smith, Meg, "The White Stones, the Quiet Walk," (poem) *Poe Little Thing* 2.

Smith, Michael Marshall, "Getting Over," *Postscripts* 2.

——, "This Is Now," *BBC Cult Vampire Magazine*.

Smith, R. T., "Gypsy Fiddle," (poem) *Georgia Review*, vol. 58, issue 1.

Sng, Christina, "The Art of Weaving," (poem) *Flesh and Blood* 14.

Snyder, Lucy A., "Installing Linux on a Dead Badger: User's Notes," *Strange Horizons*, April 5.

Somers, Jeff, "The Defragmentation of Thomas Crane," *The Urban Bizarre*.

Sparks, Cat, "Last Dance at the Sergeant Majors' Ball," *Borderlands* 3.

Speegle, Darren, "Buoyancy," *Gothic Wine*.

——, "Chasing Fuseli," Ibid.

——, "Colibri," Ibid.

——, "End of the Line," Ibid.

——, "Merging Tableaux," *Horrorfind*.

Stanley, Barbara, "Bitsy," *Subnatural*.

Stanley, Nelson, "Pit Bull," *Trunk Stories* 2.

Steensland, Mark, "The Barn," *Not One of Us* 32.

Sterzinger, Ann, "Amy," *The Urban Bizarre*.

Stiles, Paula, "In the Bush," *Albedo* 28.

Straley, John, "Lovely," *Powers of Detection*.

Stroh, Harley, "The Devil's Last Dance," *Space and Time*, spring.

Stuart, Kiel, "On the Language of Alligator Twins," *Electric Velocipede* 7.

Sullivan, John, "You're Only Insane Girl Twice," *Flytrap* 2.

Swanwick, Michael, "The Word That Sings the Scythe," *Asimov's*, Oct./Nov.

Taaffe, Sonya, "Another Coming," *Not One of Us* 32.

——, "Apocalypso," (poem) *Mythic Delirium* 10.

——, "An Eclipse of Raven," (poem) *Dreams and Nightmares* 68.

——, "Expiration" *Vestal Review* 19.

——, "Festivities," *Lunatic Chameleon* 3.

——, "The Laying-Out," (poem) *Mythic Delirium* 11.

——, "Lilim, after Dark," (poem) Ibid. 10.

——, "Retrospective," *Not One of Us* 31.

——, "Sekhmet in the Ruins," (poem) *Lunatic Chameleon* 4.

——, "Tzaddik," (poem) *Mythic Delirium*, 11.

Tarr, Judith, "The Hermit and the Sidhe," *Emerald Magic*.

Tate, James, "Letzeburgesch," (poem) *Agni* 60.

Tate, Lisa, "The Loch," *Midnight Street* 3.

Taylor, Terence, "Plaything," *Dark Dreams*.

Tem, Melanie, "The Car," (poem) *The Devil's Wine*.

——, "Woman Wailing," (poem) Ibid.

Tem, Steve Rasnic, "An Ending," *A Walk on the Darkside*.

——, "This Is the Last Time I'm Telling the Truth," (poem) *The Devil's Wine*.

——, "Yesterday," *Quietly Now*.

Tem, Steve Rasnic and Melanie Tem, "Empty Morning," *The Many Faces of Van Helsing*.

Tennant, Peter, "The Beautiful Dead," *Midnight Street* 2.

Tessier, Thomas, "The Infestation at Ralls," *The Many Faces of Van Helsing*.

Thielbar, Melinda, "The Ghost of Me," *Weird Tales* 336.

Thomas, Jeffrey, "The Abandoned," *A Walk on the Darkside*.

——, "The Color Shrain," *Punktown: Third Eye*.

——, "Damask," *Honey Is Sweeter than Blood*.

——, "Honey is Sweeter than Blood," Ibid.

——, "The Tripod," *Terror Tales* 2.

——, "Willow Tree," *Inhuman* 1.

Thomas, Lee, "Anthem of the Estranged," *A Walk on the Darkside*.

——, "Before You Go," *Chizine* 21.

——, "Pierce," *Circus/Carnival* (CD-ROM).

Thomas, Scott, "Song to a Sleeping City," *Punktown: Third Eye*.

Thompson, Ryan Michael, "False Idols in a False Sun," *The Parasitorium*.

Thorson, Maureen, "Too Late Now," (poem) *Lit* 9.

Tidhar, Lavie, "The Curious History of the Micro-Cynicon," *Fortean Bureau* 18.

Tinti, Hannah, "Bloodworks," *Animal Crackers*.

———, "Miss Waldron's Red Colubus," Ibid.

Travis, J. J., "The Dark Inside," *All Hallows* 36.

Tremblay, Paul G., "All Sliding to One Side," *The Last Pentacle of the Sun*.

———, "Colonel Evans' Last Mission," *All Hallows* 36.

———, "City Pier," *Compositions for the Young and Old*.

———, "Dole as Ribbit," Ibid.

———, "Reaching," Ibid.

———, "Role Models," Ibid.

Trimm, Mikal, "The Clockmaker's Wife," (poem) *Star*Line*, Sept./Oct.

———, "The Game of Not Knowing," (poem) *Dreams and Nightmares* 69.

Tullis, Scott, "The Death Knell," *Nemonymous Four (Part 3)*.

Tumasonis, Don, "Crossroads," *A Walk on the Darkside*.

———, "A Short Tragic History of Road Mishap Mystery," *All Hallows*, Oct.

Tuttle, Lisa, "*My Death*," (novella) chapbook.

Urbancik, John, "Beneath Midnight" (novella) *New Dark Voices*.

Uubie, Norman, "The Fish Cypher of Michel de Nostradam," (poem) *Triquarterly* 119.

Valente, Catherynne M., "Gingerbread," (poem) *Music of a Proto-Suicide* (chapbook).

———, "Vitia Capitalis," (poem) Ibid.

van Dyk, Amber, "Sour Metal," *Alchemy* 2.

———, "Storyville," *Rabid Transit: Petting Zoo*.

Vance, Michael, "Blind Faith," *Maelstrom, Volume 1*.

VanderMeer, Jeff, "The City," *Secret Life*.

———, "The Compass of His Bones," Ibid.

———, "Secret Life," Ibid.

Van Pelt, James, "Echoing," *Asimov's*, Dec.

Van Velde, Vivian, "Morgan Roemar's Boys," *Gothic!*

Vaz, Katherine, "Your Garnet Eyes," *The Faery Reel*.

Vaughn, Carrie, "The Bravest of Us Touched the Sky," *Talebones* 29.

Vernon, Steve, "Al Wood Dreams of the Sun," *Nightmare Dreams*.

———, "Harry's Mermaid," Ibid.

———, "Jugular," Ibid.

———, "Moving Lines," Ibid.

Vick, Edd, "Choice Cuts," *Electric Velocipede* 6.

Vukcevich, Ray, "Glinky," *F&SF*, June.

———, "Human Subjects," *Amazing Stories*, 603.

Waldrop, Howard, "The Wolf-man of Alcatraz," SCI FICTION, Sept. 22.

Warburton, Geoffrey, "Ms. Found in a Hotel Pigeonhole," *Supernatural Tales* 7.

Ward, Lucy A. E., "In the Greenhouse at Olfuston Park," (poem) *The Horror Express* 3.

Warner, Matthew, "Angel's Wings," *Tales from the Gorezone*.

Watson, Ian, "Lambert, Lambert," *Weird Tales* 335.

Weber, Richard D., "Jack in Green," *Black October*, vol. 1, issue 5.

Webster, Bud, "September," (poem) *Mythic Delirium* 10.

Wedel, Steven E., "Murdered by Human Wolves," (novella) chapbook.

Wentworth, K. D., "The Secret Language of Flowers," *Flesh and Blood* 15.

Westerholm, Jim, "Madeleine," *Zahir* 3.

What, Leslie, "Why a Duck," *All-Star Zeppelin*.

——, "2:30," *Strange Horizons*, Dec. 13.

Wilce, Ysabeau S., "Metal More Attractive," *F&SF*, Feb.

Wilhelm, Kate, "His Deadliest Enemy," *Ellery Queen's Mystery Magazine*, March/April.

Willard, Nancy, "An Accident," (poem) *Hudson Review*, vol. 57, no. 2.

Williams, Conrad, "Alsiso," *The Alsiso Project*.

——, "Game," (novella) *Chapbook*.

——, "Nest of Salt," *Use Once, Then Destroy*.

Williams, David, "Girl with a Cat," *All Hallows* 36.

Williams, Liz, "Indicating the Awakening of Persons Buried Alive," *Electric Velocipede* 6.

——, "The Marsella," *Electric Velocipede* 7.

——, "Skindancing," *The Banquet of the Lords of Night and Other Stories*.

Williamson, Chet, "A Father's Tears," *Quietly Now*.

——, "The Pebbles of Sai-No Kawara," *F&SF*, Feb.

Wilson, Mehitobel, "Close," *Damned*.

——, "Parting Jane," *A Walk on the Darkside*.

Witcover, Paul, "Left of the Dial," (novella) *SCI FICTION*, Sept. 1.

Wolfe, Gene, "Calamity Warps," *Realms of Fantasy*, Apr.

——, "Golden City Far," *Flights*.

——, "The Little Stranger," *F&SF*, Oct./Nov.

——, "The Lost Pilgrim," *The First Heroes*.

——, "Monster," *Amazing Stories*, Sept.

——, "Prize Crew," *Postscripts* 1.

Wolfman, Marv, "The Last Man on Earth," *Strange Bedfellows*.

Wunderlich, Mark, "Device for Burning Bees and Sugar," (poem) *Post Road* 8.

Ya Salaam, Kalamu, "Alabama," *Crossroads*.

Yolen, Jane, "Musings about Seth," (poem) *Mythic Delirium* 10.

Yourgrau, Barry, "Have No Fear, Crumpot Is Here," *Gothic!*

Zivkovic, Zoran, "Compartments," *Postscripts*, summer.

Zoboi, Ibi Aanu, "Old Flesh Song," *Dark Matter: Reading the Bones*.

The People Behind the Book

Horror Editor **Ellen Datlow** is the editor of *SCI FICTION*. She was the fiction editor of *Omni Magazine* for seventeen years, and has edited numerous anthologies, including *Vanishing Acts* and *The Dark*. She has also collaborated with Terri Windling on the first sixteen volumes of *The Year's Best Fantasy and Horror*, *Sirens*, the Snow White Blood Red fairy tale series, *A Wolf at the Door*, *Swan Sister*, *The Green Man*, and *The Faery Reel*. She has won many awards for her editing, including seven World Fantasy Awards, The Bram Stoker Award, the 2005 Locus Award, and the 2002 Hugo Award. She lives in New York City.

Kelly Link is the author of two collections, *Stranger Things Happen* and *Magic for Beginners*. Her short stories have won the Nebula, Tiptree, Locus, and World Fantasy Awards. She is also the editor of the anthology *Trampoline*. **Gavin J. Grant** and **Kelly Link** produce a twice-yearly zine, *Lady Churchill's Rosebud Wristlet*, and publish books as Small Beer Press. Originally from Scotland, Gavin moved to the U.S.A. in 1991. He has been published in the *Los Angeles Times*, the *Hartford Courant*, *Time Out New York*, *SCI FICTION*, *Strange Horizons*, *The Magazine of Fantasy and Science Fiction*, and *The 3rd Alternative*, among others. Link and Grant live in Northampton, Massachusetts.

Media critic **Edward Bryant** is an award-winning author of science fiction, fantasy, and horror, having published short fiction in countless anthologies and magazines. He's won the Nebula Award for his science fiction, and other works of his short fiction have been nominated for many other awards. He's also written for television. He lives in Denver, Colorado. His story collection *Flirting with Death* (Cemetery Dance Publications) will be published soon.

Comics critic **Charles Vess**'s art has graced the pages of numerous comic and illustrated books for over twenty-five years. His comics work has appeared in, among other publications, *Spider-man*, *The Sandman*, *The Books of Magic*, and his own self-published *The Book of Ballads and Sagas*, and his art has won him two Will Eisner Comic Industry Awards among many other kudos. In 1999, Charles received the World Fantasy Award for Best Artist for his illustrations in *Neil Gaiman and Charles Vess's Stardust*. His latest graphic novel is *The Book of Ballads* (Tor), which is enjoying great critical acclaim. For current information, visit his Web site: www.greenmanpress.com. He lives amidst the Appalachian Mountains in southwest Virginia and enjoys his "simple" life very much.

Anime and manga critic **Joan D. Vinge** is the two-time Hugo Award–winning author of the *Snow Queen* cycle and the Cat books. Her most recent novel is *Tangled Up in Blue*, a novel in the Snow Queen universe. Her novels *Catspaw, The Summer Queen,* and *Dreamfall* have recently been reprinted by Tor Books. She's working on *LadySmith*, a prehistorical novel set in Bronze Age western Europe. She lives in Madison, Wisconsin.

Music critic **Charles de Lint** is a musician specializing in Celtic music, a folklorist, and a music reviewer. He is also the World Fantasy Award–winning author of a number of fantasy novels and shorter works, especially stories set in the fictional city of Newford. He and his wife, MaryAnn Harris, live in Ottawa, Canada.

Series jacket artist **Thomas Canty** has won the World Fantasy Award for Best Artist. He has painted and/or designed covers for many books, and has art-directed many other covers, in a career that spans more than twenty years. He lives outside Boston, Massachusetts.

Packager **James Frenkel**, a book editor since 1971, has been an editor for Tor Books since 1983, and is currently a senior editor. He has also edited various anthologies, including *True Names and the Opening of the Cyberspace Frontier, Technohorror,* and *Bangs and Whimpers*. He lives in Madison, Wisconsin.